A Bride's
Agreement

Five Romances Develop Out of Convenient Marriages

A Bride's
Agreement

DiAnn Mills
Elaine Bonner, Ramona K. Cecil,
Nancy J. Farrier, JoAnn A. Grote

BARBOUR BOOKS
An Imprint of Barbour Publishing, Inc.

Our mission is to publish and distribute inspirational products offering exceptional value and biblical encouragement to the masses.

 Member of the
Evangelical Christian
Publishers Association

Printed in the United States of America.

Contents

THANKS TO A LONELY HEART

by Elaine Bonner

CHAPTER 1

He glanced around as he tied his horse to the hitching rail. Steven Barnes had looked down this dusty little street many times in the past few years. There was the feed store with the wagons out front waiting to be loaded with seed and grain. Across the street stood Hall's General Mercantile and as usual Mr. Hall was standing at the door leaning on his broom visiting with a customer. The bank, the café, every building in town was like a familiar friend to him.

The Coffee Cup Café had been painted white many years ago but the sand storms of west Texas had taken their toll. The steps creaked as Steven's boots made contact, and the wooden porch seemed to groan under the weight of a lone man walking across its weathered surface. Steven removed his cowboy hat and slapped it against the leg of his jeans sending sand flying in every direction before he opened the door of the café.

The little bell above the door of the Coffee Cup Café tinkled, and Emily Johnson looked up to see who her next customer would be. Steven Barnes was a familiar sight. He had come into the café many times over the past five years, but something about him was different this time. Emily could sense something was wrong. He rode his horse into town from the Bar Eight Ranch a couple of times a month, and he'd always been willing to pass the time of day with her before. She didn't know a lot about him except that he was married and had some children. For some reason, he had left them back in east Texas. He never talked about them much and would change the subject quickly if anyone mentioned them.

Occasionally, he would sit at one of the tables and read what appeared to be a letter. Emily couldn't help noticing the faraway look that would come over him at those times.

Today, as he seated himself on one of the stools at the counter, Steven Barnes was definitely preoccupied. Although she didn't know a lot about his personal life, he was always friendly, and she had always been fond of his sense of humor. But today there was no laughter in him. She poured him a cup of coffee and asked, "How are you today, Steven? Sure is a beautiful day, don't you think?"

"I'm okay, and the weather's fine I guess," he responded as he picked up his cup and took a sip.

Emily busied herself wiping tables for a few moments, then walked back behind the counter and tried again to engage Steven in conversation. "I noticed the big annual barbecue for the Bar Eight is next Saturday." She wiped her hands on the white apron covering her blue gingham dress as she continued. "I guess things are pretty busy out your way. Must be a lot of hustle and bustle to get ready for an event like that."

"I reckon there is," he replied without enthusiasm. "I don't get involved in that sorta thing too often. Chances are I won't be here next Saturday anyhow."

"You planning a little trip out of town, Steven?" Emily asked.

"Not just a trip," he confided. "I'm leaving for good."

A look of surprise flashed on her face as she inquired, "I don't mean to be nosy, but I know you have family in east Texas. Are you going home?"

His face turned pale. "Well, I'm going back to east Texas. I don't know if I can call it home anymore. Maybe I don't have a right to call it home." Steven's voice became shaky, and Emily could see his hands were trembling as he continued. "At any rate, I got word that my wife passed away a few weeks ago. A friend wrote me. He said that if I didn't get in touch with the county judge soon, my kids would become wards of the county. Seems a neighbor lady is helping take care of them now, but I've got to get back."

"Steven, I'm so sorry to hear about your loss," Emily said sincerely. "It must be very hard for you being so far away at a time like this. How many children do you have?"

"Five," he replied. "Four boys and a girl."

Emily could not tell by looking at his face what he was feeling, but she was hearing something in the sound of his voice. She thought it sounded like sheer terror. He must be scared stiff to think about going home to five children he hadn't seen for at least five years, having to take the sole responsibility for raising them.

"Have you ever been married, Emily?" Steven asked, drawing her out of her thoughts.

"Yeah, I was once," she answered. "My husband was killed right after the turn of the century in an accident. I guess that makes it about eight years ago now." It didn't seem like that long, and yet, in some ways, it seemed like a lifetime. "That's when I started working here." Emily paused and refilled Steven's cup.

"Thanks," he said, then looked at Emily as he asked, "Have you ever thought about getting married again?"

"Sure I have. But I guess I'm just too picky. And besides, the pickings aren't so good here," Emily answered.

On the outside she was smiling when she answered him. But the truth of the matter was Emily was so lonesome sometimes that she could hardly stand it. She had no children and no family, and she ached for a man in her life. She had loved her husband very much, and after his death, she had thought she would never be able to love again. But for quite some time, she had felt she was ready to welcome someone into her life. The trouble was, no one was beating down her door. The only so-called proposal she'd had was from a man twice her age. He lived in a shack on the edge of town and was looking for someone to take care of him in his old age. He was probably the only person in town worse off than she was. At the age of thirty, Emily was beginning to give up hope of ever finding anyone. She was trying to accept her lonely heart and learn to live with it.

"Do you like kids, Emily?" Steven asked.

"Yeah, I like kids," she replied. "My husband came from a big family. I loved to help care for his nieces and nephews before we moved out here."

Emily was saddened once again, thinking about Jim's family. She had completely lost touch with them after his death. They seemed to just forget all about her. Maybe she was a sad reminder of the son they had lost.

Again Steven's voice brought her back to the present. "Emily, I have a proposition for you," he stated matter-of-factly. "I need someone to help me care for my children and take care of the house. Would you consider marrying me and coming to east Texas with me?" Steven stared into his coffee cup as he continued. "Now this would be a marriage in name only. I wouldn't expect you to be a wife to me, just a mother to my children."

Emily dropped the cup she was holding, shattering it into pieces. The breaking glass startled the two older gentlemen seated at the table in the corner, the only other people in the room. One of them called out, "Hey Emily, Lon'll dock your pay for that." Emily forced a smile back at the old fellow, but she couldn't speak. She looked at Steven. "What did you say?"

"I offered you a job and asked you if you'd be willing to marry me," he responded. There was no emotion in his voice and his face was void of all expression.

This certainly was not the proposal she had hoped for. There was no soft moonlight and certainly no bells ringing. Just a straightforward business deal. She knew Steven didn't love her, and she had known from the start he was a married man, so she had never thought of him in such a way.

"Of course I'd provide for you," Steven said. "I have a pretty good farm, and with a lot of work I think it could pay off. You'd get your room and board and whatever else you needed. I'd provide for you like a wife. I just wouldn't exercise my husbandly rights."

"Steven, you can't be serious. We don't know each other well enough to get married," Emily finally choked out.

"Like I said, I'm not asking you to be my wife. This is strictly a business deal. I'm really just offering you a job. I'm just offering to marry you to make it look respectable."

Stunned by his blunt reply, Emily muttered, "Steven, I don't know what to say. An offer like this needs some thought. Can you give me a little time?"

"I'm leaving early Friday morning. I need to know soon enough to arrange things with the preacher. I'll be back in town Wednesday morning. Can you decide by then?"

"I'll have my answer for you Wednesday."

Emily watched as Steven left the café, got on his horse, and rode off. She couldn't believe she had asked for time to think about his proposal. Why hadn't she just given him an answer then and told him no. What a ridiculous proposition! How could she even consider it?

Sure she wanted to get married, but she was hoping for a better deal than this. Steven wasn't even actually proposing marriage; he just wanted a mother for his children. After being alone all these years, she couldn't see herself raising five children. Wednesday she would just have to say thanks but no.

After the supper crowd was gone and the café cleaned and ready for breakfast the next morning, Emily locked up and went to the boardinghouse. Although Mrs. Jenson, the owner, invited her to play a game of cards, Emily politely refused, saying she was too tired.

She entered her lonely room, which had been her home for almost eight years. It wasn't fancy, but it was clean and comfortable. She had an iron bed frame with a soft mattress. The table by her bed held a white glass lamp with pink roses on the base; beside the lamp sat a picture of her and Jim on their wedding day. She sat on the bed as she picked up the small frame.

Staring at the picture and touching Jim's face, she said in a soft voice, "Oh, if only you hadn't left me. We had such a perfect love. I want that same feeling again. I ache to be loved like you loved me. To know that someone cares about me." Tears began streaming down her face, and with a trembling voice, she continued to speak to the picture. "Jim, I don't want to spend the rest of my life alone. What do I do? I know Steven doesn't love me, and I'm not in love with him, but what if this is my last chance? I don't want to spend the rest of my life alone and lonely. What should I do?"

She was tired and began to get ready for bed, but her mind kept racing. Steven and his unique proposal dominated her thoughts. As she lay in bed, she asked the Lord for guidance. This afternoon as she had stood in the café and watched Steven ride away, she had made up her mind to tell him no. But as she lay in the darkness talking with Jesus, she started to get confused. Surely God couldn't want her to marry a man she barely knew and didn't love.

She lay awake most of the night. *This is crazy,* she thought. *I've got to work tomorrow. I have to get some rest.*

The ache of loneliness continued to fill Emily's being. There were many questions to consider. She and Steven didn't love each other, and that was no basis for a marriage. Emily didn't even know if Steven believed in God. How could she even consider his proposal? Loneliness was the only reason she could come up with to leave Abilene and marry a man with whom she shared no love.

Of course, she wasn't real sure of her future here. Lon Blackstone had mentioned several times lately that he was getting too old to keep running the café. What if he closed it; then what would Emily do? Maybe if she thought of Steven's offer as just a job, she could make a better decision. After all, Steven had made it very clear that it was a job, not a marriage he was offering her.

Emily didn't know what time it was when she finally drifted off to sleep. She was abruptly awakened by a loud knock on her door and a voice yelling, "Emily, are you sick? You're late for work."

Startled, Emily answered, "No, I'm fine, Mrs. Jenson. I just overslept. I'll be down in a minute."

Jumping from the bed, Emily splashed some water on her face and hurriedly dressed. She pulled her hair up in a quick bun and ran out the door. As she walked into the café, Mr. Blackstone, the proprietor, was already frying bacon, and a customer was seated at the counter.

"You're late," Mr. Blackstone smiled. This was the first time in the seven and a half years Emily had worked for him that she hadn't been on time. "Did you have a late date last night?" he asked.

"You know me, always out on the town," she laughed. "I'm sorry I'm late. For some reason I couldn't get to sleep last night."

"Have a lot on your mind, do you?" he questioned.

"Oh, something like that," she answered, turning to the customer seated at the counter. "Can I get you a refill on that coffee, Pete?"

"You need someone to talk to or a shoulder to cry on, Emily?" Lon asked seriously.

"Maybe later." She went to wait on the two gentlemen who had just entered the café.

Emily knew if there was one person in the world she could talk to and count on it was Lon Blackstone. He had been almost like a father to her over the past few years. She knew she could tell him her dilemma, and he would be straightforward and honest with his opinions.

The little café had a very busy day, and Lon stayed until three o'clock, instead of leaving as usual at two. Before he left, he poured two cups of coffee and turned to Emily. "Girl, let's sit down and rest a minute. We deserve it."

After they seated themselves at a table, he looked at Emily and asked, "Care to tell me what's going on?"

"Someone asked me to marry him yesterday." That was the first time she had said it out loud, and it sounded strange.

"That's wonderful! But who is it? I didn't know you were seeing anyone special."

Emily sat quietly without responding to his questions.

"If you don't mind me saying so, you don't seem as excited as a girl should be when she gets a proposal of marriage," Lon observed.

She looked at Lon. "Let me tell you the whole story and please don't say anything until I'm finished."

Lon nodded and Emily cleared her throat as she began. "Steven Barnes came in here yesterday and told me he had just found out his wife had died. He said he has to go back to east Texas to take care of his children. Seems they will become wards of the county if he doesn't get back there soon. Well, he asked me to marry him. Actually, he offered me a job. He wants me to help him raise his children. He said we would get married for appearances only. It would be a marriage in name only."

Lon listened patiently as she finished the story. "What are you going to do?" he asked.

"Right after he left I thought, 'how stupid, why didn't I just tell him no.' I decided right then and there that I would tell him no thanks when he comes back for his answer. But, for some reason I couldn't stop thinking about his proposition. That's why I didn't get any sleep last night."

Lon, a dedicated Christian, asked the question she expected: "Have you prayed about this?"

"Yes, I have," she answered. "And the more I pray, the more confused I become. I have thought about getting married again for a long time. But silly me, I always thought in terms of marrying someone I was in love with. I thought God promoted that idea. One thing I do know for sure, Steven Barnes is not in love with me. I have never thought of him in terms of marriage either. The thought of five children really scares me, too."

Lon looked thoughtful. "God does want there to be love in a marriage. But you said Steven made it very clear that this would be a marriage in name only, that he was really offering you a job. I have known a few couples whose love came after marriage. They got married for some good reason or another without being in love, but the love grew with time."

"So are you saying that if I marry Steven just to help him raise his children, that eventually we might fall in love?"

"That could be a possibility. You know some folks start out in marriage just being friends. As a matter of fact you have to be friends with the person you marry for a marriage to last. Do you like Steven? Are you friends?" Lon asked.

"I like him," Emily responded. "I don't know if you could say we're friends. The only place I've ever seen him is here."

"When do you have to give him your answer?"

"Tomorrow," she replied. "You sound as though you think I should accept."

"Not at all," he stated. "But I do think you should consider all sides. Since you didn't give him an immediate no, then the proposition must not have sounded all bad to you. You said the more you pray about it the more confused you become. Maybe God knows something you don't. Just make the decision you think is right for you, and I'll stand by you all the way. There is something for you to consider—do you know if Steven is a fellow believer?"

"That is a concern; I don't know. But since this is a job and not a marriage, if he isn't a Christian, his children might really need me. They would need someone to instruct them in the ways of the Lord."

Lon left her alone with her thoughts. Emily had really thought Lon Blackstone would think that Steven should be horsewhipped for making such a proposition to her and that she should tell him no thanks! Instead, she was even more troubled, if that were possible. It looked as though it would be another long night in her lonely room.

∞

Late the next afternoon, Emily heard the door open. Looking up from the counter, she saw Steven. Maybe for the first time in all these years, she really looked at him. He stood a little over six foot tall and he had brown hair and blue eyes. He was not the best-looking man she had ever seen, but he wasn't bad, not bad at all.

What was she thinking? She had to keep everything in perspective. She had to remember he didn't want her for his wife, just as a mother for his children.

Steven walked over and sat down on a stool at the counter. "Could I get a cup of coffee?"

"Sure." She wasn't about to say anything first; he had to bring up the subject. With trembling hands, she poured his coffee.

He drank almost the whole cup before he spoke again. "Well, have you thought about my offer?"

"Yes, I have. Actually I have thought of nothing else the past two days," she replied.

"Have you come to a decision?" he asked calmly.

Her heart was pounding and her knees were shaking. She felt as though she was gasping for air. When she finally found her voice, she answered weakly, "I have a couple of questions first."

"Okay, what are they?"

Still with trembling voice, Emily asked, "Steven, are you a Christian?"

Steven drank another sip of coffee and then answered. "I believe in God. Used to even call myself a Christian. But I don't go to church much. Guess I sorta got out of the habit."

That was not the answer Emily had hoped for, but it would have to do. She went on to her next question. "Why are you here and your family still in east Texas?"

"I left to find work," he choked out.

"But why did you never go back home?" Emily pried.

"I kept thinking just a little more time, a little more money to send home. Before I knew it, too much time had gone by, and I wasn't sure I had a home to go to anymore."

"Surely your wife and children wanted you back more than they wanted the money you were sending," Emily suggested.

Steven looked aggravated. "Don't be too sure of that. Are you concerned about my leaving you someday?"

"To be honest, that did cross my mind. I'm not sure I'd want to be left alone with children that weren't mine."

Reaching into his jeans pocket, Steven pulled out a wad of bills and shoved them across the counter to Emily. "That's my month's wages. Take it and put it away. You can use it for a little security. I know I can't convince you that I would never dump my kids on you, but at least that would be enough to get you by for a few weeks. As soon as we get back to east Texas, I'll have the judge draw up papers as to who will care for the children in the event of my death or disappearance. Does that ease your fears?"

"I guess so," Emily mumbled. "But you don't have to give me this money. I know you'll probably need it for the trip."

"No, you keep it. I hope I've answered enough questions." Steven sounded agitated. "Now, are you going to accept the job or not?"

Emily hesitated just a moment, then answered, "Yes, Steven. I'll accept the job and I will marry you."

She had said it! She had accepted his proposal. She could hardly believe her ears. Had she really told Steven Barnes she would marry him?

His expression never changed. "I'll go talk to the preacher and see if he can marry us tomorrow. Can you be ready to leave early Friday morning?"

"Sure, I guess so."

He never said I'm glad you said yes or even thank you. It really didn't seem to matter at all to him one way or the other. She hadn't expected him to kiss her or even embrace her, but he could have at least smiled. Instead she got nothing!

"I'll be back after I talk to the preacher to let you know what time the ceremony will be," he stated as he walked out the door.

Emily had to sit down before she fell down. Her knees were about to buckle under her, and the butterflies in her stomach must have turned into birds. Really big birds. She couldn't believe she had actually said yes. Well, there was still time to change her mind.

She was still sitting down when Steven returned a few minutes later.

"The circuit judge is in town. I ran into him on my way to the preacher's. In light of the circumstances of our marriage, I decided to ask him to perform the ceremony. Is that okay with you? He can do it about three o'clock tomorrow."

Still in a state of shock, Emily replied, "That's fine with me. Where will the ceremony be held?"

"That's a problem," he said. "There isn't a courthouse here, so I guess we'll have to use the sheriff's office. It really doesn't matter. Do you want me to pick you up here or at your boardinghouse?"

"The boardinghouse, I guess," she responded. "I'll go and talk with Lon now and tell him I'm quitting. I sure hate to leave him in a bind, but maybe he'll understand."

"I'll see you tomorrow about fifteen till three," was all Steven said before he left.

Emily closed the café and walked over to the Blackstones'. As she walked, she tried to sort out her feelings. She didn't know what to say to these people. They had been so good to her. She sure hated not being able to give them more notice. She knew they would be happy for her if she were truly in love, but as it was, she couldn't explain why she was marrying Steven. Loneliness was the only explanation.

Emily arrived at the house, summoned up her courage, and finally knocked on the door. "Emily, my dear, do come in. What brings you by here tonight?" Helen asked as she invited Emily into her home.

By this time Lon had come into the room. Emily made herself as comfortable as she could on the sofa, then she began. "I have come to share some news with you." She tried as best she could to put a smile on her face and enthusiasm into her voice when she added, "I'm getting married."

"Oh my dear, that's wonderful! Who is the lucky fellow?" Helen wanted to know. When Emily didn't immediately reply, Helen added, "I didn't know you were seeing anyone."

Shyly, Emily began to explain. "It's Steven Barnes. He asked me to marry him, and I accepted. The problem is, we're getting married tomorrow, and then we're leaving early Friday morning for east Texas. I'm so sorry I couldn't give you more notice. You two have been so good to me; I really hate leaving you in a bind."

"This is all very sudden, isn't it? I didn't know you and Steven had feelings for one another. You never mentioned it," remarked Helen.

Lon had not said a word. "I might as well tell you the whole story," Emily said. "Steven asked me to marry him so I could go and help him raise his children. It seems his wife recently passed away, and now he's left with the task of being a father and a mother. As you know, he hasn't even been a father lately. I guess he just didn't want to face them alone, so he asked me to help him. This will be a marriage in name only. I am to help with the children and take care of the house."

"It seems to me those are jobs he could have hired someone to do. He didn't have to marry himself a nanny and housekeeper," Helen angrily stated.

"Actually Helen, he did hire someone to do those jobs—me. The marriage is just for appearances," Emily informed her.

"But—" Helen began before Lon cut her off.

"Helen, that's enough. I know Emily has considered this very carefully. I know she feels she's doing what's right for her. What time is the wedding?" he inquired. "We'd like to be at the church to see you married—if that's okay?"

"There is no one I'd rather have at my wedding than the two of you," Emily answered. "The wedding is at three tomorrow afternoon, but it isn't going to be at the church. Steven thought under the circumstances he'd ask the circuit judge to marry us. The ceremony's going to be in the sheriff's office."

"At the sheriff's office!" Helen exclaimed. "That will never do! Lon, you get in touch with that judge and tell him the wedding will be here. At least a living room is more pleasant than a sheriff's office. I'm sorry, Emily. I know I'm butting in, but we'd love for you to be married in our home."

"Oh Helen, that would be so wonderful. It would be a lot nicer and warmer here. Thank you so much," Emily said with tears in her eyes.

"Lon, you find the judge and tell him about the change in plans," Helen instructed.

"I'll tell him. I know where to find him. He always stays at the same place. You don't worry about a thing, Emily. Helen and I will take care of every detail. You just bring Steven over here."

"You don't think Steven will mind the change in plans, do you?" Helen asked, with concern in her voice.

Emily looked at her and replied, "I don't think so. But after all, it is my wedding, too. I should at least get to pick the place for the ceremony. You two are so wonderful. How can I ever repay you for your kindness?"

"Kindness never has to be repaid," Lon stated. "You just be happy. That's all we want for you."

Emily hugged both her friends and left. She would have never made it these last seven and a half years if it hadn't been for Lon and Helen. Not only had they given her a job, but they had been like parents to her. She would miss them terribly.

∞

Back in her room at the boardinghouse, she began to load her few personal belongings into her trunk. Mrs. Jenson had been very surprised to hear her news. She'd wished Emily well and even refunded the balance of her month's rent as a wedding gift.

Emily had very few possessions, and she didn't need long to pack. She didn't know where she would be spending tomorrow night. Steven hadn't mentioned it. She figured she would stay here, but just in case, she would be packed and ready to go. She laid out her best blue dress to be married in. This was nothing like her first wedding when she was so in love.

She had hardly been able to wait to marry Jim. He was her handsome prince and loved her with all his heart. She had been sure of that. She had worn a traditional white dress, and her father had walked her down the church aisle. It had been a wonderful day.

Her mother wasn't there, for she had died when Emily was a baby. Her father had never remarried, and he passed away just a year after her marriage to Jim. Still, she and Jim had a wonderful but short marriage. They had shared only five years together, but she had been left with nothing but happy memories. It seemed those memories would have to last a lifetime now. She was sure there would be no happy memories made tomorrow.

∞

Emily was awakened by the sun shining through the window onto her face. She didn't know how long it had been since she had slept this late. Of course she had no idea what time she had finally fallen asleep; she hadn't slept much in the last two nights.

She got up and washed her hair so it would have plenty of time to dry. She had decided to try to fix it a little special today. Although it wouldn't matter to Steven, it might make her feel better.

Mrs. Jenson was more than willing to help, but there was nothing Emily could think of for her to do. They spent the morning visiting together, but Emily couldn't bring herself to tell Mrs. Jenson all the details of her marriage. She loved her, but she knew Mae Jenson was one of the biggest gossips in town. Emily let her think that she and Steven had a mutual affection for each other and had decided to get married since he was having to leave town. Mae thought Emily was very noble for having said yes to a man with so many children.

After lunch, Emily went upstairs to dress and work on her hair. She fixed it, looked at it, then took it down and tried again. After a couple more tries, she noticed it was getting late. This time would have to do.

When she put the last pin in, she admired her handiwork. She had pulled most of her hair up but had let some soft curls fall around her face. The outcome was rather flattering. No one except Jim had ever accused her of being pretty, much less beautiful, but today she didn't look half bad.

She put on her dress and made a final inspection, pleased with what she saw. She would try to feel good about herself, no matter what happened today.

Mrs. Jenson called to her from the foot of the stairs. Knowing Steven must have arrived, Emily took a deep breath and started down the steps.

He was waiting for her in the parlor.

"You look lovely," Mrs. Jenson said, giving Emily a hug. "I wish you and Steven the best."

Steven looked on and said nothing. Finally he told Mae good-bye, then turned to Emily. "We'd better be going."

He opened the door, and Emily walked out into the sunlight. Once outside and safely out of earshot of Mae, Emily said, "There's been a small change in plans. The wedding is going to be in the home of Lon and Helen Blackstone. When I went over there last night to tell them I was leaving, they just insisted. I hope you don't mind."

"No, that's fine with me. You did tell the judge, didn't you?" he asked.

"Lon said he would take care of that for us."

They walked the rest of the way in silence. Emily was praying the entire time, *God, please let me be making the right decision.*

Lon greeted them at the door, extending his hand to Steven. "Congratulations, Steven. You're getting a wonderful girl."

Steven shook his hand and thanked him weakly. Emily noticed the vase of fresh flowers on the mantel, and from the fragrance in the air, she detected that Helen had baked this morning. Emily certainly hoped they hadn't gone to a lot of trouble. She didn't know how Steven would react.

The judge was already there waiting for them. Steven turned to him and said, "I guess it's time we get started."

"An eager bridegroom. I've never met a man yet that wasn't in a hurry to get the wedding ceremony over," the judge teased. He walked over and stood in front of the mantel. "If you two would just stand in front of me here, we'll get started."

Emily was in a daze, not from happiness but from fright. She still couldn't believe she was doing this. But she must have answered all the judge's questions to his satisfaction, although she didn't really hear what he was saying. When the judge asked Steven for the ring, Steven's face went pale. Getting a ring had never crossed his mind. Emily saw his despair and discretely slipped the small gold band that Jim had given her off her hand, then handed it to Steven. He in turn handed it to the judge, who was somewhat bewildered by this time. The judge continued with the ceremony, and Steven slipped the ring on her hand. Then came those words: "By the authority vested in me by the state of Texas, I now pronounce you husband and wife. You may kiss your bride."

What would Steven do now? Just ignore it, shake her hand, what? To Emily's surprise, he leaned down and kissed her lightly on the cheek. Her stomach did flips. She was completely amazed that his faint kiss could do that to her. Emily reminded herself she had to keep her emotions in check. This was not a true marriage, and she must not forget that.

"I hope you two don't mind, but I took the liberty of making a small cake and fixing some punch," Helen announced. "If you'll excuse me, I'll go get it."

"May I help you?" Emily asked anxiously.

"I'd be delighted for you to keep me company in the kitchen if you'd like," Helen answered.

Once in the kitchen, though, Emily sat down. She was relieved to have the ceremony over and to be away from Steven for a moment.

"You shouldn't have gone to so much trouble for us, Helen," said Emily. "But I really do appreciate it. You have made this day much more pleasant."

"You are very welcome, my child. I'm just so sorry that this day isn't more special for you in every way," Helen remarked. "Now let's go join the menfolk and enjoy some of my cake."

The cake and punch were delicious. The conversation on the other hand was lacking. The judge excused himself as soon as he finished his refreshments. Lon then began questioning Steven about east Texas and his farm. Emily learned for the first time that his place was near a town called Tyler. Steven said Tyler was about the same size as Abilene. She also learned that it would take them almost two weeks to get there. At least now she had a little more information about her future.

Steven announced that it was time to leave and turned to Emily to ask, "Would you like me to walk you back to the boardinghouse or do you want to stay and visit with your friends for a while?"

"I think I'll just stay here," she said, fighting back the tears. He seemed so cold and unfeeling.

"Okay. I'll pick you up at sunup in the morning." He thanked Lon and Helen for their hospitality and left. He said no more to Emily.

It was a few moments before Emily could gain her composure and speak. "I want to thank you both again for everything you've done. I'll be going now. I just wanted to say good-bye to you in private."

Lon wished Emily well, gave her a big hug, and walked into the kitchen. Helen just stood there a moment before she spoke. "I'm afraid you've cut a very rough road out for yourself. Please remember we love you and are here for you if you ever need us. I know Steven said he didn't expect you to be a wife to him, but you'll be on the road for almost two weeks. You never know what can happen in that length of time. You take care of yourself and be prepared for anything."

"I believe Steven will hold true to his word about this being a business deal instead of a marriage. I'll just take it one day at a time and leave it all in the Lord's hands," Emily assured her. "I love you both, and as soon as we get there, I'll write you. I'll send you my address because I expect you to keep in touch." Emily hugged her friend, then turned and walked out the door.

She could no longer hold back the tears as she walked toward the boardinghouse. She wondered what people would think about a bride staying alone on her wedding night. This was not the normal chain of events, but this had not been the normal wedding.

∽

Back at the boardinghouse, Mae inquired if her husband would be joining her later.

"No," Emily replied, trying desperately to hide the fact that she had been crying. "He still has some things he has to finish up at the ranch. We'll be leaving at first light in the morning. I probably won't see you then, so let me say good-bye now. Thank you for everything you've done for me. You've always gone above and beyond a landlady's call of duty."

They wished each other farewell, then Emily walked up the stairs to her lonely room one last time. It was early, but she was very tired and didn't feel like eating any supper. As she changed into her night clothes, the tears that had just started to flow on the walk home began to come in a storm now. She couldn't remember ever feeling so lost and alone; no one should feel this way on their wedding day, or any day for that matter. Lying across the bed, she sobbed and tried to pray, but the words would not come. Night had fallen when she finally drifted into a restless sleep.

CHAPTER 2

Emily awoke with a start, disoriented for a moment. She shook her head and wiped her eyes to clear the cobwebs away. Maybe she had just had a bad dream. But no, letting her eyes open, she realized she was in her room at Mrs. Jenson's boardinghouse. And the cold hard fact was that she was married to Steven Barnes.

She stood and walked over to the window. Gazing out over the sleepy little town, everything looked the same. Nothing much ever changed here, but she knew her life was changing completely.

The sun was just barely appearing over the horizon, and she knew Steven would be there soon. She still couldn't believe she was Mrs. Steven Barnes. Her stomach churned. She couldn't remember ever being this frightened. *God,* she prayed, *please give me strength for whatever lies ahead.*

Hearing a buckboard pull up, she raced down the stairs, hoping to let Steven in without waking Mrs. Jenson. As she reached the bottom of the stairs, however, she heard Mae greet Steven.

"Come in, Steven," Mae was saying. "You certainly are out early this morning. I guess you're anxious to pick up your bride and be on your way."

"Yes'm, I am. We have a long trip ahead of us. Is Emily up?" he asked.

"I'm here. I heard you pull up." Emily came into the hallway. "Mae, I'm sorry we got you up so early."

"You didn't wake me," Mae replied. "I wanted to see you off. I have breakfast ready if you'll eat a bite."

"You shouldn't have gone to all that trouble," Steven responded. "I had something before I left the ranch."

Mrs. Jenson turned to Emily. "Well, you haven't eaten, and you need something in your stomach before you start off on such a long trip."

Emily could tell by Steven's expression that he didn't want to wait while she ate breakfast. And as nervous as she felt, she was afraid that food would just make her sick. She turned to Mae and tried to smile and sound excited. "You really shouldn't have gone to so much trouble. I'm so excited this morning, I'm afraid I couldn't eat a thing."

"I'll tell you what I'll do. I'll just wrap up some biscuits and bacon for you to take. You may get hungry in a couple of hours." Mae headed for the kitchen.

"That would be wonderful," Emily said. "Steven, I'll show you where my trunk is." They turned and started for the stairs.

Emily opened the door to her room and pointed to her trunk. "Is this all you have?" Steven asked.

Emily chuckled and said, "Yeah, I travel light."

Steven apparently failed to notice the humor in her statement, as he ignored her. *This is going to be a very long trip,* Emily thought to herself.

Steven picked up her trunk and left. Emily looked around one last time, then walked out and closed the door. She silently said farewell to Emily Johnson and hello to Emily Barnes. Whoever Emily Barnes was or would turn out to be was still unknown.

Mrs. Jenson was waiting on the front porch with a small basket. Emily hugged her, thanking her for all she had done.

Steven looked impatient when Emily finally walked out to the wagon. He helped her up onto the seat and then climbed up beside her. Popping the reins, he started the horses down the street. Emily turned and waved good-bye to Mrs. Jenson and to her life in Abilene.

The March morning was clear and bright as they started their journey. A nice breeze was blowing, and Emily was grateful that they were traveling now rather than during the blazing hot summer. After they had traveled several miles, however, Steven still had not said a word. Emily tried to decide how to start a conversation with him.

"How long do you think it will take us to get to your place?" asked Emily.

"Barring any trouble, and if we don't have to stop too many times, we should be there in about twelve days," he replied.

"Tell me about the place. What's it like?" Emily hoped this question would lead to more than a one-line answer.

"Not much to tell. It's a farm."

Emily was very frustrated. She could not bear sitting next to this man for twelve days in this wagon and not at least be able to carry on some kind of conversation. She continued to ask questions, and he continued to give as brief answers as possible. Finally the sun was high in the sky. Her stomach was beginning to let her know that she hadn't sent it any food since the wedding cake and punch yesterday.

"It must be about noon," Steven finally said. "I guess we can stop and rest a spell and have a bite to eat. I need to water the horses."

"That would be wonderful," Emily replied. "I would really like to stretch my legs. And I am getting hungry."

There weren't a lot of trees in this part of Texas, but they stopped near a small patch of grass by the side of the road. Emily was glad for time to walk around. Steven said he was going to take a walk down the road a little piece, and Emily decided that was very considerate, since it allowed her a little time to herself.

By the time Steven returned, she had spread a blanket in the small shade cast by the wagon and gotten out the food that Mae Jenson had fixed. Steven sat down on the edge of the blanket and helped himself to a biscuit without saying a word. She wondered if it was her or if it was just the time and place; maybe he was so used to spending time alone out on the range that he had forgotten how to converse with another human being.

The afternoon was the same as the morning: They rode in silence. It would have at least been nice if she could have enjoyed the view, but there wasn't much to see here, for the land was flat and empty. Occasionally she would see a jack-rabbit or a tumbleweed would blow by, but that was about as exciting as it got. It was a long afternoon, and Emily decided she would have to find some way to occupy her time or she would go crazy before they arrived in east Texas.

At sundown, Steven stopped for the night. He gathered wood for a fire, and Emily started to prepare supper. She fixed a small stew, and they enjoyed it with the last of the biscuits from Mae. Much to her surprise, Steven did tell her the stew was good.

"You can sleep here," Steven said, laying out a bedroll close to the wagon. "I'll be over there if you need me." He walked over about fifty feet and laid out the other bedroll.

Emily pulled her Bible out of her trunk and sat down. She was reading the Bible through as she had done several times before, and tonight's passage was Psalm 23. The verses had never meant so much to her or seemed so real. Tonight she thought she knew just what David had felt when he wrote this psalm; this trip was like walking through "the valley of the shadow of death." David couldn't have felt any lonelier when he wrote those words than she was feeling right now. *Lord, please be my Shepherd,* Emily prayed. *Please follow me all the days of my life.*

⚭

Every day was the same. Emily tried desperately to carry on a conversation and each time failed miserably. She had known loneliness before, but nothing compared to what she was feeling now. Emily realized that loneliness seemed to intensify when you were with someone who apparently didn't want to be with you.

To occupy her time, she began to keep a journal, recording her thoughts and observations along the way. On day seven of their journey, she observed that at least the scenery was beginning to change. There were trees along the roadside and a lot of grass. The green was beautiful, and the wildflowers added a sprinkle of color here and there.

Emily had been so caught up making entries in her journal that she almost didn't realize Steven was speaking. "We should get to Fort Worth late this afternoon. I thought we would get a hotel room and spend the night there if that's okay with you."

Emily couldn't believe her ears: Steven was talking to her! She was sure he didn't actually want her opinion, since she knew he had already made up his mind. "That sounds great to me!" she responded almost too enthusiastically. "To tell you the truth, it won't hurt my feelings at all to get to sleep in a real bed for a night. And a bath sounds like heaven."

They arrived in Fort Worth about four-thirty that afternoon. The town was bigger and busier than Abilene, with lots of shops and, of course, a saloon or two. Steven stopped the wagon in front of the hotel, then helped her down, and they walked inside. It wasn't fancy, but it did look clean and well-cared for.

After Steven registered, Emily followed him up the stairs and into a room. She looked at the big double bed. One room, one bed.

"I'll go get your trunk and bring it up." Steven started toward the door.

"There's no need to bring the whole trunk," Emily replied. "There's a small blue cloth bag on top that has everything in it that I'll need."

Steven was back in just minutes with the bag Emily requested. "I'm going to take the wagon to the livery stable and get the horses taken care of. The clerk said the bath was two doors down, and he already had the girl fill the tub with clean hot water. You get cleaned up, and I'll be back later."

Steven left, and Emily immediately headed to the bath. She locked the door and took off her clothes. Quickly, she climbed into the tub. She couldn't remember ever having felt so dirty, and it was heavenly to sit in a tub of hot water. She lay back in the tub and closed her eyes.

She couldn't help but wonder about the one room and the one bed. What did Steven have in mind? He had talked to her more since their arrival here than he had the whole trip. Could he have decided that he would exercise his rights as a husband after all? He certainly had made no attempt out on the trail. What would make him decide to now? She couldn't help but be a little nervous about it, but right now a bath and getting her hair washed was all she cared about.

When she got back to her room, the bed looked so inviting she decided to stretch out for a little while. She didn't know how long she'd been asleep, when she heard a knock at the door. Sleepily she asked, "Who is it?"

"Steven," answered the voice from the other side. "May I come in?"

She walked over and quietly replied through the closed door, "Steven, I'm sorry. I fell asleep. I'm not dressed."

"Well, I'll be in the dining room. Why don't you get dressed and join me there," he invited.

"That would be nice. I won't be long."

She listened as he walked away. *Did he just ask for my company,* she wondered. *Don't be silly, he just knows you have to eat, and you can't very well cook for yourself in a hotel room.* Emily dismissed her thoughts as she hurriedly dressed and fixed her hair. She looked in the mirror and was not too displeased with what she saw. Seven days on the road had given her a rosy complexion.

She walked into the dining room and saw Steven sitting at a table alone. As she approached the table, he stood and pulled a chair out for her. She noted he did have good manners and also that he had taken a bath and shaved. She couldn't help but notice how nice he looked, and she got that strange feeling again. A kind of nervous, jittery feeling. When she came back to reality, she realized the waitress had approached and Steven was giving her his order.

"Emily, what would you like?" Steven asked.

"Oh, a steak sounds good to me, too," she replied, then added, "with potatoes and greens."

The waitress left, and Emily looked around the room. "This is a nice place. It's much larger than our little café back home and much nicer."

"I guess so," Steven stated. "I just hope the food is as good. I hate to spend money on bad food."

Emily watched him for a moment and realized he appeared as nervous as she felt. Her mind began to play tricks on her. Did Steven get the same little funny feelings she got from time to time? Could he be thinking about her as a woman?

Stop it, Emily, she thought to herself. *You knew from the start this was not a real marriage. Don't start kidding yourself now. He's never given the slightest indication that he's interested in you as a woman. Yet he did get just one room with one bed, and after all he is a man. . . .* She was once again lost in her own dream world when the food arrived.

They exchanged very few pleasantries over their meal. The food was good, and Emily just enjoyed the fact that she didn't have to cook or clean up afterwards.

"How much farther to your farm?" Emily asked.

"It's still about a five-day journey from here," he replied. Looking at his watch, he noted, "It's getting late, and we need to get an early start in the morning. I'll see you to the room."

Steven pulled her chair out, and she stood and started toward the door. That funny feeling was back again. Was he just walking her to the door or was he planning on going through the door? Her hands were sweating and her knees were weak. Her heart was racing like crazy. She could handle sleeping fifty feet from him in the wide open spaces, but sleeping only a few feet or possibly a few inches from him was something else entirely. Why was she feeling this way? *This is not a marriage—it's a job,* Emily reminded herself. She had never had any special feelings for Steven Barnes. He was just a man who came into the café from time to time. Why was she feeling this way now? Maybe simply because it had been a terribly long time since a man had held her in his arms, and she ached to be held and loved again.

They arrived at the door, her heart still pounding. What should she do? What was he going to do? "You get a good night's rest, and I'll call for you first thing in the morning," Steven said. "Be sure and lock the door," he added as he walked away.

Emily walked inside and locked the door. *How stupid of me,* Emily thought. *Of course Steven had no intentions of coming into the room and staying the night. The man barely speaks to me.* She slowly got ready for bed, on the verge of tears, though she really didn't know why. Was she relieved he didn't come in? Or was she disappointed?

She lay in bed and tried to figure out what was going on with her. All those years she had known Steven, she had thought of him as a married man and therefore unavailable. She had never looked at him with romantic eyes— but now she was married to him. Although he had made it perfectly clear that theirs was a marriage in name only, her lonely heart apparently had not totally accepted that.

She remembered her marriage to Jim and how much in love they had been. She remembered how very special those first few days and weeks were and how they could not get enough of each other. That was the only standard for marriage she had, and this was nothing like that. She guessed her heart just remembered and wanted that kind of relationship again, but she seriously doubted she would ever know that kind of love with Steven Barnes. Apparently, it would take a miracle to even get him to carry on a conversation with her.

She would just have to make sure she kept her emotions in check so she would not get hurt. She would learn to be as indifferent as Steven and remember that this was a job, not a marriage.

∞

Emily awoke early the next morning, glad to have slept in a real bed. She knew she had the cold, hard ground to look forward to for the next few nights.

She was dressed and ready to go when Steven knocked on the door. "Good morning," she said as she opened the door. "Did you sleep well?"

"Morning," he replied. "I slept okay. Are you ready to go?" His usual impatience was showing.

"All ready," she answered, trying to keep a happy tone in her voice.

"Thought we'd get a bite of breakfast before we head out," he offered. He picked up her bag and led the way to the dining room.

They had eggs, bacon, and biscuits with cream gravy for breakfast, a hearty meal that left Emily stuffed. When they walked outside, the wagon and team were waiting, and they began the day's journey.

∞

The scenery was getting prettier. More greenery and more trees. The day went by as the days before had.

On the morning of the eleventh day, Emily asked, "Steven, tell me about the children. I'd like to know a little bit about what to expect."

He sat quietly for a few minutes, then he cleared his throat and began. "It's been five years since I've seen them, you know." Emily sat quietly and let him continue. "The oldest is Matthew. He'd be about sixteen now, a man. Probably he has been doing a lot of the work around the farm. I figure he's been the man of the house. The next boy is Mark. My wife—Becky—had a thing for Bible names. Mark's fourteen. He was always real quiet, liked to read a lot. Then there's Luke and John. They're twins. Luke is the leader of the two, John follows him. When you see one of them, you see them both. They're ten. Then comes Sarah. I guess she's seven now. She was just a baby when I left. I can't tell you much about her. She was the spitting image of her momma the last time I saw her. Becky told me in her last letter that Sarah really liked school."

Steven sat quietly. Emily thought she had seen a couple of tears run down his cheek as he talked about his children. She knew he had left to find work, but why had he stayed away so long? Would she ever learn the answer to that question and all the other questions she had about this man? She could see a lot of hurt on his face. Possibly a lot of regret. All she could do for him at this point was pray for him, and maybe God would heal the hurt. She knew she had to pray for the children, too. She wasn't sure what she had gotten herself into, but she knew whatever lay ahead would not be easy for any of them. Emily pulled out her pad and pencil and began to write.

Day 11
 Steven told me about the children today. I am very nervous about the prospect of becoming caretaker of five children. I wonder what they will think of me. This is the most frightening thing I have ever faced thus far in my life. I hope I never face anything worse. According to Steven's time-table, we should be arriving in Tyler tomorrow. So I will have to face the five judges either tomorrow or the next day. I pray for God's guidance and comfort.

⬭

Late in the afternoon, they came into the small town of Tyler. Steven turned to Emily and explained, "We're gonna spend the night here. It's about a half day's ride from here to the farm. I thought we could stay here and get cleaned up so we would be presentable when we get there. I also have to let the judge know I'm back and am gonna assume full responsibility for my kids."

Steven checked them into a hotel. It was much smaller than the one in Fort Worth, but it was clean. Once again Emily got to soak herself in a nice tub of hot water. She just sat and relaxed, for she knew, starting tomorrow, her life would change. She wasn't sure it would be for the better.

"God, give me the courage to get through tomorrow," she prayed. "I lift Steven and all five of his children up to You. Give us all the courage to survive whatever lies ahead."

CHAPTER 3

The wagon came to a stop. The house was large, with a front porch that stretched the length of the house. A swing hung on one end of the porch, and firewood was stacked on the other. The house looked as though it had never been painted. Toys were scattered across the yard's patches of grass, and a lone rosebush stood at the end of the porch. The one redeeming factor was a large oak tree beside the house that would shade it from the hot afternoon sun.

Emily looked around, realizing that everything familiar was gone from her life. Here she sat in front of a strange house, beside a man she hardly knew, about to embark on a life filled with uncertainty. The trip had been a long one, and it seemed years, not weeks, since they left Abilene. Now, sitting in front of this dark house in east Texas, she wondered once again if she had made the right decision.

The front screen door opened and out walked five children, their eyes fixed on the wagon, their faces cold. There was not a smile among them. Steven helped Emily down from the wagon and then opened the gate. As she walked toward the porch, no one said a word.

A heavyset woman stepped out the door, her hair pulled back in a bun, her face lined by years of hard work. She dried her hands on her apron as she spoke. "Heard you were coming home. You're a little late, don't you think?" She turned and walked back into the house.

Steven looked at his children. His faced showed sheer terror. Emily could tell he had no idea what to say or do.

The terrible silence was finally broken by Sarah. "Are you our daddy?" she asked.

Steven cleared his throat and with an unsteady voice answered, "Yes, I am, Sarah. My, how you've grown. You're a beautiful young lady now."

He then spoke to Luke and John and received a quiet hello and weak handshake from each of them. Steven extended his hand to Mark. "Hello, Mark. It's good to see you." Mark stood still and stared at his father.

Matthew finally spoke. "Are you here to stay or just passing through?" His tone was bitter.

"I'm here to stay," Steven replied. He hesitated, chewing on his lip. "I—I'm sorry about your mother. I would like for all of you to meet Miss Emily

Johnson. She has come to take care of you."

Emily couldn't believe her ears. How could he be so cruel as to say sorry about your mother, here's someone to replace her, all in the same breath? And what was that he called her, Emily Johnson? He hadn't even introduced her as his wife. Well, that was fine with her.

"Hello, children, I'm happy to meet each one of you," Emily said.

The children never moved and never said a word. They looked as though the wind had been knocked out of them, as though their world had just come to an end.

Emily glanced around as they entered the house. Some of the furnishings had obviously been in the family for years. The place had a homey atmosphere, and some people would probably find it cozy and welcoming. But Emily didn't. She didn't know if she would ever feel welcome in this house.

"Come on, I'll show you where the kitchen and the washstand are so you can freshen up," Steven said.

Emily followed close behind him. In the kitchen she saw the plump lady from the brief encounter on the front porch.

"Emily, I'd like for you to meet Alice Bentley. Alice, this is Emily Johnson. Emily will be taking care of the kids."

"Pleased to meet you, Miss Johnson," Alice responded. Then looking at Steven, she asked, "If she's gonna take care of the kids, what are you gonna do?"

"I'm gonna see if I can make a go of this farm and support this family," Steven answered sharply.

"Do you know how many times Rebecca prayed that she would hear those words from you?" Alice asked. "No, you don't, because you haven't been around. She worked herself into an early grave trying to hold on to this place, waiting for the day you would come home. Well, now you're here, but she's not here to see it." Alice turned to stir the pot on the stove.

Steven's face reddened. He turned to Emily and said, "Through that door on the back porch you should find water and a wash pan."

Emily left the room, and Steven sucked in a deep breath. He turned to Alice and stated firmly, "I don't have to explain anything to you or anyone else. What happened was between me and Becky. I'm back. I will resume my role as father and head of this household. Is that understood?"

"Oh, I understand you all right. I just don't think you understand. Those kids have lost the only parent they have known. They don't know you or that woman you've brought here to raise them. The job will require a lot of patience, care, and understanding. I've never seen much of that in you. I can't judge her; I don't know her." Alice kept right on preparing dinner.

"You don't know me either," Steven remarked as he walked out on the back porch. He turned to Emily and said, "See if you can help Alice with dinner. I'm gonna unhitch the team." As he walked away, Steven tried to hide the tears he knew were filling his eyes.

∽

"Can I help you with anything, Mrs. Bentley?" Emily asked.

"The name's Alice. You can peel those potatoes if you like. Tell me about yourself, Emily."

"There's not much to tell. I've been a widow for eight years. I was working in a café in Abilene when I met Ste—I mean Mr. Barnes," Emily answered.

"When did you and Steven get married?" Alice inquired.

Emily dropped the potato she was peeling and turned as white as a sheet. She finally found her voice and replied, "What makes you think we're married?"

"That little gold band on your hand for one thing. And, no matter what I think of Steven, he isn't going to bring an unmarried woman into this house to live with him and his children and cause more gossip," Alice answered. "Of course there will be talk that Steven brought a new bride home when his wife was barely cold in her grave."

Emily could tell that was Alice's opinion, and she couldn't blame her. She didn't know why she hadn't thought of that sooner. Of course people would think she was the reason Steven didn't come home to his family. They would think she was a home wrecker, that Steven had met her while he was away, and they had probably lived in sin.

"It's not what you think," Emily began. "We are married, but in name only. Steven used to come into the café a couple of times a month and drink coffee. We'd pass the time of day, but that's all. I hardly know him. There was nothing between us before our marriage, and there has been nothing between us since. He married me, but only so I would come here and take care of the house and help raise the children. I'm not sure we're even married in name, since he introduced me as Emily Johnson."

"If it's not love, what made you marry him and come all this way to raise five kids you don't even know?" Alice asked.

With a faraway look in her eye, Emily said, "I don't know. I have asked myself that a million times over the last couple of weeks. I guess part of it, or maybe all of it, was loneliness—and the fact that it's not really a marriage but a job. I'm a nanny and a housekeeper, with just the title of wife."

Emily paused; she didn't know how much she should share with this woman, but for some reason she decided to continue. "I have no children and no family, just me. For the first few years after Jim died, I didn't want to find anyone. I had been so in love with him, I didn't think I could ever love anyone else again. But, after a time I began to long for someone in my life. But for some reason I remained alone. I had begun to resign myself to the fact that there would never be anyone for me. I guess when Steven made me his proposition, I thought this might be my last chance at having a family and not dying a lonely old woman."

"I'm afraid you've cut a very rough row to hoe for yourself. It's hard enough raising children with two parents who love each other and support each other. I'll just have to pray extra hard for each one of you," Alice said.

"I know prayer is the only thing that will help this situation." Emily sighed. To change the subject, she asked, "Tell me something about yourself, Alice."

"I've been a neighbor and friend of the Barneses since they first moved here about fifteen years ago. Matt was just a baby. I helped deliver the other four. Rebecca Barnes was one of the finest women I've ever known. I love these kids just like my own grandchildren. I've been helping out ever since Rebecca got sick. My husband and boys have helped out around the farm ever since Steven left."

Alice paused and turned the chicken she had frying on the stove, then continued. "I've been taking care of the kids since Rebecca died, but the county decided since I wasn't blood kin, they'd have to step in and take over. That's when Steven was contacted."

Very timidly Emily asked, "Tell me about Steven."

"I'm afraid anything I tell you will be biased," Alice said, "but here goes. As I said, they moved here about fifteen years ago. They tried to make a go of the place and for the first few years did pretty good. Then I don't know just what happened. We had a drought one year and their crops failed. They had the five kids, and I think it was just more than Steven could take."

Alice took a sip of coffee, then continued. "There seemed to be a change in Steven about that time. He had seemed like a pretty happy fellow, but he got to where he was gloomy all the time. They say you don't know what goes on behind closed doors, but I don't see how anyone could not have loved Rebecca. Anyway, Steven just up and left one day. Rebecca said he had gone to find work, and just as soon as they got a little ahead, he'd be back. That was five years ago. I never heard her say one bad word about the man in all that time. She'd just say he was doing the best he could."

"I knew he had a family," Emily remembered, "but he never spoke much about them. He never spoke much about anything. Our conversations usually consisted of the weather and local events."

Alice looked at the clock. "We'd better get dinner on the table or those kids will be starving."

∽

Out in the barn, Steven had unhitched and fed the team. Now he just sat there on a bale of hay with his head in his hands, tears running down his cheeks.

Lord, I have no earthly idea what to do. I don't know if You even hear me after all I've done. I deserted my family, and now after all this time I have to be a father to my kids. How can I expect them to respect me after what I've done to them? I don't ask anything for myself, Lord, but show me what to do for the kids.

How long had it been since he prayed? He wasn't a church-going man. Oh, he had gone on occasion, and he did believe in God. As a boy he had followed Christ, but he hadn't prayed in years. Now it seemed the only thing he could do.

He thought about his situation. Why did he marry Emily and bring her here? What on earth could he have been thinking? He didn't know her and his kids certainly didn't. But it had seemed like a good idea at the time. He knew she was a good woman and a God-fearing woman. But why Emily? Why didn't he just wait until he got here and then find someone to help out around the house and with the kids? Maybe somebody that the kids knew. He had just made everything harder by bringing her. But it was too late now. He would just have to make the best of a bad situation.

He had made things clear to Emily that this was a marriage in name only. She shouldn't expect him to be a husband to her, and he wouldn't expect her to be a wife to him. He doubted he could ever be a husband to anyone again, not after he had failed so miserably with Becky. He had lived with the guilt of being a poor husband and father for so long it had become a permanent companion to him.

His next step would be to tell the kids that Emily was his wife. He didn't know why he hadn't told them up front, but now he had no choice. He knew they wouldn't take it well—but then they weren't going to take anything about this situation well. He heard the dinner bell and slowly headed toward the house.

The kitchen table was long, with chairs at each end and benches along the sides. Steven walked to the head of the table and pointed Emily to the chair at the foot of the table. "Emily, you sit there."

With rage in his voice, Matt cried, "That was Momma's place."

Without any emotion in his voice, Steven stated, "Now it will be Emily's place."

Trying to calm the angry seas, Emily responded, "I'd be happy to sit on the side or anywhere. It really doesn't matter to me."

"You kids might as well know now. I should have told you in the beginning. Emily is my wife and will be treated with the respect the woman of the house should have." Steven's voice was emphatic. He looked at Emily as if he were giving a command. "Emily, sit at the foot of the table."

The silence was deafening; you could have cut the air with a knife. Finally, the children took their usual places around the table, with Sarah sitting to Emily's right. Alice sat down to Emily's left with the two older boys. Steven picked up the fried chicken and served himself, then began to pass the plate.

"Aren't we gonna say the blessing?" Sarah asked.

Steven flushed and looked helplessly at Emily, then at Alice. Alice took the cue and asked, "Whose turn is it to say grace?"

Very shyly, Luke replied, "It's mine."

"Okay, bow your heads, and, Luke, you say the blessing," Steven instructed.

Luke began, "Dear Lord, we thank You for this food and for the hands that prepared it. We ask Your blessings upon this house." He hesitated a moment and cleared his throat as if trying to decide whether to continue. He then finished, "And everyone that dwells herein. Amen."

The meal was very quiet. No one seemed to know what to say or do. Emily wasn't even sure of what she was eating. She and everyone else went through the motions of the meal.

Steven finally spoke. "What's your usual routine around here after dinner?"

Bitterly, Matt replied, "We do our chores."

"I was hoping you'd be a little more specific," Steven replied.

"Okay. Mark and I have been trying to fix the fence around the garden. Some of the posts have rotted out and the fence is falling down. We were going to work on it this afternoon." In a short tone, he added, "Is that all right with you?"

Looking him in the eyes, Steven answered, "It's fine with me. Do you need some help?"

Staring right back at his father and never batting an eye, Matt replied, "We've gotten along without your help for all these years. I think we can manage this afternoon just fine! We can certainly mend a fence without your help!"

Nothing more was said. Steven finished and left without saying anything to anyone. Emily was probably the only one that noticed he barely touched his food. He certainly didn't have the appetite of a farmer. Alice began clearing the table. As soon as she and Emily had washed the last dish, she turned to Emily and said, "I sure hate to do this to you, but I have to get home and care for my own family. They made do with sandwiches for dinner, so I need to fix them a good supper. You should have plenty of leftovers for supper. You'll just have to heat them up."

"Thank you for everything," Emily told her. "I do hope we can become friends. I know I can't take Rebecca's place, and I don't want to. I would like to create a place for myself, though, and I hope folks will give me the chance."

Alice just smiled. Emily could tell she had reservations and that it would take time. Based on the brief time she had known Alice, though, Emily believed her to be a fair-minded person. "If you have any questions, give me a holler," Alice said. "I just live up the road a piece."

Emily walked Alice to the front door and watched as she disappeared down the road. Now she was truly on her own, and she was terrified. She turned around and wondered what to do first. She was sure Steven had brought in her trunk, but she had no idea where he had placed it. It would feel good to get out of her traveling clothes, but she didn't know where to go. This was supposed to be her new home, and she had never felt more like a stranger anywhere.

The front door opened into a large hallway. In the hall was a daybed, hat rack, and small dresser, neat but dusty. She turned and to her right was a large family room, with a big fireplace on the opposite wall. A large braided rug lay on the floor in front of it, with a sofa, two big overstuffed chairs, a rocking chair, and several straight-back chairs scattered throughout the room. The room looked lived in but not messy. It, too, was a little dusty.

Pictures stood on the mantel. One of the whole family showed that Rebecca had been a pretty woman, small, a little frail looking in the picture. Steven had been a handsome young man. He didn't smile in the picture; as a matter of fact, only the children were smiling, while Steven and Rebecca looked very solemn. Emily wondered how long before he left this picture had been taken. Sarah was in the photograph, so it couldn't have been long, Emily deduced.

Another picture caught her eye, a wedding picture. In this picture the two people had big smiles on their faces. Steven was even more handsome here and Rebecca more beautiful. Emily knew she could not compare with Rebecca. Emily was anything but beautiful, and she certainly wasn't small and frail, though she preferred to think of herself as being from much hardier stock. She could just hear the folks now, asking each other what Steven could have seen in her when he had Rebecca waiting for him at home. Oh well, somehow she would get through all this and folks would realize she didn't steal Steven away from Rebecca.

She walked across the hall and opened a door. Her trunk sat in the middle of the floor, near an iron bed. This must have been Rebecca's room, Emily realized, looking at the silver comb and brush with a small hand mirror that lay on a dressing table. The room Steven had shared with her when he lived here. She opened the wardrobe and found it filled with clothes. The room had apparently not been touched since Rebecca died.

A trunk stood in one corner, and Emily thought about exploring it, but she decided against it for now. The wardrobe was full, so she would just leave her things in her trunk for the time being. As she removed one of her work dresses from the trunk, she knew she would have to talk with Steven about Rebecca's things. She frowned uneasily while she changed her clothes. This must be the room Steven intended her to use, but she wasn't sure it was big enough for both her and the memories she could feel here.

Exploring the rest of the house, Emily found one other small bedroom downstairs that appeared to be Sarah's. Upstairs were two rooms where obviously the boys slept. She decided to look around outside next. She would have liked a guide for this tour, but apparently that was not to be.

She found the well-stocked smokehouse, then walked through the chicken yard. From the looks of things, fresh eggs and fried chicken would be plentiful. She could see a couple of milk cows out by the barn, so there would be fresh milk and butter.

Emily could see the two older boys working on the garden fence, but she decided not to approach them. She heard children laughing in the distance. The noise sounded as though it was coming from the front of the house, so she moved that way. When she rounded the corner, the children spotted her and immediately stopped their play.

A big collie dog was in the yard with the children. "What's the dog's name?" Emily inquired.

"Precious," answered Sarah. "She's my dog; we got her when she was a baby and I help feed her and take care of her, so she's mine."

Emily smiled. "She's a beautiful dog. It looks like you've taken very good care of her. I can tell she loves you very much."

"She follows Sarah everywhere she goes," Luke added. "Momma always said she didn't have to worry about Sarah if she was off somewhere because Precious would take care of her."

"It's nice to have a friend like that. One you can depend on to always be by your side," Emily replied. She had a sad faraway look in her eye. Right now she would love to have a friend, just someone she could talk to.

Her thoughts were interrupted by Sarah's voice. "Since our father married you, are you our mother now?" All three children looked very anxious to hear the answer to that question.

"I know you children loved your mother very much, and I know I could never take her place," Emily said gently. "I just hope that in time I can become your friend. I would like for each of you to be my friend. I don't know anyone here, and I sure could use a friend right now."

John looked very puzzled. "I didn't know grown-ups had friends," he remarked. "What do they do with friends? They're too old to play games."

"There's lots of things to do with friends besides just play. Friends are people you can share all your secret thoughts with. Someone you can just talk to when you're lonely. Grown-ups need friends just like children do," Emily answered.

The children sat in silence, then Luke finally spoke. "I guess maybe we could be friends. What is it you would like to talk about?" he asked.

"Why don't each one of you tell me about yourself and what you like to do. What foods you like to eat. Just anything you can think of about yourself," Emily said.

The children started sharing their likes and dislikes, and Emily was enjoying their visit so much that she completely let the time get away from her. Suddenly, she realized it was getting late, and she had better get supper on the table.

She had just gotten everything warmed and ready when Steven came in, followed closely by Matt and Mark. Matt yelled for the younger children and soon all were seated around the big table. Supper was just as quiet as dinner had been. When they finished eating, only Sarah stayed to help Emily with the dishes. Emily wondered where Steven was; she really needed to talk with him and get a few things settled.

She found him sitting alone on the front porch and she cleared her throat before she began. "I don't mean to intrude, but there are a few things I need to know. Little things like what time do you want meals served? Where am I to sleep? Also, how much authority do I have with the children and assigning them chores? I just want to get things clear from the start so we have as few problems as possible."

In his usual monotone fashion, Steven began, "We'll get up about sunup, and you can start breakfast. We'll eat after the milking's done. Dinner will be about noon and supper about sundown."

He let out a long sigh, then continued. "You'll sleep in the front bedroom, the first door on the left. You have complete authority with the kids. You can assign them whatever chores you feel necessary. You'll run things like the lady of the house would do."

Steven had answered all of her questions, but he never looked at her. He just sat there staring down the road. Emily wondered if he was wishing he could take off down that road again and never look back, because right at this moment that was what she would like to do.

Emily decided this was not a good time to approach the subject of Rebecca's belongings. She sat in silence, looking up at the heavens and thanking God for getting her through this first day. She was dreading going to bed in that room.

CHAPTER 4

Emily lay in bed for hours wondering how she would ever make things work. She may have made a little progress with the three youngest today, but she knew it would take a long time to make friends with Matt and Mark. Steven, well, that was a whole different story. How would she ever break through the barrier he had built around himself? Even though Emily considered this a job, she hoped to bring the children and their father together, but she could not foresee this group becoming a family anytime soon.

The loud crow of a rooster awakened Emily the next morning. She found Steven straining milk as she walked into the kitchen.

"Good morning," she said. "I'm sorry if I overslept."

"You didn't. I'm just up a little early," he replied.

"I'll get breakfast started." Emily put the coffee on to brew, found the flour, and started to make biscuits. The door opened and in walked Matt. He grabbed the milk pail and started for the back door.

Steven stopped him. "The milking's done for this morning."

Matt gave him a long, cold stare, then turned and walked out of the room. Steven poured himself a cup of coffee and sat down at the table.

Emily fried bacon and scrambled eggs. Her biscuits turned out exceptionally well, she thought. The kids straggled in one by one and seated themselves at the table.

"Momma always gave us a choice of how we wanted our eggs cooked," said Mark under his breath. "And her biscuits were a lot better."

"I'm sorry if the breakfast is not to your liking. No one was here when I cooked the eggs, so I couldn't ask anyone how they wanted them," Emily said as nicely as she could. "Mark, how would you like your eggs prepared next time?"

Mark flushed, and his eyes shot daggers at her. "I prefer them fried."

"If everyone will be patient with me, I will try my best to learn your likes and dislikes." Emily's voice was polite but firm.

Steven acted as though nothing had transpired. Emily knew for now she was on her own with the children. He certainly wasn't going to help her in any way.

Pausing between bites of egg, Steven said, "I noticed all the fields have been plowed and planted except that back five acres. Is there some reason it was left out?"

"We're not going to plant it this year. The cotton we planted back there didn't do good," Matt answered. "Uncle Clyde said to let it rest a year, and that's what we're gonna do."

"What kind of deal do you have with 'Uncle Clyde' on the rest of the crops?" Steven inquired.

"A seventy-thirty split. We get the seventy cause we take care of the fields. He just helps us till and plant and harvest," Matt replied. "Do you have a problem with that?"

"No, I don't have a problem with that. But now that I'm home, I think we can do the work ourselves and we won't have to impose on him." Steven's tone was firm. He then added, "And we are going to plant the back five acres."

Matt's face turned red. He slammed his fist on the table and yelled, "We haven't been imposing on him. He has been paid for his help from the sale of the crops. Uncle Clyde said let those back five acres rest this year, and that's what we're gonna do. I think he knows more about farming than you do. He didn't run away when his farm flopped the way you did!"

Steven just sat there and let his son finish. Then he spoke. "I think you're forgetting who owns this farm, young man. And I also think you're forgetting who the father is around here. I will not tolerate this kind of behavior from you."

Infuriated by his father's remarks, Matt blew up again. "Me and Mark have been doing all the work around here while you've been gone. And doing a good job of it, too. Now you just waltz in here and take over and expect us to bow to your wishes and respect you as a father. Well, that's not gonna happen, mister. You walked out on us and left us to fend for ourselves, and we did. No thanks to you."

Matt had to catch his breath, but he continued. "You couldn't handle it when things were bad. Now that things are going good, you expect to come back and take up where you left off. You weren't man enough to turn things around yourself. You let us do it for you. Now you want the benefits from it. We've worked hard for this place, and we're not gonna let you ruin it or take it away from us."

Matt was shouting at the top of his lungs. Steven didn't try to defend himself. He didn't do anything. Matt stomped out of the room and slammed the back door. Steven sat there a moment, then he, too, got up and left. Emily noticed his shoulders seemed to sag a little lower than usual. She couldn't help but wonder why he had let his son talk to him that way. She surmised that Matt had probably put into words a lot of the feelings Steven had about himself.

Slowly, everyone filed out one by one except Sarah. "I'll help you with the dishes," she said. "I always used to help Momma."

"Thank you, Sarah." Emily smiled. "I would love to have your help and your company. After we finish the dishes, maybe you could help me round up the dirty clothes. I need to do some washing."

"I'd be glad to, but we shouldn't have too much. Miss Alice washed day before yesterday," Sarah said. "You should know that Monday is wash day."

True to Sarah's word, the children didn't have a lot of dirty clothes, but Emily needed to wash hers anyway. She was sure Steven had some as well. She saw something sticking out from under the daybed in the hall. Pulling up the spread, she noticed Steven had pushed his things under it. This must be where he had been sleeping. Emily was surprised to find it a little unnerving to know that just a wall separated them at night. She pulled his clothes out and added them to her pile.

Sarah helped her gather wood for the fire and get the wash pot set up. After an hour, the washing was finished, and it was time to start dinner.

"Sarah, would you like to help me get dinner ready?" Emily asked.

"I sure would! I like to cook." Sarah grinned from ear to ear.

It was the first genuine smile Emily had seen in quite a while, and it was really nice to see. "Since you're gonna help me, I think I'll have time to make a big peach cobbler for dessert."

Sarah's smile got bigger and brighter. "Oh boy. Let's get started. I can hardly wait for dessert."

"Sarah, don't you kids go to school? I love having your help, but isn't this a school day?" Emily inquired as they began their meal preparations.

Softly and rather shyly, Sarah answered, "We do go to school, and this week is the first time we've missed in a long time. Uncle Clyde found out in town last week that Daddy should be getting here real soon, so Matt said we were gonna stay home for a few days and keep an eye on things. I don't know what we're supposed to keep an eye on, but I guess Matt and Mark do."

Emily got Sarah started washing potatoes. "Miss Emily," Sarah asked after a moment, "what is my daddy like? I don't remember him at all, and Momma never talked about him much. I used to ask Matt about him, but he would just say he didn't remember. Will you tell me about him?"

Emily was silent. She didn't know how to answer the child's question. She didn't know Steven herself. What could she say to this little girl? Sarah looked at her with such a trusting face. Emily couldn't tell her she just married her daddy without knowing him and came here to take care of them—or could she? She said a quick prayer and asked the Lord for guidance.

Emily began, "Sarah, I haven't known your father very long. He is a very nice man, and he loves you children very much. Right now he just doesn't know how to show it. He has been away so long and all of you are kind of like strangers to him. Just like he's a stranger to you. You'll have to give each other time. You'll all have to try to get to know one another again. Just like you will all have to get to know me, and I will get to know you. We all just have to be patient." Emily knew she had not answered the little girl's question, but she hoped Sarah would drop the issue.

"I like you, Miss Emily," Sarah said. "But I'm not sure about Daddy. He doesn't seem very friendly. He seems mad all the time. And Matt's mad now, too, since Daddy got here. I don't think Matt and Mark like him very much."

The child seemed to have a lot of insight into the situation. "They have a lot of things to work out between them. I don't think your daddy is mad, Sarah. He just has a lot on his mind right now." Emily added, "We'd better get that peach cobbler started if we want it to be ready for dinner." She hoped that would get Sarah's mind on a different subject, at least for a while.

After they had gotten the cobbler in the oven, Sarah set the table. "Would you like me to ring the dinner bell?" Sarah asked. "I'm really getting hungry."

Emily laughed. "Yes, of course. I'd forgotten we had to do that. You go right ahead."

Sarah went to the back porch and gave the dinner bell a nice long ring. Emily dreaded for everyone to come in. So far mealtime had not been the most pleasurable of experiences around here.

The boys all came in, washed up, and took their places at the table. Steven was nowhere in sight. They waited a few minutes for him until finally Emily asked, "Whose turn is it to say grace?"

"It's mine," Sarah said, and she began. "God is great; God is good; let us thank Him for our food. And please help Daddy and Matt not to be mad at each other. Amen."

Emily looked up and saw Steven standing in the doorway. "We waited, but the food was going to get cold, so we started without you. I hope you don't mind."

Visibly shaken by his daughter's prayer, Steven took his seat at the head of the table. "I'm sorry I'm late."

He picked up the ham, took a piece, and began to pass it around the table. He said nothing else. No one talked. *You'd think that the silence would be better than the yelling at breakfast was,* Emily thought, *but it's the loudest quiet I ever heard.* If this continued, no one would ever get to know anyone around here.

"Can we have dessert now?" Sarah asked with a big smile on her face. "Miss Emily made peach cobbler."

"Of course we can. Will you help me serve it?" Emily asked.

"Boy, that sure was good," Sarah said as she finished her cobbler. "It was as good as Momma's."

Matt shot daggers at Emily and shook his head. Under his breath he mumbled, "Not everybody will be that easy to win over."

Another appetizing and nourishing meal was over. Once again, Steven had eaten very little, and Emily's appetite certainly wasn't what it had been. At this rate she and Steven would both lose a few pounds. She did note that although Matt and Mark were not friendly toward her or complimentary to her food, they left little on their plates.

∞

By twilight, the kids were all in their rooms. Steven had disappeared right after supper. Emily went out on the front porch for a while to get some fresh air.

She was sitting in the porch swing when she heard someone whistling, not a tune, just a monotone whistle. She looked up and saw Steven come around the corner of the house. As he rounded the corner, he spotted her and stopped.

"Beautiful evening," Emily observed.

"Yeah, I guess so," he hesitantly answered as he started to walk off.

He stopped when Emily spoke again. "Steven, could I talk to you for just a moment?"

He turned. "Go ahead."

"Steven, I feel uncomfortable in Rebecca's room. All of her things are still in there. Her clothes are in the closet and even her comb and brush on the dressing table." Emily didn't know what to say now. She hoped he would jump in and help her out.

After a considerable silence, he finally said, "I'll take care of it." Then he walked off.

Steven would take care of it—but when? She would just have to wait and see. She got up and went to her room. She read her Bible, then turned out the light. As she lay in the darkness, she once again asked God to help her through another day. She also prayed for Steven and each one of the children.

She asked God to please help Steven show some love and affection toward his children.

She heard the front door open and footsteps in the hallway. Steven was going to bed right outside her door. She had gotten that strange feeling again that morning as she washed his clothes with hers. This cold, seemingly unfeeling man was causing her all kinds of grief and discomfort.

She couldn't help but think about him lying in this very bed with another woman, and that disturbed her. Why should that bother her? She had no claims on the man. With the darkness surrounding her, she wondered what it would be like to be held by Steven. She tried to make the feelings go away, but loneliness lay heavy on her heart. Emily began to pray for God to keep her heart pure. Although legally she was married to the man, she wasn't sure she was in God's eyes.

∞

Emily was awake early. This morning she would start her duties on time. She was glad there was a connecting door from her room to the kitchen, so she didn't have to go through the hall and pass Steven's sleeping form if he were still in bed.

She was making biscuits when Matt came in with the milk. He had apparently been determined Steven wasn't going to do his chores this morning.

"Good morning, Matt." Emily smiled warmly. "How would you like your eggs this morning?"

Matt grunted something unintelligible without looking at her. He finished straining the milk and left the room without a word.

Watching him as he exited, Emily whispered to herself, "Good morning, Emily. I'll take my eggs any way it's easier for you to fix them. You're so kind to ask." Then she thought, *Lord, please keep me from popping that rude young man up beside the head.*

Steven came in and poured himself a cup of coffee and sat down at the table. He looked very tired, like he hadn't gotten much sleep either. She couldn't remember ever seeing anyone look so unhappy.

"Good morning, Steven," she greeted. "Did you sleep well?"

After a big yawn, he said, "Morning. I slept okay."

She would ask him the magic question and see what kind of response she could evoke from him. "How would you like your eggs cooked this morning?"

"Any way's fine with me," he responded, not to her surprise.

The children all wandered in as she set a plate of fried eggs on the table.

Mark looked at the eggs, then at her, but there was of course no thank you from him. After the first bite, he did whisper softly, "I prefer them sunny-side up."

There was just no way to please this crew, so why did she try? She might as well make some more trouble, so she remarked, "I know this may be none of my business, but today is a school day. Since all of you have missed the last couple of days, don't you think you should go today?"

"We're taking the week off," Matt quickly replied.

"Is this some kind of a holiday?" Steven inquired.

"No, we're just taking the week off to be around here," was Matt's response.

"Well, that's very kind of you to want to be home with me and Emily, since we just got here," Steven said nonchalantly. "But I would much rather you kids go to school. An education is very important."

Emily was stunned. Was there a hint of humor in his voice? This was wonderful. She couldn't help but throw a little smile his way when he glanced at her. *Be still my heart,* she thought. Was that a little grin she saw almost touch his lips?

Matt started to argue, but Steven stopped him before he could begin. "There will be no discussion. You kids will go to school today."

They all got up to leave, but Sarah was the only one that said anything. "The breakfast was real good, Miss Emily." With her head down as she passed her father's chair, she said, "Bye, Daddy."

Steven turned her way. "Bye, Sarah." His voice trembled.

After the children left the kitchen, Emily prepared lunches to send with them to school. Steven rose from the table when the front door slammed behind the children. As he started out the back door, he called, "Don't fix dinner since the kids aren't here. I'll grab something when I come in later."

Emily watched him go. Then she turned to her chores. After spending the morning cleaning, she decided to take a break and explore the lane she had seen behind the barn.

∽

Steven came in to grab himself a biscuit and a piece of bacon and found the house deserted. This would be a good time to clear Becky's things out of the bedroom. He found an empty trunk in the attic and took it into Becky's room. He took down her dresses one by one from the wardrobe and neatly folded them and placed them in the trunk.

Lying on the top shelf was something wrapped in an old sheet. Pulling it down, he accidentally dropped it on the floor. As he picked it up, he noticed it was Becky's wedding dress. Holding it, he remembered how beautiful she had looked wearing it the day they were married. They were so happy then. What had happened to them? Fighting back the tears, he knew the answer to that question and blamed himself for the whole thing.

He had to finish this task before Emily returned. He cleared off the dressing table and looked around for anything else that might need removing. He picked up a small box from the table and looked inside. There he found a small locket. Opening it, he saw a picture of himself and one of Matt. He had given this to Becky right after Matt was born. More tears threatened.

He sat down in the rocking chair, clutching the locket in his hand. He and Becky had been happy at one time. The day he married her, he thought, was the happiest day in his life. But the day Matt was born, that was so special. When he held that little bundle in his arms, he had never felt such joy and love.

They had a good happy life until he forced Becky to move here to the farm. This had been his dream, not hers. He had wanted a farm and had sold everything they had to make his dream come true. Then he had run out on his dream and his family. Tears flowed freely. How could his family ever forgive him? How could he ever forgive himself?

Quickly, he closed the locket and tucked it back in its little hiding place. He put it away inside the trunk. Seeing nothing else he felt he should remove, he closed the trunk and carried it up to the attic.

∽

As Emily sat in the living room that evening, mending a pair of John's overalls, Sarah came in and asked, "Emily, do you go to church?"

"Why yes I do, Sarah," Emily replied. "What makes you ask that?"

"Well, we go to church, too, and this Sunday is Easter. I was hoping you would go with us." Sarah took a long breath, then began again. "I usually get a new dress for Easter. Momma always made me one, but I guess this year I'll just wear my old one."

Emily looked at the little girl standing there so innocently. She was the only friend Emily had here, and Emily could already tell she was a treasure among treasures. Emily had a lump in her throat when she responded to Sarah's plea. "Sarah, I would love to go to church with you Sunday. I appreciate your thinking about me and asking me to go with you. Maybe if we talk to your daddy, he would give us enough money to buy some material, and I could make you a new dress for Sunday."

"Oh Emily, that would be wonderful! But we don't have to talk to Daddy. Momma had lots of material. It's in a trunk in her room. Come on, I'll show you." Grabbing Emily's hand, Sarah pulled her through the door into the bedroom.

Sarah walked to the trunk sitting in the corner by the fireplace and opened the lid. She began pulling out piece after piece of material. The little girl's excitement grew with each new discovery. Emily wondered why anyone would purchase so much material, but she guessed that didn't matter. Sarah was so excited that Emily couldn't help but get carried away in her enthusiasm.

They looked at every piece in the trunk. There was every color imaginable, plus the notions to go with them. Some of the material looked to be the weight and texture for heavy curtains or upholstery. Sarah finally decided upon a piece with small pink flowers in it. It was a good choice because it would be lovely with her soft blond hair and her sky blue eyes.

Sarah smiled. "There should be enough material here for you to make you a dress, too. Momma and I always had a dress alike on Easter."

Emily was completely caught off guard by Sarah's comment. The little girl was so sincere, and she surely didn't want to hurt her feelings. "Sarah, that is very sweet of you. I would love to have a dress to match yours, but since this is Friday, I'm afraid I'll only have time to make one dress. I want you to have a new dress, and I'll make me something later."

That satisfied Sarah for now, and Emily was grateful for that. Emily took Sarah's measurements, then asked the little girl to bring her one of her dresses so she could fashion a pattern. Sarah rushed from the room and was back in no time with her Sunday best in hand. Emily noted the stitching; Rebecca had been very handy with a needle and thread. Well, Emily would just do her best and she considered that to be pretty good. She had never sewn for a little girl before, but she looked forward to the challenge.

Sarah told her good night, and Emily decided to start her project tonight. Her little nap after her walk had rested her, and she wasn't tired right now. She had noticed the treadle machine sitting in front of the window, and now she would check it out and see if it was in working order.

As she walked toward the machine, she noticed Rebecca's vanity set was missing from the dressing table. She opened the wardrobe and found it empty. Steven must have cleared everything out while she was gone this afternoon. He said he would take care of it, and he had wasted no time in doing so. She must remember to thank him for his consideration.

She quickly unpacked her belongings, hanging her clothes in the wardrobe.

She placed her comb and brush on the dressing table, and she gently picked up the wedding picture of herself and Jim. Running her fingertips lightly across Jim's face, her mind began to wander again to days gone by. The what-ifs came back. Like, what if Jim hadn't died? Would they have had a place like this, maybe a little girl like Sarah? What if Jim were here right now? She knew her life would be different. Happiness would have filled her life if Jim were here.

Stop it! she said to herself. Jim was gone; she was here, and she would have to make the best of things. Emily could not change the past and had very little control over the future, but she could do something about the present. She could get started on a dress and make one little girl very happy.

Emily found the sewing machine in good working order. That would make her job much easier. She began to fashion a pattern in her mind, and using Sarah's dress for guidance, began to cut what she saw in her mind's eye. She got each piece cut to her satisfaction, then moved a lamp close to the machine and started to put the pieces of her puzzle together.

She heard the screen door open and knew that Steven was going to bed. She couldn't stop her heart from skipping a little beat, but she did try to ignore it. She forced herself to keep her mind on her sewing, not on Steven.

The clock struck 2:00 a.m., and she realized she had been at this for about six hours. She was pleased with what she lay out on the bed. This morning she would have Sarah try it on so she could pin up the hem and make any alterations that might be necessary. Emily could hardly wait to see the expression on the little girl's face. But right now she had to get some sleep.

∽

The rooster crowed all too early. It seemed Emily had barely laid her head on her pillow when she heard his unwelcome cry. It was Saturday, and the morning routine would be the same except that the children would not be going to school.

Steven was sitting at the table drinking a cup of coffee when she walked into the kitchen. "Sorry if I overslept," she apologized.

He looked up from his coffee and remarked, "I heard you up late last night. I thought I heard the sewing machine."

"You did. I hope it didn't bother you. I was making Sarah an Easter dress."

"Easter dress. Is it almost Easter?" Steven queried.

"Tomorrow's Easter Sunday," she answered. "Sarah invited me to go to

51

church with her. I'm thankful she's warmed up to me. She is really a precious little girl."

Emily finished the biscuits and slid them into the oven. The kids straggled to the table one by one, except for the twins, who always came in together.

When breakfast was drawing to an end, Steven said, "I would like you boys to help me finish plowing and planting that back five acres this morning."

Then came the expected silence. Finally, Matt broke the tension by saying, "I thought I told you Uncle Clyde said not to plant that part this year."

"Matt, I thought I made it clear to you that I'm the father around here. I know what Clyde says. I agree that we don't need to plant cotton in that area, but I was thinking of planting corn there. And that's what we're gonna do."

"If you want to plant it, fine! But don't expect us to help you," Matt argued.

Steven looked at Emily, then around the table and said, "If you'll excuse us, Matt and I need to step outside and have a little talk." Steven stood and motioned for Matt to join him.

"What's he gonna do?" asked Sarah after they had gone. A look of fear showed on her face.

Mark mumbled something about his father trying to prove who was boss. The twins looked almost as frightened as Sarah. Emily tried to calm their fears by saying, "It's okay. Your dad just wants to talk to Matt, and he didn't want there to be any more yelling at the table. You kids go on and play while I clean the kitchen."

∞

Outside, Steven and Matt stood toe to toe and stared at one another for what seemed like an eternity. Steven finally began. "Matt, we need to get things straight right now. I know you've been the man around here for quite a while. And from what I can tell, you've done an excellent job, but I'm back now. I'm back whether you like it or not, and we need to learn to work together."

Steven stopped. He really didn't know what to say to the young man at this point. He remembered a lot of long talks they had when Matt was a boy, but now he was grown. He wouldn't have let any man talk to him the way Matt had talked to him, but Steven couldn't help but think that he deserved Matt's wrath. For the sake of the farm and the others, though, they had to at least come to an understanding.

Steven started again. "Look, I know you're mad at me and probably at this point you even hate me. And I can't say that I blame you. But we need to learn to at least work together. We both want to be able to take care of this family, and for that to happen, this farm has to make it. Let's just try to work the fields together and harvest the crops when the time is right. You don't have to like me to do that."

"I don't have to do anything with you," Matt responded. "You have no right coming back here and trying to take over. You walked out on us without so much as a good-bye. We never heard from you until you showed up here Tuesday. Don't expect me to welcome you with open arms." The contempt in his voice came through loud and clear.

Steven never batted an eye. "Well, let me put it to you this way. I am the father; you are the son, whether you like it or not. My word will stand. What I say goes. Is that clear?"

"Yes sir!" Matt turned and fled.

For a moment, Steven just stood there. What did Matt mean, they never heard a word from him? He had written Becky regularly, at least at first. And he had sent money every month since he left five years ago. Did she not ever tell the kids that or show them one of his letters? Maybe someday he could talk to Matt about that rationally. But he doubted that it would be any day soon.

CHAPTER 5

Easter Sunday, and what a glorious day! The sun was bright; the birds were singing; the flowers were blooming; all was right in God's world. At least those were Emily's first thoughts when she awoke that morning. Then she remembered where she was, and she knew hardly anything was right in this house.

She looked at the clock and realized she had plenty of time before anyone had to leave for church. Maybe a special breakfast this morning. The family arrived as she set a steaming plate filled with light fluffy pancakes on the table.

"Good morning. And a glorious Easter morn it is," Emily said in the most cheerful and convincing tone she could muster.

"Good morning, Miss Emily," Sarah chimed. "I'm gonna wait until after breakfast to put on my beautiful dress. I didn't want to get it dirty."

Emily looked around the table as she asked, "What time do we have to leave the house in order to get to church?"

Matt and Mark looked at each other, then Matt sharply questioned, "Do you plan on going to church with us?"

"Yes, Matt, I do," Emily answered firmly. "I always attended church back in Abilene. Sarah asked me to attend with her this morning, and I'm going to."

Silence once again struck the Barnes clan at the dining table. Matt and Mark both looked as though they might be ill. Sarah looked confused by the whole exchange, and Steven and the twins appeared not to notice anything but the pancakes.

Emily decided to break the silence. "I'm really looking forward to meeting some of my new neighbors. Is church at eleven here? What time do we have to leave?"

"Church starts at eleven, and it's two miles down the road. It depends on how fast you can walk as to how early you have to leave," Matt replied.

"Matt, we always take the wagon to church," Sarah reminded him.

"If I have to go to church, I'm not riding in the same wagon she's in. We'll take the wagon, but she can walk." Matt left the room.

Nothing more was said. Emily cleaned the breakfast dishes, then went to her room to dress. She guessed she had better leave by ten-thirty. Maybe someone would at least tell her which direction the church was. She didn't remember passing one when they arrived here, but she had been so nervous that day she could have missed it.

Emily walked out on the porch. Sarah was dressed and sitting in the porch swing. "Emily, could you help me with my hair bow?"

The wagon pulled up at the front gate as Emily finished Sarah's hair. Matt yelled, "Ya'll come on. It's time to go."

Just as he yelled, Steven rounded the corner of the house and walked up to the wagon. "Matt, it's really nice of you to drive everyone to church this morning," he commented, opening the gate for the twins.

"I told you I'm not riding in the same wagon as that woman!" Matt said angrily.

"Then I guess you'd better step down from there because Emily's riding to church in this wagon." Steven stepped up on the wheel and took the reins from the young man.

Matt refused to budge. In a commanding voice, Steven declared, "You either get down on your own, or I'll pull you down."

"I'd like to see you try." The words were barely out of Matt's mouth before Steven grabbed him by the collar and in one fell swoop picked him up and set him on the ground.

Everyone gasped, but no one was as surprised as Matt himself. He was on the ground before he knew what happened. He stood there dumbfounded.

"Now, young man, you can walk to church." Steven turned and looked at Mark and the twins, who were already in the back of the wagon. "If there's anyone else who feels he is too good to ride in the same wagon with Miss Emily, this would be the time for you to step down."

The twins stayed right where they were, but Mark climbed down from the wagon. He walked over and stood beside Matt.

"Emily, Sarah, I'm driving you to church," Steven called to where they stood on the porch.

Steven assisted Emily up into the wagon, then picked up Sarah and set her on the seat beside Emily. He climbed up beside the ladies and slapped the reins. The horses started down the road.

∽

The church was a small white building with a tall steeple. Just as it came into view, the church bell began to peal out the call for all to come worship. Emily wasn't too sure any of this family was in a worshipful mood, but she knew there couldn't be a family there who needed it more. Steven pulled the horses to a stop and jumped down from the wagon. He lifted Sarah out and set her down gently on the ground.

After helping Emily down, he said, "I'll be waiting out here when the service is over to drive you home."

Without another word, he climbed back up in the wagon and drove away. Sarah took Emily's trembling hand and led her toward the open doors of the church.

A hush fell over the crowd gathered outside the doors as they approached. Emily deduced that the tall slender man standing on the steps greeting everyone was the minister.

Sarah pulled Emily toward him. "Brother Kirkland, this is Emily. She's living with us now and taking care of us."

The minister extended his hand. "Hello, Emily. I'm Thomas Kirkland. I'm very happy to have you worship with us this morning."

The tone of his voice and the kindness pouring from his eyes almost made Emily feel welcome. "Thank you, Reverend Kirkland. I'm happy to be here," was all she could manage to respond.

When the service was over, Sarah shot out the door with her friends and Emily was left standing alone in the midst of strangers. Finally a familiar face, Alice Bentley, walked up to her.

"It's good to see you, Emily," Alice greeted as she extended her hand. "How's everything going?"

"I guess it could be worse, but I'm not sure how," Emily answered honestly.

A crowd of curious onlookers had joined them. Alice began to introduce Emily to each of them. There were no warm smiles among them, just a few grunts. She noticed Alice introduced her just as Emily, never mentioning her last name. Oh well, she would try not to be judgmental. It would take time for these folks to get to know her. She had to be patient and give them the time.

Outside, Steven waited by the wagon. A couple of men had wandered over and were talking to him, seeming genuinely happy to see him. She thought she even spied a grin on Steven's face, but she didn't want to keep him waiting, so she strolled over to where he stood. As the men left, Steven called the children. They all boarded the wagon and started home.

"Everyone just loved my dress, Emily. Thanks for making it for me." Sarah looked up at her father, as if wanting him to say something to her. But as usual, he maintained his silence.

Emily had caught a glimpse of Matt and Mark just as the service ended. They were headed out the back door. She was glad they had come to church even if they didn't want to be seen with her. Today's message was one everyone needed to hear. It was too bad Steven hadn't joined them, but she would continue to pray for all of them.

Emily had tried to make Easter dinner a special occasion. She had put a tablecloth and the fancy dishes on the table. But nothing she did made any difference. The boys never refused to eat, but there was always some whispered comment about how their mother did things. Of course they whispered it loud enough for Emily to hear. Steven never ate much and never commented on the quality of the food. Sarah was the only conversationalist during mealtime.

Emily was determined that she would not let this gloomy family bring her spirits down today. She would keep in mind that this was Easter, that her Lord arose from the dead today, and she would rejoice and be glad.

∽

The days dragged on. Nothing seemed to change. The children would go off to school, and Steven would head out for the fields. He would always tell her not to worry with dinner for him, but she would always make sure she left something easily accessible to him. She filled her days with household chores and long walks exploring the territory.

She had been in this place a month, and the only friend she had made was Sarah. Today she decided she must do something about it. She had attended church every Sunday, but no one had made an effort to become her friend. Alice greeted her each time she saw her, and today Emily decided she would make the first move to win Alice's friendship. She changed into a clean dress, grabbed her bonnet, and started down the road.

The Bentley residence was a well-kept white house with a white picket fence around the yard. Emily knocked on the front door, and Alice welcomed her inside.

"I hope you don't mind me dropping by unexpectedly. I just had this terrific hunger to visit with another woman," Emily explained.

Alice replied warmly, "Not at all. I should be ashamed of myself for not getting by your place to see how you were getting along. Let's go out in the kitchen. I just made a pound cake and some fresh lemonade."

The kitchen was a large room, much like Emily's. But something about it felt much different. The cabinets were painted white and a pretty curtain hung over the window. Some fresh-cut daffodils sat in a vase in the center of the table. The room and the lady reigning over it made you feel at home. That was the difference between Emily's kitchen and this room.

Alice poured them each a glass of lemonade and cut two pieces of cake, and the two ladies began to talk. Emily poured out her heart to Alice. She told her about the power struggle between Matt and Steven. How they all seemed to hate her, with the exception of Sarah and maybe the twins. She told Alice how lonely and miserable she felt.

Emily was really struggling and suffering to make a family out of complete turmoil. Her heart was showing on her face as she shared with Alice.

"You've mentioned how everyone feels about you and how you feel about them. That is, everyone except Steven. What's going on with the two of you?" Alice questioned.

"Absolutely nothing," Emily replied. "There's no conversation, no nothing between us. Most of the time it's as though he doesn't even notice that I'm there."

Surprised, Alice asked, "You don't talk about anything? Not even the children?"

"He occasionally gives me some kind of instruction. And if I ask him a direct question, he'll answer it with as few words as possible."

"We've got to get you out of that house and involved with other people," Alice announced. "Day after tomorrow is our quilting day at the church. You're going with me. We all take a sack lunch and quilt and visit all day. It'll be a good chance for you to get to know some of the ladies and for them to get to know you."

"I'm not so sure they want to get to know me," Emily replied timidly. "They're pretty standoffish at church."

"Oh, hogwash. If I can change my mind about you, anybody can. I'm one of the most stubborn old women there." Alice laughed.

It was good to share laughter with someone again. They spent the rest of their visit just getting to know one another.

"Oh my, would you look at the time. I've got to get home. The kids will be coming in from school, and I've got to start supper," Emily said. "You'll never know how much this visit has meant to me. You'll have my friendship for life because of the time we have spent together today."

Alice embraced her newfound friend, then walked her to the door. "Don't forget, day after tomorrow. I'll pick you up about nine o'clock."

"I'm looking forward to it," Emily called as she opened the gate.

∞

As Emily finished her chores the next morning, she made another resolution. Her visit the previous day with Alice had turned out so well she decided to try something new today. Today she would make a picnic lunch and take it out to Steven. She knew where he was today. She had seen him working the field behind the barn.

Filling the basket with fried chicken, potato salad, and fresh baked bread, she headed out to find him. She stopped by the well first and pulled up the bucket where she had lowered a jug of freshly brewed tea earlier to cool. She wrapped it in towels and started toward the barn.

Emily found Steven hoeing the rows of cotton just as she had expected. Hearing her call his name, he laid down his hoe and walked over to her.

"Something the matter?" he asked.

"No. I was in the mood for a picnic. It's no fun to have one by yourself, so I hoped you'd join me," Emily explained.

She spread the blanket in the shade cast by the barn and began to unpack the tempting morsels. She never gave Steven a chance to refuse.

Taking the large glass of cool tea she offered him, he drank it down without taking a breath. "That really hit the spot," he remarked.

She filled his glass again and handed him a plate of food. He actually seemed to relax a little.

"I don't know much about cotton, but those plants certainly do look healthy," she observed.

"Yeah, as long as we get a little rain now and then, we should make a good crop."

Steven ate more than she had seen him eat since they arrived here over a month ago. He even grinned a little when she offered him a piece of the pound cake she had baked that morning.

"Pound cake's my favorite," he said softly.

This was the most pleasant meal Emily had enjoyed in a long time. The conversation wasn't extensive, but it was pleasant. The thing she enjoyed most was there was no arguing and no one commenting under their breath about how Momma would have done it.

She packed up the basket while Steven folded the blanket and handed it to her. He seemed very nervous and was fidgeting like a schoolboy on a first date. She almost laughed, but she thought he was very cute.

"The meal was very good. Thank you," he said as he picked up his hat and started back to work.

Emily was pleased with the way this new adventure had turned out, too. Not nearly as dramatic as yesterday, but the least little improvement with Steven was progress. She could hardly wait until tomorrow. Maybe meeting the ladies of the church at a social function would be friendlier than at the worship service. She could only pray her third new adventure would turn out as well as the first and second.

∽

She was waiting on the front porch with her sack lunch when Alice drove up in her buggy the next day. When they pulled up in front of the church, Emily could tell by the number of buggies that quilting days must be well attended.

Inside, the quilting frames had already been set up and a couple of ladies were already busy stitching. As Emily and Alice entered, a hush fell over the crowd. It wasn't just Emily's imagination; all eyes in the room were on her. Alice took a firm grip on her arm, probably to keep her from fleeing the lion's den.

Alice pulled her forward as she spoke. "You girls remember Emily Barnes. I asked her to join us today. She's been in our community for a while now, and we all need to get to know her better. And we have to give her a chance to get to know us, too."

Alice directed Emily to the chair next to hers. "Emily, I'm sure you don't remember everyone's name, so let me introduce you again. To your left is Suzie Atwater, and the lady next to her is our preacher's wife, Rosemary Kirkland."

Alice continued until she had introduced her to everyone seated at the quilt. Emily picked up her needle and thimble and began to stitch. All eyes were still glued on her. She knew that not only did she have to win approval for herself at these quilting functions, but her stitches had to pass their critical eye, too.

Apparently her stitches met with their approval. Their eyes finally were drawn to the squares in front of them and they began to sew. Conversations could be heard all over the room, but Alice was the only person who talked with Emily.

Emily decided to try another daring adventure and proceeded to engage Suzie in conversation. This adventure failed miserably, so she continued with her quilting. At Rosemary's suggestion, they broke for lunch. Most of the women went outside and sat under the shade of the big trees to eat their lunches. Much to Emily's surprise and delight, Rosemary Kirkland joined Alice and Emily as they sat down.

"I hope you don't mind my butting in on the two of you." Rosemary's voice was friendly.

"No," Alice said. "We're delighted to have your company."

The ladies opened their lunches and began to chat. It seemed a big revival was planned for the month of June and Alice was in charge of arranging the meals to feed the pastor and visiting preacher. Emily gathered that the church family took turns feeding the ministers during the two weeks of the revival.

Emily had sat quietly during the ladies' conversation and Rosemary finally addressed her. "Alice tells me you're from Abilene. I've never been that far west. It must have been a hard decision for you to leave your home and come so far to start life all over."

"It was a very hard decision. One I didn't take lightly. But it seemed like the right thing to do at the time," Emily told her.

"Did you grow up in Abilene?" Rosemary inquired.

"No. I grew up in El Paso. My husband and I moved to Abilene about ten years ago. When he was killed, I just stayed on there. It's been home to me for quite a while," Emily confided.

Rosemary had a natural way of making folks feel comfortable. Emily hadn't meant to share so much of her personal life with her so soon, but she was glad she had.

Rosemary continued. "You certainly were young to be left a widow. It must have been hard on you. I'm sure your family would have loved to have you move back to El Paso."

"I didn't have any family left there. My mother died when I was a baby, so it had just been me and my dad. Daddy died right before Jim and I moved to Abilene." Emily couldn't believe she was sharing so much of her past with this woman. Before long she would be telling her the truth about her relationship with Steven.

The trio looked up from where they were sitting and noticed that most of the ladies had gone back into the church. Deciding that they had better do the same, they picked up their belongings and went inside.

∽

The quilting bee ended about two o'clock. As Alice and Emily were getting ready to drive off, Rosemary yelled for them to wait. Running out to the buggy, she said, "Emily, that big white house you see over there, that's the parsonage. I want you to come and visit me anytime. I would truly love to be your friend."

Emily found it difficult to respond. She felt the tears welling up inside. "Thank you. I would love to be your friend, Rosemary."

"I'll be looking for you to stop by before long," Rosemary called as the two drove away.

Alice waited a few minutes before she said anything. "Emily, Rosemary is very serious. She wants to be your friend. She's a wonderful person, and I figure a lonely person at times. You may have noticed she and Brother Kirkland have no children, so I'm sure she gets lonely. She tries to keep busy with church activities, and she's always the first one there during an illness or a crisis. You'd do well to cultivate her friendship."

"I could tell that she's a very special person. I hope we can become good friends. I think it might take awhile before anyone else wants to call me their friend. The other ladies didn't overwhelm me with their eagerness to get to know me."

"Give them time. They're all nice ladies, just prone to be a little gossipy and nosy. They'll come around once they get to know you."

The next day, Steven rode into Tyler and went directly to the bank, where he was shown into Calvin Meyers's office. Calvin was president of the bank and probably one of the most influential citizens in town.

"Steven Barnes, I'm glad you're back. It sure is good to see you," Calvin greeted as he extended his hand.

"It's good to see you, Calvin. I just need to know what the finances look like for the farm."

"It's in good shape. Just like the last report I sent you. Actually you may not have gotten that report. I mailed it a little over a month ago, so you'd probably left. I'll show you my copy of it." Calvin pulled a pad out of his desk and handed it to Steven.

"Thanks. I also want to tell you how much I appreciate you looking after things all that time I was gone." Steven looked over the figures on the pad Calvin handed him. "Things are in much better shape than I'd hoped. Looks like the place did much better without me around."

"You wait just a minute. You might not have been here, but you had a lot to do with the success of that farm," Calvin quickly pointed out. "When you left and stopped by here and appointed me guardian of your place and your family, I took that job very seriously. I've known you all your life. We grew up in the same community, and I knew if you were leaving you had good reason. Not a month went by that you didn't send money to care for your family. You had a big part in how well the place did."

"Oh, I know I sent money. Anybody could do that. I wasn't here for my family. I should have come home."

"Yeah, you should have come home. But I know better than anyone why you didn't. If you had left Rebecca in charge of things, you wouldn't have had anything to come home to. That woman could go through money faster than anyone I've ever seen." Calvin shook his head. "I also know she made your life miserable after you bought the farm. She sure was good at pouring on the charm for everyone else though. After you left, she played the part of deserted female to the hilt."

"I did desert her. She had a right to play that part. When I left I only planned to stay gone just long enough to get us back on our feet financially. But as time went by, I couldn't bring myself to come back. I felt like such a failure. Not only as a farmer, but as a husband and father, too."

"When you wrote and asked me to find someone to sharecrop or rent the land, I knew then you weren't coming home," Calvin confessed.

"You really picked wisely when you chose Clyde Bentley to farm the place."

"I talked to Clyde, and he agreed to do it and to teach the boys to farm so they could eventually take over. Clyde is your friend, Steven. He knew what Rebecca was really like, too. He could see how she rode you and never let you forget how you dragged her to that godforsaken place."

"Look, Becky's not all to blame here. I knew what she was like when I married her. I should have never taken her from the life she was accustomed to. She never wanted to be a farmer's wife. The farm was my dream. And I couldn't even hold on to it," Steven sadly admitted. "There is something I don't understand though."

"What's that?" Calvin asked.

"Matt told me the other day that they never heard from me after I left. That's just not true. In the beginning, I wrote to Becky regularly. I didn't write so much the last couple of years, but I did at first. Now why would Matt think I didn't keep in touch with them?"

"I'm sure Becky planned it that way. Most anybody you ask will say she never said an unkind word about you after you left. She got more sympathy that way, and everyone thought she was a martyr." Calvin paused a moment. "Now she talked a different story to me. She didn't like having to come to me for money, and she called you some rather choice names in this office. As for the kids, she just let them think you left without a word, and that she didn't know where you were."

"She always knew how to get in touch with me. I have her letters to prove it." Steven sighed.

"You better hold on to those letters. You may be forced to prove it to your kids some day." Calvin grinned just a little as he asked, "Tell me about this new Mrs. Barnes I've been hearing about."

"And what have you been hearing?"

"Gossip is that she's the reason you didn't come home. Most folks have you living in sin with her for the past five years," Calvin informed him.

"Boy, they couldn't be farther from the truth on that one." Steven sighed again. "I don't care what anyone else thinks, but I'll tell you what really happened."

"You don't have to. You know I don't believe rumors," Calvin assured him.

"I know I don't have to, but I want to. I really need to talk to someone about this. A couple of days after I got your letter about Becky's death and about the kids, I went into the café where Emily worked. I used to go in there whenever I'd go to town. We were acquaintances, that's all. We'd pass the time of day, and she always had a smile for everyone who came in. Anyway, that day I just asked her to marry me. Actually I made her a business proposition. I knew she was a good, God-fearing woman, and I explained my situation to her. I told her this would be a marriage in name only. She accepted. I don't know why, but she said yes. I knew Becky would want the kids raised by someone like her."

"Are you sure you asked her to marry you because Becky would want the kids raised by someone like her? Or do you want the kids raised by someone like her?"

"I was sure at first now I don't know. She is a remarkable woman." Steven smiled as he thought about Emily. "I have to stand firm though. I can't be a husband to anyone. I'm no good at that job."

Calvin frowned. "Steven, you made some mistakes. We all make mistakes. You can't beat yourself up forever over the past. The past is gone and you can't do anything about it. You can, however, do something about the present and possibly make the future better for yourself and your family. Don't throw your chance for happiness away. You deserve to be happy."

The men sat in silence for a short while. Steven was thinking about what Calvin had just said. He didn't feel he deserved to be happy. He had been a lousy husband. Becky had told him that often enough. He knew he would never be father of the year, either, but he could keep his children fed, clothed, with a roof over their heads. He would expect nothing for himself. He would have to pay for his mistakes.

Calvin interrupted his thoughts. "As for you not being a good husband, well, I thought it took two to make or break a marriage. I know you did your best. Maybe if you would have had more support from Becky, things would have been different. Look, Steven, you made some mistakes, but God forgives.

All you have to do is ask for His forgiveness. He'll wipe the slate clean for you if you'll let Him. He'll allow you to forgive yourself, too."

"Calvin, I messed my life up, and now I've got to live with it. I think God gave up on me a long time ago. Thanks for the sermon and everything else." Steven stood and extended his hand to Calvin.

As Calvin shook Steven's hand, he replied, "Just remember, I'm your friend. I'm here if and when you need me." He smiled. "I'm gonna come out to your place one of these days and meet that remarkable woman that's your wife in name only."

Steven shot him a half grin as he turned to go. He had one more stop to make before he started back to the farm—the judge's office, where he needed to fix out a paper on the kids just as he'd told Emily he'd do. He had broken a lot of promises in the past, but from now on he would do his best to keep all promises he made, starting with this one to protect Emily.

Afterward, in no big hurry to get home, Steven kept the horse at a slow trot. His mind was spinning as thoughts of Emily filled his head. He had done remarkably well until now at keeping her at a safe distance; he couldn't start thinking of her as his wife. He couldn't fail at marriage twice.

Feeling the sunshine warm on his back and smelling the clean fresh air lifted his spirits a little. "The picnic the other day was really nice," he thought out loud. He could picture Emily as she came out to the field with the basket. It was such a relaxing moment, and so peaceful. Emily seemed to have a way of making things peaceful for him.

"Stop it, Steven," he said to himself. "You can't do this to yourself. She's just here to help with the children and take care of the house. She never agreed to be your wife. You've got to remember that!"

The other thing nagging at him was what Calvin had said about the Lord forgiving him and allowing him to forgive himself. He just couldn't see how that was possible. He had made such a mess of things, no one could forgive him. His kids certainly hadn't, and God couldn't either. Maybe if he worked hard enough and the farm continued to have success, maybe he could earn his children's forgiveness. But at this point he just wasn't good enough to be in God's presence. He had no right to ask God for anything.

CHAPTER 6

On Sunday after church, Alice approached Emily. "Would you consider having the ministers over for a meal during the revival?" she asked.

"Oh Alice, I don't know. Our meal table is still a battlefield. I sure wouldn't want a preacher hit by a stray bullet."

"Just think about it. I have one spot left and I can't seem to get anyone to fill it. It's the noon meal on the first Friday. The visiting preacher is coming alone, so you would just have him, Rosemary, and Brother Kirkland. Maybe you could talk it over with Steven."

"I'll do my best. How soon do you have to know?"

"You can let me know Wednesday at prayer meeting. The revival starts next week. If I don't get someone else to take that spot, then I'll have to feed them three times instead of two."

It seemed silly not to be able to invite guests to your home. But Emily still didn't feel like it was her home. She took care of the house and prepared the meals, but she didn't feel at home. She would talk to Steven, but Alice hadn't given her much time.

∞

The children were all in bed or at least in their rooms. The house was quiet, but Emily wasn't ready to turn in. She slipped out on the porch and sat down in the swing. Nature's symphony was in fine form that evening. The crickets and frogs appeared to be having a competition to discover who could sing the loudest.

The sound of Steven's monotone whistle grew louder, and Emily looked up to see him walk around the corner. He jumped when he saw her sitting there.

"I'm sorry if I scared you," she apologized.

"I just wasn't expecting anyone to be out here this time of night," he said. Sitting down on the edge of the porch, he remarked, "The breeze sure is nice tonight."

"It certainly is."

Steven gave her a long look, and Emily caught a glimpse of something in his expression, something she could put no name to. He wiped his forehead, as though he were suddenly hot. The evening was rapidly getting warm, Emily thought as she looked at Steven sideways. She was suddenly very aware of every little movement he made; she fought a sudden crazy yearning to be held close to him in his arms. The air that was once cool and inviting now seemed a little stifling.

She cleared her throat. Someone had to break this spell before it was too late. "Steven, I need to ask a favor of you."

"What is it?"

"Alice asked if I would have the preachers over for a meal during the revival. I would really like to do it for her. She's been so kind to me, I would like to help her out with this."

"Emily, you don't have to ask my permission to have people over. This is your home, too, you know. It may be a little awkward, but this family should be able to behave for one meal."

"Thank you very much, Steven. I'll let Alice know."

This was a side of Steven Emily hadn't seen. Being sensitive was not a trait he had been putting on display recently. It was very nice, very nice indeed. She noticed that the air hadn't cooled off at all.

"I guess I'd better turn in. It's getting late," Emily said as she rose from the swing. She felt weak in the knees.

"Good night," Steven whispered as she walked by him.

"Good night," she returned.

∽

The revival began. The visiting preacher, Brother Lemons, was a dynamic speaker, and the brush arbor that had been built for the revival was filled every night. The whole community seemed to have turned out—except for Steven. He drove them to the services and picked them up, but he never stayed. Emily was very disappointed. On Friday morning, Steven told the children that the ministers and Rosemary were coming for dinner. He instructed them to be on their best behavior.

The clergy and Rosemary arrived and were shown into the living room, where Steven played the gracious host. Emily was very proud of him.

"Whatever you're fixing smells delicious," Rosemary said, coming into the kitchen.

"It's ham. I hope you haven't eaten it every day this week."

"As a matter of fact, we haven't had it at all. It will be a welcome change. Although all the meals have been great," Rosemary acknowledged. "Sarah, the table looks lovely."

"Sarah is my right hand around here," Emily said, giving Sarah a smile. "I think everything is ready. Sarah, do you want to ring the dinner bell for the boys while I go get the menfolk?"

The meal was not as bad as Emily had feared. The children were quiet but well behaved. Brother Lemons was a wonderful conversationalist and drew everyone in at one time or another.

After the meal, Brother Lemons turned to Steven and commented, "I don't believe I've seen you at the service this week, Steven."

Emily almost dropped her cup of coffee. She couldn't believe the minister was so blunt. She wondered what Steven was going to say.

"No sir. You haven't. I don't go to church much. Brother Tom can testify to that," Steven chuckled. Brother Lemons's question didn't seem to offend him at all.

"I want to ask a favor of you. You've shared your home and the bounty from your hard work with me, and I want to share my service with you. Actually it's not my service, it's the Lord's, but He and I want you to come. Will you do that for me?" Brother Lemons was looking directly at Steven, waiting for an answer.

"I'm not gonna lie to you and tell you I'll come. But I will think about it."

∞

Emily was glad to have some time alone with Rosemary. They had become good friends over the past weeks, and Emily had been able to share her heart with Rosemary.

"Tell me, are things any better? Steven seemed real relaxed at dinner," Rosemary said, as she and Emily washed the dinner dishes.

"There's been no major breakthrough, but there hasn't been as much quarreling either. Steven was very nice about me having you over to eat. He really surprised me. I've never seen him talk to anyone as much as he did at lunch with Brother Lemons and Brother Tom," Emily confided.

"I really hope things work out with the two of you. I think you could make a good life for yourselves and the kids. I know you're in love with him. And from what I saw today, I think he may be falling in love with you."

Emily's stomach flip-flopped. She carefully dried the soap from her hands before she answered. "What makes you think I'm in love with Steven?"

"The way you look when you talk about him. You may not realize it yourself, but you love him."

Emily poured them both a glass of lemonade and sat down at the table. "Oh, I realize it all right. I just don't like to admit it to myself, much less anyone else." Emily took a sip of her lemonade, then continued. "At first I thought my feelings were just because it had been so long since I had a man in my life. You know the kind of feelings I'm talking about."

Rosemary laughed. "Yes, I know. Just because I'm married to the preacher doesn't mean I don't experience those kind of feelings. We are very much in love with each other, and we are very loving."

"I tell myself I shouldn't have those feelings for Steven. I know we're married, but yet we aren't. I also realize that it is probably next to impossible for anything to change between us. He has built a wall so high and so thick around himself that no one can get through." Emily sighed.

"I wouldn't be so sure about that. I noticed him looking at you a couple of times when he thought no one would see, especially you, and what I saw has possibilities. I say the man is falling in love with you. He probably won't admit it even to himself right now, but he certainly has feelings for you," Rosemary told her friend.

"Steven is carrying around a big load of problems that he has to work out before he can love anyone. Right now he can't even let anyone love him," Emily commented as she prepared a tray with glasses and a pitcher of lemonade. "We'd better carry some of this lemonade out to the men."

They visited with the men on the porch, and just before the visitors left, Brother Lemons once again asked Steven to the services. Steven still wouldn't commit himself; he just smiled.

"I'll be praying for you, Steven," Brother Lemons called as he mounted the wagon.

∞

That evening Steven drove the family to the service as usual. He dropped them off and left, but before he got very far down the road, he abruptly stopped the wagon. He kept hearing a little voice telling him to turn the wagon around and return to the meeting. The little voice was insistent. It nagged him until he finally obeyed.

He returned to the meeting, but he parked the wagon out of sight. He stood under a tree near the arbor, where he could still hear and see but yet remain undetected. There was singing and shouting the likes of which he hadn't heard in years. When Brother Lemons started to speak, Steven stood spellbound.

The preacher spoke of forgiveness. He said that God would forgive all our sins. We don't have to clean ourselves up for God—God does the cleaning for us. His message said all a person has to do is to ask God's forgiveness and He gives it freely. God will take our burdens and carry them for us. We don't have to be weighted down anymore.

Steven stood there thinking. Could this be true? Would God forgive him for all he had done? This preacher had said almost the same thing Calvin had told him that day in the bank. Could it be that someone was trying to get through to him?

The final hymn was being sung. "Just As I Am" was ringing through the night. The words of the song were almost the same as the preacher had spoken: God takes you just as you are. Steven wanted forgiveness. He wanted to know peace in his life. He had lived with this guilt long enough, and he didn't want it any longer.

Steven fell to his knees right there beside the tree. He prayed, "God, forgive me for all my sins and my mistakes. I want peace in my life. I want You in my life." That was all he could get out. The tears began to flow like rain washing his soul clean.

The service ended and Steven made his way to the wagon. A part of him wanted to shout from the rooftops what had happened. Another part wanted to keep silent and enjoy the peaceful feeling for a while. The silent part won.

∞

The next week everything was the same around the farm except for the look on Steven's face. Ever since Friday night, he'd been wearing a peaceful look that Emily had never seen before. He even smiled occasionally, which was a rather unusual condition for him.

Sarah noticed the change in her father. "What's happened to Daddy?" she asked Emily. "He doesn't look so unhappy anymore."

"I'm not sure," Emily answered. "But I noticed something different about him, too. I think maybe he has asked Jesus to come into his life."

Sarah looked confused. "Wasn't Jesus his friend before? I thought Jesus was everyone's friend."

"He is," Emily assured her. "But you've heard the preacher talk about forgiveness and asking Jesus into your heart. Jesus doesn't just force Himself into your life. You have to ask Him to come in. A person also has to ask forgiveness for their sins and wrongdoings before Jesus can forgive them."

"And you think that's what Daddy did? He asked God to forgive him for his sins?" Sarah puzzled. "Did Daddy do something real bad?"

"No, sweetheart, I don't think your daddy did anything real bad. I think he just had a lot of problems on his mind. And I think he thought he did some things he shouldn't have done."

"I sure hope he feels a lot better now. Maybe I'll ask him if Jesus is his friend now."

"Maybe we had better wait until he feels like telling us about it. It may be something he wants to keep to himself for a little while," Emily said.

"I don't understand. If Jesus is his friend now, shouldn't he want to tell people about it? The preacher said that you should tell people about Jesus being your friend."

This was turning into one of those discussions with questions that could become difficult to answer to a child's satisfaction. But Emily would try.

"Some people have a hard time talking about their friendship with God. It's much easier for them to show other people by the way they live their lives. You know—by going to church, helping other people, loving their family. Even by the look on their face. You and I noticed a different look on your daddy's face."

"Yeah, but Daddy doesn't go to church."

The questions continued to get tougher. "Well, it's not absolutely necessary for a Christian to go to church. They should go so they can fellowship with other Christians and renew their faith. You know church for a Christian is like food for your soul. You have to eat food to stay alive, and if you go to church, it helps you grow stronger in your faith."

"Well, shouldn't Daddy go to church so he can grow stronger?" Sarah continued her inquisition. "Will his faith die if he doesn't go?"

Emily was going to have to come up with some answers that didn't lead to more questions. This child's curiosity was getting the best of her.

"As I said, church is good for you, but you don't have to go. You can read your Bible and pray without going to church. That can help you grow as a Christian also."

"I've never seen Daddy read his Bible and he only prays real short prayers at the table." Looking thoughtful, Sarah quietly added, "I wonder if Daddy has a Bible?"

"It isn't necessary for someone else to see you read your Bible or hear you pray. It's only necessary for God to see and hear you."

Sarah seemed satisfied with Emily's answers for the time being, but Emily was afraid a lot more of these endless question sessions lay ahead.

∞

Steven drove the wagon to service every night the next week but left as usual, or so it appeared. He would park the wagon out of sight and walk back and stand in the shadow of the trees.

Friday night came, and the revival would be over after the service that night. When Emily walked out to get into the wagon, she noticed Steven had on a clean shirt and pants. He had never cleaned up to drive them to church before. Emily prayed that this was a sign that he would join them for the service that night.

Arriving at church, Steven helped the women from the wagon. He then offered Emily his arm. The duo walked to the brush arbor, with the younger children following close behind them. A large crowd had already gathered, which meant the back pews were filled. As the procession marched down the aisle, all heads turned, and a hush fell over the congregation.

Emily had been in a state of shock from the moment Steven had offered her his arm. She realized that she had a very tight grip on him, but she was afraid to let go for fear of falling over.

Steven stopped at a pew close to the front, and everyone sat down. Emily was finally able to take a deep breath, but she was still unable to speak. She just looked up at Steven and smiled. This was the first glimmer of hope that someday they might actually become a family.

Brother Lemons preached a powerful message that night. He talked about the meaning of families and the obligation of the father to be the spiritual leader. Emily saw that Steven listened intently, a puzzled frown on his face.

∽

When the service ended and the invitation was given, Steven fought an incredible battle. He felt the pull to go to the altar and confess before God and this company his newfound hope. But his pride and the devil were standing in his way. Finally, just before the last verse of the closing hymn, he made the short walk to the altar. He fell on his knees, and the ministers joined him.

"Thank you for caring enough to pray for me," Steven said as he embraced Brother Lemons at the altar.

"Steven, my boy, I'm not the only one that cares for you. You will never know how many prayers have gone up for you," Brother Lemons informed him. "Although your battle is just starting. I know you still have a lot of things to get straight at home. It won't be easy and it won't happen overnight. You will have to be persistent, even when you feel all is lost. Just remember, in the end the victory will be worth the battle. My prayers will remain with you and your family. Also remember, Brother Kirkland will be here to help when you need him. And you will need him." Brother Lemons smiled. "So be man enough to ask him to be your friend and to allow you to cry on his shoulder."

After the service, most of the folks made their way to Steven and shook his hand. He was welcomed warmly back into the fold by the majority, although there were obviously a few skeptics in the crowd.

The ride home that evening was very quiet. Steven didn't think he had ever seen the stars shine brighter. The moon lit up the way like a brilliant torch. It was a grand and glorious evening! If only this feeling could last forever. He felt as though all of his problems had melted away. That, of course, was not true. Four of his problems were riding in the wagon with him, while two walked home. He would just have to pray for God's guidance on how to make things right with his family.

Unable to sleep that night, Steven walked out onto the porch and found Emily sitting in the porch swing.

"It's beautiful tonight. Don't you agree?" Emily asked.

"One of the prettiest I've seen in a very long time," Steven confessed.

"Your decision tonight was the answer to a lot of prayers. I'm real happy for you," Emily said as her eyes filled with tears.

Steven wanted to share his contentment with this woman who shared his name. But no matter how much he wanted to, he wouldn't allow himself to do it.

"Thank you," was all he managed to respond.

CHAPTER 7

It was a hot and humid summer day and nothing pressing had to be done. After breakfast Steven told the twins that if they would help him dig up some worms, they would head to the creek for a little fishing. He had decided that a fishing trip might be a way to start winning over the twins.

Emily had never witnessed so much excitement from the two little boys. They grabbed their hats and headed to the barn to fetch a shovel. It was difficult for Emily to picture so much enthusiasm over little crawly things.

Watching the three of them almost running down the lane lifted Emily's heart. She was glad Steven was finally making an effort to get to know his children.

"Since the boys are fishing today, you and I should think of something special to do," Emily told Sarah.

"What could we do? I don't like to fish," Sarah informed her.

"I don't care much for fishing either." Emily smiled. "I was thinking more of something we girls enjoy doing. Why don't we look through all that material in the trunk and see if we can't find enough to make you new curtains for your room."

"Really? You mean I can help make them?"

"Sure. I was about your age when I started to learn to sew," Emily said.

"Sarah, do you know why your mother had all of this material?" Emily questioned, as they looked through the trunk.

"Somebody sent it to her. Every so often a big package of material would come. I asked her who sent it and she just said it didn't matter."

"Why didn't your mother make it up into clothes?" Emily asked.

"I don't know. She made us new dresses at Easter and the boys a new shirt sometimes. I guess she didn't like to sew very much. Now what about my curtains?" Sarah's tone told Emily she didn't want to answer any more questions.

Emily removed one of the worn curtains from the window to use as a pattern and let Sarah cut the first panel as she watched. Sarah was almost as excited about her curtains as she had been months ago about her Easter frock. They cut and stitched until time for dinner. Sarah rang the dinner bell for Matt and Mark, but the two older boys never came in.

∞

After the fishermen returned with a bountiful catch, Sarah went out on the back porch and found her father washing up. Grabbing his arm, she cried, "Daddy, come to my room. You've got to see what Emily and I did today."

"Let me dry my hands," he answered, taking the towel from the hook.

"We made new curtains, Daddy, see," Sarah instructed as the two entered her room. "Aren't they beautiful? Emily let me sew a whole bunch on them."

"They certainly are pretty," Steven said, looking into the innocent face of his daughter. "Looks like the two of you did a terrific job."

Steven smiled at his little girl as she took his hand and started pulling him back toward the kitchen.

"Daddy likes my curtains, Emily," Sarah announced.

"They're really nice," Steven said, then asked, "None of you would happen to know where my horse is, would you? It's not in the barn."

"Maybe the boys let it out to pasture," Emily suggested.

"Where are Matt and Mark?" Steven asked.

"We haven't seen them all day," Emily responded. "They didn't come in for dinner and they haven't been around the house all afternoon."

When the family sat down for supper, Matt and Mark still hadn't arrived. They waited awhile and then started eating without them. They were just finishing their meal when the two strays wandered in.

They had begun to help themselves to the food on the table when Steven asked, "Do you boys know what time meals are served around here?"

"Yes sir," Mark replied.

"When the dinner bell rings you know to drop what you're doing and come in. Do you not?"

"We didn't hear the bell," was Matt's reply.

Steven asked them where they had been and if they had taken his horse. The boys gave limited responses to his inquiries and he informed them that if they made it a practice to be late for meals, they would go hungry.

"The meals are prepared and on the table on time. The least you can do is show up on time to eat them," Steven stated firmly.

The boys offered no response to his proclamation. They continued to fill their mouths and their stomachs.

∞

As Steven relaxed on the porch after supper, Sarah came out to join him. She had her hands behind her back as she approached her father.

"Daddy, would you read me a story?" she asked in her sweetest tone.

Delighted, Steven responded, "I guess so. Do you have a particular story in mind?"

Sarah held her hand out to her father as she said, "I'd like to hear a story out of here."

Steven took the book from her and smiled as he read the words *"Holy Bible"* on the front cover. "What story would you like to hear from this book?"

"It doesn't matter to me. You pick one," Sarah told him.

"Let's go into the living room, where we can sit by the lamp to read," Steven suggested.

As he sat himself in the large rocking chair, Sarah climbed into his lap. He opened the Bible to First Corinthians, the thirteenth chapter, and began to read. As he read the words of the chapter on love, a warmth began to fill his being, yet a sadness lingered there also.

Sarah had laid her head on his shoulder. He hadn't held this child in his arms since she was two years old. Tears falling from his eyes, he put the Bible on the table and hugged his daughter.

Seeing his tears, Sarah asked, "Daddy, why are you crying?" Getting no response, she added, "I love you, Daddy."

As she laid her head on his shoulder, he softly kissed the top of her head and whispered, "I love you, too, Sarah." He continued to hold her until she fell asleep in his arms.

This man who had been so unfeeling, so isolated within himself, had finally let someone into his world. Sarah lay limp and peaceful in her father's lap. Apparently, she had finally gotten what she had wanted: a daddy. The thought made new tears prick Steven's eyes.

"I'll get her dressed for bed if you'll take her to her room," Emily offered as she walked into the living room.

Steven smiled at her and stood with Sarah in his arms. He carried her to her bedroom and laid her gently on her bed. For a moment he looked down at the angelic face. He could never make up for all the years he had missed, but he would try to make the future the best that he could.

Leaving Sarah's room, Steven went upstairs and found the twins wrestling on the floor of their room.

"It's time for you boys to be in bed," he said.

"Yes sir, we were headed that way. Just got a little sidetracked," John confessed.

"Well save some of that energy for tomorrow. I need you two to help me in the fields," Steven told them.

"You mean we can go to the fields with you?" Luke asked. "We never got to do that before. Matt always said we were in the way."

Steven leaned over to tuck the boys in and assured them, "You won't be in my way. I think it's time you boys started to learn how to farm. Now get to sleep." He blew out the lamp on his way out the door.

Steven paused a moment in front of Matt and Mark's door, but he didn't feel he would be welcome in that room. *God*, he prayed, *please show me how I can win their respect. Maybe even their love.*

∞

Emily was in the swing when Steven stepped out on the porch. "Get everyone tucked in?" she asked.

"Well, three of them. The other two will have to tuck themselves in," he responded.

"Oh, they'll come around," she assured him. "You just have to be patient with them."

"I have a feeling those two will push patience to the limit. I'm not sure Job could have survived them. They make pestilence look pleasing."

"Steven, they're not that bad. They just have a lot of anger built up inside. We just have to get through that wall of anger and then we'll find the young men inside."

"I think anger is too mild a word. Hate seems to fit better," said Steven.

They sat in silence for a while before Emily bid him good night and went inside. The same little voice that had made him stop the wagon and go back to the camp meeting started nagging him again. This time it was talking about Emily. It told him he was an idiot to treat such a special lady this way. It told him that he needed to work on his relationship with Emily before it was too late.

It was a very persistent little voice, but for tonight he managed to ignore it, or at least put it off. He kept telling himself, and the little voice, that it was much more important to get everything straightened out with his kids first. Steven's experience told him that this would not be the last time he heard the not-so-gentle nudging from inside his soul.

∞

After breakfast the twins left for the fields with Steven, and Sarah ran out to play. Emily found herself alone in a house where she still felt like a guest. There had to be something she could do to make it feel more like her home.

She decided to start with the living room. Rolling up her sleeves, she gave the room a good scrubbing. Then she rearranged the furniture. The windows were covered with worn shades, and she decided to make curtains. She would start on that right after dinner.

After dinner, Emily set about her task. If she worked really hard, she could get most of the curtains finished so she could surprise everyone after supper.

Using the material from Rebecca's trunk, she made simple, straight curtains. She devised a way to hang them on the windows with some nails and heavy string. She made tie backs so she could pull the curtains open and let the light into the room. Pleased with her handiwork, Emily could hardly wait for everyone to come home.

Emily had supper ready when the family came in. As everyone started eating, Sarah commented, "I like the new curtains in the living room and the way you did the furniture."

"Thank you, Sarah," Emily responded.

With a look that could kill and a voice to match, Matt asked, "What did you do to the living room?"

"I just rearranged the furniture and made some curtains," Emily replied.

Matt jumped up from the table and ran to the living room. Angrily, he began to rip the curtains from the windows. Steven went after him and grabbed his son by the shoulders.

"Matt! Stop this!" he demanded. "What do you think you're doing?"

"What gives her the right to change my mother's house? She has no right to be here at all, and for that matter neither do you! Why don't you just get out?" Anger and hatred flowed from the bitter young man.

Without thinking, Steven spun Matt around and almost hit him, but Emily grabbed his arm before he could deliver a blow.

Looking Matt in the eyes, he demanded, "You will apologize to Emily for this outburst and for destroying her hard work."

"I'll never apologize to her!" Matt shouted as he struggled to release himself from his father's grip.

Steven took Matt by the collar and escorted the young man to the barn where the razor strap should be hanging.

<hr />

After Steven and Matt left the house, Emily began to pick up the curtains. Matt had only torn them off two of the five windows, but as Emily picked up the last panel, she sat down on the floor and began to sob. She couldn't hold back the tears any longer. Tonight was the last straw. She didn't know if she could go on, or even if she wanted to.

Sarah walked over to Emily and put her little arms around her shoulders. "Don't cry, Emily. I'll help you put the curtains back up."

Emily looked up and saw the twins standing before her. "Yeah, we'll help, too."

These precious little children! She knew she had to keep trying for their sakes. Drying her eyes on her apron, she said, "Thank you, all of you. I would really appreciate your help."

Evaluating the damage, Emily realized all Matt had done was break the string that had been supporting the curtains. They were easily fixed and reattached to the windows.

"What do you think Daddy's gonna to do to Matt?" Sarah asked.

"He's gonna belt him good," Luke proclaimed.

"Now kids, you have to leave the discipline up to your father. Matt behaved very badly and your father will talk to him about it," Emily said.

"Yeah, he'll talk to him with a belt," John chimed in.

About that time the back door opened and in walked Matt, followed closely by his father. Matt did not give the impression that he had enjoyed his conversation with his father. Steven stopped and washed his hands before he entered the kitchen.

Matt was headed out the doorway leading into the hall when Steven's voice stopped him. "Matt, just where do you think you're going?"

With a stubborn cutting edge to his voice he replied, "To my room, sir!"

"I don't think so. My memory appears to be better than yours. I think you've forgotten to do something."

"And what might that be, sir?"

"Matt, do we need to make another trip out to the barn to refresh your memory?"

Giving his father an "I'll get you for this one day" look, Matt turned to Emily and bitterly spit out, "Sorry."

It was apparent to everyone that he really wasn't sorry. But he did say it. Clearly, Matt was in a power struggle with his father. Whether Steven wanted it that way or not, he would just have to prove he was man enough to handle the job of father.

꿍

Steven came around the corner of the house and spotted Emily sitting in the porch swing as usual. He sat down on the edge of the porch.

They sat for a long time in silence before Steven finally spoke. "I want to apologize for what Matt did tonight. The room looks really nice."

"There's no need for you to apologize. You didn't do anything. I should have been more sensitive to their feelings. I should have realized how hard it is for them to have someone else come into their mother's home and take over."

Steven couldn't hear her crying, but he could see her body tremble in the moonlight. "Emily, you've bent over backwards to be sensitive to everyone and not hurt anyone's feelings. This is your home now. Rebecca doesn't live here anymore."

Emily's sobs seemed to deepen with every word Steven said. Crying women had never been a specialty of his, and Steven didn't know what he should do. What he wanted to do was take her into his arms and hold her, but he couldn't allow that. Instead, he reached into his pocket, pulled out his handkerchief, walked over, and handed it to her.

Emily took it and tried to dry her eyes, but it was no use; the tears wouldn't stop flowing. The main valve had been turned on and there was no way to shut it off this time. Steven stood helpless. She looked like a child sitting there. What had he done to this lady? He had brought her from her well-known world to a world that was strange to them both. He could stand it no longer; sitting down beside her in the swing, he took her into his arms. He held her while the rest of the water flowed over the dam. He could feel the dampness of her tears through his shirt. He had no words of comfort; he just held her.

Neither of them knew how long they sat there. Emily's tears eventually ceased, but Steven continued to hold her. She finally lifted her head and looked into his eyes. "Thank you. I needed that."

"I didn't do anything," he replied gruffly.

"You did more than you'll ever know."

Looking into her eyes, she looked so helpless and vulnerable. He wanted to kiss her, but before he gave in to the urge, he stood up and left her sitting alone in the swing.

"If you're feeling better, I'm going to make one last round to check on things and then I think I'll turn in," he stated.

"You go ahead. I'm okay. I'll turn in soon," she told him.

Steven walked off. There was nothing to check on; he just needed to walk some of this tension off. He could hear his little voice in the distance, like it was coming up behind him. He turned and said out loud, "Now you just wait. Don't start with me tonight. I still need to take care of my children first before I can think of myself and my needs." Why had he said that? Was he beginning to need Emily?

His little voice couldn't help but answer his question and it stopped Steven in his tracks, for it was as audible as if someone was standing right there. "Yes, Steven. You are beginning to need Emily, and furthermore, you're in love with her." His little voice had a lot of nerve to tell him something like that and then just leave, but that's exactly what it did, and Steven was left alone with his thoughts.

Emily found it difficult to fall asleep that night. Her mind was swirling and her heart was pounding. It had felt so good and so right to be in Steven's arms. She was proud of the way he was getting close to his children, the younger ones at least. If they could get close as a couple, maybe they could become a real family. She was in love with the man and there was nothing she could do to change that now.

CHAPTER 8

Emily was in the midst of her morning chores as her mind replayed the events of the night before, over and over again. That morning at breakfast Steven had acted no differently toward her. She didn't know what she had expected, maybe a smile. There was nothing. She really needed to talk with someone. Maybe she could visit Rosemary Kirkland this afternoon.

Steven had some work to do around the barn that afternoon, and this gave Emily the perfect opportunity to visit Rosemary, as he would be close in case the children needed anything.

Steven was repairing a harness when she entered the barn. "Steven, I'm going to visit Rosemary Kirkland for a little while," Emily informed him.

"Okay," he said. "I'll hitch the buggy for you."

Steven hitched his little gray mare to the buggy and brought it around to the front of the house, where Emily waited. He took her arm and helped her up into the seat.

As she started to drive away, he looked at her and smiled. "You be careful."

It was such a little thing, such a common statement. But his smile and his concern meant the world to Emily. She was a goner, and she knew it.

Rosemary was sitting on her front porch shelling peas when Emily arrived. Emily greeted her, then pulled up a chair and sat down.

"It's good to see you. What brings you up my way in the middle of the week?" Rosemary asked.

"I just needed a little female conversation," Emily confided. "Have you got another pan? I'll help you shell these peas while we talk."

Rosemary disappeared into the house and returned with a pan for Emily. Emily quickly filled it and began shelling the peas.

"Is there something special you wanted to talk about?" Rosemary asked.

Emily blushed as she spoke. "Oh, nothing special."

"Let me guess. Could the subject be about six-foot-three and weigh about 190 pounds? Tell me, has there been some new development?" Rosemary questioned.

"Am I so obvious? You always seem to know when Steven's on my mind."

"It's not that hard to figure out. I'd bet Steven's on your mind most of the time," Rosemary teased.

Emily blushed again. She told Rosemary about the events of the past few days, beginning with Steven's newfound affection toward Sarah and the twins. She ended with Matt's outrage the previous evening.

"It sounds as though Steven's beginning to take his role as a father seriously. I'm very happy to hear it," Rosemary noted. "I agree that he still has a long way to go before he wins over Matt and Mark, but I think he can do it. My question now is, has he started taking his role as a husband seriously?"

"I had a small glimmer of hope last night. I'm probably making too much out of it, but it really meant a lot to me at the time. After the fiasco ended and all the kids were in their rooms, I went out and sat in the porch swing. The whole evening had been a nightmare. I had only wanted to turn the house into a home and all I accomplished was to turn it into a battlefield again. Steven walked up and sat down on the porch." Emily paused for a moment; she didn't want to start crying now.

"He apologized for Matt's behavior and I told him he had nothing to apologize for. I should have been more sensitive of everyone's feelings. I know it's hard for the children having a stranger come into their mother's home and take over."

"You told Steven that you should have been more sensitive?" Rosemary wanted to know.

Emily nodded, then continued. "Steven tried to make me feel better by telling me that I'd tried to protect everyone's feelings and that it was my home and I could fix it like I wanted. He said Rebecca didn't live there anymore. Well, that's when I couldn't hold it in any longer. I sat there and cried like a baby. I was so embarrassed, but I couldn't do anything about it."

"You shouldn't have been embarrassed. Steven was right. It is your home now, not Rebecca's," Rosemary tried to comfort her friend.

"You're both wrong. Rebecca Barnes lives in every corner of that house. She lives in the faces of her children and she still occupies the place in Steven's heart that I'm rightfully entitled to. I didn't want to cry in front of him, but with every word he uttered I cried harder."

"What happened next?" Rosemary asked.

"Steven offered me his handkerchief, then he sat down beside me in the swing and held me in his arms until I finished crying. For just an instant I felt safe and secure and maybe a little loved." Emily had tears in her eyes once again.

"I don't think you're making too much of this. Steven has to care about you. If he didn't, he would have just let you cry alone. Tell me, how did he act this morning to you?"

"Like he always does. It was as though nothing had happened last night. But this afternoon when I left to come over here, he hitched the buggy for me. And when he helped me up onto the seat, he smiled and told me to be careful." Emily giggled. "Boy, I'm really grasping for straws now, aren't I?"

"Not really," Rosemary affirmed. "If it were anyone else smiling and telling you to be careful, I'd think nothing about it. But this comes from a man who, up until very recently, barely acknowledged you existed. Any small gesture becomes very significant when it comes from him. Now about his holding you last night—did he release you as soon as you stopped crying, and what happened when he did let you go?"

Emily thought a moment, then answered, "Well, actually he held me for a little while after my crying had stopped. And just for a moment, after he released his hold, I thought he was going to kiss me. But he didn't. He excused himself and left."

"That's very promising." Rosemary set down her pan of shelled peas. "Let's go have some lemonade and move this conversation into the kitchen."

Rosemary poured two glasses of lemonade and set a plate of cookies on the table. "I told you I saw something in Steven's eyes the day we had lunch with you," Rosemary said. "I really believe he's starting to have feelings for you but is afraid to act on them. I think maybe he's afraid of marriage."

She took a cookie, then continued. "Most folks around here thought Rebecca Barnes was wonderful, but I've got a hunch that all was not what it was made out to be. There was just something about her attitude. I heard her make a few comments about Steven that made me wonder if he didn't kind of have a rough time at home. It could be he feels like a failure as a husband and is afraid to try it again."

"Rosemary, how do you come up with all this insight on people? I know there's something in his past that's haunting him. And I know there was some reason why he didn't return home after he earned enough money to get the farm out of debt. But I just don't know what the answers to those questions are." Emily sipped her lemonade, then thoughtfully added, "If a man's happy at home, then why would he stay away for five years?"

"That's my point exactly. If Rebecca was such a wonderful wife, then why didn't her husband come home? Now either she wasn't so wonderful or he's just a scoundrel. I didn't know Steven before he left, but from what I've seen of him since his return, I don't think he's a scoundrel."

"Okay, so his marriage was far from perfect and he's afraid to try it again. So where does that leave me? Looks like my chances might be pretty slim." Emily sighed.

"Not necessarily. You know a horse can be a little skittish, but he can still be broken. You just have a fellow who's a little gun-shy, but he can be brought around with proper handling."

"Look, you're talking to the wrong woman. I'm about as inexperienced as they come at handling men," Emily confessed.

"You were married before, so you had to have won at least one man's heart. That makes you experienced. Anyway, mostly you just have to be yourself. Steven is falling for you already. You just have to give him a little push."

"And how do you suggest I push?"

"Take every opportunity when you're alone to flirt a little. Let the man know you're interested. He's probably afraid of rejection, so he won't make a move. Let him know in subtle little ways that he won't be rejected."

"Do you want me to throw myself at him?" Emily asked.

"No! You know how to flirt, surely. Just be extra nice to him. Give him the opening and see what happens. This man's your husband, not some total stranger."

"He's almost a total stranger. I know very little about him. And just because we have a piece of paper that says we're married doesn't mean we're husband and wife."

"Look, you'll figure out what to do as the opportunities present themselves. Just follow your instincts. Pray about it; I have a strong feeling that the Lord is on your side."

Emily heard the clock in the other room chime the hour. "I've got to go. It's almost suppertime. I didn't realize we'd talked so long. Rosemary, thank you for listening and for all your advice."

Rosemary stood and gave her friend a hug. "Everything is going to work out. You just wait and see. You two are in love and love always finds a way."

As Emily drove home she thought about Rosemary's advice. How could she flirt with Steven? She hadn't flirted in so long she was afraid she would make a fool of herself. Well, she would just play it by ear, and she knew praying about it certainly wouldn't hurt.

∞

It was a hot July evening and Emily really wanted to sit out in the porch swing, but this evening she was nervous. What if Steven was out there? How would she act? She went to her room, but it was too warm to go to bed. She peeked out the door before she walked out on the porch and saw no one. She eased onto the swing. Finally a little wind began to stir, and she relaxed until she heard that familiar whistle. But there was something a little different about the whistle this time. It was no longer monotone; Steven was actually whistling a tune.

"Sure feels hot this evening," Steven said as he sat down on the edge of the porch.

"Sure does," she replied. She hoped they were both talking about the weather. "How are the crops doing?"

"Pretty good, considering. The corn should be ready to gather next month. I'm gonna have the boys clean out the corncrib next week. Looks like we're gonna have a good year. We should sell enough cotton to take us through the winter and planting next year."

This was very nice, Emily thought. They were actually having a conversation. "The twins were really excited about helping you today, and Sarah's thrilled at the attention she's been getting from you."

"It feels good to be a father again. I didn't realize how much I'd missed them," Steven said. "I'd tried for so long not to think about the kids too often. Of course they have changed so much." His voice broke and he stopped talking.

Even in the moonlight, Emily could tell he was crying. She didn't know what to do. He might be embarrassed if he knew she could see his tears. "Steven, you have to put those years you were away behind you. You can't change the past, and you can't control the future. You just have the present, so make the best of the time you have now."

"I just wish there was something I could do about Matt and Mark. I wish they didn't hate me so much. Emily, what can I do to make things up to them?" Steven lifted his head and looked toward her.

Taken off guard by his question, she took a moment to respond. "Why don't you try sitting them down and talking to them. Just let them say what's on their minds and then you tell them what's on yours. Once everything is out in the open, maybe it won't look quite so bad and at least you'll know what you're dealing with."

"I don't know if I've got enough courage to sit down and talk to them face to face. There's so much anger there. It might be dangerous."

"Maybe you need a third party to be present. Someone who could be impartial. You might think about talking to Brother Kirkland. Maybe he would sit down with the three of you or at least give you some advice on what to do."

"That sounds like a good idea. I'll think about it. Well, it's getting late. I guess we'd better go in." Steven stood and stepped up on the porch. He opened the door and allowed Emily to walk in first.

Emily stopped when she got to her bedroom door. "Good night, Steven."

"Good night, Emily. I hope you sleep well." Steven smiled at her.

Emily lay awake for hours. That strange feeling wasn't just in her stomach tonight; it was in her heart as well. They had talked on the porch almost like a husband and wife would. He had even asked her advice. It had been wonderful.

"Oh Lord, just let our relationship grow. Let us become a family in every sense of the word," Emily prayed. She also hoped and prayed that in the not too distant future she would feel Steven's arms around her again. And she couldn't help but wonder what it would be like to be kissed by this man she was falling in love with more and more every day.

After church on Sunday, Steven approached Brother Kirkland and invited him to drop by that afternoon. Steven explained that he needed to talk with the preacher.

It was about two o'clock when Rosemary and Brother Kirkland arrived, and Steven suggested they all sit on the porch since it was such a warm afternoon.

After chatting a few moments, Brother Kirkland suggested, "Steven, why don't you give me a little tour of your place. I'd like to see what you've done with it."

"Sure, I'd love to. If you ladies will excuse us," Steven said as he stood to leave.

Emily watched as Steven disappeared toward the barn. "I think Steven wants to talk about Matt and Mark. He even asked my advice the other night about what he should do with them. I suggested he talk to Brother Tom."

"That sounds hopeful, him asking your advice about something," Rosemary observed.

"We had a very nice talk. It was the first time we'd ever really carried on a conversation. But those few isolated moments on the porch are still all we share." Emily's tone was wistful.

"Well, that's better than it was. Maybe those few moments will become more frequent, until they just happen all the time," Rosemary encouraged.

∞

The men had passed the barn and headed down the lane. There was a fallen log by the side of the path and Brother Kirkland stopped and took a seat. "Steven, what's on your mind?"

"A lot of things," Steven confessed. "But mostly what I wanted to talk to you about was Matt and Mark. I've made real progress with the younger children, but those two are so bitter, I can't break through the wall they've built around themselves. Brother Kirkland, I need some advice on how to handle them."

"First of all, call me Tom. I don't want to be just your pastor—I want to be your friend. Secondly, can you give me a little background? I wasn't here when you left. I'll admit, I've heard various stories about your departure and why you stayed away. But I don't believe much unless I hear it from the source."

Steven really needed to unload on someone and maybe Tom Kirkland was the right person. "Well, this farm had always been my dream," he began. "My parents ran a little general store and were very successful at it, but I wanted to be a farmer. When I finally got my dream, I thought everything would be wonderful from then on. How wrong I was. Everything went pretty well for the first few years, but then it all fell apart. The weather didn't help. Most folks lost money that year. Anyway, the only thing I could come up with was to leave here and go find work so I could meet the mortgage. So that's what I did."

Steven paused, then continued. "I just kept drifting farther west until I wound up in Abilene. That's where I spent the last five years. Sarah was just two when I left, and Matt was eleven. I'm sure it was the hardest on the older boys. The younger ones were too young to know what was going on. I wrote to Rebecca regular at first, but I sent money every month the whole time I was away. I just couldn't make myself come home. I really missed the kids and wanted to see them, but I guess not bad enough, or I would've come back."

"Steven, when you left, you did what you thought you had to do to keep body and soul together. I don't see that you did anything wrong by leaving. I'm sure it was hard on everyone at that time," Tom stated. "You said you really missed your kids, but I noticed you didn't mention your wife. I get the feeling maybe your marriage wasn't as happy as most folks thought it was. Am I right?"

"It wasn't Becky's fault. I forced her to move out here. She didn't want to be a farmer's wife. Life was real hard for her. She had grown up in a rather well-to-do family, and farm life wasn't her cup of tea."

"Why didn't she go back to her family after you left and didn't come home?"

"After we moved here, her father turned the family business over to her brother and he squandered it all away. It broke her parents' hearts. I guess you could say they were left penniless. She blamed me for that, too. Her father didn't like me from the start, so even if we had been there, he wouldn't have given his business to her. He didn't want me getting my hands on any of his money."

"Did Rebecca blame you for all her misfortunes?"

"I was to blame for most of them. She never wanted a big family. But I'm the one that kept getting her pregnant. She didn't want to live on a farm, but I moved her to this place. Then I left her alone to raise five children that she didn't really want in the first place." The burden of guilt was so great that Steven couldn't continue. He had ruined Becky's life, and now he had to pay for it.

"Steven, you're not to blame for everything that was wrong in Rebecca's life. It takes two people to have children. Did you force yourself upon her?" Steven shook his head. "Well, she was a consenting adult and your wife. Maybe the farm was your dream, but did you force her here at gunpoint? Did you discuss it with her before you made the move here?" Tom asked.

"We talked about it a great deal. I sold my father's store after he died and we agreed to try this for five years. After the five years were up, we talked about it again and decided to stay."

"Sounds to me like she willingly made a decision to stay here. You didn't force her, she made the choice."

"Then why did she blame me for everything? When times were hard, why did she tell me it was all my fault?" Steven questioned.

"Some people find it impossible to accept responsibility for anything. They always have to put the blame on someone else for their misfortunes. Maybe that's what Rebecca did and you were the only one around she could blame."

"She seemed to delight in telling me what a lousy husband and provider I was. But when we were out among folks, she would act like the perfect obedient wife." Steven hesitated, then continued. "Something has bothered me since I got back: In an argument one day, Matt said that they never heard from me after I left. That's just not true. I wrote. Becky always knew how to get in touch with me. Is it possible she never told the kids?"

"That's entirely possible. That would have let her continue to blame you for any problems she had. To the general public, she never said an unkind word about you, and of course that won her a lot of sympathy. But it sounds to me like that was just her normal routine. At home she was telling you what a terrible husband you were, but in public she was singing your praises. Then she just continued the same pattern after you left."

"I let that woman destroy all of my self-confidence. I knew I was a terrible husband and would never be able to make any woman happy." Steven sighed.

"What about Emily?" Tom asked. "What kind of husband does she think you are?"

Steven couldn't help but chuckle. "Emily doesn't think of me as a husband. I don't know how she thinks of me. Probably as the biggest heel in the world."

Tom looked completely baffled. "What do you mean?"

"Emily and I are married in name only. When I found out I had to return to be father and mother to my children, I guess I was just too scared to face it alone. Emily worked in a little café I used to go to occasionally. I knew she was a kind and good woman, so I asked her to marry me and help me raise my children. I made it clear to her that she and I would have no relationship. I don't know how that woman has put up with me and these kids. Matt and Mark are rude to her, and I haven't treated her much better. For the most part, I just ignore her, although that's getting more difficult every day."

"What do you mean?" Tom asked.

"Maybe it's just the fact that I'm lonely or that there hasn't been a woman in my life for a very long time. But I find myself drawn to her. And right now, I need to work things out with my kids before I do anything about my personal needs."

"I'd say the first thing you need to do is to forgive yourself for your mistakes. God has already forgiven if you've asked Him to. Next, quit blaming yourself for Becky's unhappiness. I'm sure you made some mistakes as a husband; we all do. But you couldn't be the cause of everything wrong in her life. Steven, it's okay for you to be happy. You don't have to be miserable the rest of your life. You missed a lot of time with your kids, and you can't make up for that time. You need to ask their forgiveness. Tell them you're sorry for staying gone so long. Then you all have to get on with living today."

"But do you think Emily and I could possibly have a future after all this?"

"Yes, I do. You may have gotten married without really knowing each other, but you can make this work if you really want to," Tom encouraged.

"And just how do we do that?" Steven questioned.

"Maybe you need to court your wife and get acquainted. Who knows, you might realize you like each other. You might even find yourself in love."

Steven wanted to get off the subject of Emily and back to the original topic. "We've talked about everything but what I originally wanted to talk to you about. What do I do about Matt and Mark? Emily suggested I sit them down and get everything out in the open. But when they hate me so much, that's a pretty scary proposition. So she suggested maybe a third party should be present."

"I think sitting down with them face-to-face is a splendid idea. And if you're asking me to be the third party, I'd be happy to. Do you have any proof that you and their mother corresponded during those years you were away?"

"I still have the letters she wrote me. I don't know if she saved any of the ones I wrote her or not. Calvin Meyers, at the bank, can verify I sent money each month. He also knew where I was the whole time. Before I left, I asked him to be in charge of the finances of the farm. Becky wasn't very good at managing money."

"We will allow the boys to vent all their anger, then you can present them with your side. We don't want to destroy their feelings about their mother, but they have to know that their father does care about them and always has. It'll be rough on everyone, and things may not get better right away. But at least the boys will have the truth and can sort out their feelings."

The men sat silently for a time before Tom spoke again. "Steven, you have a rough time in front of you, but you've already come through a very hard time. Now that you have God on your side, you will survive. Why don't we pray together? Then we'll go back to the house and join the ladies."

❧

On Tuesday morning, Calvin Meyers came out to the farm. Emily led him into the living room and he took a seat in one of the big overstuffed chairs. "Is Steven around today?" Calvin asked. "I knew I'd be taking a chance finding him nearby—but I would really like to talk with him."

"You're in luck. He's in the field behind the barn," Emily informed him. "I'll get Sarah to run out and tell him you're here."

They chatted until Steven entered the room a few moments later. "Calvin Meyers, what brings you out this far? Are you here to foreclose on my farm?" Steven joked.

"I might just try that. The bank could make a good profit off this place.

It's really looking good," Calvin teased.

"Have you been telling my wife any nonsense about me? Emily, don't believe a word this fellow tells you." Steven smiled at Emily.

Emily was too shocked to respond. She couldn't believe Steven had actually referred to her as his wife. Maybe they were making progress.

After talking for a while, Steven asked, "Since your bank has quite an investment in this place, would you like to take a little look around?"

"You bet. Emily, will you excuse us?" Calvin asked.

"Sure, I've got to get dinner finished. You're welcome to stay for dinner if you'd like," she offered.

"That sounds wonderful, but I have to get back to town. Maybe another time. It's been a pleasure meeting you." He shook her hand.

Once out of earshot, Steven asked, "So, what do you need to talk to me about?"

"Matt and Mark came to see me the other day," Calvin replied.

"That must have been the day they were late for supper and the day my horse was missing out of the barn. They were very vague about their whereabouts."

"Well, they came to see me. It seems they're concerned that you aren't very sincere in your dedication to them or this place, and they wanted to know how they could protect their interests. And of course their mother's money." Calvin paused to see what Steven's reaction to this bit of news would be.

"Those boys really dislike me. I knew their anger was strong, but I didn't know it went this deep. What did you say to them?"

"I hope I didn't overstep my boundaries. I told them you had sent money every month you were away. I also told them you'd made me caretaker of your finances. That you didn't have to come home if the money was what you were interested in, since it was your money and you could've gotten it anytime."

Calvin paused again and waited for a response. When Steven offered none, he continued, "Just as you suspected, the boys are under the impression that their mother didn't know where you were or how to get in touch with you. I explained that their mother and I always knew how to reach you and that I sent you a monthly statement on the finances of the farm. I also informed them that their mother heard from you, too. That didn't go over too well."

"I'm sure it didn't. They're so angry with me for leaving and then you tell them something they don't want to hear about their mother, the only parent they've had for a long time. I know it's got to hurt to think the one person you could count on lied to you. Calvin, why would she do that?" Steven puzzled.

"I don't know. Rebecca did some strange things. I guess she thought that if you ever came home, she'd have some leverage with the kids. She would be the good guy for hanging around and you'd be the bad guy for deserting them. The only problem is, now she's gone—so the boys don't think there is a good guy."

"Any suggestion on how I might become the good guy to those two?"

"I think you need to sit down and talk to them. Show them the letters you have from Rebecca. Let them know you didn't just desert them. That you stayed in touch."

"I hate to have to destroy their image of their mother."

"Steven, you can point out that although their mother's judgment wasn't the best in the world, she did love and care for them. But the bottom line is, their mother's gone and you're here. You're all they've got now. They have to forgive you and get on with their lives." Calvin turned to his friend. "I don't envy you this job, but you've got to talk to them."

"I know I do. Emily gave me the same advice. I also talked to Tom Kirkland about it. He has agreed to sit down with me and the boys and be a mediator. After what you've told me, I guess I shouldn't put it off any longer. I know how Daniel must have felt before he was thrown into the lions' den."

"You can handle it," Calvin said. "I've seen you weather tougher storms."

CHAPTER 9

Steven drifted in and out of a restless sleep, thinking about the upcoming talk with Matt and Mark. But what really kept him awake was the thought of courting Emily. When morning finally came, he wandered into the kitchen. Breakfast smelled especially good this morning, and Emily looked especially nice. Steven was sure she probably looked this way every morning, but he had just been too blind to notice. Well, maybe he could throw a little courting in on the side while he arranged to have his talk.

"Good morning, Emily. Breakfast smells almost as good as you look," Steven announced as he took a cup from the cupboard and poured himself some coffee.

"Thank you," Emily said softly.

Steven gave her a big smile as he sat down at the head of the table.

∞

Emily couldn't help but smile as she did her morning chores. She even found herself humming a joyous tune. She was amazed at how the slightest attention from Steven made her mood brighter.

"Emily, you sure are in a good mood," Sarah noted as she threw the chickens another handful of corn. "Did you get some good news or something?"

"No. I'm just in a good mood today. It's such a lovely day, it makes me want to sing."

∞

Brother Tom was away from home when Steven dropped by the parsonage, so he left a message with Rosemary. Since Steven could do nothing about his boys today, he decided to try a little more courting. Stopping at the general store, he got Wilma Jenkins, the storekeeper, to pick out the notions Emily would need to make a dress with the material he chose. He would surprise Emily this evening after the children had gone to bed.

As Steven approached the corner of the house, he realized that he looked forward to seeing Emily sitting on the porch swing. In the early days he had been somewhat uncomfortable when he found her sitting there. But he had to admit that he could have ended his evening strolls elsewhere if he'd been that uncomfortable.

That evening, instead of sitting down on the edge of the porch, Steven went into the house. In a few moments, he reappeared with a small bundle in his hand.

He handed the package to Emily. "This is just a little something to thank you for everything you've done since we got here. I'm sorry it's taken me so long to say thanks."

Emily slowly reached out for the package. "Steven, you shouldn't have, but thank you. I don't think I've ever received a gift when it wasn't a special occasion." Her trembling fingers struggled to untie the string.

She ran her fingers lightly over the soft material. The moon was bright, but she couldn't distinguish the color. Smiling, she said, "I'm sure it's lovely, but I'll have to go in to the light to see the color."

"It's lavender, with little white flowers," Steven informed her as he sat down on the edge of the porch. "I realized you hadn't asked for anything since we got here. I thought you might like a new dress."

"That's very thoughtful of you. I can hardly wait to get it made. I hope I can finish it before Sunday." Steven could hear the excitement in her voice as she spoke.

"I've been very thoughtless toward you. If you need anything for yourself you can charge it at Jenkins's store. If they don't have what you need or want, then we can go into Tyler to get it. If you ever need money, don't be afraid to ask. Actually, I've been thinking, why don't you keep the money from the sale of the eggs? That way you'll have a little cash you can call your own, to do with as you please."

"That's very generous of you, but it's not necessary. I make do okay."

"I know it's not necessary, but I insist. I don't want you to do without things." Steven chuckled as he added, "I'm a successful farmer and my wife shouldn't have to make do. She should have whatever she wants."

"My, all this wealth could go to my head," Emily chuckled.

Looking at her he said, "Seriously. I'm sorry for not being more sensitive to your needs. And I'm eternally grateful for everything you've done for me and my family. You've also taken more than your share of abuse not only from me but my kids as well."

By the time Steven finished, Emily was in tears, but they were happy tears this time. They sat in silence for a while, neither knowing just what to say.

After a moment, Steven said, "Emily, I never did ask you, but did you spend your own money on the material for the curtains in the living room and Sarah's Easter dress? If you did, I want to pay you for them. I know I should've asked sooner, but it didn't really dawn on me until today, when I was looking for that material for you."

Emily shook her head. "There's a big trunk in my bedroom full of material. Sarah showed it to me when I told her I would make her a dress. I asked Sarah about it, and she said that someone had sent it all to her mother, but Sarah didn't know who it was."

Steven was quiet for a short time. "I thought it looked familiar. I sent a lot of material home through the years. Stuff to make Becky and Sarah dresses and the boys shirts, you know, for their birthdays and Christmas and such. I even sent a few pieces for curtains and slipcovers to brighten the place up. I guess Becky didn't like my taste in fabric."

"You have excellent taste. But you either sent an awful lot of material or Rebecca made up very little of it."

"Well, before I take all the credit for the selection, I should tell you that Mable Truman, the dressmaker in Abilene, helped me pick out most of it. I had thought Becky would make it up into things for the kids and then she could truthfully tell them that their daddy hadn't forgotten them on their special days."

Not knowing what else to say, Emily finally asked, "Steven, have you thought anymore about having a talk with Matt and Mark?"

"I talked to Tom about it last Sunday, when he and Rosemary came by. I went to see him today to set up a time to talk to them, but he wasn't home. Calvin told me yesterday that the boys had been to see him, both of them mad as hornets. From what he said, I need to talk to them as soon as possible."

They talked a little longer, neither of them in a hurry to go inside. They both agreed that he couldn't put off his talk with his sons any longer.

∞

The family was seated at the breakfast table the next morning when they heard a knock at the door. "I'll get it," Steven said.

Opening the front door, he saw Tom Kirkland standing on the porch. "Rosemary told me you stopped by yesterday. I figured it was about the boys, so I wanted to get here as soon as I could," Tom told him.

"Thanks for coming so quickly. I've got a pretty urgent situation on my hands," Steven explained.

As the two sat down on the porch, Steven began to explain what Calvin had told him. "So the boys think you've come back for the money and are going to run off with everything they've worked so hard for?" Tom observed.

"Yeah, I guess so. Plus, they think I completely deserted them."

"Well, let's see if we can straighten any of this mess out." Brother Tom squared his shoulders.

The men went into the kitchen and found the family just finishing breakfast. Emily poured coffee for the two men as they seated themselves at the table.

As Matt and Mark rose to leave, Brother Tom stopped them. "Would you boys mind staying a few minutes? Your father and I would like to talk to you."

Hesitantly, the boys sat back down. Emily took the three younger children with her outside to do the morning chores, keeping them occupied while the others talked.

Steven had no idea how to begin, so he was grateful when Tom broke the ice. "Boys, your father spoke with me the other day. He's very concerned about the relationship—or I should say the lack of a relationship—between the three of you. It seems since his return you three have not been able to come to terms with your feelings. So this morning we're gonna try to get everything out in the open so we can deal with it." Tom paused and looked at the Barnes men before going on.

"I know you boys are angry," Tom continued, "and that's only natural, but keeping that anger inside doesn't do anyone any good. Least of all you. Matt, you start. I want you to tell your father just how you feel about him and this whole situation."

There was silence. Finally Matt began; once the feelings started to surface, the words rolled out like water flowing over a dam. "I'm mad, real mad. You walked out on all of us. You didn't care what happened. We worked hard to save this farm and to have a place to live. All boys my age have to help out around their places, but I didn't just have to help out—I had to run the place. I had to do your job. Momma told me I was man of the house and I had to take over for you, so I did."

Matt caught his breath and continued. "You left without so much as a good-bye. I just woke up one morning and you were gone. Momma said she didn't know why or where you went. She said she guessed you went to find work. But we never heard from you again."

Steven listened as his son vented his anger and hatred. His heart broke to think that Rebecca had been so bitter as to turn his children against him. He didn't know if he could find the words to explain his feelings and actions; he didn't know if he could change their minds about him. But he had to try.

Silently, Steven said a prayer, and then he began. "I didn't just run out on you. Your mother and I talked about my going for a long time, and it seemed to be the only solution. The drought had wiped us out that year and our savings were gone. I had only one choice as far as I could see—leave here and go find work so we wouldn't lose the farm and our home. I looked in on you boys before I left. You were sleeping so peacefully, I just couldn't bring myself to wake you. I wanted to remember that peaceful look on your faces."

The boys appeared to be listening, but Steven couldn't tell much from their blank faces. He continued, "I started working my way west, and each time I went through a town I would mail your mother a letter. When I finally settled in Abilene, I wrote her on a regular basis and she answered my letters."

Brother Tom didn't have to ask for a response; Matt jumped right in. "No one heard from you. Momma said she didn't know where you were. Why would she lie to us?"

"I don't know why your mother said that, but it's not true. She always knew where I was. I also sent messages in my letters to you kids. And I sent money every month to Calvin at the bank," Steven defended.

Finally, Mark spoke. "Why did you wait until Momma died to come home? Was Emily the reason you couldn't come home sooner?"

"I don't know why I didn't come home. The longer I stayed gone, the easier it was to stay away and the harder it became to think of coming back. I had asked Calvin to get someone to farm the place, and he asked Clyde to do it. Clyde was willing to take on the job and to teach you boys. From Calvin's monthly reports, I knew the place was doing much better without me than it ever did with me, so I just stayed gone. I was a coward and I was wrong for staying away."

Mark wasn't satisfied with his father's answer. "What about Emily? Is she the reason you didn't come back?"

Steven shook his head. "Emily is not the reason. I've heard the gossip about her and me, but that's what it is—gossip. Emily and I are just now starting to become friends," Steven told his sons. "I hope someday that our friendship will grow into something more. Emily is, and will continue to be, a part of this family. I pray that you two will learn to accept her as such. You can't blame her for my faults and shortcomings."

His answer hadn't fully satisfied Mark's curiosity. "If Emily isn't the reason you stayed away and you had no other reason, then why did you come back at all?"

"I got news that your mother had died and that you children were gonna become wards of the county. I couldn't let that happen. Whether you believe it or not, I never stopped loving you kids."

"Then why didn't you stay in touch?" Matt wouldn't drop that issue. He just couldn't believe his mother had lied to him all those years.

Tom had remained silent throughout the conversation so far, but now he spoke. "Steven, go get the letters."

Steven went out into the hallway. As he got down on his knees and reached under his bed to retrieve the bag that contained the letters, he noticed a small box shoved all the way back against the wall. He had pulled the bundle of letters from his bag and started to walk back in the kitchen, when his little voice told him to look inside that box.

He pulled the bed away from the wall, picked up the box, and looked inside. There were his letters to Rebecca, tied neatly with a small ribbon. Stunned for a moment, he stood there in silence, staring at the contents of the box. Rebecca hadn't told the children about his letters, but for some reason she had kept them. Now he had absolute proof that he had not completely forgotten his family—but what was his proof going to cost his sons? Steven finally managed to make his legs carry him back to the kitchen where his judges awaited.

He laid the letters Rebecca had written him in front of Matt and then sat down. Matt began to thumb through them. Frowning, he picked up one, opened it, and read. When he had finished reading, he laid the letter down. His hands were trembling and the tears had started to trickle down his face.

"Why would she lie to us? She was our mother. Why would she make us think our father didn't love us anymore?" Matt asked between sobs.

"Son, I don't have the answer to those questions. But I can tell you, I do love you and I always have. I never stopped loving you and I never forgot about you." Steven cleared his throat. "I found this under the bed in the hall when I went to get the letters your mother wrote to me." He set the little box containing his letters on the table.

Mark began to examine the letters his mother had written while Matt opened the box. Matt picked up the neatly tied bundle and flipped through them. There was letter after letter that his father had written to the family while he was gone. His tears began to flow even more furiously.

"Why would she lie?" Matt cried.

"Matt, we don't know why she did it," Brother Tom explained. "No one can explain it. But I know your mother loved you. She was very wrong in not telling you the truth about your father's whereabouts, but you have to forgive her. You have to forgive your father, too. It's time to put the past behind you and start over."

"Forgive?" Matt choked. "You want me to forgive? I find out I've been lied to by the one person I thought I could trust, and I'm supposed to forgive her? My father deserts me without so much as a good-bye, much less an explanation, and I'm supposed to forgive him, too. Preacher, you're crazy!"

Matt gathered all the letters from the table and placed them in the little box, tucked it under his arm, then walked out the back door. Steven started after him, but Tom stopped him. "Steven, let him go. He needs some time alone to sort things out."

Steven turned around. Mark was still seated at the table, and Steven walked over to him and sat down on the bench beside him. He placed his hand on his son's shoulder. "Mark, I love you," was all he could say. Mark fell into his father's arms. Steven held him as they both cried. At least one son had forgiven him.

Tom stayed and talked with Steven and Mark until almost dinnertime. Matt had still not returned when Tom finally had to leave.

"He'll be back when he gets things straight in his mind," Tom said. "You come get me if you need anything." Looking at Mark, Tom added, "If any of you need to talk, feel free to stop by the parsonage anytime."

As Steven walked Tom outside and watched him leave, Emily appeared. She looked up at Steven and he dropped into the swing, his shoulders slumped. Quietly, she sat down beside him.

"Well," Steven sighed, "Mark seems to forgive me but Matt just walked off. I showed them the letters their mother had written to me, and by some strange coincidence, I found the letters I had written to Rebecca. They had been under the bed in the hall all this time. I showed them to the boys, too. Matt took all the letters and left. Tom says he just needs some time alone to sort things out. I sure hope that doesn't take too long."

"I'm sure that's it," Emily said. "It's just a lot for him to digest all at once. We'll pray he works things out soon."

"Emily, he looked so unhappy. His whole world came apart. He doesn't feel he can trust anyone anymore. I'm afraid I've lost him for good."

"Remember the prodigal son? He came back, and so will Matt. You just have to pray and have faith."

Steven frowned. "The prodigal son left because he was greedy and wanted to try things on his own. He didn't leave because he felt everyone had betrayed him. And he also knew he would be treated fairly by his father when he returned. Matt feels alone and betrayed. He doesn't trust me. What if he doesn't come back?"

Emily reached over and took Steven's hand in hers. Looking into his eyes, she said, "Steven, he will come home."

Matt still hadn't returned when the family finished supper. Steven looked around the table. "Do any of you have any idea where Matt might have gone?"

"There's a spot down by the creek where he goes a lot, but I already looked there. There was no sign of him," Mark answered.

"What about friends? Does he have any friends that he might go see?" Steven continued his interrogation.

"He doesn't have many friends," Mark answered. "He's been too busy being the man around here. He hasn't had time for friends. The only place he might go would be Uncle Clyde's and I checked there, too."

After the children left, Steven looked at Emily with desperation in his eyes. "Emily, I can't just sit here. I've got to do something. I'm gonna go have a look around."

"It's getting late. You be careful," she warned as he went out the back door.

Emily checked on the children, trying to reassure them that Matt would be okay. Even Mark seemed to welcome her attention tonight.

Emily was really more worried about Steven at this point than Matt. She knew Steven was still blaming himself for everything that was wrong in this family. She couldn't sleep, and since the evening was so warm, she kept vigil from the porch swing. As she waited she lifted Steven and Matt up to God in prayer.

The hours went by and there was still no sign of Steven or Matt. The mosquitoes forced Emily to move her vigil to her bedroom. She lay down, but sleep would not come, so she continued to pray. Somehow God would make this right; He could take an impossible situation and make it work out for everyone. She didn't know how He would turn this one around, but she knew He could and she continued to pray.

The clock on the mantel had just chimed 1:00 a.m. when Emily heard the front screen door squeak. She jumped up, put on her robe, and rushed out into the hallway. Steven stood there all alone. His mood seemed even darker than it did when he left.

"No sign of him?" Emily asked.

"Nothing. But I didn't really have much hope of spotting him after it got dark. I sat down by the creek and prayed and tried to figure out why I'd done the things I did. Why didn't I come home? I knew my kids needed me even if Rebecca didn't."

Steven slumped down on the side of his bed. "I would cry, but the tears are all gone. I knew winning the hearts of my older sons wouldn't be easy, but I never expected this. I've never felt so helpless in my life. Emily, why did I desert my family?"

"Steven, I don't have any answers for you. You're the only one who can answer all those questions. If you search deep down inside, I think you'll remember why you acted as you did."

Emily's voice was tender, and Steven knew the words she spoke were true. No matter how much he loved his children, he realized, his love for their mother had died a slow, painful death. Once he was away from her destructive criticism, he just couldn't force himself to come back. Not for anyone. He would have stayed and continued to endure her bitter remarks if the opportunity had never presented itself for him to leave; he would have even continued to defend her right to say them, and he would have gone on taking the blame for making her life miserable. But the opportunity came to go and he took it. Deep inside, he had been relieved to escape. Now he had to take responsibility for his actions.

Steven looked up into Emily's understanding face. Seeing the love in her eyes, he didn't feel quite so alone. He stretched out his arms and Emily walked into them. He held her around the waist and put his head on her chest. She stroked his cheek tenderly as she placed a soft kiss on the top of his head.

"I really made a mess out of everything," he sighed.

"There's nothing you can do about the past. It's done. You have to start from now. God has forgiven you because you asked Him to. Now forgive yourself. Start right now being the best father you can and your children will accept you for what you are now."

Afraid to look up into Emily's eyes, Steven asked, "What about being a husband? Can I start that from right now, too?"

"I don't see why not," Emily answered.

Steven stood and tilted her head up toward his face, then placed a warm tender kiss on her soft lips. He felt comforted just holding her in his arms. Steven released his hold and gave her one more gentle kiss before telling her good night. As he settled into his bed, he said one more silent prayer for Matt's safe return.

CHAPTER 10

Steven was saddling his horse to go search for Matt when Mark came up behind him. "Dad, I want to go with you."

Steven was startled by the sound of someone behind him, but he was more startled by someone calling him Dad. He turned around.

"I'd like for you to come. You know Matt's hiding places better than me." Steven put his arm on his son's shoulder. "It'll be good to have you along, son. Families have to stick together at a time like this." Mark's arm around his waist told Steven that the young man agreed.

☜☞

Steven and Mark had searched everywhere. They had enlisted the help of Clyde Bentley and his boys, but they still had had no luck. Steven knew it was well past suppertime, for the sun was setting over the trees. He had sent Mark home earlier and given him instructions to tell Emily he would be in later.

"Steven, we're losing the light," Clyde said. "We'd better call it a day. Matt's a smart kid. He knows how to take care of himself. He'll come home just as soon as he has everything straightened out in his head."

"Unless he's better than his father at straightening things out, he may be gone a long time. I still can't seem to get things straight in my mind. Clyde, you didn't see his face when he left. His whole world had been destroyed. He doesn't think he can trust anyone anymore."

"I'm sorry about that. I didn't know Rebecca had told those kids she didn't know where you were. I knew Matt was very angry at you, and he didn't want to talk about you at all. But I just thought he was mad about your leaving. I had no idea she was filling their heads with such nonsense." Clyde shook his head. "Seems she told everyone whatever story best suited her fancy. She had most of the community believing she was the deserted wife. Poor Rebecca, they all thought. My Alice was a staunch supporter. She wouldn't even listen to me when I tried to tell her different."

"Well Clyde, I did desert her. I left and didn't come back."

"Yeah, you left all right. But you didn't desert her. She knew you was going, and she knew why you was going. She also knew where to find you. Deserting is when you just up and leave without a word to anyone. You didn't desert. I caught Rebecca's temper a few times myself. That was one vicious woman when she got mad or things didn't go her way." Clyde looked thoughtful. "If she'd been my wife I'd probably left long before you did."

"I didn't know anyone but me had ever seen that side of her. She was always the loving and charming wife out in public. It was only in private that she would show her more emotional side," Steven remembered.

"Well, she showed it to me. She got real mad the first year I farmed your place. She wanted to pay me a small wage instead of sharing the profits, and she was fit to be tied when she found out she had no say in the matter. She raked me and Calvin over the coals."

"I'm sorry. You shouldn't have had to go through that. I should've come home and taken care of my own responsibilities, not pawned them off on you and Calvin," Steven said.

"Look, you're not responsible for Rebecca's actions. If she treated you anything like she treated me and Calvin, you had to go for your own sanity."

"Oh, her wrath was something I endured every day. It wasn't so bad until we moved here, to the farm. Before that it only happened occasionally. But she hated this place so much that she despised me for bringing her here. Before things got so bad I offered to try and sell and move back to Henderson, but she refused. By then her brother had taken over the family business and lost everything. I guess torturing me seemed like a better alternative than going back to her hometown and facing her family's shame." Steven paused; these were not pleasant memories.

"If Rebecca had only been willing to work with you, ya'll could've had a good life. You have five beautiful children and you could have really made a go of this place. A marriage can't work, though, if the partners aren't willing to work together and do a lot of compromising. A man needs a good woman behind him, and a woman needs an understanding and loving man."

How right Clyde was. He and Rebecca had never had the ingredients for a happy marriage. She had made him feel worthless and he had made her miserable. Now he was trying to salvage what was left of the mess they had made of their lives. Their marriage had never been good, but they had produced five wonderful children, and with God's help, he would be a father to them at long last. And maybe, just maybe, he could be a husband to Emily.

"We'd better head toward home. We'll get an early start in the morning if that kid doesn't show up tonight," Clyde suggested.

"Thanks for all your help," Steven said. "We've pretty much covered this area. There's no telling where he's at by now. I guess I'll go into Tyler tomorrow and talk to the sheriff. Maybe he can contact some of the surrounding areas and turn something up."

The men said their farewells and Steven headed home along the creek bank, leading his horse. He had walked about a mile when he heard a rustling in the bushes. Cautious, he stopped and watched for some wild animal to appear. Instead, Matt walked out of the darkness and almost ran into his father before he noticed he was there. Startled, the two stood in silence, staring at each other.

"Matt!" Steven finally cried. "Son, we've been looking everywhere for you. I've been worried out of my mind." He started to embrace his son, but Matt pulled away.

"I've just been trying to sort things out in my mind," Matt replied.

"Well, were you able to do that?"

"Not really. I still have a lot of unanswered questions."

Steven picked up a small twig and began to nervously break it into small bits. "Can I answer any of your questions?"

"Will you be honest with me and tell me the whole truth?" Matt quizzed.

"I'll try," Steven promised.

"Well, I remember how much fun we used to have. You would take me fishing, and we even camped out by ourselves a few times. Then one morning I woke up and you were gone. I didn't know why. You were just gone. Why didn't you tell me good-bye?"

Steven leaned against a tree for a moment, then squatted down and picked up another twig. As he raked the stick across the ground, he said, "I have those same fond memories."

His voice trembled as he searched for the words to explain his actions to his son. "It was just as I told you. The drought that year almost put us under. I had sold the general store I had inherited from my folks and put a down payment on this farm. The rest of that money I had put in savings and it saw us through even when the farm wasn't doing so good, but it was all gone. Your mother and I talked about our options and together we decided that I should leave and go find work. I could work to get enough to pay off the mortgage and set a little aside for a rainy day. So I left."

Matt sat down on the ground in front of his father. He said nothing, but Steven knew he was waiting for the rest of the explanation.

"I don't know why I didn't talk to you. I have no excuse. I was terribly wrong. Things were really bad for me. I felt like a complete failure. I had failed your mother, you kids, and myself. I was so caught up in self-pity that I couldn't see what anyone else might be feeling. I did go into your room the morning I left. You and Mark were sleeping so peacefully, I just didn't have the heart to awaken you."

Steven stopped. He had to be completely honest. "That's not exactly true. I was too big a coward to wake you up. I knew if you were awake I would have to do a lot of explaining before I left and I was too big a chicken to do that. That peaceful expression of your faces was a whole lot easier to live with than the questions would have been. Your mother told me she would explain everything to you after I left."

"I read your letters," Matt muttered.

"Then you know I did try to explain some of my actions to you in the letters. Of course that didn't do much good since you never saw them until yesterday."

"I blamed myself." Matt's voice quivered. "I thought that if I'd helped out more around the farm, then things wouldn't have gotten so bad and you wouldn't have run away."

"Matt, none of it was your fault. No one could help the drought. It was just one of those things farmers sometimes have to face. I did what I had to do about the farm. Where I fell short was in the way I handled things with my family."

"After you got enough money to pay the mortgage, why didn't you come home then?"

Steven sighed heavily. He knew he couldn't whitewash things and make them believable. He had to be perfectly honest with his son. "Your mother and I had a very bad marriage. It wasn't all her fault, and it wasn't all my fault. As I told you, I felt like a failure. Your mother never liked living on a farm, and she never let me forget I was the one who insisted we move here and give farm life a try. As time went by, we grew further and further apart. I felt like I had ruined her life."

Steven sighed. "Everything I touched I ruined. My marriage, the farm, everything. So the farther I got from east Texas and the bad memories, the easier it was to stay gone." He looked at his son. "Now don't get me wrong. You kids were never bad memories. You were the only things in my life that made sense. But for me to come back to you meant I had to come back to your mother, and I wasn't man enough to do that."

The night was still. Steven could hear Matt's slow breathing, and once or twice he thought he detected a sob. The quiet surrounded them for several minutes.

"Matt, you're too young to understand the relationship between a man and a woman. My staying away had nothing to do with you kids. It was all because I felt like a failure. Your mother made me feel that she would have been better off if she'd never laid eyes on me." Steven paused before he added, "When Clyde started helping you boys farm the place, you did so much better than I'd ever done, I decided all of you were better off without me. It was self-pity. I was full of it. I know that now. I felt really sorry for myself, so I stayed away."

"So you didn't love Momma and that made you stay away from all of us."

"That's putting it bluntly, but in a way I guess it's true. But if you read my letters, then you know I never stopped loving you kids. It was just your mother. If someone continually tells you what a loser you are and what a lousy husband and father you are, you eventually start to believe them. I had finally started to believe Becky. I thought you would all be better off without me around. So when I left, I just stayed gone."

Once again silence hung over them for a few moments while Steven struggled and prayed about what to say next. "Matt, I was wrong. I made the biggest mistake of my life. Not coming back to my family was the worst mistake ever. Please forgive me. I can't change the past, but maybe if we start over, start from right now, we can have a good future."

Matt was silent a long moment. Then he said, "I guess I can understand a little about why you did what you did. I thought all night about why Momma lied to us. Either she wanted to make our lives miserable or she really hated you. I noticed in your letters each time you wrote a special note to us kids. You said you missed us, but you never said you missed Momma. I also noticed in her letters, Momma never said she missed you or asked you to come home. I read the ugly remarks she made about being better off without you. Then I started remembering a few times I'd overheard the two of you."

Matt stood, then walked over and leaned against the tree behind Steven. "I remember one time before you left. She called you a lousy husband and provider and said that you were worthless. I didn't understand it all, but I knew she didn't like you very much. You never said anything back to her. You never defended yourself. You just let her yell and call you names."

"I'm sorry you heard any of our quarrels. A child shouldn't have to hear his parents argue."

"I didn't really hear you argue. You never said anything. She did all the yelling. Why didn't you defend yourself?"

"It's like I told you. I'd come to believe that what she said was true. I believed I was a lousy husband and father. I no longer felt like a man."

Steven stood and faced his son. "That's not true any longer. Several weeks ago, I gave my life to Jesus and He's showing me I am worth something. I know with His help we can be a family. And I can learn to be a good father. It won't happen overnight, and it'll take a lot of patience and understanding on all our parts. It will also require some forgiving on your part."

"So if I can forgive you, then everything will be okay?"

"No, Matt. Everything won't be okay. But it will be a start."

"So, after I forgive you, do I have to accept Emily as my mother?"

"Emily doesn't want to replace your mother. But I think if you would give her half a try, she could be your friend. She is a part of this family now."

Matt frowned. "I can't make any promises, but I'll work on forgiving you. As for Emily, that's a different story."

"Well that's not exactly what I'd hoped for, but we'll consider it a start. Now what do you say to going home before they send out a search party for the two of us?" Steven suggested.

CHAPTER 11

Steven awoke with the sound of the rooster crowing. A multitude of tasks awaited him since he had abandoned his chores for the last couple of days. He dressed, then headed to the barn to do the milking. Just as he reached the barn door, it opened and out walked Matt with a pail full of milk.

"Well, good morning. You're certainly up early," Steven observed.

"I decided that since I'd probably been the cause of you getting a little behind in your work I'd get started early and help you catch up," Matt stated. "I noticed that the woodpile is really low. We'd better get started laying some in for the winter."

"You're right about that, son," Steven said. "Let's go in and get the milk strained and have breakfast so we can get started. I thought I'd let the twins help today," he added as he took the pail of milk from Matt.

Emily and Sarah hurriedly cleaned the kitchen. Emily was anxious to get started on the new curtains for her bedroom and a new dress for herself from the material Steven had given her. Sarah took her doll and went outside to play. Precious, her faithful dog, stayed continually at Sarah's heels as she baked mud pies for her doll.

Emily put a pot of black-eyed peas on to cook and a pound cake in the oven to bake before she pulled out her sewing. She knew her pound cake was Steven's favorite. She spread the cloth out on the kitchen table and carefully cut each piece. She would do as much as she could this morning and hoped that as soon as dinner was over she could finish at least one of her projects.

Stopping her sewing for the morning, Emily finished the preparations for lunch. She prepared baked squash, new potatoes, fried okra, corn on the cob, and a big pan of cornbread. She still had fresh tomatoes and cantaloupe to complete the meal. Sarah rang the dinner bell as Emily lay the spread on the table.

Once the dinner dishes were washed and put away, Emily returned to her sewing. She cooked enough that morning so all she would have to do to get supper on the table was warm the food, that would enable her to sew right up until the last minute.

When her curtains were at last complete, she stood back and admired her handiwork. She was very pleased with what she saw. Her old bedspread still covered the bed, although it didn't go with the curtains as well as she would have liked. At least now the room felt more like it was hers. She hoped that before long the room would no longer be just hers.

Emily thought back to the night before last when Steven had kissed her. There had been no more such displays of affection. She knew he had been very hurt and upset that night, and she prayed that his turning to her had not been just because of the misery he felt. She hoped he kissed her because he wanted to.

∽

It was a very hot day and Steven was having trouble keeping his mind on his work. Not because of the heat, but because his thoughts kept going to Emily. She had been so loving and understanding the other night. Emily had been there for him during his time of need. But most of all he couldn't get that kiss out of his mind.

As he picked up an armload of firewood and started toward the wagon, he very distinctly heard his little voice, *Steven, now that you have things basically under control with your children, are you going to get started on building a relationship with Emily? You keep stalling and making excuses. You have a terrific lady just waiting to be your wife and you keep acting like an idiot. It's time to get into the game.*

"I know. I know," Steven said aloud before he remembered there was no one there. He then began to develop a plan. He and Emily were married, but they didn't really know each other. He would continue with what he had half-heartedly started and court his wife. Maybe a walk after supper would be a good way to begin.

∽

After making sure the younger children were ready for bed, Emily let herself relax. The sun was low in the sky, but there was still at least an hour of daylight left as Emily walked out the front door. Steven was seated on the edge of the porch, leaning against one of the posts.

Before she could sit down in the swing, Steven asked, "Are you too tired to take a little walk with me?"

A little surprised by his question, she softly replied, "No. That's sounds nice."

"From the looks of those clouds in the distance, we may get a little shower later tonight," Steven observed, as they started down the lane toward the creek.

"We could use some rain. Maybe it would cool things off a little," Emily returned.

Their words were few and far between, but the silence was not awkward. As they continued their lazy stroll, Steven reached over and took Emily's hand in his. Just the touch of his hand made her stomach flip and her heart race. They stopped at the widest part of the creek, just a few yards upstream from the spot Emily had come to think of as her private sanctuary. Steven picked up a small stone and threw it across the water.

"I guess you think that was pretty good," Emily teased.

"It skipped three times even on this narrow creek," Steven returned. He offered her another stone. "Think you can do better?"

Emily took the stone and closely examined it before she gave it a toss. "Five skips," she bragged.

"Four and a half. That last one fizzled out, so I'm being generous even calling it a half," he returned.

"That's still one and a half better than you," she quipped.

Steven searched and found two more flat stones. "Okay, let's throw together and go for distance and number of skips."

The two stones made five skips each across the water, but Emily's outdistanced his and landed at the water's edge on the opposite bank.

"Just where did you learn the skillful art of stone skipping?" he asked.

"On the banks of the Rio Grande. My daddy used to take me to the river. He could skip a stone farther than anyone I've ever seen."

Steven seated himself on the soft grass and Emily joined him. "Tell me about your father," he said.

"There's not much to tell. My mother died when I was a baby and Daddy raised me. He worked hard all his life and never had much to show for it. He was a kind, honest, loving man. He couldn't give me much in the way of worldly possessions, but he gave me lots of love. He kept the two of us fed and sheltered. He never remarried, although he had lots of opportunities. Every widow and old maid in town was after Daddy and he took advantage of their eagerness to please him. He got them to teach me to sew and cook. He could cook, and he taught me all he knew, but he thought I could benefit from a woman's influence." Emily couldn't help but chuckle.

"The most important thing about my father, though, was the fact that he was a Christian. He loved God, and you could see that love in everything he did."

Night had fallen as they started back toward the farmhouse. Steven held her hand for the entire walk home. The house was dark with the exception of a light shining through Matt and Mark's window. Hidden in the shadow of the house, Steven took Emily in his arms and kissed her soundly.

∽

"Emily, why did Matt run away?" Sarah asked Emily as they were doing chores the next morning.

"He was upset," Emily responded. She didn't know how much she should explain. Stepping on Steven's territory was not what she wanted to do, but knowing Sarah, she would have to give the child a fairly thorough explanation.

"What was he upset about?" Sarah continued.

"I guess he was sort of mad at your daddy," Emily said, still certain the child would not be content with that answer.

"Why was he mad at Daddy?" Once again, Sarah's relentless pursuit of the truth was at work.

Emily decided she might as well give Sarah the only explanation she could. "You probably don't remember when your daddy lived here before with you kids and your momma. But Matt does, and he has been very angry with your daddy for leaving. Your daddy and Brother Tom sat down and had a long talk with Matt and Mark the other day, and your father tried to explain to the boys why he left. Matt got really upset and went off by himself to think things through. Now he's home, and maybe everything will be better between your daddy and Matt."

"Why did Daddy leave?" Sarah prodded.

"Sarah, I can't answer any more of these questions. You will have to ask your father why he left. I wasn't around at that time and he's the only one who can tell you that."

That must have satisfied the little girl's mind, for the persistent questioning stopped for now.

∽

Emily laid aside the garment she was sewing and started outside to round up the kids for bedtime. She only got as far as the front door when she heard Steven's and Sarah's voices on the front porch. Sarah had her father cornered and was grilling him on the reasons for his disappearance.

Steven obviously didn't know how to answer Sarah's questions. Emily prayed for his guidance, and then quietly returned to her sewing for a little longer.

∽

Steven explained about the drought and why he left to find work, but nothing he said seemed to satisfy Sarah. Her questions kept coming. She was like a hound that had a coon treed, and Steven was the coon. No way was he leaving that porch until she was satisfied with his answers.

"Sarah, I don't know how to explain to you why I didn't come home for so many years. Sometimes grown-ups make bad mistakes and bad decisions. My staying away was a bad decision. I love you children very much and I never stopped loving you. I thought about you all the time I was away. I wondered what you looked like and how big you had grown. But I just couldn't come home. I should have though." Steven looked into Sarah's eyes.

He looked for reassurance that she was understanding what he was trying to tell her and that she was satisfied with his explanation. Instead, he saw confusion in her face.

"But why couldn't you come home?"

Steven was beginning to sweat now. Oh, how he wished someone could get him out of this hot seat. He looked around, hoping to see some help coming from somewhere, but he was alone with his interrogator. Where was that little voice when he needed it? It had been persistent about butting into things in which Steven didn't want interference, but now when he could use some help, the voice was silent.

Steven decided to try a slightly different approach. "Sarah, have you ever been afraid?"

"Yeah. I'm afraid of snakes. Mark scared me with one once. It was just a garden snake, but I was really scared," Sarah offered.

"Okay. Do you know what it means to let someone down? To have someone disappointed in you?"

"Uh-huh. One time I was supposed to help Momma fix supper, but I was playing and forgot to come in. She was really mad at me and said she was disappointed in me. It made me feel really bad." Sarah's little face was sad.

"Well. When I left here I was really scared. I was afraid I would lose the farm. And I thought I had let everyone down. I thought your mother was very disappointed in me. So I stayed away. I guess you could say I was hiding. I was afraid of facing your mother and you kids because I thought I let you down." Steven stopped talking and looked once again at Sarah.

Her face showed signs of understanding. "You must have felt really bad. I'm sorry you felt that way." She got on her knees in the swing so she could hug Steven's neck. "Daddy, you didn't disappoint me. I love you and I sure am glad you're home." She released her hold on her father.

Tears filled Steven's eyes. If everyone could be as forgiving as this small girl, the world would be a much better place. Giving Sarah a hug and a warm kiss on the cheek, he said, "I love you, too, Sarah. Now, I think it's time you went to bed. It's past your bedtime."

The little girl gave her daddy a big smile as she hopped from the swing and disappeared through the front door.

∞

Emily heard the screen slam and laid down her sewing. Steven was still seated in the swing when she walked through the door. Looking up at her, he motioned for her to come sit beside him. After she had seated herself next to him, Steven reached out and took her hand.

"I wish you'd come out a little sooner," Steven proclaimed.

"I heard you and Sarah talking and thought I'd leave you alone. I thought you might need some time to yourselves," Emily returned.

"That child doesn't let up when she wants an explanation about something," Steven remarked.

"I know. I've been through a couple of her relentless question sessions. It's about time you had your turn," Emily said as she let out a soft giggle.

"There's an evil side to you that I've never seen before," Steven responded as he turned to look at Emily.

His smile told her he was joking so she quipped, "I think it's only fair that you get your share of answering her questions."

"Well, you could have at least come to my rescue when you heard her interrogating me," Steven continued with the lighthearted teasing.

"You weren't around to help me. Turn about's fair play, I always say."

"Like I said, you have an evil streak," he joked as he dropped her hand and slipped his arm around her shoulder.

Emily struggled to keep her voice steady as she asked, "Well, did you satisfy her curiosity?"

"I hope I did. She seemed satisfied. At least for now," Steven answered as he drew Emily just a little closer to him.

It felt good having Emily next to him. The emptiness he had felt for so many years was beginning to lessen. Without removing his arm from her shoulders, Steven reached over with his other hand and picked up Emily's left hand. He ran his finger over the gold band on her third finger. A cold shiver went through him. He had slipped that ring on her hand, but it wasn't his ring. He had been so unfeeling that day. How could a fellow ask a lady to marry him and then forget to buy a ring?

As the memory of that day began to flood his mind, Steven wondered why Emily had ever consented to marry him. He recalled the look on her face as she slipped Jim's ring off her finger and handed it to him to place back on her hand. He didn't understand why she hadn't fled out the door at that very moment.

Sitting there beside her now, he was certainly glad she hadn't. With her beside him, his lonely heart was being warmed and filled. As he continued to stroke her hand, a new and very unexpected feeling overcame him. He was jealous. The ring on her finger wasn't his; it had originally been placed there by another man. Emily had probably never taken it off until the day she slid it off for him to place back on her finger.

For the first time Steven realized he didn't like the thought of her ever being with another man. He knew from what she told him that she had loved Jim very much. Would she ever feel that way about him? He would do his best to make sure she did. And someday, someday soon, he prayed, he would replace the ring she now wore with one of his own.

Emily's voice broke into his thoughts. "It's getting late," she said. "I guess I'd better go inside."

Steven wasn't ready to let her go, but for now he knew he had to. "Yeah, I guess you're right," he responded.

Emily stood, but Steven didn't let go of her hand. He rose from the swing and pulled her into his arms. As she looked into his eyes he covered her mouth with his.

"Good night," Steven said as he released his hold on her. "Have sweet dreams," he continued as he opened the screen door.

"Good night," she whispered. As she passed in front of him through the door, she paused and gently touched his cheek. She gazed deeply into his eyes as she murmured, "My dreams should be very sweet tonight."

As Steven watched her disappear into her bedroom and close the door, he knew his dreams would be very sweet, too. That is, if he was ever able to get to sleep.

CHAPTER 12

On Saturday evening, Steven walked out behind the barn and found Emily sitting on a fallen log.

"So this is where you are," he said as he sat down next to her.

"I just wanted a little quiet time, so I started to take a walk. I got this far and realized that maybe I didn't want to be completely alone after all. So I sat down here to try and figure out a way to get you to join me for an evening stroll."

"You didn't have to work so hard at figuring out how to get me to join you. All you had to do was ask."

"Well, I knew you were tired so I didn't think you'd be interested in a walk this evening," Emily said softly.

Taking Emily's hand in his, Steven told her, "I am tired but not too tired to take a walk with you."

Never letting go of her hand, Steven stood and pulled Emily to her feet. They strolled farther down the lane, hand in hand. Steven couldn't remember ever enjoying time like this with anyone. Becky would have thought evening strolls down a country lane were boring. Steven was learning that nothing he did with Emily was boring.

As they walked, Steven began to tell Emily about his dreams for the farm. He spoke about someday building a bigger barn. He hoped to have several cows to milk and more horses, just for the pleasure of raising horses. His voice became excited as he talked.

"I want this place to shine. I want my kids to be proud of their home. And someday I want at least one of them to want to take over and call this home for their family." Steven stopped and stood still a moment. He gazed up at the stars, then turned to Emily. "Emily, what kind of dreams do you have?"

Emily was quiet for what seemed like a long time. Finally she spoke. "Your dreams sound very nice. I'd kind of like to share them if that's okay."

"I sort of had that in mind," Steven replied shyly. "Someday I'd like to build us a new house. One with a big kitchen. Lots of space for the family to gather. One that is bright like sunshine. One so that when anyone walks into it, they can tell that it is your kitchen."

Emily was silent for another long moment. At last Steven prompted her, "Emily, would you like a new house with a big kitchen?"

116

"It sounds wonderful." He thought her voice trembled a little. "But I'm happy with what I have now. I don't have to have anything big and showy. I don't think the kids do either. It's not the house that makes the home."

"I know. And I realize we still have a long way to go before we can call our place a real home. I also know we have a lot of work left before we're a family. But Emily, sometimes you just have to dream." Steven took a few steps away from her and began to survey his surroundings. "Emily, I like what I see here, but there's still a lot of work to do. Not only to the farm but to the people that live here. Sometimes I get so anxious I have to just stop and visualize things the way I would like them to be. Do you know what I'm talking about?"

"I think I do."

"I can see a big white house. A pretty white house, with flowers all around. A big front porch. The perfect place to gather with the family. And for the grandkids to play later on."

He took Emily's hand and started back toward the house. He spoke again, but this time in a much softer tone. "Emily, I have other dreams, too. I also picture that someday we'll be a family, a real family. That my children will be proud to call me Dad. That Matt and I will work side by side, together in harmony, and that he'll even enjoy it."

"Well, that dream seems to be getting very close to being a reality," Emily observed.

"Yeah. We've made progress, but we've still a ways to go." He hesitated, then added, "In my dream, you're a part of the family, too."

"That part may be a little farther away. At least as far as Matt and Mark are concerned. Luke, John, and Sarah all accept me and even love me. But Matt and Mark are different stories."

Steven squeezed her hand. "They'll come around. It'll just take a little more time." Steven wanted to continue with his dream and tell Emily that his dream included her in the role of his wife, but he lost his nerve before the words would come out.

◯◯

As they ate dinner on Sunday, Sarah asked, "We are going to the social at the Spragues', aren't we? It's a lot of fun. Last year was the first time I ever got to go. They have games and everything for the kids. And dancing for the grown-ups. We are going, aren't we, Daddy?"

"I hadn't thought much about it," Steven replied. "But I guess we can if everyone wants to."

"Oh boy! Emily, you want to go, don't you?" Sarah asked.

Music filled the air as Steven and the family arrived at the Spragues' big red barn. The laughter echoed as the fiddle rang out with the beginning chords for a square dance. The wagon had barely come to a stop before the twins and Sarah were off to join their friends. As usual, Matt and Mark had refused to come with the family. Steven helped Emily down, and then with pride on his face, he escorted her inside.

As the square dance ended and the first notes of a waltz came through the air, Steven took Emily in his arms and guided her across the floor; everyone else seemed to disappear; it seemed as though they were the only two people in the place. Sometime between the time Steven had asked Emily to marry him and now, they had fallen deeply in love.

They shared dance after dance with one another, waltzes and square dances alike. Steven did manage to tear himself away from Emily long enough to dance with his young daughter, and Emily in turn shared a dance with both Luke and John. Matt and Mark were both in attendance having ridden their horses to get there, but they didn't acknowledge that their dad and Emily were present.

Steven was abruptly torn away from his wife for a few moments by some of the men who wanted to discuss the upcoming harvest. Rosemary found Emily sitting alone and joined her.

"You and Steven look really happy," Rosemary commented.

"Yes, we are. I'm starting to feel like a wife. Well, almost. At least I'm starting to feel like someday soon I'll be a wife."

"How are things with the boys?" Rosemary asked.

"Things seem to be pretty good between them and Steven. But I'm still very much an outsider as far as they're concerned. They only speak to me when they absolutely have to. I don't know what else to try to win their friendship."

"I don't have any advice for you. I've never been in that situation. All I can do is tell you to keep trying and continue to be patient. I'll keep praying for all of you."

"Thanks. I need all the prayers I can get."

"And just why do you need so many prayers?" Steven asked as he walked up beside his wife.

Smiling broadly, Emily replied, "Just because I'm married to you."

Steven took her teasing in stride and returned, "Just for that remark, you may need even more prayers. How about another dance?"

⌒

The entire crowd was disappointed when the Spragues announced the final song of the evening. Steven pulled Emily into his arms and whirled her around the floor. He wished he could make this evening last forever. He wanted her in his arms always. As the music ended, he reluctantly released her and they bid farewell to their hosts and friends.

A full moon lit their way home and cast a romantic glow on the evening. The children were fast asleep on some blankets in the back of the wagon before they had gone a mile down the road. Steven slowed the horses to a walk, then pulled Emily close to him.

Softly he whispered, "You really looked beautiful this evening."

"Thank you."

"I really had a good time. It was wonderful to hear you laugh so much." Steven stammered as he continued, "I wish I could make tonight last forever."

A lump as big as Texas filled Emily's throat as tears of happiness began to trickle down her cheeks. She finally whispered, "So do I."

She laid her head on Steven's shoulder and he lightly kissed her hair.

"I know it's late, but could we go out on the porch for just a few minutes?" Steven inquired after they had gotten the kids tucked in for the night.

"Sure. I'm so happy I don't think I could sleep anyway."

Matt and Mark arrived home just as they walked outside. "Did you boys have a good time?" Steven asked. "I sure did."

"Yeah, everyone could tell you had a good time. You made a fool of yourself with her all night," Matt snarled as he went into the house.

"Wait just a minute, young man," Steven snapped.

Emily grabbed his arm and said, "Let him go. Don't let him ruin this evening, please."

"You're right. I'll have a talk with him tomorrow. I don't want anything to spoil my mood tonight."

They sat in the swing and Steven held Emily in his arms. As they gently swayed back and forth, Steven confessed, "I guess it's become pretty obvious how I feel about you. My son says I made a fool of myself over you. Well that's fine with me. I plan on making a fool of myself on a regular basis from now on." He pulled Emily closer and encircled her with his arms. "I love you, Emily."

He'd said it. He had finally put what was in his heart into words. "I love you," Steven repeated. He then turned her face to his and kissed her gently.

"I love you, too, Steven," Emily whispered, and they shared another kiss.

After she went inside, Steven walked back out into the night air and took deep breaths of the clean fresh air. Each night it got harder and harder to tell Emily good night at her door. And knowing that only a wall separated them made his heart beat out of control every night. Tonight he had to get control of himself before he did something he would regret later. He loved Emily; he didn't doubt that for a minute, but he wanted to give that love time to grow before he took her as his wife. He prayed for God to give him the strength he needed, and he thanked God for the love that he had found with this very special lady.

∞

Emily leaned against the closed door of her empty bedroom. Never before had the room felt more empty or her heart more full. She longed to have Steven come through that door with her, but she knew they weren't ready for that yet. Their love was young, and they had to give it time to grow before they could consummate it as husband and wife.

As she lay in bed, Emily thanked God for the love she had found with Steven. She even thanked Him that she had been so lonely that she accepted Steven's outrageous offer when he had made it.

∞

In the morning Emily was in the kitchen preparing breakfast when Steven came in and set the milk bucket on the cabinet. He walked up behind Emily and encircled her waist with his arms. He placed a kiss on her cheek and whispered, "Good morning. Did you sleep well?"

"Good morning to you. I slept very well, thank you. How about you?"

Emily turned to face Steven as he informed her, "I had very pleasant dreams."

Steven and Emily were engaged in a warm good morning kiss when Matt entered the room. "Don't tell me we have to start putting up with this disgusting behavior?" he griped.

Upset at being so rudely interrupted, Steven returned, "I don't consider what I was just doing disgusting behavior. It's perfectly normal for a man to kiss his wife good morning. And it's not any of your concern in the first place."

"Well, if you have to do it, you could do it somewhere where the rest of us don't have to watch," Matt shot back.

"Excuse me. But this is my home and I'll kiss my wife wherever and whenever I please. You'd better get used to it because there's gonna be a lot more of it from now on."

Matt gave the back door a slam as he left the kitchen. Emily had remained silent throughout the confrontation, and Steven noticed the bewildered look on her face.

"I'm sorry about that. I didn't mean to embarrass you." He reached to take Emily in his arms.

Emily pulled away. "I wish my presence didn't cause such a problem for Matt. It made me very uncomfortable to have him catch us kissing and make such an issue out of it."

"Look, Matt will just have to learn to deal with it. Please don't let his attitude cause you to pull away from me. I love you, Emily. We're just getting our relationship on a solid footing. Don't back off now. I don't think I could take that." He paused a moment, then continued. "I'll slow down if I'm going too fast for you. I don't want you to be uncomfortable about anything. I won't demonstrate my feelings for you except in private if that's the way you want it. I guess I was still just a little carried away from last night."

Emily could hear the sincerity in his voice and see something akin to panic in his eyes. "Emily, just tell me what you want," Steven pleaded.

"I want our relationship to grow. I like for you to kiss me. It just made me a little uncomfortable for Matt to make such a big deal out of it. He made me feel like a kid getting caught by a father."

"I'll try to be more discreet from now on. It won't be easy though. I've fallen deeply in love with you and I'd like to shout it from the rooftops. I want the whole world to know that I love Emily Barnes and she loves me. You do still love me, don't you?"

"Very much," Emily answered.

Steven took a look around the room, then gave Emily a quick kiss on the lips.

CHAPTER 13

One more day of logging and they would have enough wood to take them through the winter, Steven estimated. He and Clyde had carefully calculated what the two farms would use and had decided that if they did as well today as they had the past few days, they should have wood to spare.

Matt and Clyde's son Jacob were using a two-man saw to fell a tall pine tree. They had made their cut and thought they knew exactly which direction the tree would fall. As they cut, the tree cracked and started falling in the opposite direction from what they had anticipated. Matt cried, "Timber!" Steven looked up just in time to see the massive tree coming down on him. He turned to run but stumbled. The tree fell, pinning him underneath.

Clyde dropped his ax and hurried to Steven's aid. Matt was already there. "Steven, where are you hurt? Can you tell?" Clyde called.

"It's my left leg. I can't move it at all."

Clyde began to shout instructions, and with his expertise, they skillfully cut the tree away and freed Steven's leg. One look told Clyde that his friend's leg was badly broken, but his first concern was to stop the bleeding. A branch from the tree had punctured Steven's thigh and he was losing a lot of blood. Clyde used his bandanna for a tourniquet and tried to get the blood flow under control. He also put a splint on the lower part of Steven's leg. Jacob and Matt unloaded the firewood from the wagon so Steven could be taken home.

∽

Emily saw the procession coming up the road, and her heart dropped to her feet. She ran down the road to meet them and saw Steven lying in the wagon covered with blood. "I don't think it's as bad as it looks," Clyde tried to assure her. "I've already sent for the doctor."

Once at the house, Emily had them carry Steven into her room. After making him as comfortable as they could, Emily cut away what was left of Steven's pants leg.

Steven had remained conscious throughout the whole ordeal. The pain was excruciating, but he was obviously determined to be strong. He reached for her hand. "Kind of a mess, isn't it?"

She looked into his eyes. He couldn't hide the pain from her, but she loved him for trying to make her feel better even now. "Yeah. You really did a good job. Now let me try and get this wound in your thigh cleaned and dressed."

"How about a little kiss first? A kiss would help the pain go away."

Emily smiled as she leaned over and gently kissed her husband. "I'm afraid my kisses aren't that powerful, but if you think they help, I'll be more than happy to oblige you."

She tenderly began to clean the wound in Steven's thigh. The bleeding had almost stopped for the time being. Dr. Emerson arrived and examined the wounds, then sent Emily out of the room when he got ready to set the bone. She cringed when she heard Steven's cry as the doctor pulled the bone into place.

Clyde and the doctor emerged from the room. Dr. Emerson gave Emily instructions on how to care for Steven's wounds and handed her some powder that would help ease his pain. "Be careful with that powder, but he'll need it for a couple of days," Dr. Emerson said. "Give him some now and he should sleep for a while. I'll be by tomorrow. If you need me before that, send for me."

Emily pulled the rocking chair up next to the bed that evening and made herself comfortable. Steven was asleep. She had no intention of leaving Steven's side this evening. She reached over and took his hand in hers and drifted off to sleep still holding his hand.

She was abruptly awakened by Steven's moaning and thrashing about. Quickly she spooned more of the medication into his mouth. When she did, she noticed his head was hot. The wound on his thigh had started bleeding again, she discovered, and she changed the dressing as the doctor had instructed. Then she began to bathe Steven's face with a cool washcloth. Steven continued to toss and turn and started to mumble in his restless sleep.

"Emily, where are you? Don't leave me," Steven cried.

Tenderly, Emily whispered, "Steven, it's okay. I'm right here."

She continued to bathe his face with the cool cloth. As she gently stroked his forehead, she spoke softly to him in a effort to calm his restless slumber. Steven would relax for brief intervals, but then the thrashing, moaning, and mumbling would start again. Emily couldn't understand everything he said, but at times she knew he was telling Matt it was okay, he knew he didn't mean to do it. She didn't know what Matt didn't mean to do, but it seemed very important to Steven that his son know he understood.

Other times Steven called Becky's name. He kept saying something about being a lousy husband and father. Once he told Rebecca that things had changed and he could be a good husband now to Emily.

Then there were times that he cried for Emily. He continued to beg her not to leave. Emily did her best to comfort him. She had tried for what seemed like hours to get his fever to come down, but her efforts were in vain. The doctor had told her to expect him to run a temperature, but he was burning up, and it became evident that the medicine the doctor had prescribed was doing little to ease the pain.

Emily quietly opened Matt's door and walked over beside his bed. She softly called his name. "Matt. Wake up."

Sleepily, Matt opened his eyes and grunted, "What do you want?"

"It's your father. I think he's getting worse. I need you to go get Doc Emerson."

Without another word, Matt jumped out of bed and grabbed his clothes. He was out of the house in no time and headed for the barn to saddle the horse.

Emily continued with her futile efforts to comfort Steven and ease his pain. Time passed very slowly as she waited for Matt to return with the doctor. When they finally arrived, Dr. Emerson once again cleaned Steven's wounds. He pulled out several more fragments of tree bark. Then he poured something that smelled like whiskey into the wound. When he did, Steven screamed with pain. Emily quickly answered the cries of the children and offered comfort and explanations to them.

"Will Daddy be okay?" the three younger siblings asked.

"The doctor's here now. Your daddy will be fine. Let's all pray and ask God to make him well soon." Emily was doing all she could to comfort the children and ease her own mind at the same time. After the little family group had asked God to pour out His healing blessings upon Steven, Emily left Matt and Mark in charge of the smaller children and went to be with her husband.

"How is he, Doctor?" Emily asked as she entered the bedroom.

"That leg's got a pretty nasty infection, but he's a strong fellow. He'll be all right."

The doctor stayed until well after sunup. He cleaned and dressed Steven's wound several times during the course of his visit. By the time he left, he was satisfied with the way the injury looked and Steven appeared to be resting comfortably.

Emily was exhausted on her feet, but she was not leaving Steven's side. Matt and Mark had fixed the children's breakfast and had taken care of the morning chores. Clyde and Alice also came by early that morning.

"Emily, I'm here to help," Alice announced. "Just tell me what you want me to do first."

"That's very sweet of you, but I know you have your own family to look after," Emily returned.

"We'll get by. You need me right now, so here I am. That's what friends are for. I'll start lunch." Alice finished her little speech, then left the room.

Emily continued to sit in the rocker at Steven's bedside. She would hold his hand and bathe his face whenever he became restless. Occasionally, during his quiet moments, Emily would drift off into a light sleep, but the slightest movement from Steven would awaken her.

"Emily, you have to get some rest. You won't do Steven any good if you collapse," Alice stated when she brought Emily a glass of lemonade. "It's almost lunchtime, and I'll bet you haven't had any sleep since before Steven got hurt."

"Oh, I nap here in the chair when he sleeps," Emily said.

"Why don't you go lay down. I'll keep an eye on him," Alice offered.

"Thanks. But I can't leave him right now. I have to be here when he wakes up."

After lunch Brother Tom and Rosemary stopped by. They both tried without any success to get Emily to rest; she still insisted she had to be by Steven's side.

Emily stayed at Steven's bedside that night, and finally she fell asleep with her head lying on the edge of the bed beside him. The clock on the mantel had just chimed 3:00 a.m. when Emily felt Steven's hand caressing her hair. She lifted her head, and for the first time in almost two days, she looked into his blue eyes.

"You look very tired," he whispered.

"Well, you look wonderful." She took his hand in hers and gently kissed his fingers.

"How long have I been out?"

"Almost two days. You gave me quite a scare."

Steven gently stroked her cheek. "I'm sorry. I didn't mean to. Have you been here the whole time?"

Smiling, she looked into his eyes and whispered, "Where else would I be? I had to make sure you were okay."

"I love you, Emily Barnes."

"And I love you, Steven Barnes. Don't you ever scare me like that again."

"I'll do my best not to. Come here." Steven motioned for her to sit on the bed beside him. She carefully sat down on the edge of the bed and Steven pulled her into his arms. She gently put her head on his chest.

"You have to get some rest," Steven instructed Emily. "Who'll take care of me if you collapse?" He smiled.

"I'll get some rest. Don't you worry. Now that I know you'll be all right, I can rest."

"Good. I have to be all right. I have too much to live for now."

Emily slid back into the rocking chair. Seeing a grimace flood Steven's face, Emily asked, "Did I hurt you?"

"Just the jiggling of the bed. I'll be okay," Steven assured her as he took her hand.

For the most part he held her hand gently but rather frequently would give it a firm squeeze. Emily could tell by the expression on his face and the glassy look in his eyes that he was in pain. She picked up the powder the doctor had given her and mixed it with water, then spooned a dose into Steven's mouth.

Steven insisted that she go lie down, and she assured him that she would just as soon as he fell asleep. She sat by his side and held his hand until the medicine lulled him into a restful slumber. Finally assured that Steven was doing okay for the moment, Emily went out into the hallway and stretched out on the bed. She left the bedroom door open so she would be sure to hear Steven if he called out or became restless. Before she drifted off to sleep, she thanked God that Steven was better and prayed for his speedy recovery.

∞

The next morning Emily was awakened when she heard Steven moving around in his bed. His soft moans continued to make her heart ache. She wished desperately that she could take his pain away.

As she entered the bedroom, Steven opened his eyes. "Good morning," she whispered as she leaned down and kissed him gently on the cheek.

"Good morning. You look a little more rested. You did lie down like I asked, didn't you?"

"Yes. I stretched out on your bed. I feel just fine. Now, would you like a little something for breakfast?"

"I am a little hungry," Steven acknowledged.

"That's a good sign. I'll go see what I can find for you to eat."

"Oh, would you tell the kids that I'd like to see them? Especially Matt."

"Sure." Emily started into the kitchen.

"How's Daddy?" The question came from all five children seated at the kitchen table.

"Well, why don't you go ask him yourself. He wants to see you."

Everyone but Matt jumped to their feet as Emily cautioned, "Now keep the excitement down. Your daddy still doesn't feel very good, so be quiet and don't bounce on the bed."

Matt sat in silence and continued to pick at his breakfast.

"Matt, aren't you going in? You father especially asked to see you," Emily stated.

"He probably wants to yell at me."

"Matt, I don't know what the problem is, but he kept calling to you in his sleep the other night. He kept repeating over and over that it wasn't your fault. He wants to see you. I think you should go in and talk to him. Whatever it is you think you've done might not be so bad if you talk to him."

Matt leaned his elbows on the table and buried his face in his hands. "I caused his accident. I'm the reason he almost died."

Matt's shoulders began to tremble. Emily didn't know what to do. This young man had always shown such contempt for her, she didn't know if he would accept her consolation.

Emily finally walked over to Matt and placed her arm around his shoulder. "I'm sure it's not as bad as you think. I know your father doesn't blame you. Even if you were responsible in some way, your dad would forgive you. Matt, he loves you."

Surprisingly, Matt didn't pull away from Emily's touch or her comforting words.

"I am to blame. The tree fell the wrong way and pinned him under it. I must not have made the cut right or it wouldn't have fallen like that."

By now his whole body shook with sobs. Emily drew him into her arms. "Matt, it's okay. Your daddy's going to be fine. You can't keep blaming yourself. You have to go talk to him. You can't avoid him forever, you know. I know you'll feel better if you just talk to your father."

Emily wasn't sure Matt was aware of what he was doing, because he turned, wrapped his arms around her, and laid his head on her shoulder while the last of his tears spilled down his face. When the other children entered the kitchen, Matt quickly came to his senses and pulled away from Emily.

"Matt, Daddy wants to talk to you," Mark informed him.

Matt drew in a deep breath and walked toward the bedroom door.

∞

"Matt. Son, come over here and sit down." Steven indicated the chair next to his bed.

Reluctantly, Matt took the chair his father offered.

"Matt, you're probably feeling pretty bad, but I just want you to know this isn't your fault."

"How can you say that? I must have made my first cut wrong, so the tree fell on you."

"Matt, sometimes those pine trees have a mind of their own and fall where they want to. You didn't do anything wrong. You couldn't help what happened. Now quit blaming yourself. Once again I won't be able to live up to my responsibilities, so I need you to take over for me."

"It's not your fault this time that you can't do your job. Just tell me what you want me to do."

"Well, harvest starts next week. It'll be up to you to handle it. I know you can do it, because you've done it before. I really wanted to help this year, but that's out of the question now."

Matt lifted his head and met his father's eyes. "It's okay, Daddy. You worked hard in the fields. Whether or not you help harvest doesn't matter. The crops are still yours."

"Thank you, son. That means a lot coming from you. I'll be counting on you to see that everything gets done."

Steven extended his hand to his son and this time Matt grasped it firmly. They had come a long way since that first day on the front porch.

CHAPTER 14

Matt and Mark worked from sunup to sundown in the cornfields. The corn had dried and was ready to be pulled. Some of it they would store in the corncrib to use to feed the livestock through the winter; the rest they would shell so it could be milled into cornmeal. Clyde and his sons helped out, splitting their time between their own crops and the Barneses' fields.

Emily and the twins shelled corn until their hands were bleeding. Emily didn't realize how many ears a person had to shell to fill a five-pound bag with kernels. She was very grateful when Clyde brought his corn sheller over for them to use. Luke and John took turns placing the ears of corn into the contraption and pulling the handle down to remove the kernels from the cob. Sometimes it took both of them to pull the handle, and Emily relieved them from time to time.

Doc Emerson dropped by at least once a week to check on Steven. After two weeks of bed rest, Steven was getting restless, and he was grateful when Doc Emerson brought him a pair of crutches. He then could go out onto the porch and do more than his fair share of corn shelling.

As the weeks passed, Steven's leg improved, but the doctor still insisted that he keep his weight off it and use the crutches. The cotton was ready to pick, and Matt and Mark went at it with a vengeance. On the second day of picking, Emily stated that she would be joining the boys in the fields. After listening to the many protests from the Barnes men, she put her foot down and went to the field just as she planned. Emily had picked a little cotton in her youth, but very little. She had forgotten what a difficult and backbreaking job it was. Matt and Mark were each finished with a row before she got halfway down hers. But nothing discouraged her; she refused to give up. She would not let these little cotton balls get the best of her.

She felt Matt and Mark watching her. "Even Luke and John pick faster than she does," she heard Matt mutter.

"Yeah," Mark answered. "But I never saw Momma out in the fields, no matter how little help we had. She never pitched in the way Emily does."

∞

Steven accompanied his family to church on Sunday. He couldn't manage getting up onto the seat, so he rode with the younger children in the back of the wagon.

Just as they started to drive off, Matt and Mark came out the front door and Matt called, "Wait up. Mark and I want to ride with you."

Steven was so overcome that he couldn't speak.

As the boys got to the wagon, Emily looked at Matt. "Matt, would you drive?"

"Yes ma'am, I'd be glad to," Matt answered. Then he climbed up into the seat next to Emily.

Steven was bursting with joy. It seemed at last they would be a family. When they arrived at church, Steven noticed the tears on Emily's face.

Steven offered thanks to the Lord for the blessings of the day. He prayed that they would become a close family, that his children would love and accept him as their father, and that they would love and accept Emily as their friend, if not their mother. He also prayed for God's guidance in the final step of making Emily his wife.

∞

The next morning as the family finished breakfast, they heard a loud commotion out front. When they went to investigate, they found most of their neighbors standing in the front yard.

"Steven, Emily, we're here to get the rest of your cotton picked. You're our friends and our neighbors, and we're here to help," Brother Tom said as he walked up on the porch.

"That's very kind of you," Stephen said to the crowd, "but I know most of you have harvests of your own. You don't have time to do mine, too."

"We discussed it after church yesterday. We decided that if we all pitch in, we can get everyone's done and no one will lose anything. We'll start with yours, then move on to the next field. We're a community, and for this harvest at least, we're going to work as one. After everyone's cotton is picked, then we'll pitch in and get it to the gin," Clyde explained.

Alice stepped forward. "Don't think you're getting off for free. You have to feed this bunch. But we ladies are here to help cook. Can you handle that, Emily?"

"With pleasure we can handle that," Emily answered.

The men headed to the fields and the ladies went into the kitchen. The old adage that too many cooks spoil the stew certainly failed to be true that day. The ladies talked and laughed as they worked to prepare a meal that would feed the field hands. Preparations were well under control when Emily decided to slip away for a few minutes and see if she could find Steven. He had disappeared right after the men left for the fields.

She found him in the barn sitting on a bale of hay. "What are you doing out here all alone?"

"Actually, I started out to feel sorry for myself but instead wound up counting my blessings. When we first arrived here, would you have ever believed that something like this could have happened?"

"Things were different then. It did appear hopeless and dark. Thank God, He is still able to change lives and mend broken hearts. He's also able to change folks' opinion about other people and circumstances."

Steven was silent for a moment. "You know, the day we arrived here, I sat in this very spot and had a long talk with the good Lord. That was the first time I had talked to Him in years. I asked Him to help me be a father to my children. At the time I was just praying that I would be able to keep food on the table, clothes on their backs, and a roof over their heads. I didn't think I could ever be a real father to them. I didn't think I deserved to be a real father to them. But look how He answered that prayer."

He paused, then said, "Emily, it's amazing. First He saved my soul and forgave me of my sins. Then one by one, He gave me back my children. Isn't God good?"

"Yes, Steven. God is very good. He has given me the family I didn't think I'd ever have."

He turned to face her. "There's one other thing. That first day, I talked to God about you. I couldn't figure out why on earth I asked you to marry me and come back here with me. I was certain that day that I could never be a husband to you, not when I had felt like such a failure as a husband. I didn't believe any woman could ever love me or want me as her husband. But look how God answered that prayer. He gave me back my confidence and He gave me you. He knew before either one of us that we were meant to be together."

"God does work in mysterious ways."

The dinner bell rang, and Steven sighed. "Emily, I have some things I want to say to you, but right now is not the time or the place." He stood with the aid of his crutches and offered her his hand, then pulled her to him and kissed her. "I love you, Emily."

"And I love you, Steven."

∞

The weeks passed. Harvest was just about over and everyone would have a good year. Doc Emerson had been out and told Steven he could start bearing weight on his leg. Slowly, he graduated from crutches to a cane.

Since he was no longer confined, Steven insisted on helping get the cotton to the gin. Everything was getting back to normal in the Barnes household. Actually it was better than what had been normal.

Matt and Mark had become a part of the family since the Sunday they had ridden in the wagon with the rest of the group. There was still some tension between the boys and Emily; the boys had been so angry at her for so long, they had never gotten to know her. They couldn't help but act as though she were still a stranger among them. But at least now they were willing to give her a chance.

Steven had begun calling the family together each evening after supper to have a short family devotional. God was bringing them together at long last.

By late November, the weather was cool but not freezing, since east Texas didn't have a lot of miserably cold weather. Emily remembered the day in the barn when Steven had told her he had some things to say to her but it wasn't the right time. That had been almost two months ago, and she was beginning to wonder if he had changed his mind. They hadn't spent much time alone since then. Sometimes she wondered if he was avoiding her.

The devotion time was over and the kids were all tucked into their beds, or at least safely in their rooms. Emily was making sure the firebox in the kitchen was sufficiently stocked for the morning when she turned and saw Steven standing in the doorway staring at her.

"Do you need something?" she asked.

"No. I was just watching you." He hesitated, then added, "That's not the truth. I do need something."

"What?"

"You. I need you, Emily Barnes. Would you be willing to put on a sweater and join me on the front porch for a little while?"

Emily gave him a big smile. "Sure."

Once seated in the swing, Emily noticed that Steven appeared nervous. He fidgeted in the swing, seemingly unable to get comfortable.

Finally, Emily asked, "Steven, is something wrong?"

Steven didn't answer right away. He fidgeted in the swing and shuffled his feet on the floor some more. Emily was beginning to worry, when he finally spoke.

"I've been wanting to talk to you, but I haven't been able to get my courage up until now."

"What's so important that you have to rake courage up before talking to me? You should know by now you can talk to me about anything."

"I know that. But this is different. It's about us."

Emily's heart began to pound. She didn't know if she was excited or nervous or a mixture of both. Not wanting to interrupt his train of thought, she sat silently and waited for him to continue.

"Emily, I'm very much in love with you and I want you to be my wife." Steven paused again, picked up Emily's left hand, gazed into her eyes, and asked, "Emily, will you marry me?"

"Steven, I'd be happy to marry you, but have you forgotten? We're already married."

"I know we stood before a judge and that legally we are man and wife. But I don't want that cold, heartless ceremony to be the start of our marriage."

Steven began to run his thumb over the gold band on her hand. "And I want my ring on your finger. It hurts me to think that I was so unfeeling that day that I would take another man's ring and place it on your finger. I want a new start. I want to forget that time ever happened. We met, and now we have fallen in love. I want you to be my wife in every sense of the word, but I can't take you as mine until we've been married in a church by a minister of God. I want to proclaim my love and devotion for you before God and everybody. Emily, will you marry me?"

"Oh Steven. I feel the same way. Yes, yes, I'll marry you!"

Steven pulled Emily into his arms and kissed her. "When do you want to have the ceremony?" Steven asked.

"Anytime. The sooner the better."

"Let's go talk to Tom first thing in the morning."

When Emily got to her room, she removed Jim's ring from her finger. She gently placed it inside her small jewelry box, knowing she would never wear that ring again.

She walked to the bedside table and picked up the wedding picture of her and Jim. She gazed at it lovingly, then tucked it away in a bureau drawer. She had no feelings of emptiness or remorse. Emily knew Jim was smiling down on her. He would be happy that she had found true love once again.

CHAPTER 15

The next morning, Steven and Emily went to see Tom Kirkland. Tom answered Steven's knock. "Come in. What brings you two to my doorstep?"

"We need to talk to you if you have a minute," Steven answered as they followed Tom into the house.

Emily blushed a little as Steven explained, "We'd like you to marry us."

"I thought you were already married," Tom said with a puzzled look on his face.

"Legally we are. But now we would like to be married in God's eyes. You see we want to start our marriage out right. We want to be married in church with our friends and family present."

"That's wonderful!" Tom exclaimed. "I'd be honored to marry you." He stood and offered his hand to Steven as Rosemary embraced Emily.

"When do you want to get married?" Tom inquired.

Steven looked at Emily and asked, "How much time do you need?"

"Well, I'd like to make myself a new dress for the occasion. A couple of days at least."

Rosemary jumped up and exclaimed, "Just a minute! I have a wonderful idea. Emily, follow me."

Emily followed Rosemary down the hall into a bedroom. Rosemary opened the wardrobe and pulled out a hanger covered with a sheet. As she pulled the sheet off, she revealed a beautiful ivory-colored dress covered with lace.

"Emily, I'd be honored if you'd wear my wedding dress. It should fit you. Here, try it on."

"Oh Rosemary, it's beautiful. But I couldn't."

"Sure you could. Come on, try it on."

"But I can't get married in a dress like that. I've been married before."

"That's nonsense. Anyway, this dress is ivory, not white. And you and Steven are already married, you're just repeating your vows. This would be your something old. Please, it would make me so happy."

"It's beautiful. If you're sure it'll be all right, I'd love to."

Emily slipped off her dress and slipped into the wedding gown. "It's perfect," Rosemary said. "You look beautiful. Now let's get a date set, and the sooner the better."

"My feelings exactly," Emily responded. "I have one more favor to ask of you. Will you be my matron of honor?"

"I'd love to!" Rosemary exclaimed.

When they returned to the living room, Rosemary's eyes were shining. "Well, the dress is taken care of, so let's set a date."

"Well, tonight's prayer meeting, so we could announce it then and ya'll could be married Friday night. That's day after tomorrow. Can you be ready by then?" Tom asked.

"Sounds good to me," Steven answered.

Emily gave her approval as Rosemary said, "Why don't you leave the arrangements up to me? I want to decorate the church and I know Alice will want to help. You two don't worry about a thing. Just let me handle it."

As they got up to leave, Rosemary gave one last instruction. "Emily, why don't you plan to spend Thursday night with us? You know you're not supposed to see the groom on your wedding day."

"But..." Steven started to speak but Rosemary cut him off.

"Now, no buts about it. You can survive one day without her. Besides, it'll take us most of the day to get her prettied up for the wedding."

Emily and Steven called the children into the living room that same day after school. After everyone was seated, Steven said, "As I told you kids when Emily and I came here, we were married in Abilene. But now we want to be married again and this time in church. We want to really be husband and wife, and we want to start our marriage out right. So we're getting married Friday evening at six o'clock at the church."

Steven had barely finished his speech before the three younger children started to cheer. Even Matt and Mark extended their hands in congratulations, and then they embraced Emily.

Steven asked Matt to stay for a moment after the family meeting broke up. When they were alone, Steven asked, "Matt, I would like for you to be my best man."

"You want me to stand up for you at your wedding after all the trouble I caused you and Emily?"

"I can't think of anyone I'd rather have. You're my eldest son, and I want you at my side when I marry the woman I love."

"I'd be happy to stand up with you, Dad." Matt glanced toward the mantel and saw the wedding picture of Steven and Rebecca. Walking over, he picked up the little framed picture in his hand. "Dad, if you don't mind, I'd like this picture. She will always be my mother, and I'll always love her. I'll probably never understand the things she did, but I think I can live with that now. Your and Emily's picture should be here now."

With tears in his eyes and a lump as big as Texas in his throat, Steven hugged his son. "Thanks, Matt. You have become a young man who I'm very proud to call my son."

"And I'm proud to call you Dad," Matt returned.

∞

As soon as supper was over Thursday night, Steven brought the buggy around to drive Emily to the parsonage.

"I'll miss you tonight," Steven said as they slowly made their way down the road. "I've become accustomed to knowing that you're just in the next room."

"I'll miss you, too," Emily replied.

"After tonight I don't plan on spending any more nights without you. And I won't be sleeping in the hall."

Emily blushed, but he could see that the thought had great appeal to her. She tucked her arm through his and put her head on his shoulder.

"Matt has finally accepted both of us," Steven said softly. "I don't know if you noticed or not, but yesterday he removed mine and Becky's wedding picture from the mantel. He said that that place now belonged to you and me."

"Oh, Steven, isn't God wonderful? We will truly be a family now."

When Steven stopped the buggy in front of the house, he jumped down and then helped Emily to the ground. "I'd like a good-night kiss now. I probably won't be able to get one later." Emily obliged him, and then he walked her to the door. After briefly greeting Rosemary, Steven stepped off the porch. He stood alone in the darkness and watched Emily as she disappeared into the house.

"Thank You, Father God, for all the blessings You've poured out on this undeserving farmer," Steven prayed. He mounted the buggy and drove off into the crisp autumn night.

∞

Emily awoke. It was her wedding day. This time she was very much in love with the man and he was in love with her. Life was wonderful. Before she ever got out of bed, she thanked God for all the blessings He had bestowed upon her. And she especially thanked Him for Steven.

There was a gentle knock on her door, and Rosemary entered carrying a tray with pancakes, syrup, eggs, and coffee. "I think a bride deserves breakfast in bed," she said as she set the tray on the table beside Emily.

"This is just too much to ask for. I've never had breakfast in bed before," Emily acknowledged.

Rosemary sat with Emily while they planned out their day. Emily would get her hair washed while Rosemary went over to the church and helped Alice and a couple of the other ladies get everything ready. Then Rosemary would come back and help Emily style her hair. They would have the afternoon to talk and visit like young girls.

∞

Steven didn't think he had slept a wink all night long. He was up early and got the milking done. He even managed to prepare an edible breakfast for his family. It was unbelievable to him that after all these years he found himself so desperately in love.

All day his thoughts were of Emily. Early in the afternoon, he slipped into the bedroom that tonight he would share with his wife. He filled the wood box so they would be able to have a cozy fire all night and moved in his few personal belongings and put them away. Although it was the room he had once shared with Rebecca, he was amazed to discover no unhappy memories were lingering anywhere. In the past few months, this had truly become Emily's home. He could feel her presence in every corner, like a warm and loving feeling. His heart raced with anticipation at the thought of spending the rest of his life with Emily. Once again he thanked God for Emily.

∞

The church was filled with friends. Steven nervously waited outside for his cue that the ceremony was about to begin. He repeatedly asked Matt if he had the ring. Each time Matt patiently assured him he did, but his efforts to calm his father were in vain.

As the music started, Tom, Steven, and Matt entered the church through the side door. The front doors opened and Rosemary slowly walked down the center aisle.

The wedding march resounded and the congregation rose. Emily appeared at the door holding on to Clyde's arm. As Emily walked toward Steven, the love he had for this woman poured out from him. Tears sparkled in Emily's eyes.

This ceremony was nothing like the first. Their love for each other not only surrounded them but touched everyone gathered there. On this perfect autumn Friday evening, they discovered the true meaning of the vows they were pledging to one another. Their love had truly made them one.

After the ceremony, everyone was invited to Clyde and Alice's for cake and punch. Before the evening got too late, Steven suggested to Emily that they say good night to everyone and make their way home. To Emily's surprise, the children gathered around them and kissed them good night and wished them well. It seemed that Steven had arranged for the kids to stay with Clyde and Alice until Sunday.

Steven tied the buggy to the fence when they got home and walked Emily to the door. Once at the door, he picked her up and carried her across the threshold. He built a small fire in the fireplace in the bedroom, then excused himself and went to unhitch the team. Emily took advantage of the time alone to change into her nightgown and robe.

When Steven returned, he removed his tie and coat, and he and Emily sat on the rug in front of the fire. As they sat facing one another, Steven gently stroked Emily's cheek. "I'm so thankful I asked you to come with me to east Texas. Whether it was misery, loneliness, or just plain fear of facing my children alone that made me ask you to marry me the first time, I don't really know. But I'm very thankful that you agreed. I'm also grateful that I've had the opportunity to get to know you, first as my friend and now as my wife."

"Yes." Emily sighed with contentment. "I'm thankful that I accepted your offer, even though I tried to think of it as just a job in the beginning. Because I was so lonely for a family again, I agreed to come to a strange place with a man I hardly knew. But God in His great wisdom and mercy has made something beautiful out of something that could have turned out so bad."

Emily reached into her robe pocket and pulled out an envelope. She handed it to Steven.

"What's this?" he asked.

"Remember the month's pay you gave me before we left Abilene? That's it. It's now the start of our savings to make the dreams we have for this place a reality."

A smile covered Steven's face as he took his bride in his arms. "I guess we can say thanks to lonely hearts, we're together. But a relationship that started out of loneliness and misery is ending in love. I do love you, Emily Barnes."

"And I love you, Steven Barnes."

EPILOGUE

Emily stood in the doorway of the living room and watched her husband talking to their six-month-old baby girl. Could it have been almost three years since she came to this house? And three years ago that's what it was—just a house, full of unhappy people. Now it was a home full of love.

"I hate to interrupt your conversation with Mary Elizabeth, but if we don't hurry we'll be late. The train is due in at three o'clock you know," Emily told Steven.

"I know. Mary and I were just discussing how excited we were that Matt was coming home from college. He hasn't gotten to meet his little sister yet." The baby gave her daddy a big smile because he spoke every word directly to her instead of looking at his wife.

"Well, let's go. The others are in the wagon," Emily said, trying to rush the stragglers.

"Daddy, Momma, are you two coming?" Sarah called from the back of the wagon. "We're gonna be late."

"We're coming," Steven called as he and Emily walked through the front door. "Matt will wait if we're not there when the train comes into town."

∞

"Do you see him?" Mark asked. He was craning his neck, trying to see past each passenger who was exiting the train.

The last passenger off was Matthew. He was a handsome young man and cut a magnificent figure standing there in his boots, jeans, cowboy shirt, and hat. As he stepped onto the platform, he was accosted by the happy group of family eager to greet him.

"It's good to have you home, brother." Mark grabbed Matt and gave him a bear hug.

"It's good to be home. Luke, John, you two must've grown a foot since I left last fall," Matt told the twins.

"Only about six inches," John replied with a grin as he and his twin brother greeted Matt.

"Matt," Sarah squealed as she jumped into the arms of her big brother. "I missed you."

"I missed you, too, baby sister. And you have turned into a pretty young lady since I left."

"Thank you, but I'm not your baby sister anymore. Come on. You've got to see Mary Elizabeth." Sarah pulled her brother by the arm over to where their parents stood with the baby.

"Welcome home, son," Steven said as he hugged Matt.

"It's really good to be home," Matt returned. "Now let me see my little sister."

"Mary Elizabeth, this is your big brother Matthew," Emily introduced. Emily handed the bundle to Matt.

"You're beautiful," Matt exclaimed. Right on cue, the baby gave her brother a warm smile. "Oh, look, she likes me and she's already got a tooth!"

"Of course she likes you. We've told her all about you. She's been very anxious for you to get here. She's ready to be spoiled by someone new," Emily told Matt.

"Thank goodness she looks like you, Emily." Matt gave his stepmother a smile, then leaned over and kissed Emily on the cheek. "Are you doing okay?"

"I'm fine. Especially now that all my family is back together. Even if it is for just a few weeks," Emily returned.

"Hey, enough of this. I think we can continue the rest of our reunion at home over some of Emily's chocolate cake," Steven said as he picked Matt's bag up off the platform.

"Emily's chocolate cake? I think I can handle that." Matt started toward the wagon with Mary Elizabeth in his arms.

"It's good to have our family together again," Steven whispered to his wife.

"Yes. I'll treasure these weeks since Mark will be leaving with Matt when he goes back to school," Emily wistfully commented.

"I guess the new house will just have to wait until we get our kids educated," Steven said.

"That's okay. I don't need a new house. I've already got the perfect home."

A Bride's Sweet Surprise in Sauers, Indiana

by Ramona Cecil

CHAPTER 1

Sauers, Indiana, April 1849

Have you lost your senses? My *Vater* will shoot you!" Fear for the young man standing before her bubbled up in Regina Seitz's chest.

A deep laugh rumbled from Eli Tanner, but the cacophony of his father's horse-powered gristmill behind them quickly swallowed the sound. The nonchalant grin stretching across his handsome face told her he did not share her concern. "Your pa is a reasonable man. He may run me off his farm and give me a tongue-lashing in German, but I doubt he would shoot me for taking you to a box supper at Dudleytown."

"He might if you take me without his consent and without a chaperone." With all her heart, Regina wished her words were true. In her seventeen years, she couldn't remember a longer, colder winter than the one their little farming community had just endured. Now that the harsh weather had finally given way to a warm and glorious spring and with Lent and Easter behind them, she looked forward to occasions like this Saturday's gathering at the Dudleytown School to socialize with friends her age. And of all the boys in the county, she could think of no other she would rather have squire her to the event than Eli. But Eli hadn't seen the thundercloud form on Papa's face last September after her sister Elsie's marriage to her non-German husband, William. Eli hadn't heard Papa's booming voice ring like a death knell, proclaiming that he would never again sanction the marriage of a daughter to a non-German.

Eli took Regina's hands in his, sending a thrill through her. He drew her away from her pony cart and into a slice of shade closer to the mill's weathered gray walls. She still could hardly believe she had caught the eye of Eli Tanner. And she probably would not have if his previous sweetheart hadn't eloped with a young farmer from Driftwood—something she would never understand. For with his broad shoulders, thick shock of auburn hair, and green eyes that almost matched the spring's new growth all around them, the miller's son was, in Regina's estimation, the handsomest boy in all of Jackson County.

But he wasn't German, or even of German descent. And there lay the problem.

"I want to court you, Regina." At the passionate tone of Eli's voice, Regina's heart throbbed painfully. "Sooner or later, your pa must be told."

"He will not consent to it." Regina shook her head and hung it in despair. Tears welled in her eyes at the unjustness of it. "Papa is determined to have a German farmer for a son-in-law. Someone he can hand the farm down to." A cool breeze swept through their shady nook, and she shivered. But Eli's strong fingers wrapped warmly around hers, sending heat radiating up her arms and chasing the chill away.

Eli shrugged his shoulders. "Your pa will get over it. You said he was unhappy at first when your sister Sophie married that wheelwright and moved to Jennings County and again last fall when Elsie married the dry goods merchant from over in Washington County. But he never shot them." Chuckling, he bent and plucked a handful of blue violets from a lush patch of sweet grass. "In fact, if memory serves," he said as he rose and tucked a couple of the flowers behind Regina's ear, his face so close to hers that his warm breath stirred her hair, "he threw both your sisters rip-roarin' weddings. He accepted their choices for husbands, so he should at least let me take you to a box social."

Regina hated the bitterness welling up inside her. She loved her sisters and was glad for their happiness. But it seemed so unfair that she should be punished because they hadn't chosen German farmers for husbands. She nodded, wanting to believe Eli. "It is true. Papa did give in to Sophie and Elsie. But I am his last chance to get a German son-in-law. I do not think he will give in so easily this time."

"Maybe not easily, but he will give in. You are his youngest and prettiest daughter." Grinning, Eli touched his finger to the end of her nose. "But unless he changes his mind by this Saturday, it will not help us for the box supper. So you must tell your folks that you are going with one of the girls you know, like Anna Rieckers or Louisa Stuckwisch."

Regina gasped. "Lie to Papa and Mama? You want me to break *Gott's* commandments? I could never! My parents trust me. I would never go behind their backs. And even if I were foolish enough to try, someone would be sure to tell them I was there with you. Then Papa would never agree to let you court me and would probably lock me in the house until I am thirty!"

Eli's green eyes flashed, and for an instant a scowl furrowed his brow. But the stormy look passed as quickly as the clouds scooting across the midday sky, and his face brightened again. The lines of his features softened as he gazed at her. "You should always wear violets in your hair. They look good against your light hair and make your eyes look even bluer."

Regina's anger at his suggestion that she deceive her parents evaporated as she basked in his compliment.

"Eli!" Sam Tanner's stern voice barked from the mill door. "You got those bags of flour loaded?"

"Comin', Pa!" Eli called while keeping his gaze fixed firmly on Regina. He thrust the fistful of violets into her hand. "Just think about it, Regina. I'll be waitin' behind your barn at ten o'clock Saturday morning if you change your mind." He started toward the mill then turned back to her. "But I won't wait long."

Regina watched his broad back as he strode toward the mill's door. Something in the tone of his voice when he uttered those last words made her wonder if he intended a larger meaning than just the social event Saturday. She had no doubt Eli would not wait for her forever. And despite his optimism that Papa would change his mind, she doubted it. Not without strong convincing.

With a heavy heart, she climbed to the seat of the pony cart, flicked the reins down on the black-and-white mottled hindquarters of the little gypsy pony, and headed for home. Ever since January, when Eli began showing interest in Regina, she'd spent countless sleepless nights trying to think of ways to convince Papa to give up his obsession about marrying her off to a German farmer. But aside from simply rejecting every prospective suitor her parents suggested, Regina had yet to come up with any argument to dissuade Papa from his quest. And now with the coming of spring and Eli eager to declare his intentions, she could see her chances for happiness slipping away. On the bright side, Papa had at least stopped trying to push her toward every unmarried German farmer in the county between the ages of eighteen and fifty. But she couldn't believe he had given up entirely. He would likely begin again with his matchmaking when a new crop of German immigrants arrived.

That thought reminded her of the letter she'd picked up earlier at the schoolhouse where the community's mail was delivered. In her excitement to see Eli, she'd nearly forgotten about it. In the nearly eighteen years since her family had arrived in America, Papa and Mama had made it their life's mission to assist in the emigration of others from Venne, their old village in the kingdom of Hanover. So although it was common for Papa to receive letters from German families planning to immigrate to Sauers, he would doubtless be cross if she were to misplace or lose such a missive.

As the pony cart bounced along the rutted road to her family's farm, she gazed out over the countryside. Rolling fields of newly turned sod filled the April air with the earthy scent of spring, while milk cows grazed in verdant pastures spread over the landscape like acres of green velvet. She couldn't blame anyone for wanting to leave the cramped farms of Hanover for the abundance of fertile land here in Jackson County, Indiana.

She glanced down at the letter nestled in the basket on the seat beside her. It was postmarked Baltimore, Maryland, a regular port for immigrant ships from Bremen, Hanover. Picking it up, she examined the letter more closely. Scrawled in the top left-hand corner of the envelope was the name Georg Rothhaus. It sounded vaguely familiar. Most likely, Papa had mentioned the name in passing as a recent correspondent.

As she turned into the lane that led up to their two-story, hewn-log house, she stuffed the letter into her skirt pocket. Dismissing the letter, her mind raced. How might she best broach the subjects of the box supper and Eli to Mama and Papa?

Inside, her *Holzschuhe* clomped on the puncheon floor of the washroom that ran the length of the rear of the house.

"Is that you, *Tochter*?" Mama called from the kitchen a few steps away.

"*Ja*," Regina called back as she slipped off her wooden shoes. She smiled. Since Sophie and Elsie had married, Mama no longer had to specify *which* daughter.

The smell of simmering sausages and onions wafted through the kitchen doorway, making Regina's mouth water. Papa would be in soon for the midday meal. She padded into the kitchen in her stocking feet, praying God would give her the words to soften her parents' hearts toward Eli.

Mama glanced over her shoulder from her spot in front of the straddle-legged woodbox stove. "Did you get the flour?" With the back of her hand, Mama brushed from her face a few wisps of chestnut-colored hair that had pulled loose from the braids pinned to the top of her head. Regina had often wished that like Sophie and Elsie, she had inherited Mama's lovely brown hair instead of the pale locks more closely resembling Papa's.

"Ja, Mama. Two bags, like you asked. They are too heavy for me to lift, so I left them in the cart."

Regina heard the back door close then the sound of heavy steps on the washroom floor. Papa had come in for dinner. This was the perfect opportunity to present Eli in a good light. "Mr. Tanner's son, Eli, put the bags of flour in the cart for me, Mama. Wasn't that nice of him?"

Mama stopped pushing the meat and onions around in the skillet with a wooden spoon and grinned. "Ja, but that is his job, no?"

"Well, yes. I suppose." Regina's voice wilted. This was not going as well as she'd hoped.

"Do you mean these bags of flour?"

Regina turned to see Papa standing in the kitchen doorway, sock-footed with a bag of flour on each of his broad shoulders.

He carried them to the pantry and plopped them on the floor, sending up plumes of pale dust. When he turned back to Regina and her mother, his smile had left, and his expression became stern. He rubbed the blond stubble along his jawline. "Ja, Regina, your *Mutti* is right. If Tanner or his *Sohn* had made you carry such heavy bags of flour, I would not be pleased. I would have to have words with them for sure."

With Papa getting his hackles up and talking of being displeased with the Tanners, Regina decided this might not be the best time to press her case about Eli. Thinking how she might change the subject, she remembered the letter.

She pulled the envelope from her skirt pocket and held it out to him. "Look, Papa, a letter came for you."

A look of anticipation came over Papa's broad face as he took the letter from her fingers. With impatient movements, he tore open the envelope. As he perused the pages, a smile appeared on his face and gradually grew wider until his wheat-colored whiskers bristled.

"*Gott sei Dank!*" His pale blue eyes glistened. Rushing to Mama, he hugged her and kissed her on the cheek. "Catharine, *meine Liebe*." Then, turning to Regina, he hugged her so hard she could scarcely breathe, lifting her feet clear off the floor. Setting her back down, he kissed her on the forehead as if she were five years old. "Meine Regina. *Mein liebes Mädchen*."

Stunned, Regina stood blinking at her usually undemonstrative father. Though she didn't know anyone with a deeper, more abiding faith in God, she couldn't remember hearing him actually shout out praises to the Lord. And he certainly wasn't one to openly show affection.

"Ernst, what has come over you?" Mama's brown eyes had grown to the size of buckeyes.

Still beaming, Papa gazed at the pages in his hand as if they were something extraordinary. "*Mutter*, you must prepare the house. We will be having very important guests soon."

"Who could be so important?" Mama gave a little chuckle and peered around Papa's shoulder at the missive. "Are we to host President Taylor or Governor Dunning?"

Papa shook his head. "*Nein*. Even more *wunderbar*." Now he looked directly at Regina, a tender look bursting with fatherly affection. "Georg Rothhaus is coming and bringing his son Diedrich. Our Regina's intended."

CHAPTER 2

Diedrich faced the stagecoach, dread and excitement warring in his stomach. Shouldering the little trunk that held all of his and his father's worldly goods, he took a resolute step off the inn's porch.

He could hardly believe that their long journey was about to come to an end. But what end? His stomach churned, threatening to reject the fine breakfast the innkeeper had served them less than a half hour ago. According to the innkeeper, they were within a couple hours' drive of the little farming community of Sauers and Diedrich's prospective bride.

A firm hand clapped him on the shoulder. "Today we shall reach our new home, Sohn." Father's confident voice at his side did little to still the tumult raging inside Diedrich. Father was not the one facing matrimony to a girl he'd never met.

The thought made Diedrich want to turn around and go back into the inn. But he could not retrace the thousands of miles that lay between this Jackson County, Indiana, and his old home in Venne, Hanover. And even if he could, he'd only be returning to the same bleak choices that had prompted him to agree to the deal Father had made with Ernst Seitz—conscription into the army or sharing the meager acres of farmland that barely supported his brothers and their families.

Father's hand on Diedrich's back urged him toward the waiting stagecoach. Willing his feet to obey, Diedrich stepped toward the conveyance as if to the gallows. The gathering canopy of storm clouds above them seemed an ominous sign. In an attempt to quell the sick feeling roiling in his stomach, he reminded himself of his own secret scheme to avoid the matrimonial shackles *Fräulein* Seitz waited to clap on him.

In their two and a half months aboard the bark *Franziska*, Diedrich had spent many hours alone in his stinking, cramped bunk. Day and night the ship had pitched and rolled over the Atlantic, keeping Diedrich's head swimming and his stomach empty. During those agonizing hours, it wasn't thoughts of a bride he'd never met that had given him reason to endure the hardships, but thoughts of the California goldfields and the riches waiting there for him. Gold nuggets, the newspapers said, just lay on the ground waiting for anyone with an industrious nature and an appetite for adventure to claim their treasure and realize riches beyond their wildest imaginings. But Diedrich couldn't get to the gold in California without first getting to America. And it was Ernst Seitz's generous offer to pay Diedrich's and Father's passage in exchange for Diedrich marrying *Herr* Seitz's youngest daughter that had gotten them to America.

In all his twenty-one years, Diedrich had never prayed longer or more earnestly than he had during that sea voyage. As the apostle Paul had charged in his first letter to the Thessalonians, Diedrich had virtually prayed without ceasing. And many of his prayers were petitions for God to somehow release him from the bargain Father and Herr Seitz had struck without breaking the girl's heart or dishonoring Father.

Guilt smote his conscience. No virtue was more sacred to Father than honor. And Father was an honorable man. How many times had Diedrich heard his father say, "A man's word is his bond"? Scheming behind Father's back to figure a way to break the word bond he had made with their benefactor didn't sit well. But at the same time, Diedrich couldn't imagine God would bless the union of two people who had no love for each other.

The wind whipped up, snatching at the short bill of his wool cap and sending a shiver through him. He handed the trunk up to the driver to secure to the top of the coach while Father practiced his English, carrying on a halting conversation with their fellow travelers—a middle-aged couple and a dapperly dressed gentleman. Barbs of bright lightning lit up the pewter sky, followed by a deafening clap of thunder. All five travelers hurried to board in advance of the storm. They'd scarcely settled themselves in the coach when the heavens opened, pelting the conveyance with raindrops that quickly became a buffeting deluge.

Sitting next to the door and facing his father, Diedrich settled back against the seat. The next instant a whip cracked, the driver hollered a hearty "Heyaa!" and the coach jerked to a roll. The other passengers began to talk in English. Diedrich understood only an occasional word, but the conversation seemed mostly centered on the weather. The woman, especially, looked worried, and Diedrich shared her concern. Herr Seitz had written that the roads were particularly bad in the springtime and often impassable.

Father leaned forward and tapped Diedrich on the knee. A knowing grin began a slow march across his whiskered face. "Why so glum, mein Sohn? You look as if you are going to the executioner instead of into the embrace of a lovely young bride."

Diedrich tried to return Father's smile but couldn't sustain it.

Father's expression turned somber. "It was to save you from conscription that we came, remember? Who knows if King Ernest can keep Hanover out of the revolution." He shook his head. "I would not have you sacrificed in the ridiculous war with Denmark." Moisture appeared in Father's gray eyes, and Diedrich hoped their fellow travelers didn't understand German.

Leaning forward, he grasped his father's forearm. "I am grateful, Father." And he was. This time his smile held. Although for many years Father had shared Diedrich's dream to come to America, Diedrich knew the heartache leaving Venne had cost his parent. He would never forget how Father had hugged Diedrich's brothers, Johann and Frederic, as if he would never let them go. How the tears had flowed unashamed between the father and his grown sons and daughters-in-law at their parting. Hot tears stung the back of Diedrich's nose at the memory. But as hard as it had been to say those good-byes, he knew the hardest parting for Father was with the five little ones—knowing that he may never see his *liebe Enkelkinder* again this side of heaven.

Father shook his head. "Nein. It is not me to whom you should be grateful, mein Sohn. We both owe Herr Seitz our gratitude." A grin quirked up the corner of his mouth, and a teasing twinkle appeared in his eye. "Not only did he send us one hundred and fifty American dollars for our passage, but he will give you a good wife and me a fine Christian daughter-in-law."

The coach jostled as a wheel bounced in and out of a rut, and Diedrich pressed the soles of his boots harder against the floor to steady himself. Bitterness at what he was being forced to do welled up in him. And before he could stop the words, he blurted, "You do not know if she is a fine Christian woman or if she will make me a good wife, Father."

Father's face scrunched down in the kind of scowl that used to make Diedrich tremble as a child, though his father had never once lifted a hand against him in anger. "I may not know the daughter, but I know the Vater. Any daughter of Ernst's would be both a good wife and a fine Christian woman." Father's stormy expression cleared, and his smile returned. "And Ernst says she is pretty as well."

Diedrich crossed his arms over his chest and snorted. "Every father thinks his daughter is pretty."

Father yawned then grinned, obviously unfazed by Diedrich's surly mood. "You were too small, only a *kleines Kind* when the Seitz family left Venne for America. But I remember well Ernst's bride, Catharine, and she was *eine Schöne*. And their two little ones were like *Engelchen*. I have no doubt that your bride will be pretty as well."

Diedrich shrugged and turned toward the foggy window. Learning that Regina Seitz's mother was once a beauty and her sisters had looked like little angels as children did nothing to squelch his growing trepidation. But arguing with Father would not improve his mood. And that was just as well, for the sound of a muffled snore brought his attention back to Father, whose bearded chin had dropped to his chest and eyes had closed in slumber.

With Father dozing and the three other passengers engaged in a lively conversation in English, Diedrich turned his attention toward the window again. The rain had stopped. At least he didn't hear it pattering on the roof of the coach now. Peering through raindrops still snaking down the glass, he gazed at the green countryside speeding past them. If all went as he planned, it would matter little whether Regina Seitz was ugly, a beauty, or simply plain. By autumn, Diedrich should be on his way to California and the goldfields. But if things didn't go as he planned. . . No. He would not even consider the alternative. *Dear Lord, please do something to stop this marriage.*

Suddenly the coach came to a jarring halt, jolting him from his prayerful petition. Through the coach window, he could make out the front of a large white house. Apprehension knotted in his stomach. They had arrived. As he gazed at the building before him, he still could not help marveling at the size of the houses here in America. Though some were small and crudely made of logs, many others, like the one framed by the coach's window, were far larger and either made of brick or sided with thin planks of wood called clapboards. At least the Seitz home would have plenty of room for him and Father.

Sitting up straight, Father blinked and yawned. He stretched his arms as far as the coach's low ceiling allowed. "Why are we stopping?"

"I think we have come to the end of our journey." Diedrich had scarcely gotten the words out of his mouth when the coach driver opened the door at his elbow. Diedrich climbed out first, followed by Father, while their fellow passengers exited by the opposite door.

Back on the ground, Diedrich stretched his legs and arms. Though he did not look forward to the meeting that would soon take place inside the house before him, he was glad to leave the cramped quarters of the conveyance behind him. Coaches were clearly not built for the comfort of people Diedrich's height.

"Come on up to the porch, folks." The driver closed the coach door and ushered everyone up to the house's front porch. He balled his fist as if to rap on the door, but before he could, it opened, and Diedrich's jaw went slack.

A pleasant-faced young woman stood in the doorway. Though not stunning in looks, she was by no means ugly. In fact, the only remarkable thing about her was her distended middle, which clearly revealed she was in the family way.

Diedrich's heart plummeted. So it wasn't that Herr Seitz desired a German farmer for a son-in-law; he simply needed a husband for his daughter. Anger coiled in his midsection. Had he and Father endured an excruciating journey of two and a half months to now be played for fools?

He glanced at Father, whose wide-eyed expression reflected his own shock.

"Guten Tag." The girl dipped her head in greeting then stepped back to

allow her guests entrance. "Please come in." She ushered them into a spacious room furnished with several benches and chairs, some arranged on either side of a large fireplace.

Motioning for everyone to sit down, she began speaking rapidly in English. As he had in countless other such situations since his arrival in America, Diedrich caught only an occasional word. "Coffee" and "bread" suggested they would be offered food. The next moment a man of about thirty years entered the room from the house's interior.

The young woman smiled up at the man, who now stood beside her and rested his hand on her shoulder. Again the woman spoke and Diedrich understood only two of her words, but they were the most important ones: "Husband" and "Gerhart."

The coach driver spoke to the man and nodded toward Diedrich and Father, who sat together on one of the benches that flanked the fireplace. This time, the word "Deutsch" caught Diedrich's attention.

The man smiled and nodded. He stepped toward them, and Diedrich and his father rose. "Guten Tag," he said, reaching his hand out to each man in turn. "I am Gerhart Driehaus, and you have already met my wife, Maria." He cast a smile in the woman's direction as she waddled out of the room. "I understand you wish to go to the home of Herr Ernst Seitz."

"Ja," Diedrich and his father said in unison. As Father made the introductions, relief spilled through Diedrich, followed quickly by remorse for having mentally maligned their benefactor. Though he still planned to avoid marrying the man's daughter—or anyone else for that matter—he was glad to have no evidence that Herr Seitz had been dishonest with them.

Herr Driehaus cocked his head southward. "The Seitz farm is but two miles from here. Rest and enjoy some coffee and Maria's good bread and jelly while I hitch my team to the wagon. Then I will take you there."

Diedrich and his father uttered words of thanks. What a joy to converse again in their native tongue with someone besides each other—something they'd done little of since leaving the German community in Cincinnati.

Fifteen minutes later the coach departed the Driehaus home with the other passengers, leaving Diedrich and his father behind. Refreshed by steaming cups of coffee and light bread slathered with butter and grape jelly, Diedrich hoisted their little trunk into the back of Gerhart Driehaus's two-seater wagon. Father sat in front with Herr Driehaus while Diedrich took the backseat.

Soon they left the main thoroughfare and headed south down a hilly road. In places, the mud was so thick and the ruts so deep and filled with water that

Diedrich feared the wagon would become bogged down. But the four sturdy Percherons plodded along, keeping them moving.

As they bounced along, splashing in and out of ruts, Herr Driehaus pointed out neighboring farms, and he and Father talked about crops and weather. The sun had come out again, causing the raindrops on tender new foliage to sparkle like diamonds. The clean scent of the rain-washed air held a tinge of perfume from various flowering bushes and trees. Suddenly the notion of living in this place didn't seem so bad to Diedrich, at least through the spring and summer. But if he didn't want to live here for the rest of his life, he would have to be as quick and agile as the little rust-breasted bird that just flew from a purple-blossomed tree along the roadway, showering Diedrich with raindrops.

"We have come to the home of Herr Seitz." With the announcement, Herr Driehaus turned the team down a narrow lane as muddy as the road they'd left. At the end of it stood a neat, two-story house with a barn and several other outbuildings surrounding it. Though just as large, this house, unlike the Driehaus home, was constructed of thick hewn logs, weathered to a silvery gray. A large weeping willow tree stood in the front yard. Bent branches sporting new pale green leaves swayed in the breeze, caressing the lush grass beneath.

Despite the serene beauty of the scene before him, a knot of trepidation tightened in Diedrich's gut. In a few moments, he would come face-to-face with the girl who expected to soon become his wife.

The lane wound between the house and the barn, and Herr Driehaus finally brought the wagon to a stop at the side of the house. They climbed to the ground, but as they stepped toward the house, a shrill scream from somewhere behind them shattered the tranquil silence.

They all turned at the sound. When Diedrich located the source of the noise, his eyes popped. A mud-covered figure emerged from the thick mire of the fenced-in barn lot. Only her mud-encased skirts identified her as female. She took a labored step forward, and her foot made a sucking sound as she pulled it out of the mud. But when she tried to take another step, she fell onto her knees again, back into the thick pool of muck. Emitting another strangled scream, she glanced over her shoulder. It was then that Diedrich noticed a large, dark bull not ten feet behind her. With his snout to the ground, the animal made huffing noises as he pawed the mire, sending showers of mud flying. The bull obviously didn't like anyone invading his domain.

Terror for the hapless female gripped Diedrich. In another moment, the great animal would be on her, butting and tramping her into the mud. Casting aside his coat and hat, he raced headlong toward the barn lot.

CHAPTER 3

H–help!" Regina struggled to pull her foot from the thick, black mud. But the harder she tried, the deeper she sank. Her heart pounding in her ears, she glanced over her shoulder at Papa's bull, Stark. The huge dark beast had trotted to within feet of her. With his head lowered, he snorted and pawed at the sodden ground. His big eyes, dark and malicious, fixed her with an unwavering glare. What would it feel like when his head struck her like a giant boulder? Would she feel the pain when his horns pierced her body and his sharp hooves slashed at her flesh? Or would the first butt of his mighty head have already sent her to heaven where the scriptures told her there was no pain?

Determined not to learn the answers to the questions flashing in her mind, she managed to pull enough air into her fear-paralyzed lungs to let out another scream. Where was Eli? Couldn't he hear her? As perturbed as she had been that he'd surprised her in the barn after she had explicitly told him to stay away, the knowledge of his nearness helped to quell her growing panic. Surely he would hear her calls and come to her rescue.

The ground shook as Stark trotted closer. It almost seemed a game to the bull, like a cat that had cornered a mouse.

Finding strength she didn't know she had, Regina pulled one foot from the black ooze, but the other foot refused to budge, and she fell face forward again in the muck. Pushing herself up with her palms, she came up spitting unspeakable filth. If Eli had already left, maybe she could get Papa's attention. Mustering all her lung power, she let out another strangled scream.

Suddenly, she looked up to see a tall, broad-shouldered figure racing toward her. Clean shaven and lithe, the man was definitely not Papa. . .or Eli. Instead, she got the impression of gentle gray eyes that reminded her of her soft, warm flannel, filled with concern. Straight brown hair fell across his broad forehead and his strong jaw was set in a look of determination.

Relief spilled through Regina as the stranger scooped her up in his arms. Murmuring reassurances, he ran with her toward the barn lot's open gate. The next several seconds passed in a series of sensory flashes. The clean scent of shaving soap filled her nose as she rested her face against his hard chest. Against her ear, she heard the deep, quick thumping of his heart like the muffled beats of a distant drum. The sound of his voice, rich and deep, uttered words of assurance as he strode toward the house, cradling her securely in his strong arms.

At the back door, he set her gently on her feet before Mama, whose face registered an ever-changing mixture of shock, fear, horror, and dismay. Gingerly grasping Regina's mud-drenched shoulders, Mama uttered unintelligible laments in tones that reflected the varied emotions flitting across her face.

Glancing over her shoulder, Regina managed to catch a parting glimpse of her rescuer before Mama whisked her into the house. Now covered in the mud she had deposited on him, he stood stock still, his kind gray eyes regarding her with wonder and concern.

A half hour later, Regina slid down in the copper tub and groaned. The clean, hot water into which Mama had shaved pieces of lye soap was now tepid and brown from mud and other unpleasant things on which Regina didn't care to speculate. If not for the grimy contents of the bathwater, she might be tempted to slip beneath the surface and not come up.

She shivered, remembering the angry look on the bull's face. Countless times she had taken that same shortcut from the barn to the house without any such mishap. But in her desperation to keep Papa from discovering her and Eli together in the barn, she hadn't considered that the rain had turned the barn lot into one huge mud puddle.

She scowled at a sliver of straw turning lazy circles atop the scummy surface of the water. It was all Papa's fault. If Eli were allowed to court her in the open instead of having to sneak around and surprise her in the barn like he did today, she wouldn't be sitting in the bathtub in the middle of the week washing off unspeakable filth. She wouldn't have had to disappoint Eli by missing the Dudleytown box supper last Saturday. She also wouldn't have had to tell him of Papa's plans to marry her off to a stranger. She had expected Eli to be unhappy and perhaps even angry at her news. But she hadn't expected him to demand she elope with him right away.

She sighed. For the past week, she had prayed for God to deliver her from the plans Papa and Herr Rothhaus were making for her future. And though a part of her longed to give in to Eli's demands, she couldn't believe God would want her to run away without a word to her parents. Such an impulsive action would doubtless break their hearts. Perhaps that was why God hadn't allowed her to give Eli an answer. For at that moment they'd heard the sound of a wagon approaching. Sure that Papa had returned from his trip to Dudleytown, she had instructed Eli to hide in the barn until the wagon was out of sight while she headed to the house through the barn lot.

She ran the glob of soap over her wet hair, working up a lather. On the other hand, by not leaving with Eli, she may have missed a window of escape God had opened for an instant. At least then she wouldn't be trapped in her upstairs bedroom, washing off barnyard muck in preparation for meeting the man Papa had chosen to be her future husband.

At the thought, her cheeks tingled with warmth. In truth, she may have already met him. *Diedrich Rothhaus.* Was it possible that the man with the strong arms and kind gray eyes was the one to whom Papa had promised her? Her heart did an odd hop. For days now, she had dreaded his coming. Nearly every night she drenched her pillow with her tears, praying that God would cause the man to decide to stay in Baltimore or Cincinnati—anywhere but here in Sauers.

The fractured memory of her rescuer flashed again in her mind. She tried to assemble the bits and pieces into a clear picture, but they refused to come into focus. Yet she knew without a doubt that the man she had left covered in mud at the back door did not fit the picture of the Diedrich Rothhaus she had conjured up in her apprehensive imaginings. But of one thing she was sure. The stranger who had carried her to the house spoke German.

"Du bist jetzt sicher." Yes. The words he had spoken so gently, assuring her of her safety, were not English words but German.

The door opened a crack and Mama slipped into the room with Regina's best dress draped over her arm. Her face, pruned up in a look of dismay, did not bode well for Regina. "I have brought your Sunday frock." Her voice held the stiff tone that always preceded a scolding.

Laying the dress and a bundle of small clothes on Regina's bed, she stepped to the side of the tub and shook her head. "I still cannot imagine what you were doing in that barn lot. You know how muddy it gets when it rains. And how many times has your Vater warned you to stay away from that bull? I cannot bear to think what might have happened if Stark had got to you." Her voice cracked with emotion, smiting Regina with remorse. "I thank Gott He sent that brave young man to save you." She pulled the ever-present handkerchief from her sleeve and dabbed at her watery eyes. "If not for Diedrich Rothhaus, we might be having a funeral instead of planning a wedding."

Regina groaned inwardly. So the man who rescued her *was* the man Papa had chosen for her husband. Her pulse quickened, but she forced her attention back to her mother, who, though stronger than most women Regina knew, did tend to be overemotional at times. "It is sorry I am, Mama. I did not think—"

"And you are usually such a thoughtful Mädchen." Shaking her head, Mama sniffed back tears, obviously not finished with her rant. "And as thankful as I am that young Rothhaus was there to get you away from the bull, how embarrassing that the first time your intended sets eyes on you, you are covered in mud!" She shook her head again and pressed her hand to her chest. "When I told your Vater what happened, I thought he would collapse right there in the kitchen. And he might have, but he did not wish to embarrass our family any further in front of Diedrich and Herr Rothhaus."

Diedrich. If only she could form a clear image of him in her mind. But it didn't matter what he looked like, or even that he had rescued her. The question remained—who would rescue her from him?

Mama helped Regina out of the tub and wrapped her in a cotton towel. "Poor Diedrich," her lamentations continued. "By the time he handed you to me, he was nearly as muddy as you were. Your Vater is helping him to wash and change into the spare set of clothes he brought with him." As Mama's voice grew more frustrated, she rubbed the towel over Regina's skin harder than necessary.

"Ouch!" Regina snatched the towel from her mother's grasp and stepped away. When would Mama and Papa stop treating her like a child? "I'm not a *Kind*, Mama. I can dry myself." At the hurt look on Mama's face, guilt nipped at Regina's conscience. Mama meant well, and besides embarrassing her and Papa in front of the Rothhauses, Regina *had* given her parents a terrible fright. She sighed, and her tone reflected her penance. "I am sorry I fell in the mud and what's-his-name had to pull me out." Though by now Regina knew the man's given name as well as her own, she couldn't bring herself to say it. "But I am not the one who asked him to come. And as I have been telling you and Papa for the past week, I do not want to get married! Especially to someone I have never met."

Mama cocked her head. Some of her earlier anger seemed to seep away, and she gave Regina a caring, indulgent smile. "I know this is happening very fast for you, Regina. But you know that your Vater and I want the best for you, and the Rothhauses are good people. Once you get used to the idea, I am sure you will be happy." Her smile turned to a teasing grin. "After all, you must marry someone, and Diedrich *is* very handsome. And he must have a brave and good heart to have gone in there with that bull to carry you to safety."

Or he is just very stupid. Regina decided to keep that thought to herself as she stepped into her bloomers and pulled her petticoats over her head.

Mama walked to the dresser and picked up Regina's hairbrush. "Do you want me to brush and plait your hair? We want to show your intended and his Vater how very pretty you are when you are clean."

Mama might as well have run her fingernails across a slate board for the way her comment sent irritation rasping down Regina's spine. The thought of parading in front of Diedrich Rothhaus like a mare he considered buying was beyond irksome. But at the same time, Mama's words planted the seed of a plan in Regina's mind. A plan that nurtured a tiny glimmer of hope inside her. Perhaps falling in the mud was not such a bad thing. Maybe it was part of God's plan to rescue her from a loveless marriage.

Regina put on her Sunday best dress of sky blue linen and fastened the mother-of-pearl buttons that marched down its front. "*Danke*, Mama, but no." She gave her mother the sweetest smile she could muster. "I am sure you have things to do in the kitchen. I will be down to help you in a few minutes."

Tears glistened in Mama's eyes as she gazed at Regina. "What a beauty you are, liebes Mädchen. She hugged Regina and kissed her on top of her damp head, sending a squiggle of shame through Regina. "I would not be surprised if Diedrich Rothhaus insisted on setting the wedding date within the month."

Instead of bringing comfort, the compliment ignited a flash of panic in Regina. *Dear Lord, give me time to convince Diedrich Rothhaus that I am not someone he would want to marry.* As Mama left the room, closing the door behind her, Regina sent up her frantic prayer. Then she calmed herself with thoughts of her budding plan designed to thwart the life-changing one her parents had foisted on her.

Gazing into her dresser mirror, she watched her brows slip down into a determined frown. If Diedrich Rothhaus refused to marry her after all the money Papa had spent to bring him and Herr Rothhaus here from Venne, surely Papa would relent and let her marry Eli or whomever she chose. All she had to do was make herself repugnant to Diedrich Rothhaus.

She plaited her damp hair into two long braids. But as she brought them up to attach them to the top of her head as she normally did, she paused. Instead, she tied the ends of each with a blue ribbon as she used to do when a child, letting them dangle on her shoulders. She might as well put her plan into action immediately. Young Herr Rothhaus would doubtless find a girl who looked twelve far less appealing than one who looked Regina's age of seventeen.

～

Diedrich splashed tepid water from the tin dishpan onto his face, rinsing off the lye soap. Herr Seitz had brought him into this long narrow room between the back door and the kitchen to wash up before taking Father on a tour of the farm.

With his eyes scrunched shut against the stinging water and soap, he reached for the cotton towel *Frau* Seitz had left for him on the side of the washstand. He couldn't get his mind off the girl he'd carried to safety little more than a half hour earlier. Behind his closed eyelids, he saw again her big blue eyes wild with fear, shining from her mud-covered face. The face of his future wife? Though the image that lingered in his mind could not be called attractive, it was more than compelling. Something about the look in her eyes had made him want to protect her, reassure her.

Burying his face in the towel, he scrubbed as if to scrub the image from his mind. He must be daft. Did he want to end up like his brothers, growing old before his time trying to eke out a living farming with too many hungry mouths to feed? No. He hadn't come all the way to America to become snared in the same trap into which his brothers had fallen before him. He must stick to his plan and let nothing—not even a pair of large, helpless blue eyes—distract him from reaching the California goldfields and the riches waiting there for him.

He dipped a scrap of cotton cloth into the tin basin of water and washed off the mud that still clung to his hands and arms. At the pressure of the cloth on his skin, he felt again the soft curves of the girl's body in his arms. She had fit as if she belonged there. Despite the cool spring air that prickled the skin of his bare torso, heat marched up his neck to suffuse his face.

At a creaking sound on the stairwell to his left, followed by what sounded like a sharp intake of air, Diedrich turned. What he saw snatched the breath from his lungs as if Alois, the strongest man in their village, had punched him in the stomach. The prettiest girl he'd ever seen stood as if frozen three steps from the landing. Her hair, the color of ripe wheat, hung in two braids on her shoulders. They made her look younger than her obvious years. But there was nothing childlike about her gently curved figure. Her blue frock matched her bright blue eyes, which were at least as big and round as Diedrich remembered from the barn lot and seemed to grow larger by the second. Her pink lips, which reminded him of a rosebud, formed an O.

It suddenly struck Diedrich that he was standing before her shirtless. Glancing down, he watched a bead of water meander down his bare chest to his stomach. He snatched his waiting clean shirt from a peg on the wall beside the washstand and held it against him to cover his bare chest. He opened his mouth to utter a greeting, but his throat had gone dry and nothing came out. He cleared his throat. Twice. Had he lost all his senses? She was just a girl. Regina. For months he had tried to fashion an image to attach to the name. But nothing he had ever envisioned approached the loveliness of the girl before him.

She remained still and mute. Fearing she might fly back up the stairs, he tried again to speak. This time he found his voice. "Are you all right?"

"Ja. Danke." She finally stepped down to the floor, though she stayed close to the stair rail as if to keep maximum distance between them. "Thank you for helping me. . .out of the mud." Though she spoke with a hint of an American accent, her German was flawless.

"*Bitte sehr*. I am glad you were not hurt. Forgive me." Turning away from her, he hurriedly shrugged on his shirt and began buttoning it up, praying she would still be there when he turned back around. She was.

"I am Regina." Unsmiling, she took a couple of halting steps toward him.

"I am Diedrich. Diedrich Rothhaus." Without thinking, he reached out his hand to her.

In a tentative movement, she reached out a delicate-looking hand that ended in long, tapered fingers and touched his palm, sending tingles up his arm to his shoulder. An instant later, she drew back her hand as if she'd touched a hot stove. Looking past his shoulder, she glanced out the open door behind him. "Papa and Herr Rothhaus are back from looking at the farm. You may join them outside until Mama and I call you for dinner."

She slipped past him and headed for the kitchen, leaving him feeling deflated. Not once had she smiled, and no hint of warmth had softened her icy tone. Instead, her stilted voice had felt like a glass of cold water thrown in his face.

Fully revived from the odd trance that had gripped him at first sight of her, Diedrich gazed at the spot where her appealing figure had disappeared. As beguiling as her face and form, Regina Seitz was an enchantress chiseled from ice. His resolve to find a way out of this arranged marriage solidified. And if his prospective bride's chilly reaction to him was any indication of her feelings in the matter, obtaining his goal might not be as difficult as he'd feared.

Stepping outside, Diedrich headed to the relatively dry spot in the lane where Father and Herr Seitz stood talking and laughing.

"Ah, there you are, mein *Junge*." Herr Seitz clapped Diedrich on the shoulder, his round face beaming. "I was telling your Vater, I have *wunderbare* news. On my way back from Dudleytown, I met Pastor Sauer on the road and told him about you and my Regina. He is looking forward to meeting you and Herr Rothhaus and will be happy to perform the marriage whenever we like."

CHAPTER 4

Regina looked down at her plate of fried rabbit, boiled potatoes, and dandelion greens and fought nausea. Not because of the food on her plate, which she normally loved, but from Papa's enthusiastic conversation with Herr Rothhaus speculating on the earliest possible date for her wedding.

"By the end of May, we should have the planting done." Papa wiped milk from his thick blond mustache that had lately begun to show touches of gray. "The first Sunday in June, I think, would be a fine time for the wedding."

June? Regina's stomach turned over. Unless she could think of a way out of it, in six weeks she would be marrying the stranger sitting across the table from her. She looked up at Diedrich, who sat toying with his food. Did the alarmed look that flashed in his eyes suggest he shared her feelings about their coming nuptials? Her budding hope withered. More likely he found the date disappointingly remote.

"Ja." Herr Rothhaus nodded from across the table, a boiled potato poised on the twin tines of his fork. His face turned somber and his gray eyes, so like his son's, took on a watery look. "Mein Sohn and I owe you and Frau Seitz much." His voice turned thick with emotion, and he popped the potato into his mouth.

Papa clapped the man on the shoulder. "Happy we are that you and your fine son are finally here, *mein Freund*. Over the last three months, I have said many prayers for your safe passage." He brightened. "And this Sunday, I shall ask Pastor Sauer to lead the whole congregation in a prayer of thanks for your safe arrival." Then he turned his attention to Regina, and his smile drooped into a disapproving frown—one of many he'd given her since they all sat down for supper. "Again, it is sorry I am that you came all the way across the ocean to see our Regina, and she is covered in mud."

Regina groaned inwardly. Did Papa have to keep bringing it up? And how many times did he expect her to apologize for embarrassing herself in front of the two men? Out of the corner of her eye, she thought she caught the hint of a grin on Diedrich's lips, but at that moment he lifted his cup to his mouth and took a sip of milk, covering his expression.

Mama turned to her, and in the same coaxing voice she used to speak to Regina's two-year-old nephew, Henry, said, "Regina, perhaps you would like to ask Diedrich about his voyage?" She rolled her eyes in Diedrich's direction, her expectant look conveying both a summons and a warning.

Regina sat in mute defiance. There may be nothing she could do to stop her parents from forcing her into a marriage with this Diedrich Rothhaus, but they couldn't make her like it. And they couldn't make her talk to him.

At her reticence, Papa leveled a stern look at her and in a lowered voice that held an ominous tone said, "Regina."

Diedrich's glance bounced between Papa and Mama, but then his gaze lit softly on Regina's face like a gray mourning dove on a delicate branch. "A rough winter crossing, it was. But thanks be to Gott, the *Franziska*, she is a sturdy bark with a crew brave and skilled."

Regina hated that Diedrich had come to her rescue once again. Even worse, she hated how her gaze refused to leave his. And how his deep, gentle voice soothed her like the caress of a velvet glove.

The three older people launched into a conversation about the Rothhauses' journey from Venne. Though he remained quiet, a pensive look wrinkled Diedrich's brow. Then in the midst of his father recounting an incident on the flatboat during their trip down the Ohio River from Pittsburg to Cincinnati, Diedrich broke in.

"Forgive me, Vater. Herr Seitz. Frau Seitz." He looked in turn at the three older people. "I have been thinking. You are right, Vater. We do owe Herr and Frau Seitz much, as well as Fräulein Regina." His tender gaze on Regina's face set her heart thumping in her chest. "The scriptures tell us to owe no man anything. And King Solomon tells us in Proverbs that the price of a virtuous woman is far above rubies." He turned to Herr Rothhaus. "Vater, I feel it is only right that before any marriage takes place, we should work the summer for Herr Seitz. With our labor, we can at least repay him our passage." His focus shifted to Regina. "And the extra months will allow time for Fräulein Seitz and I to get to know one another—which, I think, will make for a stronger union."

At his quiet suggestion a hush fell around the table. Then the elder Rothhaus began to nod. "Ja," he finally said. "What my son says makes much sense, I think. I am not a man who likes to feel beholden."

Looking down at his plate, Papa frowned. But at length he, too, bobbed his head in agreement, though Regina thought she detected a hint of disappointment in his eyes. "In my mind, you and your son owe me nothing, Herr Rothhaus. But I understand a man's need to feel free of obligation." Smiling, he turned to Regina and Mama. "And waiting until September will give you two more time to plan the wedding, hey, *mein Liebling*?"

During the exchange Regina sat agape, relief washing through her. Vaguely registering Mama's agreement, she could have almost bounded around the table and hugged Diedrich's neck. A reprieve! It did not entirely undo the deal, but it bought her some time to put her plan into action and a real chance of escaping this unwanted marriage. She glanced up at him engaged in conversation with Papa and couldn't stop a smirk from tugging up the corners of her lips. By the end of summer, Diedrich Rothhaus would beg to be let out of the agreement.

∽

Over the next week Regina had managed, for the most part, to stay clear of Diedrich. Their only interaction was at mealtimes and after supper when everyone sat together in the front room listening to either Papa or Herr Rothhaus read from the Bible. To her parents' chagrin, Regina began taking less care with her appearance. Only on Sunday and when she took her pony cart past the mill on the road to Dudleytown did she make sure that her hair was neatly plaited and her dress clean and mended.

A smug grin lifted her lips as she fairly skipped through the chill dawn air to the barn, swinging her milk bucket. The sunrise painted streaks of red and gold in myriad hues across the blue-gray of the eastern sky. The sight would normally be enough to brighten her mood, but this morning she had even more reason to smile. So far, her plan to turn Diedrich against her seemed to be working. Only rarely did she catch him looking her way, and she doubted the two of them had shared a dozen words since his arrival. On Sundays when the five of them all rode to and from St. John's Church together, Regina was careful to sit between Papa and Mama. And during the week, the men spent their days in the fields plowing and planting while Regina and her mother worked around the house.

Her grin widened. This morning she had taken her plan to discourage Diedrich even further. Time and again over the years, Mama had reminded Regina and her sisters that a man would often overlook appearance if his wife was a good cook. Regina had noticed that Diedrich and Herr Rothhaus were usually the first up and out of the house each morning, often putting in as much as an hour's work before returning for breakfast. So this morning, Regina had gotten up extra early and made two batches of biscuits, one the normal way and the other with twice the flour. It had taken some vigilance, but she made sure that Diedrich and his father got the rock-hard biscuits while she saved back the good, soft ones for her parents.

Remembering the look on Diedrich's face when he bit into one of the hard biscuits, she laughed out loud. For a moment, she actually feared he had broken a tooth. But even more encouraging was the frown Herr Rothhaus had exchanged with his son when he tried unsuccessfully to take a bite of his own biscuit. Though the two men had smiled and thanked her, they were forced to finally abandon the biscuits. Somehow they'd managed to chew most of the eggs she'd fried to almost the consistency of rubber as well as the fried potatoes she'd carefully burnt.

As she neared the barn, she hummed a happy tune, trying to think of how she might destroy another meal for the Rothhauses. No man in his right mind would marry a woman who cooked like that, and no caring father would commit his son to a lifetime of dyspepsia.

In the barn, she made her way through the dim building to the stall where their milk cow stood munching on timothy hay. "Good morning, Ingwer." She pulled her milking stool near the big, gentle animal and patted her ginger-colored hide that had inspired the cow's name. "How are you this fine morning? Will you give me lots of good milk with thick, rich cream today?"

Settling herself on the stool, Regina giggled, the happy noise mingling with the cow's dispassionate moo. "I shall be careful not to startle you with cold hands so you will not kick over the bucket like yesterday," she said as she crossed her arms over her chest and warmed her hands in her armpits.

As she bent down and reached beneath the cow, a hard hand clamped down on her shoulder, and she jerked. Her head knocked into Ingwer's side, causing the cow to moo and kick the bucket over.

Whipping her head around, Regina met Eli's angry glower. She jumped to her feet. "Eli, you scared me! What are you doing here? You know my Vater will be very angry if he finds—"

"I thought you were my special girl. Now I hear you're gettin' married." Not a trace of sorrow or even disappointment touched his green eyes. The only emotion Regina could read in his twisted features was raw fury. For the first time, she felt fear in Eli's presence.

She shrugged her shoulder away from his grasp. If possible, his face turned even stormier. He stepped closer, and for an instant the urge to run from him gripped her. But that was silly. She'd known Eli since they were children. He would never hurt her.

His fists remained balled at his sides. The rays of the morning sun filtering between the timbers of the barn's wall fell across his thick, bare forearms. In the soft light, she could see the muscles flexing beneath his tanned skin like iron springs. He leaned forward until his face was within inches of hers. "So are you gettin' married or not?"

"No, of course not. I'm not marrying anyone." Regina prayed she could make her words come true. "And I *am* your special girl."

"Not what I heard." He eased back a few inches, but his face and voice remained taut with anger. "Heard you were marryin' some German right off the boat."

Regina waved her hand through a sunbeam that danced with dust mites. "Oh, it is all Papa's idea. I knew nothing about it." She didn't know who she was angrier with—Papa for making the deal with Herr Rothhaus without her knowledge, neighbors who had trafficked in gossip disguised as news, or Eli for questioning her interest in him. "Do not believe everything you hear, Eli. I have no intention of marrying anyone, including the man Papa chose for me."

Instead of diluting Eli's anger, Regina's words seemed to stoke it. Lurching forward, he grabbed her arms. His fingers bit into her skin as he glared into her face. "You'd better be telling me the truth. I let a man take a girl from me once. I won't make that mistake again."

Regina yelped at the pain his hands were inflicting on her arms and struggled to pull away. "Ouch! Stop it, Eli. You are hurting me!"

Ignoring her plea, he pulled her roughly to him, and a ripping sound filled her left ear. Glancing in the direction of the sound, she noticed with dismay that the right sleeve of her dress had torn away at the shoulder.

"Look, you tore my dress!" Furious, she wriggled in vain in Eli's iron grasp.

His only answer was a throaty chuckle as he tried to press his mouth down on hers. But she turned her head at the last instant, and his lips landed wetly below her right ear.

"Eli, please stop it!" Tears flooded down Regina's face. Vacillating between pain, fear, and anger at his bad manners, she fought to free herself.

"Let her go, friend." Like the sound of distant thunder, an ominous warning in German rumbled beneath the deep, placid voice to their right.

CHAPTER 5

Relief and shame warred in Regina's chest as she looked over to see Diedrich's tall, broad-shouldered form filling the barn's little side doorway less than five feet away. She had no idea how much German Eli knew. But whether or not he understood Diedrich's words, Eli could not mistake the threat in Diedrich's voice as well as his stony glower and clenched fists.

Eli took his hands from Regina and stepped back. The two men traded glares, and for a moment, Regina feared a fight might ensue. Instead, Eli visibly shrank back and turned to her.

"Call off your German dog, Regina." Though audibly subdued, his voice dripped with scorn as he shot Diedrich a withering glance. "And you tell *him* not to say a word to your pa about our. . .argument, or we are through." With one last caustic glance between Regina and Diedrich, Eli turned on his heel and stalked out of the barn.

Only when Eli had disappeared through the big open doors at the end of the barn did Diedrich cross to her. "Are you hurt?" His gray eyes full of concern roved her face then slid to her bare shoulder and the ripped calico fabric hanging from it.

"No, I am not hurt." Fumbling, Regina tried to fit the torn sleeve back in place, but it wouldn't stay. She had done nothing wrong and should not feel embarrassed. Still, she did. But any embarrassment took second place to the anxiety filling her chest at Eli's parting warning. If Diedrich told Papa or Herr Rothhaus about what had just transpired between her and Eli, Papa would never allow Eli back on the farm. Stepping to Diedrich, she put her hand on his arm. "Please, do not tell Papa and Mama what you saw, or even that Eli was here. Eli is a. . .friend. We were just having an argument."

Diedrich's brow furrowed, and he glanced down at the straw-strewn dirt floor. After a long moment, he lifted a thoughtful but still troubled face to her. "To me, he did not look friendly. But unless I am asked, I will say nothing. And Herr Seitz knows he is here. The man you call Eli brought a bent driveshaft from the gristmill for your father to straighten at his forge."

Relief sluiced through Regina, washing the strength from her limbs. She grabbed the railing at the side of Ingwer's stall for support and blew out a long breath. "Gott sei Dank!" With the closest blacksmith shop at Dudleytown three miles away, it was not unusual for neighbors to bring their broken and bent iron pieces for Papa to fix at his little forge behind the barn.

"Thanks be to Gott that you were no more hurt." Only a hint of admonition touched Diedrich's voice as he bent and righted the milk bucket. When he straightened, his gaze strayed again to her bare shoulder. His face reddened, and he looked away. "You must mend your frock. I will milk the cow."

"Danke." At his kindness, Regina mumbled the word, emotion choking off her voice. *He is our guest. Of course he feels obliged to be kind.* But deep down, she knew his kindness did not spring entirely from a desire to be polite. She also knew intuitively that he would keep his word and not mention to her parents the incident between her and Eli. Turning to leave, she glanced back at his handsome profile and her pulse quickened, doubtless a reaction to her earlier fright with Eli and her embarrassment that Diedrich had witnessed the scene.

"Regina." His soft voice stopped her. "You do not want this marriage between us, do you?"

His blunt question caught her by surprise, and her heart raced as she turned around in the narrow doorway. Would Diedrich, like Eli, become enraged at her rejection? After all, he *had* sailed all the way from Venne to marry her. "No." The honest word popped out of her mouth, accompanied by an unexpected twinge of sadness.

To her confusion, instead of showing anger or disappointment, Diedrich's expression took on the same closed look she'd seen on Papa's face when he engaged in horse trading. "Neither do I want it."

Regina's jaw sagged. "But—but Papa paid your way here so you would. . .so we would—"

"I know." He winced. "Why do you think I suggested that my Vater and I work here through the summer to pay off our passage?"

"You—you said so we could get to know each other better." Her face flamed, and her eyes fled his.

"May Gott forgive my lie." His deep voice sank even further with regret.

Amazed at his words, Regina took a couple of tentative steps toward him. So all her scheming to put him off had been unnecessary? "You do not want to marry me?"

At her breathless question the emotionless curtain that had veiled his eyes lifted and they shone with both sorrow and remorse. "Please, Regina, I mean you no insult. It is not my intention to hurt you. I mean, look at you. Any man would be pleased. . ." Reddening, he shook his head as if to bring his thoughts back into focus. He took her hands in his, and the gentle touch of his fingers curling around hers suffused her with warmth. "It is not that I do not want to marry you. I do not want to marry anyone. Not until I have made my fortune."

Regina slipped her hands from his and stifled the laugh threatening to burst from her lips. "Made your fortune?" She glanced through the open doors at the end of the barn. In the distance, the morning sunlight turned the acres of winter wheat to fields of emerald. From a fence post, a cardinal flew, the sunlight gilding the edges of the bird's ruby-red wing. This farm had been her home for the past ten years since her family moved here from Cincinnati, where they'd first settled after arriving in America. After their cramped quarters in the German part of the noisy city, this place had seemed like Eden to seven-year-old Regina. And she still loved the farm with all her heart, but there was no fortune to be made here, despite what Diedrich and his father might have been told. Shaking her head, she gave him a pitiful look. "I do not know what others have told you, but you will find no fortune here. Papa has one of the most prosperous farms in Sauers, and we are certainly not wealthy."

Diedrich nodded. "You have a beautiful farm. I have been plowing for days now, and never have I seen better, richer soil than what I have found here. But I do not mean to make my fortune in Indiana."

"Then where?" Intrigued, she barely breathed the query as she drew closer.

A spark of excitement lit his eyes and his expression grew distant. "By September I hope to have paid off my passage and earned enough money to make my way to the goldfields in California." He fished a tattered scrap of newspaper from his shirt pocket and handed it to her.

Regina could barely make out the faded German words, but what she could read had a distinctly familiar ring. Since last autumn when newspapers first heralded the discovery of gold in California, advertisements like this one—only in English—had peppered every newspaper in the country. Offering every kind of provision needed by the adventurous soul willing to make the trip west, such notices promised riches beyond all human imagination, with little more effort than to reach down and scoop up gold nuggets from California's streams and mountainsides. Many young men from all over the country, including Jackson County, had hearkened to the siren's song and braved myriad dangers to make their way to the continent's western coast. And though a goodly number had lost their lives in the effort, to Regina's knowledge, not one had "struck it rich" as the papers put it.

She handed Diedrich back the scrap of paper and experienced a flash of sorrow tinged with fear. Would he be among the number to forfeit his life in the quest of a golden dream?

Diedrich tucked the paper back into his shirt pocket. "You asked me to keep the secret of your *Liebchen* from your parents. I must ask you to keep from them my plans as well."

Heat flamed in Regina's cheeks that he had guessed Eli was her sweetheart. Then anger flared, stoking the fire in her face. Despite her relief in learning that Diedrich did not want to marry her any more than she wanted to marry him, it did not excuse the fact that the Rothhaus men had lied to Papa. They had taken advantage of his generosity and used his money to come to America under false pretenses. "And when do you and Herr Rothhaus plan to tell my parents that you lied to get money for your passage here? Or will we just wake up one morning to find you both gone?"

"Nein." He barked the word, and an angry frown creased his tanned forehead. He grasped her arm but not in a threatening manner as Eli had done; his fingers did not bite into her skin as Eli's had. "You do not understand. My Vater knows nothing of my plans. He is an honorable man. He made the agreement with your Vater in good faith." His chin dropped to his chest, and his voice turned penitent. "I have deceived my Vater as I have deceived yours." He let go of her arm, leaving her feeling oddly bereft. "I know it was wrong of me, but I had no other means to get to America." When he raised his face to hers again, his gray eyes pled for understanding. "For many months, both my Vater and I had prayed that Gott would find a way for me to leave Venne for America before the army called me into service. So when the letter came from Herr Seitz offering us money for passage, it seemed an answer to our prayers." Diedrich's Adam's apple bobbed with his swallow. "My Vater was so happy that we were coming to America. I did not have the courage to tell him how I felt and to ask him to refuse your Vater's gift." He shook his head. "For months I have dreaded this moment, praying that Gott would find a way for me to get out of this marriage without disappointing both our Vaters." He swallowed again. His gray gaze turned so tender tears sprung to Regina's eyes. "But mostly, I prayed I would not break your heart."

Glancing away, Regina blinked the moisture from her eyes. So Diedrich Rothhaus was an honorable man. That was no reason for tears. And even if she wanted to marry him—which she did not—he did not want to marry her. At length, she lifted dry eyes to him. "So what do you suggest we do?"

He blew out a long breath and looked down at his boot tops, mired with the rich, dark soil of the back forty acres. When he lifted his face, a smile bloomed on his lips. Regina wondered why she had never noticed before the gentle curve of his mouth and the fine shape of his lips. "I think we should pray. I prayed I would not break your heart and Gott has answered my prayer. The harvest does not come immediately after the planting. Gott takes time to grow and ripen the grain.

So maybe we should give Him time to work in this also. I am sure the answer to our prayers will come in His season."

Diedrich's notion seemed sound. If they rushed to Papa and Herr Rothhaus now and confessed that they had no desire to marry, it would only bring discord and invite a barrage of opposition from their parents. Instead, the summer months would give Regina and Diedrich time to gradually convince their elders to dissolve their hastily cobbled plan to unite their children.

Regina nodded. "Ja. I think what you say is true. By harvesttime, the debt you and Herr Rothhaus owe to my Vater will be paid, and our Vaters will not feel so obliged to keep the agreement they made. Then when we tell them we do not think it is Gott's will that we marry, they will be more ready to accept our decision."

Diedrich stuck out his hand. "When we boarded the *Franziska*, my Vater said, 'We go to America where we can be free to live as we want.' If in this free land our Vaters can make a deal that we should marry, I see nothing wrong in the two of us making a deal that we should not."

With a halting motion, Regina placed her hand in his to seal their agreement. At his firm but gentle clasp, a sensation of comforting warmth like the morning sun's rays suffused her. Again she experienced regret when he drew his hand from hers.

He picked up the three-legged milking stool. "It is a deal, then. We shall work together to change our parents' minds and pray daily for their understanding." A whimsical grin quirked the corner of his mouth, and he winked, quickening Regina's heart. "I trust our agreement will now bring an improvement to my meals."

Regina's face flushed hotly. How transparent he must have found her feeble attempts to dampen his ardor. And even more embarrassing was learning that her efforts were entirely unnecessary. But at least she would no longer have to come up with new ways to turn Diedrich against her. Knowing she'd gained an ally in her quest to avoid the marriage Papa and Herr Rothhaus had arranged for her should make her heart soar. So why did it droop with regret?

CHAPTER 6

"There, *Alter*, does that feel better?" Diedrich lifted the last of the harness from the big draft horse's back. "At least you can shed your burden, mein Freund. I only wish mine came off so easily." What Diedrich had witnessed this morning had surely burdened his heart to a far greater extent than the leather harness and collar encumbered the big Clydesdale before him. He took the piece of burlap draped across the top beam of the horse's stall and began wiping the sweat from the animal's dark brown hide.

Anger, along with other emotions he didn't care to explore, raged in Diedrich's chest. A half day of plowing had not erased from his mind the scene he had come upon this morning in the barn. He hadn't felt such an urge to pummel someone to *Milchreis* since he was fourteen and found Wilhelm Kohl about to drown a sackful of kittens in the stream that separated their two farms. The sight of Regina struggling in the clutches of that rabid whelp she called "Eli" had made Diedrich want to take the boy's head off. At fourteen, Diedrich had plowed into eighteen-year-old Wilhelm without thought of the consequences, sending the bigger boy sprawling and the terrified cats scampering to the nearby woods. But when Wilhelm had righted himself and got the wind back into his lungs, he'd commenced to beat Diedrich until it was his face and not Wilhelm's that more closely resembled rice pudding.

Diedrich finished rubbing down the horse and tossed the piece of burlap over the stall's rail. If he had given in to his temper this morning as he had years ago with Wilhelm, the outcome would doubtless have been much different. Nearly a head taller than Eli and easily a stone heavier, he could have done serious damage to the boy if not taken his life altogether.

At the sobering thought, he blew out a long breath and shoved his fingers through his hair. Thanks be to Gott, over the past seven years he had grown not only in stature but also in self-control and forethought. Having declared his intentions, or rather the lack of them to Regina, Diedrich had no right to voice his opinion of her choice in a suitor, however brutish he considered the man. Still, for some reason, the girl to whom his father had promised him evoked in Diedrich a protective instinct he had rarely felt in his life. Twice since arriving in Sauers, he had seen fear shine from Regina's crystalline blue eyes, and twice he had felt compelled to vanquish it by coming between her and whatever threatened her.

He shook his head as if to dislodge from his mind the vision of Regina

171

struggling in Eli's arms. A new burst of anger flared within him like bellows pumping air into a forge. In an attempt to calm his rising temper, he patted the horse's muscular neck. "What Fräulein Seitz does is not my concern, is it, mein Freund?" But saying it aloud did not make it so. The thought of Regina marrying that oaf Eli concerned Diedrich greatly. How could he leave for California with a clear conscience knowing he was likely opening the door for her to stroll into matrimony with the hot-tempered youth? Still, he could see no good way out of his conundrum. He hadn't come all this way to give up his dream of making his fortune in California. And even if he weren't planning to leave Sauers, he'd made an agreement with Regina. If he reneged on their agreement and forced her into an unwanted marriage, he'd likely consign them both to a miserable life. No, his best option was to simply stick to his plan—and their agreement—and pray she would have enough good sense not to run off with the scamp.

The large horse dashed his head up and down and emitted an impatient whinny, wresting Diedrich from his troubled reverie.

"Forgive me, Freund. Of course you are right. I must take care of what Gott has given me to do and leave the rest to Him." He crossed to a pile of hay and grasped the pitchfork sticking from it, then carried two large forkfuls of dried timothy hay to the waiting stallion.

As if to say thanks, the Clydesdale expelled a mighty breath through his flaring nostrils, his sleek sides heaving with the effort. The great puff of air sent hay dust flying, and Diedrich sneezed as it went up his nose.

"Ah, there you are, mein Sohn." Father's bright voice chimed behind Diedrich, turning him around. "I thought maybe you had already gone to the house for dinner."

"Nein, Vater. As you always say, the animals feed us, so we must feed them before we feed ourselves." Glancing over his shoulder, Diedrich sent his father a smile and was struck again by the marked change in his parent since their arrival in America. It was hard to believe that Father was the same brooding, work-worn man who had raised him. From the moment they stepped off the *Franziska* in Baltimore, Diedrich had witnessed a transformation in his normally sullen father. It was as if someone had lit a new flame behind his father's gray eyes. But it was more than that. Though half a head shorter than Diedrich, Father stood taller now, and there was a new lilt in his step that belied his fifty-six years. America was good for Father.

"Ja." Father bobbed his head as he dragged his hat from his still-thick shock of graying brown hair. A good-natured twinkle flickered in his eyes. "I do say that for sure. And it is true. But I wonder if after this morning's breakfast, you are not so eager to eat the food prepared by your intended?"

"Are you?" Sidestepping the question, Diedrich ignored his father's teasing tone and use of the word "intended." Turning to hide his fading smile, he forked more hay into the horse's manger.

Father chuckled and stepped nearer, his footfalls whispering through the straw strewn over the barn's dirt floor. "Herr Seitz assures me that this morning's breakfast must have been a mishap and that his Tochter is usually as good a cook as her Mutter."

"I'm sure it is so," Diedrich said, careful to keep his face averted. Though she'd made no such admission, Diedrich suspected that Regina had ruined the meal on purpose to discourage him from marrying her. But he could not share that suspicion with Father without betraying the secret agreement he and Regina had made.

"Spoken like a loyal husband-to-be." A smile lifted Father's voice. He clapped his hand on Diedrich's shoulder, sending a wave of guilt rippling through him. "You will see. By this time next year when she is no longer Fräulein Seitz, but Frau Rothhaus, *das* Mädchen will be making *köstlich* meals for us in our own home."

Diedrich tried to smile, but his lips would not hold it. He had no doubt that Regina would be making delicious meals for someone, but they would not be for him. It scraped his conscience raw to allow his father to fashion dreams of the three of them sharing a home in domestic tranquility, when Diedrich knew it was never to be.

Father slung his arm across Diedrich's shoulder. "Come, mein Sohn. The horse has had his feed. It is our turn now." He smacked his lips. "I can almost taste that *wunderbares Brot* Frau Seitz makes from cornmeal."

As they stepped from the barn, Father stopped. Turning, he faced Diedrich and grasped his shoulders. He shook his head, and his eyes glistened with moisture. "Mein *lieber* Sohn. Still sometimes I cannot believe it is true, that we are really here." He ran the cuff of his sleeve beneath his nose. "Since you were a kleines Kind, I have dreamed of coming to live in America. I gave up thinking it would ever happen. And now in the autumn of my life, Gott has resurrected my withered dream and made it bloom like the spring flowers." He waved toward a lilac bush laden with fragrant purple blossoms growing just outside the barn.

Diedrich groaned inwardly. He did not need any more guilt rubbed like salt into his sore conscience. He forced a tiny smile. "I am glad you are happy here, Vater." He tried to turn back toward the barn's open doors, but Father held fast.

Father's throat moved with his swallow. "I am more than happy. Mein heart is full to overflowing. Soon I will have a new daughter-in-law, and in time, Gott willing, Enkelkinder to bounce on my knee. And it is you that I have to thank for making my dream come true." He gave Diedrich a quick hug and pat on the back. His voice thickened with emotion. "I do not know how I can ever thank you."

Later at the dinner table, Father's words still echoed in Diedrich's ears, smiting him with remorse. His appetite gone, he stared down at his untouched bowl of venison stew. Time and again on their walk to the house, he had been tempted to blurt out the truth. But doing so would not only humiliate Father and break his heart; it could render them both homeless as well.

He glanced across the table at Regina. In contrast to his sullenness, her mood had improved greatly. In fact, she looked happier than he had seen her. Her hair was neatly plaited and wound around her head like a halo of spun gold. Pink tinted her creamy cheeks, reminding him of the blossoms that now decorated the apple trees. Her lips, an even deeper rose color than her cheeks, looked soft as the petals of the flower they resembled. They parted slightly in laughter at a humorous comment by Frau Seitz. An unfamiliar ache throbbed deep in Diedrich's chest, and he experienced a sudden desire to know how Regina's lips would feel against his. Immediately, the memory of the miller's son trying to learn that very thing elbowed its way into his mind, filling him at once with rage and envy.

"Such a face, Diedrich. You do not like the stew?" Frau Seitz's voice invaded Diedrich's thoughts, bringing his head up with a jerk. "Regina made it herself."

He blinked at his hostess and reddened at Regina's giggle. "Yes. I mean no. *Es schmeckt sehr gut.*" A blast of heat suffused his face. As if to demonstrate his sincerity, he spooned some of the meat and vegetables swimming in dark gravy into his mouth. The stew was surprisingly tasty, but with Diedrich's worries twisting his gut into knots, it might as well have been sawdust.

"*Danke.*" Regina gave him a sly smile as if to acknowledge their shared secret, sending his heart tumbling in his chest.

At the sensation, Diedrich sucked in air and almost choked on the chunk of venison in his mouth. If he'd found having Regina as an enemy uncomfortable, having her as an ally was proving no less disconcerting. He stifled a groan that bubbled up from his chest and threatened to push through his lips. Was there ever a more wretched soul than he? For the length of the spring and summer, he'd have to pretend to Father as well as Herr and Frau Seitz that he was happily betrothed to a girl whom he had secretly agreed not to marry. At the same time, he had to keep from Father his plans to leave for California until he earned enough money to pay back Herr Seitz for his passage to America. But most importantly, he needed to somehow find a way to convince Father and Herr Seitz that he and Regina should not marry while convincing Regina that she should not marry Eli. The last thing he needed was to lose his heart to this pretty Fräulein.

CHAPTER 7

Regina stood at the edge of the plowed and harrowed garden and inhaled the rich scent of the earth. How she loved the smell of newly turned sod in the spring. Each April for the past ten years, she, Mama, Sophie, and Elsie worked together to plant this little patch of ground behind the house with potatoes, cabbage, and string beans. What fun the three of them had as they talked, laughed, and sometimes even sang together while planting the garden.

Her heart wilted as she reached down to pick up her hoe and burlap sack of seed potatoes. With Sophie and Elsie miles away in their own homes and Mama busy ironing yesterday's laundry, Regina would plant the potatoes alone this year. She stepped from the thick grass into the soft, tilled ground, her wooden shoes sinking into the sandy soil. Instead of looking forward to spending a pleasant hour with her mother and sisters, today Regina saw nothing before her but a morning filled with lonely, monotonous, back-aching work.

Heaving a sigh, she looked toward the fields beyond the barn where Papa worked with the Rothhaus men tilling the fields for planting corn. A flash of resentment flared in her chest. While the arrival of Diedrich and Herr Rothhaus had greatly lightened Papa's work, it had increased hers and Mama's. With two extra people to feed and clothe, mother and daughter no longer had the luxury of working together on many of the daily household chores. Now they often needed to work separately in order to accomplish more in the same amount of time.

Continuing to gaze at the distant field, she could make out one man behind the cultivator and another with a strapped canvas sack slung across his shoulder, obviously planting corn. Was it Diedrich? She peered through squinted eyes, but at the extreme distance, she could not tell for sure. At the thought of him, an odd sensation of pulsating warmth filled her chest—a sensation for which she had no certain name. Relief? Yes, it must be relief. Learning last week that he, too, did not want the marriage their fathers had arranged for them allowed her to relax in his presence. Now she no longer avoided him. Indeed, she found it easier to converse with Diedrich than with Eli, who was usually more interested in trying to steal a kiss than talking.

Wielding the hoe, she gouged an indention in the soft dirt. Then, taking a piece of potato from the bag, she dropped it into the hole. Careful to keep the sprouting "eye" up, she covered it again with dirt, which she tamped down using the flat of the hoe blade. After repeating the process for the length of one row, boredom set in. With only the occasional chirping of birds for company, Regina began singing one of her favorite hymns to fill the silence. "Now thank we all our Gott, with heart and hands and voices—"

"Who wondrous things hath done, in whom His world rejoices." A deep, rich baritone voice responded, hushing Regina and yanking her upright.

Grinning, Diedrich strode toward her carrying what looked like a rolled-up newspaper. "Please do not stop singing. That is one of my favorite hymns."

The odd fluttering sensation in her chest returned. "I will if you will sing it with me."

"Who from our mothers' arms hath blessed us on our way," he sang. Regina lifted her soprano voice to join his baritone in singing, "With countless gifts of love, and still is ours today."

After jabbing a stick in the ground to mark the place where she'd planted her last potato, she trudged through the uneven dirt of the garden to where he stood.

Laughing, he clapped his hands together. "Well done, if I say so myself." His expression turned apologetic. "Forgive my intrusion on your work, but I would like to ask a favor."

Curious, Regina focused on the paper in his hand as she neared. From what she could tell, it looked to be the *Madison Courier* newspaper. "I was about to take a rest anyway." Though not entirely true, she liked that her reply erased the concerned lines from his handsome face.

Diedrich unrolled the paper. With a look of little-boy shyness that melted her heart, he held it out to her. "Will you read this to me, please? I cannot ask your parents or my Vater. And Vater knows less English than I do." He narrowed his gaze at a spot near the top right side of the paper. "I recognize only the word *California*."

Taking the paper from his hands, Regina followed his gaze and focused on an article beneath a heading that read HO FOR CALIFORNIA. Scanning the article, she saw it advertised a fort in Arkansas as a place for California gold seekers to gather. A feeling of apprehension gripped her, and for an instant, she was tempted to tell him the paper was simply reporting about gold having been found in California. But he'd be sure to find out the truth eventually. And besides, wasn't Pastor Sauer's sermon last Sunday on the evil of telling untruths?

"So what does it say?" Eagerness shone in Diedrich's gray eyes.

"It says gold seekers should go to a place called Fort Smith in Arkansas." Her drying throat tightened, forcing her to swallow. "It lists all the items someone going to the goldfields will need and claims they have those things for sale. It also says the government is building a road called the Fort Smith-Santa Fe Trail to the goldfields."

"Then this Fort Smith, Arkansas, is where I should go?" His eyes sparking with interest, he took the paper from her limp hands.

Regina fought the urge to tell him no, that he shouldn't go there. Instead, she mustered a tepid smile and with a weak voice said, "Yes, I suppose it is."

Anticipation bloomed on his face, and he rolled the paper back up and stuffed it inside the waistband of his trousers at the hip. He took her hands into his, and his flannel-soft eyes filled with gratitude. "Danke, Regina." His calloused thumbs caressed the backs of her hands, and her heart took flight like a gaggle of geese. He dropped her hands, and she experienced a sense of loss.

She turned and faced the garden again. "Well, I must get back to my planting, or we will not have potatoes this year." Despite an effort to lighten her voice, it sounded strained.

"I am done with the plowing, and Vater and Herr Seitz are finishing the corn planting." He looked over the little garden patch. "I would be happy to help you finish planting the potatoes."

With her heart slamming against her ribs, her first inclination was to decline his offer. What was the matter with her? Eli was her sweetheart, not Diedrich. Besides, by the end of harvest, Diedrich would be heading for California. She looked at the hoe and the nearly full sack of seed potatoes lying in the dirt. Diedrich and his father caused her enough extra work, so why not accept his help? She nodded and smiled. "Danke. I would much appreciate that."

For the next hour, they worked together with him digging the holes and her dropping in the pieces of cut potato. As they worked, they sang hymns, and Regina marveled at how well their voices blended. When not singing, they swapped anecdotes about tending gardens as children with their siblings.

"Do you miss your brothers?" Regina asked as she placed the last piece of potato in the little gully Diedrich had just dug.

His face took on a pensive expression, and he rested his chin on the back of his hands, which covered the knob of the hoe's handle. "Ja. I do miss them."

Regina stood and brushed her palms together, dusting the soil from them. "Your brothers did not want to come here?" Herr Rothhaus had mentioned his older sons and their families on several occasions but had never said if they, too, would like to come to America.

Diedrich shook his head. "Johann, no. He is the oldest and is attached to the farm in Venne. Frederic, I think, would come, but his wife, Hilde, is with child again. Even if they had money for the passage—which they do not—she was not willing to risk it."

His comment struck home for Regina. "I was born on ship during Mama and Papa's voyage here." Her gaze panned the surrounding farm. "I am glad Mama was courageous." For a moment they shared a smile, and warmth that had nothing to do with the midday sun rushed through her.

Diedrich jammed a maple stick into the ground at the end of their last row of potatoes to mark it, then glanced up at the sky. "Now all we have to do is pray for Gott to send the sun and the rain." Grinning, he nodded toward the split log bench near the house. "I think we have earned a rest."

"So do I." Regina followed him out of the patch of tilled ground, unable to remember a more enjoyable experience planting potatoes. As she stepped from the loose soil of the garden, one of her wooden shoes sank deep into a furrow, and when she lifted her foot, the shoe stayed behind. Not wanting to get her sock dirty, she balanced on one foot and bent the shoeless one back beneath her.

At her grunt of dismay, Diedrich turned around. Seeing her plight, he hurried to her. "Here, hold on to me." He reached down to retrieve her shoe. Obeying, she slipped her arm around his waist and felt the hard muscles of his torso stretch with his movement. Her heart quickened at their nearness as he held her against him with one hand while placing the Holzschuh on her stockinged foot.

With her shoe back in place, she mumbled her thanks and stepped away from him as quickly as possible, hurrying to the bench in an effort to hide her blazing face. She tried to think of an instance when Eli had kindled an equally pleasant yet unsettling reaction in her but couldn't.

They perched at opposite ends of the bench, leaving a good foot of space between them. For a long moment, they sat in silence. The gusting breeze, laden with the perfume of lilac blossoms, dried the perspiration beading on Regina's brow.

At length, Diedrich reached behind him and pulled the newspaper from the waistband of his trousers. He looked at it for a moment then turned to Regina. "I have another favor to ask. I would like for you to teach me to read the English. I will never make it to California if I cannot speak or read the language of America."

Like all the local young people of German heritage, Regina was fluent in both German and English, having learned English in school. Switching between the two languages felt as natural to her as breathing. With German spoken exclusively at home, it hadn't occurred to her that Diedrich lacked that advantage.

She smiled. "I'm not sure how good a teacher I will be, but I will try."

She scooted closer and, bending toward him until their shoulders touched, began to point out some of the simpler words on the pages of the open newspaper. "*And.*" Dragging out the enunciation, she pronounced the word above her index finger then had him repeat it.

An obviously quick learner, he mastered the one-, two-, and three-letter words by the first or second try. So Regina moved on to some larger words but with decidedly less success, making for humorous results.

After butchering the word *prospectors* for the third time, he began guessing at its pronunciation, making the word sound sillier with each try and sending Regina into fits of laughter so hard that tears rolled down her cheeks. "Nein, nein, nein!" she gasped between guffaws, her head lolling against his shoulder.

"Regina."

At the sound of her name, she looked up to see Eli standing a few feet away and eyeing her and Diedrich with an angry glare.

CHAPTER 8

I thought you said you weren't interested in him." Despite his earlier fierce look, Eli's voice sounded more hurt than angry as he cast a narrowed glance over Regina's shoulder toward the bench she'd sprung from seconds ago.

"Diedrich asked me to teach him English, that is all." She shrugged, trying to force a light tone.

"Diedrich, huh?" Eli shot another glare past her, his voice hardening and his brow slipping into an angry V.

Despite the dozen or so feet between them, Regina could feel Diedrich's eyes on her back. Thankfully, he had not followed her across the yard to where she and Eli now stood beneath the white-blossomed dogwood tree. She desperately wished he would discreetly leave her and Eli alone, but after the two men's confrontation in the barn last week, she doubted he would. Why did Eli have to come at this very moment?

Sighing, she put her hand on Eli's arm. His tensed muscles reminded her of a cat about to pounce. Though admittedly flattering, Eli's jealousy was growing tiresome. As much as she tried to make her voice sound conciliatory, she couldn't keep a frustrated tone from creeping in. "What I told you is true." The temptation to tell him about the agreement she and Diedrich had made tugged hard. But she couldn't risk him blurting it out in an unguarded moment. "You will just have to believe me."

Eli groped for her hand, but for reasons she couldn't explain, she drew it back and crossed her arms over her middle, tucking her hands protectively beneath them. "Why are you here?"

"My uncle's barn burned near Dudleytown last night."

A wave of concern and sorrow swept away her defenses, and she reached out to touch his arm again. "Oh Eli, I am sorry to hear that. I hope your uncle and his family were not hurt."

He gave an unconcerned shrug. "Na. They're all right. Lost a couple of pigs, but they got the horses and cows out." A grin crept across his handsome face. "Thing is, Pa and some of my uncle's neighbors are plannin' a barn raisin' soon as Pa can get enough lumber sawed at the mill. He's invitin' everybody in Sauers to come." Fun danced in his green eyes, and he grasped her hands. "Your pa's already agreed to come and bring you and your ma." His smile faded briefly as he glanced behind her. "And them two fellers stayin' here with you." He focused on her face again, and his smile returned with a roguish quirk. "We can see each other all day durin' the barn raisin'. And with so many people about, I'd wager we could prob'ly slip off and get some time to ourselves and nobody would even notice."

Drawing her hands from his, she stepped back and thought she heard a stirring sound behind her. She prayed Diedrich would not feel compelled to save her from Eli's exuberance. The prospect of having to step between the two men to prevent them from coming to blows did not appeal to her. Nor did she relish the notion of explaining to Papa and Herr Rothhaus what had prompted the fisticuffs.

Thankfully, Eli made no move to recapture her hands or, worse, try to steal a kiss, which would doubtless bring Diedrich sprinting to her side.

Eli's gaze, focused behind her, tracked to the right as if following a moving object. Was Diedrich, after all, deciding to intrude on her and Eli's conversation? Or had he gone, leaving the two of them alone? Oddly, she found the second notion more disconcerting than the first.

Eli's expression sobered, and he took a couple of steps backward. "I just wanted to let you know about the barn raisin'. An' if you *are* my special girl, you can prove it by sneakin' off and spendin' some time alone with me durin' the meal." Reaching up, he plucked a blossom from the boughs above them and pressed it into her hand.

Before Regina could tell him that her parents would never allow her to do such a thing, he turned and took off at a quick trot, disappearing around the corner of the house. Opening her palm, she stared at the ivory-colored flower with its spiky crownlike center and jagged, rust-stained tips that edged its four petals. Three weeks ago on Easter Sunday morning, Pastor Sauer had suggested that the appearance of the blossoms should be a reminder of Christ's sacrifice for man's sins. Guilt pricked like a thorn at her heart. She doubted Christ, or her parents, would approve of what Eli had asked her to do.

Had Diedrich heard? Though he couldn't read English, both he and his father had displayed an ability to understand some of the spoken words. At the thought of his having overheard Eli's demand, a flash of panic leapt in her chest. She spun around to look for him, but he had gone. Instead of bringing her relief, the sight of the empty bench brought a strange forlornness.

❧

Thunder boomed, shaking the bed Diedrich shared with his father and rattling the window glass across the dark room. Wide awake, he rolled onto his side, searching in vain for a more comfortable, sleep-inducing position. The ropes supporting the feather tick mattress groaned in protest with his movements, while a white flash of lightning cast an eerie glow over the room.

Through the tumult Father slept, his snores and snorts adding to the cacophony of the storm outside. Diedrich rolled onto his back again and closed his eyes, but still sleep eluded him.

Sighing, he sat up in surrender. He swung his legs over the side of the bed and pressed his bare feet to the nubby surface of the rag rug that covered much of the puncheon floor. At supper, his concerns about Regina and her attachment to the boy called Eli had robbed him of his appetite. But now, his stomach rumbled in protest of its emptiness. In truth, it was not the raging storm but thoughts of Regina and Eli that had kept sleep just beyond Diedrich's grasp.

As quietly as possible he pulled on his trousers and shirt and padded barefoot across the room, hopeful that the sounds of the storm would cover any creaking noises his movements might evoke from the wood floor. He would rather Herr or Frau Seitz not discover him wandering about their home in the middle of the night.

Intermittent flashes of lightning guided him to the kitchen at the back of the house. But upon reaching the room, he realized he would need a more constant light in his quest for food or risk knocking something over and waking everyone in the house.

He lit the tin lamp on the kitchen table, suffusing the space with a warm, golden glow. In search of the remnants of last night's venison supper, he stepped to the black walnut cabinet where he had seen Frau Seitz and Regina store leftover food from meals. As he reached up to grasp the knob of the cabinet door, he caught a flicker of movement out of the corner of his right eye.

Freezing in place, he peered intently through the kitchen doorway that opened to the washroom. A creaking sound emanated from the enclosed stairway that led up to Regina's bedroom. For a heart-stopping moment, Diedrich contemplated blowing out the lamp and bolting to the interior of the house and his own bedroom. But before he could move, a small dancing light appeared on the back door and a shadowy figure emerged from the stairwell.

A small gasp sounded from the washroom. Unable to speak or move, he gazed unblinking at the vision before him. Fully dressed, but barefoot and with her unplaited hair cascading around her shoulders, Regina stood motionless in the threshold between the washroom and kitchen. Light from the amber finger lamp in her hand burnished her loosed tresses, making them appear as a cloud of gold around her face.

"*Verzeihst du mir.*" Finding his tongue at last, Diedrich murmured his apology. "Forgive me for waking you." He glanced at the cabinet. "I woke up hungry and thought. . ."

To his surprise, she smiled and walked to him. "It was the storm that woke me, not you." She glanced upward. "The sounds are more frightening to me upstairs with the big cottonwood tree swaying just outside the window beside my bed. So during storms, I often come down and sit near the bottom of the stairs. I was on my way down when I saw your light in the kitchen." As if to lend validity to her words, an explosion of thunder shook the house. She jerked, and for a moment, Diedrich feared she would drop the glass lamp. He eased it from her fingers and set it beside the tin one on the kitchen table.

The look of fear on her face made him want to comfort her. Protect her. Instead, he said the stupidest thing that could come out of his mouth. "It is just noise. It cannot hurt you."

Giving him a sheepish smile, she opened the cabinet, releasing the welcome aroma of roasted venison. "I know it is silly of me, but I have always been afraid of storms. Mama says I was born during a storm at sea on their journey from Bremen to Baltimore." She handed him a platter covered with a cotton towel. "My fear of storms wasn't so bad when my sisters were here and shared my room, but now that I am alone in my bed. . ." Her words trailed off as if she realized she'd said too much, embarrassing herself.

"This venison smells *wunderbar*." Rushing to her rescue, Diedrich hastened to change the subject. Why did he always feel compelled to protect her, even from herself?

She took down another plate from the pantry cabinet, and Diedrich inhaled a whiff of sourdough bread. "If you will slice the meat and Mama's good *Bauernbrot*," she said, "I will dip us each a *Becher* of milk." Darting about the kitchen, she produced two plates and a large knife then headed toward the crock of milk beside the sink.

When they finally sat together at the table with the ingredients for their middle-of-the-night repast, Diedrich propped his elbows on the tabletop and bowed his head over his folded hands as Regina did the same. Diedrich's whispered prayer of thanks was swallowed up by a violent crash of thunder. Regina gasped and jumped then visibly trembled as the sound continued to roll and reverberate around the little kitchen.

Diedrich's heart went out to her. Remembering his trepidation during an especially rough storm at sea, he understood some of her fear. He reached across the table and gripped her hand, warm and small, trembling in his. The urge to round the table and take her into his arms and hold her close to him became almost suffocating.

"You are safe." The words seemed simplistic and woefully inadequate, but they were all he could think to say. Yet despite how feckless they sounded, those three words appeared sufficient. For as the sound subsided, rolling off into the distance, a measure of fear left her eyes.

"*Danke.*" Drawing her hand from his, she glanced down, a self-conscious smile quivering on her lips.

For several minutes, they ate in silence. When a bright flash of lightning that Diedrich knew would precede another clap of thunder lit the kitchen, he tried to think of something that would distract her from the coming noise. An idea struck, and he hurried to wash down his bite of venison and bread with a gulp of milk. "How do you say *Blitz* in English?"

"Lightning," she said around a bite of bread.

"Lightning," he repeated, and she nodded.

Thunder rumbled, and she appeared to stiffen. She gripped her mug of milk so hard her fingers turned as white as its contents.

Diedrich covered her hand with his to draw her attention back to him. "*Donner.* How do you say Donner?" If he could keep her distracted, maybe she would forget to be frightened.

"Thunder." Her voice trembled slightly, mimicking the sound outside as it dissipated and rolled away.

"Thun–er." Diedrich dragged out the enunciation, intentionally leaving out the *d* to keep her focused on teaching him the word.

She smiled and giggled, a bright, almost musical sound. His heart bucked like Father's prize bull the time Frederic was fool enough to climb on the animal's back. "*Nein.*" She shook her head. "Thun–*der.*"

"Thunder," he managed to whisper, his racing heart robbing him of breath.

The wind howled and assailed the kitchen window with a blast of rain.

Regina glanced at the window. "Rain," she said. "*Regen* is rain."

"Rain," he repeated, glad to see that the fear had left her blue eyes.

For the next several minutes they ate while taking turns coming up with words for her to translate into English. Lightning flashed and thunder rumbled, but as they finished their food, she no longer seemed affected by the noise. Now fully engaged in the game, she appeared completely relaxed.

"*Scheune.*" Her voice held a challenge as she leaned back in her chair and crossed her arms over her chest.

A desire to show off sparked in Diedrich. This was one of the few English words he had learned from Herr Seitz. Answering her smug look with one of his own, he locked his gaze with hers and said, "Barn. *Scheune* in English is barn."

"*Ja!*" The word burst from her mouth on a note of glee loud enough to rival the storm's noise. Immediately, she clasped her hand over her mouth and cast a wide-eyed glance toward the doorway that led to the inner part of the house as if afraid she had woken their parents. When several seconds passed and no one appeared, a nervous-sounding little giggle erupted from behind her fingers. Rising, she gave him a self-conscious grin and gathered up their plates and mugs. "I think we should go back to our beds now before we wake our *Eltern*," she whispered.

Diedrich watched her move about the kitchen and his heart throbbed. *I cannot lose my heart to this girl. I cannot!* But his errant heart pranced on, scorning his censure. If only he knew she was safe, then maybe when autumn came he could leave for California with an unshackled heart. But that could not happen as long as Regina continued to court that brutish fellow, Eli. The concerns that had kept Diedrich awake rose up in his chest, demanding release. Somehow he must find the words to dissuade her from considering the scoundrel for a husband. *Dear Lord, give me the words that would convince her to turn away from Eli Tanner.*

When she had returned the meat and bread to the pantry cabinet and closed the doors, Diedrich walked to her and took her hand in his. He chose his words with care, as if he were picking fruit for a queen.

"Regina." He gazed into her eyes, which sparkled like blue stars in the lamplight. At her expression of questioning trust, he nearly lost his nerve. His arms ached to hold her, but that wouldn't do. Instead, he caressed the back of her hand with his thumb and swallowed to moisten his drying throat. "Regina," he began again. "I do not know how well you know this fellow, Eli. But I do not think he is a good man. It is my opinion that you would be wise to consider—"

"I did not ask for your opinion." She yanked her hand from his grasp. "You know nothing of Eli or of me." Her expression turned as stormy as the weather outside. "Just because your *Vater* and mine made a deal does not give you the right to tell me what I should do!"

CHAPTER 9

Regina stood in front of the dresser mirror and slipped another pin into the braid that crowned her head. A bright ray of morning sun dappled by the new leaves of the cottonwood tree outside her window speckled her hair with its light. Though vanity was a sin, she always liked to look her best for church. She fingered the snowy tatting that edged the collar of her blue frock. For reasons she couldn't explain, she wanted to look especially nice today. Inspecting her reflection, she smoothed down all hints of wrinkles in her freshly washed and ironed Sunday frock. She couldn't help thinking of Diedrich's comment last Sunday when he helped her onto the family's wagon for the trip to church. *"With your golden hair and blue frock, you remind me of a summer sky."*

Diedrich. There he was again. Always loitering on the fringes of her mind. More and more, she found herself thinking of him. Since the storm two nights ago, they hadn't spoken again at length. At the realization, regret smote her heart. Many times she had wanted to apologize for lashing out at him, but somehow she had not found the right moment. He had obviously gotten the wrong impression of Eli when he saw them arguing in the barn and was just trying to protect her. But his words of caution, however carefully delivered, had touched the one nerve in Regina that everyone, including Eli, had lately rubbed raw. With the exception of her eldest sister, Sophie, who had always delighted in bossing her around, Regina had been allowed the freedom to make most of her own decisions in life. Now, suddenly, everyone seemed determined to wrest that control away from her. Papa, Mama, Herr Rothhaus, and even Eli, with his demands that she spend time alone with him at the coming barn raising, all wanted to tell her what to do. She had appreciated the fact that Diedrich had not treated her in a dictatorial manner but had shown her the respect due a friend and equal. So when he voiced his opinion of Eli, it was, as Mama often said, "the drop that makes the barrel overflow."

As she remembered how she had angrily stalked away from him after he had tried so hard to quell her fear during the storm, guilt gnawed at her conscience. Her mouth turned down in a frown. Ironically, their secret pact to not get married had formed a bond between them that never could have occurred had they agreed to their parents' bargain. And now she feared she had broken that bond. She missed the easy friendliness she and Diedrich had enjoyed before she'd allowed her temper to shatter it. Oddly, her arguments with Eli had never bothered her as much as this one rift with Diedrich, possibly because she felt at fault. Though she instinctively sensed that Diedrich was not one to hold a grudge, she knew she would not be easy again until she had made amends with him. Still, she dreaded the encounter, which was sure to be awkward.

So despite the sunny day, her mood remained clouded. She usually looked forward to attending Sunday morning church service and enjoyed Pastor Sauer's sermons. But this morning she had to force her feet toward the stairs. Even anticipation of seeing friends like Anna Rieckers and Louisa Stuckwisch had not spurred her to dress more quickly. But Mama had already called up twice, warning Regina she'd be left behind if she didn't come down soon, so she could delay no longer.

When she reached the bottom step, her heart catapulted to her throat and she froze. Dressed in his best with hat in hand, Diedrich stood near the back door. She hadn't expected him to be waiting for her. Before she could say anything, he spoke.

"*Guten Morgen*, Regina." Though his lips remained unsmiling, his gentle gray gaze held no speck of grudge. If anything, his expression suggested apology. "The others have all gone out to the wagon, but I hoped we might speak alone."

"Guten Morgen, Diedrich." Her throat went dry, making her words come out in a squeak. If she was going to make amends, now was the time. She opened her mouth.

"Diedrich."

"Regina."

They spoke in near unison, and he smiled, dimpling the corner of his well-shaped mouth. "*Bitte*, you speak."

Shame drove her gaze from his face to the floor. "Verzeihst du mir. I should not have acted so rudely the other night."

"Nein." Wonder edged his voice, and he took her hands in his. "It is I who should ask your forgiveness." His thumbs caressed the backs of her hands as they had done during the storm, sending the same warm tingles up her arms. "You were right. It is not my place to say whom you should choose for friends." He grinned. "I only hope you still count me among them."

Regina wanted to laugh with glee. She wanted to jump up and down and clap her hands like when she was small and Papa bought her a candy stick at the Dudleytown mercantile. She couldn't say why, but knowing the friendship that had sprung up between her and Diedrich was still intact made her happy. But instead of embarrassing herself with childish antics, she smiled demurely and murmured, "Of course you are my friend." Turning her face to hide her smile, she focused on reaching for her bonnet on a peg by the back door.

He blew out a long breath as if he had been holding it. *"Ich bin froh."*

Glad. Yes, glad fit how Regina felt, too. She basked in his smile as he escorted her to the wagon where her parents and Herr Rothhaus sat waiting.

And the gladness stayed with her throughout the church service. From time to time, she found her gaze straying to the men's side of the church. With his Bible—one of the few things he'd brought from Venne—open on his lap, Diedrich sat beside his father, his rapt attention directed toward the front of the church and Pastor Sauer. His straight brown hair lay at an angle across his broad forehead and his clean-shaven jaw in profile looked strong, as if chiseled from stone. Regina wondered why she had never noticed how very handsome he was.

An odd ache burrowed deep into her chest. Perhaps it would not have been the worst thing in the world if Papa and Herr Rothhaus had gotten their way and she had ended up with Diedrich for a husband.

" 'And be ye kind one to another, tenderhearted, forgiving one another, even as God for Christ's sake hath forgiven you.' " Pastor Sauer's compelling voice drew Regina's attention back up to him. He paused and stroked the considerable length of his salt-and-pepper beard as if allowing time for the scripture to soak into his congregants' brains. The subject of his sermon had been directed particularly toward married couples. But the words of the scripture drew in Regina's mind a stark contrast between how Diedrich and Eli treated her.

She glanced over at Diedrich again, and the ache in her chest deepened. It didn't matter how sweet, caring, or handsome Diedrich was. Eli was handsome, too. And he wanted to marry her. Diedrich wanted to hunt for gold in California.

∞

Diedrich pumped the pastor's hand. "It was a fine sermon, Pastor Sauer."

Pastor Sauer gave a little chuckle and clapped him on the shoulder. "Danke, Sohn." Then, leaning in, he added, "And one you should remember, maybe, hey?" With a twinkle in his eye, he shot a glance across the churchyard to where Regina stood talking and giggling with two other young women. "Herr Seitz tells me you and Fräulein Seitz have decided to wait until after the harvest to wed." He nodded his head in approval. "That is *gut*. Learn your bride's heart before you wed. It will make for a more harmonious home."

Diedrich quirked a weak smile that his mouth refused to support for more than a second. He felt like a liar and a fraud. But he couldn't share his true plans with Pastor Sauer any more than he could share them with Father or Herr and Frau Seitz.

Giving the pastor's hand a final shake, he headed for the patch of shade where the Seitz wagon stood. *"Learn your bride's heart."* The pastor's words echoed in his ears.

It almost made him wish Regina *was* his bride-to-be, as everyone thought. For every day, he learned something new and wonderful about her. This morning he had learned she had a sweet heart, full of forgiveness. And if not for the beckoning goldfields of California, a life here with Regina on this fertile land would be more than enticing.

It had troubled him that yesterday she seemed to make a concerted effort to keep her distance from him, finding reasons to stay near her mother. He had surmised she was still angry with him over his comment about Eli, and didn't blame her. Of course she would have viewed his words as meddling in her personal business, and rightly so. But what had troubled him more was the look on her face this morning when she came downstairs. For one awful moment, he had seen something akin to fear flicker in her eyes. Had she stayed away from him because she thought that, like Eli, he might respond to her earlier righteous indignation with anger? The thought both sickened and angered him. He hardened his resolve to do everything in his power over the summer to open her eyes to the dangers the Tanner boy presented.

At the wagon, he turned and looked back in her direction, and his heart quickened. A wide smile graced her lovely face as she carried on an animated conversation with her friends. The morning sun turned the braids that circled her head to ropes of gold, while her calico bonnet dangled negligently from her wrist, brushing her sky blue skirt with her every gesture. She laughed, a bright, musical sound that always reminded him of a brook tripping over stones.

"Diedrich. I was looking for you." Herr Seitz put his hand on Diedrich's shoulder, jerking him from his musings. "I hope you are not so much in a hurry for dinner." He glanced over his shoulder at Father, who was sauntering toward them with Frau Seitz on one arm and Regina on the other. "Your Vater and I have agreed it is a nice morning for a drive."

As was their usual custom on Sundays, they had forgone breakfast this morning, opting instead for a larger meal after church. And though Diedrich's stomach gnawed with emptiness, his curiosity was piqued. "Ja, it is a gut day for a drive. I can wait to eat." Since their arrival nearly a month ago, Diedrich had rarely left the Seitz farm. And though his stomach might protest, he was eager to see more of the countryside.

Herr Seitz turned to his wife. "Come, Mutti. We are going to take a drive." He helped Frau Seitz to the front seat of the wagon, while Diedrich helped Regina up to the seat behind it. Diedrich and his father would sit in the last of the three seats in the spring wagon.

Frau Seitz huffed. "I know it is a nice day, but could we not take our drive after dinner? Regina and I have *Kaninchen* to fry and *Brötchen* to bake."

"The rabbit and the rolls will wait." Herr Seitz shook his head as he settled beside his wife and unwound the reins from the brake handle. "This drive is *wichtig.*"

Regina gave a little laugh as she adjusted her skirts. "You are acting very peculiar, Papa. I do not see what could be important about a Sunday drive around Sauers. But if we must go, could we take the road past Tanners' mill? It has fewer ruts than some of the other roads." Though her voice sounded nonchalant, Diedrich detected a note of stiffness about it. From his experience, her opinion of the road's surface was correct. But he doubted it was the true reason she wanted to go in that direction. Instead, he suspected she hoped to glimpse her sweetheart as they passed the mill. At that thought, he experienced a painful prick near his heart.

Herr Seitz shook his head. "We will not be going past the mill, Tochter. What I want to show you is at the west boundary of our land."

Her hopeful expression dissolved into a glum look that saddened Diedrich. Why could she not see that Tanner did not truly care for her—that no man who loved her would treat her so roughly.

When Diedrich had settled beside his father in the seat behind Regina, Herr Seitz looked over his shoulder as if to assure himself everyone was settled. Focusing his gaze on Diedrich, he grinned. "Diedrich, you should sit with Regina. I do not think your Vater will mind to have a seat to himself." Did the man have a twinkle in his eye? Herr Seitz turned back around before Diedrich could be sure.

"Ja, Diedrich. You should sit with your intended for this ride." Father gave Diedrich's arm a nudge.

Rising obediently, Diedrich made his way up to the seat Regina occupied. "Of course. It would be my pleasure." And though his words could not have been truer, he was not at all sure Regina felt the same. But to his surprise, she offered him a bright smile when he sat down beside her. And as they bounced over a rutted road that was little more than a cow path, they fell into easy conversation. Regina gleefully pointed out to him the homes of her friends, adding interesting tidbits about the families and their farms.

"Anna's family has six milk cows," she said, indicating a neat white clapboard house nestled among a stand of trees. "And since she is the only girl and her brothers hate to milk, she must help her Mutter milk all six cows every morning and every evening."

As she talked, Diedrich nodded and offered an occasional comment, but mostly he simply enjoyed watching her smiling face and the light in her eyes as she spoke about the area. Clearly, she loved this place.

After passing acres of neatly tilled fields, the wagon turned down the narrow path that marked the boundary between Herr Seitz's cornfield, which Diedrich had recently helped to plant, and a neighboring forest. At last, Herr Seitz reined in the team of horses, bringing the wagon to a stop.

"We are here." He turned a beaming face to Diedrich and Regina.

Perplexed, Diedrich sat mute, unsure what "here" meant.

Regina's tongue loosened quicker. "Papa, why have you brought us to the back end of the cornfield and Herr Driehaus's woods?"

Herr Seitz's smile turned smug, as if he knew a great secret. "These are not Herr Driehaus's woods any longer. He sold them to me last week, all twenty acres. It is on this land we will build a home for you and Diedrich and Georg."

CHAPTER 10

Stunned to silence, Regina could only look helplessly at Papa. She turned to Diedrich, but his blanched face reflected the same shocked surprise that had struck her mute.

A sick feeling settled in her stomach. She had completely forgotten that Papa had talked of purchasing this land back when Elsie was courting Ludwig Schmersal, before she became betrothed to her husband, William.

"Well, have you nothing to say?" Papa eyed her and Diedrich with a look of expectation. The whiskers on his cheeks bristled with his wide grin.

Mama saved them both. Turning to Papa, she clasped her hand to her chest and said in a breathless whisper, "Twenty acres? Can we afford this, Ernst?"

Papa waved off her concern. "Do not worry, wife. With Georg and Diedrich helping with the farm this summer, I expect the profits from the corn and wheat crop to more than cover the cost of the land." He shrugged. "Besides, since the land has not been improved and adjoins our farm, Herr Driehaus gave me and Georg a very good price: one dollar and seventy-five cents an acre."

Diedrich swiveled in his seat and gaped at his father. "You knew of this, Vater?"

Herr Rothhaus nodded, and the same smile Regina had seen so many times on Diedrich's face appeared on the older man's—except on Herr Rothhaus's face, graying whiskers wreathed the smile. "Of course. It is a fine surprise, is it not, Sohn?"

"Ja, a fine surprise, Vater." Diedrich gazed at the woods as if in doing so he could make them vanish. "But you should not have agreed to such an extravagant gift."

Herr Rothhaus shook his head. "Of course I did not agree to accept the land as a gift. I have promised Ernst that we will pay him back for the land as soon as our first crop is sold. But we cannot take advantage of the Seitzes' hospitality forever. We need a house built and ready for us when you and Regina wed this autumn."

What blood was left in Diedrich's face seemed to drain away. Regina had to fight the urge to confess all to their parents. But what good would that do? The deal had been made. The money had been spent.

To his credit, Diedrich turned back and sent a heroic if somewhat taut smile in Papa's direction. Some of the color returned to his face, and he said in a voice that belied the tumult Regina knew must be raging within him, "Danke, Herr Seitz. This will be a gut spot for a home. And as my Vater said, you will be paid back in full. I promise."

Was he thinking that he would find enough gold in California to pay Papa back? Regina could imagine Papa's face in the fall when Diedrich revealed his plans to head to the goldfields. She was glad she hadn't eaten anything this morning, for if she had she would have lost it for sure.

The ride home was accomplished in silence except for Papa and Herr Rothhaus carrying on a rather lively conversation across the length of the wagon, discussing plans about how the new house should be built.

Panic gripped Regina. Struggling for breath, she looked helplessly at Diedrich. Oddly, his expression had turned placid. Smiling, he patted her hand as if to assure her all would be well.

Regina tried to return his smile, but her lips refused to form one. She had learned enough about Diedrich to know he would pay Papa back or die trying. And that terrified her.

⌒

The next day, as she worked with her mother in the kitchen, Regina's mind continued to wrestle with the thorny problem Papa had presented to her and Diedrich.

Smiling, Mama glanced up from peeling potatoes. "You are very quiet today, Tochter. I wonder, are you thinking of your new home the men will be building soon?" As she talked, she worked the knife around a wrinkled potato covered in white sprouts, divesting it of its skin in one spiral paring. The vegetable was among the few remaining edible potatoes from last year's crop Regina had managed to find in the root cellar. She was eager to harvest the first batch of new potatoes from the crop she and Diedrich had planted, but that wouldn't be until at least July. It saddened her to think that shortly after the first potato harvest, Diedrich would be leaving for Arkansas to be outfitted for his journey to California.

"Ja, Mama. I was thinking of the house." At the stove, she offered her mother a tepid smile and lifted the lid on the pot of dandelion greens to check if it needed more water. If only she could share her concerns with Mama. But she couldn't, so better to steer the conversation in another direction. "I was thinking, too, about Pastor Sauer's message yesterday." That wasn't a complete lie. The pastor's message *was* one of the many thoughts swirling around in Regina's head as if caught up in a cyclone.

Mama dipped water from the bucket beside the sink and poured it into the pot of peeled potatoes, which she then carried to the stove. "And what about the pastor's sermon were you thinking?"

Regina gave the steaming greens a quick stir with a long wooden spoon. Assured they had sufficient water, she returned the lid to the pot. "I was thinking of the verse Pastor read from Colossians." Surely sometime in her life she had read the verse before, but it had obviously never struck her as it did yesterday.

Mama nodded. "'Husbands, love your wives, and be not bitter against them,'" she recited. Turning from the stove, she cocked her head at Regina and crossed her arms over her chest. "So what about the verse do you not understand?"

In an effort to hide her expression, Regina walked to the sink and began dumping the potato peelings by handfuls into the slop bucket, careful to keep her back to her mother. "Pastor said it meant that a husband should always treat his wife with kindness." She couldn't help thinking of Eli's angry outburst in the barn and how he had torn her dress when she tried to pull away from him. And how his demeanor and actions had frightened her. "But surely husbands get angry at their wives sometimes."

Mama's laugh surprised Regina. "Of course they get angry. Just as wives get angry at their husbands. But husbands and wives can be angry at one another and still be kind." She crossed the kitchen to Regina and gently took her arm, turning her around. "Regina, you have seen your Vater angry with me many times, but did you ever see him raise his voice to me or his hand against me?"

Regina shook her head. "Nein, never." Such a thing was unimaginable. And neither had Papa treated her or her sisters in that manner. *So why did I allow Eli to treat me so roughly?* The question that popped into Regina's mind begged an answer or at least some justification. Regina and Eli were not married. Surely he would treat her differently if she were his wife.

Mama walked to the table where the two skinned squirrels Father had shot this morning lay soaking in brine. Taking up the butcher knife, she began cutting the meat into pieces for frying. "It is only natural for you to be thinking of these things with your wedding day coming in September. Your sisters, too, were full of questions before they wed." She sent Regina an indulgent smile. "But I am confident you will have no concerns with how Diedrich will treat you. Besides being a good Christian young man, he does not seem to be one who is quick to anger. And I have seen nothing but consideration and kindness from him."

Regina agreed. Her heart throbbed with a dull ache. Everything Mama said about Diedrich was true. One day he would make someone a kind and sweet husband. But not Regina. Suddenly, the image of Diedrich exchanging wedding vows with some anonymous, faceless woman drove the ache deeper into Regina's chest.

Mama held out a crockery bowl. "Here, fetch some flour for coating the meat." She glanced out the window as Regina took the bowl. "In an hour the men will be in from the fields and expecting their dinner. So we must get this *Eiken* browned and into the oven."

In the pantry, Regina scooped flour into the bowl from one of the sacks on the floor. Her mind flew back to the day when she had fetched the flour from the mill. So much had changed in her life—and her heart—since that day. Was it only a month ago? It seemed so much longer. That day, her mind and heart had brimmed with thoughts of Eli. She remembered how her heart had pranced with Gypsy's feet as the pony bore her ever nearer to the gristmill and her sweetheart. She thought of how she had reveled in Eli's every touch and how her heart had hung on his every word. But lately, thoughts of him no longer caused joy to bubble up in her or sent pleasant tingles over her skin.

Yet she still experienced those feelings. But now the man who sparked them spoke German and had not green but gray eyes. Had Diedrich indeed replaced Eli in Regina's heart? It was true that Diedrich was kind and sweet. But he was also leaving Sauers in the fall. To allow her heart to nurture affection for him would be beyond foolish. Most likely, her waning interest in Eli was caused by her seeing him so infrequently. And that wasn't Eli's fault. Yesterday she had asked Papa to drive by the mill, hoping to catch a glance of Eli. She needed to know if the sight of him still made her heart leap when he wasn't surprising her by coming up behind her unexpectedly. And though mildly disappointed she didn't get the chance to test her reaction at seeing Eli, missing an opportunity to see him hadn't made her especially sad.

An hour later with the squirrel golden-brown in the frying pan, Mama took the corn bread from the oven and plopped it on top of the stove. She glanced out the kitchen window and gave a frustrated huff. "The meal is cooked and ready for the table. I hope the men come in soon." Shaking her head, she clucked her tongue. "With the planting done, they may have time to dawdle, but we have a day's work to do before the sun goes down."

Regina looked up from the table where she worked placing the stoneware plates and eating utensils. She agreed. Not only would she and Mama need time to clean up the kitchen after the meal, but this was washday. Outside, they had two lines of laundry drying in the sun and wind that would need to be taken down before time to begin preparing supper. "Do you want me to go call them in?"

Mama shook her head. "Your Vater and Herr Rothhaus have gone to look at the new piece of land. You would have to hitch Gypsy to the cart or ride one of the horses, and that would take too long. I am sure they are already on their way home. But Diedrich is here on the farm, fixing the lean-to behind the barn that was damaged in the storm. It would be gut if he came on in and washed up before the others arrive."

Nodding her acquiescence, Regina headed out of the house. She hadn't had a chance to talk to Diedrich in private since they learned about Papa buying the land. This would give her the perfect opportunity to find out his thoughts on the situation. The placid look that had come over his face after the initial shock of Papa's announcement still puzzled her. She couldn't imagine him heading to California in the fall and leaving his father alone with the debt. A tiny glimmer of hope flickered in her chest. Was it possible he might actually give up his dream of California gold and stay in Sauers? She wished her heart didn't skip so at the thought. Diedrich was a friend, nothing more. But her rebellious heart paid no attention to the reprimand, dancing ever quicker as she neared the barn.

Skirting the barn lot, she approached the end of the barn where the lean-to that sheltered the plow, cultivator, and other farming tools jutted out from the back of the building. As she rounded the corner of the barn, a sudden, deafening crash shattered the calm. Her heart catapulted to her throat, and she jumped back. Stunned, she stood frozen in place as her mind tried to grasp what had just happened. Slowly, a sick feeling began to settle in the pit of her stomach. Then panic, like a burst of heat, thawed her frozen limbs. As if her feet had grown wings, she rushed toward the source of the din, now quiet.

When she reached the back of the barn, her mind refused to accept what her eyes saw. The entire roof of the lean-to lay in a heap of hewn logs and lumber.

CHAPTER 11

Regina felt as if someone had squeezed all the breath out of her lungs. Heaving, she managed to pull in enough air to scream one word. "Diedrich!"

Scrambling to the debris pile, she began frantically pitching pieces of wood from the rubble. Splinters became imbedded in her hands. She didn't care. "Diedrich, where are you? Can you hear me? Are you hurt?" Sobs tore from her throat and tears flooded down her cheeks. She had to get to him. She *had* to! Scratching and clawing, she worked her way through the seemingly endless mountain of rubble, all the while calling his name over and over. Somewhere under the pile of wood he lay injured and unconscious. . .or worse. No! Her mind wouldn't accept that. Her *heart* wouldn't accept that.

"Diedrich! Tell me where you are." Somehow she lifted beams she never would have imagined she could move. Her arms burned, and her chest felt as if Papa's forge burned inside it, her heaving lungs the bellows feeding the flames.

Her mind told her she could not do this. She needed to get Papa and Herr Rothhaus to help. But her heart kept her tethered to the spot. She couldn't leave Diedrich alone. "Hold on, Diedrich. I will get you out. I will. I will!" Squeezing her words between labored breaths and ragged sobs, she tugged on a giant beam, but it wouldn't budge. The rough wood tore at her palms. She didn't care. "Dear Lord, help me to get him out. Just let him be alive." Grunting, she shoved her desperate prayer through gritted teeth as she wrapped her bruised arms around the enormous log. Clutching it in a death grip, she gave a mighty pull. But the timber refused to move more than a few inches. Her burning muscles trembled and convulsed with the effort. At last, her strength depleted, she could hold it no more and the beam settled back onto the pile of wood with a thud, taking her down with it. Gasping for breath and praying for strength, she tried again, but her muscles refused to respond. The dark shadow of defeat enveloped her, leaving her body limp and her eyes blinded with tears.

An agony Regina had never known rent her heart like a jagged knife. She would never see Diedrich's smile again or hear his voice or feel his touch. She sank to her knees on the heap of wood. Somewhere from deep within her, a tortured wail tore free. She raised her face to the sky and screamed the name of the man she realized, too late, owned her heart. "Died-rich!"

"Regina."

For a moment Regina thought she had imagined his voice. In an instant, her spirits shot from the pits of grief to the heights of joy. Diedrich was alive! But how could his voice sound so strong, so calm and unaffected from beneath the pile of wood? "Diedrich." Her heart thumping out a tattoo of hope, she peered breathlessly into a gap between the planks that she'd opened with her digging, but she could see nothing in the dark abyss.

"Regina. What has happened? What are you doing?" Suddenly, she realized the voice did not come from within the mountain of lumber but from a spot beyond her left shoulder. Jerking her head around, she saw what she'd thought to never see again—Diedrich alive and safe striding toward her.

"Diedrich." Since she'd found the dilapidated lean-to, she'd called his name with nearly every breath she'd drawn into her lungs. She'd uttered it through her sobs and screamed till her throat was raw. But this time it came out in a breathless whisper. She pushed to her feet as disbelief gave way to unmitigated elation that surged through her, renewing her limbs with strength. With fresh tears cascading down her cheeks, she ran to him. Blindly she ran, sobbing her joy, sobbing her relief. "Diedrich. Dank sei Gott." This time she breathed his name with her prayer of thanks like a benediction an instant before he caught her to him.

His strong arms engulfed her, holding her close to his heart. Clinging to him as if he might vanish were she to let go, she wept her relief against his shirtfront until it was sodden with her tears. "I thought—you were under—there. I—I thought—you were—dead." Her words limped out through halting hiccups.

"Oh Regina." His voice sounded thick with emotion. His breath felt warm against her head. She reveled in the sensation of. . .Diedrich. Still holding her securely, he pushed away from her enough to look in her face. His unshaven jaw prickled against her chin as he gently nudged her head back. For the space of a heartbeat, his soft gray eyes gazed lovingly into hers. Then slowly, as if in a dream, his eyes closed, his face lowered, and his lips found hers.

Closing her eyes, Regina welcomed his kiss. For one blissful moment, time was suspended. There was no sky, no earth. Only a sweet sensation of happiness swirling around the two of them in a world of their own as Diedrich's lips lingered on hers. Where Eli's kisses had been rough and taking, Diedrich's were tender and giving. Eli's embraces had felt confining, but Diedrich's arms were a sanctuary.

Too soon his face lifted and his lips abandoned hers. Slowly, Regina's eyes opened as if reluctantly rousing from a beautiful dream. The wonder on his face mimicked the emotion filling her chest. But then, as if he suddenly became aware of what had happened, his brows pinched together in a look of pained remorse. Releasing her, he dropped his arms to his sides and stepped back. "Regina. Forgive me. I should not have. . ." He seemed at a loss for words as his gaze turned penitent.

Of all the emotions Regina imagined he might express at this moment, regret was not among them. Anger and hurt chased away all remnants of the bliss she had felt seconds earlier, and the last drop of mercy seeped from her broken heart. Forgive him? He releases an emotion within her so powerful that it shakes her to the core then asks her to forgive him as if he had simply trod on her toes? No sir! Let him wallow in his guilt. She obviously meant nothing to him. Like Eli, Diedrich simply enjoyed kissing girls. At least Eli wanted to marry her someday.

Clutching her crossed arms over her chest to quell her trembling, she glared at him. "Mama would like you to come and wash up for dinner." Her flat tone reflected her deflated spirit. Whirling away from him to hide the tears welling in her eyes, she ran toward the house, ignoring the words of apology he flung in her wake.

Dinner passed in torturous slowness with Regina focused on her nearly untouched plate, careful to avoid looking at Diedrich. He, too, said little, speaking directly to her only once when he inquired about the condition of her now bandaged hands. Shrugging off his concern, she'd mumbled that her injuries were of no consequence, though Mama had pulled four large splinters and several small ones from Regina's palms before washing the wounds with stinging lye soap and wrapping them with strips of clean cotton. Yet in truth, she had not lied. The soreness in her hands was miniscule compared with the pain Diedrich's nearness inflicted on her heart.

Thankfully Regina's and Diedrich's reticence seemed to go unnoticed by their parents, who filled the void with praises to God for delivering Diedrich from certain death or injury and discussions of how the lean-to might be more securely rebuilt. When Regina could no longer bear their conversation, which revived the agonizing moments she'd experienced atop the ruined shed, she made her excuses and fled to the clothesline behind the house.

Her bandaged hands hampered her movements as she worked her way down the clothesline, snatching the wooden pins that secured the laundry to the twine. If she worked fast enough, maybe she could ignore the tempest raging inside her that Diedrich's kiss had loosed. But no matter how fast she worked, she couldn't escape the heart-jolting truth she could no longer deny. She loved Diedrich. With all her heart. With every ounce of her being, she loved him. Somewhere deep inside, she'd known it even before she thought she had lost him beneath the collapsed roof of the lean-to. Yet knowing that loving Diedrich was futile, she'd lied to herself, pretending her feelings for him didn't exist. But that pretense had crumbled beneath the soft touch of his lips on hers.

Anger shot a burst of energy through her arms, and she whipped a bedsheet from the line with unnecessary ferocity. What good did it do to love him when he didn't love her back and didn't even plan to stay in Sauers? Gripping both ends of the material, she gave it such a sharp snap that it cracked like a gunshot. And though the action undoubtedly sent any insects that might cling to the sheet flying, it did nothing to relieve Regina's pain and frustration.

Why, Lord, why did You allow Diedrich to come here in the first place? Most likely, Papa would have eventually relented and allowed her to marry Eli. And until today, she could have married him and lived happily. But no longer. Now she could not imagine marrying anyone but Diedrich.

Once she had thought she loved Eli. Unpinning a shirt from the line, she gave a sarcastic snort. The infatuation she'd felt for Eli compared to her love for Diedrich was like the difference between the light from her little finger lamp and the brightest sunlight. It was as if she had lived her whole life with all her senses dulled, and now they were suddenly awakened, keen and sharp.

As she folded the shirt, she realized it belonged to Diedrich. It was the shirt he had worn when he first arrived. The shirt she had pressed her face against when he carried her from the barn lot. Another stab of pain assaulted her heart, followed by a flash of bitterness. Whenever disappointments had come in life for her or her sisters, Mama would always quote the verse from Romans: "And we know that all things work together for good to them that love God, to them who are the called according to his purpose."

Regina's lips twisted in a sneer. She dropped the shirt into the basket then finished taking down the rest of the laundry. Well, she *did* love God. She loved Him with all her heart and had trusted Him all her life. And what did He do? He allowed her to fall desperately and completely in love with a man who said he didn't want to marry her. She could almost imagine God looking down on her and mocking her from heaven.

Blinking back tears, she headed for the house. As she walked, a thought struck, igniting a tiny glimmer of hope. Diedrich *had* kissed her, so he must hold some degree of affection for her. It was at Elsie's wedding last fall that she'd first set her cap for Eli. And though it had taken a few months to catch his eye, she had eventually succeeded. Perhaps, if Regina tried, she could win Diedrich's heart before harvest. With that glimmer of hope to dispel her dark mood, she stepped into the house.

In the kitchen, Mama turned from the ironing board, where she stood flicking water from a bowl onto Papa's good shirt. She rolled up the shirt and crossed to Regina, a look of concern furrowing her brow. "Ah, my poor liebes Mädchen." She patted Regina's cheek. "Your face tells me you are in pain. Are your hands hurting you so much?"

"Nein." Forcing a smile, Regina shook her head. "They are only a little sore." How she longed to tell her mother it was not her hands that pained her most but her heart.

Mama took the basket of clothes from Regina and set it on the floor then gently turned her bandaged hands palms up. "I do see two specks of blood. You should have told me that the work pained you. I could have brought in the rest of the wash."

Regina drew her hands from her mother's grasp. Though tempted to blame her sour expression on her superficial wounds, she did not care to add a bruised conscience to her emotional and physical injuries. "Truly, my hands hurt only a little. The accident upset me, that is all." Mama—always wanting to fix things. But for once, Mama couldn't fix what troubled Regina. And the less Regina talked about it, the better.

"Hmm," Mama murmured. "I still think it is best if tonight I make a raw potato and milk poultice for your hands. That should take out the soreness." Then a smile replaced her serious expression. "It was a brave and good thing you did, Tochter—trying so hard to move that wood when you thought Diedrich was underneath it. After you left the table, he asked me about your hands. He said he was *sehr* sorry you were hurt and hoped your injuries were not severe."

Regina stifled the sarcastic laugh that bubbled up into her throat. Diedrich broke her heart by saying in as many words he wished he hadn't kissed her, then worried about a couple of splinters in her hand? "I hope you eased his mind about my injuries."

Grinning, Mama gave her a hug. "I did. I also told him he is a fortunate young man to be marrying a girl who would do such a thing for him."

How Regina would have loved to see Diedrich's face when Mama said that! With great effort she reined in the cackle of mirth threatening to explode from her lips but allowed herself a wry grin. "I'm glad you did, Mama." Diedrich deserved to feel a little guilty.

Mama went back to dampening pieces of clothing in preparation for tomorrow's ironing.

"Do your hands feel well enough to put clean sheets on the beds, then?"

"Ja, Mama." Regina gathered the sheets from the basket and headed for the interior of the house and the downstairs bedrooms. The first bedroom she came to was the one Diedrich shared with his father.

As she stepped through the doorway, her heart throbbed painfully. Though the two had been here a scarce month, this room had become very much theirs. She couldn't imagine them not being here. She couldn't imagine *Diedrich* not being here. Once he left, would she ever be able to walk into this room without thinking of him? The thought drove the ache in her heart deeper.

Her gaze went to the small hobnailed trunk at the foot of the bed. What must it be like to have to fit a few precious pieces of your life into something so small then take it across the ocean to begin a new life in a strange land? One of those precious items—the little black Bible father and son had brought from Venne—lay atop the trunk. Suddenly the need to touch something that belonged to Diedrich filled her, and she picked it up. With her finger, she traced the raised lettering embossed in the black grain of the leather. So much of the gold had worn away she could barely make out the words *Heilige Schrift*.

Gold. It was what Diedrich wanted, what he dreamed of.

Her eyes misted, so she closed them. Again she felt his lips on hers and his arms holding her close against him. His words may have suggested that the kiss they shared meant nothing to him. But his caresses had told her something very different. Could she convince him to give up his dream for her? Somehow she must, or live the rest of her life with a Diedrich-shaped hole in her heart.

Heaving a sigh, she started to lay the Bible back onto the trunk when she noticed a folded piece of paper sticking up from inside the back cover. Curious, she slipped it out. Unfolding it, she saw that it was part of a map. Two circled words on the map drew her gaze. "Fort Smith." She remembered the article about the place in the *Madison Courier*. She glanced at something scribbled along the edge of the map. The words she saw penciled in the margin of the page smote her heart with another bruising blow. "California or bust."

CHAPTER 12

D iedrich swung the broadax above his head then, with a savage blow, brought the blade down on the poplar log, sending wood chips flying. A few more blows and he would have another log cut in two. After rebuilding the demolished lean-to behind the barn, he, along with Father and Herr Sietz, had worked for the past three days felling trees on this wooded land Herr Seitz had bought from Herr Driehaus. By the end of the week, they hoped to have enough timber cut to begin construction on a log house.

Though used to strenuous farmwork, Diedrich couldn't remember feeling more exhausted after a day's work than he had these past three days of cutting trees. Every muscle in his body ached, and he marveled at the stamina of the two older men who worked a few yards away, cutting branches from felled trees.

Despite the hard work and the long hours, Diedrich relished the labor. Anything to keep his mind off Regina. Yet however hard he worked, he couldn't get out of his head the image of her kneeling on that pile of lumber, sobbing his name, and tugging on a beam so large it would challenge even his strength, let alone hers. And at night, as tired as he was, the memory of her tear-drenched face as she ran toward him robbed him of sleep. He could still feel her body trembling against him. She fit in his arms as if God had made her for them, and he ached to hold her again.

But the memory that most tortured him day and night was of the kiss they had shared. In that one moment—at once wonderful and terrible—his life had changed forever. In an instant, the feelings he had tried to fend off for weeks had crashed down upon him with as much force as if he *had* been beneath the shed when it collapsed. He could no longer deny his love for Regina. But what he should do about those feelings, his mind and heart could not agree. So he worked. He worked until the blisters forming on his hands turned to calluses. He worked until his mind was too tired to think and his body too numb to feel. . .anything.

Wielding the ax, he slammed the broad blade into the log again with a mighty force, this time severing it. The two pieces of the log now joined a dozen of their fellows, each eighteen feet in length and ready to be hewn into squared beams for construction of the house's walls. The house in which he and Regina were supposed to live together as husband and wife. If only he could believe that was a possibility. He shook his head as if he could sling from his mind the images that notion formed there—tender, sweet images that gouged at his throbbing heart. He needed to keep working.

Swiping his forearm across his sweaty brow, he turned to find another suitable poplar. But then he stopped, pressed the ax head against the log, and leaned on the tool's handle. Gazing at the forest before him, he huffed out a frustrated breath. He could single-handedly cut down all twenty acres of trees and still not calm the tumult inside him.

He scrubbed his sweat-drenched face with his hand. The question that had haunted him for three days echoed again in his mind. Was it possible Regina loved him, too? Her tears and her kisses said yes. But when he had let her go, her expression had reflected very different emotions. What had he seen there? Shock? Anger? Disgust? Pain slashed at his heart. Surely she could not think he would take advantage of her fear that he'd been injured in order to steal a kiss from her. No, he couldn't believe that. He had seen her eyes close and her lips part invitingly. He had felt how sweetly, how eagerly she returned his kiss. So why had she run away from him, especially when he'd been quick to apologize for his impulsive actions? The only answer that made any sense ripped at his battered heart. She had simply gotten caught up in the moment and immediately regretted what had happened.

If only he knew for certain she felt about him the same way he felt about her, he would give up his dreams of adventure and riches in an instant. Without regret or a backward glance, he would trade all the gold in California for Regina's love. But so far, he had not mustered the courage to confront her—to demand she tell him her feelings one way or the other and put him out of his misery. For until he knew for sure, he could still nurture hope. And despite their secret bargain not to marry in the fall, maybe, just maybe, he could change her mind and win her heart away from Eli Tanner.

"You are working too hard, Sohn." Diedrich hadn't noticed his father walk up. "I know you are eager to build our home, but you must be alive to enjoy it, hey?" Chuckling, he clapped Diedrich on the shoulder.

Diedrich answered with a wry smile. If Father knew the real reason he was working so hard, Diedrich doubted he'd be laughing.

Father walked to a log that lay in a slice of shade. Sitting, he motioned for Diedrich to join him. "Ernst says his ax is getting dull and he forgot to bring a pumice stone." He waved at Herr Seitz, who waved back from across the clearing as he walked, ax in hand, toward the wagon. "He said we should take a rest while he sharpens his ax."

Sending a wave toward Herr Seitz, Diedrich sat on the log. Father leaned back against the smooth bark of a beech tree, his arms crossed over his chest and his legs stretched out in front of him with his feet crossed at the ankles. Diedrich hunched forward, his arms on his knees. For a moment, they sat quietly, enjoying the cool breezes that rustled the canopy of leaves above them and dried the sweat from their faces. Only the chattering and squawking of birds in the trees and the occasional beating of wings as the fowl took flight disturbed the silence.

At length Father angled his head toward Diedrich. "So tell me, Sohn, what is it that has been troubling you?"

Diedrich gave a short, sardonic laugh. Of course Father would have sensed his discontent. Pausing, he contemplated how best to answer. In the end, he decided to ask a question of his own instead. "Did Mama love you when you married?" Diedrich remembered Mama saying that though she and Father had known each other all their lives, their marriage was arranged by their parents.

A surprised look crossed Father's face, followed by a wince that made Diedrich regret the question. In the five years since Mama's death, Father had rarely mentioned her. He had cared for Mama deeply. Diedrich had never questioned that. And he sensed Father's silence on the subject was not due to lack of affection, but on the contrary, because he still found it too painful to touch with words. Diedrich was about to apologize for asking when Father's lips turned up in a gentle smile. Resting his head back against the tree, Father ran his curled knuckles along his whiskered jaw, a sure sign he was giving the question consideration. Finally, he said, "I don't think so, not at first."

"But she did. . .later?" Hoping he had not overstepped his bounds, Diedrich turned his gaze from Father's face and focused instead on a colony of ants marching in a line along a twig.

A deep chortle rumbled from Father, surprising Diedrich. "Oh yes. Later she did."

Emboldened by the lilt in Father's voice, Diedrich pressed on. "So what did you do to win her love?"

Another soft chuckle. "I just loved her, Sohn, as the scriptures tell us in Ephesians. 'Husbands, love your wives, even as Christ also loved the church, and gave himself for it.' Were you not listening to Pastor Sauer's sermon last Lord's day?"

"Of course I was listening. I just thought maybe you would know something I could do. . . ." Diedrich let the thought dangle. He never should have broached the subject in the first place. How could Father give him any useful advice when he had no idea Regina had already situated her affection on another?

Drawing his knees up, Father leaned forward and put his hand on Diedrich's shoulder. "I know it was a difficult thing, asking you to marry someone you had never met, Sohn, but Regina seems to be a very caring, God-fearing girl. She treats her parents with affection and respect, and I am sure she will treat you in the same manner." He grinned. "And she is very pretty, too. I do not know what more you could want."

Diedrich nodded mutely, though he wanted to say that what he wanted was Regina's full heart—that he wanted to know if by some miracle he'd been blessed to win her love, she would not look at him one day and wish she had married Eli Tanner. "Everything you say is true, but I just thought perhaps you could tell me what I might do to grow her affection for me."

Father sighed. "Do not concern yourself, Diedrich. I have seen Regina look at you with affection. In time, I am sure her feelings for you will grow to a deeper love." Then as he gazed across the clearing to the cornfield, his eyes turned distant and his voice wistful. "Just love her, Sohn. Love begets love."

Diedrich ventured a glance at Father's face and, noticing a glistening in his eyes, decided he should not pursue the conversation further. Bringing up painful memories would not help Diedrich win Regina's heart. Father said he had seen Regina look at Diedrich with affection. With that to give him courage, he would pray for God's guidance and confront Regina. At the very next opportunity to speak with her alone, he would bare his heart to her and accept whatever happened.

∽

Perched on a three-legged stool, Regina hunched over the butter churn. Gripping the handle of the dasher, she began pounding it up and down. She'd decided that the shade of the big willow in the side yard would be a pleasant spot to churn the butter. It also provided a good view of the lane.

Since the devastating kiss she had shared with Diedrich, she'd had few opportunities to encourage his attention. It hurt to realize that, if anything, he seemed to avoid her. But she couldn't really blame him. He along with Father and Herr Rothhaus had been working so hard on clearing the new land that they hardly had energy to eat, let alone make conversation. But this morning at breakfast, Papa had said by noon today they might have enough logs cut to begin work on the house. And if so, they would likely come in early for dinner. Since Regina and her sisters were little, Mama had preached that a man found nothing more captivating than an industrious girl. So at every opportunity, she wanted Diedrich to find her engaged in some kind of domestic occupation. And if they were to come home early, Diedrich was sure to see her here hard at work, making the butter he so loved to slather on corn bread.

With the willow's supple branches draping over her shoulder like a green ribbon, she hoped to present a fetching picture. A few coy smiles and the batting of her eyes had proved sufficient to catch Eli's attention. But Diedrich was a far more serious person and would likely find such antics silly and juvenile.

She sighed. If only she could talk with Elsie. Scarcely two years Regina's senior, Elsie had, until her marriage to William last September, been Regina's lifelong confidant. While Regina had never been especially close to her more staid and proper eldest sister, Sophie, Regina and Elsie had grown up playing and giggling together. Unlike Sophie, who would most likely ridicule Regina's heartache, Elsie would sympathize and know exactly what Regina should do to win Diedrich's heart.

At the distant sound of a wagon rumbling down the lane, Regina's heart hopped like a frightened rabbit. The men must have met their day's goal of felled trees. Rising slightly, she repositioned her stool so she could angle her profile for a more flattering effect.

But as the wagon neared, her heart dipped. It was definitely not their wagon or team of horses. Butter churn forgotten, Regina walked toward the lane to see who might be visiting. When the wagon came to a stop between the house and the barn, she finally recognized Elsie's husband, William. Her heart skipped with her feet as she hurried toward the wagon. She hadn't seen Elsie since Easter. It was as if God had answered her prayer before she prayed it.

Bouncing up to the wagon, she peered around William but could not see Elsie. Shading her eyes from the sun with her flattened hand, she tipped her face up to her brother-in-law. "Guten Tag, William. Where is Elsie?"

Only now did she notice the somber expression on William's face. Since he was naturally jovial, his glum look curled her heart in on itself. Regina's smile wilted. "William, what is wrong?" Fear tightened her chest and filled her mouth with a bad taste. As William climbed down, she gripped the wagon wheel to support her legs, which had gone wobbly. Once he reached the ground, the gray pallor on his drawn face was visible beneath at least two days' growth of straw-colored beard.

The quick *clop-clop* of wooden shoes sounded behind Regina, and before she could ask anything more about Elsie, Mama's stern voice at her left shoulder demanded, "Where is my Elsie? Is she all right?"

William's blue eyes brimmed with tears and sorrow. Torturing his battered brown hat in his hands, he shook his head mutely.

CHAPTER 13

illiam." Mama gripped William's shoulders and leveled a no-nonsense gaze into his eyes. "You tell me now—what has happened to my Elsie?"

William sniffed and ran his sleeve beneath his nose. Even as terror clutched at Regina's throat, her heart hurt for William, who looked suddenly older than his twenty-one years. "Doc Randolph says she was with child, but. . ." He shook his head again. A tear coursed down his scraggly cheek and disappeared into the bristle of pale whiskers. He paid it no mind. "She is restin'. Doc says she is out of danger and should be up on her feet again in a few days." His sad gaze shifted between Mama and Regina. The semblance of a smile quavered on his lips. "She was so lookin' forward to tellin' ya about the babe."

Mama pulled him into her arms as if he were Sophie's two-year-old, Henry, and had just fallen and skinned his knee. "It is sorry I am, lieber Sohn. Sometimes it is hard, but we must trust Gott. I know my liebes Enkelkind is in His arms." Letting William go, she brushed the wetness from her cheeks and offered him a brave smile. "These things, they happen. There will be more *Kinder*." Mama squared her shoulders. "I must go to her."

Regina blinked away the tears welling in her own eyes and gripped her mother's arm. "I know you want to go to Elsie, Mama, but I am not sure I am ready to take care of everything here alone. And think, is it proper for me to be here without you while Diedrich is. . ." Her face heating, she abandoned the thought. As much as she hoped to win Diedrich's affection, the last thing she wanted was to force him into a marriage because people in the community thought something improper had occurred.

Mama sighed, and her brow wrinkled in thought. "Of course you are right, Tochter. Such a thing would not be *korrekt*. I would not have your wedding day tarnished with talk of impropriety."

William shook his head. "My ma was seein' to Elsie, but then my sister's kids got sick, and she had to go help with them." He scrubbed his face with his hand. "Doc said Elsie has to stay in bed for the next several days, so I've been tryin' to take care of her and the store at the same time. It's 'bout got me frazzled. I closed the store and found a neighbor lady willin' to sit with Elsie until I can get back tomorrow evenin'. But with the doctor bills, we cain't afford to close down anymore."

"Why don't I go?" As sad as Regina was about William and Elsie's loss, she wondered if something good might come of this unfortunate situation. She had just been thinking how she would like to talk to Elsie, and this was her chance.

William nodded at Regina. "Elsie would like that. She's been pinin' for you. I think you just might be the medicine she needs to lift her spirits."

Mama bobbed her head in agreement. "Ja. You should go, Regina, and see to your *Schwester*." She smiled at William and, putting her hand on his back, guided him toward the back door. "But now we must feed you before a big wind comes and blows you away."

A half hour later, between helping Mama with dinner and making a mental list of what she'd need to take with her to Salem, Regina scarcely noticed when Diedrich, Papa, and Herr Rothhaus returned to the house. The conversation at the meal was focused on the sad news and comforting William. More than a few tears were shed around the table and many prayers went up, asking God to comfort the grieving young couple and restore Elsie to full health.

His eyes glistening, Papa paused in slicing a piece of roast pork. "We know what you are feeling, William. Do we not, Mutti?" He sent Mama a sad smile. An odd look crossed Mama's face, and though she nodded, she quickly changed the subject to what foods Regina should make for Elsie that might help to build back her strength.

Though Regina wondered about Papa's comment and Mama's reaction to it, she had more pressing concerns to occupy her mind. And one of them sat across the table from her. Diedrich had said little aside from joining his father in offering his sympathy and prayers. But several times during the meal, she thought she noticed disappointment as well as sorrow on his face when he looked at her. Most likely, he was simply sad about the news William had brought them. But Regina couldn't help hoping his glum look had something to do with his learning that she would be leaving the farm for several days.

The next morning after breakfast, when Regina came down from her bedroom with a calico sack full of necessities for her stay at William and Elsie's home, she found Diedrich waiting at the bottom of the stairs.

"Regina." His gray eyes held hers tenderly, snatching her breath away and sending her heart crashing against her ribs. For the space of a heartbeat, she thought—hoped—he might actually kiss her. Instead, he simply took the sack from her hands. Deep furrows appeared on his broad forehead. "There is something—something I have wanted to say. Needed to say. . ."

"Are you ready to go, Regina?" William came through the kitchen door into the washroom, with Papa and Mama trailing behind him.

Diedrich looked down at the floor. When he looked up, he gave her a sad smile. "Tell Elsie I am praying for her and William."

"Danke." Regina managed the breathless word as William took her calico sack from Diedrich's hands and ushered her outside.

With a thirty-mile trip ahead of them, they would need to head out as soon as possible to make it to Salem before sunset. So good-byes were quickly said all around, with Papa promising to fetch her home five days hence. Regina hugged Mama and Papa, and even Herr Rothhaus gave her a hug and a quick kiss on the cheek. But Diedrich only took her hand and, in a voice scarcely above a whisper, murmured, "*Gott segne und halte dich*, Regina," before helping her up to the wagon seat beside William. His gaze never left hers, and her heart throbbed painfully at the tender look in his eyes.

"God bless and hold you, too, Diedrich." Somehow she managed to utter the sentiment around the lump in her throat. A moment later William snapped the reins down on the horse's rumps, and with a jerk, the wagon began to roll down the lane. Away from home. Away from Diedrich. What had he been about to say before William cut him short at the back door? That question would doubtless haunt her until she returned home and got the chance to ask him.

But over the next few days, all other thoughts faded as Regina's concern for Elsie demanded first place in her mind and heart. How it had ripped at Regina's heart to see her beautiful, vibrant sister lying abed, gaunt and melancholy. That first evening, they spoke little. For a long while, they had simply held each other and cried. And when they finally did speak, the words were tearful prayers directed heavenward for the little one they would never hold.

William had made up a little straw tick pallet for Regina in the kitchen, and the next morning at the break of dawn, she was awakened by a knock at the kitchen door. A large, rawboned woman who introduced herself as Dorcas Spray, the neighbor lady who had sat with Elsie the day before, presented Regina with a fat, rust-colored rooster she'd just killed. "A good dose of chicken broth will set Elsie right," she said. Then, lamenting that she could stay only a moment, she thrust the fowl's scaly yellow feet trussed up with twine into Regina's hands, its broken neck dangling at her knees. Trying to sound appreciative, Regina had thanked the woman then spent the rest of the morning plucking, butchering, and stewing the rooster. But at noon, when she finally handed Elsie a large cup of the meat broth, her sister's smile was more than sufficient payment for her work. According to William, Elsie had scarcely eaten anything since losing the baby, so it heartened Regina to see her sipping the hot chicken broth with gusto.

"Mmm, what did you put in this, Regina? It tastes even better than Mama's." With eyes half closed, Elsie inhaled the fragrant steam curling up from the stoneware cup she cradled in both hands. The sight filled Regina with gladness. It was the first time since her arrival she had seen her sister smile. Some of the pink had begun to return to Elsie's cheeks as well, and Regina's concern for her sister's health began to abate.

"Thyme." Regina picked up the tortoise shell comb from the dresser across the room then pulled a chair up beside the bed where Elsie sat propped up with pillows. "Mama only puts in salt, pepper, and sage, but I like the taste of thyme," she said as she combed her sister's nut-brown hair.

"Me, too." Elsie grinned and took another noisy sip. Then her grin faded, and the sad frown returned. "Gunther," she uttered softly, her cinnamon brown eyes filling with tears. "If the baby was a boy, I was going to call him Gunther, after Mama's papa—our grandpapa. And if it was a girl, Catharine after Mama." Her voice broke on a sob, and Regina dropped the comb to the bed and wrapped her arms around her sister.

"And you will use those names one day," she murmured as she rocked Elsie in her arms and kissed her head. "Gott has named this one, and one day you will know the name."

Elsie sniffed and, with teardrops still shimmering on her lashes, offered Regina a brave smile and nod. She drained the rest of her broth, and Regina went back to combing her sister's hair. Though she rejoiced to see Elsie emerging from the heartrending ordeal, she suspected her sister would continue to suffer moments of sadness like the one she just experienced. She prayed that with time those painful moments would become rare and blunted.

"William has been wonderful through it all." Though still tremulous, Elsie's voice lifted bravely as Regina braided her hair. "I love him even more now, I think, than I did the day we married." Then her wistful tone turned almost playful. "And what of you and Eli Tanner? At Easter, you told me he wanted to court you."

Regina paused in tying her sister's braids with lengths of thin red ribbon. She suddenly remembered that Elsie knew nothing of Diedrich. Trying to keep her voice unaffected, she simply said, "Papa has chosen someone else for me."

Elsie sat up straighter. Her eyes grew round, and she put her hand on Regina's shoulder. "Who?" she whispered in breathless interest.

"His name is Diedrich Rothhaus. He and his father arrived from Venne last month." She told Elsie about the deal Papa and Herr Rothhaus had made, agreeing that Regina and Diedrich would marry.

Elsie hunched forward. "So tell me, what is he like? Do you like him?"

The memory of the kiss she and Diedrich had shared returned with a bittersweet pang. How could she put her feelings into words when she felt as if a cyclone were swirling in her chest? Her eyes filled with tears.

"Oh Regina. Is he that awful?" Elsie hugged her. Sighing, she sank back onto the pillows, and dismay filled her voice. "I was afraid Papa would do something like that. He was so disappointed when I refused to marry Ludwig Schmersal and later fell in love with William."

Before she thought, Regina said, "But you didn't reject Ludwig until he decided to join the army and go fight in Texas." Smote with remorse for her thoughtless comment, she cringed inwardly. This was not a time to remind Elsie that her first love had died in the war with Mexico.

Elsie smiled. "And Gott sent William to help soften that heartache for me." Her brows pinched together in a thin, inverted V. "Surely if we try, we can think of a way to change Papa's mind and get you out of this marriage."

"But I don't want out of it!" Regina blurted, eliciting a puzzled look from Elsie. Suddenly, tears rained down Regina's cheeks, and the whole tangled mess tumbled from her lips like apples from a torn sack.

At length Elsie gave a huff. "Let me get this straight. You liked Eli, but now you like Diedrich. But Diedrich wants to go to California, and Eli still wants to marry you?"

Regina nodded.

Emitting a soft sigh, Elsie reached over and took Regina's hands she had nestled in her lap. "My liebe Schwester. I can see why you are confused. But that is why Gott has given you a head to think with as well as a heart to feel with." She tapped Regina gently on the head. "I thought I loved Ludwig, too. But when he told me he was going to the war, I knew I did not want to become a widow at eighteen." She sighed. "As it turned out, I was right. And by the time we got the sad news about Ludwig, I was already in love with William." She pressed a hand to her chest and, glancing at the bedroom doorway as if to assure herself her husband was not within earshot, said, "My heart hurt when I learned of Ludwig's death, and there are times when I still think of him fondly. But if Ludwig had truly loved me, he would not have left for the army. And unless Diedrich changes his mind about going to California, I think you should forget about him and remember why you liked Eli in the first place. At least *he* will likely stay in Jackson County."

The next day Elsie's advice was still echoing in Regina's mind as she rearranged lanterns on a shelf behind the store's counter. She had offered to watch the store while William rested and spent some time with Elsie, who was feeling much better.

Though fun-loving and possessing a decidedly romantic streak, Elsie also had a good, reasonable head on her shoulders. As tightly as Regina's heart twined around Diedrich, she had to admit that her sister's logic made good sense. One kiss did not mean Diedrich loved her and wanted to marry her. If he remained steadfast in his plans to head for California in the fall, then she would know she should steer her heart back to Eli.

The little bell William had fixed to the front door jingled, and Regina abandoned her musing. William had warned that, being Saturday, the store might become busy. His prediction had proved accurate. Regina had already waited on several customers this morning and enjoyed the experience. Wondering whether she would be met by a housewife needing food staples or dry goods or a farmer needing a tool or ammunition for his rifle, she turned around and her heart hopped to her throat. Eli stood in the doorway, looking as handsome as she had ever seen him.

He sauntered toward the counter, no hint of surprise touching his roguish smile. "Heard you were here seein' to your sister." The swagger in his voice matched his gait.

"Yes. Elsie is. . .feeling much better." Regina didn't even care how he had learned she was here. Such news would undoubtedly spread quickly. She sensed, however, that he was not here out of concern for Elsie or William.

"That's good. Glad to hear it." His stilted tone held more duty than genuine concern. With an air of negligence, he picked up a pewter candle holder on the counter and studied it.

"Is there something I can help you with?" His cavalier attitude raked her nerves like a wool carder. She had to force herself not to snatch the pewter piece from his hands as if he were her toddler nephew.

"Came to Salem to get a gear wheel for the mill, so I thought I'd stop by to let you know that the barn raisin' for my uncle will be this comin' Friday. I wanted to know if you planned to be back home by then." He wandered over to a display of men's felt hats on a hat tree and began trying them on for size. He positioned a wide-brimmed black hat at a jaunty angle atop his auburn curls and shot her a devastating smile. "How do I look?"

Warmth spread over Regina's face, and her heart fluttered like it used to when she looked at him. She wanted to tell him he looked better than any man had a right to, but she suspected he already knew that. Pretending interest in the copper scales on the counter, she ignored the question about his appearance and forced a nonchalant tone. "Papa will fetch me home Monday."

He took off the hat and put it back on the tree then moseyed over to her. Easing behind the counter, he came up close to her and slipped his arms around her waist. Her first instinct was to pull away and tell him he shouldn't be behind the counter. But with many breakable items on the shelves behind them, she didn't want a tussle. "That's good, 'cause I'm plannin' a surprise for you." Without warning he pressed a hard, wet kiss on her lips then turned and strode out of the store before she could utter a reproach.

Stunned, Regina gazed at his retreating figure and absently touched the back of her hand to her mouth, which felt bruised. She couldn't guess what surprise Eli had planned for her, but instead of igniting eagerness, the prospect of discovering what it might be filled her with consternation.

⁂

Diedrich followed Herr Seitz into the Dudleytown store. A barrage of sights and smells assailed his senses. This was his first time to visit the store. Normally, seeing such a huge collection of disparate items all crammed into such a small space would have captured his full attention. But it only reminded him of Regina, and he found himself wishing he were in the Salem mercantile instead of the little Dudleytown general store.

In the two days since Regina left with William McCrea, she'd reigned over Diedrich's thoughts like a queen. The longing to see her again had become like a physical ache, throbbing day and night beneath his breastbone. Thanks be to God, Herr Seitz would travel to Salem Monday and bring her home. Home. When had the Seitz farm become home to him? He knew the answer. The moment Regina had claimed his heart. But when she did return and he managed to find a private moment with her to tell her his feelings, what if she rejected his love? Where then would he find a home? He recoiled from the thought, but forcing himself to face the possibility, he knew his only option was to stick to his original plan and head west as soon after harvest as possible.

"She is what you need, do you not think?" Herr Seitz's words jarred Diedrich from his melancholy thoughts.

Diedrich's heart raced and his eyes widened as he turned to the older man. "W–what?" Had he murmured Regina's name aloud unknowingly?

Herr Seitz held up a hammer. "You will need your own hammer for the barn raising this Friday, as well as later, building the new house, *nicht wahr*?"

"Ja." Nodding, Diedrich turned away, pretending to examine a piece of harness as heat marched up his neck to his face. Though Herr Seitz expected Diedrich to marry Regina, he was glad the man could not read his thoughts.

Smiling, Herr Seitz clapped him on the back. "Take your time and look around while I have Herr Cole gather the items on Frau Seitz's list as well as the nails we will need for our work on the house."

Returning the man's smile, Diedrich nodded. As he strolled about the store, his mind wandered back to Regina. Finding an array of iron skillets displayed on the wall, he couldn't help wondering which one she would prefer if she were choosing for their home.

"Diedrich." Herr Seitz appeared again at his shoulder, a frown dragging down the corners of his mouth. "Herr Cole does not have the nails we need, but I still must purchase from him the other items Frau Seitz wants. So if we want to get home in time to get any work done today, I will need you to go to the blacksmith shop down the street for the nails."

"*Sehr gut.*" Diedrich nodded. He had noticed the blacksmith shop when they passed it on the way to the general store.

Herr Seitz shrugged and his tone turned grudging. "Herr Rogers asks more money for his nails, but he usually has a large amount to sell." Herr Seitz pressed several coins into Diedrich's hand, and an unpleasant feeling curled in his stomach. Suddenly, he was glad Regina was not here to see her father dole out money to him as if he were a child. Since he and Father had left Venne, they'd been living off the generosity of Herr Seitz. Diedrich longed to have his own money. Money he had earned with his own two hands.

As he walked down the street, thoughts of the California goldfields once again fired his imagination. How he would love to have his own money, his own gold. But sadly, if he left Sauers for the goldfields, it would mean he had lost all hope of winning Regina's love. And no amount of gold would compensate him for such a loss.

Diedrich stopped in front of a weathered gray building. Its yawning doors beckoned, and he didn't need to read the brick-colored lettering above them to tell him he'd found the blacksmith shop. The *clang, clang, clang* of iron on iron as well as the blast of heat radiating from within the establishment told him he could be nowhere else.

As Diedrich stepped into the building's dim interior, a giant of a man with a chest like a barrel and sweat dripping from his flame red hair glanced up from his work at an anvil. Fixing his gaze on Diedrich, he said something in English, of which Diedrich understood only "friend" and "seat." But as the blacksmith accompanied his comment with a nod toward an upturned keg, Diedrich understood him to mean he should sit and wait.

He situated himself on the barrelhead the blacksmith had indicated, next to another man who also waited on an upturned box. The man beside him, dressed in buckskin and wearing a battered felt hat pulled low over his face, stopped whittling the piece of wood in his hands. Turning, he lifted a smiling, if somewhat scraggly, bearded face to Diedrich and stuck out his hand. "Zeke Roberts." His friendly grin revealed a mouth full of blackened teeth and spaces where several were missing.

Diedrich grasped his hand. "Diedrich Rothhaus." He hoped the man didn't expect to engage in conversation and wished he'd learned more English from Regina.

The man cocked his head and in flawless German said, "I detect a German accent. Do you speak English?"

Relieved not to have to scour his brain for the right English words, Diedrich held up his index finger and thumb, leaving only a small space between.

Zeke nodded. "Ah, you haven't been here long, then?"

Diedrich shook his head. "My Vater and I arrived last month. For now, we are living in Sauers with the Seitz family." Unsure about Regina's feelings, he was not inclined to enlighten Herr Roberts on the reason he and Father were brought here.

Zeke went back to his whittling. "Then I doubt you would be interested in going to California?"

The word caught Diedrich by surprise. He jerked to attention, his spine stiffening. "California?"

"Ja. Next spring, I plan to leave for the California goldfields. That is, if I can sell my house in Salem and find a couple of adventurous fellows willing to partner with me in the venture." He shot Diedrich a grin. "When I saw you walk in here, I thought to myself, now there's just the kind of young fellow I'm looking for." Then, pausing in his work with the knife, he shrugged. "But if you are settled here, I doubt you would be interested in such an arrangement." He puffed a breath, blowing shavings from the piece of wood, which was beginning to take the shape of a bird in flight.

Diedrich's heart galloped then slowed to a trot and finally limped. Mama always told him God never closed one door without opening another. Did his meeting Zeke Roberts mean Regina would reject his love and God had sent this man to provide him a way to California? Though the notion pained him, he could not dismiss it out of hand.

"So would you be interested?" Zeke gave him a gap-toothed grin.

Diedrich swallowed to wet his drying throat. Somehow he forced out the word "Possibly."

CHAPTER 14

Kneeling over the auger, Diedrich twisted the tool's handle and grunted with the effort of driving the spiral iron bit deep into the eight-by-eight support beam. But no amount of exertion could numb the pain in his heart. Sadly, it appeared he had been right about his meeting with Zeke Roberts. God was obviously preparing him for Regina's inevitable rejection. Since her return from Salem, he had noticed a decided coolness in her attitude toward him.

Several times he had tried to talk with her privately, but each time she had shied away, citing varying excuses for avoiding a conversation with him, including having to help her mother with food preparations for today's barn raising. And in the nearly six hours since Diedrich and his father had arrived here in Dudleytown with the Seitzes to help built Herr Tanner's new barn, he still had found no opportunity to speak to Regina alone.

Pausing in his work with the auger, he leaned back, resting on his heels. The sights, sounds, and smells of the construction site swirled around him, lending a festive air to the proceedings. The sounds of hammering and sawing mixed with the constant buzzing of myriad voices generated by the milling crowd. A westerly breeze brought tempting aromas from the food tables to mingle with the scents of freshly cut lumber as well as the still-lingering smell of the old, burnt barn. But despite the joyful atmosphere, Diedrich's aching heart robbed him of all celebratory feelings. And the happy cacophony around him could not drown out the incessant refrain ringing in his ears. Regina didn't love him.

Pivoting on his knees, he glanced across the barn lot to the long trestle tables covered with dishes of food. Seeking Regina, his gaze roamed the large group of women swarming around the tables. When he finally found her, a sweet ache throbbed in his chest. She threw back her head in mirth as if in response to someone's humorous comment, and his heart pinched. He had allowed himself to hope he might enjoy her smiles and hear her laughter every day for the rest of his life. But with each passing moment, that hope grew dimmer.

At least for once, he didn't see Eli Tanner anywhere near her. So far, the boy appeared to spend more time talking to Regina than helping to build his uncle's new barn. An ugly emotion Diedrich didn't care to name filled his mouth with a bad taste. If Regina was determined to marry the cur, there was little he could do about it. Still, as long as Diedrich remained here in Jackson County, he would keep a close eye on the Tanner boy, especially when he was near Regina.

"*Pass auf*, Sohn!" Father's warning to look out scarcely registered in Diedrich's brain before he found himself slammed to the ground. The next instant he felt a stiff breeze as something whizzed past his head.

When Father's weight finally lifted off him, Diedrich pushed up to all fours, spitting bits of grass from his mouth. Out of the corner of his eye, he saw Eli Tanner and another youth carrying a ten-foot-long plank—obviously the object that had nearly hit him and Father. The smirk on Eli's face made Diedrich wonder if the close call was entirely an accident.

Father, already on his feet, reached down and grabbed Diedrich's arm, helping him up. "Sorry I am to knock you down, Sohn. But when the *Jungen* came through here and began to swing that board around, I saw that your head was in the way of it. I do not want to think what might have happened if it had hit you. Only Gott's mercy saved you."

Feeling more than a little foolish, Diedrich gave his father a pat on the back. "Ja. Gott's mercy and a Vater with a sharp eye," he said with a sheepish grin.

Walt Tanner, the man whose barn they were building, rushed up and began speaking rapidly in English. Though Diedrich understood few of his words, he clearly read regret and apology in the man's face.

Herr Seitz came striding up, concern lining his face as well. Once he had assured himself Diedrich and his father were unhurt, he engaged in a quick exchange with Walt Tanner in English then turned back to Diedrich. "Herr Tanner wants to know is everyone all right? He wants me to tell you that before the Jungen brought the board through this place, he called for everyone to get out of the way. It did not occur to him you would not understand his words."

The look of sincere remorse on Tanner's face evoked sympathy in Diedrich. It was not the man's fault that his nephew and the other boy had acted carelessly. He reached his hand out to Walt Tanner, who accepted it. "Danke, Herr Tanner. My Vater and I appreciate your concern, but we are unhurt." He grinned. "Only my pride is bruised a little, perhaps."

Herr Seitz translated Diedrich's words and Tanner nodded, while a look of relief smoothed the worry lines from his face. After shaking hands again with Diedrich and his father, Walt Tanner went back to his work.

When everyone had gone back to what they were doing before the near accident, Father gripped Diedrich's arm. He glanced across the barnyard to the food tables where Regina and the other women continued to work and visit, apparently oblivious to the subsiding commotion at the building site. A teasing grin quirked up the corner of Father's mouth. "I do not know if it was your stomach or your heart that drew your attention away from the work happening around you, but you must be more watchful, Sohn." He gave Diedrich a wink. "You will have many opportunities to look at your intended in safety," he added with a chuckle.

Diedrich tried to smile, but as his gaze returned to Regina, his smile evaporated. She was laughing and talking to Eli again. Seeing her playfully bat his hand away from the food, Diedrich almost wished Father had let the board hit him and put him out of his misery. It couldn't have hurt any worse than the pain he was feeling now.

～

"Eli, I told you not to touch the food!" Regina smacked Eli's hand as he reached for a slice of Mama's raisin and dried apple *Stollen*. He seemed to have spent more time talking to her and sneaking bits of food than helping with the barn building. So far, she had seen no hint of the surprise he had promised, just his hovering presence, which was becoming increasingly aggravating.

"I'm hungry." With a lightning-fast motion, he snatched a pickled beet from the top of an open jar and popped it into his mouth. "Besides," he said around chewing the beet, "you and your ma always bring the best food." The whine in his voice turned wistful, and pity scratched at Regina's heart. Having lost his mother nine years ago, Eli probably did look forward to the varied dishes offered at occasions like this barn raising.

Regina placed a linen towel over the open jar of beets. "We will ring the dinner bell in a few minutes." She glanced across the barn lot to the spot where the skeleton of the new building was beginning to take shape. The blackened earth around the site served as a reminder of why a large part of Dudleytown as well as Sauers was gathered here.

Unbidden, her gaze sought out Diedrich. Though standing with his back to her and amid at least a dozen other men, Regina had no trouble finding him. His broad back and exceptionally tall figure made him easy to recognize. Even from this distance, she could see the muscles across his back and shoulders move beneath his white cotton shirt as he worked with the other men to stand up a section of wall. Her heart sped to a gallop. Since her return from Salem, she had tried to take Elsie's advice and shut Diedrich out of her mind and heart, but he kept nudging his way back in. She had prayed that at her first sight of Eli this morning, her heart would jump like it had when he entered William and Elsie's store. But it hadn't. In fact, compared to Diedrich, Eli appeared juvenile and almost silly. And for the past several minutes, all she'd wanted to do was find an excuse to get away from Eli. She was about to tell him she needed to go help her mother with something when Mama appeared at her elbow.

"Eli is your name, is it not?" At his nod, Mama maneuvered between him and Regina to set a towel-swathed pan of corn bread on the table. "Your *Onkel* will have a fine new barn soon, ja?"

"Yeah." He chuckled. "It will almost be worth havin' the old one burn down."

Mama frowned, and Regina had to suppress a giggle. If Eli wanted to make a good impression on her mother, he was doing a very poor job of it. Mama glanced toward the construction site, and her frown deepened. "My Ernst tells me there was almost an accident with Diedrich Rothhaus earlier. That he was nearly hit by a beam."

Regina gasped, her throat tightening. The same flash of fear she had felt when she thought the lean-to had fallen on Diedrich sparked in her chest. "Was he hurt?" Breathless, she glanced across the barn lot at Diedrich in search of any sign of injury.

Eli gave an unconcerned chuckle, and anger flared in Regina's chest. "Nah." He negligently reached over, broke off a piece of Stollen, and began nibbling on it. "His pa pushed him out of the way." He shrugged. "Uncle Walt hollered for him to move, but I reckon he didn't get it through his thick skull." He snorted, and Regina wondered why she had ever thought him handsome. "I doubt he would have even felt it if it had hit him."

Mama's look of disapproval mirrored the disgust rising in Regina. She understood that Eli viewed Diedrich as a rival for her affection. *If only that were so.* But it did not excuse his callous attitude, and Regina had no interest in making excuses for him to Mama.

Mama opened her mouth as if about to say something, but another woman pulled her away with a question about the food.

When Mama left, Eli grasped Regina's hand. "After the dinner break, come to the west side of the barn. I have somethin' I want to show you."

Regina yanked her hand from his. She wanted to tell him she had no interest in anything he had to show her. Instead, she bit her bottom lip and groped for a more diplomatic excuse to decline his invitation. The dinner bell began to ring. She cocked her head to the right where she expected the serving line to form. "You'd better get in line." She would make no promises. And after dinner, there would be enough work with the cleanup to provide ample excuse for her to avoid Eli.

"The west side of the barn," Eli reiterated. Then with a parting wink and grin, he trotted off to join the crowd of men advancing toward the food tables.

Regina's gaze scoured the group in search of Diedrich, but she didn't see him. When all had assembled, Pastor Sauer's booming voice bade everyone pause and give thanks for the repast set before them. After the prayer was finished and the last amen faded away, Regina moved to a spot behind the serving table. The men, who had worked hard all morning constructing the barn, would eat first.

While serving the dishes before her, Regina occasionally glanced down the line of male faces, looking for Diedrich. She scarcely noticed when Eli passed in front of her, absently plopping chicken and noodles on his plate and ignoring his reminder to join him later. At last, her gaze lit on Diedrich's face, and her heart danced. Sadly, she realized Elsie's advice would do her no good. It was useless to continue trying to veer her heart away from Diedrich. It belonged to him now, and she could not call it back. And unless she could change his mind about going to California, her heart was destined to be broken.

As Diedrich neared, her pulse quickened. She caught his eye, and they exchanged a smile. For an instant, she got the fleeting impression he was seeking her out as well. But even if he was, she was sure it was only because of the friendship they had built over the past month. *A friendship built on the understanding that we will not marry.*

"Hey gal, I'd like some of them chicken and dumplin's, if ya don't mind." The gruff voice pulled Regina's attention from Diedrich to the burly man in front of her. Her cheeks burning, she mumbled her apologies and dipped a generous portion of the food onto the man's plate. Did Diedrich notice her blush, and if so, did he guess her preoccupation with him had caused her discomposure? She prayed not. Somehow she must learn to control her responses to his smiles—his nearness. Until such a time as she won his heart, she must hide her feelings from him at all cost. If he ever did choose her over his dream of California gold, she needed to know he did it with a free and willing heart—not out of some dogged sense of duty.

Reclaiming a tight rein on her composure, she forced her attention back to serving food to the workmen filing along the opposite side of the table. So when she looked up to find Diedrich standing before her, her heart did a somersault. Flustered, she blurted, "I heard about the accident with the beam. I am glad you were not hurt." His face reddened, and she groaned inwardly. Clamping her mouth shut, she dipped him some of the chicken and dumplings. Embarrassing him was not a good strategy for winning his heart.

He grinned. "I was hoping you did not see that. It is clear, I think, that I need more of your English lessons." His grin disappeared, and his gray eyes searched hers. His Adam's apple moved with his swallow. "Regina, I need to speak with you privately. Perhaps when you get your food, we can sit together and talk?"

"Come on, man. The rest of us want to finish gettin' our vittles, too." A bearded man behind Diedrich shifted impatiently. Though Regina doubted Diedrich understood all of the man's words, his embarrassed expression clearly showed he comprehended the fellow's meaning.

"Ja," she managed to murmur before Diedrich moved on. Had Diedrich read the longing in her face and wanted to remind her of their bargain?

At the thought, her stomach knotted. The moment the last man was served, she abandoned the food table. She couldn't even think of eating until she found Diedrich and learned what was on his mind.

Making her way through the milling and shifting crowd, she glanced about. Diedrich hadn't mentioned where she should look for him. Suddenly, someone grabbed her hand. Looking up, she met Eli's eager expression with one of dismay. Impatience and aggravation twined in her chest. She tried to pull her hand free, but he held tight. "Let go of me, Eli! I'm looking for someone."

His forehead furrowed angrily. "You're supposed to be looking for *me*. You promised me you would spend some time with me, remember?"

She groaned. She had promised him. At the very least, she had allowed him to believe she would spend time with him. And if what he told her in the store was true, he had gone to some trouble to concoct a surprise for her. Mustering patience, she heaved a sigh. "All right. Show me your surprise." The sooner she humored him, the sooner she could search for Diedrich.

Gripping her hand so hard it hurt, Eli towed her toward a thicket that edged the woods surrounding his uncle's farm. "Let me go, Eli! That hurts." Dodging branches and prickly briars, she stumbled through the wooded undergrowth. But despite her complaints, Eli kept a tight grip on her hand. Finally, they reached a clearing, and he stopped and let go of her hand. There, across the little creek that ran through the clearing, stood a tethered horse hitched to an open surrey.

Confused, Regina turned to him. Had he bought a surrey and wanted her opinion of it? "Is this yours?"

He shrugged. "Nah. I borrowed it from my uncle."

Regina huffed her impatience. She was not about to go gallivanting around Dudleytown with Eli. "You know I can't go riding with you without Papa's permission."

Grinning, Eli took her hand again and towed her closer to the creek. "We won't need anybody's permission to ride together after today. Two miles away, there's a preacher waitin' to marry us."

CHAPTER 15

Regina's eyes popped, and her jaw sagged. Yanking her hand from his, she took two steps backward. "Have you lost all reason?"

Eli's face transformed into an angry mask. His green eyes turned stormy, reminding her of how the sky looked once when a cyclone came through Sauers. He grabbed at her hand again, but she pulled it away. "I'm tired of waitin'. We're gettin' married this afternoon, and that's the end of it!"

Raw fear leapt like a hot flame in her chest. She struggled to breathe. Surely he wouldn't force her to go with him. Then slowly, cool reason flooded back, extinguishing her fear. Even if Eli did force her to go stand with him before a preacher, no preacher she knew would perform such nuptials against her wishes.

Drawing in a deep, calming breath, she turned to him. "Eli, I cannot marry you—ever."

Hurt and anger twisted his handsome features. "You like me. I know you do. You said so."

Sadly, Regina knew he was right. She bore at least part of the blame for the predicament in which she found herself. For months she had encouraged Eli, even pursued him. Tears sprang to her eyes, and she hung her head in shame. "I am sorry I let you think I wanted. . . It was wrong of me. But I know now I cannot marry you, Eli."

He cursed, shocking her. Fear flared again. She had seen him angry before, but even the time they had argued in the barn, he hadn't cursed at her. "Quit worryin' about what your folks think, Regina. I wager they won't like it much at first, but they'll get used to the idea in time."

He stepped toward her, and she took another step back. The time had come to share with Eli what she now realized. "I have told you before I would never marry without my parents' blessing, and that is true. But it is not the only reason I cannot marry you."

Stepping closer, he held out his hands palms up. "What other reason is there?"

Unsure how he would react to her next words, Regina prepared to bolt, praying she could find her way back to the barn lot. "I cannot marry you because I do not love you. I love someone else."

Eli's face scrunched up, and his eyes narrowed to angry green slits. "And who *do* you love—Rothhaus?" He nearly spat Diedrich's surname.

"Yes," she blurted. It felt good to say it. And now that she had, she wanted to scream it. "I love Diedrich Rothhaus."

A rustling sounded a few feet behind her. She spun around, and for an instant, her heart jolted to a dead stop in her chest. Diedrich stood less than two yards away, his eyes wide and his mouth agape.

For an excruciatingly long moment, they both stood stock still, exchanging a look of stunned incredulity. The awareness in his eyes confirmed he had both heard and understood her declaration of love for him. A wave of humiliation washed through her. Her feet, which seemed to have taken root in the woods' decaying underbrush, sprang to life again. Spurred by her embarassment, they now seemed to have sprouted wings, and she ran. As she sped past Diedrich, she thought she heard him utter her name, but the ringing in her ears drowned it out. Dead leaves moist from recent rains slipped beneath her feet. Brambles clutched at her clothes. Branches stung her face and arms. She ignored it all. She didn't even care where she ended up as long as she didn't have to face Diedrich. What did he think? What did he feel? Sadness? Pity? Or worse—fear that she would break their secret agreement and force him into the marriage their fathers had bargained?

By the grace of God, she suddenly emerged from the wood into a clearing behind the building site of the new barn. Gasping for breath, she finally stopped. With her whole body trembling and her heart slamming against her ribs, she clutched a poplar sapling for support. She feared if she let go of the tree, she might crumple in a heap. But knowing Diedrich was doubtless only steps behind her lent strength to her shaky limbs. She couldn't let him find her in this state. She had to have time to compose herself and gather her thoughts before allowing him to confront her with what he had heard her say.

Drawing a deep, tremulous breath, she somehow made her way to the food tables. There she noticed Anna Rieckers wrapping a cotton towel around a large crockery bowl. Glancing up, her friend caught sight of Regina and halted in her work. A look of concern etched on her face, she stepped toward her.

"Regina, are you sick? You do not look well." She grasped Regina's arms, and Regina slumped against her, glad for the support.

"I—I don't feel well." It was not a lie. Between the shock of Eli trying to force her to elope with him and Diedrich learning that she loved him, Regina felt physically ill. She was glad she hadn't eaten anything before leaving the food tables—for if she had, she surely would have lost it back in the woods.

Anna's pale blue eyes shone with compassion. "Come. You need to sit down. Let me help you to the quilts Mama and I spread in the shade." Slipping her arm around Regina, Anna gently steered her toward a giant catalpa tree. "We are about ready to leave for home, but you can rest on the quilts until we get the wagon loaded."

Regina stopped. "You are going home?" The Rieckers would need to pass by Regina's house. Perhaps they would be willing to take her home.

Anna nodded, and a look of disappointment pulled her lips into a frown. "Ja. Papa and my brothers will stay for a while, but Mama and I need to get home and start the milking." Swiping at a strand of blond hair blown across her face by a passing breeze, she cast a longing glance toward the skeletal framework of the new barn. "I was hoping to spend more time with August, but Papa won't let him bring me home until we are formally promised."

Regina had known for months that Anna and August Entebrock were keeping company. August's name was one Papa had mentioned last fall as a possible suitor for Regina. She remembered being happy to report to Papa that the twenty-year-old farmer was courting her best friend and thus unavailable.

Anna's narrow shoulders rose and fell with a deep sigh. "You are so fortunate that your intended lives with your family. You get to see him every day."

Regina wished she could confide in Anna that seeing Diedrich every day felt at times more like a curse than a blessing. Best friends since childhood, she and Anna had long dreamed of marrying the same year and raising their families next to one another. Except for Papa, no one had been more excited than Anna to learn of Regina and Diedrich's pending engagement. It had taken all of Regina's fortitude not to share with Anna her earlier feelings for Eli and the deal she had made with Diedrich. And while she could trust her sister Elsie to keep her secret, Anna's exuberance sometimes caused her to blurt things without thinking. Regina couldn't risk the truth getting back to Papa.

Scanning the building site, Anna gave a little gasp. "Oh, there is your handsome *Verlobter*. Perhaps I should tell him you are not feeling well. He may want to take you home." She turned as if to go fetch Diedrich, but Regina clutched her arm, restraining her.

"Nein!" The word exploded from Regina's lips. At the stunned expression on Anna's face, Regina tempered her voice. "Of course Diedrich cannot take me home, Anna. That would not be korrekt unless Mama and Papa came, too."

Anna reddened, and she shook her head. "Nein, nein. Of course I did not mean that the two of you should go home alone. I was thinking that his Vater would go, too."

"There you are, Regina. I have been looking everywhere for you." Mama strode toward them, a less-than-pleased expression on her face. Despite the stern look and the censure in her voice, Regina couldn't remember being happier to see her mother. But before she could say anything, Anna piped up.

"Frau Seitz, Regina is not feeling well."

"Oh?" Mama's perturbed expression melted into one of concern. She pressed the back of her hand against Regina's forehead and then her cheeks. "You do look flushed. Perhaps you should lie down in the back of the wagon for a while."

Regina cast a hopeful look at Anna then back to Mama. "Anna and her Mutter are leaving soon. I was thinking maybe they could take me home." She turned imploring eyes back to Anna.

Anna smiled. "I will go ask Mama, but I know she would be happy to take you home."

Mama nodded, and Regina felt some of the tension drain from her body. "That would be gut, I think." Mama smiled and patted Regina's cheek. "You probably ate something that did not sit well. You should go home and rest now, and tomorrow I will give you a good dose of castor oil."

Regina shivered at the thought of the castor oil but managed a weak smile. She would drink a whole bottle of the stuff if it kept her from having to face Diedrich.

A half hour later, feeling at once foolish and deceptive, Regina stood in her own yard and waved good-bye to Anna and her mother. Eventually she would have to face Diedrich, but at least their confrontation would not be witnessed by dozens of curious onlookers.

Turning, she stepped toward the house then stopped. Though still a bit shaky from this afternoon's occurrences, the last thing she felt like doing was taking a nap. She needed to keep both her mind and body busy. Tipping her head up, she shaded her eyes with her flattened hand and squinted at the sun riding high in the sky. It was still early afternoon. She should be able to get most of her chores done before everyone came home in an hour or so.

She slipped into the washroom and exchanged her leather shoes for her Holzschuhe then grabbed the egg basket. Over the course of the next hour, she gathered the eggs, hoed the garden, and picked a mess of dandelion greens for supper. But as she headed to the barn to feed the horses and milk the cow, the tension knotting her stomach had not loosened, and she knew why. Though she'd rolled the question around in her head all afternoon, she still hadn't decided what she would say when Diedrich confronted her about her feelings for him. Clearly, she had two choices—tell him the truth and burden him with guilt or deny her feelings and lie. Her conscience recoiled from both options.

Inside the barn, she was met by the familiar and somehow calming smells of hay, manure, leather, and animals. As she approached the stall, Ingwer greeted her with a friendly moo. Bobbing her head, the cow eyed her with a quizzical look as if to ask why she was being milked so early. Grinning, Regina pulled the three-legged stool from the corner of the stall and situated it at the cow's right side. She positioned the bucket beneath the udders and settled herself on the stool. "I know it is early, *meine Alte*," she said as she patted the cow's ginger-colored side, "but milking you calms me, and I need to think clearly."

The first splat of milk had scarcely hit the bucket when Regina heard the distant jangling of a wagon and team coming down the lane. For an instant, her chest constricted then eased. Even if Diedrich wanted to talk with her alone, finding a private moment would be difficult. She went back to milking, confident she could avoid spending any time alone with him at least for the rest of the day.

"Regina." Though quiet, the sound of Diedrich's voice brought Regina upright. She slowly turned on the stool, her face blazing and her heart pounding so hard she feared it might burst from her chest. She glanced behind him, praying she would see either Papa or Herr Rothhaus. She didn't.

No smile touched his lips as he walked toward her. His soft gray eyes held an intense look she had never seen in them before. Rising on wobbly legs, she leaned her shoulder against Ingwer for support. She had no idea what to say, so she was glad when he spoke first.

"Frau Seitz said you were feeling sick. Are you better, then?"

"Ja," Regina managed to croak, her back pressed against Ingwer's warm side.

He stepped closer, his gaze never veering from her face. "I do not know much English." As he neared, he reached out and took her hands in his. At the touch of his strong, calloused hands on hers, her throat dried and her insides turned to jelly. "But I know the word *yes*, and I know the word *love*." His thumbs gently caressed the backs of her hands. "I need to know if what you told Tanner is true. Do you love me?"

Regina swallowed hard. Her mind raced with her heart. What should she say? She knew Diedrich. The memory of the words he had spoken to her weeks ago came flooding back. *"I prayed I would not break your heart."* If he even suspected he would break her heart by going to California, he would forfeit his dream. And in September, as their fathers had agreed, she would marry the man standing before her—the man she now loved. But she would not have his heart. No. She would not wake each morning with the fear of finding regret in her husband's eyes and have her heart broken anew every day for the rest of her life.

"Regina." His gentle grip on her hands tightened, and his throat moved with his swallow. "Tell me. Did you mean the words you said to Tanner?"

Her heart felt as if it was being squeezed by an iron fist, and she winced with the pain. Hot tears stung the back of her nose and flooded her eyes. Unable to hold his gaze, hers dropped to the pointy toes of her wooden shoes. *Dear Lord, forgive my lie.* She shook her head. "I just told Eli that so he would leave me alone."

He let go of her hands, and she fought to suppress the sob rising up from the center of her being. But then she felt his hands slowly, gently slip around her waist, drawing her to him. His head lowered, and his lips found hers. Reason unhitched. Her heart took control, and she welcomed his kiss. She felt as if she were floating. Were her feet still on the ground? It didn't matter. Nothing mattered but the sweet sensation of Diedrich's lips caressing hers. She slid her arms around his neck and clung to him, returning the tender pressure of his kiss with matching urgency. Then suddenly it was over. He raised his head, freeing her lips.

With all her senses still firing, Regina slammed back to reality with a jarring jolt. Feeling as limp as a rag doll, she stepped back out of his embrace and leaned against the cow, which shifted and mooed.

A smile crawled across Diedrich's lips until it stretched his face wide. "You can lie to me with your words, mein Liebchen, but your kiss, I think, tells me the truth." Still smiling, he turned and walked out of the barn.

Somehow Regina managed to finish the milking. Her mind and heart still spinning, she said little as she later helped Mama with supper. Occasionally Mama would press the back of her hand to Regina's forehead and cheeks, then, clucking her tongue, vowed to dose her with any number of herbal concoctions. Supper passed in a fog with Regina tasting nothing she ate. Diedrich, on the other hand, seemed especially cheerful and animated. She tried not to look at him during the meal, but several times he caught her eye and gave her a sweet, knowing smile that sent her heart bounding like a rabbit chased by a fox.

When everyone had finished and the older men pushed back from the table, Mama glanced at Regina's half-eaten plate of food. "I think for sure you are not well, liebes Mädchen. It is best, I think, that you go on up to bed."

Desiring time alone to ponder the many emotions raging inside her, Regina was about to agree. But before she could speak, Diedrich piped up.

"Please, Frau Seitz, if Regina feels well enough at all, I would especially like for her to join us in our evening Bible reading." The glint in his eye told Regina he knew she was not really sick—at least not sick in the way Mama thought.

Regina offered a tepid smile. "Ja. I feel well enough." She couldn't begin to guess why he might want her present for the Bible reading. Earlier in the barn, he had seen through her lie. Was he or his father planning to read scripture admonishing liars? As strange as this day had been, she was prepared to believe anything might happen.

A few minutes later, as they did each evening after supper, everyone gathered in the front room. Regina sat in her normal place on a short bench beside the hearth. Mama, as usual, settled in her sewing rocker situated on the opposite side of the fireplace. The three men pulled up chairs in a half circle facing the fireplace. Usually, either Papa or Herr Rothhaus would read a scripture, followed by a few minutes of discussion about the verses, after which one of the men would offer prayer. Then for an hour or so, everyone would discuss the day's events until daylight slipped away and yawning broke out around the group. As soon as the prayer was finished, Regina planned to make her excuses and head upstairs.

Diedrich took a chair facing Regina. Her disconcertment growing, she studiously kept her gaze focused on her hands folded in her lap. Was he, too, thinking of the sweet kiss they had shared in the barn? And why was his mood so cheerful if he thought she was in love with him?

"Vater." Diedrich turned to his father seated to his left between him and Papa. "If you and Herr Seitz do not mind, I would like to read the scripture this evening."

"Sehr gut, Sohn." Herr Rothhaus looked a bit surprised but handed Diedrich the Bible. Sensing something momentous was about to occur, Regina held her breath and braced for whatever might happen.

Diedrich opened the Bible at a spot marked by a small slip of paper. Regina noticed two other such markers protruding from the book's pages. The sight did nothing to ease her building trepidation.

Diedrich cleared his throat, and everyone became quiet. Then in a clear voice he read—or more accurately recited—from the fourth chapter of Lamentations. All the while, his eyes never left Regina. " 'How is the gold become dim! how is the most fine gold changed!' "

Regina's heart began to pound in her ears and tears misted her eyes.

He turned to another marked page. "Proverbs 18:22," he announced then read, " 'Whoso findeth a wife findeth a good thing, and obtaineth favour of the Lord.' " His voice softened as his gaze melted into hers. Now tears began to course in earnest down Regina's cheeks. But he was not finished. He flipped the pages to yet another marker and said, "Proverbs 31:10." Then, closing the book he rose, set the Bible on the chair, and walked to Regina. With his eyes firmly fixed on hers, he recited, " 'Who can find a virtuous woman? for her price is far above rubies.' Or gold."

Herr Rothhaus shook his head, bewildered. "Sohn, I do not think it says the part about gold."

"I know, Vater, but I am saying what is in my heart." Diedrich took Regina's hands in his and knelt before her. Her tears became a torrent. "Regina, mein Liebchen," he murmured. "You are mein Liebling, mein *Schätzchen*."

Regina could hardly believe her ears. Her heart sang as he declared her his sweetheart, his darling. . .his treasure.

From her seat on the other side of the hearth, Mama sniffed and dabbed her eyes with the hem of her apron. Papa and Herr Rothhaus exchanged grins while nodding their approval.

"*Ich liebe dich*, Regina," Diedrich said, his eyes shining with unvarnished adoration. "I know we have been promised for many months, but my heart needs to ask you here, in front of our parents, do you love me, too? And if we were not promised, would you still want to be my wife?"

Her heart full to bursting, Regina nodded. "Ja." The word came out on a happy sob. Still holding her hands, Diedrich stood, bringing her up with him. Taking her in his arms, he placed a chaste kiss on her cheek; then, lifting his lips to her ear, he whispered softly so only she could hear. "I love you, my darling. You are worth more to me than all the world's gold."

Mama wept openly, the sound blending with the creaking of her rocking chair. Papa cleared his throat and in a voice thick with emotion said, "I think we should hurry to finish that new house, hey, Georg?" Herr Rothhaus agreed with a hearty laugh.

All of this filtered vaguely into Regina's brain. The amazing miracle unfolding before her dominated her mind, heart, and senses, as did the man she loved—the man in whose arms she rested.

∞

For Regina, the next four weeks would pass in a blissful blur. The men hurried to finish the house before threshing time began in early July. Mama and Regina spent their days planning the coming wedding, making strawberry and cherry preserves, and tending the garden. The moments Regina and Diedrich enjoyed alone were few and precious—a tender glance or touch of their hands in passing, a stolen kiss in the washroom or behind a piece of laundry drying on the line when Regina hung out the wash. As the idyllic summer days drifted by, Regina lived for the day she would become Frau Rothhaus.

By mid-June, Mama decided it was time to begin piecing together the squares of cloth that would become Regina's and Diedrich's wedding quilt. Over the years, Mama had kept in a cedar box precious squares of cloth that held sentimental significance to the family.

This morning with the men gone again to work on the house, Regina and her mother sat together in the front room, the basket of quilting squares on the floor between them.

A gentle breeze wafted through the open front door, bringing with it the fragrance of roses and honeysuckle as well as the lulling hum of the bees that hovered around the blossoms. Working her needle along a square of cloth, Mama pressed her foot to the puncheon floor, setting the rocker creaking as it moved in a gentle motion. "I am hoping we can find a day soon when your sisters can come and we can all work together on this quilt as we did for each of theirs."

Regina looked up from the needlework in her own hands. "That might be hard to do. Elsie is always busy helping William with the store. And with baby Henry walking now, Sophie has her hands full, especially since she and Ezra moved into that big house in Vernon."

Mama frowned. "Sometimes I wish your sister did not have such grand tastes. I worry how they can afford such a nice home. The smaller house they had before would have served them well until Ezra and his brother built up their wheelwright shop, I think."

Regina agreed. She'd never understood Sophie's appetite for extravagance. To Regina, the notion of having her own home, however humble, was in itself heady. In truth, she would happily live in a mud hut as long as she was with Diedrich. But she was genuinely proud of the two-story log home he and his father were building for her. And eventually, as they gradually built on to it, her house would rival this home she had grown up in. Yet she knew her eldest sister would likely scoff at it. She remembered how Sophie had gasped in horror when she learned Elsie and William would be living in three small rooms attached to the back of their store.

Not wanting to hear another of Mama's rants about Sophie's spendthrift ways, Regina decided to steer the conversation to the quilt pieces.

She reached into the basket and brought up a bright blue square of cloth. "This was from your wedding dress, am I correct?"

Smiling, Mama nodded. "Ja, you remember well from when we made your sisters' quilts, I think."

Next, Regina held up a scrap of faded yellow material. This one, she couldn't guess. It didn't look like material from any of the dresses she or her sisters had worn as youngsters. "And what is this from, Mama? I do not recognize it."

Mama looked up, and the smile on her face vanished. Her complexion blanched, frightening Regina. She looked as if she had seen a ghost. Her shoulders sagged, and before Regina's eyes, her mother seemed to age ten years. Her brown eyes, welling with tears, held both sorrow and resignation. "I had completely forgotten I'd saved that." She exhaled a deep breath as if gathering strength. "Regina, there is something you need to know. Something your Vater and I should have told you long ago."

Regina's scalp tingled in the ominous way it often did before a storm. With fright building in her chest, she held out the square of cloth that trembled in her shaking fingers. "Mama, what is this cloth?"

A tear slipped down Mama's cheek. "It is from the swaddling blanket you were wrapped in when your mother gave you to me."

CHAPTER 16

W ell Sohn, we shall have a nice warm home, I think." Smiling, Father turned a slow circle in the center of the house's main room and eyed their handiwork.

Diedrich tugged on the ladder he'd just nailed against the loft to test its sturdiness and gave a solemn nod. In a little over a month, they had cleared an acre of land and built on it a twenty-two-by-thirty-foot log home with a full loft. Though his head told him that what he, Father, and Herr Seitz had accomplished on the house in six weeks' time was more than impressive, he still wished he could present Regina with something grander.

Father ambled to the east end of the room. There, he cast a studious gaze at the rough-hewn wall and stroked the graying whiskers that covered his chin. "Now, I think, we should begin work on furniture for our home. Ernst explained how is made the beds called *wall peg* that are built against the wall." He sent Diedrich a sly grin accompanied by a wink. "You and your bride will need a good strong bed for sure, hey?"

Heat shot up Diedrich's neck and suffused his face. "Vater!" Since that blessed evening when he and Regina had declared their love for each other, his intended had set up court in his mind and heart. Waking or sleeping, not a moment passed that he didn't find her lingering sweetly on his mind. He had enough trouble keeping his thoughts from straying beyond korrekt boundaries. He did not need Father's teasing comments making the task more difficult.

Father leaned his head back and roared in mirth. "It is only the truth I am saying."

He crossed to Diedrich and gave him a good-natured clap on the shoulder. "Your bride, too, will want *stark* furniture. After dinner, I think, we will begin to build the bed."

Diedrich glanced at the wedge of sunlight angled across the puncheon floor through the open southerly door. He nodded. "Sehr gut, Vater. My stomach as well as the sun tells me it is time we should head back to the Seitzes' kitchen for dinner." The instant the words were out of his mouth, Diedrich groaned under his breath. The way Father liked to tease him about Regina, he was liable to ask if Diedrich's stomach was the only part of him nudging him back to Regina's home. But Father only grinned and followed Diedrich out of the house, keeping all other thoughts on the subject to himself.

Outside, Diedrich closed the front door to keep out any small animals that might be enticed by the shade to amble in while he and Father were gone. Then, stepping back away from the building, he allowed himself a parting look at the house. His and Regina's home. The thought filled him with joy and a yearning for the day he would carry his love into their new home. His gaze roved over the two-story building. The front door, situated exactly in the center of the south wall, was flanked by a window on each side. One let light into the large room that would serve as their front room and bedroom. The other brought light into the kitchen. Directly above those were two more windows cut under the eaves, allowing daylight into the loft. Eventually, he would build a proper staircase up to the second story. There, God willing, he would have need to fashion bedrooms for his and Regina's sons and daughters. His gaze slid down the house's plain front facade. He also would build a long porch with a roof above it so that Regina could sit in the shade and sew, shell peas from her garden, or pare apples from the trees he would plant. Then another, even sweeter image assembled itself in his mind, and his heart throbbed with longing. How clearly he could see her sitting there on the front porch, rocking their first child against her breast while a summer zephyr played with a strand of her golden hair and ruffled the soft, pale fuzz of their babe's head.

Yes, Father was right. It was a good, sturdy house—a house he could be proud of.

At that moment, Herr Seitz appeared from the cornfield that faced the house. He had spent the morning cultivating the green stalks now chest high. Unfamiliar with the crop in his old home of Venne, Diedrich liked the plants with their feathery tassels and long, drooping tapered leaves that whispered softly as the summer breeze rustled through them. Even more, he liked the prospect of the grain that would provide them with cornmeal to make the tasty yellow bread Regina and her mother served at nearly every meal.

As Diedrich bounced along in the back of the wagon, anticipation built in both his stomach and his heart. He could scarcely wait to see Regina again. Her sweet smiles fed his spirit like her good cooking fed his stomach.

But when they finally arrived at the house, he was surprised when she didn't meet him at the back door as she often did. As he waited his turn at the washstand inside the back door, he inclined his ear, listening for her voice. But instead of hearing her normally cheerful tone as she conversed with her mother, he caught only an occasional unintelligible word mumbled in a flat monotone. At the sound, a grain of concern planted itself in his chest and quickly grew to a niggling worry. Back in April, Pastor Sauer had advised Diedrich to learn Regina's heart. This he had done. He had come to know Regina's heart well enough for him to sense when something was not right with her. When he finally entered the kitchen, her downcast expression confirmed his suspicions. Frau Seitz also seemed distant and somewhat glum. Had mother and daughter had some kind of an argument? Diedrich could hardly imagine it. Even when Regina had initially rejected her parents' plans for her and Diedrich to marry, she had never, to Diedrich's knowledge, dishonored them with a cross word.

At the table, he tried to engage her in conversation about the progress he and Father had made on the house this morning. But despite his best efforts, he could scarcely evoke the smallest smile from her. And even when she did smile, it didn't reach her lovely blue eyes, which today reminded him more of a faded chambray shirt than a cloudless summer sky. Clearly something troubled her. And though he sensed he was not the cause of her melancholy mood, the thought brought him only a measure of relief. He was gripped by a profound need to know what had stolen her joy and a strong determination to do whatever was in his power to restore her happiness. He would not go back to work on their new home until he'd seen things set right with Regina.

After the meal, Father and Herr Seitz went to the front room to let their meals settle and discuss the work on the log house. Diedrich stayed in the kitchen, quietly watching Regina and her mother tidy up after the meal. Watching them work together, Diedrich grew more bewildered over Regina's odd demeanor. He could detect no anger or tension between Regina and her mother.

When the last dish had been washed, dried, and put away, Diedrich rose. Stepping toward the two women, he held his hand out to Regina while addressing her mother. "Frau Seitz, may I have your permission to take Regina for a walk?" Frau nodded. "Ja, it is sehr gut that you talk." Regina took his hand, and for the first time since he came in for dinner, she gave him the sweet smile he'd come to expect—the smile that felt like a caress.

Her face a somber mask, the usually undemonstrative Frau Seitz gave Regina a quick hug. She and Regina exchanged a look Diedrich couldn't decipher. Then she said something very odd. "You are my daughter, liebes Mädchen. Do not forget that."

Regina's eyes welled with tears that gouged at Diedrich's heart. She gave her mother a brave smile and whispered, "I know, Mama."

At once, curiosity and concern twined around Diedrich's heart like the wild vines that sprang up among the cornstalks. The moment he and Regina stepped outside, he was tempted to stop and insist she tell him what was the matter. But better judgment counseled him to wait. To his surprise, she spoke first.

"Diedrich, let us go see the garden. Our potato plants are flowering now. We should have new potatoes to fry soon." Her voice still sounded sad and distant. Taking his hand, she led him to the bench beside the house that overlooked the garden. Regina was right. The plants looked robust and healthy. The memory of the day they had planted the potato crop together came back to Diedrich and in an odd way reinforced the bond he felt with her.

When they had settled themselves on the bench, a large tear escaped her left eye. For a moment it clung to the golden fringe of her lower lashes, glistening in the sunlight like a dewdrop. Then a blink dislodged it, sending it to the rose-pink apple of her cheek to meander down her face.

Diedrich could bear it no longer. Placing his finger beneath her chin, he gently turned her face to his. "Regina, please tell me, what is the matter? Have I done something to upset you?"

Her wide-eyed look of surprise washed him with relief. "No, mein Liebling, it is not you." Then, turning away from him again, she hung her head and focused on her hands clasped in her lap. "I—I am not who you think I am. I am not who *I* thought I was."

The last strands of Diedrich's patience frayed. He had no more interest in puzzles or guessing games. Gently grasping her shoulders, he turned her to him. "Regina, what is this nonsense you are saying? In less than three months we shall be married. You must tell me now what is troubling you."

Her chin quivered, smiting him with regret. "This morning Mama told me that she did not give birth to me."

"What?" Diedrich had never met a kinder, more caring Christian woman than Frau Seitz. He couldn't imagine her saying something so hurtful to her child. . .unless it was true. And if it was, why had she waited until now to tell Regina? But if it were true, Frau Seitz's odd comment earlier asking Regina not to forget that she was her daughter began to make sense.

Regina sniffed and drew in a ragged breath. "We were piecing together my wedding quilt." Quirking a smile, she blushed prettily, making his heart canter. "When I found a piece of material I didn't recognize, Mama's face looked so terrible I thought she was having an attack of apoplexy." Her voice turned breathless at her remembered alarm. She went on to tell him how her mother claimed it was from the blanket Regina was wrapped in when her birth mother gave her away.

"But who was your real mother, and why would she give you away?" Now Diedrich fully understood Regina's discomposure. He, too, struggled to assimilate the revelation. His heart broke for his beloved. He couldn't imagine how it must feel to learn something so shocking.

Regina sniffed again, and Diedrich had to force himself not to pull her into his arms and comfort her against him. But he sensed that she needed to tell this, and he needed to hear it. "Mama said I was born on the boat from Bremen to Baltimore to a couple named Eva and Hermann Zichwolff."

"But they didn't want you?" The thought, which seemed incredible to Diedrich, angered him.

Another tear tracked down Regina's face. "Mama said there was much sickness on the ship. Not everyone who left Bremen lived to see America."

Diedrich nodded. He knew he and Father were very fortunate that during their voyage to America the *Franziska* had experienced no losses.

Regina kept her gaze fixed on her hands, which she wrung in her lap. "My Vater. . .my natural Vater." She stumbled on the words as if she couldn't believe she was saying them. "He died two weeks before I was born and they buried him at sea. A few days after I was born, Mama also gave birth to a baby girl." She shook her head sadly, and her voice took a somber dip. "But her baby lived only a few hours." After pausing to draw in a fortifying breath, Regina continued. "When they docked in Baltimore, many of the German immigrants were taken into homes of German-speaking people there. Eva, the woman who gave birth to me, spoke passable English. Not having a husband to take care of her and. . .me, she began looking for domestic work. Mama said Eva was given the opportunity to work for a very wealthy Baltimore family. But the family said she could not bring me." Regina shrugged. "Eva remembered that Mama had lost her child and would be able to provide me with nourishment, so she took me to her."

Smiling bravely through her tears, Regina patted her chest. "Mama's heart still hurt very much after losing her baby girl. She told me that when she took me as her own, it helped to soothe that hurt." She dabbed at her tear-drenched face with her apron hem. "Mama did say Eva cried when she gave me away."

Diedrich's heart bled for everyone involved, but mostly for Regina. He grappled for words that might bring her comfort. Gently stroking her arms from shoulder to elbow, he finally said, "I would say Gott has blessed you doubly. He gave you to a birth mother who cared enough to find you good, loving parents when she couldn't keep you. Then He not only gave you a wonderful Mama and Papa but two sisters as well."

More tears flooded down Regina's face. "You do not mind, then, that I was born Regina Zichwolff?"

Diedrich grinned. "Your name could be Regina *Schlammpfütze* and I would love you just the same." Giving her the surname of Mudpuddle reminded him of the first time he set eyes on her, and he couldn't help a chuckle. She giggled through her tears, making him wonder if perhaps they were sharing the same memory.

Then, turning serious, he cupped her face in his hands and gazed deeply into her lovely cerulean eyes. "It is sorry I am, mein Liebchen, that you have had such a shock today." He brushed away her newest tears with his thumbs. "But it makes no difference to me or the life we will soon have together." Then he smiled as another revelation struck. "Except that if your life had not happened as it did, I would not have you here in my arms. I think, even then, while Gott was taking care of you, He was also thinking of a four-year-old boy named Diedrich in Venne, Hanover."

This brought a smile to her lips, and he had to kiss them, lingering perhaps a moment or two longer than might be considered proper. When he finally forced himself to let her go, she smiled, and her eyes opened slowly as if from a pleasant dream. "I do love you, Diedrich," she murmured.

He had to kiss her again. He finally left her humming happily in the garden as she checked for potatoes big enough to harvest. Though he was stunned by what he had learned, Diedrich's heart was full. He prayed that his love would always be sufficient to vanquish every sadness in Regina's life as well as nurture her every joy.

When he stepped into the house in search of Father and Herr Seitz, Frau Seitz informed him that Father had already headed back to the new house and Herr Seitz had gone to check the maturity of the wheat crop. She grinned. "They did not want to disturb your talk with Regina."

With a quick word of thanks he turned to leave, but Frau Seitz took hold of his arm, halting him. "How—how is Regina?" Concern dulled her brown eyes and etched her forehead.

Diedrich smiled and squeezed her hand. Thinking of what this woman had meant to Regina and all she had done for her over the years, he wanted to thank her. Instead, he said, "Regina is happy that Gott has blessed her with a wonderful Mutter and Vater."

Frau Seitz's eyes glistened with unshed tears. She patted his hand. "And Gott will bless her soon with a wonderful husband."

Giving Frau Seitz an appreciative nod, he headed for the back forty acres and the new house. Father had taken the wagon and team, so Diedrich would have to either hitch the little gypsy pony to its cart or walk. Since it was a pleasant day and his spirits were high, he decided to make the nearly two-mile trek on foot.

As he walked, he remembered the name of Regina's birth parents. Herr Seitz had said many of their fellow passengers on the boat they had taken to America were also from Venne. He must ask Father if he knew of the name Hermann Zichwolff.

When he stepped into the house, Father turned from pounding a peg into the narrow gap between two logs on the east wall. He angled a grin toward Diedrich. "I was wondering if you would come back to help me with this bed, or if you had decided to spend the rest of the day holding hands with your Liebchen."

At his father's glib comment, Diedrich experienced a flash of anger. But Father had no knowledge of the emotional turmoil Regina had endured today.

Diedrich walked to his father. "Regina learned something upsetting today. I did not wish to leave her until her heart had calmed." He then shared with his father what Regina had told him.

An odd, almost wary look crossed Father's face. "So of whose blood is she?"

Diedrich couldn't imagine why Father would care. "Do you know the name Hermann Zichwolff? He and his wife, Eva, were Regina's natural parents."

Father's face blanched so pale it looked as if it were covered in flour. Then his face turned to a shade of red so deep it became almost purple. In all his life, Diedrich had never seen his father in a rage. But no other word fit the look of fury that twisted his father's features into someone Diedrich didn't recognize.

Balling his fists, Father fixed Diedrich with a murderous glare, his eyes nearly popping out of his head. "I forbid you to marry that girl! As long as I am alive, I swear it will not happen!"

CHAPTER 17

Disbelief, confusion, and pain swirled in Diedrich's chest like a cyclone. In all his twenty-one years, he had never raised his voice to his father in anger or spoken an insolent word to him. But at this moment, it took all his strength of will not to do both. He strained to hold his raging temper in check, his tense muscles twitching with the effort.

Three stilted strides brought him to his father. He held out his hands palms up in a helpless gesture. "Why, Vater? Why would you say such a thing? Was it not for me to marry Regina that we came across the ocean to America?"

Some of the anger seemed to drain from Father's face, and a glimmer of regret flashed in his eyes. He blew out a long breath as if to regain control of his emotions. His expression begged understanding. In a measured voice he said, "I know you have grown fond of the Mädchen, Sohn, but—"

"Fond?" Diedrich almost spat the word then chased it with a mirthless laugh. "Fond, Father?" He tapped his chest so hard he expected to later find it bruised. "I love Regina with all my heart. You yourself heard me declare it, did you not?"

A stubborn frown etched wavy lines across Father's broad forehead. "But that was before we knew Ernst had tricked us."

Diedrich fought the urge to scream. Had Father gone mad, or had he? Or had they both lost their senses? He struggled to understand. "Please, Vater, tell me how you think Herr Seitz has tricked us."

Another fierce look of anger flashed in Father's eyes like jagged lightning. "He lied to us, Sohn! He told us she was his daughter. And now I find that she is the daughter of. . ." He abandoned the thought as if it were too abhorrent to put to voice, and his face screwed up like he smelled something fetid.

Clearly, for some unknown reason, Father held hard feelings against Regina's birth father. But the man was dead and had been for nearly eighteen years. Nothing would change Diedrich's love for Regina or budge his determination to make her his wife. But for him to convince Father that Regina's parentage made no difference, he needed to understand why Father felt as he did. "Father, who was Hermann Zichwolff?"

Father winced and jerked as if he'd been physically struck. Then his shoulders slumped, and he trudged over to the pair of three-legged stools beside the fireplace. Perching himself on one, he motioned for Diedrich to take the other.

Diedrich obeyed, praying that with the telling, Father might rid himself of the ill feelings he'd evidently held against the man for years.

Father leaned forward, his clasped hands resting on his knees. "Do you remember hearing me speak of your Onkel Jakob?"

"Ja." Diedrich remembered Father mentioning his brother, Jakob, only a handful of times. But by the glowing tones Father had used, Diedrich had surmised that Father had idolized his older brother. Beyond that, Diedrich knew little about his late uncle except that he had died young, fighting in the army of the emperor Napoleon.

Father angled a glance up at Diedrich. "You know that Jakob died in the battle of Wagram in 1809." Diedrich nodded. "But what you do not know is that he should not have been there."

Though curious at Father's comment, Diedrich said nothing, respectfully waiting for Father's tale to unfold.

Father rubbed his palms along the tops of his thighs. "When I was but twelve, my Vater—your *Großvater*—wanted to buy twelve milk cows." He gave a sardonic snort. "He said we would become wealthy dairymen. But he had no money to buy the cows, so he went to the local moneylender, Herr Wilhelm Zichwolff, and asked if he would loan him the money. Herr Zichwolff agreed to loan Vater the money but insisted he put up our farm as collateral."

Father paused and cleared his throat, and Diedrich sensed he had come to a painful part of the story. "Within six months," Father continued, "half of Vater's new cows sickened and died, and when the time came to pay Herr Zichwolff, he could not. Vater begged Herr Zichwolff to give him more time so his remaining cows would have time to produce, but Herr Zichwolff would not." Remembered anger hardened Father's tone. "Then, like now, young men were being forced into the army. But at that time, it was Napoleon's army." Father cocked a sad smile toward Diedrich. "Jakob was eighteen and the right age to go to the army, but since farmers produced food for the army, the boys from farms did not have to go." His lips twisted in a sneer. "But the sons of moneylenders were not exempt, and Wilhelm's son, Hermann, was ordered to go fight for Napoleon." Father's body seemed to stiffen as he pressed his hands against his knees. Diedrich knew that if a man of means was called to serve in the army and didn't wish to go, he could pay someone else to serve in his stead. Sensing what was coming next, he swallowed hard and waited for Father to continue.

Father rose and walked to the open front door and gazed out over the corn-field as if he could see all the way back to Venne. For a long moment, silence reigned, interrupted only by the happy chirping of birds and the soothing drone of bees. At length, Father spoke. "Herr Zichwolff told Vater his debt would be forgiven if Jakob went to fight in Hermann's place." Father sniffed, and his voice broke with emotion. "Vater had no choice. If Jakob refused to go to the army, Herr Zichwolff would take our farm, and we would be left homeless. So Jakob went." His voice sagged with his shoulders. "And three years later, Jakob died fighting in the battle of Wagram."

Imagining how he might feel if someone had done to Johann or Frederic what the Zichwolffs had done to Uncle Jakob, Diedrich could understand some of Father's anger and grief.

Now an angry growl crept into Father's voice. "For many years, Hermann lived free and like a king on his Vater's money. Finally, at the age of forty, after he had squandered much of his family's wealth, he took a wife." Father shook his head. "You cannot know the relief, the joy I felt when I learned that the reprobate and his Frau were leaving Venne for America. I could shut the Zichwolffs from my mind forever and never have to think of them again."

Father slowly turned away from the open door and stepped back into the room. He suddenly looked far older than his fifty-six years.

Diedrich slid from the stool and crossed to his father. "But why did you never tell me this story before?"

Father shuffled back over to the east wall and picked up the stout hammer. "When Jakob was killed, I vowed never to speak the name Zichwolff again. And until today, I had kept that vow."

Somehow Diedrich needed to make Father understand that the despicable actions of Wilhelm and Hermann Zichwolff had nothing to do with Regina.

He stepped toward Father. "Father, I know how you must feel. It was a hateful and cowardly thing that Herr Zichwolff did to our family, but it was not Regina's fault. It happened long before she was born."

When Father spoke, his voice drooped with his countenance. "I know, Sohn. But that does not change the blood that runs through her veins or my feelings about it. I wish it were not so, but I cannot change how things are." Picking up one of the stubby pegs he had fashioned earlier from an oak branch, he placed the sharpened end at a chink between the logs and gave it a mighty pound, driving it into the crevice.

"But Vater. . . ." Pain and frustration hardened Diedrich's voice. His heart writhed at the thought of having to choose between Father and Regina. "You know Regina. Not so long ago, you were telling me what a good Christian girl she is. She is the same girl today as she was then."

Father shot him a fierce glance. "To me, she is not the same. And you will *not* mingle our family's blood with the blood of Hermann Zichwolff. I will not have it!"

All his life, Diedrich had loved and admired his father. He never knew a kinder, more God-fearing or honorable man. And until this moment, he would not have imagined he could feel the kind of disdain for his parent now souring in the pit of his stomach. Watching Father nonchalantly return to his work after declaring Regina unfit to be his daughter-in-law and the mother of his grandchildren fed the rage boiling in Diedrich's belly. To his horror, he had to suppress the urge to pummel his sire.

He thought of every scripture about forgiveness Father had taught him over the years. Though mightily tempted to throw them back into his father's face, he resisted, not wanting to sin himself by breaking the commandment that bade him honor his father and mother. Instead, he decided a more prudent and less confrontational tack might be to remind Father of his obligation to Herr Seitz. He had never known Father to let a debt go unpaid.

Diedrich grasped his father's shoulder, turning him to face him. "But what of the debt we owe Herr Seitz? We still owe for our passage." He waved his hand to indicate the building around them. "And now we also owe him for this house and this land."

Father slammed the hammer to the floor with a clunk and gave a derisive snort. "Ernst Seitz lied to us. To my mind, our bargain is void, and I owe him nothing!"

Diedrich noted that Father had chosen to omit the prefix Herr when he mentioned their benefactor's name—a definite insult. "You may not feel you owe him, Father, but I do. I owe him much." He raised his voice, no longer concerned about keeping a civil tone. "And what about the food you eat and the bed you sleep on? Are they not the charity of Herr Seitz?"

His father shoved past him and stalked to the open front door. "Do you not think I would return to Venne this moment if I could? At least there I have sons who honor me. And I have my own land." He narrowed a glare at Diedrich. "The land Jakob died to keep in our family's hands and out of the hands of Wilhelm and Hermann Zichwolff." The instant he uttered the name, he spat into the dirt outside the front door.

"But you cannot go back, Father." Now Diedrich's voice dripped with insolence and he didn't care. "So you will sleep in Herr Seitz's bed and eat Herr Seitz's food until I have worked enough to earn back our passage and the cost of this land."

Father swung back to Diedrich, his face an ugly mask of fury. "I will not set foot in his house again! I will live here, in this house we have built with our own hands." He held out his hands, his curled fingers calloused and gnarled with years of work. "And to pay for my food, I will find other work here in Sauers. Surely one of our neighbors could use an extra pair of hands."

Tears stung the back of Diedrich's nose, and he swallowed the lump that rose in his throat. "You can do whatever you want, Father, but I will not forsake Regina. Not for you, not for anyone."

Father's eyes glistened with unshed tears, and he stared at Diedrich as if he had never seen him before. "Then I shall have but two sons, for you shall be dead to me."

CHAPTER 18

Warring emotions clashed in Regina's chest as she led Gypsy from the barn. The shaggy pony almost pranced as she stepped into the sunlight pulling the little cart behind her.

Regina paused to rub the pony's velvety nose. "I am excited about going to see Anna, too, Gypsy, but I wish I could have seen Diedrich before I left." Twenty minutes earlier, Anna's brother Peter had appeared at the back door with news that his mother was ill. As each other's closest neighbors, it was common practice for Regina's family and the Rieckers to call on one another for help. Peter had assured Regina that his mother wasn't seriously ill, just down with a touch of ague. But since he and his brothers were busy helping their father put up hay, Anna would need help with the milking.

Normally Regina would have jumped at the chance to visit Anna. But Mama's stunning news this morning had shaken her to the core. Mama, too, had broken down and wept bitterly, begging Regina to forgive her for keeping the circumstances of her birth secret for so many years. At that moment, Regina's only focus had been to comfort her mother, assuring her that she forgave her and loved her and Papa very much.

But later, the realization that she had been born to someone else—that a woman she never knew had given birth to her and named her Regina—came crashing down on her like a building. Somehow she had managed to hold her tears through the noon meal. From his concerned glances, she knew Diedrich had sensed something was amiss. So she hadn't found it surprising when he lingered in the kitchen and asked her to walk with him. Not only had she felt it her duty to tell him what she had learned; she had also felt the need to share her burden with him. Yet her whole body had tensed and trembled as she wondered how he would take the news. She felt silly now, thinking of her unfounded worries. She should have known such news would make no difference to him or budge his love for her.

Smiling, she remembered how he had tenderly slipped his arm around her waist and how her tension had drained away at his touch as he guided her to the bench beside the garden. Just having him near, holding her hand and listening, had calmed her as she recounted all Mama had told her. Somehow, sharing it with Diedrich had made everything right. He had even made her laugh with the comment about the name Mudpuddle.

The thought sparked warmth in her chest that radiated throughout her body.

What a wonderful husband he would be. She had hoped to have a few minutes alone with him again today to assure him that she had recovered from the shock the jarring revelation had caused her and that her heart was now easy. But by the time she helped Anna with milking and cooking supper for the Rieckers clan, she would be fortunate to return home in time for Bible reading and prayers.

The sound of quick footsteps turned Regina's attention toward the house. Mama walked toward her carrying a glass jar as quickly as her Holzschuhe allowed. "Here, you must take this good, rich chicken broth to Frau Rieckers." She handed Regina the jar of still-warm broth, which she had covered with a thin scrap of leather tied with a length of twine.

"Ja, Mama." Regina smiled and nodded. The easy relationship she had always enjoyed with her mother had returned, almost as if this morning's events had never happened.

"Regina." Glancing down, Mama paused and her brow furrowed in thought. At length she lifted her face and met Regina's questioning look with a somber one. "Of course I understand you needed to tell Diedrich about how you came to be our daughter. But I will leave to you if you want Anna or anyone else to know of it." Her chin lifted a fraction of an inch. "I and your Vater do not care if others know. It was not for any shame in you that we never mentioned how you became our daughter. It simply did not matter to us. From the moment I took you in my arms, you have been our Tochter as much as Sophie or Elsie. We have nothing for which to be ashamed."

Regina grinned. Diedrich was right. God had blessed her doubly—more than doubly. She threw her arms around her mother's neck. "Of course you have nothing to be ashamed of. And neither do I." Then a thought struck, and she eased away from hugging her mother. "I do think we should add Eva to our daily prayers," she said, wondering why it hadn't occurred to her earlier. "If not for her good judgment, I would not have you and Papa or Sophie and Elsie." A smile she could not stop stretched her lips wide. "Or even Diedrich."

Her brown eyes welling, Mama cupped Regina's face in her hand. "Ja, Tochter. I think that is something we should do." She pulled the handkerchief from her sleeve and dabbed at her eyes. "Eva, I think, would be proud of the woman you have become." As was her way, Mama's mood brightened abruptly. Her lips tugged into a grin, and her tone turned teasing. "And I think she also would approve of your intended."

Mama's words made Regina long to see her sweetheart even more. An idea sparked. Perhaps she could see Diedrich before she left for the Rieckerses' farm. "I have not seen the new house since last week. Unless you think it *unpassend*, I would like to stop by there on my way to Anna's."

Mama paused for a moment, and Regina held her breath. Such a thing might not be considered exactly proper, but she and Diedrich *were* promised, and Herr Rothhaus should be there to act as chaperone.

Mama smiled and gave her a hug. "I think that would be all right." Then her expression turned stern. "But do not stay long, and be sure to get to Herr Rieckers's farm before milking time."

Her heart taking flight, Regina scrambled to the seat of the pony cart. Grinning, she gave her mother a parting wave and flicked the reins against Gypsy's back, sending her trotting down the lane. Despite the shock Regina had experienced this morning, she could not imagine a more perfect life or a more perfect world.

She glanced upward at the azure sky dotted with a few clouds like wooly lambs swimming in a tranquil sea. Did lambs swim? She laughed out loud at her silly thought. Gypsy kept up a fast gait, the clopping of her hooves on the packed dirt mimicking the quick thumping of Regina's heart in anticipation of seeing her sweetheart.

She'd gone about a mile in the direction of the new house when she spotted a figure striding toward her down the dirt road. Diedrich. Her heart bolted then settled into a happy prance. Would the sight of him always evoke the same excitement and joy she now felt? She hoped so.

Waving, she wondered why he was heading home on foot. It was too early for him to come home for supper. Since Herr Rothhaus was not with him, perhaps he was simply in need of a tool back on the farm. As she approached him, she realized he hadn't returned her wave, and now she could see that no smile touched his lips. An ominous sense of unease gripped her.

She reined in Gypsy. "Diedrich. I am on my way to Anna's farm, but wanted to stop and see all the work you and your Vater have done on the house this week."

Still no salutation. No smile or word of greeting. A look of pain crossed his grim features and the tiny yip of unease inside Regina suddenly grew to a growling dread. "Diedrich, what is wrong? Is your Vater injured?"

"Regina, we must talk." Without invitation, he climbed to the seat beside her and took the reins from her now trembling hands. "*Linke*," he called to the pony with two quick clicks of his tongue and pulled on the left line, turning the pony and cart around.

As they veered off the road and headed across a meadow, Regina's dread became a raging fear. She gripped his arm. "Diedrich, please tell me what is the matter."

Still he said nothing. At last, he reined Gypsy to a stop in the shade of a big cottonwood tree beside the meandering stream of Horse Lick Creek. Countless wild thoughts skittered every which way through Regina's mind. Surely if Herr Rothhaus was hurt they wouldn't be sitting here but heading as fast as Gypsy's little legs could carry them toward help. Unless. . . No. She wouldn't think such things. "Diedrich!" She said his name so forcefully she startled the pony, making the animal jump and jerk the wagon. "You must tell me this minute—what is wrong?"

For another long moment, the fluttering of the cottonwood's leaves, the gurgling of the stream, and the chirping of birds filled the silence. At length, Diedrich turned from gazing over the tranquil creek and took Regina's hands in his. His face looked drawn and almost as old as his father's. His eyes—those gentle gray eyes that usually looked at her with awe and love—swam with tears and sorrow. "Regina, I do not know how to tell you this, but Vater is not coming back to the farm."

Regina heard herself gasp. Her ears rang and her head felt light. For an instant, everything around them appeared to spin. If not for Diedrich's strong hands gripping hers, she might have fallen off the cart. With tears streaming down her face, she willed strength back into her weak limbs. Her poor Diedrich. Her poor Liebling. She must stay strong for him. "Oh Diedrich, your Vater is dea—dea. . ." She could not say the word.

"Nein. Vater is well." He shook his head and patted her hand, sending ripples of relief through her. "I did not mean for you to think that." Then his handsome features twisted in a look of anguish. "But what I must tell you is almost as painful."

For the next several minutes Regina sat in stunned disbelief as Diedrich recounted the incredible story his father had told him. A wave of nausea washed over her. Who was she? From what kind of terrible people had she sprung? She fought to keep from losing her dinner over the side of the cart.

Diedrich rubbed her arms in a comforting motion as he had done earlier on the bench beside the garden. "It is sorry I am to tell you this, my Liebchen. I would have rather cut off my own arm than tell you." He shook his head, which hung in sorrow. "But I did not want you to hear of it from anyone else, even your own parents."

Regina struggled to assimilate what he had told her. Herr Rothhaus must despise her. Though Diedrich had not used those exact words, Regina could surmise nothing less. Otherwise, Herr Rothhaus would not have vowed never again to step foot in her home. The ramifications of what this could mean to her and Diedrich and their future plans together hit Regina with the same force as if someone had struck her in the stomach with a wooden club.

Her head began to spin again. As if the shocking news about being adopted wasn't enough to discover in one day, now she must face another soul-jarring disclosure. *Dear Lord, how much more can I bear?* She now understood how Job in the scriptures must have felt. Suddenly a new thought struck, and with it, a new terror that grabbed her in its bloody, gnashing teeth. Her heart—no, her whole insides—felt as if they were crumpling in on themselves. Her lungs seized, and she struggled for breath. Diedrich had brought her here to tell her he no longer wanted to marry her. Herr Rothhaus was his father. Of course Diedrich would choose him over her. With her whole body trembling, she managed to muster enough breath to say, "So you do not want to marry me now." Her words came out in a desolate tone with no hint of a question. She hated the tears streaming down her face.

Diedrich's eyes widened. "Nein." He shook his head. "I mean ja." He slipped his arms around her waist and drew her closer to him. A tender expression softened the drawn lines in his stricken face. "I love you, Regina. I will always love you. And I want you to be my wife. You are mein Liebchen," he whispered, "mein Liebling, mein Schätzchen." His voice broke slightly over the last word. But Regina thought he uttered the endearment with a touch less conviction than he had six weeks ago when he first said those words to her.

A fresh deluge of tears cascaded down her face. "But your Vater will never sanction our marriage now."

Diedrich winced as if she had struck him. The muscles of his jaw moved then set in a look of determination. "Regina, my Vater is a gut man. All my life, I have known him as a kind and just man who tries to live as our Lord would wish. I am sure when he has had time to think on it—to pray on it—he will repent of his harsh words." He heaved a deep sigh. "But for now, I must gather his things and take them to him, for he insists he will live now in the new house, apart from your family."

With that, he turned Gypsy around and headed back home. They rode in grim silence until Diedrich reined the pony to a stop between the house and barn. He handed Regina the reins then cupped her face in his hands and pressed a tender kiss on her lips. Though his eyes looked sad, he gave her a brave smile. "Do not worry, Liebchen. Gott is stronger than any problem. If we pray, I am sure He will hear our prayers and have mercy on us and change Vater's heart."

Regina tried to answer his smile, but her lips refused to support it. She watched him jump to the ground, and her heart quaked. As much as she wanted to believe him, she couldn't help wondering if perhaps this was God's way of telling her and Diedrich that He did not want them to marry.

CHAPTER 19

H onour thy father and thy mother: that thy days may be long upon the land which the Lord thy God giveth thee.'"

At the words from Exodus uttered in Pastor Sauer's resonant voice, the urge to emit a bitter laugh gripped Regina. The biblical edict seemed an impossible one for both her and Diedrich to keep. But laughing aloud in church and embarrassing her parents and Diedrich would not improve her plight. So she sat quietly, her head down and her hands folded in her lap while the silent misery that had held sway over her entire household these past nine days once again engulfed her.

Herr Rothhaus's stunning proclamation had shattered not only Regina's and Diedrich's happiness, but Regina's parents' serenity as well. Mama wept almost daily now, blaming herself for ever having disclosed the truth of Regina's parentage. Frustrated at his inability to soothe Mama, Papa seemed to stay in a nearly perpetual state of anger. Enraged that Herr Rothhaus considered him a liar and a sneak, Papa insisted that Diedrich keep his word and marry Regina. And though Diedrich's firm assurance that he had no plans to break his promise to Regina had somewhat appeased Papa, Papa's stormy mood remained.

Caught squarely in the center were Regina and Diedrich. Despite Diedrich's belief that his father's hard stance would soon soften, Herr Rothhaus showed no sign of moving in that direction. If anything, he seemed even more staunchly opposed to Diedrich and Regina marrying. As the days passed, Regina's hope of the man's attitude changing dwindled, especially since he refused to discuss the matter with either Papa, Diedrich, or even Pastor Sauer.

Morning sunlight streamed through one of the church's open windows and angled warmly across Regina's face. But neither the sun's rays nor the happy chirping of the robin perched on the windowsill could brighten her mood. The future that had once looked so sunny had now turned bleak. The commandment the pastor had read struck her as almost mocking. All her life she had tried diligently to keep God's commandments. Even when she and Diedrich had plotted together to avoid matrimony, they had not disrespected their parents. Instead, they had hoped to gradually—and respectfully—change their parents' minds. Ironically, now that they loved one another and wanted to marry, she could see no way for them to avoid breaking the commandment Pastor Sauer had just read.

Her gaze drifted to her left and the men's side of the sanctuary, and her heart ripped anew. Diedrich sat with his head bowed and his arms resting on his knees. As painful as Herr Rothhaus's rejection was for Regina and her family, she couldn't begin to imagine the agony it inflicted upon Diedrich. Her heart swelled at her darling's unwavering devotion to her. But his decision to defy his father and not cancel their wedding plans had come at a terrible cost to him. And it had proved a bittersweet victory for Regina. Daily she saw the toll that decision took on the man she loved. Though he kept up a brave face, she watched him grow sullen and gaunt. Not a day passed that he didn't assert his love for her, but rarely did she see him smile now. It was as if Herr Rothhaus had ripped a hole in his son's soul, and each day a little more of Diedrich's joy seeped out.

Guilt saturated Regina's heart. She had caused this rift between Diedrich and his father. If Diedrich sinned by defying his father's wishes, didn't Regina sin as well by allowing him to do so? But whether or not Diedrich saw his defiance of his father as a sin, Regina knew his honor would never let him break off their engagement. But if she broke it off, wouldn't she dishonor Papa as well as break her heart and Diedrich's in the bargain? A greater question loomed. Did she even have the courage to break her engagement and send away the man she loved?

Out of the corner of her eye, she caught Anna Rieckers exchanging smiling glances across the aisle with her intended, August Entebrock. To her shame, Regina experienced a stab of jealousy. She'd learned of her friend's engagement only minutes after Diedrich told her that his father had forbidden their marriage. Hearing Anna bubble with excitement about her engagement had driven Regina's hurt even deeper. She had tried hard to set her own heartache aside and rejoice with her friend but had ended up weeping in Anna's arms and spilling the whole awful story to her. And Anna had comforted her, faithfully following the apostle Paul's charge to "weep with them that weep." Sadly, Regina knew that her own concerns had prevented her from living up to the other part of the scripture and rejoicing with Anna as wholeheartedly as she should have.

More guilt. How many sins had Regina committed over the past two weeks? She didn't want to consider the number. *Dear Lord, forgive my transgressions.* But would He forgive her if she purposely continued to sin and to cause Diedrich to sin as well?

Despair settled over her like a dank fog. *Dear Lord, show me the way. Tell me what I should do.*

"'And Jesus said unto her, Neither do I condemn thee: go, and sin no more.'" Pastor Sauer's voice filtered into Regina's silent prayer. The words of the scripture echoed in her ears, and her heart throbbed with a painful ache. She'd asked for

God's direction. And though she may not like the answer, He had given it. Now she just needed the courage to see it through.

The rest of the service passed as in a fog for Regina, the pastor's voice melding with the drone of the honeybees that buzzed around the hollyhocks blooming outside the church's open windows. At last the pastor invoked the benediction, and the congregation filed out of the church—the men first, followed by the women.

Regina's heart felt like a lump of lead in the center of her chest. Though everything in her screamed against it, she knew what she had to do.

Following Mama outside, Regina mumbled an absent pleasantry as she passed Pastor Sauer at the door. While Mama went to talk with Frau Rieckers, who seemed well recovered from her bout of ague, Regina glanced around the crowded churchyard for Diedrich. She saw no reason to prolong the misery. Like the time last month when she got the splinters in her hands, the ones she and Mama pulled out quickly hurt much less than those they had to extract slowly. As Mama had said, "Better short pain than long pain." The same wisdom applied now.

Her gaze roved over the crowd milling about the churchyard. At last she spied Diedrich, and her heart clenched. He and Papa stood together talking with Herr Entebrock and Herr Rieckers and their sons. Regina knew that Papa's encouragement had meant a lot to Diedrich in the wake of his own father's rejection. And Papa had taken Diedrich to his heart as a son in a way he never had with Sophie's husband, Ezra, or Elsie's William. Papa would doubtless take the news of the broken engagement as hard as Diedrich would.

Regina's grip on her resolve slipped, and she swallowed hard. Drawing a fortifying breath, she started to take a step toward the men when someone grasped her arm.

"Regina." Anna's blue eyes were round, her face full of urgency. "I was hoping I would get a chance to talk with you." Tugging on Regina's arm, she pulled her to the side of the church. "I thought I should tell you. August said that Diedrich's father has been working this week on their farm." Glancing down at the ankle-deep grass as their feet, she caught her bottom lip between her teeth. "I thought. . .if you would like. . .I could ask August to talk to his Vater. Maybe Herr Entebrock could intercede—"

"No." Though her heart crimped at her friend's eagerness to help, Regina shook her head. She gave Anna's hand a quick squeeze. "I appreciate you trying to help, Anna, but I do not think such a plan would be wise—or necessary."

Anna gave a frustrated huff. "But you said Herr Rothhaus will not talk to your Vater or Pastor Sauer, or even to Diedrich as long as the two of you are promised." Her shoulders rose and fell with her sigh. "I know you said Diedrich still wants to marry you despite his father's objection." She frowned. "But you are so sad, and it is not right that you should be sad planning your wedding. We must do something to change Herr Rothhaus's mind so he will give you and Diedrich his blessing. Then you can be as happy planning your wedding as I am planning mine." Then her honey-colored brows slipped together and her eyes narrowed suspiciously. "What do you mean by 'not necessary'?"

Regina sighed. She'd told Anna everything else. She might as well tell her what she had decided to do. Bracing for the negative response she knew was coming, she blurted, "I'm going to break my engagement to Diedrich."

Anna's eyes popped to the size of tea saucers; then her face crumpled in a pained look. "But why, Regina?" She held out her hands palms up. "All you've talked about since the Tanners' barn raising is how much you love Diedrich and how you can hardly wait to marry him." The disappointment in Anna's anguished tone smote Regina with remorse. "We promised each other we would have both our weddings in September. You and Diedrich will stand up for me and August; then August and I will stand up for you and Diedrich." It hurt Regina to disappoint her friend, but she might as well get used to the reaction. Telling Mama and Papa would be no easier. Yet as much as she dreaded telling her parents, that trepidation paled compared to the notion of telling Diedrich. Her heart quaked at the thought.

Regina clasped Anna's hands. "Didn't you hear Pastor Sauer? If Diedrich and I marry against his father's will, are we not dishonoring him?" The weight of her sorrow pulled her head down like an iron yoke. "I cannot make Diedrich sin by disobeying his father."

Anger flashed in Anna's eyes, and she snatched her hands from Regina's. "Are you daft, Regina? Don't be foolish. It is Diedrich's father who is wrong, not you or Diedrich. Didn't you hear Pastor Sauer read Colossians 3:21? 'Fathers, provoke not your children to anger, lest they be discouraged.'" Crossing her arms over her chest, she snorted. "I'd say that fits exactly what Herr Rothhaus has done."

Regina couldn't help a grin. She hadn't expected to get a double sermon this morning. And though it warmed her heart to see her good friend's willingness to leap to her defense with such fierce abandon, she couldn't entirely agree. "One sin does not cancel out another, Anna. Besides, how can Diedrich change his father's mind if Herr Rothhaus will not talk to him? And Herr Rothhaus will not talk to Diedrich as long as Diedrich and I are promised."

Sniffing back tears, she gave Anna a hug. "Diedrich still loves me, Anna, and

I love him. Gott willing, our engagement will not stay broken long, and he will be my Verlobter again soon." She forced a smile. "Diedrich assures me that after his Vater has had sufficient time to think about it, he will repent. Just pray he is right and that Gott will help Diedrich change his Vater's heart." Anna opened her mouth as if to make another objection, but Regina held up her hand and Anna closed her mouth. "I know what I am doing is right, Anna. If it is Gott's will, we will both have our September weddings."

Giving a nod of surrender, Anna swiped at a tear meandering down her cheek. At the same moment, Regina glanced over Anna's shoulder to see a smiling August Entebrock walking toward them. Stepping away from Anna, she grinned and whispered, "Dry your eyes. August is coming."

To her credit, Regina felt only joy and not a speck of jealousy as she watched Anna and her tall, blond *Verlobten* walk hand in hand toward Anna's mother.

"They make a nice-looking *Paare*, do they not, mein Liebchen? Almost as nice looking as us." At Diedrich's soft voice and the touch of his hand on her back, Regina jerked.

"Ja. Almost." Her heart turning cartwheels, she pivoted to face him. Somehow she managed to muster a decent smile but wished her voice didn't sound so breathless. It was the first time since his father had disowned him that she'd heard even a hint of a tease in Diedrich's voice, and it did her heart good.

He slipped his arm around her waist, and from force of habit, she leaned into his embrace. Would the change in their formal relationship affect their familiar one? She prayed it wouldn't, but feared there was no way it could not. He began to guide her toward the wagon. "August tells me that he and Anna are planning a September wedding as well." His voice, which had begun on a light tone, ended on a sad one. Had August also mentioned to Diedrich that his father was working on the Entebrock farm?

Stopping, she swiveled to face him. She might as well pull out the emotional splinter now. "Diedrich, there is something I need to talk with you about."

"Oh, there you two are." Mama bustled up and took hold of Regina's arm. "I would love to visit more, but we have that turkey Vater killed yesterday roasting in the oven. We must get home soon to see to it, or it will be as dry and tough as leather."

Instead of annoyance, Regina felt a rush of relief at the intrusion. She couldn't break her engagement to Diedrich with Mama, Papa, and half of St. John's congregation looking on. She needed time alone with him to fully explain her reasoning. Perhaps they could find a private moment together after dinner.

As they headed down the road toward home in the wagon, talk turned to the upcoming threshing of the wheat crops around Sauers and Dudleytown. Every summer the community came together, everyone helping each other harvest their wheat crop. And with the new threshing machine Herr Entebrock bought this spring, the work should go even quicker this year. In exchange for help harvesting his own wheat crop, he had promised the use of his machine to his neighbors as well.

Regina loved threshing time. It was like a big party that moved from farm to farm and went on for a month or more. The women of the community gathered in the kitchen of the host farm and put together fantastic meals for their men, who labored long hours in the fields. She especially enjoyed when everyone came to her family's farm. Would she and Diedrich ever host a threshing at their own home? Her heart pinched at the thought. Not unless God changed Herr Rothhaus's heart and mind. And at this point, it was beginning to look like it might take a miracle.

Sitting beside her, Diedrich absently laced his fingers with Regina's as he talked with Papa. His thumb gently caressed the back of her hand, sending pleasant tingles up her arm. Her heart throbbed painfully. She fought the urge to cling to him and weep. They loved each other. It was not fair that she must let him go to have any chance of their gaining his father's blessing. She prayed she wouldn't have to let him go forever.

Blinking back tears, she lifted her face to the warm breeze as Papa turned the wagon into the long lane that led to their house. If Diedrich caught her crying, he would want to know why, and this was not the time or place to tell him.

As they neared the house, the sight of a wagon and team parked between the house and barn swept away Regina's anguished thoughts.

Mama gripped Papa's arm and gave a little gasp. "Ernst, is that not Sophie and Ezra's team? And why would they have chairs and feather ticks in the back of the wagon?"

Mixed emotions swirled in Regina's chest at the prospect of seeing her eldest sister. Though she itched to hold her baby nephew, Henry, she and Sophie could rarely share a room for a half hour without getting on each other's nerves. She had often wondered how she and Sophie could be sisters and yet be so different from each other. But since she had learned they were not blood sisters, their different personalities made a little more sense.

When they had all climbed down from the wagon, Sophie appeared from a wedge of shade beside the house. Glancing behind Sophie, Regina could now see Ezra playing with two-year-old Henry on a quilt spread out on the grass.

Mama beamed as she hurried toward the little family. "Sophie, Ezra, it is wunderbar that you have come. Where is my kleines Henry, my liebes Enkelkind?" But as Sophie neared, the distraught look on her face wiped the smile from Mama's.

Practically running the last few steps, Sophie threw herself into Mama's arms and sobbed. "Oh Mama, Papa. You must help us. We are desperate!"

CHAPTER 20

Feeling slightly awkward, Diedrich stood behind Regina, cupping her shoulders with his hands to silently lend his support. Obviously something was not well with her eldest sister and family. The last thing Regina needed was another emotional blow.

Frau Seitz hugged her eldest daughter and murmured words of comfort while alternately begging her to explain the cause of her distress. The woman's husband walked toward them, their young child perched on the crook of his arm. No hint of a smile touched Ezra Barnes's bearded face, which looked haggard and drawn.

Herr Seitz's frowning glance bounced between his distraught daughter and his son-in-law. "Sophie, Ezra, you must tell us now. What is the matter?"

Frau Seitz gently pushed Sophie away enough to look into her tear-reddened eyes. "Sophie, what is wrong?"

Sophie sniffed and for a moment appeared to get a better grip on her emotions. "We—we have been put out of our home." The last word dissolved into another wrenching sob.

Ezra, his eyes also red-rimmed, approached his wife and rubbed her back with his free hand. In a gentle tone that held only a hint of scolding, he said something to her in English. Diedrich wished he had worked harder to learn the language.

The toddler, whom Frau Seitz had called Henry, whimpered and sucked his thumb so hard he made soft popping noises. Diedrich's heart went out to the little boy, who appeared at once confused and frightened. Fidgeting in his father's grasp, he began to whimper louder, and Regina reached up and eased him from Ezra's embrace.

Rocking the child in her arms, she whispered comforting hushes while brushing soft brown curls from his round cherubic face. "Shh, mein lieber Junge, shh." She bounced him in her arms and patted his back then kissed his rosy cheek.

At the sight, Diedrich's heart turned over. In a flash, he caught a glimpse of what their future might hold, and a sweet longing pulsed in his chest. What a wonderful mother she would make. How he would love to drive her back to St. John's Church this minute and ask Pastor Sauer to join them in holy matrimony. But too many things needed to be resolved before that could happen, including whatever plagued Sophie and her little family.

Herr Seitz harrumphed. "We must all go in the house and talk, I think."

258

Moving as one, the group headed to the house. When everyone had situated themselves around the kitchen table, a slightly more composed Sophie, speaking in German, began to explain the family's plight.

"You know that Ezra's brother, Dave, brought him into his wheelwright business shortly before we married." Frau and Herr Seitz nodded, worry lines etching deep crevices in their faces. Sophie drew in a ragged, fortifying breath. "Lately, business has not been good." She sniffed. "A new wagon shop opened on the other side of town. Their operation is larger, and they began to undercut us in price." She gave her husband a brave smile. "Dave never liked it that Ezra fixed wheels for people on promise of payment. And when business fell off, it irritated him even more." Her fingers trembled across her cheek, wiping away a tear. "They argued all the time. Then Dave began to claim that money was missing from each day's till and accused Ezra of taking it."

Frau Seitz pulled the handkerchief from her sleeve and handed it across the table to her daughter, who wiped her eyes and delicately blew her nose. "Well, one thing led to another. Ezra and Dave got into a terrible argument, and Dave fired Ezra."

Regina shifted a squirming Henry on her lap. "But surely when Dave calms down, he will listen to reason. Perhaps you are being too hasty."

Diedrich couldn't help wondering if Regina was mentally comparing Ezra's situation with his brother to Diedrich's feud with his father.

Sophie shot Regina a scornful glare and snorted. "Don't you think we tried to reason with him?" she snapped. "He fired Ezra two weeks ago. We've been trying to reason with him ever since." Her face crumpled again, and she began to weep in earnest. "Because money was so tight, we had gotten way behind on our note for the house. By the time Dave fired Ezra, we had already missed three payments. So when Tom Pemberton down at the bank found out that Ezra had lost his position, he told us he couldn't float us any longer and said we would have to move out so the bank could resell the house."

Frau groaned. "Oh Sophie. Why did you not tell us sooner? Why did you let things get so bad?" She shook her head. "I was afraid something like this might happen. I knew you should not have bought such an expensive house."

Sophie sobbed, and Ezra gathered her in his arms. "We thought business would get better," she mumbled from her husband's shoulder. "We never imagined Ezra would be out of work."

Herr Seitz shook his head and put his hand on his wife's arm. "None of that matters now, Catharine. The past is the past. It is gut that Ezra has a skill. I am sure he will find work soon." In the midst of all the gloomy faces, his brightened.

"For now, you will live here with us, and Ezra can help me and Diedrich with the threshing and putting up the hay."

He rose, and everyone followed. With a smile that looked strained, Herr Seitz glanced at Diedrich and Ezra. "Now we must give the kitchen to the *Frauen* so they can make us dinner." Lifting Henry from Regina's lap, he headed to the front room, and Ezra and Diedrich followed.

There, Herr Seitz and Ezra conversed in English with Herr Seitz translating in German for Diedrich. Henry played on the floor with a ball of yarn his grandfather had found in Frau Seitz's sewing basket. Though he didn't feel it proper to ask, Diedrich couldn't help but wonder where everyone would fit in the house.

Later, a somber mood reigned over the noon meal, lightened occasionally by Henry's rambunctious antics. Mostly the conversation was in English, which Diedrich assumed was for Ezra's benefit. Still far from proficient in the language, Diedrich struggled to follow what was being said. Between the little he could glean and what Regina translated for him, he gathered that the talk stayed mostly on the upcoming threshing. For each time Ezra's brother's name was mentioned, Sophie would begin to weep.

Diedrich understood Sophie's distress. But Regina's reticent attitude both perplexed and troubled him. She scarcely looked at him. And when she did, her eyes welled with tears. Even more worrisome was his sense that her sadness didn't entirely spring from her sister and brother-in-law's problems. In the churchyard she had said she needed to talk with him about something. Could whatever was on her mind earlier be the cause of her odd behavior? He was determined to talk with her privately after dinner and find out.

After the meal, Diedrich again joined Ezra and Herr Seitz in the front room while the women tidied up the kitchen. Sitting quietly, he only half listened as the other two men discussed the Barneses' financial problems. His mind kept drifting to Regina, wondering what she might have wanted to discuss with him.

"Diedrich, I—I need to talk with you." Her voice from the doorway surprised him, bringing him upright in his chair. He experienced a flash of alarm at her grim tone and the odd way her gaze refused to hold his.

His heart pounding with trepidation, Diedrich sprung from his seat. Mumbling an apology to Herr Seitz and Ezra, he carefully sidestepped Henry on the floor and followed Regina into the kitchen, where Sophie and Frau Seitz still worked. With her head bowed and her arms crossed over her chest, Regina stalked purposefully through the kitchen and out the back door. His concern growing with each step, Diedrich trailed behind, trying to think of anything he might have done or said to upset her.

Lengthening his steps, he caught up with her at the corner of the house. He put his hand on her shoulder, bringing her to a stop. "Regina, what is it? Tell me what is the matter."

Finally, she turned. The tears welling in her blue eyes ripped at his heart. Obviously he had misjudged the extent to which Sophie and Ezra's situation bothered Regina.

He drew her into his arms. "It will be all right, mein Liebchen. Your Vater is right. With Ezra's skills, he is sure to find work as a wheelwright soon. Until then, Sophie, Ezra, and Henry have a home here with family who love them." It felt good to hold her in his arms and comfort her.

To his surprise she pushed away from him. She shook her head, tears streaming down her cheeks. "I am not upset about Sophie and Ezra." She made impatient swipes at the wetness on her face as if angry at herself for crying.

Diedrich's bewilderment mounted along with his feelings of helplessness. "Then why *are* you crying, Liebchen?"

She stepped away, and fresh tears flooded down her face. "Please, you must not call me that."

"But why?" Diedrich took her hands in his. He couldn't guess what might be troubling her, but he couldn't comfort her until he found the cause of her anxiety. Her pain-filled eyes stabbed at his heart. He rubbed the backs of her hands with his thumbs. "Have I done something to upset you? If I have, I beg your forgiveness—"

"Diedrich, I must break our engagement." With that astounding declaration, she slipped her hands from his. Turning, she walked toward the garden bench he had begun to think of as theirs.

Feeling as if someone had punched him hard in the stomach, Diedrich stood stunned, unable to think or move. When his frozen limbs thawed and his mind began working again, his thoughts raced. He followed her to the bench and sat down beside her, praying she did not mean the words she had said. Surely they were simply a result of the several emotional blows she had suffered over the past couple of weeks.

He tried to capture her hands, but she pulled them away and folded them in her lap. Frustration tangled with the pain balling in his chest. "Why, Regina? Why would you say such a thing?" Had she decided she didn't love him after all? He couldn't believe it. Gripping her arms, he forced her to meet his gaze. His heart writhed. "Do you not love me, Regina? Is that what you are saying? You no longer want to marry me?"

The agony in her lovely eyes both tortured him and gave him hope. "Nein. That is not what I am saying."

Diedrich thought his head would explode. Having earlier watched Ezra Barnes deal with Sophie's tears, he felt a comradeship with the man. Mustering his patience, he blew out a long breath. "But if you still love me, why do you wish to break our engagement?"

Regina sniffed, making Diedrich regret the sterner tone he had taken. "It is not that I *wish* to break our engagement. I feel I *must* break it for now, if we are ever to have the chance to marry."

Diedrich's temples throbbed. He strove to keep a tight rein on his patience. "You are speaking nonsense, Regina. Either you want to marry me, or you don't."

New tears sketched down her face, smiting him with remorse. "Weren't you listening to Pastor Sauer's sermon?" She folded her arms over her chest as if to close herself away from him. "By defying your Vater and keeping our engagement, are you not dishonoring him?"

Diedrich winced at her words that reminded him of his painful separation from Father. Not a moment passed that their estrangement didn't gouge a fresh wound in his heart. Every day as he worked in the hayfields with Herr Seitz, he expected to look up at any moment and see Father striding toward them, smiling and waving his hand. But so far, it hadn't happened. More than once Diedrich had started toward the new log house with the intent to confront Father and try again to make him see reason. But each time he had turned back, fearing his efforts would only result in doing irreparable damage to their fragile relationship. Only Regina's love and his faith that God would eventually soften Father's heart had kept him going. It hurt him that Regina lacked the patience to wait for God to work.

Since her hands remained folded and tucked firmly against her body, he gently grasped her arms. "Regina, it has only been two weeks. I am sure that Vater will repent and give us his blessing soon. Besides, if we break our engagement, he will have less reason to change his mind. I have faith that Gott will change Vater's heart if we only pray and have patience."

Scooting back away from his grasp, she waved her hand through the air, barely missing a black and orange butterfly flitting past. "And you think your Vater will one morning wake and decide on his own that what he is doing is wrong, and he will then come and give us his blessing?"

Diedrich ignored the hint of scorn in her voice. "Perhaps it will happen that way. How can I know how Gott will work?"

She huffed. "But that is just it. Don't you see? Gott uses us to do His work.

Your Vater loves you, Diedrich. When he sees that what he is doing is making you sad, there is a much greater chance he will change his mind about us marrying." She grasped his forearm, and her crystal-blue eyes, which matched the sky behind her, pleaded for understanding. "But as things are, he is *not* seeing you. He can put you and me out of his mind and go on being stubborn as long as he wants. So if you can go to him and honestly tell him that we are no longer planning to marry, he will talk to you again. Then you will at least have a chance to convince him to bless our marriage."

Pondering her words, Diedrich rubbed his chin, already sprouting new stubble since his early morning shave. Her reasoning made some sense. But it also forced him to consider the possibility he had so far refused to face. What if Father never repented and gave them his blessing? No. He would not consider that. He trusted God to change Father's mind, and Regina needed to do the same. "You may be right. Perhaps I can more easily change Vater's mind if I can talk with him. But to me, breaking our engagement is like saying to Gott that I do not trust Him." Another thought popped into his head to bolster his argument. "Besides, I promised your Vater we would remain engaged. If we do not, are we not dishonoring *him*?"

For a moment, Regina's pale brows knit together in thought, giving him hope. But she shook her head. "I do not think it is the same thing. Papa would be sad if we broke our engagement, but he knows we cannot marry without Herr Rothhaus's blessing. He would understand."

Frustration built like rising steam in Diedrich's chest. He wanted to throw up his hands and tell her that none of this mattered because in a few days Father would doubtless change his mind. Instead, he couldn't resist trying another line of reasoning in an attempt to make her see things his way. "But by your thinking, we were dishonoring both our fathers when we decided not to marry after they had agreed between them that we would." He arched an eyebrow at her. "Yet as I remember, you had no scriptural objection to our plan."

Her face pinked prettily, and he couldn't stop a grin. What fun it would be to mentally spar with Regina for the rest of his life.

A challenge flashed in her blue eyes, and her unflinching gaze met his squarely. "And do you remember what our plan was?"

"To convince our fathers we should not marry." The words popped out of his mouth before he thought and was met by her triumphant and somewhat smug smile.

She nodded. "That is so. And if we convinced them, then we would not be disobeying or dishonoring them by not marrying."

Blowing a quick breath of surrender, he gave her a sad smile. "You are a formidable opponent, Regina Seitz." Yet he was prepared to surrender only this one skirmish—not the entire war. "I still believe by remaining engaged, we will sooner turn Vater's thinking and win his blessing."

She swiveled on the bench and looked across the potato patch with it plants now sporting white blossoms. For a long moment, she seemed to focus her attention on a bluish-gray bird with a snowy belly perched on a fence post beyond the garden. The bird's head darted about as if following some unseen insect. Then, giving a bright whistling call followed by several chirps, he took flight. When he had gone, Regina sighed and pressed her clasped hands into the well of her apron between her knees. "So you do not believe you are dishonoring your Vater?"

"Nein." He blew out a breath. "I do not know." Why did she feel the need to force him to think of things he would rather not consider? He couldn't keep the irritation from his voice. "But Vater is the one who is wrong. It is not from any belief that we are poorly matched that he is against our marriage, but because he refuses to forgive your birth Vater and Großvater." He gazed down at her lovely face, and his heart throbbed with love for her. He had to make her understand. Cradling the side of her face with his hand, he gentled his voice. "I know you want to do as our Lord commands, but I think you are wrong in this."

She shook her head sadly, and his heart plummeted. Her eyes glistened with welling tears. "When you heard me tell Eli that I loved you, I knew you would give up your dream of going to California and marry me so as not to break my heart. That is why I lied and told you I didn't love you." A tear beaded on her lower lash then slipped down her petal-soft cheek. "I did not want to wake each morning wondering if that was the day I would see regret in your eyes."

Diedrich stifled a groan. Surely she didn't think he still harbored dreams of heading west. "Regina, I told you. All the gold in California means nothing to me now. You are all that matters to me."

She gave him a weak smile. "I believe you. But even if you are right about the commandment and we would not be dishonoring your Vater by remaining engaged against his wishes, you still need to mend the rift between the two of you. I want your Vater to give us his blessing, but I want him to give it with a full heart, not because he feels forced to give it. I want our family to be whole and full of love, not riddled with anger and resentment." She kissed him on the cheek, her warm breath sending tingles down his neck and spine. "I love you, Diedrich. But for now I must break our engagement. Go to your Vater and tell him so. Then pray that with Gott's help you can change his mind about us marrying. Because until your Vater gives us his blessing, I cannot promise to marry you."

CHAPTER 21

These are some of the nicest cherries I have seen in a long time." Sophie smiled up from her work of pitting the bright red fruit at the far end of the table. "Did they come from that little tree at the east end of the barn?"

Using the back of her wrist, Regina brushed a strand of hair from her face before applying the rolling pin to a lump of pie dough. "Yes. Mama said she was surprised at how nice they are after we had such a cold winter." Her heart smiled with her lips. She couldn't remember spending a more amiable hour with Sophie. In fact, Regina noticed that her eldest sister's attitude toward her had sweetened considerably since Easter, when Sophie and her family had last visited. Regina couldn't have been more surprised when Sophie suggested that Mama play with Henry outside while she and Regina work together making pies for the threshing at the Entebrocks' farm Monday.

Sophie worked the paring knife's sharp point into another plump cherry and deftly plucked out the pit. "I did notice at Easter that the tree was covered with tight buds." She gave Regina a sideways glance, and her next words tiptoed out carefully. "That must have been just before Diedrich and Herr Rothhaus arrived."

At Diedrich's name, a painful longing pricked Regina's chest. "Ja," she managed to murmur. She hadn't seen Diedrich since she broke their engagement almost a week ago. In fact, he had left shortly after their conversation. Papa and Mama had racked their brains trying to figure the best sleeping arrangement in order to make room for Sophie, Ezra, and Henry. They decided that Regina should give the young family her larger upstairs bedroom, which she had once shared with Sophie and Elsie. But that put both her and Diedrich downstairs, which would not be proper. Then Diedrich took Papa aside, informing him that Regina had broken their engagement and explaining why. Confident his father would accept him now that he was no longer betrothed to Regina, he suggested that Regina take his downstairs room and he would move to the new log house with his father.

At Diedrich's news, surprise, chagrin, and sorrow had flashed across Papa's face in quick succession. In the end, with a sigh of resignation and a look of profound disappointment, he had reluctantly agreed with Diedrich's suggestion. Regina sniffed as hot tears stung the back of her nose and filled her eyes. She smashed the rolling pin down hard on the dough. In one afternoon, she had broken the hearts of the two men she loved most in the world.

Sophie rose and came around the table to put her arm around Regina's shoulders, startling her with the tender gesture. "Forgive me, Regina. I didn't mean to upset you by mentioning the Rothhauses." She patted Regina's shoulder. "I know this has all been very confusing for you. I blame Papa." Irritation edged her voice. "He never should have made such a deal with Herr Rothhaus in the first place. Why, Mama says he didn't even tell her about it until the letter came saying Herr Rothhaus and his son were on their way."

Regina sniffed and gave her sister a brave smile. She knew Sophie meant well, but she could never make herself wish Diedrich had not come into her life. "It is all right, Sophie. I believe Gott will use Diedrich to soften Herr Rothhaus's heart."

Sophie stiffened and stepped away from her. "Hmm." She pressed her hand to her chest, and her voice turned breathless. "I must say, I am still stunned by it all myself. When Mama told me how she and Papa had adopted you, I nearly fell over." She shook her head and clucked her tongue. "And on top of it all, there is that awful business about the Rothhauses and your real Vater."

A flash of anger leapt in Regina's chest. A faceless man by the name of Hermann Zichwolff may have given her life, but in her mind, Papa would always be her real father. "Papa is my Vater just as he is your Vater." She hated the defensive tone in her voice.

Sophie gave an odd little giggle and waved her hand in the air. "Of course Papa is your Vater. You know what I mean."

Regina wasn't sure she did but decided to let it go. She hated to spoil the amicable mood she and Sophie had enjoyed together this afternoon.

Another little giggle warbled through Sophie's voice. "It is a bit funny though, since Elsie and I always thought you got your blond hair from Papa." She sashayed back to her end of the table. Dipping a tin cup into the sack of sugar, she scooped out a heaping cupful and poured it over the cherries she had pitted.

"I suppose." Regina wished Sophie would find something other than Regina's adoption to talk about.

Sophie reached into the sack of flour and grabbed a handful, which she sprinkled over the sugared fruit. "For a girl who was always a bit of a dull goose, you certainly have turned into a bundle of surprises. When we were here at Easter, Elsie was convinced you had set your cap for that Tanner boy." Another giggle. Shriller now. "Then two weeks later, I get a letter from Mama saying you are engaged to someone just arrived from Venne."

Regina hoped she was imagining the snide tone that seemed to have crept into Sophie's voice.

Sophie paused in mixing the flour into the cherries to shoot Regina a critical glance. "Be careful with that dough, Regina. Rolling it too hard will make it tough." Suddenly, her demeanor brightened. Her lips quirked in a sly grin, and her voice turned teasing. "Eli Tanner, is he not the miller's son? An exceptionally handsome boy, if memory serves."

Regina shrugged as she transferred the pie dough to two waiting pans. Once she would have agreed. But she had glimpsed meanness in Eli's character that now made him ugly to her. Regina was no happier with Sophie's new subject of conversation than her last. She almost blurted that Diedrich far surpassed Eli in both looks and character, but Diedrich was another subject she would rather not discuss with Sophie.

Humming gaily, Sophie picked up the crockery bowl of prepared fruit filling and carried it to Regina. With the bowl tucked between the crook of her arm and her waist, she plucked out a cherry and popped it in her mouth. Her brows knit in deliberation as she chewed. After a moment, she picked out another cherry and held it out to Regina. "Here, taste this and tell me if you think it is sweet enough."

Regina couldn't remember the last time Sophie had asked her opinion on anything. Reveling in her sister's uncharacteristically congenial mood, she acquiesced, opening her mouth to accept the sugar- and flour-coated cherry Sophie dropped on her tongue. The earthy taste of the flour and the sugar's sweetness blended perfectly with the tart fruit to induce a pleasant tingle at the back of Regina's jaw.

Regina gave her sister a smile and nod. "I think you have it just right, Sophie," she said as she munched the cherry. "Ezra must think he married the best pie baker in three counties."

Sophie chuckled and raked the cherries into the dough-lined pans with a wooden spoon. "Well, whether or not he thinks so, he at least had better say so." She angled a grin up at Regina. "You learned from Mama, just like Elsie and I did. I am sure whomever you marry will like your pies as much as Ezra likes mine."

Whomever I marry. Regina stifled a sardonic snort. It was inconceivable to her to imagine making pies for, keeping house for, living with, and loving any other man than Diedrich. The past six days had crept by in agonizing slowness. The week she had spent helping Elsie, she had missed Diedrich. But then she had still guarded her heart, expecting him to leave for California. Since then, she had allowed him to claim her heart completely. So since their parting Sunday afternoon, the longing to see his face—to touch his hand—had become a palpitating ache in her chest. It burrowed ever deeper, intensifying by the day. Sunday she was so sure she had done the right thing. Now she wondered. Torturous thoughts darted about in her head like a hound after a warren of rabbits. Did Diedrich miss her, too? Did he lie awake at night trying to bring her face into focus in his mind? Had he yet broached the subject of Regina to his father? Did he even plan to? No. She must not think that way. *Please, Lord, give Diedrich the right words to change his father's mind and heart.*

At least tomorrow was Sunday. Surely he would come to services and she could see him then. But if his father came, too, it might be difficult for her and Diedrich to find a chance to talk.

Sophie looked up from cutting strips of dough for the pies' latticed tops. "I must commend you on your good sense, Regina. It was very wise of you to break off your engagement to Diedrich."

Regina swiped at the tears welling in her eyes. "Then you do not agree with Mama and Papa and Diedrich? They feel if I hadn't broken our engagement, Herr Rothhaus might be forced to examine his heart more closely and thus change his thinking."

Sophie dropped the paring knife to the table with a clatter. Turning, she took Regina by the shoulders and fixed her with a stern look. "Regina, I know that Mama and Papa do not agree with us, but they are just disappointed and are not thinking clearly. I am absolutely certain you did the right thing. In that, you must believe me." Her brown eyes intensified until they looked almost as black as coal. "Whatever you do, you must not reinstate your engagement to Diedrich. Nothing good can come of it."

"You mean I shouldn't reinstate it without his Vater's blessing." Though she knew it was an oversight on Sophie's part, Regina couldn't bear to leave the thought where her sister had left it.

Sophie let go of Regina's shoulders and turned to face the table again. With a flip of her wrist, she waved a flour-covered hand through the air. "Of course," she said lightly. "You know what I mean."

Moving to Sophie's side, Regina began placing the strips of dough over one of the pies, weaving them into a lattice design. It heartened her to know that she had an ally in Sophie. At the same time, it caused an uneasy feeling in her breast. She had trusted her parents' guidance all her life. The only time she had ever questioned a decision of theirs was when Papa had chosen Diedrich for her husband. And now she could see that even in that, Papa was right. In trying to prevent Diedrich from opposing his father, Regina had no choice but to oppose her own parents. So although she was glad Sophie understood her thinking and supported her, it didn't make her feel any better about her decision.

∽

"Do not look so glum, Sohn." Father pressed his hand on Diedrich's shoulder and every muscle in Diedrich's body tensed.

Shrugging off his father's hand, Diedrich shifted on the low stool where he perched near the hearth with the open Bible on his lap. "I am not glum, Vater. I am but reading the scriptures." May God forgive his half-truth. His melancholy mood was far beyond glum. And gazing unseeing at a printed page while his mind was two miles away with Regina could not in truth be called reading.

The past week had proven a test of Diedrich's patience, faith, and fortitude. Facing Father and admitting that Regina had broken their engagement was hard enough. But seeing the look of relief and joy the announcement brought to his parent's face had torn his heart asunder. He would have turned on his heel and walked back to the Seitz farm that instant, if not for his father's happy tears and welcoming outstretched arms. It had irked Diedrich to be made to feel like the prodigal son when he knew he had done no wrong, but at least he and Father were talking again. And his and Regina's future happiness depended on his rebuilding a relationship with his father.

Father gave a sigh of contentment as he eased down on the seat of the rocking chair he had built during Diedrich's absence. Besides working each day at the Entebrock farm, Father's industry over the past weeks was evident in the several pieces of new furniture that now graced the house. "And which of the scriptures are you reading?"

Diedrich blinked and focused on the open book draped across his knee. A few minutes earlier, he and Father had endured another quiet supper during which the tension between them was thicker than the two-day-old stew they had dined upon. For the moment, their fragile and often uneasy truce seemed dependent on an unspoken agreement not to mention Regina. So in an effort to discourage conversation with his father and to be alone with his thoughts, Diedrich had simply opened the Bible and pretended to read. He glanced at the top of the open page and said, "Proverbs." He wished he had managed to keep the tone of surprise from his voice. Fortunately, Father didn't seem to notice.

Leaning back in the chair, Father emitted a contented grunt and folded his arms over his stomach. "Ah, Proverbs. *Prima.* There is much wisdom there."

Diedrich was tempted to say that perhaps Father could benefit from Solomon's wisdom. But he bit back the retort. To the best of his ability, he'd tried to stay respectful in his words and actions toward Father, trusting that God would bless his efforts and soften Father's heart toward Regina.

Father rocked his chair forward. "Read to me some of what you have been reading."

Caught unprepared, Diedrich scanned the open page. He angled the book to better catch the waning daylight streaming through the front window. His gaze lit on the thirteenth verse of the fifteenth chapter. "'A merry heart maketh a cheerful countenance: but by sorrow of the heart the spirit is broken.'"

Father's brow furrowed deeper with thought, and he absently grazed his chin whiskers with his knuckles. "Read more."

Diedrich dutifully sought the fourteenth verse and began reading. "'The heart of him that hath understanding seeketh knowledge: but the mouth of fools feedeth on foolishness.'"

Father flipped his hand in the air, indicating Diedrich should continue reading.

"'All the days of the afflicted are evil: but he that is of a merry heart hath a continual feast.'"

With a long sigh, Father rocked forward, his hands gripping the curved arms of the rocking chair. "I have been thinking, Sohn. This country we have come to is much bigger than the county of Jackson or even the state of Indiana."

Diedrich feared the direction his father's thoughts seemed to be taking. But he would let him have his say.

Craning his neck around, Father glanced out the front window. "There are many other German settlements besides this one in many other states." Looking down, he blew a quick breath through his nose. "The scriptures are right. It is not gut for a man to be sad. Because Herr Seitz did not deal with us honestly, your heart is sad." Hanging his head, he shook it in sorrow. "I did not bring you here to be sad."

Diedrich wanted to scream that he would not be sad if Father would only give him and Regina his blessing to marry. But quarreling with Father would not help his cause. So instead, he said, "I am not sad, Father." And at this moment, he told the truth. He was furious. Unable to sit and listen to any more of Father's musings, he stood abruptly, forgetting the Bible on his lap. The book dropped to the floor with a thud.

Father bent to pick it up, and a folded square of yellowed paper fluttered to the floor. He began to unfold it. "What is this?"

For an instant, Diedrich's heart caught with his breath. He knew exactly what Father held in his hand. He had long forgotten about the map to the California goldfields that he'd tucked in the pages of the Bible. Diedrich heaved a resigned sigh. "It is a map showing the way to the goldfields in California." None of it mattered now, so he no longer saw any reason to keep his earlier plans hidden from Father.

Father's eyes popped, and his jaw sagged as Diedrich told how he had secretly planned to avoid the marriage Father and Herr Seitz had arranged between him and Regina. Diedrich huffed a sardonic snort. "I was going to make us rich." His lips tugged up in a fond smile, and his voice softened with thoughts of Regina. "But then I found something far more valuable here." For a moment, Diedrich worried that Father might make an unkind comment about Regina—something he would never abide.

But the distant look in Father's eyes suggested he had stopped listening. His eyes wide, he perused the map. A smile crawled across his face until it stretched wide. With a sudden burst of laughter, he slapped his hand down on his knee. "That is where we should go, Sohn. I believe Gott put this idea in your head because He knew things would not go well for us here with Herr Seitz." His eyes sparked with a look of excitement Diedrich had not seen in them since they first embarked for America.

Diedrich was about to say he had no intention of going anywhere without Regina when Father popped up from his seat and pressed his hand on Diedrich's shoulder. His smile still splitting his face, Father gazed at the map in his hand and bobbed his head. "Ja. When we have earned enough to pay Seitz for our passage, he can have back his land and this house. We will go to California as you planned."

CHAPTER 22

oward. The word echoed in Diedrich's head as if hollered down a well. He bent and scooped up an armful of ripe wheat. Snagging another handful of the cut grain from the field, he absently wound slender stalks around the bundle he held in the crook of his arm, making a sheaf. Pitching the sheaf into the waiting wagon, he glanced up at the morning sky. Blue. Blue as Regina's eyes. The wheat reminded him of her hair. His heart ached to its very center.

Pausing, he dragged off his hat and ran his forearm across his sweaty brow. He glanced across the wheat field dotted with workers toward the Entebrock farmhouse situated beyond the barn. He could barely make out the white clapboard structure half hidden by several large maple trees that surrounded it. Somewhere in the kitchen, Regina worked with the other women of Sauers, preparing the noon meal. The moment he and Father arrived this morning, Diedrich began searching for her face among the gathering crowd. But just as he caught a glimpse of her climbing down from the Seitzes' wagon with her mother and sister, Father had stepped to his side and steered him toward Herr Entebrock's new Whitman thresher, eager to show him the workings of the machine.

Coward. Diedrich loathed the thought of branding himself with such an onerous label. Yet what else could he call himself when he had allowed the fear of his father's ire to keep him from the woman he loved?

He pitched another bundle of wheat toward the wagon with such force it almost sailed over it. Saturday evening when Father found the map on which Diedrich had drawn the route to the California goldfields and vowed the two of them should go, Diedrich had not disputed him. Not once since reconciling with Father had he stated outright that he still wanted to marry Regina. Instead, by his silence, he had allowed Father to think he had abandoned the notion of ever making her his wife. Although he realized the prudence of keeping his own counsel and not risking an argument and possibly another estrangement from Father, his reticence felt ignoble.

Anger and shame twisted in his gut like the straws he twisted around another bundle of wheat. "Coward." This time, he mumbled the word aloud in a guttural growl that sounded to his own ears like the snarl of a wounded animal. Surely the word fit his actions yesterday at church.

For days he had looked forward to Sunday and the opportunity to see Regina again. The two weeks Diedrich and his father were estranged, Father had not attended St. John's Church. He had even rejected Pastor Sauer's and Ernst Seitz's efforts to speak to him about his hard feelings toward Herr Seitz. So it had come as somewhat of a surprise when Father announced that he would be accompanying Diedrich to services.

Remembering his dismay at learning he would not be attending services alone, guilt nipped at Diedrich's conscience. Although glad that Father would be in the Lord's house, he had hoped for an uninhibited opportunity to speak with Regina. Instead, he and Regina were forced to hide their affection for each other when in Father's sight. They had managed to exchange a precious few sweet glances during the service and later across the churchyard. The memory of those tender looks filleted Diedrich's heart.

But at least the pastor's sermon on forgiving neighbors seemed to have some positive effect on both Father and Herr Seitz. Immediately following the service, Herr Seitz had approached Father and asked his forgiveness. He vowed he had never intended to trick or defraud Father or Diedrich in any way. And claiming no knowledge of Father's feud with the Zichwolffs, he explained that having raised Regina from infancy, he had simply always considered her his daughter. Father had grudgingly accepted Herr Seitz's explanation and handshake, and the men had parted; if not exactly friends, then at least not sworn enemies.

At the sight, hope had sparked in Diedrich's chest that Herr Seitz might have actually cracked the wall of malice Father had built against Regina. But while Father forgave Herr Seitz for not divulging Regina's heritage, he had made it clear he still could not sanction a marriage between Diedrich and Regina. At that statement, Diedrich had seen anger flash in Herr Seitz's eyes—anger that had matched Diedrich's own emotion at Father's words. Yet both he and Regina's father had failed to champion her in voice. Diedrich understood Herr Seitz's reluctance to cause a row in the churchyard while his family and neighbors were within earshot. Diedrich, too, was hesitant to jeopardize the two men's fledgling reconciliation.

Diedrich's heart writhed in anguish and shame. Still, he should have gone to her as he'd wanted, taken her in his arms, and declared his love for her in front of Father and the entire congregation. He should have shouted his intentions to make her his wife regardless of the consequences.

In fact, he had tried to sneak a moment with her while Father was busy talking with the Entebrock men on the other side of the churchyard. But before he approached the spot where she'd stood huddled with her mother, sister, and Anna Rieckers, she had glanced up and spied him coming. Her face had blanched then turned crimson. Frowning, she had shaken her head and turned her back to him. She might as well have buried a knife to the hilt in his heart. But as much as it hurt to see her spurn him, he knew she was right. Antagonizing Father at this juncture would gain them nothing and would likely destroy any hope of earning his blessing.

How Diedrich wished that he and Regina could simply elope as young Tanner had tried to entice her to do at the barn raising. The thought of making her his wife and whisking her away from all impediments to their happiness was almost intoxicating. It reminded him of a poem Mama used to read to him when he was little. The German translation of a Scottish ballad, the poem told of a knight named Lochinvar, who stole away his lady love from beneath the noses of those who would keep them apart.

He crushed another armful of wheat against him so hard he heard the stalks snap. Was he courageous enough to do anything so gallant? But even if he was, he knew Regina would never agree to leave behind her parents or this place she loved so well.

Blowing out a long breath, he tied another sheaf and slung it into the wagon. So far, he had failed Regina. He had failed them both.

A hard hand came down on his shoulder from behind. "Surely you are not already winded, Sohn." Father's chortle rasped down Diedrich's spine like a wood file. While Diedrich's mood had vastly deteriorated over the past week, Father's had greatly improved, especially since he began making plans for them to leave Sauers for California.

Reminding himself of the wise saying "A steady drip carves the stone," Diedrich forced a tepid smile. Though Father's heart had turned to stone toward Regina, Diedrich was determined to wear it down. And he would accomplish that only in little drips, not in one deluge.

∞

Regina carried a large bowl of mashed potatoes to one of the trestle tables set up in the Entebrocks' yard. As she had done countless times today, she scanned the slice of field beyond the barn for Diedrich. But the distance was too great to discern the features of the workers who looked like moving specks on the pale background of the wheat field.

Heaving a sigh, she set the bowl on the table with a thud. What good would it do her to see Diedrich when she couldn't talk to him, touch him? None. How bittersweet to see him from a distance yet know that for him to come any closer would be to risk further angering Herr Rothhaus. Had she not tortured her heart enough yesterday at church?

When she had seen Papa and Herr Rothhaus talking and shaking hands in the churchyard, her heart had leapt in her chest. For one blessed moment, she'd thought surely Herr Rothhaus had repented and all would be well. But later, Papa's glum face had told her before his words that it was not the case.

Tears filled her eyes at the memory of her disappointment. Papa's cross demeanor later had not helped. All the way home he had scolded her for what he deemed her impulsive act of prematurely breaking off her engagement to Diedrich. Papa argued that if she and Diedrich had stood firm and shown their determination to marry, Herr Rothhaus would more quickly relent. He contended that since he and Mama continued to bless the union, it would put pressure on Herr Rothhaus to do the same. Though she saw some merit in Papa's argument, she still felt in her heart she had taken the correct route. Yet her longing to speak openly to Diedrich—to touch him—had grown so palpable that the temptation to acquiesce to Papa's wishes had been strong. Only Sophie's whispered encouragements to stay her course had given Regina the strength to remain resolute.

The sound of women's voices behind Regina jolted her from her reverie. In a moment, someone would ring the dinner bell and the men, including Diedrich, would head in from the fields. Her heart quickened at the thought. Hopefully the two of them could find a moment together away from Herr Rothhaus's sight.

"We have made a lot of good food, hey, Tochter?" Mama's bright voice broke into Regina's thoughts. "I must be sure to tell Diedrich that you and Sophie made the cherry pies."

Managing a sad smile, Regina turned and hugged her mother. Despite the many times she had begged her not to blame herself, she knew Mama still harbored guilt for her role in causing the trouble between their family and Herr Rothhaus. "Danke, Mama. I do think the pies turned out very nice."

Mama's expression and voice softened. "Regina." She took Regina's hand and gave it a pat. "Keep trusting in Gott and praying." Her brown eyes glistened with welling tears. "Your Vater is right, you know. Gott has bound your heart with Diedrich's. It is wrong of Herr Rothhaus to withhold his blessing for selfish reasons. And if we pray, I am sure in time he will see he is wrong." She gave her a coaxing smile. "Today, I think, would be a wunderbare time to tell Diedrich that you want again to be his *Verlobte*."

Regina sighed. She saw nothing to be gained in plowing this same ground all over again, but Mama seemed determined to do so. "Mama, did you not always tell me two wrongs do not a right make?" She took her mother's hands and gave them a gentle squeeze. "You know I love Diedrich and want to one day become his wife. You also know I pray every day Herr Rothhaus will repent and accept me as his *Schwiegertochter*." She hated the fresh tears welling in her eyes. "But what if he stays stubborn and will not change his mind? Would you have me wait until the day of our wedding to break our engagement?"

Mama shook her head. "Of course not. But the harvest is three months away. There is plenty of time for Gott to change Herr Rothhaus's mind."

Regina stifled the urge to scream. She must find a way to make Mama understand the folly in her and Papa's thinking without being disrespectful. "And it is only on how to help bring that about that we disagree, Mama. I love you and Papa, and I have always obeyed you. But to my thinking, remaining engaged to Diedrich without his Vater's blessing makes no more sense than if I would try to hitch Gypsy to the back of her cart instead of the front and ask her to push it rather than pull it. And Sophie agrees with me—"

The clanging of the dinner bell cut off Regina's words. When it had stilled, Mama glanced at the throng of women bustling about the tables, placing the last dishes before the men arrived. A look of consternation crossed her face. "We shall talk about this again later, Tochter." She patted Regina's hand again. "But I am believing Gott will hear our prayers and make a way for you and Diedrich to marry." Her countenance and her voice turned stern. "And my faith is strong enough to believe Gott can do that with you and Diedrich engaged just as easily as if you were not." With a brisk nod, she stepped away to relieve Helena Entebrock of one of the two pitchers of lemonade in her hands.

The jangling of teams and wagons brought Regina's gaze up to the barn and the wheat field beyond. On foot and wagon, the men began streaming around the west corner of Herr Entebrock's barn toward the house. Regina's heart quickened as she scanned the male faces for Diedrich's. When she found him, her heart skipped. Walking beside his father, he lifted his head and laughed then clapped his father on the back. Obviously, father and son had shared a joke. At the sight, Regina's heart throbbed painfully, and her resolve deepened. She prayed Mama was right, and God would soon change Herr Rothhaus's feelings about her. But despite her parents' wishes and her own yearning to reinstate her engagement to Diedrich, she couldn't risk causing another rift between Diedrich and his father.

∞

Poking his fork beneath the golden layer of flaky piecrust, Diedrich snagged a cherry. He popped the fruit in his mouth and glanced down the long row of tables situated in the shade of four sprawling maple trees, praying he might catch Regina's eye. But he could no longer find her face among the women hovering around the table and assisting the diners. Disappointment dragged down his shoulders. By now most of the men had finished their main meal and, like him, had moved on to the desserts. Several of the women had begun carrying stacks of dirty dishes back into the house. Regina must have joined them when he wasn't looking.

Savoring the dessert, he couldn't help a secret smile, knowing Regina had helped to make it. The pie reminded him of her, both sweet and tart. Like yesterday at church, she'd kept her distance from him today. And again, they'd only managed to exchange a few smiles and glances. But he was glad, at least, that her mother had found a moment to stop him on the way to the dessert table and mention that Regina and her sister had made the cherry pies. Hopefully he would get a chance to compliment her on them before he had to head back to work.

Emitting a contented sigh, Father pushed back his chair. "That pie looks sehr *schmackhaft*, Sohn. I think maybe I will have a piece myself." Chuckling, he patted his stomach. "That is, if I can find an empty spot to put it in."

Diedrich pushed another bite of pie into his mouth to hide his grin. If Father knew Regina had made the pie, he wouldn't touch it. A flash of mischief he couldn't resist struck. "Ja, Father, you must taste the pie. Be sure to get a piece of the cherry. I know it is your favorite, and I have never tasted a better piece of cherry pie than this one." Knowing he spoke the truth helped to assuage his guilt for the trickery.

While Father headed to the dessert table, Diedrich gathered up their dirty dishes. He would risk being teased for doing women's work for a chance to see and maybe even speak to Regina.

Stepping into the house, he poked his head through the kitchen door. A blast of heat almost as intense as that from a forge slammed him in the face, nearly taking his breath away. Giving the room a cursory perusal, he could not find Regina among the shifting swarm of females squeezed into the small, stifling space. As hot a job as he and the other men had out in the field, Diedrich didn't envy these women their task. He would much rather be outside where at least he could catch a passing breeze to cool the sweat from his brow. It amazed him that anyone could breathe in here, let alone produce the wonderful meal he had helped to consume. Beyond that, the cacophony of chattering female voices resembled the buzz of a giant nest of angry hornets. After only a minute or so, his head began to pound from the racket.

Thankfully, he and Frau Seitz caught sight of each other at the same time. Somehow she squeezed through the crazy quilt of moving skirts and made her way to where he stood at the kitchen door.

He handed her the pile of dishes. "I would like to speak with Regina. Do you know where I might find her?"

Smiling, she pushed a sweat-drenched lock of brown hair from her forehead. "Ja. Henry was fussing, so she took him outside to show him some kittens. On the west side of the house, I think."

"Danke." He nodded his thanks and turned to go, but she grasped his arm, halting him. Her smile had vanished, and her expression held an odd mixture of sadness and hope. "Diedrich, Herr Seitz and I are praying you will yet become our Sohn."

"Danke, Frau Seitz. I am praying the same." Emotion thickening his voice, he gave her a quick hug then left before he embarrassed himself. Less than three months ago, he had prayed he might avoid becoming this woman's *Schwiegersohn*. Now to one day become her son-in-law was his fondest wish.

Outside, he hurried toward the west side of the house, his heart keeping pace with his quickened steps. As he approached the corner of the building, he heard Regina's unmistakable giggle. "Do not do that. You know better." Another giggle. "No, you are getting no *Küsse*. Now away with you."

Her words stopped him cold. For a moment he stood frozen as hurt and anger twisted in a putrid wad of jealousy in his chest. To whom could she be talking so sweetly and playfully denying kisses? Then he grinned at his own foolishness. Frau Seitz said she had taken Henry outside to play. She was obviously talking with her little nephew.

But when he rounded the corner of the house, his heart jolted. Out of the corner of his eye, he caught a glimpse of a male figure disappearing around the other end of the building. All that registered was a flash of auburn hair and a green shirt. Who had worn a green shirt today? His mind raced. He couldn't think.

"Diedrich." Regina's breathless voice yanked his attention from the now vacant end of the house to her flushed face. Her eyes were wide. Her hair had come loose from its pins and dangled in two braids on her shoulders.

"Who was here? I heard you talking with someone." Diedrich tried to keep his voice light but couldn't prevent an accusatory tone from creeping in.

She glanced over her shoulder. Did he imagine the flash of guilt in her eyes? "No one is here but me and Henry." No hint of guile tainted her voice, helping to ease the suspicious thoughts fermenting in Diedrich's mind. She walked over to where the toddler sat beneath a maple tree, digging in a loose patch of soil with a wooden spoon. A liberal amount of the dark, sandy dirt covered the little boy's face and hands, as well as his white cotton gown.

"No, Henry. I told you, do not do that. Your Mutti will be angry with both of us for letting you get so dirty." Regina's laugh sounded a tinge nervous as she picked up the squirming child and swiped uselessly at the dirt and grass stains on his gown.

At her admonishment, remorse smote Diedrich's heart. Her chiding words to Henry now nearly matched what Diedrich had heard her say a moment ago. She had obviously been talking only to the child. Even her mention of kisses made perfect sense in the light of rational thought. As much as Regina loved her little nephew, Diedrich doubted she would have wanted the imp to kiss her until she could wash his face and hands. Shame sizzled through Diedrich for his uncharitable thoughts. He understood now what Solomon meant when he wrote in the sixth chapter of Proverbs, "For jealousy is the rage of a man."

"*Tante* Gina." Henry bopped Regina on the head with the wooden spoon.

She leaned away from the boy and rubbed the top of her head. "Henry, you must not do that." But the giggle warbling through her voice seemed to render the scold ineffective.

Laughing, Henry raised the spoon, poised to strike again, and Diedrich eased the utensil from the boy's chubby fingers. "Nein, you must not hit your Tante." He stifled a chuckle but couldn't stop his grin.

Whimpering, Henry squirmed harder in Regina's arms. He reached out a grimy hand for the spoon—now safely in Diedrich's possession—and made grabbing motions with his fingers.

"Nein. You can only have the *Löffel* if you do not hit your Tante." Diedrich fought to retain a stern face as he had done so many times when disciplining his own nieces and nephews. He prayed that this grubby cherub would one day become his nephew as well.

Heaving a resigned sigh, Regina lowered the toddler back to the spot beneath the tree. "You might as well play there. I don't think you can get any dirtier."

Chuckling, Diedrich handed the spoon back to Henry, who promptly used it to attack a cluster of tiny anthills.

Regina turned a sweet smile to Diedrich. She put her hand on his bare forearm, sending pleasant tingles dancing over his skin. "I'm glad you found me. I hoped you would."

At her tender touch and longing gaze, Diedrich's heart pounded out a quick tattoo like the triple-time cadence of a military drumbeat. He ached to hold her. Instead, he captured her hands. "I have missed you."

"And I have missed you." Her blue eyes glistened up at his. Her soft, sweet lips—he knew how soft, he knew how sweet—tipped up in a sad smile.

The yearning to take her in his arms and kiss her grew so powerful Diedrich could no longer resist it. Dropping her hands, he slipped his arms around her waist.

She stepped back out of his embrace and a pained expression furrowed her delicate brow. "Papa said Herr Rothhaus has not yet relented."

"No, not yet." At the admission, Diedrich swallowed down a bitter wad of regret. He recaptured her hands. "We must give Gott time to work, Liebling."

She nodded, but her gaze drifted from his to where Henry sat gleefully dispatching ants with his spoon.

The dinner bell began to ring, signaling it was time for the workers to return to the fields and the threshing machine. At the sound, Diedrich and Regina exchanged a desperate look. They would likely not see one another for at least another week and a half when the threshers moved to the Seitz farm. A determination stronger than anything Diedrich had ever felt shot through him. He would not leave her without the taste of her kiss on his lips.

He stepped toward her, praying she would accept his embrace. The next moment she surprised him by throwing her arms around his neck and pulling his face down to hers, now drenched in tears. For one blissful moment, nothing mattered to Diedrich but Regina's sweet caresses. A resolve to be her unfailing champion solidified in his chest.

With a sudden movement that jarred him back to reality, she let him go and stepped back away from him. "You must go. It would not be good if your Vater saw us together." She glanced nervously from one end of the building to the other. Then she snatched up Henry and, ignoring the child's whimpering complaints, turned and strode toward the back of the house.

A whirlwind of emotions swirled through Diedrich as he watched her walk away. He must no longer sit passively by and wait for God to change his father's heart and mind. *Dear Lord, show me how to soften Father's heart.*

With his prayer winging heavenward, he headed toward the east side of the house where the other men were gathering, some already making their way back to the wheat field. As he glanced around for his father, a familiar, knobby hand gripped his shoulder, turning him around.

Father's eyes sparked with excitement, and his whiskered face beamed. "Where have you been, Sohn? I have wunderbare news to tell you."

Diedrich ignored the question. "What news, Vater?"

"The miller, Tanner, and his boy came for some bushels of last year's wheat that Herr Entebrock needed to move out of his granary to make room for the new grain."

Diedrich shrugged. "Ja. That is good news, I suppose. There will be plenty of room in the granary for the new crop of wheat." Could Father be entering his dotage at the age of fifty-six?

Father chuckled and shook his head. "Nein. That is not the good news. Herr

Tanner mentioned to Herr Entebrock that he is looking to hire an extra man to work at his mill." He shrugged. "Sweeping up, seeing to the horses, those kinds of jobs."

Diedrich started walking toward the field, and Father fell into step beside him. "And did he find someone?"

"Ja. Is that not exciting?" Father bounced along with an extra spring in his step.

Diedrich grinned, indulging his parent's odd merriment. "Ja, that is gut. The scriptures instruct us to rejoice with those who rejoice. But I do not see why Tanner's success in finding a worker should be exciting to you."

Father stopped and took hold of Diedrich's arm, compelling him to stop as well. "I did not say? Why, because I am the man he has hired, Sohn."

While Diedrich struggled to digest what Father had just told him, Father nudged his arm. "There they go now." Grinning, he swung his arm in a wide arc as two men in a wagon passed them. Diedrich had not seen the older man before, but he had seen the younger one. It was Eli Tanner. And he was wearing a green shirt.

CHAPTER 23

Regina heard and smelled the town of Salem before she saw it. Tucked back in the stuffy confines of Sophie and Ezra's Conestoga wagon, she could see little in front of their team of horses. The arched frame supporting the wagon's canvas cover presented only a limited, thumbnail-shaped vista. But the noise of horse and wagon traffic, the halloos of passersby, and the smell of roasting meat told her they were finally nearing their destination. The distant sound of gunshots suggested some Fourth of July revelers had already begun their evening's celebration.

Leaning back against the wagon's side, she stretched and yawned. Beside her, Henry remained sleeping on his pallet, his rosebud lips making popping sounds around the thumb he perpetually kept in his mouth. Gazing at the sleeping toddler, she smiled fondly. The child's habit of sucking his thumb had built up a callus on the digit where his teeth constantly raked across the skin. At Mama's insistence, Mama, Sophie, and Regina had started rubbing the boy's thumb several times a day with bitter herbs to discourage his thumb-sucking habit. But for once, Regina didn't begrudge Henry his familiar comfort. The thirty-mile trip from Sauers to Salem had been a taxing one. They had left home at dawn, and now the lengthening shadows told Regina it must be at least five in the afternoon. Aside from the half hour they had taken near Vallonia to eat their midday meal and feed and water the horses, they had kept up a punishing pace in order to arrive in Salem before nightfall.

Ezra glanced over his shoulder into the wagon's interior. "We are almost there, Regina. Better wake the boy."

Beside Ezra, Sophie's shoulders rose and fell with her sigh. "Praise be to Gott! My whole body aches, and I am sure I must be bruised from bouncing for miles on this hard seat."

A moment before Ezra brought the horses to a stop, Regina had glimpsed the sign over William and Elsie's store. Reaching out to gently rouse her sleeping nephew, she had to agree with Sophie. Yet despite the grueling journey, she was glad for the chance to get away from home for a couple of days.

She had not originally planned to join Sophie and her family on their trip to visit Elsie and William. But after all that occurred at the Entebrocks' threshing two days ago, she needed time away from Mama and Papa and their constant insistence that she should reinstate her engagement to Diedrich. So when Sophie invited her to join them, Regina had jumped at the offer, though she suspected Sophie mainly wanted her along to help care for Henry.

But if she had hoped the trip would be a respite from her thoughts of Diedrich and her worries about their relationship, she soon learned she was mistaken. On the contrary, the long hours in the back of the wagon had provided ample time for her mind to wander to Diedrich and their parting kiss. Her heart fluttered at the memory. But as precious as their few minutes together were, that tender moment had made their parting again all the more painful. And as long as Herr Rothhaus forbade their marriage, such stolen moments, however sweet, were futile. Perhaps that was why Diedrich had not initiated the kiss. A finger of disappointment squiggled through her. After witnessing the congenial scene between him and his father, she couldn't help wondering if Diedrich had even mentioned her name again to Herr Rothhaus. Also, something about Diedrich's attitude when he first appeared around the corner of the Entebrocks' house bothered her. The way he had looked behind her and the suspicious tone in his voice when he asked who she had been talking with still rankled. For an instant, his demeanor had reminded her of Eli's jealous behavior. In fact, she later heard that Eli and his father were at the Entebrock farm that afternoon, though she hadn't seen them. Could Diedrich have imagined she'd spent time with Eli? At the memory of the kiss they shared, she dismissed the thought. Diedrich knew her heart.

Waking, Henry whimpered and began to cry. Regret smote Regina, and she turned her full attention back to her young charge. Helping him to sit up, she patted his back. "It is all right, my sweet Junge. Are you ready to see your Onkel William and your Tante Elsie?"

"I would say not." Irritation edged Sophie's voice from behind the wagon where she stood peering in at her little son. "With a soiled gown and diaper, you are not fit to see anyone, Henry. I would have thought your Tante Regina would have your diaper changed and a fresh gown on you by now."

Regina jerked. Lost in her own thoughts, she hadn't noticed her sister climb down from the wagon seat and come around to the back of the Conestoga. She hurried to untie Henry's soggy diaper and replaced it with a fresh one from the basket that held his clean clothes. She gave a little laugh. "I guess the wagon ride has made us both sleepy, hey, Henry?"

While Regina dressed Henry, Sophie stood looking on, her arms folded over her chest. "Ezra has gone into the store to let William and Elsie know we have arrived."

Buttoning Henry's fresh gown, Regina made funny faces until she had the toddler laughing. She couldn't understand why Sophie always seemed eager to let

Regina, their mother, or even Ezra tend to Henry. She gently brushed the sweat-damp curls from the child's forehead. If God ever saw fit to give her such a sweet child, even Mama would have to beg to tend to him.

Handing a freshly dressed Henry to his mother, Regina climbed out of the wagon.

Sophie shifted the child to her hip, her mood seemingly as improved as her son's. "I am so excited to see Elsie. And I do hope Ezra can get a job here at the wagon factory."

In her letter inviting them to Salem's Fourth of July celebration, Elsie had mentioned that a new wagon factory had just opened for business here. Assuming they would need wheelwrights, William had suggested Ezra apply for a job. Of course, Ezra was eager to explore the possibility. Sophie, too, had gushed with excitement, saying how wonderful it would be to live near Elsie.

Regina gave her sister an encouraging smile. "I'm praying for that, too." And she meant it. At the same time, guilt tickled her conscience. Of course she genuinely wanted Sophie and her family to be financially secure and happy in a home of their own again. But she couldn't deny that she also looked forward to them moving out of the home she shared with her parents. For the past three years, Regina had enjoyed a respite from her eldest sister's criticisms and bossy ways. And though Sophie had treated her more kindly since moving back to the farm, she still had a tendency to get on Regina's nerves. There was simply no denying that she and Sophie got along better with some distance between them. And though Salem wasn't quite as far from Sauers as Vernon, it *was* a full day's drive.

Sophie leaned toward Regina. "I must say, I was surprised that Elsie seemed in such good spirits in her letter." She shook her head sorrowfully. "Poor Elsie. Maybe seeing Henry will cheer her after her"—she glanced around as if to assure herself no one else was within earshot and lowered her voice to a whisper—"miscarriage."

Regina groaned inwardly. "I am sure Elsie will love getting to see Henry again, but you don't need to whisper, Sophie. Elsie had a miscarriage, not some sort of unmentionable disease." Why was Sophie so prudish about such things? Even when she was expecting Henry, it had taken her a full five months to admit she was in the family way. And then, she might have waited until the child's birth to reveal her happy news if Mama hadn't mentioned during one of the couple's visits that Sophie seemed to have gained weight since her wedding. At Mama's comment, Sophie had turned beet red. Then, taking Mama aside, she had privately whispered she was in the family way. Regina grinned, remembering how she and Elsie had jumped up and down upon learning of the coming blessed event. Clapping their hands, they had chanted, "Baby, baby, we are going to have a baby!" until their mortified sister turned purple-faced and begged them to hush.

Sophie reddened and glanced around again. "Well, of course she didn't have a disease. But one must be discreet when mentioning"—she lowered her voice again—"women's problems."

Regina stifled a giggle at Sophie's priggish attitude. She was tempted to say that Elsie's miscarriage was not strictly a "woman's problem" since William had suffered the loss of a child as well. But antagonizing Sophie would not make for a good start to their Independence Day celebration.

At that moment, Elsie popped out of the store and came bounding toward them, her arms outstretched and happy tears glistening on her smiling face. It did Regina's heart good to see her sister's healthy glow.

Elsie hurried to hug Regina first. "Regina, I'm so glad you came, too!" Taking Regina's hands, she bounced on the balls of her feet and giggled. "I was so happy to get your letter saying your Diedrich chose you over California."

Regina returned Elsie's hug and gave her a tepid smile. Several times she had thought to write Elsie again and share all that had happened since Diedrich's declaration of love. But she couldn't bring herself to reveal in a letter the jarring news of learning about her adoption and the trouble it had caused for her and Diedrich. "I am glad to see you looking so well, Schwester."

Fortunately, in her exuberance, Elsie didn't seem to notice Regina's abrupt change of subject and immediately turned to hug Sophie and Henry. Easing Henry from Sophie's arms, Elsie swung her little nephew up in the air, making him giggle. "My, Henry, you have grown into such a big Junge since I last saw you!"

Regina smiled. Maybe Sophie was right. Seeing Henry did seem to cheer Elsie.

Perching Henry on her hip, Elsie headed for the store. "Come, *Schwestern*. While William and Ezra are gone to check on that wheelwright job for Ezra, we can catch up on all our news, and you can both help me prepare our picnic meal for later. Then when the men return, we can head to the Barnetts' farm for the pig roast and later the fireworks." Turning to Henry, her eyes grew big. "Do you want to see the fireworks, Henry?"

Henry nodded enthusiastically and clapped his hands, though Regina was sure the little boy hadn't the first notion what fireworks were.

A few minutes later, the three sisters were chatting away in Elsie's little kitchen as they assembled the picnic meal. Regina's recent familiarity with the room allowed her to work with speed and confidence, while Sophie fumbled through drawers and shelves, constantly asking direction from Elsie.

Bouncing Henry on her hip, Elsie moved about the kitchen offering her sisters one-handed assistance with the preparations. She stepped to the table where Regina stood mixing together the ingredients for potato salad and peered over her shoulder. "Mmm, that *Kartoffelsalat* smells wunderbar, Regina."

Sophie turned from poking around in the shelves of Elsie's cabinet. Her face pinched up in a look of annoyance. "I am sure she makes potato salad exactly the way Mama taught us all to make it, Elsie." Her voice, if not exactly derisive, was as flat and dry as an unbuttered pancake.

"Perhaps." Elsie picked a snickerdoodle cookie from a basket on the table and handed it to Henry, who had begun to fuss. "But you should have tasted the broth she made for me when I was abed. Of the three of us, I do think Regina has most inherited Mama's gift for cooking."

Sophie turned from the cabinet. "But she's not—" If Regina didn't know better, she might have interpreted the quirk at the corner of Sophie's lips as a sneer. "Oh, you do not know, do you, Elsie?"

"Know what?" Elsie's expectant smile swung between Sophie and Regina.

Anger and dismay leapt in Regina's chest at Sophie's thoughtlessness. This was not the way she had wanted to tell Elsie what their mother had disclosed about Regina's birth. But she was determined that Elsie would hear it from her lips, not Sophie's.

Blowing out a resolute breath, Regina pulled a chair out from the table. "You should sit down for what I must tell you, Elsie."

With a quizzical look on her face, Elsie sat. Henry wriggled from her grasp and slid to the floor then toddled across the room to his mother. Elsie gave a nervous giggle. "What could you possibly have to tell me that I must sit to hear?" Suddenly her brown eyes grew large, and her voice turned breathless. "You are not married already, are you?"

Regina shook her head and gave her sister a sad smile. "Nein. I only wish that was the news I have to tell." Swallowing down the lump that had gathered in her throat, she recounted the fantastic tale Mama had told her when they had worked together on Regina's wedding quilt.

If possible, Elsie's eyes grew even wider. Her jaw went slack, and she looked at Regina as if she hadn't seen her before. Having never been close to Sophie, it hadn't bothered Regina so much for her eldest sister to learn they were not connected by blood, but Elsie was a different matter. Until this moment, Regina hadn't feared her revelation would diminish Elsie's love for her, or that Elsie would see her as anything other than her sister. But now she hated to think the news might weaken the special bond she and Elsie had always enjoyed.

Tears welled in Elsie's eyes, and she sprang from her chair to embrace Regina. "Oh my liebe Schwester, what an awful thing for you to learn." Then, pushing away from Regina, she took her hands. Her chin lifted, and her face filled with almost defiant loyalty. "I do not care how you came to be my sister. You are my sister, and you will always be my sister. Blood doesn't matter." She glanced over at Sophie, who was brushing cookie crumbs from the front of Henry's gown. "And I know Sophie feels the same way."

Sophie quirked a smile that vanished so quickly Regina almost missed it. "Of course," she mumbled as she continued brushing at Henry's clothes. "But it is too bad Herr Rothhaus does not feel as you do, Elsie."

It stung that Sophie didn't enthusiastically reiterate Elsie's sentiment, but Regina dismissed the omission, considering it but another of Sophie's oversights.

Elsie gasped, and her forehead pinched in anger. "You mean Diedrich does not want to marry you because you were not born to Mama and Papa?"

Regina shook her head, eager to correct Elsie's wrong impression of Diedrich. "Nein. Diedrich still loves me and wants to marry me." But even as she said the words, a faint but insidious voice whispered inside her head. *Does he still love me?* And if he did, why hadn't he tried harder to change his father's mind about her?

Elsie blinked. "But Sophie said Herr Rothhaus—"

"Diedrich's Vater," Sophie said in a matter-of-fact tone as she reached into the cabinet. "Ah, here are the jars of sauerkraut."

Regina explained to Elsie the callous way in which her birth father and grandfather had treated Herr Rothhaus's family. The retelling stung the open wound on her heart as painfully as if she'd squeezed lemon juice into it. She sniffed back the tears. "So Herr Rothhaus has forbidden Diedrich to marry me. And unless Gott helps Diedrich change his Vater's mind. . ." Unable to finish the thought, she shook her head.

Elsie's expression turned indignant. "What those men did was terrible, but it happened before you were born. How can Herr Rothhaus blame you?"

Stifling a sardonic snort, Regina fought a wave of despair. "Because I am of their blood. And I cannot change that."

Elsie gripped Regina's hands, and her voice turned resolute. "Then we must pray that Gott will change Herr Rothhaus's heart. As our Lord promises us in Matthew 21:22, 'And all things, whatsoever ye shall ask in prayer, believing, ye shall receive.'"

At the familiar scripture, Regina's frustration burst free. She yanked her hands from Elsie's. "But I *have* been praying, and nothing has happened." Not wanting Elsie to see the flood of tears cascading down her face, she turned her back. She hated the anger in her voice but couldn't keep it out. "When Diedrich defied his Vater and refused to break our engagement, Herr Rothhaus disowned him. I did not want to cause Diedrich to sin by dishonoring his Vater, so I broke our engagement. I also thought if Diedrich could talk to his Vater again, he would have a better chance of changing Herr Rothhaus's mind about me. But so far, he hasn't been able to." *Or won't.*

Elsie marched around to face Regina. Grasping her shoulders, she forced her to meet her gaze. "Then for whatever reason, it is not Gott's time to change his mind. With Gott, all things are possible. He will give us the power to do whatever we need to do." She cupped Regina's face in both her hands as Mama might do. "Gott will give Diedrich the power to change his Vater's mind. If we pray believing that will happen, it will happen."

Swiping at her tear-drenched face, Regina nodded. Despite the pain it had caused Regina to recount her heartache, sharing it with Elsie had also lightened her burden. Besides Mama, Regina knew of no one who could storm heaven with prayers on Regina's behalf more forcefully or with more sincerity than Elsie could. She sniffed. "At first I believed Gott would change Herr Rothhaus's heart. But nothing has changed, and I'm beginning to wonder if it will ever happen."

Elsie's mouth tipped up in an encouraging smile, and she patted Regina's hand. "You must have faith, Schwester."

Regina went back to mixing the potato salad that didn't need more mixing. Faith. Could Mama be right that Regina's lack of faith was hindering God's working? "Mama says by breaking my engagement to Diedrich, I am showing a lack of faith. She and Papa think if I reinstate our engagement, Herr Rothhaus would see how committed Diedrich and I are to each other and would soon relent and give us his blessing."

Sophie, who had remained quiet, crossed the room in three quick strides. "Nein!" Alarm filled her face. Elsie and Regina exchanged surprised looks. As if gathering her composure, Sophie squared her shoulders and cleared her throat. When she spoke again, her voice was tempered and her words measured. "I have told you, Regina, you are doing the right thing. And I am sure Elsie will agree with me." She shot their sister a look that defied contradiction.

Elsie blinked. "I—I can see virtue in both ways of thinking. . . ."

Sophie gripped Regina's shoulder, and her expression turned almost fierce. "Under no circumstances should you reinstate your engagement unless Herr Rothhaus grants you and Diedrich his blessing."

Her sister's repeated advice did not surprise Regina, but the passion with which she imparted it did.

Elsie ambled across the room to extract Henry from the bottom of the cupboard. A thoughtful frown creased her forehead. "Of course Diedrich should not defy his Vater. But I can see Mama's point."

Sophie crossed her arms over her chest and assumed a wide, dictatorial stance. Her stern look reminded Regina of the expression on Sophie's face when she scolded Henry. "To even contemplate marriage without the blessing of both families is inviting disaster, Regina."

Regina wondered if Sophie had forgotten Papa's reluctance to allow Ezra to court Sophie. Only Ezra's sound Christian upbringing and his unimpeachable work ethic had swayed Papa from insisting Sophie marry a German farmer instead.

Looking down her nose at Regina like a strict schoolteacher, Sophie tapped her foot on the floor. "Since Ezra and I married, I have heard of three girls—all from good Christian families—who married against the wishes of their parents or their husbands' parents." Her right eyebrow arched. "All ended very badly."

Elsie's eyes widened. "What happened to them?"

Regina stifled a groan. For the life of her, she could never understand why Elsie was always so quick to take Sophie's bait and beg for her to repeat gossip. Surely Elsie knew their sister was itching to tell the tale.

"Well," Sophie began, a smug look settling over her face. "I heard of one couple who married against the young man's family's wishes." She snapped her fingers. "Within one month, he had left her and gone back to his parents. The poor girl had no choice but to return humiliated and scandalized to her own parents' home." Her voice lowered. "Of course the girl was ruined after the divorce. No decent man would go near her."

Elsie shook her head in sorrow. It was enough to spur Sophie on.

Sophie's eyes sparked as if she relished the tale she was about to impart. "And then there was the girl who defied her parents and eloped with her young man." She clucked her tongue. "Her parents sent the sheriff after them all the way to Madison. They had the young man arrested for stealing their horse, though the girl said it was hers. The young man went to jail, and the girl was sent to live with a maiden aunt in Louisville." Bending down, she whispered, "They say the poor thing wasn't right in the head after that."

Regina couldn't figure out how people knew the state of the girl's mind if she lived as far away as Louisville. But she had no interest in encouraging Sophie by inquiring.

Sophie's brow scrunched, and she tapped her lips three times as if gathering her thoughts. "And of course there was the couple who—"

"Sophie, please. I'd rather not hear any more." Regina's nerves bristled. Though she was sure Sophie's intention was to save her and Diedrich from a similar tragic ending, her sister's gossiping made her skin prickle. Turning away from Sophie, she swathed the bowl of potato salad in a linen towel and tucked it into a waiting basket.

Sophie sniffed, a sure sign her feelings had been bruised. "Well," she snapped, "they died."

Elsie gasped.

Fearing Sophie would feel compelled to recount grisly details of the grim story, Regina hurried to change the conversation to the possible job opportunity for Ezra. But although listening to Sophie's tragic stories had made her squirm inside, she couldn't deny the cautionary tales had made an impression. Sophie's words kept echoing in her head. *"Within one month, he had left her and gone back to his parents."* Diedrich had known Regina for less than three months. But he had known his father all his life. However much he loved her, she couldn't expect his allegiance to her to be stronger than what he felt for his parent. Sophie had solidified Regina's resolve. She must not reinstate her engagement to Diedrich until Herr Rothhaus found it in his heart to bless their union. And if not. . . No, she must not think that. If only she had the faith of Mama and Elsie. *Dear Lord, help my unbelief.*

Elsie covered a basket of dishes and eating utensils with a towel. "I do hope Ezra gets that job, Sophie. It might be a little crowded, but William's Mutter has two upstairs rooms she doesn't use. I'm sure she would rent them to you until you could find a home of your own here in Salem."

Just then, William and Ezra strode into the kitchen wearing wide smiles. Ezra snatched Henry from his spot on the floor and swung him up in his arms. "There is my little man." Giggling, Henry grabbed a wad of his father's shirtfront in his chubby hand and said, "Dada, Dada."

Sophie hurried to her husband, her face tense. She gripped his arm. "What did you learn?" Her voice sounded breathless.

Ezra's smile stretched so wide Regina feared his lips might split. "I start in two weeks."

"Praise Gott!" Sophie sank to a chair, all the starch gone out of her. Her hands trembled in her lap.

Regina and Elsie sent up their own prayers of thanks, and hugs and kisses were exchanged all around.

Ezra held up a hand palm forward in a gesture of caution. "The pay won't be nearly what I was making as part owner of my own shop. But if the factory makes a go of it here, there will be plenty of opportunity for advancement."

Sophie stood, and some of the tension returned to her features. "If they make a go? You mean the factory might not stay here?"

Ezra offered a nonchalant shrug, seemingly unfazed by his wife's concern. "Well, there is no guarantee, of course, but people are always needing wagons."

Appearing somewhat satisfied with her husband's answer, Sophie pressed her hand to her chest as if to suppress her jubilant heart. "At least it is a stable job for the present, and you can continue to practice your trade." Her lifting mood seemed to pick up steam, and she brightened. "Now if we can just find a house here, we could be moved within the month."

It was on this happy note that, a few minutes later, they all piled into Ezra and Sophie's Conestoga with baskets of picnic fare and traveled a mile's distance to the farm of a man named Jim Barnett.

At the end of a long lane, they pulled into a grassy expanse beside a large, weathered gray barn. Sitting in the back of the wagon, Regina rested her chin on her forearm draped across the wagon's backboard and gazed out at the deepening gloaming. The setting sun painted streaks of pinkish-orange, purple, and gold across the darkening blue-gray sky. In a deep blue strip beneath the colorful hues, the first star of the evening winked at her like the eye of a playful angel. Was Diedrich back at the new house admiring the same view? At the wistful thought, warmth filled her. How she longed to share all the sunsets of her life with him—to stand beside him at twilight as they gazed together on the evening's first bright star. But unless God softened Herr Rothhaus's heart. . .

The wagon jolted to a stop, yanking her from her musings. Several other wagons and teams had already arrived, and dozens of people milled about the area. Roast-pork-scented smoke filled the air, teasing Regina's nose. As she climbed from the wagon, she spotted the smoke's origin. At the edge of a fallow field, two blackened patches of ground glowed red with smoldering embers. Above the embers stood iron spits on which two whole hogs roasted to dusky perfection.

Will jumped from the back of the wagon then helped Elsie and Sophie to the ground. "Mmm." He rubbed his belly. "Can't wait for a plate of that roast pork." Mimicking his uncle, Henry, perched on his father's arm, rubbed his own belly, drawing a laugh from his elders.

Regina helped Sophie and Elsie spread quilts over the grass a few yards from the wagon, where they would have an unobstructed view of the fireworks later. As she headed back to the wagon for the basket that held their eating utensils, she noticed Ezra and William standing near the wagon and shaking hands with a scraggly bearded man wearing a fringed deerskin shirt.

"Zeke Roberts," the man said around the corncob pipe in his mouth as he pumped William's hand.

William introduced himself and then Ezra. "This is my brother-in-law, Ezra Barnes. He and his wife and baby and my wife's other sister have come down here from Sauers to join in our celebration this evenin'."

"Is that right?" Regina heard the man say as she reached into the wagon for the basket of utensils. He gave a throaty chuckle. "You fellers wouldn't know a young feller up there in Sauers by the name of Diedrich Rothhaus, would ya?"

At Diedrich's name, Regina froze. As far as she knew, Diedrich had never been to Salem. How could he know this man?

When Ezra explained that Diedrich was living on land owned by his parents-in-law, the man guffawed. "Well, I'll be switched!"

At his exclamation, a chilly foreboding slithered down Regina's spine. She stood as if paralyzed. A series of soft pops told her the man had paused to draw on his pipe.

A snort sounded, followed by Zeke's voice. "Why, young Rothhaus has agreed to join up with me and head to the Californee goldfields next spring."

CHAPTER 24

Regina pummeled the steaming bowl of potatoes with punishing blows of the masher. At least her frustration would make for some of the smoothest mashed potatoes served at today's threshing. Shortly after dawn, the threshers began arriving at the farm. She'd hoped to find a moment to speak to Diedrich alone and confront him with what she'd heard Zeke Roberts say. So far, she hadn't seen Diedrich today. But she had no doubt he was working somewhere in the field loading wagons with bundles of wheat and would appear in the yard with the other workers when the dinner bell rang. Diedrich still owed Papa a summer's worth of work on the farm, so whether or not his father decided to come, Regina was sure Diedrich would participate in today's threshing. And before the dinner break was over, she was determined to learn why he hadn't informed Roberts he was no longer interested in going to California. That is, if he *was* no longer interested.

She plopped another golden dollop of butter atop the potatoes then beat the melting lump into the snowy mound until it disappeared. In the week since Salem's Independence Day celebration, Zeke Roberts's words had tumbled around in her brain, tormenting her thoughts and robbing her of sleep. When she'd recovered from the immediate shock of hearing the man's claim that Diedrich planned to accompany him to California, she had confronted him, intent on learning the details behind his astonishing comment. But Roberts had seemed unable to remember the exact date he'd met Diedrich in the Dudleytown smithy. Regina surmised it must have been while she was in Salem caring for Elsie. But even if that were so, how could Diedrich promise Roberts he would travel with him to California next spring then a few days later pledge his love to Regina and promise to stay here in Sauers with her? Finding scant satisfaction in the man's vague answers, she'd leveled a relentless barrage of mostly fruitless questions at him until William finally took pity on Roberts and escorted Regina back to their picnic spot, little the wiser for her efforts. Wielding the masher, she punished the potatoes again.

"You have them mashed enough, I think, Tochter." Mama maneuvered through the shifting maze of cooks to stand beside Regina at the kitchen table. "We want mashed potatoes, not potato soup." She glanced across the room to where Sophie bent over the baskets of dishes and eating utensils Helena Entebrock had brought earlier. Sophie appeared to be sorting through the dishes and other tableware donated by all the families in the threshing ring specifically for use at threshing dinners like today's. She was likely gathering place settings to take outside to the makeshift sawhorse tables Papa and some of the other men had set up in the yard earlier.

Mama handed Regina a stoneware plate. "Here, cover those potatoes with this and put them on the stove to stay warm. Then help your sister set places at the tables."

"Ja." Regina nodded, happy for the opportunity to escape the hot kitchen for a while.

When she and Sophie had loaded four baskets with enough dishes and utensils for twenty-two settings, they gratefully headed outside into cool, welcoming breezes and the shade of the old willow tree.

Though reason told Regina that Diedrich was beyond her sight, she couldn't help turning her face in the direction of the wheat field.

"Have you talked with him yet?" Sophie's tone was matter-of-fact as she transferred a plate from the basket to the table.

"Nein." Regina didn't need to ask whom Sophie meant. All the way back from Salem, Sophie had railed about how inconsiderate it was of Diedrich not to have mentioned to Regina his conversation with Zeke Roberts. Regina had defended Diedrich, saying it was likely all a misunderstanding, but she couldn't help sharing a smidgen of her sister's sentiment.

Sophie placed a knife and fork at either side of the plate. "I do think you are sehr wise not to reinstate your engagement to Diedrich." She shrugged. "Who knows what is ever in men's heads?" With a light laugh, she tapped her own noggin.

Regina had thought she knew what was in Diedrich's head and his heart. But now she wasn't so sure. Yet she declined to comment, not wanting to encourage Sophie. For reasons that remained murky to Regina, Sophie seemed to have taken a negative view of Diedrich.

For the next several minutes, Regina and Sophie worked together quietly. After a while, Regina noticed her sister glancing toward the house. She assumed Sophie was checking to see when the women might begin to exit the back door with dishes of food.

Suddenly, Sophie gave a little gasp. "I'd better go check on Henry." With that, she took off toward the house at a quick trot.

Regina shook her head and gave a little snort. She would never understand Sophie. Regina herself had put Henry in his little trundle bed for a nap less than half an hour ago, leaving young Margaret Stuckwisch to watch over him. Usually

Sophie never checked on Henry until he had slept at least an hour. And this morning, before the women began cooking, Sophie had handpicked Margaret to look after Henry, even commenting on how mature the girl seemed for twelve years old. So it seemed odd Sophie would suddenly become uneasy about Henry.

Abandoning her effort to decipher what had motivated Sophie's abrupt departure, Regina reached in the basket for another plate. The touch of a hand—a hard, definitely male hand—on her shoulder brought her upright. Whirling, she met Eli Tanner's smiling face.

His smile slipped into a lazy grin. "I was hopin' I'd get a chance to talk to you alone."

Regina frowned, wondering why Eli had decided to join the group of threshers. Or perhaps he had not come for that reason at all. Despite his reason for being here, he was not a welcome sight, and she couldn't think why she had ever considered him handsome or dashing. At the present, the only emotion he elicited from her was aggravation. "What do you want, Eli? I have work to do."

His jaw twitched, but his grin stayed in place. His green eyes held an icy glint. "Mr. Rothhaus—the old German man who works at our mill—said you gave his son the mitten." Cocking his head to one side, he lifted his chin, planted his feet in a wide stance, and crossed his arms over his broad chest. "So since you ain't promised now, I thought I'd give you another chance and ask your pa if I might come courtin'."

Had Herr Rothhaus encouraged Eli to come and make another offer for her hand? Fury rose in Regina's chest. How dare the man meddle in her affairs! Diedrich's father had obviously not changed his mind about her and was trying to get her out of his son's life for good. Well, she wouldn't have it. And she wouldn't have Eli now either, even if he offered her a mansion and untold wealth—which, of course, he couldn't. Though tempted to take out her anger on the silly young swain before her, Regina got a firm grip on her temper. Herr Rothhaus may have even led Eli to believe Regina would be open to entertain his attentions. She fought for a calm, dispassionate voice. "I am sorry if Herr Rothhaus gave you the wrong idea, Eli. But my feelings have not changed since your Onkel's barn raising. And it would do you no good to talk to Papa. He will tell you the same."

Eli snorted, and his grin twisted into a sneer. "Still stuck on the old man's son, huh?" He gave a derisive laugh. "Won't do you any good. Old Rothhaus ain't never gonna agree to you marryin' his boy. And accordin' to him, he and his son are headin' out west to the goldfields come spring." Another scornful chuckle. "He told me how you wasn't born a Seitz but come from bad people." With a slow, lazy look, he eyed her from head to toe, making her squirm and her stomach go queasy. Then he gave a disinterested shrug. "Don't matter none to me though. A German's a German, to my way of thinkin'. But I doubt if all the other fellers around Sauers would see it the same way." His smirk made her want to slap his face. "I'd advise you to give my offer another think, or you're liable to end up an old maid."

Any remnant of affection she might have held for Eli vanished. Eli Tanner was a slug. It seemed impossible that she had ever entertained the notion of marrying him. Her body trembled with the effort to contain the rage surging through her. She balled her fists so tightly her fingernails bit into her palms. Tears sprang to her eyes, but she quickly blinked them away. She would rather take a beating than have Eli think his words had hurt her.

Piercing him with her glare, she schooled her voice to a tone as dead flat and icy as a pond on a still January morning. "Like I told you before, my heart is already situated. And if I cannot have the man I love, I will have no one." She skewered him with an unflinching glare. "And I would rather live happily alone for the rest of my life than spend even an hour with you."

He winced, and for an instant his haughty mask crumbled. Regina experienced a flash of remorse for the satisfaction the sight gave her. Her words had found their mark. Eli might be a vain and cocky slug, but she *had* once encouraged his attention.

He sneered. "One day you'll be sorry." With another snort and a derisive parting look, he turned on his heel and stalked across the yard toward the barn and, she supposed, the wheat field beyond.

As she watched him walk away, a sob rose up in her throat. Not from regret for what she had said to Eli. She had meant every word. The anguish that gripped her sprang from Eli's claim that Diedrich and Herr Rothhaus planned to leave Sauers for California. Had Diedrich given up trying to change his father's mind? Could it be true they were planning to leave next spring? Zeke Roberts thought so.

Somehow she managed to finish her task as the dinner bell began to ring. With her head down to hide her tears, she started back to the house as a line of women streamed out of the back door, their hands laden with steaming dishes of food.

Panic flared. She needed time to think and compose herself before facing anyone, including Mama, Sophie, or even Anna Rieckers. Her mind raced to think of a spot where she might escape for a moment of solitude. On impulse, she headed toward the far side of the house and the half-log bench by the little vegetable garden. With the sun directly overhead, the short shadow cast by the house barely reached the bench.

Sinking to the hard seat warmed by the sun, she hugged herself, trying to still her shaking limbs. She had told Eli the truth, except for one thing. If she lost Diedrich, she would not live happily. She couldn't imagine her life being happy or even contented without him in it. New tears filled her eyes and cascaded down her face. Diedrich had accused her of not giving God time to work. Now it seemed he had given up on God working altogether. Or had the lure of the goldfields taken first place in his heart again?

"Regina." At Diedrich's soft voice, Regina jerked. Her heart jumped like a deer at a rifle shot then bounded to her throat.

Standing, she wiped the wetness from her face. "Diedrich." Her voice came out in a squeak.

He stepped closer, and she could see the pain in his gray eyes. "I saw you talking to Eli. Is it because the two of you had an argument that you are crying?"

He had obviously misconstrued the angry exchange he'd just witnessed between her and Eli. His insinuation that she cared enough about Eli for him to make her cry rankled. Did Diedrich think she and Eli were courting again? Had Herr Rothhaus suggested to Diedrich that was the case? Indignation flared in her chest. How could Diedrich believe such a thing, even from his father? It hurt that Diedrich could think her so fickle or her love so untrue that she would entertain attention from Eli or any other man. "Nein. . .sort of."

His gray eyes turned as hard as granite. "Then it is because of Eli you are crying."

She met his look squarely. "Nein. I am crying because Eli said you and your Vater are going to California in the spring," she blurted. The floodgates holding back her emotions burst inside her, allowing fresh tears to spill down her cheeks. "And Eli was not the first to tell me you are leaving." She told him what she had heard from Zeke Roberts at the Fourth of July picnic. "So when were you planning to tell me? Next spring?"

He groaned. Two quick strides brought him to her side. "Regina, I told you the truth when I said I had no more interest in going to the goldfields. I spoke to Zeke before I knew you loved me. And I never promised him I would leave Sauers." He frowned. "If he told you I did, he is wrong. There was no deal, no handshake." He glanced down. "Only if I knew I had lost all hope of winning your love would I have considered leaving Sauers for California." His voice softened with his gaze. "I could not bear the thought of staying here and being reminded of what I had lost every day for the rest of my life." A sad smile lifted the corner of his mouth, and he took her hands in his. "But Gott had mercy on me and granted me your love." Then his smile faded, and he let go of her hands. "Or has He?"

"What do you mean?" A finger of anger flicked inside her. So he did think she was encouraging Eli's attention.

His jaw worked, and he glanced toward the garden as if allowing himself a moment to gather his thoughts and perhaps rein in his emotions. At length he turned a blank face to her, but his voice sounded tight. "When I went looking for you at the Entebrocks' threshing, I heard you telling someone not to kiss you. Then when I reached the side of the house where you were, I thought I saw Eli disappear around the corner of the house. And just now, I see him talking to you again."

If she were not so angry and Diedrich's accusations were not so completely ludicrous, Regina might have laughed. Instead, she planted her fists against her waist to stop her body from trembling with fury and glared at him. "Diedrich Rothhaus! How dare you accuse me of consorting with Eli behind your back!" She hated the traitorous tears slipping down her cheeks. "I never saw Eli at the Entebrocks' threshing. I do not know what you thought you saw, but like I told you then, I was playing with Henry. He was trying to kiss me with his dirty face, and I was telling him to stop."

To his credit, Diedrich's expression turned sheepish. Then he glanced toward the side yard, and his Adam's apple moved with his swallow. "But Eli was here with you now."

"Ja!" She puffed out an exasperated breath. "Because your Vater told him we are no longer promised, he came again to ask if he could court me."

"And what did you tell him?" A muscle in his jaw twitched.

It took all Regina's strength not to stomp off in a huff. *Dear Lord, why did You make men with such hard heads?* Drawing a fortifying breath, she prayed for patience and searched his pain-filled eyes. "What do you think I told him, Diedrich? I told him the only thing my heart would let me tell him—that I love you. And if I cannot have you, I will marry no one. I sent him away and told him never to come asking me again." She stumbled back to the bench through blinding tears. Sinking to the wooden seat, she hugged herself with her arms and stared unseeing toward the garden. "But if you cannot trust my love, I do not see how we can marry—even if your Vater gives us his blessing." Her voice snagged on the ragged edge of a sob.

He came and sat beside her and slipped his arm around her. "Forgive me, mein Liebchen." His voice sagged with remorse. "It is just that we must be apart so much. We cannot talk and share what is in each other's hearts and minds." He lifted her chin with his forefinger and turned her face to his. "I am ashamed for questioning your love, even for an instant. But you also thought I was planning again to go to California. Because we cannot talk to each other, it becomes easier to imagine things that are not so and causes us to question each other's love."

What he said made sense, but his mention of California reminded her of another question that had niggled at her mind since her conversation with Eli. "It is hard for me to believe your Vater decided on his own that the two of you should go to California. Did you tell him about your earlier plans to go out west to hunt for gold? And if you did, why would you tell him if you are not still planning to go there?"

Turning from her, Diedrich blew out a long breath. Leaning forward, he gazed out over the garden, his arms resting on the tops of his thighs and his hands clasped between his knees. "I had forgotten about the map to the goldfields I put in the back of the Heilige Schrift. One evening Vater found it." He gave a short, sarcastic laugh. "Now he is convinced this is what Gott wants us to do."

Disappointment pinched Regina's heart. "And you let him think you would go to California with him?"

Diedrich winced. "At first." His voice dipped with remorse. "It was too soon after we had made amends. I did not wish to cause another argument. But after Herr Entebrock's threshing. . ." He shook his head. "I knew I must begin to fight harder for you. . .for us." He straightened then turned and took her hands. "That evening, I told Vater I still love you and hope to convince you again to agree to marry me. I told him if I could convince you to reinstate our engagement, I would not be going to California."

Regina's heart trembled, imagining Herr Rothhaus's angry face at Diedrich's admission. The thought stole the breath from her voice. "What did he say?"

Diedrich let go of her hands and turned back to the garden. "He laughed." A mixture of pain and anger crossed his scowling features. "Not a big laugh. Just a deep, quiet laugh, as if he pitied me. He said I would change my mind come spring."

At Diedrich's words, the hope Regina had nurtured that his father would soon repent and grant them his blessing to marry, withered. "So—so your Vater has shown no sign of changing his mind about giving us his blessing?" An errant tear escaped the corner of her left eye.

Diedrich shook his head. "Nein." He said the word so softly she scarcely heard it. He brushed the tear away from her cheek with his thumb. "That is why I came looking for you. We have tried this your way. But every time I try to speak to Vater about you—begging him to find some scrap of forgiveness in his heart for you, an innocent—he closes his ears and walks away."

He stood, and she followed. In the moment of stillness between them, she could hear the other men laughing and talking as they ate at the tables in the yard. Diedrich took her hands again. "I have tried, Regina. But I am now even more convinced your parents are right. I think the only thing that will change Vater's mind is if he sees we are determined to marry." He gave her hands a gentle squeeze. The plea in his eyes ripped at her tattered heart. "Please, mein Liebling, will you not reconsider reinstating our engagement? The scriptures tell us in Hebrews 11:1, 'Now faith is the substance of things hoped for, the evidence of things not seen.' And our Lord tells us in Matthew 17:20, 'If ye have faith as a grain of mustard seed, ye shall say unto this mountain, Remove hence to yonder place; and it shall remove; and nothing shall be impossible unto you.' I am convinced Gott will change Vater's heart. But Gott is waiting, I think, for us to show our faith in Him. Regina, can you not find in your heart faith the size of a mustard seed?"

The scriptures Diedrich quoted convicted Regina, pricking her with guilt. Like her parents, Diedrich seemed sure this approach would soon turn his father's heart around. But what if it didn't? How long could Regina and Diedrich wait on the Lord to work? And what if spring came and Diedrich was forced again to choose between her and his father?

Sophie's stern admonition echoed again in Regina's mind. *"Under no circumstances should you reinstate your engagement unless Herr Rothhaus grants you and Diedrich his blessing."* She thought again of the young woman Sophie had told her about whose new husband left her and returned to his parents' home. Not for one instant did Regina think her good and noble Diedrich would do anything of the sort. But if Papa, Mama, and Diedrich were all wrong and reinstating her engagement to Diedrich did not budge Herr Rothhaus from his position, next spring everyone would once again face the same impasse. No. Breaking her engagement to Diedrich the first time had nearly ripped her heart out. She wasn't sure she'd have the courage to break it a second time. Better to take Sophie's advice and wait for Herr Rothhaus's blessing.

Regina shook her head sadly. "Nein. I wish my faith was as strong as yours, but it is not."

Diedrich's Adam's apple moved with his swallow. A look of anguish darkened his gray eyes. "Then perhaps Vater is right. Maybe there is nothing here for me in Sauers. Maybe it is best if I go look for gold in California after all."

CHAPTER 25

Squinting against the rising sun, Regina trudged numbly through the dewy grass. Diedrich's parting words yesterday afternoon played in torturous repetition in her head. Each time his words flayed her heart as if scourging it with a briar cane.

She gripped the rope handle of the bucket filled with potato peelings until the rough fibers bit into her hand. If only she could have as strong a faith as Diedrich and Mama and Papa. Of course God could change Herr Rothhaus's heart. Of this, she had no doubt. But the nagging thought that lurked in the darkest recesses of her mind slunk out again to whisper its insidious question. *Does He want to?* Though she loved Diedrich with all her heart and he professed the same for her, what if, for reasons beyond their understanding, God opposed their union? In that case, nothing they tried would nudge Herr Rothhaus from his stubborn stance.

The scripture Papa read last night from the book of Isaiah joined with her own melancholy contemplations to fill her heart with doubt. *"For my thoughts are not your thoughts, neither are your ways my ways, saith the Lord. For as the heavens are higher than the earth, so are my ways higher than your ways, and my thoughts than your thoughts."*

Gripping the bottom of the bucket, she slung the contents toward the chicken coop, scattering the vegetable peelings over the barren patch of ground. The chickens, which at first squawked and fled the barrage, batting their snowy wings in fright, now returned to greedily peck at the offering. Like the chickens, was Regina, too, unaware of what was good for her? Had God intentionally thrown up the impediment of her birth family to prevent her and Diedrich from marrying?

Her heart rebelled at the thought. Again she dragged out the question now worn and tattered from constant mulling. If God was against their love, then why did He bring Diedrich here to Sauers in the first place? And why, even against Regina's and Diedrich's own wills, did God allow their hearts to fuse so tightly?

She glanced up at the sky, lightening now to a pale blue as the sun faded the deep pink and purple hues of the waning dawn. "Dear Lord, why have You visited this heartache on me and Diedrich? Are You testing our faith as Mama, Papa, and Diedrich think, or are You telling us we should not marry?"

No answer came. Only the clucking of the chickens and the rustling of the maple trees' leaves stirred by a gentle breeze disturbed the quiet.

Heaving a weary sigh, she started back to the house, her Holzschuhe scuffing through the wet grass. How she longed for Elsie's levelheaded and unbiased counsel. Although Regina had enjoyed her time in Salem with Elsie and William, there had been no time for her and her middle sister to talk alone at length. But Elsie was thirty miles away. Perhaps she should talk to Sophie again. Although her eldest sister had made her opinion on the matter clear, she had on several occasions offered Regina a sympathetic ear. In fact, it still surprised Regina how interested Sophie seemed in Regina and Diedrich's situation. Perhaps it was the mellowing influences of marriage and motherhood, but for whatever reason, Sophie actually seemed to care about Regina and her future. After all, Sophie's advice *had* strengthened Regina's resolve, preventing her from giving in to Diedrich's pleas to reinstate their engagement. If nothing else, maybe Sophie could help ease Regina's mind about her decision yesterday.

As she approached the house, the sound of voices reached her ears. Another couple of steps and she was able to identify the voices as belonging to Sophie and Ezra. Glancing up, she realized she was standing beneath the upstairs bedroom that had, until recently, been hers. The morning air was obviously still heavy enough to carry the couple's decidedly intense conversation beyond the room's open window.

Not wanting to eavesdrop on what sounded like a spat between her sister and brother-in-law, Regina started to step away. But her sister's caustic tone of voice halted her.

"She is not even my blood sister! I tell you, Ezra, it is not right that that little pretender and a man who has been in the country less than three months should inherit Papa's land!" Sophie's words and resentful tone slashed Regina like a knife.

"You know your pa wants the land to go to a German farmer, Sophie. I am neither." Ezra's voice held a note of frayed patience.

Sophie snorted. "That is your problem, Ezra. Your view is too narrow. Look, we have a son—Mama and Papa's blood grandson. It is Henry who should inherit this farm, not two people who have no blood claim."

Despite the warm July morning, an icy chill shot through Regina. She'd always known Sophie was not especially fond of her, but the vitriol in her sister's voice stunned her. So that was why Sophie was so emphatic that Regina should not reinstate her engagement. Her positive comments about Eli as well as her criticisms of Diedrich began to make sense.

Brokenhearted at her sister's greed and ugly words, Regina wanted to slink away, but the sound of Sophie's voice again kept her rooted to the spot.

"Eli Tanner assured me that Herr Rothhaus will never allow his son to marry Regina. So all we have to do is plant the idea in Papa's mind that there is no hope of a marriage between Regina and Diedrich Rothhaus, and that Papa would be far wiser to will the land to us to keep for Henry—Papa's blood grandson."

"But next week we'll be movin' to Will's ma's house in Salem so I can begin my new job. What good will this farm here in Sauers do us when we're clear down in Salem?"

Sophie huffed. "It is like you have blinders on, Ezra! You said yourself that job might not last. This land should be my birthright, and it will be here. Think. You could start your own wheelwright shop in the barn. Eventually we could even sell off some acreage and build a proper house—a big one like we had in Vernon. You could own your own business again. And when Henry gets old enough, he could help you." Her tone turned sweet, cajoling. "Barnes and Son, Wheelwrights. It has a good sound, I think. Don't you want that one day, mein Liebchen?"

"Yeah, reckon I would, honey." Ezra's tone turned thoughtful then playful. "But I think Barnes and *Sons*, Wheelwrights, sounds even better." A soft chuckle.

Silence, then Sophie's giggle.

Regina's imagination supplied what she could not see. Her stomach churned at her sister's conniving treachery. Mama and Papa had taken in Sophie and Ezra when they were destitute. Now the couple conspired to use their baby son to steal her parents' homestead. Regina felt sick.

Moving as quietly as her wooden shoes and trembling legs allowed, she rounded the house then sprinted to the barn. There she searched and found an empty burlap sack and a shovel. Her parents and Diedrich were right. The time for inaction had passed. Regina needed to step out in faith and trust God with the rest.

∞

Kneeling on the new porch floor, Diedrich took the nail dangling from his lips and pounded it into the next board. With the Seitzes' wheat crop threshed, cleaned, and stored and the corn crop months away from harvest, he'd decided this would be a good time to begin work on a porch for the new house.

Reaching in his shirt pocket for another couple of nails, he paused and took a moment to look behind him and assess his morning's work. Redolent with the smell of newly cut poplar, the porch extended two-thirds the length of the house's front. Washed in the morning sun, the boards gleamed like gold.

Gold. His heart contracted. The word reminded him of his angry parting words to Regina yesterday. The hurt in her blue eyes still haunted him. He shook his head to obliterate the memory then lifted another board from the pile on the ground beside him and fitted it into place. She still loved him. He saw it in her eyes and felt it in her touch. She wanted to marry him as much as he wanted to marry her. He glanced up at the front of the house. His heart told him she, too, longed for them to have a future here together. Why could she not see that as long as they remained formally uncommitted, they only encouraged Father's stubbornness?

He pressed the point of a nail into the board in front of him then wielded the hammer and drove the nailhead flush with two powerful blows. But the exertion could not expel the anger and frustration roiling inside him. Despite telling Regina that he might leave for California in the spring, he knew it was a lie. As long as she still loved him, he could not leave. He felt trapped—unable to move forward, unable to move backward. The image of the Israelites gathered on the shores of the Red Sea came to mind. Diedrich understood how they must have felt with Pharaoh's army behind them and the impassable waters before them. Regina's love tethered him to Sauers. But until God provided a miracle and moved the impediment of Father's stubborn determination to cling to a decades-old grudge, Diedrich's life remained in limbo. Just as God provided a way for the children of Israel, Diedrich prayed He would grant Diedrich and Regina a like miracle.

At the distant sound of an approaching conveyance, he turned his attention to the dirt path that ran between the house and Herr Seitz's cornfield. Father must be coming home early from his work at the mill for the noonday meal. As usual, emotions warred in Diedrich's chest at the thought of his parent. Every night Diedrich prayed the next day would be the one in which God stirred Father's heart to cast off his old rancor for the Zichwolffs and embrace both forgiveness and Regina. Yet each day brought only disappointment.

As the sound grew louder, the head of the animal pulling the approaching conveyance appeared over the gentle rise in the road. Diedrich's heart quickened, matching the lively pace of Regina's shaggy little pony's feet kicking up clouds of dust. Not since the day Diedrich told Regina of Father's opposition to their marriage had she attempted to visit the new house.

Standing, he dropped the hammer to the porch floor with a clatter. *Could there have been an accident on the Seitz farm?* At the thought, he hastened his steps toward the cart as she reined in the pony.

"Regina." Reaching up, he helped her down, reveling in the touch of his hands on her waist. His arms ached to embrace her, to hold her against him and never let her go. But with no one else here, that would not be proper. And by the intense look on her face, he sensed she had come on a mission. "Is something amiss? Has there been an accident?"

"Nein." A bright smile bloomed on her face, dispelling his fears. Walking to the back of the pony cart, she lifted out a burlap sack and handed it to him.

Accepting the sack, he grinned. "What is this?" Since Father adamantly refused any food from the Seitzes' kitchen, Regina and her mother had stopped offering. So the sack's lumpy contents, which looked suspiciously like potatoes, surprised him. His curiosity piqued, he glanced inside. Sure enough, a dozen or so nice-sized new potatoes filled the bottom quarter of the sack. "Potatoes," he said unnecessarily.

"*Our* potatoes," she said with a grin. "We planted these together, and they have flourished, just as the love I believe Gott planted in our hearts for each other that same day has flourished."

She placed her hand over his, and Diedrich's heart caught with his breath. Did he dare believe the miracle he'd been praying for was unfolding before his eyes?

"Diedrich." Her eyes searched his. "Like the scriptures tell us in Galatians, 'Whatsoever a man soweth, that shall he also reap.' Gott sowed the good seeds of love in our hearts. And since we nurtured them and they grew, I believe our love is of Gott, and He will bless the harvest." She pressed her lips together and cocked her head, her eyes turning sad. "I am sorry that your Vater has decided to nurture the bad seeds of hate and bitterness. I continue to pray he will finally see how hurtful they are to him as well as to us and hoe them out of his heart. But until that day, he must reap what he has sown." She glanced down, and when she looked back up, her smile turned sheepish. "You were right. I need to show Gott I trust Him more. Today I will begin to do that. You asked me yesterday to reinstate our engagement. I am ready to do that now—that is, if you still want to marry me."

Diedrich fought to suppress the jubilation exploding inside him like the fireworks some of the neighbors had set off last week. Grinning, he put one arm around her and tugged her to his side. A flash of mischief sparked by his unquenchable joy gripped him. "Of course I want to marry you. But you must say again what you just said."

She gave him a puzzled grin, her eyes glinting with fun. "And what was it I said that you would like to hear again?"

"That I was right. I fear it may be the only time I ever hear you say those words to me."

Giggling, she gave him a playful smack on the arm, and his resistance crumbled. He dropped the sack of potatoes to the ground and pulled her into his arms and kissed her. Somewhere in the midst of his bliss, he thought he heard the roar of a sea parting.

"Diedrich!"

At the angry voice, Diedrich and Regina sprang apart. Together they turned to see Father striding toward them, his face purple with rage.

CHAPTER 26

"What is this?" Herr Rothhaus's angry glower swung between Diedrich and Regina. "I thought you were done with this Zichwolff pup, Diedrich."

Regina felt Diedrich tense. He took a half step forward as if to shield her from his father's wrath. Yet his arm remained firmly around her waist, helping to still her trembling body.

"Be very careful, Vater." Diedrich's voice, low and taut, revealed his barely controlled anger. "Regina is my future wife. I will not allow anyone, not even you, to speak to her with disrespect."

Herr Rothhaus's fists balled and a bulging vein throbbed at his temple. Regina's nightmare had become real. Would father and son come to blows over her? *Dear Lord, don't let it happen.*

Now Herr Rothhaus focused his glare on Diedrich alone. "But you told me the two of you were no longer engaged. Have you then been lying to me all this time?"

Diedrich's back stiffened. "I have never lied to you, Vater. Regina did break our engagement. And it was for your sake she broke it. As I have told you, my love for her has not changed." He looked down at Regina, and the barest hint of a smile touched his lips. His voice softened with his tender gaze. "It never has, and it never will."

Confusion relaxed the older man's rage-crumpled face. "You call her your future wife. How can that be if you are no longer betrothed?"

Diedrich's arm tightened around Regina's waist, pulling her closer. "She has finally agreed with me that reinstating our engagement may be the only way to bring you to your senses."

Herr Rothhaus's face contorted, turning myriad shades of red and purple. Regina feared he might collapse in a fit of apoplexy. He glared at Diedrich, his gray eyes bulging nearly out of his head. "My senses? My senses?" His voice climbed in a crescendo of anger. "You go behind my back and defy my wishes and now have the audacity to suggest I am not in my right mind? It is you, I think, who have lost your senses!" His murderous glare shifted to Regina. "She is a Zichwolff! I told you what they did to our family. And still you are content to let this Jezebel Zichwolff lure you into a marriage that would mingle our family's blood with that of her reprobate Vater and Großvater?"

Diedrich let go of Regina and strode toward his father. "Enough, Vater!"

True terror gripped Regina. *Dear Lord, stop this! Please, Lord, intercede.* She clutched at Diedrich's arm, but he shook off her hand and focused his fury on his father.

Diedrich's arms stiffened at his sides, and his fists clenched. His face came within inches of his father's. "From my earliest days, you and Mama taught me the scriptures. Whenever my brothers and I argued or were unkind to each other, you quoted the words of our Lord, teaching us forgiveness." His arms shot out to the sides, his fingers splayed, while his body visibly shook with emotion. "How, Vater? How could you teach us Christ's words concerning forgiveness when your heart was filled with hate and unforgiveness?"

A look of shame flashed across Herr Rothhaus's face, but his defiant stance did not budge. He rose on the balls of his feet until he stood almost as tall as his son. His eyes blazed with anger. "You dare to call me a hypocrite? You insolent pup!"

In one sudden movement, Diedrich spun on his heel and bounded to the porch then disappeared in the house. For a second, the fear that had gripped Regina eased. Had Diedrich left to cool his temper? But her ebbing trepidation flooded back as she found herself alone to face Herr Rothhaus's angry glare. The thought struck that she should climb into the pony cart and head for home. But before she could move, Diedrich shot out the front door, his Bible in hand.

He stomped to his father and waved the book in his face. "Matthew 5:44. 'But I say unto you, Love your enemies, bless them that curse you, do good to them that hate you, and pray for them which despitefully use you, and persecute you.' Matthew 6:14 and 15. 'For if ye forgive men their trespasses, your heavenly Father will also forgive you: But if ye forgive not men their trespasses, neither will your Father forgive your trespasses.' Mark 11:25. 'And when ye stand praying, forgive, if ye have ought against any: that your Father also which is in heaven may forgive you your trespasses.'" He smacked the book's leather cover, and Regina jumped at the sharp report that split the air like a rifle shot. "I memorized them just as you taught me to do, Vater. I have tried all my life to live by these words, and I thought you tried to live by them, too. Now I find I am wrong. These words mean nothing to you."

In a flash, Herr Rothhaus reached out and struck Diedrich's cheek with the flat of his hand. Regina gasped. Diedrich's whole body seemed to shudder, but he held his ground. She was glad she stood behind him and could not see his face. But she could see Herr Rothhaus's. And for a fraction of a second, the older man's expression registered shock at his own impulsive action.

For a moment, Herr Rothhaus's eyes glistened but quickly dried and turned stone-hard again. "I am your Vater! I never allowed you to disrespect me when you were growing up, and I will not allow it now." He shook his fist in Diedrich's face. "I will not tolerate being judged or called a hypocrite by my own Sohn!"

"I call you nothing but Vater." Diedrich's voice cracked, and his shoulders slumped. "I have bent over backward to remain respectful while you shattered my life and Regina's life with a laugh and a shrug. I do not stand in judgment of you. I will let Gott and your own heart do that." His voice sagged with his posture as his anger seemed to seep away, replaced by sadness. Pressing the Bible into his father's hands, he turned, and Regina's heart broke. His gray eyes held a vacant look, and three angry red streaks brightened his left cheek.

As Diedrich walked toward Regina and the pony cart, Herr Rothhaus stomped after him. "Do not call me Vater," he hollered. "You are not my Sohn! Now get out of my sight and take the Zichwolff whelp with you!"

Diedrich did not reply as he helped Regina up to the cart's seat then climbed up beside her and took the reins. They rode halfway home in silence.

At last, feeling the need to say something, Regina put her hand on Diedrich's arm. "I am sorry." Even to her own ears, the words sounded inadequate. "I should not have come. I—"

"Nein." Diedrich reined Gypsy to a halt. "You did only what I asked." As if unwilling to meet her gaze, he stared at the road ahead. "I am sorry you had to see that. And for the unkind things my Vater called you." He winced. "What you saw is not the man who raised me. I have never seen this man, and I pray I will never see him again."

Regina's heart writhed for her beloved. She prayed God would give her words to comfort him. "I know, my Liebling. Today, I did not see the Herr Rothhaus who came to our home in April. That man is kind, gentle, and caring. Today, I saw only hate. Hate is ugly, and it can make even those we love ugly." Turning to him, she reached out and pressed her palm against his wounded face. "I pray God will root out the hate from your Vater's heart so we can again see the gut man we know and love." Her words made her think of Sophie's treachery, and her heart experienced a double sting.

Diedrich's Adam's apple bobbed. He didn't reply, making her wonder if he didn't trust his voice. Instead, he touched her hand still on his cheek then turned his face against her palm and kissed it. Taking the reins back in hand, he clicked his tongue and flicked the line on Gypsy's back, setting the pony clopping along the road again.

As they turned into the lane that led to the house, he glanced over at her. "What made you change your mind?"

The memory of Sophie's hateful words rushed back to sting anew. Regina felt a deepening kinship with the man she loved. Today they had both experienced painful disappointment in people close to them. She fidgeted, reluctant to repeat what she had heard while eavesdropping. But since it affected Diedrich as well as her, she decided he had a right to know what Sophie was plotting. After recounting the conversation she'd heard this morning between Sophie and Ezra, Regina twisted the fistful of apron she'd been wadding in her hands. "I always knew Sophie wasn't especially fond of me, but I never imagined she disliked me so much." Rogue tears stung her nose, forcing her to sniff them back. "How could she act so sweet to me, when all the time she hated me?"

Diedrich shook his head and patted her hand. "I do not know, my Liebchen, just as I do not know how my Vater could let hate turn him into a man I do not recognize. But nothing is impossible with Gott. We must pray for Him to soften Sophie's heart as well as Vater's."

As they neared the house, Papa emerged from the big, yawning doors at the end of the barn. At the sight of Regina and Diedrich together, a look of pleased surprise registered on his face. He quickened his steps and met them between the barn and the house. Standing eye-level with Regina and Diedrich on the cart's low seat, he glanced between the two, his smile widening. "Has Herr Rothhaus changed his mind, then? Praise be to Gott!"

"Nein, Papa." Shaking her head, Regina reached out and gripped her father's arm to stifle his celebration. At Papa's puzzled look, Diedrich supplied the gist of what had just taken place outside the new log house.

Papa scowled and shook his head. "It is sorry I am to hear it." He pressed his hand on Diedrich's shoulder. "But you did the right thing, Sohn." A wry grin lifted the corner of his mouth. "It is never wrong to remind even a parent of Christ's commandments. Whatever your Vater may have said in anger, I know he loves you. In his letters to me, I could tell he was desperate to get you to America and out of reach of conscription. We must pray your words take root in his heart and that Gott will change him here and here." He tapped his chest and then his head. Turning to Regina, he patted her cheek. "It is happy I am that you have decided to trust Gott, Tochter. It is not always an easy thing to do." He glanced upward. "But Gott will reward your faith."

Regina smiled and hugged Papa. Though she had shared with Diedrich Sophie's selfish and deceitful plans, she prayed she could spare Papa and Mama ever learning of them.

Papa helped Regina down from the cart, and the three of them walked to the house together. "Your Mutter will be interested to hear of your news," he said as he opened the door for Regina. But when they trooped into the kitchen, Mama was not in sight. Instead, it was Sophie who turned from mixing corn bread batter in the large crockery bowl.

Upon seeing Diedrich with his arm around Regina, Sophie's eyes widened. To her shame, Regina experienced a flash of satisfaction at the dismay on her sister's face.

Papa crossed to Sophie. "Where is your Mutter? We have news to tell her."

Sophie blanched and opened her mouth, but nothing came out. She glanced toward the doorway that led to the interior of the house just as Mama emerged with Henry in her arms.

"What news?" Mama took in the three of them and gave a little gasp. With trembling arms, she lowered her squirming grandson to the floor. Her dark eyes swam with unshed tears, and she clutched at her chest. "Herr Rothhaus has repented. Praise be to—"

"Nein, Catharine." Papa stepped to her side and gently explained what had transpired.

The joy left Mama's face, and Regina was struck by the stark contrast between Mama's crestfallen expression and Sophie's hopeful one.

The starch returned to Mama's frame, and she lifted her chin. "But it is a beginning. Gott is working, I think."

"Ja." Papa nodded then turned to Regina and Diedrich. "When Georg sees you are determined to wed, he will relent and bless your union." He smiled, his countenance brightening. "And soon I shall have a gut German son-in-law to inherit my farm."

Everyone chuckled but Sophie. Whirling on the group, she stomped her foot, and her face turned stormy. "It is not fair!" She glowered at Papa. "Regina is not even of your blood, yet *she* gets the farm simply because she is willing to marry the man you handpicked for her?" Casting a scathing glance at Diedrich, she snorted. "Why, you scarcely know him." She stomped her foot again. "It is not fair, I say! I am the oldest and your blood daughter. *I* should inherit with my son—your blood grandson." With a flourish of her wrist, she gave Regina a supercilious wave. "Not that spineless little pretender." She wrinkled her nose as if she smelled something bad. "She's not even my sister!"

Though Sophie's sentiments came as no surprise to Regina, her sister's outburst and subsequent venomous diatribe stunned her. Regina and her sisters, including Sophie, had never before disrespected their parents in such a blatant manner. Diedrich stiffened at Regina's side. With his arm protectively around her back, he slid his hand up and down her left arm in a comforting motion.

Regina was sure he understood little of Sophie's words, and wondered if Sophie had chosen to deliver her tirade in English for that very reason. Yet Sophie's angry demeanor and disdainful looks left little doubt as to the subject of her ire.

"Sophie." Mama uttered her eldest daughter's name with a disappointed sigh.

Papa stiffened, and his brow lowered in a dark scowl. "Enough, Sophie! Regina is my Tochter, the same as you are." He strode to Sophie, and for an instant, fear glinted in her eyes. But when he spoke, his voice was calm, and his words measured. "It is sad I am, Tochter, that you are so bitter toward the Schwester Gott has given you. Your Mutter and I have always tried to deal fairly with you and your Schwestern." He shook his head and held out his hands in a helpless gesture. "You knew when you married Ezra I wanted to give the land one day to a farmer—a farmer with ties to the Old Country."

Sophie's eyes welled with tears, and Regina's heart went out to her. She could see how Sophie must feel much like Esau of old when his mother and brother contrived to deprive him of his birthright. But as Papa pointed out, Sophie, like Esau, had willingly forfeited any claim to the land when she married Ezra.

Sophie lifted a defiant yet trembling chin. "But I fell in love with Ezra."

Papa put his hand on Sophie's shoulder. "And so it was right for you to marry him. But he is not a farmer. And Henry, too, may well decide to follow his Vater and become a wheelwright or practice another trade altogether." He gave Sophie a fond, indulgent smile. "Because your Mutter and I give the farm to Regina does not mean we love you and Elsie any less. Like now, you, Ezra, and Henry, as well as Elsie and William, will always have a home here if you need one. But Ezra and William are not farmers. It is sorry I am that you think your Mutter and I are unfair to want the land we bought and worked on all these years to go to a daughter and Schwiegersohn who will farm it as we have."

Papa's eye twinkled, and he quirked a grin at Regina. "I do not know what I would have done if Regina, too, had settled her heart on a merchant or a wheelwright or. . .a miller."

At the word "miller," Regina's heart jumped, and heat flooded her face. Had Papa suspected her earlier infatuation with Eli? She ventured a glance up at Diedrich's face. His lips were pressed in a firm line, and his gaze skittered to the floor.

"But praise be to Gott," Papa continued, "Regina has settled her heart on Diedrich."

Sophie sniffed and folded her arms over her chest. Her rigid demeanor suggested she was not yet ready to surrender the argument. "But Herr Rothhaus may never grant them permission to marry. And Henry may grow up and decide to be a farmer. At least *he* is your own blood."

Mama, who had remained quiet but attentive to the exchange between Papa and Sophie, now glanced around the room, her attention clearly detached from the ongoing conversation. "Henry. Where is Henry?"

CHAPTER 27

Everyone stopped and looked around the kitchen, but Henry was not there. Sophie shrugged. "He has probably crawled into Regina's bed again to take a nap. You know how he loves to do that. I'm sure I will find him there." She headed for the house's interior with Mama on her heels.

Papa checked the washroom without success, and fear flickered in Regina's chest. Though she suspected Sophie was right and Henry was fast asleep in her bed, she wouldn't be easy until she knew he was safe. She held her breath, expecting any second to hear her sister or mother announce they had found him.

Instead, Sophie's voice from inside the house turned increasingly frantic as she called her son's name. The next moment she burst into the kitchen, her face white and her eyes wild. "He is nowhere. I can find him nowhere." Her voice cracked, and she began to tremble.

Mama appeared behind her, looking as pale and shaken as her daughter. She turned desperate eyes to Papa. "Ernst, he is not in the house."

The flicker of fear in Regina's chest flared. It was not unusual to occasionally lose sight of the active toddler, but until this moment, they had always quickly discovered his whereabouts.

Sophie clutched her heaving chest. "My baby! My kleines Kind. Where could he be?" Her words came out in breathless puffs, and Regina feared her sister might swoon.

As Mama and Sophie embraced, Papa slowly pumped his flattened hands up and down. "Now, now, we must stay calm. He cannot have gone far. We will find him in a bit."

Despite Papa's assurances, Sophie began to sob in Mama's arms. At that moment, Ezra came in from cutting hay. His face full of alarm, he rushed to Sophie and Mama. "What is wrong?"

Turning from Mama, Sophie gripped her husband and sobbed against his neck. "He–Henry. We cannot find Henry. . .anywhere."

The alarm on Ezra's face grew as he patted his wife's back. "Has anybody looked upstairs?" The tightness in his voice revealed his concern. "I caught him climbing up there yesterday."

At his suggestion, Regina flew up the stairs, wondering why no one had thought of it sooner. But a quick perusal of the room revealed no Henry. She checked under the bed and in the wardrobe—every nook and cranny where a two-year-old could hide. As each spot revealed no Henry, Regina's heart began to pound, and rising panic threatened to swamp her. Downstairs, she could hear the others scurrying around. Soon the whole house rang with a discordant chorus of people calling the little boy's name.

 ⟲

Regina hurried downstairs, and Diedrich met her at the bottom step. Fear stole her breath, and she could only shake her head at his hopeful look. Now true terror gripped her, and her whole body began to shake. Both the front and back doors were propped open to allow a cooling cross breeze. While everyone was focused on the argument between Sophie and Papa, Henry had obviously exited the house through one of the open doors. But which one? She thought of Papa's bull, Stark. The well. Even her gentle pony, Gypsy, tethered beside the lane, could be lethal to a two-year-old if the child crawled between the pony's hooves and the animal impulsively kicked out. A shudder shook Regina's frame.

Diedrich grasped her shoulders and fixed her with a calm and steady gaze. "We will find him, Regina. Gott will help us find him. You must believe that."

Unable to speak, she nodded. Fear paralyzed her brain until she couldn't even fashion a coherent prayer.

"Everyone outside!" At Papa's booming voice, everyone jerked to attention then scrambled for the back door. Regina was glad for Diedrich's strong arm around her waist, lending support to her quavering limbs.

Sophie and Ezra stood fixed, their gazes darting around. They looked as if they would like to go in all directions at once, but their inability to do so kept them rooted in place.

Papa began suggesting places Henry might hide. Diedrich held up a hand. "Wait." At his quiet but firm voice, everyone turned to him. "I think we should first pray for guidance. Gott knows where Henry is. If we ask, He will keep the *kleinen Jungen* safe and lead us to him."

Papa nodded. "Ja. You are right, Sohn. We must first go to Gott in prayer."

Forming a circle, everyone joined hands, and Papa began in a strong voice, thickened by emotion. "Vater Gott, You know where our little Henry is hiding. We ask You to keep him safe and direct us as we go in search of our precious Kleinen." When he referred to Henry as their precious little one, Papa's voice cracked, and Diedrich stepped in to utter a hearty "Amen."

Even before the word had faded away, everyone scattered. Over the next few minutes, they checked the well, the chicken coop, and the outhouse. When they all gathered empty-handed at the back door again, Sophie looked pale, shaken, and on the verge of collapse. Regina suspected she looked much the same as the terror in her chest grew to a growling monster.

Diedrich glanced toward the barn. "We have not yet checked the barn."

Mama sank, a trembling mass, to the built-up flat stones that edged the base of the well. At Diedrich's suggestion, she gasped and gripped her chest, rekindled fright shining from her worry-lined face. Her voice turned breathless. "The horses. The cow. Stark is in there." She lifted her terror-stricken eyes to Papa as if pleading for him to contradict Diedrich. "Not the barn, Ernst. Henry is only a baby. He surely could not have gone as far as the barn, do you think?"

Papa pressed a reassuring hand on her shoulder and shook his head. "Nein. I'm sure he is playing with us and hiding, or has fallen asleep in a place we have not yet thought of."

Despite Mama and Papa's denials, Diedrich continued to glance toward the barn, a look of urgency animating his features. "Still, it is worth looking, I think. Once when my little niece Maria was about Henry's age, she hid in the barn for two hours before we found her."

Regina sensed something was tugging Diedrich toward the barn. They had prayed for God to guide them. To ignore what could well be divine nudges seemed beyond foolish. She trusted Diedrich's instincts. "I agree with Diedrich, Papa. I think we should look in the barn."

Deliberation played over Papa's anguished face. He obviously questioned wasting time on a fruitless search in what he considered an unlikely spot. At the same time, she suspected that Papa also was wondering if God had planted the hunch in Diedrich's mind. At last he nodded. "Ja. We shall look in the barn." At his pronouncement, he and the others followed Regina and Diedrich to the large, weathered structure across the lane.

As they stepped into the building, Regina blinked, trying to force her eyes to more quickly adjust to the dim light. With trepidation, she turned her attention to the big bull's stall. To her relief, the large animal stood sedately munching hay and flicking away flies with the brushy end of his tail. The cow, too, was all alone in her stall, as were the two huge Clydesdales.

As she walked beneath the hayloft, a shower of hay dust filtered down, accompanied by what sounded like a faint giggle. She looked up and gasped as her heart catapulted to her throat. Perched on the edge of the loft with his bare legs dangling over the side beneath his gown, Henry looked down on them, his angelic expression keen with interest.

Afraid to speak or even breathe, Regina gripped Diedrich's arm. He followed her gaze and tensed. Mama, Papa, Sophie, and Ezra all gave a collective gasp.

"How on earth. . ." Ezra uttered the words Regina was sure filled everyone's minds.

The answer stood propped against the loft. Evidently, Henry had somehow managed to climb the long ladder either Papa or Ezra had left there. Regina cringed, imagining the toddler's precarious climb, his unsteady feet at times stepping on the hem of his gown in the course of his ascent. Her heart nearly stopped at the thought. But somehow God had helped the little boy to safely scale the ladder and reach the summit.

Sophie gripped Ezra's arm. "Do not just stand there, Ezra. Go up and get him!"

Ezra hesitated. "I don't know, Sophie. I don't want to scare him. He might. . ." Leaving the thought to dangle like Henry's legs, Ezra dragged his hand over his mouth. Beads of sweat broke out on his forehead.

Papa turned from Mama, who clung to his arm, and cupped his hands around Sophie's shoulders. He kept his voice low and calm, though it sounded brittle enough to break. "Ezra is right, Sophie. We must be careful not to frighten him."

Sophie huffed. "Oh, for goodness' sake! If no one else will go, I will." She headed toward the ladder. "Mama is coming, Henry."

"Mama." Henry leaned forward, evoking another collective gasp from the adults below. Sophie froze with her foot on the ladder's bottom rung.

Regina's heart stuck in her throat. She gripped Diedrich's arm and prayed. *God, please help us find a way to get him safely down.*

Ezra grasped Sophie's shoulders, gently moving her aside. "I'll go up."

With both hands pressed against her mouth, Mama leaned against Papa, who held her tight—ready, Regina was sure, to shield her eyes should the unthinkable happen. Regina clung to Diedrich as well, but he disentangled himself from her grasp. "Go to your Schwester." Confused and a little hurt that, unlike Papa with Mama, Diedrich had chosen to withdraw his support from Regina, she nevertheless went to embrace Sophie. With both her husband and son in peril, Sophie would need someone to support and comfort her.

As Ezra began to scale the ladder, Sophie's body shook even harder than Regina's. "Stay still, Henry," she called up in a tremulous voice. "Papa is coming to get you."

"Papa, Papa." Henry turned and drew his feet up under him, eliciting more sharp intakes of air.

Ezra quickened his steps. "No, Henry. Stay still."

Laughing, Henry pushed up to a standing position and toddled toward his father, his bare feet treading treacherously close to the loft's edge. Regina clung to Sophie, afraid to watch the proceedings and yet unable not to.

Now at the top of the ladder, Ezra reached out toward his son, curling his fingers toward him in a beckoning gesture. "Come here, Henry. Come to Papa."

Henry came within a fingertip's length of Ezra's reach. For a moment, the fear gripping Regina eased its stranglehold on her throat. But instead of walking into his father's arms, Henry laughed and turned as if he thought Ezra was playing a game with him. He lifted a chubby foot. Time froze with Regina's heart as the little boy teetered on the loft's edge. A look of terror contorted Ezra's face. Lunging, he reached out and swiped at his son's gown. He missed. Collective gasps punctured the air. A strangled scream tore from Sophie's throat as Henry's little body tumbled over the edge.

CHAPTER 28

Regina's mind went numb. Turning Sophie from the sight, she pressed her hand against the back of her sister's head and drew Sophie's face against her shoulder. If she could do nothing else, she could save Sophie the memory of witnessing the death of her child. At the same time, Regina buried her own face in Sophie's shoulder. Weeping quietly, she held tightly to her sister's body, now racked with sobs. Then with sudden awareness, she realized the only sound in the barn was that of her and Sophie's weeping. She hadn't heard the dreaded thud of Henry's little body hitting the barn's dirt floor or a rush of footsteps toward the site of the tragedy. No one else was weeping or wailing with grief.

Pushing away from Sophie, Regina opened her eyes. Dread filling her, she peered hesitantly over Sophie's shoulder at the spot where she expected to find Henry's lifeless form. But to her amazement, instead of the gruesome sight she'd imagined, she saw Diedrich grinning with Henry cradled safely in his arms. She nearly collapsed with relief. Now she understood why Diedrich had pushed her away. He'd hoped to position himself to catch her nephew should Henry fall. Regina's heart swelled. Every time she thought she couldn't love this man more, he proved her wrong.

Ezra scrambled down the ladder. And as if in one motion, he, Mama, and Papa all rushed to Diedrich and Henry. Only Sophie remained with her back to the group, doubled over and sobbing into her hands.

Regina gripped Sophie's forearms. "Sophie, look. Henry is safe. Diedrich caught him."

Sophie opened her eyes and blinked, disbelief replacing despondency on her face. She turned slowly as if afraid to believe Regina's words. Then, seeing they were true, she ran and snatched her baby son from Diedrich's arms.

"Henry," she mumbled against his curly head as she clutched her son's squirming form to her breast and rocked back and forth. "Don't you ever scare Mama like that again!" Her chide warbled through her sobs.

Ezra rushed to his family and enveloped them in his arms. Mama wept softly and caressed Henry's head, cooing comforting hushes to her grandson, who had also begun crying.

Papa gripped Diedrich's hand. "Danke, Sohn." His voice quivered, and his eyes watered. Regina couldn't remember the last time she'd seen Papa weep.

With red eyes and a soppy face, Ezra disengaged from Sophie and Henry then strode to Diedrich and grasped his hand. Sniffing, he ran his shirtsleeve under his nose. "I'm not good with words, but 'thank you' doesn't seem enough for what you did."

Papa translated, and Diedrich gripped Ezra's shoulder and grinned. "Bitte sehr, mein Freund. But it was Gott who dropped Henry into my arms. I am just the vessel He used."

Sophie finally relented to Mama's petitions and handed Henry to his grandmother, who smothered the little boy with kisses. Henry, who had stopped crying but still looked confused about all the commotion, fussed to get down. But Mama shook her head and held tightly to him. Papa guffawed and tousled the boy's mop of brown curls as the three of them headed out of the barn.

With her head down and her shoulders slumped, Sophie scuffed over the straw-strewn floor to join her husband. Wringing her hands, she finally looked up to face Diedrich and Regina. Shame dragged down her features, making her appear old. "*Herzlichen Dank*, Herr Rothhaus, for what you did for our Henry." A flood of tears streamed down her face, but she paid them no mind. "If not for you, Ezra and I might be preparing to bury our son." The last word snagged on the ragged edge of a sob. Ezra put a comforting arm around her shoulders, but she shrugged it off. Straightening, she sniffed back tears and lifted her quavering chin. "There is something I must say to you both, and I must say it now," she said in German, her voice breaking. "I am so ashamed. I have been mean and greedy." A new deluge of tears washed down her face.

Regina's heart turned over at Sophie's agony, but it also warmed in anticipation of her sister's repentance. Her impulse was to tell Sophie an apology was not necessary. But she knew it was—not only for her and Diedrich's sakes, but more importantly for Sophie's.

Sophie's throat moved with her swallow. Apologizing had never come easily to Regina's eldest sister. "Earlier, I said some unkind things to you. I ask you to forgive me." Now she focused her gaze squarely on Regina's face. A fresh tear welled in her left eye and perched on her lower lid for an instant before trailing down her cheek. "Regina, please forgive me for saying you are not my sister. You *are* my sister. I was so awful to you. And you have been so sweet and kind to me. I realize now that blood is not important. Family is important, and we are family. I hope you can forgive me. I will try to be a better sister to you in the future."

At Sophie's penitent words and demeanor, Regina's heart melted. She knew what the admission must have cost her naturally unyielding sibling. She gathered Sophie in her arms. "Mein liebe Schwester. Of course I forgive you."

After a moment, Sophie pushed away from Regina and turned to Diedrich.

"Herr Rothhaus, I said some very unkind things about you, too. I am sorry for them. Will you please forgive my unkindness?" Regina noticed Sophie's use of the courtesy title Herr in addressing Diedrich, an unmistakable token of regard.

Smiling, Diedrich took Sophie's hands in his. "Of course I forgive you, just as our Lord taught us to forgive."

Regina wondered if Diedrich was thinking of the scriptures he had quoted earlier to his father.

Wiping away her tears, Sophie stepped back into Ezra's embrace. "Danke, Herr Rothhaus." She glanced between Regina and Diedrich. "Ezra and I have not yet congratulated you on your engagement. We would like to do that now." She turned to Diedrich. "I look forward to having you as a brother. Please believe me when I tell you I will be praying that happens soon."

As Regina and Diedrich thanked Sophie for her kind sentiments, Regina was reminded of the scripture from the book of Hebrews that Mama liked to quote. "For whom the Lord loveth he chasteneth." Mama often warned, "When Gott wants our attention, He will get it one way or another. Those who ignore His whispered chide may have to feel the sting of His willow switch across their knuckles." God had obviously gotten Sophie's attention. And to Regina's mind, the fear of losing a child was quite a sting across the knuckles.

⁓

Over the next week, Regina and Sophie grew closer than Regina had ever imagined they could. And if she had harbored any doubt that her sister's repentance was genuine, Sophie squelched it as the two worked together in the upstairs bedroom, packing away the Barneses' things for their trip to Salem. Regina stopped her work to impulsively hug her sister. "I will miss you all so much."

At that, Sophie sank to the feather mattress and dissolved into tears. When Regina tried to comfort her, she confessed her scheme to convince Papa to will the land to her and Ezra instead of Regina and Diedrich.

"I don't know what came over me," Sophie said before blowing her nose into the handkerchief Regina handed her. "You and Diedrich are far more suited to farm life than Ezra and I. I would much rather live in town." She sniffed and mopped at her eyes. "I just wanted some security—a home no one could take away from me." With her head hung low, she twisted the handkerchief in her lap. "I know it doesn't excuse what I did, and I wouldn't blame you if you hated me."

Her heart crimping, Regina rubbed her sister's back. "Of course I don't hate you. You are my Schwester. I love you." Though cheered by Sophie's confession, Regina decided it might be best not to reveal her prior knowledge of the plan. "Everyone wants security, Sophie. But nothing in life is secure. That is why we must have faith in

Gott. I had to learn that, too. Diedrich and I have no assurance Herr Rothhaus will ever give us his blessing to marry, but we have faith that he will."

Sophie hugged Regina and promised to pray fervently for God to convict Herr Rothhaus as He had convicted her.

But two days after Sophie, Ezra, and Henry left for Salem, Regina's own faith began to flag. Though she, Diedrich, Mama, and Papa prayed daily for God to soften Herr Rothhaus's heart, they still heard nothing from him. And he had not appeared at church yesterday.

Sighing, she bundled up the sheets she'd stripped from her bed and headed downstairs, where Mama had begun heating water for the wash. Regina had preached to Sophie about faith, and now she must listen to her own counsel. Even when it seemed impossible, God, in one stroke, had protected Henry and changed Sophie's heart toward Diedrich and Regina. If God could do that, He could also change Herr Rothhaus's heart. She remembered the scripture Pastor Sauer read yesterday from the third chapter of Ecclesiastes. "To every thing there is a season, and a time to every purpose under the heaven." Just as Monday washday followed Sunday's day of rest, God surely appointed a specific time for each of His tasks as well. Still, she prayed He might hurry up and deal with Herr Rothhaus soon.

As she stepped into the washroom, a knock sounded at the back door. A man's shadow stretched across the open doorway. Papa and Diedrich were out cutting hay, but of course, neither of them would feel obliged to knock.

She dropped the sheets at the bottom of the stairs and stepped to the door. When the figure of the man came into view, dismay dragged down her shoulders. "Eli, I told you not to come around again. Diedrich and I are engaged—"

"I'm not here about that." His somber features held no hint of his usual cocky demeanor. "I'm here about Diedrich's pa—old man Rothhaus." He jerked his head toward the lane where Sam Tanner sat on the seat of a buckboard. "There's been an accident." Grimacing, he twisted his hat in his hands. "He's hurt bad. Real bad."

CHAPTER 29

Diedrich paused in his work with the scythe. Resting the curved blade on a mound of timothy hay he had cut a moment before, he leaned against the tool's long handle. Only one more half acre to cut. And if the weather stayed dry, he and Herr Seitz should be able to get all the hay put up in the mow by the end of the week.

Sighing, he lifted his sweaty face to the cool breeze and gazed at the fluffy white clouds the wind chased across the azure sky. He couldn't imagine a more idyllic scene. And indeed, to a casual observer, his life would undoubtedly seem ideal. He'd won the love of his life, and her entire family—even including Sophie—all wanted him to be part of their family. In the space of two months he could possibly claim Regina for his wife and at the same time become co-owner of the best farmland he'd ever had the privilege to work.

But the regret twisting his insides reminded him of the threatening cloud of uncertainty that still overshadowed his hopes for a happy future. Without Father's blessing, his dreams of a life with Regina on this land he had come to love could very well evaporate like the shifting clouds above him. Although Regina had agreed to reinstate their engagement, he couldn't expect her to wait forever. What was more, he knew his father's stubbornness. Father had never tolerated even a whiff of disrespect from any of his sons. And Father had undoubtedly seen Diedrich's outburst eleven days ago as a rank display of disrespect. Not since Diedrich was a child and received a disciplinary swat on the backside had Father struck him—and never before on the face.

He instinctively rubbed his unshaven cheek. The initial sting had long faded, but the memory of the blow still reverberated to his core. Diedrich's heart felt as if it were being ripped asunder. Thoughts of giving up either Regina or Father were equally abhorrent. *Dear Lord, don't make me choose. Please, God, don't make me choose.*

"Diedrich! Papa!"

At the sound of Regina's voice, Diedrich whipped his head around. The sight of her bounding toward him over the hay field lifted his glum mood while piquing his curiosity. It was too soon for dinner, so he couldn't guess what might have brought her all the way out here to summon him and Herr Seitz. And at the moment, he didn't care. He was just glad to see her. Though the distance between them still made it hard to discern her mood, he imagined her smiling face and his own lips tipped up in anticipation.

But the next moment her face came into clear view, wiping the smile from his face. Her blue eyes were wide and wild with fear. No hint of a smile brightened her terrified expression.

Dropping the scythe, he trotted toward her. He caught her around the waist, and her torso moved beneath his hands with the exertion of her lungs. "Regina, what is the matter?" He knew she and her mother were washing laundry today. Could Frau Seitz have been scalded by hot water? "Has something happened to your Mutter?"

She shook her head then pulled in a huge breath and exhaled. "Nein. It is your Vater. Eli Tanner came to tell us there has been an accident at the mill." Her chin quivered, and her eyes glistened with welling tears, causing Diedrich to fear the worst. His insides crumpled at the thought of losing his father before they had the chance to reconcile.

He let go of Regina so she wouldn't feel his hands trembling. Though he longed to ask the dreaded question pulsating in his mind, her words had snatched the breath from his lungs. His chest felt as if he'd been kicked by one of the Clydesdales.

Herr Seitz loped up in time to hear Regina's news. "Tell us, Tochter. What has happened?" He grasped her shoulders, and she drew in another ragged breath.

"Eli said Herr Rothhaus was chasing a raccoon from the mill and slipped on some grain on the floor. He fell and hit his head on the millstone." A large teardrop appeared on her lower lashes and sparkled in the sun like a liquid diamond perched on threads of spun gold. At any other time the sight would have melted Diedrich's heart, and he would have pulled her into his arms to comfort her. But not now. Instead, an icy chill shot through him, and his arms hung helplessly at his sides.

"Regina, you must tell us." Herr Seitz's voice, though firm, turned tender—coaxing. "Does Herr Rothhaus still live?"

She nodded, and Diedrich's knees almost buckled with his relief. The plethora of questions crowding his mind tumbled from his lips as from an overturned apple cart. "Where is he? How badly is he hurt? Can he speak? Has anyone gone to fetch a doctor?" He hated the harsh, interrogating tone his voice had taken, but he couldn't keep it out. If Father died before he could reach him and reconcile, Diedrich would never forgive himself.

Regina blinked, and Diedrich glimpsed a flicker of fear in her eyes. It seared his conscience. Her forehead puckered as if in confusion, or was it pain? She narrowed a harder, unflinching look at him. "He is at the house. He is alive but not fully conscious. Eli has gone to Dudleytown for the doctor, and his Vater is helping Mama settle Herr Rothhaus onto the downstairs bed." Her voice sounded rigid—formal. It was as if they were suddenly strangers.

No one spoke as the three strode to the house together. Regina didn't look at Diedrich, and her father walked between them. In more ways than one, Diedrich could feel the distance between him and the woman he loved lengthening by the minute.

When they reached the house, Diedrich didn't stop to wash up but rushed to the downstairs bedroom he and Father had shared when they first arrived at the Seitz home. Father lay on the bed with the quilt pulled up to his chest. The clean white cloth encircling his head bore a crimson stain at the forehead above his left eye. Was it just the light, or had Father's salt-and-pepper hair turned even grayer in the week and a half since Diedrich last saw him? His eyes were closed, and his face chalk white. Frau Seitz sat at his bedside. Her expression anxious, she patted his hand while continually calling his name. If not for the tiny rise and fall of Father's chest, Diedrich might have thought his spirit had already left his body.

Diedrich rushed to his father's side and took his hand. A parade of memories flashed through his mind—his father's smiling face as he swung Diedrich up on a horse for the first time; his tender expression, compassionate voice, and gentle touch as he picked Diedrich up and brushed him off when he fell. The rancor in Diedrich's heart from his recent dispute with his parent faded. Father had always taken care of him. He would now take care of his father.

With tears blurring his vision, he knelt by the bed and rubbed his father's weathered hand. "Can you hear me, Papa?"

Father moaned and rolled his head on the pillow, igniting a flicker of hope in Diedrich's chest. But no amount of prompting evoked a more coherent response. For what seemed like days but was probably less than an hour, Diedrich stayed at his father's side alternately praying and trying to rouse him. Little conversation occurred. Regina and her parents and Sam Tanner hovered nearby, quietly praying. At last, Eli appeared with a middle-aged man in dress clothes carrying a black leather satchel.

With Herr Seitz translating, the man introduced himself as Dr. Phineas Hughes. He pulled up a chair next to the bed, displacing Diedrich, and handed Regina his dusty, short-top hat. First, he lifted Father's eyelids one at a time and peered into them. Then he removed the bandage from Father's head and examined the wound. Despite the bluish-purple lump rising on Father's forehead, the doctor pronounced the wound superficial and of no grave concern. The problem, he surmised, was any unseen damage that might have occurred to the brain in the fall.

Diedrich fought the urge to pepper the physician with a barrage of questions, deciding it best to wait and allow the man to make a full examination. So he held his peace as the doctor took a sharp instrument from his satchel and poked the bottom of Father's foot. At the touch, Father moaned, rolled his head, and drew up his knee. Though ignorant of medicine, Diedrich took Father's response and the doctor's "Mm-hmm" as encouraging signs.

Returning the sharp instrument to the satchel, Dr. Hughes then took out a wooden tube with a bell shape on one end and an ivory disk on the other. He placed the bell-shaped end on Father's chest and pressed his own ear to the ivory disk. Slipping his watch from his plaid waistcoat, he watched the face of the timepiece as he listened. At length, he put away both the tube and the watch. While Diedrich waited with bated breath, the doctor sat upright and emitted a soft harrumph. "Well, his heart sounds strong." He shook his head. "But that he has not yet regained full consciousness is troubling."

Standing, he picked up his satchel then retrieved his hat from Regina. "There is really nothing more I can do. His healing is in God's hands now. We know very little about the workings of the brain, and such injuries are unpredictable. All we can do is to wait and observe." He shot a glance at Regina and Frau Seitz. "Keep the head wound clean and bandaged, and someone should sit with him until. . ." Clearing his throat, he looked down. When he looked back up, he gave Diedrich a kind smile. "Just keep a watch on him. And it would not hurt to talk to him. It has been the experience of some physicians that such patients do seem to hear and understand in some way. It is thought by some who study these cases that conversation can actually help stimulate the brain and bring the patient back into consciousness." He plopped his hat on his thick shock of graying hair. "Let me know if there are any changes. We should know one way or another within forty-eight hours."

As Herr Seitz interpreted the doctor's words, a crushing dread gripped Diedrich. The doctor's prognosis seemed to be Father would either recover or die in the next two days.

Bidding the group good day, Dr. Hughes exchanged handshakes with Diedrich and Herr Seitz then left the house with young Tanner.

With the doctor's departure, a somber pall fell over the room, and an overwhelming sense of guilt and despondency enveloped Diedrich.

∽

Regina's heart broke for Diedrich. Only the two of them remained in the room with Herr Rothhaus. Mama had left to gather more cotton cloths for bandages, while Papa saw Herr Tanner to his wagon. Seeing Diedrich slumped in the chair beside his father's still form, his face crestfallen and drawn, she was filled with a desire to comfort him. She pressed her hand on his shoulder. "Gott will hear our prayers and heal him. We must have faith."

He shrugged off her hand, sending a chill through her. The cold look he gave her felt as if he'd stabbed her through the heart with an icicle. He gave a sardonic snort. "My faith is all used up, Regina. I prayed Gott would change Vater's heart—not stop it. When I asked Him to remove the obstacles preventing us from marrying, I never expected Him to answer by taking Vater from me." His lips twisted in a sneer, and his voice dripped with sarcasm. "But Gott has given us what we asked, has He not? Soon there will likely be no impediment to our marrying."

A pain more excruciating than any she had ever felt before slashed through Regina. Though reason told her Diedrich's hard words were born out of crushing worry for his father, she also knew they came directly from his heart. Diedrich blamed their love and, by extension, Regina, for his father's condition. Whether Herr Rothhaus lived or died, a marriage between her and Diedrich had become impossible. Tears filled her eyes and thickened her voice. "Pray for your Vater's recovery, as I will be praying. But there will be no marriage. I am releasing you from our engagement."

As she turned to leave the room, she harbored a glimmer of hope Diedrich might utter a word of objection. But he stayed silent, extinguishing her hope and plunging her heart into darkness.

For the next twenty-four hours, Herr Rothhaus's condition remained unchanged. Diedrich never left his side except when Regina came into the room to change Herr Rothhaus's bandage or feed him warm broth from a cup, which he oddly took only from her hand. She had insisted on shouldering much of Herr Rothhaus's care, initially out of a sense of scriptural duty. He hated her. And his hatred had robbed her of any hope for a happy life with Diedrich. But she did not want to hate him back. She had seen the pain hatred inflicted on Sophie and then later the freeing power of forgiveness. Though Herr Rothhaus could inflict an injury on her heart, she would not allow him to inflict one on her soul. Also, she hoped by caring for his father, she might earn back a measure of Diedrich's regard. But she hadn't expected to so quickly find her heart blessed by the moments she spent with Herr Rothhaus. She soon ceased to equate the gentle man she cared for like an infant with the angry man who had hurled insults at her. At the same time, Diedrich's altered demeanor toward her ripped at her heart. The moment he spied her coming, he'd leave the room with scarcely a word or a glance. It hurt to think he could not even bear to share the same space with her.

Despite Diedrich's rejection, Regina found solace in ministering to his father. Although Herr Rothhaus gave no sign of awareness, the fact he took the broth in a relatively normal manner with her holding the cup and wiping drips from his chin encouraged her. Remembering the doctor's advice, she talked to him, prayed, recited encouraging verses of scripture, and even sang hymns as she cared for him.

Two days after the accident, Regina had just finished giving Herr Rothhaus his supper of broth. As she dabbed the remnants from his mouth and chin whiskers with a cotton towel, she recited scriptures about healing. "'For I will restore health unto thee, and I will heal thee of thy wounds, saith the Lord.'" She bowed her head over her folded hands. "Dear Lord, I ask You to heal Herr Rothhaus. Please restore him to full health—"

"Regina." Diedrich's soft voice halted her in midsentence. Opening her eyes, she looked up to find him standing in the doorway, gazing at her. His gray eyes—as soft as the morning mist—held a tenderness toward her she thought she would never see again. "I surrender."

She could only sit gaping, confused by his ambiguous comment. "Surrender what? I do not understand."

He stepped into the room. "I surrender to you—to my love for you." He crossed to where she sat and, taking her hands in his, knelt before her on one knee. "Regina, when I learned of Vater's accident, I feared he might die without us reconciling." He glanced at his father's face and grimaced. "I still do." He swallowed. "I blamed you. And I tried to close my heart to you. But it is no use. You have become too much a part of it—too much a part of me." He gave her a sad smile. "I could not bar you from my heart last spring when I thought I wanted to go to California. I should have known I could not do it now."

He glanced at his father again, and his eyebrows pinched together in a frown. "You were right. Vater made his choice. I have done much praying." His lips quirked in a wry grin. "Like Jacob of the scriptures, I have wrestled with Gott about this situation. In my own guilt, I blamed you for the rift between me and Vater. That was wrong of me—as wrong as it was for Vater to blame you for what your birth Vater and Großvater did against our family."

Regina held her breath. The lump of tears gathering in her throat rendered her mute. What was he saying? Was he choosing her over his father?

Diedrich's thumbs caressed the backs of her hands, sending the familiar thrill up her arms. "You did not repay your sister's trespasses against you with meanness or spite but forgave her as our Lord bade us to do. In the same manner, I have watched you tenderly care for my Vater after the unkind way he treated you." He shook his head, and his eyes brimmed with emotion. "Where could I find another woman like you? I know now whatever happens"—he glanced once more at his father's face—"*whatever* happens, I must make you my wife. I cannot bear the thought of living my life without you. My Vater may be against our marriage, but I feel with all my heart Gott is for it. Please say again you will marry me."

Before she could answer, a faint voice intruded.

"Angel."

At once, Diedrich sprang to his feet and rushed to his father's bedside. But Regina stepped back. If Herr Rothhaus was truly rousing from his two-day stupor, Diedrich's face should be the one he saw first—not Regina's.

Diedrich sat on the chair beside the bed and grasped his father's hand. "Vater, it is Diedrich. Did you say something?"

Herr Rothhaus's head rolled back and forth on the pillow. "Angel," he murmured again. His eyelids fluttered then half opened. He peered at Diedrich from beneath drooping lids. "Diedrich, mein lieber Sohn. You are in heaven with me, then?"

Diedrich smiled and shook his head. "Nein, Vater. And neither are you. Two days ago, you fell at the mill and hit your head on the grinding stone. We feared Gott might take you, but He has heard our prayers, and you are still with us here on earth."

Herr Rothhaus scrunched his face, and his head rolled more fiercely on the pillow. "But there was an angel with me. She sang *schöne* hymns and spoke words from the Heilige Schrift."

At his words, Regina's heart pounded, and she fought the urge to flee the room. It appeared Dr. Hughes had been right when he suggested patients with head injuries like Herr Rothhaus's might actually hear and have some awareness. What would Herr Rothhaus think if he knew hers was the voice of the angel his muddled brain had heard?

Diedrich glanced at Regina then turned back to his father. "Vater, I believe the angel you speak of is Regina. She has cared for you since Herr Tanner and his Sohn brought you here to the home of Herr Seitz after your accident."

Herr Rothhaus's right hand clenched, wadding a fistful of quilt. For a long moment, he said nothing. Tension built in the room like a coming storm. Regina's breath caught in her throat, and she braced for his angry outburst.

Instead, when Herr Rothhaus spoke again, his voice was small, weak, even contrite. "Bring her, Sohn. I want to see her."

Turning to Regina, Diedrich curled his fingers toward his palm in a beckoning gesture. "Come."

Regina hesitated as fear gripped her. She did not want to ignite another ugly scene like the one they experienced in front of the new house a few days ago. But the steady look in Diedrich's eyes assured her of his unwavering protection, and she tentatively approached the bed. As she stepped into Herr Rothhaus's view, her heart thudded. How would he react?

To her surprise, a gentle smile touched his lips. His watery eyes looked sad, and his face appeared ancient, tired. "Forgive me, liebes Mädchen. I was wrong." His gaze shifted from her face to Diedrich's. "I must ask your forgiveness, too, Sohn. You were right. I had forgotten the lessons our Lord taught us in His Word." Reaching up, he fingered the bandage around his head. "It took you and Gott together to knock the sense back into my head." The quilt covering him eased down as he breathed out a deep sigh. "I am tired of carrying the burden of hate in my heart. It has grown too heavy," he murmured as if to himself. "Too heavy and too costly."

A tear slipped down his weathered face, touching Regina deeply and forcing her to wipe moisture from her own cheeks. Herr Rothhaus looked up at Diedrich, his eyes full of contrition. "I do not want to lose you, mein Sohn." He turned a sad smile to Regina. "Or the chance to have an angel Schwiegertochter." Then his gaze swung between them. "You have my blessing to marry." He grinned. "But you must wait until I am strong again. I want to stand beside my Sohn as he takes a wife."

Smiling, Diedrich rose from the chair and slipped his arm around Regina. "Do not worry, Vater. Regina and I will marry in September, as we agreed the day we arrived here. By then you will be stark, like Herr Seitz's bull." He shot Regina a knowing grin. At his veiled reminder of their first meeting, she couldn't hold back a merry giggle.

Herr Rothhaus's voice turned gruff. "Now both of you go and let me rest so I can heal."

Diedrich grinned, and Regina bent and pressed an impulsive kiss on her future father-in-law's cheek. Her heart sang with anthems of thanksgiving for the answered prayers and miracles God had wrought over the past several minutes.

With his hand around her waist, Diedrich guided Regina outside. There they met Mama coming in from the garden with a basket of vegetables on her arm and shared the joyous news with her.

Mama wiped away tears. "Praise Gott!" Her expression quickly turned from relieved to determined. "After two days of broth, I must make Herr Rothhaus a proper supper."

When Mama had disappeared into the house, Diedrich led Regina to the garden. Regina gazed over the vegetable patch where bees buzzed and butterflies flitted around the verdant growth of potato and cabbage plants as well as vines of beans entwined around clusters of sapling poles. Her full heart throbbed with a poignant ache. Here she and Diedrich had shared so many significant moments in their relationship over the past several months, and now she sensed they were about to share another.

He took both of her hands in his, and she cocked her head and grinned up at him. "Why have you brought me here?" She gazed into his eyes—those same flannel-soft gray eyes that had made her feel safe last April in the bull's pen.

He didn't smile, but a muscle twitched at the corner of his mouth. "To hear your answer."

It suddenly occurred to her that Herr Rothhaus's awakening had distracted her before she could answer Diedrich's proposal. Mischief sparked within her, and a playful grin tugged at the corner of her mouth. Feigning weariness, she gave an exasperated huff. "Diedrich Rothhaus, I have agreed to marry you twice before. Must I say it again?"

"Ja, you must." He sank to one knee and lifted an expectant look to her, while an untethered smile pranced over his lips. "So, Regina Seitz, will you agree to be my wife?"

At his repeated petition, Regina's heart danced with happy abandon. Blinking back renegade tears, she fought to affect a bored pose while bursts of joy exploded inside her. "Ja," she drawled. "Since your Vater now agrees, I suppose I must marry you. But our Vaters promised us months ago, so my answer should be no surprise."

Grinning, he stood and let go of her hands. "Then this, too, should come as no surprise." Pulling her into his arms, he kissed her until her toes curled. Suddenly September seemed excruciatingly distant.

"Well," he murmured as he nuzzled his face against her hair, "did I surprise you?"

"Nein," she managed in a breathless whisper.

His voice against her ear turned husky. "Then I must try harder to surprise you."

Regina leaned back and smiled up into her future husband's handsome face. "Only if all your surprises are as sweet as the last one you tried."

He pulled her back into his arms and tried again.

CHAPTER 30

Sauers, Indiana, September 1850

Regina bent and reached into the oven to extract the pan of freshly baked corn bread. The sweet aroma tickled her nose as she gingerly grasped the hot pan with the cotton pot holder. Noticing the quilted square of cloth's stained and singed condition, she couldn't suppress a smile. Over the past year, Sophie's wedding gift had seen much duty.

As she plopped the pan on top of the stove, strong arms encircled her waist. Twisting in Diedrich's embrace, Regina smiled up at her husband. She slipped her arms around his neck. Would his touch ever cease to send delicious shivers through her? She couldn't imagine such an occurrence. "I should make you wear your Holzschuhe in the kitchen so you cannot sneak up on me, *mein Mann*," she teased.

Grinning, he nuzzled her cheek with his prickly chin, filling her nostrils with his scent and firing all her senses. "But then I could not surprise you, and you know how you love surprises." His lips blazed a searing trail from her jaw to her mouth and sweetly lingered there.

When he finally freed her from his kiss, she still clung to him, reveling in his closeness. No, she would never become immune to Diedrich's caresses. "You can no longer surprise me with kisses," she challenged breathlessly.

Stepping back, he reached into his shirt pocket and pulled out an envelope. "Ah, but I have other means by which to surprise you."

Intrigued, she plucked the already-opened envelope from his fingers. "What is this?" She looked at the name printed on the envelope's top left corner. "So what is so surprising about a letter from your brother Frederic?"

"Look at the postmark." His grin widened.

"Baltimore, Maryland?" It took a moment for the significance to register.

Diedrich beamed. "Frederic and Hilde and the Kinder are now in America. They should arrive in Jackson County within the month."

Regina's heart thrilled at her husband's joy. Separation from his beloved brother had remained the one spot marring Diedrich's otherwise flawless contentment. Her smile turned fond. "That is wunderbar, mein Liebchen. I am excited to meet my *Schwager* and *Schwägerin*." Not to be outdone, she decided to share her own piece of news. "Frederic, Hilde, and their children are not the only additions to our family we are expecting."

At Diedrich's puzzled look, Regina stifled a giggle. "Mama stopped by while you were gone. She got a letter from Sophie today saying Henry will be getting a little brother or sister soon." She laughed. "Mama wondered if helping Elsie with her and William's little Catharine made Sophie want another little one of her own."

Diedrich chuckled. "Soon our Vaters will have more Enkelkinder running around than they will know what to do with. And since Ezra and Sophie bought Herr Roberts's big brick house in Salem, they will have plenty of room for even more Kinder."

Regina perused Frederic's letter. "Have you told Papa Georg yet about Frederic and Hilde?"

He nodded. "Ja. On my way back from Dudleytown, I stopped by the mill to deliver to Herr Tanner a letter from Eli." He grinned. "Vater is sehr excited about the news." His grin disappeared, and his gaze skittered from hers, signaling a measure of unease. "Eli and Herr Roberts believe they have discovered a rich vein of gold on their claim near San Francisco." The tiny lines at the corners of his mouth tightened. "Perhaps you will think you should have married Eli after all. You could be a *wohlhabend* woman now."

She cupped his dear face in the palm of her hand. "I am glad for Eli and Herr Roberts, but I married the right man. And I *am* a wealthy woman." She turned to cut the cooling corn bread. If his face held a tinge of regret, she would rather not see it. "And if you had joined Herr Roberts instead of Eli, the gold would be yours."

He grasped her waist and turned her around. His soft gray gaze melted into hers. "Gott has given me more treasure here in Sauers than Eli will ever find in the hills and streams of California." He bent to kiss her, but before their lips touched, a soft mewling sound that quickly became a full-throated cry halted them.

Regina sighed and slipped out of her husband's grasp. "I must see about our Sohn."

Diedrich followed her to the doorway between the kitchen and front room. "Perhaps he is hungry."

"Nein." Regina shook her head. "I just fed and changed him a few minutes ago."

By the time they reached the front room, the baby's crying had stopped, and the cradle was empty. As Diedrich and Regina shared a look of alarm, the sound of quiet singing wafting through the open front door turned Regina's sharp concern to mild curiosity. On the porch, they found Papa Georg in the rocking chair, cradling his swaddled grandson in his arms and softly singing a hymn.

Papa Georg stopped singing and looked up at them. "Jakob and I are just enjoying the nice day," he whispered, glancing down at the now sleeping infant. "So since we require nothing at the moment but each other's company, maybe the two of you could find something else to do." Grinning, he went back to rocking and singing, while Jakob's rosebud lips worked around his tiny thumb.

At the sight, Regina's heart melted. A little more than a year ago, she would not have imagined witnessing such a scene. Her eyes misted at the culmination of all her prayers. The words of Psalms 100:5 echoed through her heart then winged their way heavenward in a prayer of thanksgiving. *"For the Lord is good; his mercy is everlasting; and his truth endureth to all generations."*

Diedrich and Regina shared a look, and their smiles turned to wide grins. Diedrich nodded. "Sehr gut, Vater. We will leave you alone with your *Enkel*."

Inside the house, Diedrich took Regina's hand. He glanced at the kitchen door then at the stairway that led to the loft. "The corn bread is baked, and you won't need to start dinner for at least another half hour. And I can't do any hammering, or I may wake Jakob. So what should we do?"

Her heart full, Regina grinned up at her husband. "Surprise me."

As he towed her toward the stairs, Regina knew that whatever surprises the years might bring, as long as she and Diedrich were together, life would be sweet.

Sonoran Secret

by Nancy J. Farrier

CHAPTER 1

Arizona Territory, 1870s

Eduardo Villegas twisted the tip of his mustache, then smoothed it back into place. In the distance, a cloud of dust heralded the arrival of his bride-to-be. Soon his lonely evenings would end.

"You look a little nervous, my friend. Are you sure you want to go through with this?"

Eduardo glanced over at his friend and pastor, Matthew Reilly. He shrugged, then continued to stare down the road. "I gave my word, Pastor. Besides, the Lord clearly showed me this is the right thing to do."

Deputy Quinn Kirby, another friend of Eduardo's, chuckled. "I know you can trust God. Trusting Diego Garcia is the problem."

"What's to trust? He promised to give me his daughter, Teresa, in marriage. After the wedding, I'll forgive the debt he owes me. It's as simple as that."

"With Diego, nothing is ever easy. That's why I'm here." Quinn brushed his fingers across his holstered pistol. "I wasn't sure Diego would even show up."

Eduardo frowned as the buckboard lurched into view. Quinn knew Diego too well. Diego would do anything to cheat on a bargain. Eduardo didn't know how else to settle the debt between them, short of bringing in the law. When Diego approached him with the idea of marriage to one of his five daughters as a way to pay what he owed, Eduardo prayed about it, then agreed to the arrangement.

Now, Matthew was right. He felt like turning around and running as fast and far as he could. What had he gotten himself into? Did he really hear God saying he should marry Teresa Garcia? He didn't even know the girl. *Lord, I'm a little nervous about this. Please let me know if this is part of Your plan for my life.*

As the wagon clattered to a stop in the grove of trees that straddled the Villegas and Garcia properties, a calm descended over Eduardo. He nodded in satisfaction, knowing God answered his prayer with His peace.

Diego Garcia stepped down from the wagon, then turned to take the hand of the young woman clad all in white. The long dress rustled in the quiet as she eased over the side of the wagon. Eduardo couldn't be certain from this distance, but he thought his bride might be missing her shoes.

"Thank God, it's a cool day," Matthew whispered to Eduardo. "Otherwise your wife-to-be would melt in all of those clothes."

Eduardo bit back a smile, knowing the truth of Matthew's words. In the Arizona Territory, the sun could be merciless. Long-sleeved dresses and gloves in the summer would bring heatstroke in a short time. The heavy veil that covered Teresa's head and blocked out fresh air must be suffocating, despite the cool day.

Diego leaned close to his daughter, speaking words too quiet for the others to hear. She stiffened and took his proffered arm. They moved toward Eduardo. He wondered if he detected reluctance in Teresa's steps. Brides are always nervous and unsure, he admonished himself. After all, he'd only spoken to the girl once over a year ago. He remembered her as being a little saucy. She wasn't beautiful, but pretty enough. There were worse things than having a wife who wasn't a beauty. Eduardo recalled her being sturdy. She would be able to work hard and have his children.

Lord, Eduardo lowered his eyes, hoping his friends weren't watching, *I'm trying to have faith in You. I know in my head that Your plans for me are right, but I don't want a wife who's only good for working and bearing children. I want someone who loves You, a wife who will be a friend.*

"Well, here is my future son-in-law." Diego's low, gravelly voice grated on Eduardo's taut nerves.

Looking up, Eduardo stared at the woman encased in white. The long, thick veil, concealing any evidence of her features, draped to cover nearly to her elbows. White, beaded gloves, tucked into the long sleeves of her gown, hid even her small hands from his sight. Eduardo took a deep breath. Part of him was relieved, but part of him wanted to rip the veil away and see how Teresa felt about this marriage. Would she be able to love him? Could he learn to love her? He could clearly recall the way his mother and father looked at one another, their eyes glowing with unspoken feelings. Anger knotted his stomach at the thought of his parents' needless deaths. As if sensing his mood, Quinn nudged him. Eduardo tamped down the rage, refusing to allow it to boil over right then.

Matthew cleared his throat. "Diego, I'm surprised your wife and other daughters didn't wish to attend the wedding. Are they coming later?"

Diego grinned and shook his head. His greasy mustache trembled with the movement. "My wife wasn't feeling well this morning. She needed the other girls to stay home and help her." He pulled his daughter forward a few steps. "Shall we get this over? Eduardo, I'm keeping my end of the bargain. Do you have the papers releasing me from my debt?"

Lifting the envelope in his pocket, Eduardo nodded. "They're right here. I'll hand them over as soon as the ceremony is done." He could almost feel Quinn's approval at his caution.

Diego's beady eyes fastened on the envelope. He licked his lips. "You know, you are getting quite a wife here. Perhaps we should add a little something to even things out on my end of the bargain."

Quinn shifted forward. Eduardo lifted his hand to stop his friend.

"Diego, my father was very generous in his help to you and your family. Your debt to my father, and now to me, is worth more than everything you own. Over the years, you have paid nothing against this debt. I am trying to be just as charitable by agreeing to forgive what you owe me. I believe that is enough of a bride price for your daughter."

Quinn stepped forward, his hand resting on the grip of his pistol. "If you don't think Señor Villegas is right, then he and Pastor Reilly can return your daughter home, and I'll escort you into Tucson. I've got a cozy little cell for you. In fact, I would prefer to have you behind bars."

Sweat beaded on Diego's brow. He held up his hand. "No, Señor Villegas is being very generous. My daughter is pleased to marry him." He pushed her white-gloved hand toward Eduardo. "Please, let's begin the ceremony."

Matthew opened his Bible and cleared his throat. "Would you like me to use your full name, Señorita Garcia?" Her head shook from side to side. The veil fluttered.

"My lovely girl is very nervous. Without her mama and sisters, she gets shy. Just Señorita Garcia will be fine."

Matthew frowned and glanced at Eduardo.

Eduardo gave a brief nod, stepped over beside Teresa, and took her hand in his. She seemed shorter than he remembered. Her fine-boned hand didn't feel as sturdy as he thought it should. A vague sense of unease swept through him, then was gone as quickly as it had come. Eduardo tensed, trying to pin down the strange sensation before giving up, convincing himself that he, too, had a case of nerves. He straightened, took his hat off, and handed it to Quinn.

Matthew flipped through the Bible until he reached the book of Ephesians. His strong voice rang out with the words written to husbands and wives in the fifth chapter. " 'Wives, submit yourselves unto your own husbands, as unto the Lord. . . .Husbands, love your wives, even as Christ also loved the church, and gave himself for it.' " Eduardo wondered if he would be able to love his wife as Christ loved the church. That kind of love would take work and commitment.

All his life, his parents had talked to him about the importance of marriage. He was prepared to do his best to love and cherish Teresa.

When Matthew asked Teresa to repeat the vows, she remained silent. Shifting to the side, she turned her head toward her father. The veil rustled.

"I'm afraid my daughter is unable to speak. If you will say the words, she will nod her acceptance."

"Why can't she say the vows?" Quinn's question carried a tinge of distrust.

"Ahh! You know these women. Flighty creatures, they are at times." Diego's strained smile didn't set Eduardo at ease. "My daughter, when she gets nervous, she has trouble talking."

"With some women that would be a blessing."

Teresa stiffened at Quinn's mumbled words.

"It's okay." Eduardo wanted to get this over. "Just get on with this, Matthew." He wanted to add that, the sooner the marriage ceremony was finished, the faster Diego Garcia would be off his land.

Matthew proceeded to recite Teresa's vows. She nodded her assent. Eduardo said the vows and slipped his mother's wedding ring over his bride's gloved finger. Her hand quivered like a leaf in the breeze. The ring stopped partway up. He knew she could put it on right later. He gave her hand a light squeeze, trying to reassure her.

"I now pronounce you man and wife."

Diego slapped Eduardo on the back. "Well, son-in-law, I reckon it's time to get those papers out and hand them over."

"What happened to kissing the bride?" Quinn leaned forward, his gaze focused on Diego.

A nervous laugh bubbled out of Diego. "I need to get back to my wife. She's sick, you know." He held out his hand to Eduardo. "If you give me the papers, my daughter can change, and I'll be getting home."

"What do you mean, your daughter can change?" Eduardo couldn't keep his apprehension in check any longer.

Waving a hand in the air, Diego forced a laugh. "Oh, you see, this is her mother's wedding dress. This gown must be kept for her sisters."

"Then we'll return the dress later."

"No, I think my wife would be too upset if I returned without her gown. She considers it very precious."

Eduardo fought the urge to roll his eyes. He pointed to the thick stand of trees behind him. "She can go over there and change while we sign the papers."

Diego rushed to the wagon and came back with a bundle of clothes tied with string. Teresa moved off to more privacy. Quinn pushed forward as Eduardo pulled the debt release papers from his pocket.

"Diego, I don't like the sound of this. Something isn't right. If you've tricked Eduardo in any way, I'll make sure you regret it."

"Please, Señor Kirby. I have brought my daughter to Señor Villegas as I promised. You have been here for the whole ceremony. What have I done wrong?"

Quinn growled and stepped back. Eduardo opened the papers, scratched his signature in the appropriate place, and handed them to Diego. After a quick glance, Diego shoved them down in his shirt and headed for his wagon.

"What about Teresa's clothes?" Eduardo gestured toward his own wagon, brought for the purpose of transporting whatever she'd brought with her.

"Thank you for reminding me." Diego whirled around and stalked off into the trees after Teresa.

"Do you want us to stick around?" Quinn's narrowed gaze followed Diego's retreating back.

"I'll be fine." Eduardo tried to sound sure of himself. "I know Kathleen is expecting you home before dark. It's a long ride back. Thanks for coming out." Eduardo clapped Quinn on the back as he walked with him toward his horse. After all the trouble Diego Garcia caused in town, Eduardo knew Quinn had plenty of reasons to be suspicious.

⊗

"Fealdad, where are you?" Diego's words hissed through the air.

Fealdad Garcia shivered. Fear clenched at her heart. She smoothed her skirt and shook her ratted hair so the tangles would conceal most of her face. *Fealdad*—"ugliness." That's what her name meant, and that's how she had to appear so her father wouldn't take out his ever-present wrath on her again. As far back as she could remember, she'd been treated differently than her sisters. While they were coddled, she did chores. When excuses were made for their mistakes, she was beaten.

She thought of the man who was now her husband. She'd only seen him from a distance once, when he visited their house to talk to her father about some business. Until today, she hadn't known how handsome he was. He had the thickest, blackest hair she'd ever seen—the kind that made her want to touch it. A long, straight nose and square jaw gave him a rugged, strong appearance. His deep brown eyes drew her in. He'd looked at her with such kindness. Oh, she hoped he would be kind to her.

"Girl, I'd better find you soon, or you'll regret hiding from me." Papa's voice sounded like the warning of a venomous snake.

The sinister threat made her fingers fumble. She slipped her shawl over her head, picked up the neat pile of wedding clothes, and stepped through the thick brush into his path.

"About time." He growled out the words as he jerked the white garments from her. One of the beaded gloves dropped. Fealdad snatched it before the garment reached the dirt. She slipped the glove on top of the pile of clothes, wishing her father would go. His black eyes took on a feral gleam as he looked at her. Fealdad stood her ground, refusing to let him see the terror she felt. He loved to hit her. He always had.

"Diego, I need to get back. I have chores to do." From the sound of his voice, Eduardo was growing impatient.

Diego stared a moment longer. His lip curled into a snarl. "We're glad to be rid of you, girl. You've never been any good for anyone. You don't do anything right. Ugly and stupid, that's what you are. Villegas thinks he's gotten one over on me, but I'm the one who wins." He pivoted and strode away through the trees. Coming to a halt, he turned and came back. He grabbed her wrist tight enough to make her gasp.

"Your husband is waiting for you." He gave a leering grin. "I'm sure he can't wait to see his lovely bride."

Fealdad tugged at her wrist. Dread clutched her heart. How could she face Eduardo? What man, no matter how kind he was, would want an ugly, worthless person like her? Would he beat her like Papa had? Would she be the cause of him turning to drink as she had with her father? Her insides turned liquid. Her legs felt limp. Stumbling behind her father, she didn't look up until he came to a halt. The polished boots in front of her didn't move. The pull of Eduardo's gaze was like a physical force, moving her chin upward. She lifted her head, hoping this time might be different, hoping she might see some sort of love and acceptance from a man instead of resentment.

Eduardo looked confused. He glanced at her father, then back at her. What might have been surprise or disgust flashed across his face. His eyes narrowed. Anger darkened his gaze. She closed her eyes. Eduardo wouldn't be any different from her father. Had she gone from one horror to another?

"What kind of trick are you trying now, Diego? This isn't Teresa. Where is my wife?"

CHAPTER 2

This is your wife." Diego thrust her forward. "You married my daughter, Fealdad—Señorita Garcia."

Eduardo's hand flashed across Fealdad's vision. She ducked. Eduardo grabbed Diego's shirt in his fist and dragged him forward. "What are you trying to pull here? You know we agreed that I would marry Teresa. You never mentioned any of your other daughters."

Her father tugged at his shirt with one hand, trying to free himself. Eduardo twisted his fist, knotting the material tighter against Papa's throat.

"Señor Villegas." Papa's face began to darken; his voice sounded raspy and strained. "I never promised you Teresa, only one of my daughters. I have kept my word on this."

Eduardo glanced over his shoulder, as if wishing his friends were still there. The muscles in his jaw bunched. Fealdad could almost see his teeth grinding, chewing on the rage over this deception. He pulled her father closer, until they stood nose to nose.

"You will get off my land. Don't you ever come here again. Is that clear?"

Papa nodded, gasping for air. The wedding dress dropped in the dirt. His fingers began to claw at Eduardo's hand. Eduardo released him with a shove, sending him sprawling onto the ground beside the garments. Her father scrabbled to get away, his chest heaving.

"Diego."

Fealdad watched as her father froze. She'd never seen him afraid of anyone before.

"*Sí* Señor Villegas?"

"Don't forget these." Eduardo nudged the now-filthy gown with the toe of his boot. "I don't want any reminders of you left on my land."

Her father scrambled to gather the clothes. Finished, his gaze flicked to Fealdad.

"She stays." Eduardo's growl sent a shiver of fear through Fealdad. "Before you go, I want to know what kind of name Fealdad is. Why would you call your daughter ugliness?"

Standing, Papa backed away toward his wagon. "Look at her. We only named her for what we saw. She will work hard for you though, Señor." He hesitated. "At least you will have peace and quiet with her. Fealdad can't talk, or at least, she hasn't spoken since she was very young."

With that announcement, her father whirled and raced the short distance to the wagon. After flinging the precious wedding clothes in the bed, he climbed up to the seat. Fealdad didn't know what to do. If she ran after him, would her father take her back home? Would that be better than staying with a husband who had been cuckolded into marriage with a girl he didn't want? How could she stay with Eduardo when he expected someone pretty and talkative like Teresa?

"Come along." Eduardo gripped her elbow none too gently, steering her toward the buggy waiting in the shade. "We may as well get on home."

Straightening her shoulders, Fealdad went with her new husband, hoping he couldn't see how terrified she was. Anger still raged in his eyes. At this point, only her compliance would keep her from a beating. She knew that from years of experience.

"Why didn't you bring any clothes?" Eduardo's hold eased as he stopped by the buggy. She stared at the ground, knowing he waited for an answer, yet unsure how to communicate with him. She shrugged, then cringed inwardly, waiting for the slap that would follow.

"Is Diego right?" He lifted her chin until her tangled hair fell back, and their gazes met. "Can you talk?"

She shook her head. Fear clenched at her heart.

"Are we supposed to go get your things?"

She shook her head again.

His eyes narrowed. "You mean you have nothing to bring? No clothes except what you're wearing?" He raised a hand.

Her eyes widened. Panic swept through her. Although she tried not to, she flinched away from him. His grasp on her arm tightened.

"Get in." He released her long enough to grab her waist and lift her onto the seat.

Before she could react, he untied the horse and sat down beside her. She edged as far away from him as she could, hoping he wouldn't notice. His fingers were white on the reins. Did he want to throttle her, or her father? A chill rippled down her spine. She couldn't help feeling sorry for Eduardo. He'd married her in good faith, thinking he was getting Teresa. Now, here he was stuck with an ugly bride who had no clothes and couldn't even talk. He must hate her. She closed her eyes. This wasn't how she pictured beginning a marriage.

The ride to Eduardo's house seemed long. The sprawling adobe house nestled among some large mesquite and cottonwood trees. Off to one side stood a barn, complete with a blacksmith forge at one end. Some corrals and a fenced pasture surrounded the buildings. A smaller house and a long, narrow building—possibly a bunkhouse—were farther away.

Eduardo pulled back on the reins, stopping the horse. He turned to Fealdad. "I can't call you Fealdad. I don't care what your parents named you. I can't do it. Do you have another name?"

All her life she'd only been Fealdad. She shook her head.

"Then I'll call you Chiquita, for now. As tiny as you are, that will be fitting." He climbed down and reached up for her. She tensed. Some of the anger seemed to have gone from him, but she knew how fast a man could be filled with rage.

"Go on in the house. I'll put the horse away. I've got business with my foreman." Eduardo started to turn away, then halted. He looked at her. She could see the tightness in his jaw again. "I'll not hold this against you. I knew how Diego was before I agreed to this marriage." His clipped words buffeted her and felt as painful as a physical blow. He swatted the horse on the rump. The animal snorted.

Fealdad watched him swing into the buggy and drive toward the barn. *Chiquita*. She rolled the name around in her head. All her life, she'd been called ugly and stupid. Eduardo called her "tiny." He was right. He wasn't tall, but she only reached his shoulder. A seed of hope sprouted as she questioned if maybe she had misjudged him. Maybe he wouldn't be an angry drunk like her father. Maybe he wouldn't hate her.

∞

The sorrel mare tried to dance away from Eduardo as he undid the harness. He knew she could sense his distress. He wanted to throw something or hit someone. He hadn't been this angry in a long time. How had he let Diego dupe him like this? Sure, he hadn't known Teresa well, but the day he met her, she had been laughing, talking, and staring at him with her big, dark eyes. That look reminded him of the flirtatious way his mother used to glance at his father. That was the main reason he'd agreed to the marriage and released Diego from his debt. He wanted to have what his parents had.

Tying the horse to a ring in the wall of the barn, Eduardo began to brush her down. The familiar motion soothed the mare and, after a while, him. He put his face against the reddish-brown neck and breathed deeply. The familiar animal scent calmed him further. Pushing away, he sighed, finished the brushing, and put the mare out in the pasture. She cantered away, nickering at the other horses standing in the shade of some mesquite trees.

He strode back into the barn and put the tack away. Sudden weariness washed over him, dulling the anger. This was his wedding day. He'd waited a long time for this day, and now it seemed like everything had gone wrong.

A low whicker of greeting came from a stall at the far end of the barn. El Rey. His new stallion, named "King" because he would be the start of a new line. He heralded the beginning of a longtime dream of Eduardo's.

"Hey boy." Eduardo rested one hand atop El Rey's withers as he stroked the baby-soft nose. El Rey sniffed his hand and whooshed a warm breath as if disappointed. Eduardo chuckled. "Spoiled, aren't you? I don't have a treat this time."

El Rey didn't seem to mind as Eduardo began to rub his ears. The horse leaned into Eduardo. Since the death of his father, Eduardo had only the animals to talk to. He'd never had other family. Although his foreman, Rico Gonzalez, had been around since Eduardo's father started the ranch, Eduardo hadn't been close to Rico. They could talk about business matters, but that was the extent of their relationship.

"I got married today, El Rey." Eduardo knew the quiet drone of his voice wouldn't be heard from any distance. "I now have a wife I didn't ask for, and I don't know what to do. She can't talk to me. I don't know how we'll ever communicate, but I gave my word. I can't go back on that." He ran his fingers through the horse's walnut-colored mane, working out a tangle.

"I'm not even sure what she looks like. She's so ragged, like one of your mares who's been run through the brush for days." Guilt stabbed him. Here he was comparing his bride to an animal, talking to a horse as if he expected advice on marriage from the beast.

The picture of Feal. . .Chiquita in her clean, but very worn, clothes rose in front of him like a specter. The dress hung on her thin frame. Her hair, washed but uncombed, fell across her face in matted tangles as if she were trying to hide. Fealdad. That's what her family had always called her. Is she so ugly? He didn't really know. When he'd lifted her chin to make her look at him, all he'd really seen were her golden-brown eyes, rich and sweet, the color of late summer honey. The thought warmed him. For a moment, he wanted to stalk back to the house and demand one more look.

Most of the time, she'd kept her scarf over her head. She was small. The top of her head barely came to his shoulders. Her hands, although work roughened, were fine boned and slender, with fingernails short and free of dirt. If she kept herself so clean, then why did she dress so ratty?

The sudden image of her ducking when he reached to grab Diego came to him. When Diego started to touch her, she flinched from him, too. Eduardo had been around enough mistreated animals to know what caused a person to do that. Someone had hit Chiquita often enough to make her wary. Was it Diego? His wife? Anger coursed through Eduardo at the thought of a child being treated that way. Did they punish her for not talking? The cause didn't matter. There were other ways of discipline than beating.

El Rey nudged his hand, and Eduardo patted the horse's neck. He had to admire Chiquita though. If she had been beaten and was afraid, she still had a lot of spunk. Although she flinched and had ducked from him once, most of the time, she held herself straight, with an air of determination that impressed him. She wasn't one to run just because she was afraid. She had strength of character. He could see that in her reaction to Diego and her refusal to back down from him.

"Eduardo?" Rico's voice called from outside the barn.

"In here."

The foreman came into the barn carrying a cloth-covered platter. Eduardo gave El Rey a final pat and headed down the aisle to meet Rico.

"Pilar sent you some food." Rico held out the dish. "She says your bride won't have time to fix something, and she's cooking, anyway."

"Tell her thanks." Eduardo took the warm plate from Rico. Pilar, Rico's wife, did most of the cooking for the *vaqueros* who worked for Eduardo. Until now, Eduardo usually ate the evening meal with them. He found it hard to work all day and still have time to cook. Pilar never seemed to mind his joining them.

"I guess I'd better take this inside." Once again, guilt stabbed at Eduardo. He'd meant to clean the house before bringing his wife home. Instead she'd been welcomed by a mess. He'd only fired the stove enough to boil some coffee this morning. He'd been too nervous to eat. Even the dishes from yesterday's breakfast still waited. Last night, he'd been so tired, he hadn't found the strength to do much of anything.

"Have you heard from Lucio and Tomás?" The two ranch hands were out checking on some of the cows that were calving. Although most of his cattle were range-bred, Eduardo still liked to keep an eye on them. Between Apaches stealing them and wild animals preying on them, they bore close watching, especially during calving season.

Rico shook his head. "They should be back today. If not, I'll send Jorge to check on them."

The two parted. Eduardo turned toward the house. A tendril of smoke rose from the chimney. Chiquita must have started a fire. He quickened his pace, wanting to get to the house before she began to cook, since they already had a meal prepared. The smell of beef and chilies seeping through the cloth made his stomach rumble. The late spring sun warmed his back.

Opening the door, Eduardo maneuvered into the house with the awkward platter of food. Pilar must have sent enough for them and everyone on the ranch. He almost smiled. Did she think he married a giant of a woman who could eat like a horse? She would be in for a surprise. He doubted if someone the size of Chiquita could eat much. She probably ate more like one of the chickens than the larger animals.

Chiquita's back was to him when he entered the kitchen. She was studying something held in her hands and didn't act like she'd heard him. He eased the plate of food onto the table, noting with surprise the amount of work she'd done in the short time she'd been there. The floor was swept clean, water was warming for washing the dishes that were stacked by the washtub, and in passing through the main room, he could see that she'd straightened his mess there.

"You've been hard at work."

Chiquita gasped and whirled around. The object in her hands crashed to the floor, splintering into pieces. Her hands flew to cover her mouth. She started to step back, then her back stiffened. She stood her ground, staring at him through a fall of matted hair.

"No." A wave of anger swept over Eduardo. She'd broken his grandmother's statue of the Madonna and Child. His mother prized that over anything else in the house. As a boy, he was never allowed to touch the precious figure.

"Do you have any idea what you've done?" He could see her slight cringing as he shouted the words. Even knowing she expected him to hit her didn't dim his anger. He had very little of his family left, and she'd just ruined a part of that.

Chiquita knelt and began to gather the larger pieces with trembling fingers. Eduardo strode over and pulled her to her feet. "I'll clean this up." He snarled the words. Deep inside, he hated what he was doing to her, but he couldn't seem to stop. He could feel a shudder go through her. He loosened his grip on her arm. She stepped back. He bent down and picked up the largest piece of the sculpture, the child's face. Rage coursed though him. He flung the piece against the wall. The tiny features exploded.

Chiquita flinched. Her slender fingers clutched her skirt. She squared her shoulders again, as if knowing what would be coming next.

CHAPTER 3

"Eduardo." The kitchen door began to vibrate as someone pounded an urgent rhythm. "Eduardo, hurry. Come quick."

Dragging his gaze from the fear and resignation he could sense in his wife's stance, Eduardo rose and jerked open the door. Anger raced like lightning through his veins. "What?"

Rico bent over, gasping for breath. He pointed toward the bunkhouse on the other side of the barn. "It's Tomás. You have to hurry. There's been an accident. One of the cows gored Lucio. Tomás came to get the wagon to bring him home. Hurry." Rico didn't wait, but turned and sprinted back the way he'd come.

Stepping outside, Eduardo hesitated, his hand on the latch. He glanced back at Chiquita. He could barely make out the gleam of her tawny eyes through the hanks of hair over her face. Her fingers still clenched her skirt, but her shoulders were squared and her head held high. Remorse fought a battle with rage. Eduardo shook his head.

"I don't know when I'll be back. If you need anything, go to Pilar. You'll find her down at the cabin by the bunkhouse." Slamming the door, Eduardo raced after Rico. By the time he reached the barn, Jorge and Tomás had the wagon hitched and the horses saddled, including a fresh mount for Tomás. There would be no time to waste if they were to save Lucio.

"Where'd you leave him?" Eduardo shot the question at Tomás as they mounted.

"Up there, near the base of the mountains." Tomás pointed to the east.

"Tomás and I will ride ahead. Rico, bring the wagon. Jorge, stay here and keep an eye on the ranch."

"Wait." Pilar trotted from the house, a bulky package in her hands. She lifted the cloth-bound parcel up to Eduardo. "Bandages, medicine, some food. You may need them."

Eduardo secured the bundle behind him on the saddle and nodded his thanks to Pilar. Motioning with his head, he kneed his gelding and raced from the yard, Tomás at his side.

The horses were breathing heavily by the time Eduardo pulled them down to a walk. As much as he wanted to get to Lucio, he knew they couldn't risk overtiring their mounts. Tomás pulled up beside Eduardo.

"What happened?"

"You know the narrow gorge—the one that's impossible to get to the bottom because it's so steep?" Tomás waited until Eduardo nodded. "One of the cows had her calf on the edge of the gorge. The minute the little one would roll over, down he would go. Lucio had me distract the mama while he went to pull the calf to a safer place."

Tomás wiped the sweat from his face with his bandana. "That cow was a mean one with horns a mile wide. She ran at me like one of the bulls in a bullfight." He frowned. "The look in her eye should have killed me."

Eduardo gripped the reins until they dug into his hands. He wanted to shout at Tomás to get on with the story, yet he knew the importance of letting the events unfold in the young man's mind. Tomás pushed his sombrero back a little. His eyes mirrored the horror of the story he was telling.

"Lucio raced in and jumped from his horse. He grabbed the calf to pick it up. The edge of the gorge gave away. His foot dropped down. He almost went over the side with the baby. I could see him scrabbling to get up. I tried to keep the mama's attention, but the minute she heard her little one cry, she forgot about me. I've never seen a cow move so fast. Lucio didn't have a chance."

A look of panic crossed Tomás's face. Eduardo reached over and squeezed his shoulder. Tomás tried to smile, but only grimaced. "That cow, she hit him hard. I think the only thing that saved him was that she knocked him clear across the gorge so she couldn't follow."

Eduardo nodded, seeing in his mind the steep gorge, only two feet wide, but about thirty feet deep.

"I jumped my horse across and got to him right away. That mama kept bellowing, running back and forth along the edge on the other side."

"Where did she get him?"

"Her horn caught him below the shoulder on the right side. If she'd caught him low or on the left, he would probably be dead right away."

A twinge of pain lanced through Eduardo's chest, as if he could feel Lucio's suffering. "Did you get the bleeding to stop?"

"No señor." Tomás shook his head, his face pale. "I took off my shirt and tore it to make a tight bandage. I don't know if Lucio was able to stay conscious. He was losing a lot of blood. We have to hurry." Tomás urged his horse to a faster pace.

The rest of the trip, they rode in silence. Despite his concern for Lucio, Eduardo couldn't help thinking about what had happened at home. Once more, his anger had gotten the best of him. He'd just made the determination to change because of Chiquita, then he'd gone in and thrown a fit over a piece of pottery that didn't really matter. Yes, his mother had prized the object, but he hadn't—at least, not until Chiquita had broken it.

He knew he'd scared her, yet she was willing to stand her ground. Admiration welled up once again. When this emergency was taken care of, he would have to sit down and talk with her. He frowned. How was he to do that? She couldn't talk. Could she read and write? He knew better than that. Very few ranch people were educated. His parents insisted he go to school in Tucson, making him one of the few learned people around here.

He would see. Maybe Chiquita would want to learn. In the evenings, he could teach her the letters. When she knew enough, they could communicate through writing, even though she couldn't verbalize anything. Surely she would want to do that.

"We're almost there." Tomás pointed ahead.

Glancing over his shoulder, Eduardo could see Rico on the wagon, far below and behind them. He must be pushing the team to even be in sight. Rico would come up a longer route to be on the same side of the gorge as they were. The trip home could be a little slower, but getting to Lucio fast could be the difference between life and death.

The cow lowed, a threatening sound, as she stood over her calf. Lowering her head, she shook her sharp horns at them, as if warning that they would get the same as Lucio if they dared to come close. Urging his horse to a canter, Eduardo jumped the narrow cleft, Tomás just behind him. Lucio lay on the ground, still and limp.

Swinging from the saddle, Eduardo ignored the angry sounds coming from the heifer across the gorge. He knelt beside his ranch hand. The ground around Lucio still looked damp and stained from his blood.

Eduardo's breath froze. He placed a hand over Lucio's heart, then bent over to place his ear on the man's chest. A slow, faint rhythm made him sigh in relief. Lucio still lived. Eduardo strode to his horse and retrieved the bundle Pilar sent with him. Untying the corners, he pulled out what he needed.

"Bring me a canteen."

Tomás, who had knelt beside him, jumped to obey. Eduardo ripped Lucio's shirt, exposing the wound so he could get a better look. The hole appeared enormous. The edges were ugly and torn. Lifting Lucio, Eduardo could see the place in the back where the cow hit him with such force that the horn went completely through. He'd lost a lot of blood, and it still seeped from the wound. Pulling the shirt away caused the flow to increase a little.

By the time Rico arrived with the wagon, Eduardo had done as much as he knew how to help Lucio. He was still unconscious, pale, and sweating. He'd moaned a few times as Eduardo worked, but he hadn't wakened. The bleeding had stopped and hopefully wouldn't start again on the trip home. Rico would drive as carefully as he could over the rough terrain.

Time would tell if the man would live. They needed to get him back to the ranch as quickly as possible, where Pilar could take over. She had considerable skill patching up wounded ranch hands. She even helped care for the injured animals. If Lucio lived through the journey home, he would stand a good chance of surviving.

"Should we chance the trip home or wait until morning?" Rico glanced at the late afternoon sun. They wouldn't be able to make it back before dark. "I threw in some bedrolls. We could make Lucio comfortable. Maybe by morning, he'll be able to travel better."

Eduardo frowned. "By morning, fever could set in. If we get him back tonight, Pilar can start treating him for infection. I put on the leaves she sent to draw out the dirt, but that may not be enough."

Rico nodded. "You're right. If that wound gets infected, he'll never make it. Let's go."

By the time the lights of the ranch came into view, Eduardo's anger had long faded. Exhaustion and guilt weighed heavily on him. Hunger, too, gnawed at him. He hadn't eaten the food Pilar sent them earlier, although he hoped Chiquita had taken the time to eat. He wasn't sure how he could tell her he regretted his earlier actions, but he had to try. As soon as Lucio was settled, he would go home and face his bride.

⟳

When the door slammed shut, Fealdad felt the concussion throughout her body. She began to shake. Would Eduardo get over his anger, or would he beat her when he came home? Sometimes Papa told her he would beat her, then waited, as if the anticipation added to his satisfaction. He seemed to delight in making her agonize before he began to pummel her. Was Eduardo the same way? His anger had been strong enough.

She watched from the window as the horses and wagon disappeared from the ranch. The woman—Pilar, Eduardo called her—glanced at the house. Fealdad stepped to the side so Pilar wouldn't be able to see her. Right now, she didn't want to have this woman coming to the house. She felt as ugly and stupid as her name. Chiquita. Eduardo might call her that, but she didn't feel any different.

The smell of food tickled her nose. She walked to the table and lifted the cloth from the tray there. Her mouth watered as the appetizing smells wafted up. Reaching out, she brushed her fingertips against a warm tortilla. How she longed to eat just a little, but she couldn't. Eduardo would be even angrier to know that she was eating his food when she hadn't done her work. Brushing the cloth back into place, she turned to see if the water was hot enough to begin washing.

Hours flew by as she did the dishes, cleaned the floor, and gathered clothes to begin washing them the next day. Eduardo's house was much bigger than her parents' with its tiny area that barely held the family. Here, the rooms were spacious and plentiful. Besides the kitchen, main area, and bedroom, there were two other rooms with beds—evidently for company. She wondered if Eduardo had a lot of people who came to visit. Did he have family near here? She didn't know anything about her husband.

Much of the house was in a state of disorder, like it hadn't been given a good cleaning in a long time. Dust, thick enough to draw pictures in, covered most of the furniture. The unused bedrooms were the worst, but Fealdad knew she couldn't clean everything in one day. The rugs felt gritty as she walked across them. Tomorrow, she would have to take them outside and beat them, along with doing the laundry.

In the bedroom that must be Eduardo's, Fealdad found a treasure: books. A shelf along the wall held more books than she thought were in the world. Glancing around to make sure she was alone, she crossed the room to stand before them. Reaching up to touch one, her fingers trembled. She stopped short of making contact. Does Eduardo know how to read?

For as long as she could remember, she'd wanted to learn to read. Her mother could read a little and had taught the other girls what she could. Fealdad never had time for the lessons, although her mother constantly scolded her for missing them. Once in a while, she would hear the girls recite some of their letters and she would try them out, silently rolling the sounds across her tongue.

Heart pounding, Fealdad rested her hand on the shelf next to the books. How many were there? She gazed up and down the long row. More than she could count from the few numbers she'd picked up here and there. It would take her a week just to look through all of them.

A bold idea tempted her. Her heart began to pound. She brushed her hair back from her eyes. Glancing at the door, she made a decision. Trotting back to the kitchen, she peered out the window. There was no sign of wagons or horses returning in the gathering dusk. If the hurt man was far away, Eduardo could be gone all night. Even if they came back soon, surely she would hear the noise of their arrival.

Creeping back to the bedroom, she took a deep breath and tugged one of the precious tomes free. Opening the pages, she lifted it to her nose. The smell of paper and dust made her sneeze. A smile lifted the corners of her mouth for a brief moment. The letters were grouped together in tight rows, marching in two columns down each page. How did anyone decipher which letter was which? How could she ever sort them into words? Running her fingers over the print, she couldn't help wondering what message the writer wanted to convey.

Putting up the first book, she eagerly drew a second from its perch. This time, she gasped as the pages opened. Pictures greeted her. Drawings of animals, mostly birds and wildlife, captured her. She sank to the floor, held spellbound as she turned one leaf after another. The drawings looked as if they could walk out of the book at any moment, they were so lifelike.

Dark settled in. She went to find a lamp so she could continue with her discovery. Eduardo and his men hadn't returned. She assumed they'd traveled too far and wouldn't be back tonight. She knew she should decide where to sleep, but the magic pictures wouldn't let her go. Time flew past, and she ignored the sounds in the background because she was so caught up with the book on her lap.

A loud thump vibrated the floor. She jumped. Her heart began to hammer loud enough to drown out any other noise. She clutched the book to her chest. The bedroom door swung open. Eduardo stood there, his face haggard and grim.

"What are you doing?"

She knew he would swagger across the room in a moment and begin to strike her. She had to protect the book. She stood and backed away, fumbling for a place to put the volume of drawings. Eduardo began to stride toward her. For a moment, she felt a whimper of fear, then she straightened, waiting for the inevitable.

CHAPTER 4

Tiny flames of fury sped through Eduardo's veins as he approached Chiquita. If Diego were standing before him, he would wring the man's neck. How could anyone treat a child so poorly that she lived in fear of his every action? This had to stop now. He'd seen her flinch as he started across the room. She was waiting for him to begin hitting her.

Lord, help me say this the right way. I don't want to instill more terror. Eduardo took the book from Chiquita and set it on the edge of the bookshelf. Taking her hands in his, he could feel the trembling she couldn't control. He wanted to draw her into his arms, to let her know he wouldn't hurt her. She'd been wounded so many times—most likely by Diego—that Eduardo knew she wouldn't trust him.

With one hand, he swept back her tangled locks and lifted her chin. Her eyes were closed, her lips compressed so tight they were nearly colorless. He could tell her teeth were clenched tight, as if she was ready for him to do his worst. Closing his eyes for a moment, he tried to calm his wrath at Diego, lest she think his anger was directed at her.

Letting out a deep breath, he traced the curve of her jaw with his thumb. A single tear welled up at the corner of her eye. Had Diego done this, too, just to torment her before the violence began?

"My father bought a horse once."

Her eyes snapped open, studying him, full of fear. Her breath came fast and ragged.

"He didn't need the mare, but he saw the owner mistreating her. The man would get her on a lead and beat her for no reason. Dad said he heard from others how the man would take out his frustration on the poor beast." Eduardo continued the soft caress along Chiquita's jaw.

"You would think that horse would be grateful to be away from such a terrible master." He frowned at the memory. "Instead, she would bare her teeth when we came near. Whenever we groomed her, she had to be well tied, because she would always try to bite or kick. That mare was ruined because some man thought he could treat her as mean as he wanted. I worked with her for a long time before I could get her to trust me a little. She never could relax around anyone else."

A tear trickled down Chiquita's cheek. Eduardo caught it with his thumb, brushing the moisture away. She didn't seem to notice.

"A horse is an animal. You can't explain to an animal that you're different. We kept her for the rest of her life, treating her the best we could.

"I've seen the signs, Chiquita. Someone hasn't treated you right, but I want you to know that you're safe here. Maybe you can't talk, but I know you can hear." He sighed. "I know I have a temper, but I promise you I'll never hit you. My parents raised me to respect others, especially women."

Lowering her gaze, Chiquita turned her face from him, trying to hide. She looked like she wanted to be anywhere but here, with him.

Eduardo released her hand and stepped back. He knew she was still scared. He wanted to give her some room. *How can I make her understand? She's terrified, Lord. Help me make her see that I'm different from Diego.*

"I see you like books. Do you know how to read?" He motioned at the bookshelf.

Chiquita glanced at the volume he'd taken from her. Her fingers curled in her skirt, clutching the worn material. She gave her head a quick shake.

"Would you like to learn?"

Her eyes widened. Her gaze sought his for a moment, the golden depths glinting in the lamplight, before she looked away again. Eduardo wanted to grin in satisfaction. For that moment, he'd seen such a longing that he knew this was something she wanted without her telling him so.

"Maybe tomorrow evening, we'll try learning some of the letters. I'll see if I can rustle up a slate to use. For now, I'd like to get something to eat. It's been a long day."

The haunted look returned to Chiquita's eyes as she edged around him to the door. Once past, her steps continued, quick and determined. Eduardo followed her to the kitchen more slowly, wondering how he could make her understand she was safe here.

A crash reverberated through the air, followed by a small sob. Stepping into the kitchen, Eduardo noticed the slump of Chiquita's shoulders. The door of the stove hung askew. He groaned. He meant to fix that before getting married, but he hadn't had the time.

"Here, let me help."

Chiquita jumped. She whirled around, backing away from him. The embers from the fire in the stove flickered to life, flaring as Chiquita moved.

"Stop!" Eduardo leapt forward. He grabbed her up. She weighed almost nothing. He whirled her around. Greedy flames attached themselves to her skirt. The crackle and pop from the stove echoed like shots in the panicked stillness surrounding them. He beat the flames with his hand, hoping he wouldn't burn Chiquita. The heat stung, but he paid no attention.

Rolling the folds of the skirt over on the fire, Eduardo squeezed, smothering them out. Chiquita had stiffened like a board. Tremors ran through her body. Eduardo almost pulled her close, then realized she must be afraid.

"I'm not mad. Your clothes caught on fire. I was only putting them out before you got burned. Are you all right?" He frowned at the ragged skirt with the blackened hole down the length of it. Chiquita clutched the edges together.

"I'm not sure those clothes shouldn't be burned anyway. Let's eat. Afterwards, I'll see what I can find for you to wear, since you didn't bring other clothes." Turning back to the stove, Eduardo stirred the fire, then maneuvered the door closed. "This thing has been giving me fits. I'll try to fix it in the morning before I leave so you won't have to worry about the door falling off."

He glanced over his shoulder. Chiquita seemed frozen in place—a waif so thin and frail, he wondered how she could stand. She must have thought he was angry about the stove and was trying to beat her. All he wanted to do was save her from the fire.

"Did you have some of the food Pilar sent over earlier? I left the platter on the table."

She shook her head, her hair once again covering her face. Smelling the spicy scent of chilies, Eduardo opened the door of the warming oven to find the mounded plate of food. Grabbing a towel, he pulled out the dish.

"The plates are in that cupboard." He indicated the shelves nearest the sink. "I'll bring in some fresh water from the well while you get the table ready." Striding from the house with the bucket swinging from his hand, Eduardo could feel his frustration mounting. *Lord, how am I going to do this? I'm carrying on a one-sided conversation. She's terrified of me. I'm gonna be walking on eggshells to keep from startling her. I don't think I can do it.*

When he carried the sloshing bucket back into the house, Chiquita waited at the side of the table nearest the head chair. The table had one plate, fork, and cup resting where he usually sat.

"Where's your plate?"

Chiquita kept her gaze lowered. She shook her head.

"Did you eat earlier?"

She hesitated, then shook her head again.

The bucket clanked as he set it down and dropped the handle. Chiquita winced. Eduardo crossed to the cupboard and brought out another plate. In silence he readied a place for Chiquita so she would be seated close enough that he could fill her plate. The girl had to get some meat on her bones. Filling two glasses with the cool water, he plunked them down on the table.

"Sit down." He hadn't meant to growl, but he was getting fed up. Wasn't she used to eating with the family? Did she have to eat scraps like a dog?

Chiquita slid into the chair he held for her, careful to keep her scorched dress from gaping. She still trembled from the scare. Placing his hands on her shoulders, Eduardo ignored the way she flinched.

"Chiquita, you need food. I don't know why you didn't want to eat with me, but my parents always ate together. They enjoyed one another's company. I hope someday we can be the same way."

Seating himself, Eduardo bowed his head to pray. Chiquita already had her head bowed, but then she'd been that way most of the time he was around.

"Do you pray at mealtimes?"

She flicked a glance at him. She seemed puzzled, almost as if she didn't know what he meant.

Eduardo couldn't help sighing. "That's all right. I'll say the prayer, and you can listen."

A few minutes later, he lifted the covering from the fragrant meal. Although dried a little from the long wait to be served, everything looked delicious. He served Chiquita first, careful not to give her too much. He didn't think she would eat, but with a quick glance in his direction, she picked up her fork and began.

After their silent meal ended, Eduardo left Chiquita to clean up while he lit a lantern and went into one of the back rooms. Putting the light next to an old trunk, he ran his hand over the scarred surface before lifting the lid. A whoosh of musty lavender air greeted him, the scent reminding him so much of his mother, he almost looked around for her. Kneeling down, he began to remove the various items packed there. The things he wanted, he put in one pile; the rest, he packed back into the trunk. His mother wouldn't have minded giving some of her things to her daughter-in-law. In fact, being able to do so would have delighted her.

Gathering the items he'd chosen, Eduardo picked up the lantern and headed back to the kitchen. Looking through his mother's things had stirred memories, reminding him of the loneliness that had become his constant companion since his parents' deaths. His heart ached. He wasn't sure marrying Chiquita would ease the ache at all.

∞

Chiquita dipped warm water from the reservoir at the side of the stove. The sight of scorched clothing made her wrinkle her nose. She could still feel the sting of the burns on her leg. She hadn't wanted Eduardo to know about them. The memory of him hitting her, trying to put out the flames, jarred her. At first, she'd thought he had finally behaved like her father. She'd done something so wrong, he couldn't help but beat her.

That hadn't been true. Instead, he'd put out the fire before she was hurt badly, then apologized as if the whole thing were his fault. He didn't blame her at all. He hadn't been mad about her looking at the books either. A spark of excitement flared in her heart. Would he follow through with his suggestion? Would he teach her to read? Hope, even in the face of a lifetime of disappointments, wouldn't die.

Supper had been so hard. She'd never been allowed to eat with the family. Only after they were finished and gone from the room could she sit down and eat of the few leftovers. Sometimes her father would deny her that, saying she had too much work to do to waste time on eating. She didn't want to displease Eduardo, but the idea of eating at the same time he did was daunting.

He'd remained so silent. She'd wanted him to tell her if the vaquero who'd been hurt was all right. She wanted to know all about Eduardo and his family. Who was Pilar? What was she like? How Chiquita longed for her tongue to be loosened, but she knew that wouldn't happen. She didn't think she'd ever really talked.

Finished with the dishes and cleanup, Chiquita listened to the quiet of the house. Where had Eduardo gone? Moving close to the flickering light of the lantern, she pulled apart the scorched place in her skirt. Small blisters dotted the red area on her thigh. She shuddered. A few times over the years, Papa threatened to burn her. The thought always brought terror. If not for Eduardo's quick reaction, she might have been burnt badly enough to die. How could she ever thank him? Did this mean she could trust him?

She thought back to the early afternoon, right before Eduardo had to leave. When he threw the piece of pottery against the wall, she'd been sure he was just like her father. The rage in his eyes looked the same. Looking back, she couldn't help but think he might have resorted to violence if his foreman hadn't come to fetch him.

Then, when he'd come home, he'd acted like a different person. He'd been kind, seeming to know what she'd suffered with her father. She was confused. What was Eduardo—tender and compassionate or violent and hate-filled?

"Chiquita?" Eduardo called from the other room. She quickly pulled the material of her dress over the burns on her leg.

Hurrying to the main room, Chiquita stumbled to a halt. Eduardo stood by the desk in one corner of the room. Beside him lay a pile of clothing. He smiled and pointed to the clothes.

"These were my mother's. I know she would have wanted you to have them." He lifted one of the dresses from the pile, letting the pale yellow material unfold. Chiquita gasped at the simple beauty. She'd never seen anything so pretty before. How could Eduardo expect her to wear something this nice when she worked all day?

"This one can be for the times when you go visiting or when we go to town." He shrugged. "That won't be often, but I remember my mother saying that every woman needed something beautiful, even if she didn't get to wear it much." He folded the dress and placed it on the desk.

"The darker ones will do for everyday work." Plucking up a light gray gown, he held it up for her to see. "My mother was about the same height as you, but she wasn't as slight. You'll probably need to alter them some." He hesitated. "Do you know how to do that?"

Chiquita nodded, amazed at his generosity. She'd never had more than one gown at a time, and Eduardo was offering at least five dresses at once. Her family would be amazed. Of course, her sisters and mother had more than she did, but none of them owned this many clothes.

Moving the pile of dresses, Eduardo stopped and looked uncomfortable. He cleared his throat. "I. . .um, got some of my mother's underthings for you." He gestured at the remainder of the stack. Under the tan, his face took on a ruddy tint. "There are a couple of nightdresses, too."

Clearing his throat again, he straightened and faced her. "In the morning, I'll bring in enough water for you to take a bath while I'm gone." He looked stern, but not angry. "I've explained to you that I'm different from Diego. I want you to stop hiding." He strode across the room toward her holding something in his hand.

Chiquita's insides quivered. She wanted to flee. She stiffened and waited.

Eduardo stopped in front of her. "Look at me, Chiquita." He waited until she met his gaze. "This is for you to use tomorrow. I'm glad you've kept yourself clean, but I'll expect you to have your hair brushed when I get home tomorrow afternoon."

Chiquita glanced down at his hands. He held out a brush and mirror such as she'd never dreamed existed. Silver, inlaid with turquoise, gleamed in the light. Spots of tarnish stained the handle in places. Eduardo must have kept the set put away after his mother's death. She couldn't possibly use something

360

so fine. What if she dropped the mirror and broke it? Would Eduardo be upset then? Would that be the time he would hit her? He'd been so angry this morning when she broke a simple figurine. What would he do over something this valuable?

She backed away, shaking her head, holding her hands palm outward to him. He understood. She could see the hurt in his eyes for a moment before anger took over. His jaw clenched. He spun around, took the set to the desk, and set them down with a clack that made her heart leap.

"I'm going to bed. You can stay in the bedroom down the hall. You don't have to stay with me until we get to know each other better." He stalked off to his room and slammed the door. She froze, wondering if the anger would grow until he sought her out to ease his rage.

CHAPTER 5

The sun shining in her eyes woke Chiquita the next morning. She stretched, enjoying the luxurious feeling of sleeping on a mattress covered with sheets and enough blankets to keep her warm. At home, she always slept on a thin pallet on the floor of the room she shared with her sisters.

She jerked upright. The sun was shining. She was late. Eduardo would be expecting her to fix coffee and his breakfast. After throwing back the covers, Chiquita stumbled from the bed and searched for her clothes. She'd carried Eduardo's mother's things into the room and had worn the simplest nightdress. Picking up her own scorched clothing, she wrinkled her nose. The burn spot in the skirt gaped open. She couldn't wear this again. She glanced at the pile of beautiful gowns. How could she ever wear one of those?

Discarding her dress, she ran her hand over the colorful pile of garments. Treating them with care, she chose the plainest brown one and put it on. The length would have been right, but the rest of the dress sagged. She could easily end up tripping over the hem if she wasn't careful. No help for it; she would have to wear this for now. Later in the day, she could take the time to make the fit better.

Chiquita rushed to the kitchen, holding up the skirt to keep from falling. A pot of coffee stood on the back of the stove. A skillet and dirty dishes showed that Eduardo had already eaten and gone. She couldn't feel his presence in the house. She closed her eyes and moaned. He would be furious by the time he came home tonight. How could she have slept late? She needed to make a good start of this marriage, or she would be doomed to a life of pain from him being angry with her.

Stretching up, she peered out the window at the barn and other outbuildings. They appeared deserted. He'd mentioned yesterday having to go take care of some business. He had planned to leave early, so she was too late to try to make up for oversleeping. She sighed and turned to the work at hand, ignoring the twinge of hunger in her stomach. There was too much to do to take time for eating. Perhaps if she spent the day working as hard as she could, he wouldn't be so enraged with her tonight.

A plan began to develop in her mind. She would work hard all day, then fix a supper that would wait for Eduardo's return. Then she would bathe, comb her hair, and don the yellow dress that belonged to his mother. Husbands must be different from fathers. Maybe if she made herself neat, as well as clean, he wouldn't be so repulsed like Papa and would be merciful. She would never be beautiful, but perhaps she could be pleasing.

∞

"Eduardo, my friend, come inside where we can talk out of the sun." Antonio Soza strode from his hacienda to greet Eduardo. They were neighbors, although their ranches were several miles apart. Eduardo often consulted with Antonio on matters of business.

"Pepito, take Señor Eduardo's horse for some water." Antonio dispatched the young boy with a wave of his hand. "Come, my friend. Maria will bring us something refreshing."

The dim interior of the adobe house felt cool after the warmth of the day. Eduardo removed his hat and wiped the beads of sweat from his forehead. A cool drink would be welcome.

"So, I'm surprised to see you." Antonio tugged at his full beard as he led Eduardo into his living room. He motioned to a chair. Eduardo sat down, placing his hat beside him. Antonio grinned. "When I sent the message for you to come over today, I didn't realize you were getting married yesterday. Congratulations, my friend. When am I to meet the lucky bride?"

They were interrupted by Maria, one of Antonio's helpers in the house. She brought them glasses of lemonade. Eduardo took a long drink of the tangy liquid before he spoke. "I married one of Diego Garcia's daughters."

Antonio's heavy eyebrows arched. "Why did you do that?"

"As you know, Diego had a debt to pay. Now he doesn't, and I have a wife."

"I don't know. I can't think of anything good to say about that man, so you watch yourself." Antonio frowned. "A lot of us would like to know where he came up with the money for his ranch. He doesn't work, he isn't wealthy, yet he could afford land that the rest of us struggled to get. Something doesn't smell right."

"I know. My father used to say the same thing."

"I've met Diego's daughters. Which one did you marry? Teresa? She's the oldest. I seem to remember the others would be too young."

Eduardo explained how Diego tricked him into marrying his other daughter, the one who couldn't speak.

"I've seen this girl before." Antonio stroked his beard, his brow furrowed. "Diego came over here with his family a couple of times when the girls were younger. They called this girl Fealdad. Am I right?"

Eduardo nodded. "I refuse to call her by that name. She can't tell me anything else to call her, so I chose Chiquita, because she's so small."

"That's a good name." Antonio nodded. "She was always a tiny thing and very pretty. I don't know why they referred to her as ugly. Diego and Lupe, his wife, used to treat her differently than the others. I asked Diego about it once. He said she was rebellious, and that was the only way to control her. I never saw the rebellion myself. She seemed to be quiet and obedient any time they were here." He smoothed his hair back. "The last time they came as a family, I saw Diego hit her for no reason. I confronted him and told him to stop. We had quite a fight. The poor girl looked terrified. I'm afraid Diego may have taken out his rage on her. The thought makes me sick."

Antonio rubbed his hands down his face. "I've often thought that I should have done something. A father has a right to raise his children as he sees fit, but to beat them for nothing is beyond reason. I didn't know what I could do though. I planned to keep an eye on the situation, but Diego never brought them back. She was such a young girl then, just a little waif."

"From the way she acts, Diego didn't stop abusing her. She's a brave one. She stands her ground, but I can tell she's afraid," Eduardo said.

Antonio's gaze seemed to bore into Eduardo. "Be gentle with her. I believe she'll be a treasure if you do. She isn't like the rest of that family. Even back then, there was something a little different about her."

Taking another sip of his lemonade, Eduardo pushed thoughts of Chiquita away. He didn't want to remember the way he'd behaved yesterday. He'd been so ashamed, he'd left home earlier than planned so he didn't have to face her. If Diego had mistreated her for so many years, how would she ever manage to be around him with his temper? This morning, before he left, he'd gotten angry with Jorge for a minor mistake that shouldn't have mattered. He sighed. That was another one he would have to apologize to when he returned home. He set the empty glass on the floor beside his feet.

"You asked me over for a reason, Antonio. I know it wasn't to discuss my marriage."

Antonio chuckled. "That's true. I wanted to talk cattle." He leaned forward, a sudden eagerness in his face. "I know you've sold some livestock to the cavalry. Right now, they're the best market in Arizona for our beef. Have you heard the news?"

Eduardo shook his head. "What news?"

"The government is going to start buying cattle from more than one person. So far, James Patterson has had a monopoly on the trade with them. He buys most of the cattle from Henry Hooker." He waved a hand as Eduardo started to protest. "Yes, I know, he's bought a few head of my beef, too, but not enough. Now though, we have a better chance."

"My friend at the fort, Conlon Sullivan, told me it might be a good idea to begin building up my herd. This must be the reason I haven't seen him for a while, or I'm sure he would have given me the news."

"I have something I want you to read and consider." Antonio crossed to a desk and brought Eduardo an eastern newspaper. "This article is about a breed of cattle developed in England. They're not as rangy as ours are. They put on weight easily. According to this article, we could vastly improve our herds by bringing in a few of these bulls."

Eduardo glanced through the article and frowned. "I don't know. Our criollos are tough. They're bred for the desert. They forage and can live among the cactus."

"But Eduardo, the criollos are little more than horns and hide. The cavalry wants some meat to feed their troops." Antonio laughed. "I think Herefords are the cows of the future."

Eduardo grinned. "If we bring in some of these fancy bulls, they'll be just like the fancy eastern men that come out here. They won't know how to adjust."

"You could be right, but I'd still like to try it. I think if we can improve our cattle, we'll have a chance to do better in the market. We might even consider shipping some to California. There's always a need for beef there." Antonio glanced at the door. "Ah, here's Maria to tell me lunch is ready. Join us, and then I can show you the changes I've made since you were here last."

After lunch, Antonio gave Eduardo a tour of the small chapel he'd built behind his house. He told of plans to build a schoolhouse someday so that the ranchers in the area would be able to get their children an education. As Eduardo was mounting to leave, Antonio reminded him once again to read the paper about the Hereford bulls.

"I hadn't thought about improving the cattle, but I have thought about the horses. The cavalry doesn't like our smaller mounts. They have so much gear to carry, they want a taller, sturdier horse. When you have the time to visit, I'll show you my new stallion. He's the first in a new line." Eduardo couldn't keep the pride from his voice. He touched the brim of his hat and cantered from the yard. The sun hung low in the west. He would have to hurry to be home by mealtime. The road home was a long one.

∞

The warm water felt marvelous to Chiquita's aching muscles. She'd done more than a day's work today. She hadn't seen or heard from Eduardo all day.

Instead, she'd washed clothes and cleaned the house, which most likely hadn't been cleaned in ages. Out behind the house she'd found a clothesline, so she'd taken the time to beat the rugs before doing the laundry. The whole house smelled fresher.

A pot of beans bubbled on the stove. Fresh tortillas were folded in a towel, keeping warm for Eduardo. Now, all she had to do was make herself more presentable. Her resolve from this morning was wavering. How could someone so ugly ever be presentable?

She found a cake of scented soap among the things Eduardo had laid out for her. The sweet, flowery smell filled the room. Never had she bathed with something so enchanting. The thought of pleasing Eduardo warmed her. She couldn't help but dream that he would like her so much, he never yelled or hit her. She sighed and began to scrub her skin. That was only a fantasy and would never happen.

By the time she climbed from the tub, the water had cooled. The sun outside dipped low, almost behind the mountains. Eduardo would be home soon, and she had to do something about her hair. He'd said he wanted it brushed.

Before bathing, she had done a quick job of taking in the side seams on the yellow dress. Now she slipped it on. The gown fell just right, as if it had been made for her. Crossing to the table, she touched one finger to the inlay on the silver brush. How she wished she had a different one to use! This one might be too fragile. She couldn't bear to ruin Eduardo's mother's special things.

Leaving the mirror alone, Chiquita picked up the brush, careful to wrap her fingers tight around the handle. She left the mirror face down. All these years, Papa told her so many times how fortunate she was to not have to see herself. She believed him and couldn't bear to look.

The mat of tangles resisted her efforts, but she was stubborn. Little by little, they came free. By the time she finished, her hair had dried. It hung to her waist, not as thick as Teresa's, but still full enough. The sides showed a slight wave when they fell forward. Would Eduardo like her hair this way? She felt so vulnerable without the tangles to hide behind.

Outside, a horse whinnied. Chiquita hurried to the window. Eduardo rode up to the barn and dismounted, acting stiff from a long ride. Rico met him, and they spoke for several minutes. She wondered if they talked about the injured man and wished she knew if he was okay. Eduardo led his horse into the barn. He would be inside soon, expecting a meal. After being gone all day, he would be hungry.

Chiquita's hands shook as she put the bowls on the table. Earlier, she'd brought in fresh water for drinking. She ladled some in glasses and put them near the bowls. Peering out the window, she still couldn't see Eduardo coming. Maybe he didn't want to face her. Maybe he was still angry with her for sleeping so late and would come in raging mad.

Her hands shook. She walked back to her room to brush her hair one more time. She glanced at the mirror. Should she look? What if she were as repulsive as her father said? How could she face Eduardo? How could she stand the thought of him being saddled with an ugly wife when he was so handsome?

His lean face swam before her. Dusky brown eyes, the color of the road after a rainstorm, twinkled in her memory. He had hair darker than mesquite bark and a mustache that curved in a graceful arc around his mouth. She felt the burning in her cheeks. When he smiled at her yesterday, he'd been the most handsome man she'd ever seen. She wanted to see him smile some more.

"Chiquita?" The kitchen door slammed shut. Heavy footsteps echoed in the quiet house. Her heart pounded. Would he be angry? She forced her legs to move. The walk down the hallway to the living room felt like miles.

"Chiquita, are you ready to eat? I'm starved. I've been..." Eduardo stopped talking as he turned and saw her standing near the hall. His eyes widened. His mouth dropped open. In two quick strides, he crossed the room to stand before her. Chiquita forced herself not to flinch.

Eduardo cupped her cheek and tilted her head until she met his eyes. He stared in silence. She wanted to groan. This meant she was as ugly as Papa said. She stepped back, breaking Eduardo's hold. Tears brimmed in her eyes, threatening to spill over. She turned to run and hide. In midstep, Eduardo gripped her from behind. She was trapped.

CHAPTER 6

Breathing came hard for Eduardo. He felt like a drowning man, gasping for air, as he stared at the vision across the room from him. When he arrived home, he couldn't believe the change in his house. The air smelled clean and fresh as a spring day. Everything sparkled from the work she'd done. He had no idea how she'd accomplished so much. Then, when he turned and saw her, he became speechless, as tongue-tied as a young boy. He didn't remember moving, but suddenly he stood in front of her, cupping her cheek in his hand.

The yellow dress was perfect for her. Her creamy, tan skin took on the tinge of ripened wheat, and her eyes sparkled with a look of shy pleasure. Her hair hung to her waist. The soft tendrils he touched were the same color as cocoa. For the first time he could clearly see her face. She had an adorable, slight cleft in her chin and a small mole above her lip on the left side. Her neck was long, straight, and slender; her whole frame, willowy.

He cupped her cheek, needing to touch her. She seemed so fragile, yet with enough spirit to give her an uncommon strength. Tears filled her eyes. She pulled away and took a step back. She wanted to run. Why? Did she believe him to be unhappy with her? He couldn't let her go. Grabbing her arm as she turned, he pulled her to him.

"Chiquita." His voice came out in a husky whisper. "Don't run." He eased her around to face him.

She looked up at him, her eyes sparkling with tears. He could see the doubts there, and the underlying fear. "Chiquita, you aren't beautiful." She looked down and tried to pull away before he could finish. "Wait." He put his arms around her to keep her from going. A tremor shook her.

"Let me finish. You aren't beautiful—you're exquisite." He ran his hand through her fine hair. Up close, in the light, he could see golden highlights woven throughout. Soft waves curled along the edges. The scent of lavender soap drifted up to him.

Chiquita's eyes were enormous, the tears shimmering. She had such a look of hope, it broke his heart. Once more, anger at Diego welled up inside him; but he pushed the rage away, lest Chiquita sense his feelings and think they were directed toward her.

"I don't know how your family could have called you that horrid name. I've never seen any girl as pretty as you." He smiled. Her eyelids drifted almost closed, as if she were enjoying the caress of his hand over her hair. Had anyone ever touched her in gentleness? He doubted that.

His stomach let out a loud growl. Chiquita's eyes widened again. He chuckled. "I can smell the beans and tortillas. If I don't get to eat them soon, I'll be too weak to walk to the table."

A ghost of a smile lifted Chiquita's lips. He released her, took her hand, and led her into the kitchen. Eduardo shook his head. He couldn't seem to quit staring at her. Whoever would have thought that tangled mess of hair hid such beauty? He was beginning to believe he'd gotten a gem in this marriage. God had been looking out for him, even though he doubted that yesterday.

After supper, Eduardo went back to search again through his mother's things while Chiquita cleaned up in the kitchen. He thought he remembered his mother packing away the old slate that he used to practice writing the alphabet. Near the bottom of the trunk, he found the things he needed. He grinned. Tonight, he planned to begin teaching Chiquita to read. She seemed to have few blessings in her life, and judging by the look in her eyes yesterday, she would consider learning to read a wondrous gift.

When he came out of the room, Chiquita was seated in the living room with one of his mother's old dresses, preparing to take in the seams. She glanced up as he came into the room.

"Oh no you don't." He strode to her chair, took the sewing from her, and pulled her up. She cringed, the look of fear haunting her eyes. Eduardo sighed inwardly. He'd forgotten how fragile she was. The slightest wrong move had her thinking he was like her father. He could see that in the way she reacted.

"Hey, what did I tell you?" He stroked his thumb over her silken cheek. "I won't hurt you. I want you to come over to the desk with me. I'll bring another chair, and we'll start your lessons."

Her eyes widened. She glanced at the things in his hand.

His lips twitched. "Yep, you guessed it. You're going to learn to read. Every evening, we'll spend a little time practicing." He pursed his lips. "Of course, I'm not a teacher, and it will be harder when you can't talk." He gave a slight smile. "But we'll manage. That is, if you want to."

She nodded. Her hair shimmered in the light. Her eyes shone, the closest he'd seen her to happy since she'd arrived. They sat side by side at the desk. He began to show her the letters. She caught on fast, copying them, her head bent forward in concentration.

Eduardo found himself distracted by the perfect curve of her jaw and the slight blush on her cheeks. When she glanced up at a long pause, he felt his face warm. He cleared his throat, trying to recall where they were. Chiquita gave him a puzzled look. She couldn't understand his hesitation. He knew she'd never had anyone admire her before. She probably couldn't fathom why anyone would.

"I think that's enough for tonight." Eduardo almost smiled at the look of disappointment on Chiquita's face. "If we try to do too much at one time, you could get confused. Have you ever heard the Bible read?"

Her brows drew together. She shook her head.

Eduardo rose and stretched. "Why don't you go back to your sewing, and I'll spend some time reading aloud. My father used to read the Bible to us at night and sometimes from other books, too. If you'd like, we can do that."

A look of amazed anticipation made Chiquita's face glow. While he found the place he wanted to read, she hurried to pick up the dress. When she gave him a puzzled glance, he understood and explained why he wasn't starting at the beginning of the book. He turned to the book of John and began to read.

∞

Smoothing the soil around the seeds she'd planted, Chiquita sat up and stretched her back. She couldn't believe how much her life had changed in the last week, since she'd married Eduardo. For the first time, she was beginning to relax and enjoy living.

She still feared Eduardo. Often during the last week, he'd lost his temper over little things that had gone wrong. On each occasion, she'd been terrified he would begin to hit her. She tried hard not to show her fright because just knowing she was afraid used to give her father satisfaction as he hit her. So far, Eduardo hadn't been violent with her at all, but she didn't trust him to continue that way. Papa had shown her how men treated women.

In the evenings, Eduardo continued to teach her the alphabet. She knew all the letters now. Last night, he taught her a couple of simple words. Then, when he got out the Bible to read, he let her look on the page and find the words she learned. She'd been so excited, she could hardly sit still. Soon she would be able to read by herself.

The ache to be able to read had grown over the past week. Growing up, there had never been any mention of the Bible. Mama had a small niche outside the house. She and her other daughters went there to pray sometimes, but Chiquita had never been allowed to join them. Now Eduardo read her fascinating stories about a man named Jesus who lived long ago. She'd never heard of Him or the miracles He did. She couldn't wait to hear the end of the story of His life. Eduardo explained that the Bible was about Jesus and His love for all people. Although she couldn't imagine Him loving her, she wanted to find out what happened to Him.

She patted the last of the seeds and dipped water from the bucket to pour over them. Her braid tumbled over her shoulder, and she flipped it back, relieved to finally have her hair in manageable form. Two days earlier, Eduardo had taken her outside to show her the overgrown garden plot his mother once tended. He brought out seeds that were old but should still grow. She'd spent most of the time since then planting and watering. When he found out she wanted to put in the garden, despite the lateness in spring, Eduardo enlisted the aid of his ranch hands, Jorge and Tomás, to turn the earth with shovels. Chiquita loved the feel of the dirt spilling through her hands and the excitement when the sprouts began to grow.

"I see you're done with the planting."

Chiquita jumped and whirled around to face Eduardo. Her breath caught in her throat. Would she always fear his approach? Could she ever learn to trust him?

"Here, let me help with that." Eduardo took the bucket from her and finished watering the newly sown seeds. "There you go." He nodded at the rows. "You've done a fine job. I look forward to the produce. I've depended on Pilar for too long."

Eduardo headed for the house, and Chiquita followed. Glancing at the hills, she couldn't help wondering at the feeling she'd had of being watched. She wondered if Eduardo felt it, too. She wasn't used to him being home this early. He usually spent most of the day on the range with Rico or with one of the hands, checking the cattle or seeing to the horses. The sun was sinking in the sky, but there were still at least three hours of daylight. She hadn't even started to fix dinner. What if he expected his meal early? She fought the panic welling up inside.

"I thought maybe you would like to see the rest of the ranch buildings. You've been here a week and still haven't met any of the hands or Pilar. She's anxious to meet you."

Her heart pounded at the thought of meeting other men. Even getting to know Pilar didn't interest her. After the way her mother and sisters treated her, she had no idea what to expect from this woman. She scrubbed vigorously at the washstand, uncertain how to let Eduardo know she didn't want to meet anyone else. She couldn't hurt his feelings. What if her unwillingness to meet his employees made him angry?

Smoothing the wisps of hair that had pulled free from her braid, Chiquita faced Eduardo, trying her best to smile. As they walked across the yard, Eduardo caught her hand in his. She flinched, wanting to pull away, but she knew that wouldn't be right. Eduardo hadn't hurt her so far. Why couldn't she relax and enjoy his company? He was bright and interesting. He was certainly handsome, yet something held her back. She knew it was his tendency to lose his temper. No matter how hard she tried, she couldn't trust someone who exploded in rage over every little thing that upset him. Papa had done that.

"I want to tell you about the plans I have for this ranch." Eduardo nodded at a pasture with mares and long-legged foals. "My father always raised cattle and had a few horses for use on the ranch. I wanted to spend time to improve our mustangs, and I have. We now supply the cavalry in Tucson with quite a few of its mounts."

Chiquita watched the mares cropping grass while their babies cavorted and raced around the pasture in total abandon. They weren't big horses, but they were well put together. They looked much stronger and sturdier than her father's nags.

"The lieutenant at Fort Lowell in Tucson, who's a friend of mine, spoke with me about what the cavalry needs. These horses, while sturdy and good at working cattle, aren't as good for the men who need to carry enough provisions for two weeks. They need mounts that will carry them and all of their necessities."

He turned toward the barn and tugged on her hand. She followed him into the dim interior. The place smelled strongly of horse, hay, and the leather from the tack.

"This is El Rey." Eduardo stopped beside a stall at the end of the aisle. The horse inside nickered and thrust his head over the wooden partition. "He will be the start of a new line of horses for us." Pride warmed Eduardo's tone. He rubbed the horse's head, running his hand under the dark mane.

"When I bought him a few months ago, I also bought a mare of this same breed. She gave birth to his foal this week. They're out in the pasture to the west. I'll take you to see them after you meet Pilar and the boys."

Chiquita had never seen such a beautiful horse. His liquid brown eyes stared down at her. His muzzle was dark, but the rest of his coat was the color of light copper. The sunlight coming down the passageway made him gleam like fire. His mane and tail were deep brown, and his face had a blaze of white. Although taller than the mares in the pasture, El Rey appeared as graceful as a dancer. Chiquita couldn't help stroking the soft muzzle. His warm breath feathered across her hand while the few whiskers tickled her palm.

She glanced up to find Eduardo watching her. She lowered her hand and stepped back. Maybe he didn't want her to touch such a valuable animal. His grip on her hand became firm. He pulled her back to him.

"You don't have to be afraid—of him or of me."

She could hear the twinge of hurt in his voice and regretted moving away. All her life, she'd wanted to ride, but she hadn't been allowed near her father's horses. Oh, how she wanted to ask Eduardo if he would teach her to ride.

As if he understood her thoughts, Eduardo spoke. "Have you ever ridden?"

She shook her head. Her hand crept up once more to touch the stallion's nose.

"Then we'll have to change that. We're pretty busy right now, but by next week, I should be able to take the time to show you how. Once you learn, you can go with me on shorter rides. Would you like that?"

She drew in a sharp breath. This man was full of miracles. First he gave her new clothes, then he taught her to read, and now he offered to teach her how to ride a horse. She wanted to pinch herself and wake up from the dream, before she believed it was real.

"Señor! Señor Villegas." A young man galloped up to the barn and jumped from his horse. His breath came in gasps.

"What is it, Tomás?" Eduardo strode down the aisle, still holding Chiquita by the hand. She trotted alongside.

"The foal." Tomas panted, trying to catch his breath "The newest one. You must come."

"What's happened?" Eduardo's grip on her hand grew tight. She could see the anger building and wanted to leave, but couldn't.

"It's dead, Señor. A puma must have found the foal lying down and killed him while the mama was grazing."

"Dead?" Eduardo glared at Tomás as if the death were his fault. He gripped her hand like a vise. She wanted to cry out, but she knew if she did, Eduardo's rage would turn on her. "The cougar came that close to the buildings?"

"Sí Señor." Tomas backed away a few steps. "Rico says you must come to the pasture." He turned and trotted away.

The set of Eduardo's shoulders and the clenching in his jaw spoke louder than words. Now that they were alone, he would unleash his wrath on her. She tensed, fighting the urge to lean as far away from him as his hold allowed.

CHAPTER 7

Furious, Eduardo watched Tomás gallop back toward the pasture where Rico would be waiting. If he had the puma there, he would wring its neck with his hands. He could almost feel the bones crunching. He heard a moan. The sound seemed to pierce the wall of his wrath, and he turned. Chiquita stood beside him, her face pale, her golden eyes dark with fear.

He glanced down. Remorse washed away some of the anger as he realized he'd been squeezing her hand. "Chiquita." He gasped as he looked at her fingers mashed together in his. He let go, intending to look and see if he'd hurt her, but she leaped away. Backing against a stall, she began to edge down the walkway to the door, her enormous eyes following his every move.

"Chiquita, wait." He stretched out his hand to her. She flinched and moved back another pace. Eduardo let his hand drop to his side. He knew he could reach her before she got too far, but she would believe he was coming to beat her. If he was to ever win her trust, he would have to learn patience. The ache in his heart over the loss of this foal was pushed to the background, replaced by the guilt of what he'd done to his wife.

"I know I hurt you. I'm sorry." Eduardo twisted the tip of his mustache. "I am not a man who causes women pain. In my anger at the puma for killing this colt, I forgot I still held your hand." He stopped. She eased a few more steps toward the door.

"Go on to the house, Chiquita. I'll be in after a while." He wanted to say they would talk about this and clear the air, but she couldn't talk. How would they ever be able to communicate if all she did was look at him with those doelike eyes? She usually didn't even nod her head; she just watched him.

He waited as his wife slipped out of the barn and hurried across the yard to the house. Striding to his horse he'd hitched outside, Eduardo could feel the rage building. He'd put a lot into these horses. Purchasing the pregnant mare and the stallion was an investment. He needed this foal to build his herd. He couldn't afford to have some hungry cat preying on his livestock.

Rico, Tomás, and Jorge were huddled around the torn carcass when he rode up. Eduardo dismounted, his horse jittery as he caught the smell of puma and death. Holding the reins in a firm grip, Eduardo moved to where Rico stood.

"Tomorrow, we'll plan to spend the day in the saddle. I want to find this cat.

I can't afford to lose more stock." His clipped words caused the men to step away from him. He ignored that and continued. "Pilar can watch Lucio, can't she?"

Rico nodded. "He's doing much better. So far, he doesn't have any infection and should be back to work in a few days."

"Leave the foal here. If the cat comes back to feed during the night, we'll get a much fresher trail for the dogs to follow. We'll all meet at first light and begin tracking." Eduardo swung up on his restless horse. The gelding danced sideways, wanting away from the terrifying scents.

Taking a last look at his ruined dreams, Eduardo headed home. He had some work to do around the stable before he went to the house. He also wanted to look in on Lucio and talk to Pilar about going to see Chiquita tomorrow while they were gone. Maybe Pilar could make her understand he wasn't a monster.

Even though rage still coursed through him, he determined to be as gentle as possible with Chiquita. He would teach her as he usually did and read the Bible. Maybe she would begin to see that he hadn't meant to hurt her. She sure didn't want to listen to his apology.

☙

The chilly dawn air sent a shiver through Eduardo as he stepped outside the next morning. The lantern swinging at his side threw a ring of light around his feet as he headed to the barn to begin seeing to the gathering of the supplies they would need. He wanted to make sure the horses and dogs were fed and ready by sunrise. Tomás and Jorge were probably already seeing to the chores, but he wanted to make sure. Today, this puma would die. He couldn't have one coming so close to the house. Not only were the foals in danger, but the people could be as well.

"Mornin'." Eduardo greeted Tomás as he entered the barn. The sleepy-eyed young man was forking hay to the horses. Small wisps of chaff drifted in the air, illuminated by the glow of the lantern. Eduardo hung the bail on a hook and went to check on El Rey. The stallion greeted him with a soft whicker.

Jorge came out of the back of the barn where they milked the cow. He carried two pails, one two-thirds full of milk, the other about half full. He handed the smaller bucket to Eduardo to take to Chiquita while he took the other to Pilar to use for the men's breakfast.

"I think soon the other cow will drop her calf. Then we will have more milk to share," Jorge informed Eduardo before leaving the barn.

The eastern sky had paled to gray by the time Eduardo got back to the house. He carried the milk inside. The handle thumped as he released it. Chiquita stood at the stove, stirring the eggs. Tortillas warmed at the side. Eduardo's stomach growled. He'd been pleased to find Chiquita was an excellent cook. After the first day, she was always up and fixing his coffee and breakfast when he came back in from doing chores.

"Good morning." He tried to ignore the way she flinched when he came near. Their school lesson hadn't gone well last night. She'd been so afraid of him, that when he finally did get her to sit by him, she trembled the whole time. He'd ended up fighting his anger and frustration at her lack of belief that he wouldn't hurt her. Rather than show more ire, he ended the session early and read to her from the Bible for a while before going to bed early.

"That smells good." He took a deep breath. "We'll probably be gone all day after the cougar. Stay close to the house until we come home. I don't like the idea of one of these cats coming so close to the buildings. It might be injured and looking for easy prey, so don't go out, all right?"

Chiquita nodded and dished up his breakfast. She began to strain the milk while he ate. He could see the dark circles under her eyes. She hadn't slept well last night. Did she think he would come in the middle of the night and start beating her?

Lord, I have no idea how to make her understand that she isn't the cause or the satisfaction for my anger. Shame swept over him like a wave. He remembered his mama telling him uncontrolled anger was a sin. When he'd thrown fits as a boy, she used to read a verse from the book of Ephesians about anger. Back then, he'd managed to contain his temper, but since the death of his parents, wrath became easier than peace. He'd allowed fury to replace the joy in his life. He didn't smile much at all anymore. He couldn't recall the last time he'd truly laughed.

Finishing his meal, Eduardo could see the pink on the horizon. The sun would be up any time. He carried his dishes to the washtub, trying to not feel hurt over the way Chiquita moved away from him. "I'm heading out." He lifted his hat from the hook. "I'll see you this evening."

◌

Watching Eduardo stride across the yard to where Rico and the two hands waited with the horses and dogs, Chiquita couldn't help rubbing her hand. She hadn't wanted Eduardo to know it still hurt. Maybe it was only the memory that hurt. He hadn't squeezed hard enough to break anything. The fear kept her awake most of the night.

She frowned. She'd planned to go up on the hill today where she'd seen some yucca cactus. They needed some soap, and the yucca made the best. The men thundered out of the yard, followed by the loping dogs. Surely, if they were chasing the cougar, the cat wouldn't dare come anywhere near the house. It would head for the hills to hide from the baying of the hounds. Gathering the cactus should be safe by this afternoon. Besides, she would be in sight of the house at all times.

In midmorning, a knock sounded on the door. Chiquita froze, the cleaning rag dangling from her hand. Who could be here? Maybe if she were quiet, they would leave. She didn't want to see anyone. The knock came again, followed by a woman's voice calling her name. Chiquita crossed to the door, her heart in her throat.

A middle-aged woman stood outside. Her face, brown and creased from years in the sun, carried a smile that seemed genuine. She appeared pleased to see Chiquita, not at all the way Chiquita's mother and sisters would look at her.

"Hello, Chiquita. I'm Pilar Gonzalez, Rico's wife. Eduardo asked me to stop by and see you, since you didn't get to come over yesterday." She held out a covered plate. "I brought some empanadas. If you have some coffee, we could spend a little time together."

Chiquita moved back to let Pilar in the house. She gestured to the kitchen. Her hands shook as she filled the empty coffeepot and put it on the stove.

"You are just as pretty as Eduardo said you were." Pilar set the plate on the table and stepped over to Chiquita. Pilar studied her, making Chiquita want to run and hide. Would this woman see how ugly she was and tell Eduardo's men?

Pilar smiled. "I can't see a thing of Diego or Lupe in you. I've seen the other girls. You don't look like them either. I think you got most of the beauty in the family, but don't tell them I said that."

Pilar continued to talk as the coffee boiled, then perked. Chiquita got out cups for the two of them and poured the aromatic brew. She sank into a chair across from Pilar. As Pilar lifted the cloth from the plate she brought with her, the scent of the pastries made Chiquita's mouth water.

"Eduardo told me you can't talk." Pilar took a small bite, then a sip of coffee. "Have you ever been able to speak?"

Chiquita didn't know what to do. In the recesses of her mind, she could recall a time when she spoke to her sister, Teresa; but the memory was so vague, she always thought it might be a dream. She shrugged.

Pilar gave Chiquita's arm a feathery touch. "I know about Diego. I know he treated you terribly. I think perhaps your mother and sisters did, too." She gave her a sad smile. "I want to be your friend. I want you to know that not all people are like the family you came from. My Rico would never dream of hitting me. He's always kind and loving." She tilted her head. "Sometimes he gets mad at me or at something else, but he would never hurt me. Getting angry is part of being human. What we do with that anger depends on who we are. Do you understand that?"

Chiquita nodded. She couldn't swallow past the lump in her throat. Was Pilar telling her the truth? Could Eduardo be angry and not hurt her? Could she trust him?

"I remember when Rico and I first married and began to work for Eduardo's father and mother. One day, a man named Diego came with his family. They were moving onto some land that bordered the Villegas ranch. They had two little girls with them." She paused, looking past Chiquita, as if seeing the picture of the people. "The oldest girl was just walking. She tried to go everywhere. The younger girl, the prettiest baby I've ever seen, laughed and jabbered at her sister the whole time they were here. Lupe tried to get her to hush, but she wouldn't listen."

Pilar's gaze sought Chiquita's. "I believe you were that baby, Chiquita. I think you have the ability to talk, but you were treated so terribly, you forgot how. Will you let me be your friend and help you? Please?"

A tear dripped on the table. Chiquita hadn't realized she was crying. Was this true? Someday, would she be able to talk? For years, she hadn't wanted to speak, but now she found she did want to. She longed to be able to read aloud like Eduardo did. If she had children, she wanted to read to them. If she could talk, she would say things to Eduardo when he wasn't angry.

She wiped the wetness from her cheeks and looked up at Pilar. She was crying, too. Pilar stood and held out her arms. With a sob, Chiquita stepped into her embrace. She'd never felt anything so sweet.

∽

The afternoon sun felt good on Chiquita's shoulders as she climbed the hill to dig the yucca roots. She carried a large cloth to bundle them in so she wouldn't get dirt all over. She hadn't accomplished much work this morning, but she'd had a marvelous time with Pilar. The foreman's wife told her a lot about Eduardo and the ranch. She talked about Diego and Lupe and how everyone questioned where they got the money for their house. It was an unsolved mystery to many people in the area. Chiquita only shrugged. She had no idea.

A couple of times during the early afternoon, she thought she'd heard the baying of dogs; but the sound had been so faint, she dismissed it as her imagination. She wondered how Eduardo and the men were doing. There was always danger when hunting an animal like a cougar. When cornered, they could be very vicious.

She was wrapping the yucca roots in the cloth when she heard the baying of the dogs. She wondered how they could get this close without her hearing them. The ground shook with the thunder of horses' hooves. Chiquita dropped to the ground, huddled close to the base of the yucca, grateful that this desert plant didn't have the sharp stickers that many others did.

An animal snarled. The barking became frenzied. She began to shake. A gunshot came so close, she started. She curled in a tight ball. The animal's growl was cut off. Rocks rattled down the hillside. Chiquita raised her head a few moments later to see Eduardo and his men standing near her at the crest of the hill, staring down the other side.

Eduardo turned to look back at the house. His gaze locked on Chiquita. His face darkened in anger. "What are you doing? Didn't I tell you not to go outside today?"

She trembled, the kind things Pilar told her about Eduardo almost forgotten.

CHAPTER 8

This had to be the cagiest cat he'd ever tracked. Eduardo and Rico shook their heads and pushed the horses harder as the trail wound back toward the hacienda. All day, the puma had tried to lose them, but the dogs were too well trained. Although they'd been slowed down a few times, they were closing in now.

Up ahead, the dogs' barking became frenzied and high-pitched. Eduardo urged his tired mount to a gallop. Racing up a hilltop near the house, he could see the cougar stretched out at a dead run. The cat would want to find a place with rocks at its back to face down the enemy. There weren't any places like that close to here. Eduardo pulled his rifle from the scabbard. He wanted to be ready as soon as he could get off a clean shot. This beast wouldn't be allowed to get any closer to his home.

For a moment, his thoughts strayed to Chiquita. Amazing how protective he felt toward her already. He enjoyed having someone there when he came in at night. Although she didn't talk, Chiquita's presence warmed the house. She cooked and cleaned better than any woman he'd ever known. His clothes that were worn or torn were now mended with small, neat stitches that she made while listening to him read the Bible. All he'd seemed to repay her with was his short temper.

All day, he'd been consumed with guilt over the way he'd hurt her last night. During the hours on the hunt, he let Rico take the lead most of the time while he hung back and prayed about his anger. He couldn't bear to see the hurt and fear in Chiquita's eyes again. His parents always had joy. He'd begged God to replace his rage with that same joy. Maybe if he tried hard enough, he could teach Chiquita to be content with him.

The puma spun around at the top of the hill and snarled at the approaching dogs. Eduardo reined his gelding to a halt and raised the rifle. The cat stayed motionless a moment too long. In the middle of his growl, Eduardo's bullet sent the cougar tumbling down the side of the hill, away from the house. All he could feel was relief that the animal hadn't ended up in his backyard, scaring Chiquita.

Swinging down, Eduardo followed Rico to the place where the cat disappeared. Rico held his gun ready in case Eduardo's shot hadn't been enough. The puma lay motionless in a pile of rocks at the bottom of the hill.

Eduardo couldn't believe how close this animal had come to his home, his wife.

Turning, he started to look down the other side of the hill at the house below. Something beneath a tall yucca caught his eye. He found himself staring at Chiquita, who huddled in a ball like a terrified child. She'd disobeyed him. She put herself in danger by coming out here while they were hunting this cougar.

His fists clenched. He could feel the anger begin to course through his veins. As if he were outside himself, he watched as he began to stride toward Chiquita. Her eyes widened, then closed as if she knew a beating was coming. Eduardo didn't slow his pace, but his prayers from earlier that day seemed to brush away the building rage. Instead, he only felt relief that she hadn't been hurt by the puma. In his mind, he could almost picture the horror of finding her injured or killed. Even worse was the thought that one of the bullets, intended for the cougar, might have struck Chiquita by accident since they hadn't known she was there. He didn't think he could live with himself if he'd done that.

Eduardo scooped Chiquita up off the ground. He pulled her against him. She came without resistance, although he could feel the rigidity of her muscles. Wrapping his arms around her, he began to stroke her back, her hair, speaking in a low, soothing tone. He glanced at Rico and motioned with a nod of his head for the foreman to take the horses and dogs and put them up. For a long time, Eduardo held Chiquita. Bit by bit, he felt her relax as she must have realized he wasn't going to hurt her. At last she rested against him, her cheek pressed to his chest. Eduardo thought he could remain like this forever. How had this woman become so important to him so soon? Dare he hope that someday he would come to love her?

"Are you all right?" Eduardo still held Chiquita tight. He picked off some of the plant debris tangled in her long hair. She nodded against his chest. He doubted she'd ever been shown simple affection like this before. "I think we should go back to the house. I'll carry the yucca for you."

He released his hold. She hesitated, then stepped back. For a change, her eyes weren't filled with fear, only uncertainty. She studied him, then her lips lifted a bit, as if she were trying to smile at him but didn't know how. After picking up the cloth bundle, Eduardo held out his hand and waited. Chiquita stared at his outstretched hand. She glanced up at him. He thought she would reject his offer, but very slowly she lifted her hand and let him wrap it in his own. Together they set off down the hill to the house.

∞

By the time Eduardo finished the evening chores, Chiquita had supper ready. She'd used dried chilies and some early squash Pilar gave her to make a stew. The smell of green chili filled the house, and Chiquita found she was looking forward to spending time with her husband tonight. Always before, she anticipated learning more of her letters and hearing the Bible read aloud. Tonight, she wanted to be with Eduardo.

When he pulled her up off the ground today, she thought for sure he would hit her for disobeying, and she knew she deserved the beating. Instead, he simply held her like a child who needed comforting after a terrifying ordeal. All her life, she'd longed for someone to do that, but Mama had never shown the least bit of affection for her. Papa only showed the opposite. Not once had they touched her without that contact hurting. She'd seen the way they treated the other girls, though. Teresa, Pabla, Sancia, and Zita all were treated as special. Only Chiquita was different. She had no idea why.

Watching out the window, she could see Eduardo stopping to talk to Rico before coming to the house. What had happened to him today? She thought for sure he was angry with her, but then he showed such kindness. After yesterday, she hadn't believed it possible. Puzzled, she tilted her head to one side, studying him. She couldn't define what, but something about him had changed. He stood, talked, and walked a little different, but she couldn't figure exactly how.

He waved at Rico and turned toward the house. Ambling along, he paused to look at the pasture, then up at the sky as if he had all the time in the world. Peace. That was it. He appeared to have a peace within that he hadn't had yesterday. Usually, he strode everywhere he went like he couldn't take the time to be distracted from the work at hand. Tonight, he seemed to not care about distractions. He was taking the time to see the beauty of life around him.

Dishing up the bowls of stew, Chiquita finished the preparations for the meal. The door opened, and Eduardo clomped into the room. He took a deep breath and let it out with a sigh.

"I could smell those chilies all the way across the yard. My stomach almost beat me to the house." He smiled at her, and she felt her face warm. She ducked her head, not sure what to make of the change in him or of the new feelings swirling through her.

During the meal, Eduardo chattered more than her sister, Teresa. He told of the hunt, his dreams for the ranch, and Lucio's amazing recovery. He spoke about his meeting last week with Antonio Soza and their talk of improving the cattle herds. She could barely keep up with the changes in conversation. She longed to be able to join in.

That evening, Eduardo sat closer to her than usual as they worked on learning a few new words. She tried to concentrate, but for some reason, his presence distracted her. Fear wasn't the problem. She found herself wanting to lean closer to him. When his hand touched her shoulder, she jumped as a shock raced through her. She met his gaze, and he smiled. Chiquita couldn't look away. Those dusky brown eyes were filled with emotion. This time, she knew he wasn't angry.

Chiquita stood. Her chair tipped over and clattered to the floor. She held her breath. Eduardo set the chair back in place. He didn't seem at all upset with her. Warmth flooded her. She had the sudden desire to run outside to cool off in the night air. What was happening to her? Was she getting sick?

"I think we've worked on this long enough." Eduardo rose and began to put away the slate and books. "Do you feel up to listening to some more Bible reading?"

She nodded and moved to the safety of the chair where her mending waited. As Eduardo read in his rich, deep voice, she tried to understand this Jesus. At first she'd been awed and afraid when she heard that Jesus was a man. She'd always been so frightened of her father. She didn't know how she could trust a God who became a man. Hearing the stories about Jesus, she came to realize He was different in many ways from Papa. Even when confronted by an adulterous woman, who probably deserved the severe punishment the men wanted to mete out, Jesus had forgiven her. He asked her to sin no more. That had been bothering Chiquita. She wanted to ask someone to explain to her what sin was. She had an idea, but didn't fully understand. Did everyone sin, or only certain people? For some reason, she felt an urgency to find out.

"I believe I'll turn in early tonight." Eduardo put away the Bible. "Today was a long one, and I want to take you riding tomorrow, if you'd like to go."

Chiquita's heart leapt. Her hands trembled with excitement as she folded the shirt she'd almost finished mending. Tomorrow she would find out what it felt like to sit on a horse. She used to dream about the wind in her face as she raced away on a horse. Sleep was a long time coming as her whole body tingled with excitement. Her mind kept replaying scenes from the afternoon and evening. She drifted off, thinking about what tomorrow would bring.

Before Eduardo returned with the milk the next morning, Chiquita had breakfast ready to put on the table. The coffee, perked before he left the house to see to the chores, had been kept warm. She couldn't stand still but continued to pick things up, putting them in different places, then moving them back just for the sake of something to do.

The door creaked open. Eduardo clomped inside. "Mornin'." He lifted the pail of milk onto the counter by the sink. "I have a couple of chores to see to before we can go for a ride."

Chiquita turned away to fuss with the forks and plates on the table. She didn't want him to see the disappointment in her eyes. From experience, she knew he had only promised her this treat as another way to hurt her. Her father used to do this all of the time. He would promise something, only to back out later. He always grinned as he watched her misery. She'd learned never to believe him, but after yesterday, she'd thought Eduardo would be different. Now she knew better. She couldn't bear to see his triumph when he knew how much he'd wounded her.

"Hey, wait a minute." Eduardo caught her by her shoulders and turned her around. "I didn't say we wouldn't ride. Rico needs to show me something." He ran his thumb under her eye, catching the tear that trickled out. "Besides, you've got some work to do before you can get on a horse." He grinned at her puzzled look. "It's a surprise. I'll tell you about it after breakfast. I'm starving."

She didn't know whether to trust him or not. This could be another trick. Papa would have done something like this if he'd thought of it. Even though her mind said she couldn't trust Eduardo any more than she could trust Papa, Chiquita's heart told her different. Eduardo seemed to genuinely care about her and about others.

After taking care of the milk, Chiquita dished up the eggs and fresh tortillas, adding extra chilies to Eduardo's breakfast, as he liked. He smiled as she set the steaming plate in front of him. When she sat down, he reached for her hand. This time, when he prayed, he kept a secure hold on her. She could barely concentrate on his words as the shock of his touch ran up her arm. At the end of the prayer, he let go. Although her hand still remembered the feel of his, she felt bereft and alone.

They ate in silence, Eduardo eating like a man who'd done a full day's work, while she picked at her food. She couldn't get her mind off what he planned to do next. "While you clean up, I have to get something." Eduardo scooted his chair back from the table. "I'll be right back."

Chiquita couldn't finish her breakfast. What would he do now? Was this surprise something nasty, or would it be a wonderful one as she used to dream about? Before she had the dishes washed, Eduardo returned. His contagious grin made him look so young and handsome, her breath caught in her throat. She couldn't look away from his gaze. This was the way the man of her dreams used to look at her. Her heart thudded, feeling like it might beat out of her chest.

"Here you go." Eduardo thrust a bundle of cloth at her. "Why don't you see if you can get this ready by the time I return?"

Tearing her gaze from his, Chiquita saw, for the first time, what he carried. The amber skirt and blouse glowed in the sunlight that streamed through the window. Threads interwoven in a pattern throughout gave the outfit a shiny appearance. She'd never seen anything so rich and beautiful. Her eyes widened as Eduardo held the clothes out for her to take.

"My mother only got to wear this a few times when she went riding. I thought the color would match your eyes." He hesitated and glanced away. "You could get the alterations made while I see what Rico needs. I'll be back in about an hour. Will that be enough time for you to get ready?"

The full skirt dragged at her arms as she let Eduardo drape the material over them. She couldn't possibly wear something so rich. What if she fell and it tore? Would that trigger Eduardo's wrath? Her eyes were drawn to his warm gaze. As she clutched the incredibly beautiful outfit to her, she could see something in his eyes. Was it admiration? For her? He smiled, and she forgot her reservations. She would do anything he asked.

He stepped close. She couldn't breathe. Eduardo brushed a hand over her hair, making her scalp tingle. "I can't wait to see you when you have this on. I'll hurry back, Chiquita."

CHAPTER 9

Clinging to the saddle with both hands, Chiquita looked like a wooden statue. Eduardo quickly found out that teaching a woman to ride would be a challenge. After he'd lifted Chiquita into the saddle, Pilar came and talked to her about how to keep her feet in the stirrups and how to shift her weight. He could tell Chiquita hadn't realized how far off the ground she would be. Her face had paled at first, even though the gelding she rode was small and stood still. Chiquita couldn't seem to get the hang of going with the gait either. She needed to learn to relax and move with the horse.

"You're doing fine." Eduardo smiled down at her. He rode his stallion, El Rey, knowing the horse needed some exercise. El Rey pranced sideways.

Chiquita's gelding snorted and nodded his head. Chiquita tensed. She gave Eduardo a wide-eyed glance.

"He's just feeling El Rey's excitement." Eduardo patted the big stallion's neck. "They'll calm down soon." He reined El Rey closer to her.

"Here, straighten your back. Let go of the saddle. Hold the reins like this." Eduardo took her hands and turned them, showing her the way to have the most control. "You won't fall. Pilar gave you good advice about how to shift your weight with the movement."

Slowly, Chiquita eased back in the saddle. Her face began to lose the look of uncertainty. She even managed to take her gaze off her mount for a minute and look at him.

"That's the way." He smiled. "See? As you loosen up a little, you begin to feel the movement. Now go with him, not against him." He pointed at the gelding, indicating they should become a team. "You have good balance already."

Chiquita sat even straighter. Eduardo ached for her. The slightest compliment meant so much to her. He could see the same thing when he touched her. Her reaction, although fearful at first, now seemed to be amazement. She couldn't seem to understand that someone could touch her in kindness or love.

Love? Eduardo frowned. Where had that thought come from? He couldn't possibly love Chiquita. He hadn't known her long enough. Yes, he felt protective of her. He could still recall the stab of fear when he saw her lying on the ground yesterday. He thought she'd been hurt. He'd never felt such intense relief before as he did when he found out she was all right. Despite those feelings, he couldn't possibly love her.

El Rey pranced ahead, and the gelding quickened his pace. Chiquita smiled. She looked more relaxed already.

"I think you're going to be a natural rider." Eduardo couldn't quit watching her. Since he'd walked into the house and seen her wearing that riding outfit, he'd been entranced. Even her hair had some of the same color threads woven throughout, and they gleamed in the sunlight. Like a princess in the stories his mother used to tell him, Chiquita now rode proud and erect.

"Would you like to try going a little faster?"

She smiled and nodded. He eased them into a slow canter, not wanting to try the rougher trot. Her mouth rounded in an O of surprise. Within moments, she relaxed once more and gave him a tremulous smile. This was the happiest he'd seen her. Even her eyes glowed. He hadn't had this much fun in years.

For the next hour, Eduardo alternated between walking and cantering the horses. He took them in a roundabout circuit, not wanting to stray too far and tire Chiquita on her first ride. She would be sore enough tomorrow without riding too long. As they walked the horses back toward the ranch house, Eduardo veered off the path, motioning to a stand of trees near the bank of the San Pedro River.

Under the shade of the cottonwood trees, he dismounted. Lifting Chiquita down, he held her for a moment to steady her. She started to move her legs, then gave him a surprised look. He chuckled.

"Walking feels funny after you've been on a horse for a while."

She nodded and took a couple of hesitant steps. Eduardo secured the horses, then took Chiquita's hand. Her troubled gaze told him she didn't understand what they were doing.

"I want to show you something."

She seemed to understand the solemnity of the occasion. Eduardo could feel her hesitancy as she followed him down an overgrown path through the grove of trees. Thick grass, drying now because of the lack of recent rains, tugged at their legs as they passed by. Ahead, a short fence outlined the family burial ground. Chiquita stiffened. She slowed, and when Eduardo glanced back, he could see her reluctance to go in with him.

Pulling her close, Eduardo stood by the fence. He wouldn't push her to go where she didn't feel comfortable.

"I don't know why I brought you here. I haven't come to visit in a long time." Regret filled Eduardo as he recalled how his mother used to come every week to clean the weeds and keep the gravesites nice. She wouldn't like the way things looked now.

Chiquita tugged on his hand. Her forehead wrinkled in a puzzled frown. She gestured at all the small markers and the two bigger ones.

"These are all my family." Pointing to the long row of tiny crosses, Eduardo could feel the old sadness creep over him. "My parents had ten children. I'm the youngest. The first nine didn't live past infancy."

Chiquita's quick intake of breath startled him. She stared up at him, her eyes wide and tear-filled.

"I remember Mama saying that when she found out she was expecting me, she didn't even want another baby. She thought if she lost another one, the pain would kill her right then and there." He paused, trying to swallow around the lump in his throat. "She used to come down here once a week. She'd plant flowers in the spring, then tend them all summer long. I think she liked to talk to her children." He could feel her questioning gaze. "Oh yes, she loved me. In fact, she probably loved me too much. She and my dad were almost too careful with me. They were so afraid they would lose me." He gave a sad smile. "I'm probably spoiled by all their attention. I sure do miss them."

Chiquita tugged on his hand. Leading him to the gate, she motioned for him to open it. He followed her inside. She went from one small cross to the next, touching each one, as if in greeting. When she came to the two larger markers, she stopped and turned to look at him.

"Those are my parents." He reluctantly followed her to the graves. "They died four years ago. I was off with Rico and the vaqueros, getting some cattle rounded up for sale. Only my parents and Pilar were at the ranch." He turned away, blinking his eyes to clear the moisture.

"When we came back, we found a renegade band of Apaches had attacked. My parents were dead. Pilar had been outside. She heard the commotion and managed to hide. We were all devastated."

He couldn't say more. The silence stretched taut. Even the birds grew quiet. Chiquita's touch was so light that, at first, he thought he'd imagined something. Then he realized she was offering him comfort. Her small hand began to rub light circles on his back. Warmth enveloped him. Eduardo turned.

She stared up at him. Tears pooled in her eyes. She pointed at the largest cross, then at herself.

"Did you know my father?" Eduardo recalled several times when his father had to have dealings with Diego. Perhaps that was what Chiquita was trying to say. She nodded, confirming his thoughts.

Taking his hand, Chiquita brought it to her cheek. Her eyes begged him to understand. Eduardo frowned. He nodded.

"My father was kind to you, wasn't he?" Her eager nod confirmed what he'd said. "That's why you remember him. There weren't many people who were nice. Am I right?"

She nodded again. Turning away from him, she touched the cross at his father's grave. Tears trickled down her cheeks. Eduardo could only imagine the pain she must be feeling, if a stranger was the only one she could recall ever treating her with kindness. Anguish, not only for her but also for himself and his lost family, nearly made him groan with pain. He must have made a sound. Chiquita turned. He wasn't sure how it happened, but she was pressed tight against him. Her arms wrapped around his waist in a fierce hug, like she wanted to give him all the comfort and strength she could.

He held her, relishing the peace that flowed over him. "I was so angry when my parents died. Over the years since then, I've grown angrier and harder to be around. I didn't even realize what I was doing." Eduardo's voice rasped in the quiet. "Only when I saw what my rage did to you, did I understand that I had to change. I'm not perfect, Chiquita. I may still get upset sometimes, but I will never hurt you. I want to learn to be happy." He held her away. Her tawny eyes gazed at him full of wonder. "Will you help me? Will you give me time to change?" Her nod of agreement made him want to shout with joy.

∞

Following Eduardo back to the horses, Chiquita didn't know what to think. These feelings were so new. Never in her life had she felt the need to comfort someone. She'd always been the one hurt, and no one ever showed sympathy to her. She wasn't sure how she knew what to do. She'd only done what she thought would be nice. A soft touch in times of distress had been a dream of hers.

This was strange to her. How could she be willing to trust any man? She almost felt like a traitor to herself. After her father's cruel trickery, she knew better than to lower her defenses around Eduardo, but she couldn't seem to help her actions. His admission of his need for help and forgiveness tugged at her heart, breaking the barriers even more. Holding Eduardo felt so right and so good. She hadn't wanted to let go of him. What was she to do?

The one thing she longed to do was talk to Eduardo. Every day, the desire seemed to grow. After her visit with Pilar, Chiquita tried to recall a time when she used to talk. There were vague memories of playing with Teresa. She thought she might have spoken then, but the fuzzy recollection could be just her wanting this so bad. Maybe this was another of her dreams.

When they got to where the horses were cropping grass, Eduardo put his large hands on her waist and lifted her up into the saddle. She could feel his strength. For a moment, she almost reached out to run her hand across his broad shoulders. Catching herself, she worked at arranging her skirt instead. She had to be careful. Maybe this was a trick of his. He acted nice now, but when she became vulnerable by caring for him too much, then he could hurt her even more.

"Are you enjoying the ride?" Eduardo reined El Rey around and started toward home. He glanced back for her answer. She couldn't help but nod. Riding was delightful, and she couldn't wait to do more.

When they emerged from the trees, Eduardo slowed, waiting for her to come alongside him. "I need to talk to you about what Rico told me this morning." He frowned and gazed off at the hills to the east. "We think someone has been watching our house."

He held up a hand at her fearful look. "No, I don't think there's any real danger. It's probably some drifter riding through, although they usually come on down and ask for a meal or work."

A chill trickled down Chiquita's back. Glancing around, she hoped no one was watching them now. The gelding snorted and danced a few steps. Chiquita grabbed the saddle to keep her balance.

"I didn't tell you to scare you." Eduardo reached out to pat her horse. "I only want you to be careful and stay close to the house. Don't gather food alone. If you need to go and I can't go with you, then I'll have one of the vaqueros accompany you." He shrugged. "This is probably nothing, but I want you to be safe."

His smile eased Chiquita's trepidation. She wanted to ask what sign they'd found. Who watched them? How close were they? A sense of unease dimmed the brightness of the day. Although she'd been enjoying the outing, she couldn't wait to get back to the safety of the house.

Closing her eyes, Chiquita forced her tense muscles to relax. For years, she'd done this exercise when her father delighted in frightening her. She refused to let him get pleasure from knowing how terrified she was, so she would put on a brave front. She could do the same now. She didn't want Eduardo to think her a coward. Threats had been a way of life for her for years, and she wouldn't let an unknown peril ruin the life she had now.

She tried to focus once more on her memories. If Pilar was right, and she used to talk, why had she stopped? For the first time in years, she allowed herself to recall her difficult early years. Pictures floated through her mind—bits and pieces of agony: Mama, with her hand raised to strike, her face red with rage; Papa, the sadistic smile on his face as he hurt her. Teresa and, later, her other sisters as they stood wide-eyed, watching her torment.

"Hey, are you all right?" Eduardo's touch made her jump. She almost lost her seat in the saddle. He grabbed her, his concern evident. "I must have kept you out riding too long. You look tired."

Wrapping the reins around the saddle horn, Eduardo reached for her. Her breath came in shallow gasps. The horrible memories were too recent. What did he intend to do? She stiffened, preparing for the worst. Then, looking into Eduardo's eyes, she relaxed. He didn't mean to hurt her. He wasn't like Papa. She had to believe that.

Taking a firm grip on her waist, Eduardo lifted her. His gaze never left hers. Her heart began to pound, this time not from fear. Time slowed. She couldn't take her gaze from his face—his eyes, his mouth. She lifted a hand to caress his cheek. Never before had she felt like this. She wanted his strong arms around her, to lay her head against his chest and hear his strong, steady heartbeat.

Time stood still as Eduardo drew her close. She could feel the warmth emanating from him. Her pulse raced. Eduardo's smile faded, replaced by a look of intensity. He began to lower his face toward hers as he settled her in front of him.

Chiquita's gelding let out a scream. Pain shot through Chiquita. She gasped. El Rey jumped. Eduardo yelled, clutched her close, and kicked El Rey into a full gallop. The pain increased. Her leg was on fire. Dreamlike, Chiquita looked down. The feathered shaft of an arrow protruded from her thigh.

CHAPTER 10

Panic coursed through Eduardo. He dug his heels into El Rey's sides, urging the big horse to go faster. They flew across the ground toward the ranch house. He tried to ignore the droplets of blood dripping from the hem of Chiquita's skirt. Holding her tight, he prayed she would be okay. Her eyes were squeezed shut, her face pale and beaded with sweat.

Apaches! They'd attacked again. For the last two years, things in Arizona had been fairly quiet. Why were they attacking now? This didn't make sense. The Indians knew the cavalry would be out after them in force. They didn't venture into this area anymore. *Please, God, let her be okay. Help me get her home safely.*

The gelding raced beside him, laboring to keep up with the longer-legged stallion. Blood ran from a wound on his withers. The arrow must have grazed him before striking Chiquita's leg. That was why the gelding had squealed. His eyes were wild with fright as he worked to keep up.

Guilt pricked at Eduardo's soul. He thought of the nights they'd spent together as he read the Bible to Chiquita. He could tell from the intensity of her interest that she'd never heard the Bible before. He'd started reading in the book of John to give her an idea of why the Bible had been written. *Lord, I knew she didn't know You, yet I haven't taken the time to explain the Gospel message to her. Oh, God, if she dies, I won't be able to bear it. Please give me the chance to introduce her to You. I know she's interested. Help her understand.*

El Rey seemed to sense the urgency of the moment. He stretched out and ran as if his, not his mistress's, life depended on it. Eduardo knew the longer the arrow stayed in her leg, the more the risk of infection. Even the jarring of the hard run could cause bleeding they would be unable to stop. His arm tensed as he held her close, trying to keep her from being jounced too hard.

He glanced over his shoulder. Were the Indians following? Where were they? He hadn't seen or heard any sign of them. Would they attack the ranch next? Living this isolated always meant running the risk of this type of attack.

The ranch buildings came into view. El Rey's breathing was labored, but Eduardo couldn't let him stop just yet. The gelding had fallen behind. Eduardo began to yell as he raced into the barnyard.

"Rico! Rico, gather the men." He pulled El Rey to a sliding stop. "Pilar, come quick."

Rico ran from the stables, followed by Tomás and Jorge. Pilar appeared in the doorway of her cabin. Seeing him holding Chiquita, she came running as she dried her hands on her apron. Lucio ran out of the bunkhouse, one hand clutching his side. The gelding thundered into the yard, his reins flapping, the whites of his eyes showing. Jorge caught hold of him.

"Rico, Tomás, get your guns. Chiquita's been shot by Indians. I don't know if they're behind me or not, but we have to be ready." Eduardo reined El Rey toward the house. "Pilar, get your medicine. Meet me at the house. We have to get this arrow out."

Pilar wheeled and raced back to her house. The men all went for their guns. Eduardo knew they would do their best to protect the ranch while he saw to Chiquita. At the house, he eased off of El Rey, still holding Chiquita. She moaned as he landed on the ground with a thump. Leaning back against his horse, Eduardo got a better hold on her, careful of her injured leg.

Striding to the door, he heard Pilar coming. She reached his side in time to lift the latch for him. Her breath came in ragged gasps as she waited for him to enter first. He strode through the house to the bedroom where Chiquita had been sleeping, ignoring the questioning glance Pilar gave him.

"I can take care of her if you want to go see to the men." Pilar was all business as she began to examine the way the arrow had pierced the skirt and gone into Chiquita's leg. Eduardo hesitated. She gave a quick nod at the door. "I'll take good care of her."

Stepping outside, Eduardo stayed in the shadow of the house as he scanned the perimeter. No sign of Indians. El Rey stood near the door, his sides still heaving from his heroic run. Sweat matted his red-gold coat. Eduardo grabbed the reins and began to lead El Rey to the barn, where he or one of the men could care for the horse. The stallion deserved an extra measure of feed today.

Rico would be in the barn. He would have either Jorge or Tomás in the loft, watching the surrounding countryside. After the attack that killed his parents, Eduardo had been careful to keep the area close to the buildings brush-free. He didn't want to give anyone a place to hide and sneak up on them. The Apaches wouldn't have an easy time. He and his men were prepared.

He stopped just inside the dim interior of the barn to let his eyes adjust. Lucio was in the first stall with the gelding, sponging down the wound near his mane. Eduardo could see the gelding still trembled from the injury and the terror.

"Tomás and Jorge are both up there, watching. They haven't seen any sign of trouble." Rico strode toward him. "What happened?"

Eduardo began to take the tack off El Rey. "We were ambushed down near the river. We were coming out of the grove of trees where the family's buried. I didn't see or hear anything." Eduardo paused and frowned at Rico. "There's something funny about this attack."

Rico nodded. "If we don't see anything soon, we might try sending Jorge for the Elias brothers. They're the best at finding renegades."

"You're right." Eduardo led El Rey to his stall and began to brush him down. J. M. Elias knew Indians better than any other man he knew. He would gladly come and help them figure out this ambush.

⌐

Waves of pain washed over Chiquita. She'd never known this much hurt before. Had her father found some new torture? She moaned and wanted to move away. That wouldn't work. He always liked it when she showed a weakness. Gritting her teeth, she stayed as still as possible, refusing to make a sound.

Once more, Papa stabbed her leg with a hot poker. She cried out. The sound broke free without her permission. Papa would be pleased. Darkness closed in around her. She fought the blackness to no avail.

Later she awoke, coming to in a haze of torment. Pilar leaned over her, deftly winding a strip of cloth around Chiquita's leg. Something hot pressed against the flesh. Pilar glanced up. Seeing Chiquita was watching her, she smiled.

"You'll be fine, I think. The arrow went in the fleshy part of your thigh and didn't make you bleed too much." She frowned. "Of course, when I took the arrow out, you bled quite a bit. I'm sorry that hurt so much." She tied a knot in the cloth and pulled the covers over Chiquita. "You lost some blood coming home. I'm glad you fainted. That saved you from a lot of pain."

Picking up a cloth and dipping it in a bowl of water, she began to wipe Chiquita's face. The coolness felt so good, Chiquita wanted to groan with pleasure. Her face and neck felt gritty with dried sweat and dirt.

"I'll let you rest for a while with this poultice. When it cools and I have to put a new one on, I'll wash you down, too. I want you to stay still so you don't break open the wound."

Pilar gathered the soiled clothes and carried them from the room. She moved in and out, removing the dirty water and medicines she'd used. Her quick glances at Chiquita spoke aloud how concerned she was. Chiquita knew there was something Pilar hadn't told her. Had Eduardo been hurt, too?

She closed her eyes, trying to recall what happened. She remembered the ride and leaving the grove. A clear vision of Eduardo lifting her from the saddle, a strange look in his eyes came back to her. Once more, her heart reacted. What had Eduardo been trying to say to her with that look? The remembered feeling that had washed through her made her stir in bed. Hot pain jolted through her. She bit her lip, forcing her body to stay still. She still couldn't remember much past the time Eduardo had been lifting her. What had happened? Where was he?

Heavy steps clomped in the hallway outside the room. The man of her thoughts opened the door and peeked in. He smiled. Her heartbeat sped up.

"Pilar told me I couldn't come in if you were sleeping." He crossed the room. Pulling up a chair, he took off his hat and put it on the foot of the bed. "I don't usually listen to Pilar, but when she's caring for someone sick or hurt, she's like a grouchy mother bear."

"I heard that, young man." Pilar swept in, carrying a tray. "If you're going to come in here and disturb my patient, you can make yourself useful. She needs something to eat and drink." Pilar set the tray on a small table near the bed. "Don't stay too long and wear her out. She needs to rest." Giving Eduardo a warning look, Pilar left the room. Chiquita didn't know how she could be so bold and sure of herself.

Eduardo gave Chiquita a sip of water, the cool liquid easing the dryness of her throat. He cradled a small bowl of stew in his hand, acting like feeding her was awkward. She wanted to take the spoon from him and feed herself, but she couldn't get her arms to move. She seemed to have no strength.

"I promise to give you small bites." His mustache lifted as he grinned at her. "I'm sure you're curious about what happened and what we're doing now. Right?"

She nodded, eager to hear whatever he would tell her.

"Well, as long as you eat, I'll talk. When you stop, I'll take it as a sign that you're too tired to hear more." He wiggled his eyebrows, making her want to giggle. "This is my way of making you eat, so you'll put a little meat on those bones."

She obediently took a bite. The stew tasted delicious, although she wasn't hungry. She chewed slowly, hoping this would keep him talking.

"Do you remember being shot?" She shook her head, and he continued. Between giving her small bites, he recounted the story of the attack and the race for the house. He told her the measures they'd taken to see the ranch would be safe. By the time she couldn't eat another bite, he appeared to have finished his story.

"Jorge is getting ready to ride to the Elias ranch. He should be able to return with them by tomorrow. They're the best, and I know they'll help. They were the ones who found the Apaches who killed my folks."

Eduardo stood and stretched. "I think I'd better let you rest. I'll be back in later. Would you like for me to read to you tonight?" He seemed to be especially excited as he asked the question. Chiquita nodded. As he left the room, Eduardo turned and winked at her. Warmth flushed her face. What was this man doing to her?

The next day, Eduardo heard the thunder of hoofbeats as he sat beside Chiquita. That must be Jorge, returning with the Elias brothers. Eduardo smoothed the hair away from Chiquita's forehead. She'd only been sleeping for a short while. She'd lost so much blood yesterday that he was amazed at how well she was doing. She wanted to get out of bed this morning, but he and Pilar insisted that she stay put. By tomorrow, he would have to tie her down to keep her there. He smiled. He'd never known a woman with so much spunk.

Last night, he had hoped to share the Gospel message with her, but she'd been so weak, she'd gone to sleep early. He prayed to get the chance soon, but he wasn't sure she understood enough to invite Jesus to be her Savior. Since she couldn't ask any questions, he had to try to guess what she wanted to know. That wasn't easy.

Pilar hurried into the room. "Rico sent me to stay while you go talk with those men. How is she doing?"

Chiquita stirred, then quieted. Eduardo beckoned Pilar to follow him from the room so they wouldn't disturb her further. "She ate well this morning. This is the first time she's fallen asleep."

"Sleeping is good for her." Pilar nodded. "When she wakes up, I'll change the dressing. If she's doing all right, maybe she can get up a little later."

"Don't let her do too much." Eduardo knew he didn't need to caution Pilar, but he couldn't help himself. "That woman works more than three people." He and Pilar shared a chuckle before he trod down the hall and left.

When Eduardo got to the barn, J. M. Elias was examining the arrow Pilar had removed from Chiquita's leg. His brothers, Ramón, Juan, and Cornelio, conversed with him in low tones. The four brothers looked grim as they studied the wood and feathers. Rico and the vaqueros watched from a distance.

Eduardo strode toward the brothers. Dread clenched his gut. He could recall in vivid detail the conversations they'd had when his parents died. They would know how hard this must be for him. All morning, as he sat with Chiquita, he could feel his anger building. He'd tried to pray and give this to the Lord, but his feelings wouldn't go away. His wife had almost died. If the arrow had been a little higher. . . If he hadn't been lifting her from her horse. . . Those "ifs" had been running through his head since the ambush happened. Rage boiled inside him like a simmering stew.

"I'm sorry to hear this happened. We're glad to know your missus is going to be fine." J.M. spoke for the brothers. His square jaw tensed as if he, too, held anger inside. "Jorge said you haven't had anymore problems, right?"

Eduardo nodded. "Everything's been quiet."

"We took the liberty of having Jorge take us to where your wife was attacked." Señor Elias glanced at his brothers, who were murmuring among themselves as they examined the arrow. "We found the spot where the shooter hid. There was sign of one horse and one man."

Eduardo frowned. "One? Apaches don't fight like that."

"We scoured the area, looking for sign of any others that were hidden elsewhere. Jorge also talked to us about the evidence you've found that someone is watching your ranch house. He took us to that spot, too."

Rico and the vaqueros moved closer. Eduardo could tell by the tense set of their shoulders that they suspected what J.M. was leading up to. He could feel it, too. He tamped down the ire, waiting for the Apache fighter to continue.

"This arrow—" The eldest Elias plucked the weapon from his brother's hand. "This is not an Apache arrow. It isn't even a very good imitation. Someone wants you to think Indians have attacked you. We think the person who's been watching the ranch is the same one who shot your wife. This has nothing to do with renegade Apaches."

Anger burned through Eduardo, making it impossible to think. Who would do such a thing? Who would try to kill him or Chiquita? Which one of them had been the real target of that arrow? A thousand questions raced through his mind—questions for which he had no answers.

CHAPTER 11

"M orning. How's the leg?"

Chiquita sighed. Eduardo had asked her the same question every day for the last week. She still limped, and her leg was sore to touch, but it had healed very fast.

Pilar was amazed with her progress. "I've been treating wounds for years, and I've never seen anyone heal this quickly," she'd told Chiquita.

Chiquita thought the reason had to do more with the God Eduardo talked and read about, but she didn't know how to tell him that.

In the last week, Eduardo not only read to her about this Jesus in the Bible, he also talked about Him afterwards. She'd learned so much and longed to know more. Eduardo seemed to know the questions her heart wanted to ask. Last night, he talked to her about sin. He explained that every person ever born, other than Jesus, who was the Son of God, had sinned. She had trouble going to sleep last night, thinking about how she was a sinner and couldn't get into heaven because of that. Eduardo promised to tell her tonight about the special way God provided so anyone could get into heaven. She wondered what that way would be. Would she have to do some special service? Did this God require money or some sacrifice like they did in the time of the Bible? When she thought about knowing, anticipation made her anxious. She pushed the thoughts from her mind and went to tend to the milk, hoping to show Eduardo her leg was fine.

"Jorge saw the Elias brothers yesterday afternoon as they were heading for Tucson. They asked him to let us know there's no sign of any uprising."

Chiquita gave him a puzzled look. Her fingers brushed across the partially healed wound on her leg.

"I didn't tell you before. I didn't want you to worry." Eduardo tugged on the side of his mustache. "The Elias brothers are experts on the Apaches. They're sure the arrow you were shot with isn't an Apache arrow, although someone took pains to see that it looked like one."

Chiquita could feel the blood draining from her face. What was Eduardo saying? If the Indians hadn't shot her, then who did?

Eduardo crossed to her and grasped her shoulders. "I don't want you to worry. I only told you so you would be careful. You can work in the garden and around the house, but I don't want you to go any farther. No more gathering yucca or anything else. If you need something, someone will get it for you."

She could see the tightly controlled anger in his gaze. Did he blame her for this? She wanted to step away, yet she wanted him to hold her and tell her everything would be fine.

"I have to go out with Rico and the boys today. We'll be gone all day. I've asked Pilar to check in on you. If you're outside and you hear the dogs barking, get inside, okay?"

She nodded. Uncertainty made her nervous. The longing to ask questions made her throat tight. Opening her mouth, she tried to make sound come out. Fear that she couldn't succeed kept her quiet. Turning to the stove, she dished up breakfast. Today, while Eduardo was gone, she would spend some time working on her reading and writing. She could read simple words now. If she practiced and worked hard, maybe soon she could talk to him through writing.

A few minutes later, Chiquita watched as Eduardo stalked across the yard to the barn. She wished he had talked to her about what was bothering him. Ever since she'd been shot with the arrow, he'd been distant. He seemed to be holding something back from her. Her inability to express herself and ask what was wrong chafed at her.

∞

Anger simmered deep inside Eduardo. This was a different kind of anger than he'd had before. This was a helplessness to protect his family and holdings. Frustration at not knowing who was trying to hurt him constantly aggravated him, wearing away all of his defenses. He could feel himself slipping away from the Lord. He needed to turn to prayer to solve the dilemma, but he ignored the small voice nudging him in that direction. Today, he and Rico would take the others and scour the ranch, looking for sign of misdeeds. Whoever wanted to hurt him or Chiquita had to leave some sign somewhere, and he intended to find it.

They were all gathered at the barn, their horses saddled and waiting. Even Lucio had come out to see them off. He'd been disappointed when Eduardo told him he would stay and watch the ranch, but they all knew he still didn't have the strength for a full day of riding. Besides, with the threat hanging over them, someone needed to be here in case of trouble. Lucio should be able to handle most anything. He could be trusted to watch.

Eduardo took the reins of the gelding readied for him. He'd chosen not to take El Rey on this trip. He didn't want to put the stallion in any danger. He was too valuable an animal.

"Jorge, I want you and Tomás to ride across the river and scour the hills over there. Be careful. Watch for any signs of trouble, no matter how insignificant. I don't know for sure what we're looking for or who is behind this." He fixed them with a serious gaze. "Don't take any chances. At the first sign of trouble, get back here. Don't do anything foolish. Is that clear?"

"Sí señor." Jorge nodded. He and Tomás reined their horses around and loped along the road leading to the river.

Eduardo watched them go, uneasiness stirring inside. Saying a quick prayer for their safety, he turned to Rico. "Let's go. We'll take the hills behind the house. It will take longer, but I think we should stick together."

Rico nodded. "We could cover more territory if we just stay in sight of each other. That way, if something happens, we would be able to help the other one pretty fast."

"Okay." Eduardo kneed his gelding. "Let's start in the east and work our way west. That way, we'll have the sun at our backs this morning." Their horses' hooves thundered across the ground as they left the yard. Eduardo glanced at the house.

Chiquita watched from the kitchen window. Her pale countenance gave him a momentary pang of guilt. He knew she didn't understand his concern, and he hadn't wanted to fully explain. He wanted to keep from scaring her. Deep down he knew, too, that he wanted her to trust him without fear. Maybe he was being unfair, given her circumstances. How he wished she could talk to him!

By noon, they'd found no sign of anything wrong. Eduardo called a halt, swinging out of the saddle, landing on the ground with a thump that jolted his leg. The gelding stepped away, probably too tired to do more. Eduardo knew the horse could sense his mood. The boiling cauldron of rage inside him threatened to explode. He needed to figure out who was attacking him and why.

Rico groaned and arched his back, stretching to relieve the cramped muscles. Eduardo knew the older man had much more trouble spending hours in the saddle, yet he hadn't complained at all during the long morning hours. Rico rummaged in his saddlebags, pulling out the lunch Pilar sent with them. Chiquita would have sent something, too, but she hadn't been told early enough to contribute. Eduardo hadn't wanted her to know what they were doing. She'd faced enough trouble in her life. He didn't want her worrying further.

Taking off a bite of tortilla, Rico indicated the hills spread out before them. They were high enough to have a good view of the hills and valleys leading back to the ranch. The snakelike river wound through the bottom of the valley, weaving in and out of view as the mountains permitted. From up here, the large trees close to the water appeared to be a carved set of child's toys.

"Do you mind me making a suggestion?" Rico glanced at Eduardo.

"I'll take any help you have to offer. I know I'm not thinking straight." Eduardo took a drink from his canteen. "Do you think I'm imagining the threat?"

Rico's eyebrows drew together. "No. Jorge and Tomás have found too many signs that someone is watching us. At first, we didn't mention this to you. They thought it was a drifter passing through."

"You mean this has been going on longer than we thought?" Eduardo clenched his jaw.

"No, not that long. Only a few weeks." Rico waved a hand in the air as if dismissing Eduardo's concern. "The boys often find evidence that someone has spent the night in the hills near the ranch. I think these men want the safety of being near the house, but not the contact. I don't think they're dangerous or responsible for the attack on your wife." He gave Eduardo a steady look.

"So, who do you think is doing this?"

"Someone who wants to hurt you." Rico gazed out across the valley. "You and your father only have one person I know of who might do this. You are very well thought of by everyone else."

"Diego Garcia." Eduardo could feel his stomach knot. That man had been a thorn in his flesh for years. He'd thought that by marrying Diego's daughter, their conflict would be at an end. "I have no way to prove it's him."

"I remember your father saying when you have a rogue animal that needs taking care of, you track him to his lair." Rico raised his eyebrows in a questioning glance. "We aren't all that far from the Garcias' place. We could drop in and see how Diego is doing."

Huffing out a breath, Eduardo nodded. "I guess you're right. Perhaps it's time for Diego's son-in-law to visit." He twisted the strap on the canteen. "After knowing the way he treated Chiquita, I only hope I can keep my temper in check when I see him."

They finished their meal, tightened the cinches, and mounted. Eduardo led the way over the hills to the rutted road that led to the Garcia place. When he thought of confronting Diego, all he could see was Chiquita and the way she feared men because of what had been done to her. Although she had an uncommon strength, anyone who knew her at all could see the terror in her eyes whenever any man showed a force or anger about anything. She seemed to always think the anger was directed at her. Getting rid of her fear might take years.

His roiling emotions calmed as he thought of Chiquita. During the last few nights, she'd seemed so eager to hear the Bible. Last night he'd wanted to explain salvation to her, but he could see her eyelids drooping as he talked. Since she rose so early, she didn't like to stay up late. Still, she refused to go to bed while he was awake. Despite the short time they'd been married, already he couldn't imagine life without Chiquita. If only she would learn to relax around him and trust him. He had to fight this tendency to become angry.

The Garcia home was little more than a shack. The cluttered yard and shabbiness of the house lent an air of abandonment to the place. A dog slunk around the corner of the house. Eduardo could count the pup's ribs without any trouble. The poor thing looked half-starved and cowered as if it had been abused, reminding him of Chiquita. His hands tightened on the reins.

The door creaked open. Teresa sashayed out, lifting a hand to her brow to block the sun. He knew when she recognized him. She smiled, and her swaying walk became even more pronounced.

"Why, if it isn't my favorite brother-in-law." She stopped beside Eduardo's horse and gave him a coquettish look.

"I've come to see your father. Is he home?" Eduardo resisted the urge to move his horse away from Teresa. She made him uncomfortable now, although she hadn't when he met her before.

"He's gone right now. Maybe I can help you." She gave him a smile that made him pull on the reins, causing his horse to dance away from her. "Are you having trouble with Fealdad? Papa can come and give you some lessons on how to get her to do what you want."

For a minute, Eduardo had no idea what she was talking about. Then he recalled Diego using that despicable name for Chiquita. His muscles tensed as he fought down the wrath. How could he have ever thought Teresa would make a good wife?

"Where is your father?"

She took a step closer, reaching out to run a hand down his horse's neck. "I don't know. He likes to go off by himself. Says he's going hunting." She shrugged. "Ever since his cousin stopped by for a visit a few weeks ago, he's been hunting a lot."

Rico snorted. Eduardo glanced at him and could see his foreman's suspicions. Diego must be the one who watched his place and shot Chiquita. But why? Was he there now, watching the place?

Teresa's hand drifted closer to Eduardo's leg. He tugged on the reins, making his horse back away. "When your father gets home, tell him I was here."

"Wait." Teresa raised her hand.

Eduardo wheeled around and raced from the yard. Rico followed close on his heels. The ride home seemed to take forever. They took a shortcut, riding silently, looking for signs.

"Eduardo, stop." Rico's sharp tone halted Eduardo. They were on a hilltop with a clear view of the ranch house, although a very distant one. "Look at this." Rico hopped off his horse and knelt down.

Eduardo joined him. The hard dirt showed the scuffing of hoofprints, as if a horse had been tethered here for a long time.

"Can you smell it?" Rico tilted his head.

Eduardo sniffed lightly, noting the scent of horse, sweat, and something else. "Someone's been smoking here." He followed as Rico edged along the ridge. On the far side of a large boulder, several cigarette butts were squashed into the earth to make them less noticeable.

"Someone's been here recently." Rico poked at one of the cigarettes. "This one is still warm. I'd say he heard us coming and hightailed it."

"Why would they be here watching? You can't see much from here." Eduardo narrowed his eyes, trying to make out any detail in the house below them.

"If you had a spyglass like they use in the cavalry, you could see plenty."

"Let's go." Eduardo surged to his feet and strode to his horse. He couldn't explain the sudden urgency to get back to Chiquita. With every bit of evidence, this was getting more serious.

They made their way to the ranch in grim silence. Desperate thoughts plagued Eduardo. Did Diego mean to harm him or Chiquita? Was it even Diego doing this? Rage kept rearing its ugly head. As they came over the last ridge, Rico gave a cry and pointed to the yard. In front of the house stood two strange horses. Wrath blurred his vision as Eduardo kicked his mount to a full gallop.

Before the horse could slide to a stop, he jumped from the saddle and sprinted to the house. If anyone had harmed Chiquita, they wouldn't live to tell about it. He ignored Rico's shout as he jerked the door open and raced inside.

Chapter 12

The door hit the wall with a crack like thunder. Chiquita jumped to her feet. Eduardo dashed into the room, rage nearly choking him. All he could see was Chiquita's face turn white. Her mouth thinned, her back stiffened. The fear that shone momentarily in her eyes receded. Eduardo didn't slow until he stood in front of her. She was all right, only terrified of him.

Swinging around, Eduardo saw Pilar seated, holding a glass in her hand. Across the room two men sat with their backs to the sun, their faces in the shadow. One of them wore a gun. They rose. Relief flooded Eduardo, leaving him almost weak from the intensity of his ire.

"Quinn. Conlon. I didn't expect to see you here. Those aren't your normal mounts." He strode across the room and shook hands with his two friends. "What brings you out this way?"

Rico stepped inside, his stance wary. Eduardo could see his friends were puzzled at the reception they were receiving. He nodded to the door. "Perhaps we could go outside and talk."

Glancing over his shoulder, Eduardo could see that Chiquita still stood ramrod stiff, waiting for her punishment for whatever crime she thought she'd committed. "Go on out with Rico. I'll be there in a minute."

Pilar frowned at him, picked up the glasses left behind by the men, and went to the kitchen. Using slow movements, Eduardo approached Chiquita. He knew he'd scared her once again. He hadn't meant to, but he'd been so afraid something had happened to her. The thought of someone hurting her had driven him crazy, yet he didn't know how to tell her that without sounding insincere.

He touched her cheek. There was only the slightest flinching. Her pale skin felt cool. The smell of his mother's lavender soap drifted to him. "I didn't mean to startle you." Running a thumb over her lower lip, he wanted to kiss her. Would she be afraid? Unyielding as she was, he knew he shouldn't push intimacy, although with each day, it grew harder to keep away from her. He longed to take her in his arms, to whisper his love to her.

"I have to go talk with my friends. I'll explain what happened later. Please, don't think I was mad at you. I wasn't." As he spoke, she opened her eyes. Her amber gaze, still a little fearful, made him take a deep breath. He turned away before he lost all reason and forgot that his friends were outside waiting for him.

The afternoon sun cast long shadows. The squeal of a horse filled the air as some of the foals kicked and raced across the pasture. The wind, coming from the direction of the river, brought the earthy smell of moist ground. Eduardo breathed deeply, trying to rid himself of the last vestiges of anger. Quinn and Conlon waited at the barn. They watched him walk toward them.

"Do you always enter your house like it's getting ready to burn to the ground?" Quinn tried to make the question light, but Eduardo could read the seriousness in his tone. His friends hadn't understood his panic.

"It's been quite a day. Come on in the barn, and we'll sit down." He looked over at Rico. "Are Jorge and Tomás back yet?"

Rico shook his head. "I'll put up the horses." He led their mounts away, giving Eduardo the opportunity to speak with Quinn and Conlon alone.

"I've had some problems here in the last few weeks."

Quinn tensed. Conlon frowned and sat forward. "What kind of problems?"

Eduardo explained losing his new foal to the cougar, the discovery that someone had been watching them, and Chiquita being shot. "We went out today to see if we could find some evidence of who's behind this."

"Did you find anything?" Quinn asked.

"Nothing we can prove." Eduardo smoothed his mustache and told them of his suspicions about Diego Garcia. "On the way home, we found evidence on that ridge. Someone who smokes has been there. Rico thinks they might be watching the house with a spyglass. The problem is, I can't figure out why anyone would do this. Even though Diego is the only one who might be guilty, why would he be interested in us?"

"Maybe he regrets letting you marry his daughter." Quinn frowned. "Although that wouldn't explain his shooting her. Besides, I thought you were marrying Teresa. I've only seen her a couple of times, but your wife didn't look like Teresa."

"That's true," Conlon said. "I remember Teresa talking up a storm, and this girl didn't say a word the whole time we were here. Pilar did all the talking."

Eduardo sighed. "Diego tricked me into marrying his other daughter. I call her Chiquita, because the name he'd given her was so awful."

"If he tricked you, we can take him to court and make him give you the daughter you wanted." Quinn's eyes narrowed.

"No, I don't want Teresa anymore. Besides, I could never send Chiquita back into that family." Eduardo explained what he'd learned of Chiquita's upbringing. By the time he finished, both of his friends were upset.

"That explains why she never said a word." Quinn rubbed at his badge. "I don't understand why a man would do that to his own daughter. He should be put behind bars."

"You're right." Conlon stood and stretched. "Unfortunately, you know as well as I do, there isn't a court that would find him guilty of anything. He would say he was disciplining her. Men can get away with a lot in the name of correction."

"If this doesn't stop, Eduardo, I want you to come and get me. I don't have any jurisdiction out here, but maybe I can put some fear into Diego anyway."

"Thanks." Eduardo warmed at the thought of having friends willing to help out. "You never did say why you came out here."

"I saw Antonio Soza in town the other day. He told me all about some new breed of horse you have here. I came to see for myself." Conlon grinned. "Quinn tagged along because he thought if he stayed home, Kathleen would make him take care of that baby boy of his."

Eduardo chuckled and led the way to El Rey's stall. Pride surged through him as Conlon and Quinn both let out low whistles of admiration. El Rey pranced to the front of the stall. He stretched out his nose, his dark mane falling forward.

"This isn't one of your regular horses." Conlon rubbed El Rey's ears. "What is he?"

"He's an Andalusian." Eduardo grinned as Quinn and Conlon both gave him questioning glances. "The Andalusian breed began in Spain, but some were brought to South America. I read about them but only learned recently that a few had been brought this far north. After some correspondence, I managed to purchase this stallion and one mare."

"What's the advantage to the breed, besides their size?" Conlon asked.

"I wanted a horse that would be bigger because I knew that's what you were looking at for your troops." Eduardo couldn't suppress a surge of excitement. "These horses are incredible. They adapt to their surroundings well, train easily, and they have to be the best-looking horses I've ever seen. They're powerful and agile. As you can see from El Rey, these horses are known for their mild temperament, making them easy to work with. You can teach them to do anything."

Conlon chuckled. "I'm not sure you care for the horse."

Eduardo laughed. "I guess I am a little enthusiastic. The more I learned about Andalusians, the better I liked them. Their history goes back a long ways."

"How soon before you have some foals from him?" Conlon scratched El Rey's ear. The horse leaned against him.

"I bought the mare because she would foal this spring. That's the colt that was killed." Eduardo couldn't keep the anger from his voice. Losing his only purebred foal had been a loss he hadn't anticipated. There were always hazards when raising livestock, but he hadn't counted on a puma coming so close to the house.

"Now I won't have any more foals from him until next year."

"I can't wait to see them." Conlon gave El Rey a final pat. "I have to get back to town. You know, you might consider bringing your wife to Tucson for a few days. Glory and I would be happy to have you visit."

"Thanks." Eduardo walked with them to their horses. "I might do that. I'm getting pretty jumpy with all that's going on here. Besides, I don't know if Chiquita has ever been to town. She might enjoy it."

❧

On her knees, Chiquita worked her way along the row of pepper plants, pulling the young weeds from the ground. The damp earth stuck to her hands and her dress. She loved the smell and feel of the dirt and the plants growing there. She flipped her braid back over her shoulder, wishing she'd taken the time to pin it up before coming out here.

Later, she would take a bath and wash her hair with some of the soap she'd made this morning from the dried yucca roots. After grating the roots, she'd boiled them until the suds began to form. Now, the water was cooling and would be ready to use soon. She almost moaned at the chance to use the fresh soap to get clean after the hard day's work.

Her thoughts drifted. Over a week had passed since Eduardo stormed in the house to find his friends visiting. He must have been mad at her for some reason. Why couldn't she learn to trust him? He wasn't like Papa. He'd proved that over and over, yet every time he got upset about anything, she knew he would hit her. Such a good man didn't deserve a wife like her. Eduardo needed someone who wouldn't be so fearful.

In the past week, Eduardo'd been so busy. Many of the mares were foaling. Every night, he was needed to help with one thing or another. Last night had been their first night together. Eduardo read from the Bible, and she realized how much she'd missed hearing those words. He'd been so gentle as he explained more about Jesus to her. Her fingers continued to pull the weeds as she recalled Eduardo explaining that Jesus, the Son of God, had died for her. Eduardo even read the story of the crucifixion to her. When he read about

Jesus being whipped by the soldiers, she couldn't help the tears that burned her eyes. She could feel those lashes. Bending over her work, she tried to hide her distress from Eduardo, but he seemed to know anyway.

He also seemed to understand all of her unspoken questions. Had he asked the same questions of his parents? When she wondered what she had to do to be accepted by God, Eduardo began to tell her that the only way to heaven was by God's grace. That's why Jesus died, so He would be the sacrifice for her. She only had to admit her sins, which she already had. Then she needed to believe Jesus was the Son of God and ask Him into her heart.

The thing Eduardo didn't understand was that she wasn't worthy of Jesus. He wouldn't want someone as ugly and useless as her. He might have died for people like Eduardo or Pilar—those who were truly good people—but He hadn't died for her. She would have to find another way to get to heaven. The more she learned about heaven, the more she longed to go there. She felt like God was calling to her heart, but it had to be a trick. How many times had Papa told her she was worthless? Would her own father have lied to her? Even her mother and sisters had agreed. Eduardo must be wrong when he said Jesus died for everyone. Her heart broke at the thought.

Swiping at her eyes with the sleeve of her dress, Chiquita continued down the row. She put the weeds in a pile to throw into the horse pasture. If she left them lying on the moist earth, they would only take root again. Papa's words were that way. No matter how many times she tried to convince herself he had lied to her, she always remembered what he said. The roots of those words went so deep inside her, she would never get rid of them. Even in her dreams, she could hear his taunting voice.

At least here, she had a haven of peace. No one yelled at her or called her names. Eduardo paid her such sweet attention. She knew she didn't deserve him. Sitting up, she cocked her head to listen. The dogs were quiet. Birds twittered in the trees near the house. Serenity settled over her, banishing the thoughts of her former life.

Easing up from the ground, she brushed off her knees. She picked up the pile of weeds she'd gathered and carried them to the edge of the garden. She hoped to have the whole garden done in another hour. First, she needed a drink. The sun beating down had warmed her more than she thought, and now her throat was dry.

Returning to the garden a few minutes later, she smiled at her progress. The squash plants were growing fast. In a few weeks, they would have fresh squash. Her mouth watered at the thought. The beans, peppers, and tomatoes would take longer. She always anticipated eating those first fresh vegetables. Nothing tasted better.

Chiquita glanced at the sun as she knelt where she'd left off. She had plenty of time to finish this and take a quick bath before fixing supper. Eduardo had gone to see Señor Soza again today. When he came home, he would be tired. She wanted to have a bath ready for him, along with a good supper.

Seeing a weed on the other side of the pepper row, Chiquita leaned over, stretching out to reach the interloper. A plant on the far side of her exploded. Dirt flew in the air. A sharp crack sounded. She fell forward, confused at what was happening. Had someone shot a gun at her?

Rolling to one side, she struggled to get up. Her dress caught beneath her feet. She fell. A second geyser of dirt erupted. The shot rang out. The dogs went wild. She heard a shout and the sound of pounding feet.

Freeing her dress, she stumbled to her feet. Heart pounding, she raced for the house. She had to get to safety. The adobe brick on the side of the house exploded. Fragments of the dried brick stung her cheek. Racing around the corner, she sobbed in terror. Was she going to die? She wanted to call for help. She opened her mouth, but nothing came out.

Lucio sprinted toward her. He motioned frantically at the house. Didn't he understand she was trying to get inside? Bark exploded from a tree. Sharp pain raced down her arm. Tears ran down her cheeks. She slipped and fell. A sob tore free. Lucio raised his gun. The sharp crack spurred her to action.

Leaping to her feet, she reached the door. The latch refused to work. Maybe she could hide on the other side of the house. She jerked one more time. The latch came loose, and the door flew open. She tumbled inside. Running through the house, she fell to the floor by her bed. Blood dripped from her face. Had he shot her? Was she going to die?

Oh Jesus, please help me. I don't want to die without knowing You. Help me to know how I can be worthy. She curled in a ball, sobbing. Never would she be good enough for Jesus. Never.

CHAPTER 13

"Chiquita, sweetheart."

Eduardo's strong arms were lifting her from where she'd curled up on the floor by her bed. She couldn't stop shaking. He cuddled her close.

"Are you hurt?" He carried her from the dim room. She bit her lip to keep from whimpering like a child. She didn't want to go out in the light. What if someone started shooting again? The thought terrified her.

Eduardo sank into the rocking chair. For a long moment, he held her tight. Their breathing melded into one rhythm. She could smell the scent of horses and sunshine on his shirt. He must have just come home. She almost smiled at the way her mind wanted to grasp at normal thoughts when the world was spinning upside down.

"Let me see." His hand was gentle as he lifted her face from his chest. "Oh sweetheart, you've been bleeding. Did you get shot?" A hint of panic infused his voice. She tried to shake her head, but her muscles didn't seem capable of responding properly.

The front door banged open. Footsteps clattered across the floor. Chiquita wanted to snuggle into Eduardo again. She'd felt so safe there. Never before had she known that kind of comfort.

Her senses were coming awake. The arm nestled against Eduardo ached. Her cheek stung and felt swollen. Remembering the flying shards of adobe and bark, she repressed a shudder, grateful nothing had pierced her eyes.

"How is she?" Pilar sounded breathless as she reached them.

"She's been bleeding, but I can't see how bad she's hurt."

Hands turned her. Eduardo's large hands lifted her, then Pilar's smaller ones brushed across her face.

"Rico, I'll need some hot water. Jorge, bring me some fresh water for now. I need to clean off the blood and dirt to see how bad this is." Pilar barked the orders like a general. "Bring her over here, Eduardo. I'll have to undress her to make sure she wasn't shot." Pilar leaned close, her face a mask of concern. "Chiquita, can you hear me?"

In a massive effort, Chiquita lifted her head enough to meet Pilar's gaze. She tried to nod, but her body felt heavy, exhausted.

"Okay." Pilar smoothed Chiquita's hair away from her face. Somehow the braid had come undone and the waves tangled around her body. "Eduardo will bring some light, and we'll see how you are."

Biting her lip to keep from moaning at the pain, Chiquita could feel her face drain of blood as Eduardo carried her to her bed. She could tell he tried to be gentle, but every movement sent a jolt of agony through her. Something must be lodged in her arm for it to hurt this much. Had she been shot? She couldn't remember. Everything happened so fast. All she thought of at the time was getting to safety.

Pilar sent Eduardo to get the water and a rag from Jorge. While he was gone, she began to remove Chiquita's clothing. The dress, crusted in dirt, stained with blood, came away reluctantly. When she began to pull the left sleeve off the shoulder, Chiquita cried out.

Eduardo rushed into the room. "What's happening?"

"Look at this." At Pilar's grim tone, Chiquita tried to sit up to see what she'd found. The sight of Eduardo in the room when she wasn't decent made her gasp. Pilar noted the sound and jerked a cover over the top of her.

"Lucio said that the shooter hit the tree as Chiquita ran past. A piece of the wood went clear through her dress and is buried in her arm." Pilar worried her lip with her teeth. "We have to get that fragment out."

Pulling his knife from his pocket, Eduardo began to cut the material from around the wood. Chiquita could tell he wanted to rip the cloth away, but he seemed too concerned about her comfort to do something so rash. When he had the area clear, she could see the flesh puckered where the bark-covered wood had pierced her arm.

"I'll have to get this out." Eduardo sat on the bed beside her, his face serious. His eyes seemed to show a reluctance to cause her pain. Chiquita's heart ached for him. She knew without a doubt that Eduardo was not at all like Papa. Pressing her lips together, she nodded for him to continue.

With a sharp tug, the piece of wood pulled free. She could feel the blood coming out, but she didn't look. Closing her eyes, she tried to stop the tears. She ached all over. She wanted more than anything to be back in Eduardo's arms. Stunned, she realized how much she'd come to care for him. Did she love him? She wasn't sure she even knew what love was.

"Hold this tight on her arm, Eduardo." Pilar pressed a cloth to slow the bleeding. "I think this is the worst. I don't see any bullet wounds. I'll get Jorge to bring some prickly pear pads. We have to get the rest of that dirt out, and the cactus should do it."

As she left the room to give instructions to the others, Eduardo held the rag to Chiquita's arm. She gazed up at him as he touched her cheek where the adobe and splinters of tree had cut her. Anger darkened his eyes. He tensed, as if he wanted to do something about this but didn't know how. For the first time, she wasn't afraid of his anger. This time, she knew he wasn't mad at her. Instead, his gentle touch soothed her. Warmth flushed her cheeks. He'd called her "sweetheart" earlier. Never in her wildest dreams had she thought any man would call her an endearment.

A few minutes later, Pilar bustled back into the room. Behind her, Rico carried a steaming pan. He placed it on a table before leaving again. Chiquita almost sighed with relief. She couldn't bear the thought of someone she didn't know well seeing her like this.

Slipping a hand behind Chiquita's head, Pilar lifted her up a bit. "I want you to drink this tea, Chiquita. This is made with some catclaw leaves. They'll help you relax. Picking out all these stickers could take time. We'll try to be as gentle as we can."

The warm tea had an unusual taste, but Chiquita swallowed obediently. When she finished, Pilar retrieved the pan Rico had carried in earlier. With care, Pilar lifted half of a prickly pear cactus pad from the hot water. She cooled it for a minute, then molded the cut side to Chiquita's arm where the tree fragment pierced her. Taking a long cloth, she wrapped the pad to wedge it tight against the skin. Chiquita gritted her teeth to keep from crying out.

When Pilar finished, Eduardo began to wipe Chiquita's face with a warm cloth. The slow, gentle movement helped her relax. She closed her eyes as he worked to cleanse the area peppered by small splinters. The sedative in the catclaw tea began to spread a heaviness through her limbs. By the time Eduardo finished washing her face, she barely noticed as Pilar removed the shards of brick and bark one by one.

By the time they finished, Chiquita didn't think she could stay awake much longer. The strain of the afternoon, combined with the medicine, made her drift into a healing sleep. Her last memory was of Eduardo pulling a chair beside the bed, telling Pilar to go home, that he would sit with her for a while.

⚭

Cradling Chiquita's small hand in his, Eduardo couldn't help wishing he was still holding her. If she didn't need the rest so badly, he'd be tempted to lift her into his arms once more. He knew if he bumped her arm in the process, he would wake her. Checking the time, he saw he needed to take off the cactus pad, cleanse, and rewrap the wound. Pilar left explicit instructions for him to follow. The problem was, he didn't want to risk waking Chiquita. All he wanted to do was sit here and watch her sleep. His fingers longed to trace the line of her cheeks, down her long, slender neck. He could almost feel the dip of the slight cleft in her chin. The memory of touching her soft skin warmed him.

Protective feelings warred within him. He wanted to stay here to make sure Chiquita rested and recovered. At the same time, he wanted to scour the hills for her attacker. Jorge and Tomás had gone out when they'd arrived home, but they found nothing. They would go out once again, at first light, to renew the search. This time, Lucio and Rico would be with them. As soon as Pilar could come and stay with Chiquita, Eduardo intended to join his men.

God, help me. I want to take vengeance. Help me control my anger, Lord. I can't do this on my own. I want to have joy in my life, but how am I supposed to do that when all these things are happening? Please, Jesus, help Chiquita. I know she's interested in You, but I don't know what to say to her. Show her the truth about who You are.

With a sigh, Eduardo kissed Chiquita's fingers. After releasing her hand, he unwound the bandage holding the cactus pad on her arm. She moaned. He frowned. At the time, he hadn't thought much about it, but Chiquita had cried out earlier. He stopped as the memory took hold. Did that mean she could talk? Had something happened to her long ago to make her quit speaking, even though she still had the ability to do so? Knowing how Diego treated her, he knew this must be a possibility. Maybe, given time, Chiquita would be able to talk to him. Hope surged. He would have to go easy on this, but maybe— just maybe—she could.

The prickly pear pad didn't want to pull away from her skin. The juice seemed to adhere to whatever it touched, which made the cactus a worthy drawing agent. As the pad cooled and dried, most of the unwanted particles would be drawn out, and the wound would seal. Eduardo retrieved a warm rag to loosen the edges of the cactus, lifting it free. The place where the wood punctured Chiquita's arm already looked better. After washing her arm with some of the leftover catclaw tea as Pilar had instructed, Eduardo sprinkled powdered catclaw leaves over the cut and wrapped the arm.

Through the whole process, Chiquita slept, moaning only when he removed the cactus. Tucking the covers around her, Eduardo once more sat in the chair by her bed. He picked up her hand. Her fingers were cool to the touch. That was good. Pilar said to watch for fever. As long as Chiquita remained cool, he knew she would be fine.

༄

The smell of tortillas cooking on the stove woke Eduardo. He'd fallen asleep, resting his head on the bed beside Chiquita's hand. He rotated his shoulders, trying to ease out the kinks. His back felt like a herd of horses had trampled across him during the night.

Chiquita's soft breathing whispered in the quiet of the room. She had some color in her cheeks. Last night she'd been so pale, he'd been afraid for her. Touching her forehead, he sighed with relief at the coolness. He and Pilar both knew the dangers of fever.

Chiquita's eyelids fluttered a few times, then opened. She blinked, her honey gaze clouded with sleep. Her cheek, slightly swollen from all of the cuts, looked sore. Eduardo spent a long time last night thanking God that the shards hadn't entered her eye. Several of the cuts were close. She tried to smile. Her dry lips looked painful.

"Let me get you a drink." Eduardo gave her a lopsided grin. "I must look awful. I fell asleep here and haven't even washed up yet."

She started to raise her hand, winced, and shook her head. Her gaze followed him as he moved across the room to wash and bring her a drink. She lowered the cup and tried to smile. He knew from the way her mouth tightened when he moved her how much her arm hurt.

"I think Pilar is here, fixing breakfast. I'll have her come in and help you. Rico is out with the vaqueros, trying to find who shot at you. I'll grab a bite and join them while Pilar stays with you."

Chiquita's eyes widened. The faint flush left her cheeks. Her hand reached for him again, and she grimaced.

Eduardo brushed the hair off her forehead. "Don't worry. You'll be safe. We won't go far. At least one of us will be within sight of the house at all times." She leaned her cheek into his palm. He wanted to stay here forever. "I have to find out who's responsible, Chiquita. We can't live like this, with someone trying to hurt you."

Standing, he jammed his hat on his head. "I want you to rest today and follow Pilar's orders. She'll take good care of you." He winked at her. She relaxed. The corners of her mouth almost tipped up in a smile. Eduardo left the room, lighthearted despite all the troubles plaguing them.

☙

"What have you found?" Eduardo spoke before his horse came to a complete stop. Rico, Jorge, and Tomás were clustered together, examining something on the ground.

"Look at this." The two younger men moved back while Rico pointed at the dirt. "Someone's been smoking here." Rico nudged the burnt scrap of paper with his finger. "Whoever shot at your wife is the same person who was on the far ridge, watching the house. They put the same twist on their cigarettes."

Eduardo squatted down beside his foreman. His finger traced the print of a boot. "You're right. Look at this boot print. Whoever wears these walks with more of his weight on the outside of his foot, right here. See how the boot's worn?"

Rico nodded. "We think he shot at the house from here, but if so, how did he continue shooting when the Señora went around the corner? He wouldn't be able to see her then."

Eduardo stood and looked down on the house. Although a long distance, this spot afforded a perfect view of the garden area, but the angle was all wrong for the far side of the house. Whoever waited here wouldn't have been able to shoot the tree when Chiquita passed it.

"Could he have been moving as she ran?"

"No, Señor. I asked Lucio, and he claims he never saw any movement from the hillside. He would have seen him if the shooter moved."

Studying the ground, Eduardo followed the man's trail to where his horse had been tied out of sight. The deep hoofprints in the hard dirt showed how the horse raced away from this spot. *If only I'd been home, then I could have stopped this madman.*

"I don't understand how he did this. Jorge, you and Tomás follow the trail. See if you can find where he went, but be careful."

Climbing on their horses, the two young men moved off. Tomás, as the best tracker, bent over his horse's withers, watching the sign. Eduardo turned back to Rico.

"What do you think? At first I thought Diego was responsible, but that doesn't make sense. Why would he allow me to marry his daughter, then try to kill her? I don't know what to think anymore, but I'm scared for Chiquita."

Rico slapped his horse's reins against his leg. He stared across the hilltop. "I have an idea. Come on."

Eduardo followed, wondering what the older man was thinking. A few minutes later, Rico stopped and dismounted. Squatting beside a boulder, he beckoned to Eduardo. There on the ground were more scuffed prints. These footprints were different. The boots were worn in a different area.

Rico glanced up. "There wasn't one man shooting at your wife, Eduardo. There were two of them."

CHAPTER 14

"How's my favorite patient this morning?" Pilar bustled into the house as Eduardo left.

Chiquita suppressed a sigh. For the past few days, Pilar had come every morning to change the bandage on her arm. By the morning of the second day, a slight infection seemed to be setting in, so Pilar made a poultice of malva leaves. She spent the morning putting the hot oatmeal-like mixture on Chiquita's arm, waiting an hour, and then repeating the process. The hot poultice wasn't pleasant, but the infection was gone. Now, the arm itched. Chiquita knew that was a sure sign of healing.

Pilar set down her basket of herbs. "I've seen caged animals that looked happier than you do. I know you're bored to tears having to stay in the house, but Eduardo knows what's best. Until they find out who's trying to hurt you, you need to stay out of sight."

With a nod, Chiquita moved to sit down and let Pilar begin her examination. She had been bored. She wanted to work in the garden. The weeds would be so thick, she would never catch up. She also wanted to begin watching for the cholla cactus to bud so she could gather some of the buds to dry. They made a delicious vegetable or a good addition to a stew. There was much to be done, yet she was stuck in the house.

"Oh, this is looking good." Pilar probed at the scar. "Is it itching yet?" When Chiquita nodded, Pilar smiled. "As long as it isn't very sore, you'll be fine. If you start having problems, let me know. Otherwise, I think I can leave you in peace."

Panic raced through Chiquita. She'd come to enjoy these visits with Pilar. This was her only contact with anyone, other than Eduardo in the evenings.

"Don't worry. I'll still come every day and see you. Would you like a cup of tea?" Pilar laughed as she looked at Chiquita. "I promise I won't put any foul-tasting medicine in this tea. I'll even add a little honey for you, if you want."

A smile pushed at Chiquita's heart. She'd never had a friend. Pilar always talked as if Chiquita was an equal or better. Quite often she tried to defer to Chiquita, since she was the boss's wife, but the lack of verbal communication stood in their way. This past week, Chiquita had tried hard to work on her reading and writing, but she still didn't know enough to converse that way.

So many questions burned inside her—questions about Jesus and how she could become worthy of Him. For years, Mama refused to allow her to pray with her or even come near their small altar. They always said only certain people were good enough, and she wasn't one of them. Doubt had begun to creep in. She needed to ask someone about the truth.

"Here you go." Pilar carried two cups of tea from the kitchen. After handing one to Chiquita, she wrapped her hands around the other and sat down.

The warm tea felt, and tasted, delicious. The early morning still carried a chill. Later in the day, the sun would warm things up a lot, but for now, the house was cool.

Taking a sip from her cup, Pilar looked up, her gaze serious. "Chiquita, do you have any idea who would be shooting at you or why?"

Chiquita shook her head. She'd already let Eduardo know, but she was afraid he didn't believe her. A lump settled in her throat. How she wanted to reassure everyone here of her innocence in this matter! She hated that she was putting them all in danger. Most of all, she wanted to know why this was happening.

"I've wanted to talk to you about something else." Pilar swirled the liquid in her cup before meeting Chiquita's gaze. "The night we took the fragment of wood from your arm, you cried out in pain. Do you remember that?"

Chiquita shook her head. That day was mostly a blur in her memory. Any attempt to recall what happened resulted in a headache.

"Besides being afraid, you were in a lot of pain. I'm not sure Eduardo noticed you cry out, but he might have. He's very quick to catch things." Pilar leaned forward. "Chiquita, do you want to talk?"

Her breath caught. Did she want to talk? Of course she did. The problem was, she couldn't. She'd tried the last few days, when she had the house to herself. Not a sound would come out, no matter how hard she tried. Tears blurred her vision as she nodded at Pilar. Pointing to her mouth and then her throat, she shook her head.

"Have you tried to speak?" Pilar set her cup on the floor beside her feet. She took Chiquita's hands in hers. At Chiquita's nod, she gave a gentle squeeze. "Do you remember having a serious disease when you were young or perhaps an accident that would have caused you to lose the ability to talk?"

Chiquita frowned. She had only vague memories of chattering with Teresa when they were very young.

"I know you used to be able to speak." Pilar began to rub Chiquita's hands. "I also have a feeling I know how you were treated by your family. Something must have happened, maybe something that made you afraid to say anything ever again. Is that possible?"

Her heart hammered as Chiquita pondered the question. Could this be true?

"Chiquita, if this is right, that you quit talking because of the way you were treated, then perhaps when you feel comfortable here, you'll be able to overcome that fear. Don't give up. Keep trying. It will be worth the effort."

As she worked around the house the rest of the day, Chiquita couldn't get Pilar's words out of her mind. Had she quit talking because of the beatings Papa gave her? The longing that had been in her heart for days now began to swell. She wanted to sit in the evenings with Eduardo and discuss things like she knew Pilar and Rico did. Was she hoping for too much?

Dusting the books, she could almost hear Eduardo's steady voice as he read to her from the Bible. This past week, something had changed between them. It had taken her a couple of days to figure out what the change was. She had begun to trust Eduardo.

After the shooting, he'd become so concerned for her. Waking up to find that he'd slept by her bedside because of his concern had done something to her. No one ever cared about her like that before. The few times she'd been sick, she had still been expected to do work. No matter how bad she felt, she wasn't given a break.

Eduardo, though, seemed to want to pamper her. He thought she should stay in bed or rest rather than do her daily chores. She'd quickly put a stop to that. Other than agreeing to stay indoors for safety's sake, she had continued cleaning and cooking. However, because of the change in him, she'd come to trust him. She could tell when he was thinking about the shooting because anger would darken his eyes, but her fear had disappeared. Eduardo cared about her. She didn't know how she knew it—she just did.

With the chores caught up by midafternoon, an excited shiver of anticipation washed over Chiquita. Eduardo encouraged her to work on her reading and writing. Today, she wanted to take the time to look at some of the books in his room that had the beautiful pictures in them. They fascinated her. She wondered if she could make out any of the words now. She'd made great progress over the last week.

Settling on the floor in front of the bookshelf, Chiquita chose the book she wanted. This one had pictures of birds and animals that she'd never seen. Trying to make out some of the words, she lost track of time. Another world drew her in. She ignored the darkening of the room as the afternoon waned.

A creak of the floorboards in the living room startled her. She glanced at the window, amazed to see the sunlight so far gone. Eduardo must be home already. Stuffing the book back in the shelf, she stumbled up on legs that had gone to sleep. Pins and needles pricked at her as she hurried from the bedroom. She hadn't even started supper.

She rushed into the front room, almost colliding with a man. She gasped and jumped back. Groping for the doorway, she calculated her chances of getting away.

The man gave her a slow, sinister smile, his lips parting to show yellowed teeth. In one hand, he held a pistol. With a flick of his wrist, the barrel of the gun pointed at her.

Fear clutched at her. Chiquita edged a step away.

"Stay right there, señora." His dark eyes narrowed. His gaze made her want to run and hide. "They said to kill you, but they didn't say how pretty you are. I might just take you with me, instead." He closed the gap between them. Lifting the barrel of the gun, he traced it across her cheek. "I can always kill you later."

Her knees shook. She couldn't think what to do. Who was this man? Who sent him to kill her? Why? The questions made her dizzy. Closing her eyes, she hoped this was only a bad dream. Any minute, she would wake up and everything would be all right.

"Let's go." His painful grip on her arm negated the idea of this being a dream. He dragged her to the door, opened it, and surveyed the yard, his gun ready. Satisfied, he holstered the weapon. Grabbing her wrist, he began to pull her around the side of the house.

Fear gave way to desperation. She'd been mistreated all her life. Most of the time, she took what was dished out. This time, she intended to fight. Chiquita dug in her heels.

The man spun around, his gaze ugly with anger. She yanked his mustache. He yelped. Lifting her arm, she bit his hand, drawing blood. He let go.

She flew across the yard toward Pilar's. She had to get help. His feet thudded behind her. She could almost feel a bullet hitting her back. Her throat burned, her lungs ached for air. He drew closer. His breathing sounded almost in her ear. She didn't have time to get to Pilar's. Darting to one side, she heard him curse.

With a burst of speed, she sprinted into the barn. Racing down the corridor, she hopped up on a bench and fell over the barrier into a stall. Huddling in a corner, she strove to control her gasping breath so he wouldn't hear her.

"I know you're in here. You may as well not hide from me." His grating voice sent a chill through her. "Come on, honey. You can either go with me now, or I'll have to kill you. I've already been paid for that."

Clutching her knees to her chest, Chiquita wanted to pray. She'd heard Eduardo talk to his God, and with all her heart, she wished she had a God who loved her, too. She didn't want just any God, she wanted the Jesus she'd been learning about.

Jesus, why did I have to be so unworthy of You? If only You would accept me, I would love You with all my heart. She held her breath to stop the sob threatening to come out. *I'm such a sinner, Jesus. I know that's why You'll never want me. Please, if You care for Eduardo, help me, too.*

The crunch of the man's footsteps sounded outside the stall. He paused. The quiet pressed down on her. Her heart pounded, shaking her with the intensity. She held her breath.

"Why there you are." The stall door creaked as he eased it open.

Chiquita huddled tight in the straw and dirt on the floor, hoping he hadn't seen her. The yank on her hair told her different. Her eyes watered as he jerked her upright. "You didn't think you could escape me, did you?"

In an instant, his countenance went from playful to deadly. He drew her close. The smell of unwashed clothing and man gagged her. Her fists clenched tight as he began to drag her toward the door.

"I'd love to stay and play, honey, but we have to get out of here before your husband returns."

The sunlight blinded her as they left the barn. She hoped he was blinded as well. Drawing back, she flung the contents in her hand at his face. She turned her head. He cried out. Letting go, he began to claw at his eyes. Bits of straw clung to his mustache. Chiquita darted away. The door to Pilar's house flung open. Pilar stood there, a rifle in her hand. She raised the weapon as Chiquita raced up beside her. Only then did Chiquita turn to look back at the man. He faced them, pistol in hand. Even from this distance, she could see the sheen of moisture on his cheeks and knew his eyes were burning from the dirt in them.

With a snarl of rage, he swiveled around and stalked off. A few minutes later, she heard the rapid clip of hooves as his horse carried him over the hills and away from them.

Pilar dragged Chiquita through the door and set the bar in place. She almost threw the rifle down before taking Chiquita in her embrace. "I saw the gun. I thought he would kill you." The two women clung together, weeping.

∽

Later that night, Chiquita curled up in bed, trying to keep from shaking.

Eduardo had been enraged when he'd come home. Through a series of questions, Pilar had already pieced together what happened, and she told Eduardo. She hadn't allowed Chiquita to return to the house until after the men came home. Instead, Pilar gave orders for the two of them to fix supper. She'd taken charge, as if Chiquita were a young child who needed something to occupy her so she wouldn't dwell on the afternoon's terror. Chiquita had been grateful.

Now, however, the earlier events wouldn't be squelched. Her mind went from remembering, once more, the feel of Eduardo's comforting embrace, to the horror of the stranger dragging her off. More than ever, she felt a need for Eduardo. That need had been growing, but tonight, she didn't think she could bear being apart from him.

∽

Lying in bed, Eduardo stared out at the moonlit night. He could almost read by the brightness if he'd wanted to, but he knew he couldn't concentrate on reading. Longing and rage warred in his heart. When he'd heard what happened to Chiquita today, he'd been furious. How could any man have the audacity to invade his home and threaten his wife? She had never done anything to anyone. Was this someone he'd offended in the last few years? With the temper he had, he certainly might have insulted someone, but he couldn't imagine anyone he knew wanting to hurt Chiquita.

The longing came from the way his arms could remember the feel of her. Small and soft, she felt wonderful. She smelled of a clean, woman scent. He'd come to the point where he wanted to have her as his wife in all ways. However, he didn't want to scare her. With the rough treatment Diego had meted out, she still feared men. He could see that every time she was around Rico or one of the other men. He had to give her more time. He couldn't force his love on her but had to wait until she was ready.

The door to his room creaked open. Chiquita stepped inside. His breath caught in his throat. In the moonlight, the white nightdress she wore gave her an achingly beautiful appearance. Her hair, flowing free about her shoulders, shimmered with a touch of moonlight. He was afraid to move—afraid she would disappear.

She pushed the door shut. After taking two small steps toward the bed, she halted. She looked like she wanted to run.

Eduardo didn't remember moving, but suddenly he stood before her. He traced the curve of her cheek. She studied him with her wide-eyed gaze. As if in a dream, Eduardo lowered his mouth to hers in a kiss that made him forget about trouble.

421

CHAPTER 15

I'm telling you, this is the right thing to do." Eduardo could still see the hesitancy in Chiquita's eyes. "I know you don't remember going to Tucson before, but I have some friends there. You've met Conlon and Quinn. Quinn's the deputy sheriff who was at our wedding. If anyone can help keep you safe, Quinn can." Uncertainty shone in her gaze.

"Oh sweetheart." Eduardo pulled Chiquita into his embrace. He knew she didn't want to leave the ranch, but he couldn't keep her here with this threat hanging over them. He kissed her, slow and tender, trying to show her his love. She clung to him. When he ended the kiss, she relaxed against him and sighed. He grinned. He hadn't realized a man could be so content.

"Pilar will be fine, if that's what you're worried about." He stroked her back, wanting to stay like this all day. "Rico can take care of everything until we come home. He knows what needs to be done. Lucio even promised to tend to your garden." That one hadn't been easy, but the young vaquero had agreed.

"Come on. I've got our things already loaded in the wagon." He led her outside, where the others waited.

"Jorge and I'll be riding through the hills on either side of you, in case there's trouble." Rico spoke in a low voice. Eduardo and Rico had discussed the need for extra protection at least until they were through the pass. They worried that the gunman would catch them unawares on the road to Tucson.

"Keep a sharp eye out." Eduardo appreciated Rico not saying anything in front of Chiquita. He didn't want her to worry more than she already did. The long trip would be tiring enough without any added tension.

Pilar hurried to them, a basket in her hands. "I've made some lunch for you." Rico lifted the basket into the wagon while Pilar hugged Chiquita. "Don't worry. I'll see that your garden is tended. By the time you get back, you'll have some fresh vegetables waiting for you." She stepped back, blinking rapidly, lifting her hand in farewell as the wagon rattled off.

Clouds gathered on the horizon. There had been a few uncharacteristic showers in the past week. The mountains got most of the moisture. The dust from the road rose up around them. Eduardo hoped the rain would come again, but not until they reached town.

A swarm of bees flew across the road. Pulling the horses to a stop,

Eduardo waited for them to pass. Even though swarming bees were usually docile, he didn't want to get in the middle of them. Trying to appear as if he were following the swarm's flight, he scanned the hills. "That sound makes my hair stand on end." He flashed a smile at Chiquita, hoping she couldn't sense his concern. "When we get back home, I'll take one of the boys to see if we can find the hive. We can always use more honey." He couldn't see Rico, but then he'd warned him to stay out of sight as much as possible. Flicking the reins, Eduardo urged the team to start.

The horses plodded up the steep incline. He took Chiquita's hand in his. She gave him a shy smile. He wanted to stop the wagon and kiss her. Instead, he tugged her closer on the seat until they were touching. Somehow, in the last few weeks, she'd become very important to him.

"Would you like me to tell you about the people you'll be meeting?" She nodded, and he couldn't resist giving her a light kiss. She ducked her head. He grinned and gave the countryside a quick scan, knowing she wouldn't notice.

"Conlon is a lieutenant in the cavalry, stationed at Fort Lowell. His wife is Glorianna, and they have twins—a boy and a girl."

Chiquita raised her eyebrows. He chuckled.

"I hope you're not wanting me to tell you their names, because I can't remember." He shrugged. "Conlon mentioned another baby coming, too. I don't know how soon."

"Quinn's wife is Kathleen. They have a baby boy. No, I have no idea what his name is either." She gave him such a comical look that he laughed. "I'm not good with kids."

Her eyes darkened, turning solemn. He could almost see the thoughts rushing around in her head. Without relaxing his vigilance, he snuggled her closer to his side. "I've never been good with other people's children, but I can't wait to have one of our own." Although he hadn't thought about children, the possibility excited him. A picture of a little girl who looked just like Chiquita warmed his heart. What he'd said to her was true. He couldn't wait to become a father. He pushed the thoughts away. Right now, he needed to keep his wife safe from harm.

"For a long time, I thought I would never want a family."

Chiquita looked up at him, a question in her eyes.

He stared out at the cactus-covered hills, finding it hard to talk about something he'd kept hidden for so long. "You saw the family graves. You know my parents lost nine children. My mother, especially, carried that grief with her until she died." He shrugged. "I didn't want to face the losses they faced."

Her hand touched his cheek. Glancing down, he could see the brightness in her eyes. He forced a smile.

"I know. Most people don't experience death like that." Clasping her hand in his, he caressed her palm with his thumb. He cleared his throat, easing the rawness. "I better pay more attention to the road. The mountain pass can be a bit rough." He still kept her hand in his, but the road wasn't what bore watching. If anyone were to ambush them, the next few miles would be the place. A man with a gun could hide anywhere.

Chiquita leaned against him. Her gaze swept the hills, too. Eduardo regretted alerting her to the danger. For some reason, he wanted to not only protect her, but keep her from any hint of distress. When he thought of what she'd faced the other day, he wavered between rage and a feeling of failure. She was his responsibility. He needed to protect her.

The drive through the mountain pass proved uneventful. Eduardo kept a close eye on their surroundings and the rock-studded hills above them. He prayed continually, unwilling to consider the possibility that something could happen to Chiquita, not when his love for her was growing every day.

Eduardo continued to study the foothills. He caught a glimpse of Rico signaling all was fine. He and Jorge were returning home now. Eduardo could relax his vigil now. They should be safe if no one had followed them this far.

∞

A sense of unease had been gnawing at Chiquita all day. She hadn't wanted to leave the ranch. Despite the three attacks on her, she knew Eduardo would be more careful. She felt safe at the ranch. She'd never become comfortable like this at home with her parents. For the first time in her life, she looked forward to each day.

Since she'd gone to Eduardo two nights ago, he'd changed even more. Papa never showed affection for Mama like Eduardo showed her. He seemed to want to touch or kiss her all of the time. Her face warmed as she thought how much she enjoyed his attention. He made her feel beautiful and wanted. He treated her like she was the most precious possession he had. She wanted to accept and bask in his adoration, but she feared one day he would see her as unworthy. No amount of devotion could erase the fact of who, and what, she was. Someday, he would see that.

Eduardo's thumb continued to stroke her palm, pausing at times as he perused the country around them. She knew he wanted to hide his concern from her, but she had already guessed they might be followed and attacked.

Coming down off the pass, Eduardo nodded to a small stand of trees.

"There's a little spring there. We'll stop and see what Pilar packed in that basket." He smiled, his eyes sparkling. "I don't know about you, but I'm about ready to cook one of the horses."

She leaned closer, drawn by the warmth in his gaze. He had the strangest effect on her. With just a look, he could make her want to be close to him. His cheeks creased in a grin, as if he understood her roiling emotions. When they stopped for lunch, she didn't know if she wanted him to take her in his arms once more or give her some space to get her feelings under control.

"Here we are." Eduardo jumped down from the wagon, then reached up to help her down. He didn't let go, but pulled her close. His gaze turned darker. Lowering his head, he gave her a lingering kiss that set her pulse pounding.

"I'll water the horses while you set out the lunch." Eduardo's voice had an unusual huskiness to it. Chiquita tried to slow her breathing as she reached for the basket he retrieved from the wagon. Eduardo chuckled when he met her gaze. "If I kiss you anymore, we may not get to town before nightfall."

Her face flaming, Chiquita carried their lunch to a grassy, shaded spot and began to set out the food. Was this the way husbands and wives usually felt about each other? She'd never had anyone look at her or affect her like Eduardo did. Even though she feared it wouldn't last, she didn't want these feelings to ever change.

During lunch, Eduardo glanced at the sky with a concerned frown on his face. Thunder rumbled in the distance. A heavy bank of clouds had settled over the mountains to the northwest of them quite awhile ago. Eduardo stood and stretched.

"We need to get on to town before the storm moves this way. Should the water start running in the mountain streams, we might have some trouble crossing the washes if we wait too long." He strode away. Chiquita began to gather the remainder of their lunch, packing everything back in the basket.

The wagon jolted and creaked as Eduardo set a fast pace. The horses, refreshed from their break, seemed eager to get to town. They snorted occasionally. The scent of rain in the air made them frisky.

The road flattened out, flanked by heavy growths of twisted mesquite and paloverde trees. A coyote trotted into the road a few hundred yards ahead of them and paused to watch them. Like a shadow, the animal disappeared into the brush long before they arrived at the spot where he'd been.

Eduardo relaxed. She knew he thought the danger had lessened once they left the mountain pass behind. Here in the flatter land, with the thick undergrowth, an attack would be harder to commit. Once more, he took her hand, tugging to urge her to come closer to him. So content she thought she might start to purr like a cat, Chiquita leaned her head on his shoulder.

A shot rang out, shattering the tranquility. A horse squealed. The wagon jerked, throwing Chiquita off balance as the horses stretched out in a full gallop. Another shot split the air. Thunder cracked. Chiquita clutched the seat as Eduardo sawed the reins, trying to slow the runaways, to no avail.

Almost losing her balance, Chiquita caught a glimpse behind them. Her gasp alerted Eduardo. He glanced back. A rider raced after them. Even from a distance, Chiquita could see the rifle he held at the ready. Eduardo leaned forward, not attempting to slow the horses, but urging them on instead.

"Get down." His yell swept away on the wind.

The wagon bounced and jolted, threatening to toss them off at any moment. Chiquita could feel the blood drain from her face. They were going to die. One man on a horse would be faster than the wagon. If this was the man who'd come to their house the other day, she knew, without a doubt, that he would kill them. She had felt the evil in him.

Lightning flashed across the sky, followed by a clap of thunder that urged the horses to run faster. The brush rushed by in a nauseating blur. Chiquita glanced back. The gunman lifted the rifle to his shoulder. She hoped his racing mount would throw off his aim. Eduardo yanked her down so her head was on his lap. She could feel the man behind drawing steadily nearer.

Huge drops of rain began to hit them. Chiquita shivered. How far were they from town? Was there anyone to help them? She had no idea. Glancing at the rifle under the seat, she knew Eduardo couldn't use the gun and handle the team. With a pang of regret, she wished she'd been able to learn one of these skills. That might have saved their lives.

She hazarded a look behind. Something buzzed past. The man was close now. She could almost make out his face. This had to be the same man who tried to take her from her house.

Eduardo shouted something. The man lifted his gun. Chiquita had the feeling she could look directly down the barrel. Would she see the bullet as it came at her? She closed her eyes, unwilling to face the sight.

The wagon tilted, throwing her forward. Eduardo caught her, steadying her. The team, slowing very little, raced into a wide wash. Tiny streams of water ran across the roadway. Eduardo looked grim as he glanced upstream toward the mountains. The peaks had long since disappeared in the dark storm clouds.

Careening wildly, the wagon crossed the wash. The gunman's horse slipped coming down the embankment behind them. His shot went wild. He jerked the reins, managing to keep his mount upright.

Chiquita couldn't stop glancing between the road, Eduardo, and the man following them. At any second, a bullet would find one of them, and everything would be over. The man raised his rifle. Thunder cracked. The rumble seemed to continue. Eduardo flicked the reins on the horses' backs, urging them to go faster. They were surging out of the wash.

The rifle jerked. The man glanced toward the mountains. His eyes widened. Chiquita followed his gaze and gasped at the wall of water rushing at him. Eduardo yelled at the horses. They seemed to sense the danger and put forth a burst of speed. The wagon flew over the edge of the wash.

She caught a glimpse of the first wave of the flood. Brown water churned past. Uprooted trees and undergrowth spun in the rushing waves like chaff in the wind. The rider, still several yards from the bank, couldn't keep his mount upright. A tree trunk, like a mighty hammer, smacked into them. The horse screamed. Both were swept away in the torrent.

The horses, wild with panic, left the roadway. Off center, the wagon careened into a tree. Wood splintered. The world tilted. Chiquita opened her mouth in a silent scream. Thrown free, she tumbled through the brush. Limbs tore at her dress. A fleeting image of Eduardo thudding into a tree nearby faded as darkness overtook her.

Cold drops of rain splatting on her cheeks woke her. She started to sit up. Every muscle in her body ached. She groaned and sank back down. Where was she? Hazy memories and the roar of rushing water brought it all back. She jerked upright. Dizziness blurred her vision for a moment.

Eduardo—she had to find him! The roar of the floodwaters filled her with fear. What if the gunman hadn't been killed? Would he come after them? She heard a groan. Turning on muscles that burned with the effort, she spotted Eduardo a few yards away. Even from this distance, she could see the dark stain running down his face. Unable to stand, she crawled across the wet ground to reach him.

He was unconscious. The wound on his head wasn't deep but had bled copiously. Blood mixed with the raindrops and ran off into the sand. Pulling up her skirt, Chiquita ripped off a piece of her petticoat. She used a corner of the piece to wipe away the dirt from Eduardo's wound, then bound the cloth around his head. The bandage wasn't pretty but would be serviceable.

The rain came faster. She couldn't get the sight of the man being washed away out of her mind. A shudder raced through her. Thunder rumbled. The storm lumbered east. Rain still pelted down. The roar of the floodwaters captured her attention; the sight mesmerized her. She'd heard of flash floods before but had never seen the power and fury of one.

She reached back for Eduardo's hand, uncertain what to do. How far was Tucson from here? Where were the horses? She didn't want to leave Eduardo to get help, but if he didn't have help soon... She refused to think further along that line.

She could hear the sound of hoofbeats in the distance. Someone was coming. Dread coursed through her. Had the gunman survived? Was he searching for them so he could finish the job he'd started?

CHAPTER 16

The rain slowed. She and Eduardo were both soaked. His teeth began to chatter and his face held an unhealthy pallor. His lips took on a bluish tint. She knew she had to get him warm soon.

Peering through the brush, Chiquita had a good view of the road heading toward Tucson. That seemed to be the direction the horses were coming from. She was sure more than one horse approached. Had the gunman somehow found reinforcements? She crouched over Eduardo, waiting.

Four horses galloped around a bend in the road about a quarter of a mile away. Clumps of sandy mud splattered from the hooves. The riders sat erect in their saddles, not relaxed like Eduardo when he rode.

Panic swept through her. How could she hope to scare off four men? She glanced around, looking for something to help her. Wood from the wagon lay scattered through the brush, but none of the pieces would help. The basket that carried their lunch lay broken on the ground fifty feet from her. The remains of the meal had scattered in the dirt. Near the roadway, a gleam of metal caught her eye. Eduardo's rifle. With a glance at the oncoming riders, she darted for the weapon, then scrambled back to place herself between Eduardo and the men. She lifted the gun, pointing it at them.

The barrel weighed more than she anticipated. Her hands wavered as she tried to hold the gun steady. How did men do this and make it look so easy? Jamming the rifle butt into her shoulder as she'd seen Pilar do, she willed her muscles to tighten and take the weight.

The approaching men slowed. They must have seen her moving to get the rifle. They were all dressed the same, which she found odd. Although she'd spent all of her life away from civilization, she'd still encountered a few drifters who'd stopped by for a meal. None of them wore exactly the same clothing, so why did these men dress that way? They came on at a walk until they were only about a hundred yards away. They stopped, their mounts standing still, as if trained that way.

The man in the lead came forward alone. Something about him seemed familiar, but she wasn't going to let down her guard. He was still too far away to make out his features.

"Hello. We heard gunshots. Then one of my men spotted a team of runaway horses. Is there trouble?"

She centered the gun on his chest. He halted and put his hands up in a gesture of surrender. Only fifty yards separated them. Her palms were sweating, and her arm muscles were beginning to shake with the strain.

"Señora Villegas?" The man leaned forward, squinting at her. He slowly removed his cap. "I'm Conlon Sullivan. We met at your house when I came to see some horses." Without his hat, she could see the shock of black hair. Now she knew why he seemed familiar. A wave of relief swept over her. The rifle wavered, and she almost dropped it into her lap. Tears clouded her vision. These were cavalrymen. That's why they were all dressed alike.

Conlon urged his horse forward until he stopped next to them. His smile faded as he saw Eduardo.

"What happened?" Conlon swung off his horse and bent to examine her unconscious husband. "Were you thrown from the wagon?" She nodded. He stood, waving his men forward. His bright blue gaze met hers. Concern etched his brow.

"We're here to help, señora. The fort isn't far. I'll send someone for a wagon to take you there."

The wait seemed interminable. Conlon and one of his men checked Eduardo over. She thought they were trying to see if he'd broken anything in the fall. The lieutenant undid the bandage, examined the cut, then rewrapped the wound. By the time a large wagon rattled to a stop, Chiquita was shaking like a leaf in the wind. She tried to force herself to stop shivering, but the chill wouldn't leave.

"My men and I will get Eduardo into the back, and we'll drive you to the fort. We have a good hospital there." Conlon lifted the rifle from the ground beside her and handed it to one of his men.

She refused to sit on the seat with the driver. Instead, she sat in the back with Eduardo's head on her lap. He hadn't come to, but he groaned and gritted his teeth when they moved him. Blood soaked the cloth around his head. She smoothed his hair, traced the lines of his face, hoping her touch would wake him or at least be a comfort.

By the time they reached the fort, Chiquita's teeth were clenched tight to keep them from chattering. She couldn't remember ever being so cold. She barely felt the hands that helped her from the wagon, holding her when her legs refused to support her weight. They escorted her into a building full of unusual smells. Conlon told her this was the hospital. The doctor there would take care of Eduardo.

"Glory, thanks for coming." Conlon smiled at the petite redheaded woman who swept through the doors not long after they arrived. Chiquita, huddled in a blanket someone had thrown around her, tried to smile but failed miserably.

"Hello." The woman plopped into a chair beside Chiquita. "I'm going to take you to our house. It isn't far from here. Alicia, my helper, is heating water for you to bathe in. You need to warm up after the soaking you've gotten. Then, we'll find some clean, dry clothing for you." She glanced up at her husband.

"Señora Villegas." Conlon squatted next to her chair. "I know you didn't speak when Quinn and I were at your house the other day, but if you could tell us what happened, that might help Eduardo. Can you?"

Fear rose up to choke her. Eduardo might die because of her inability to talk. She opened her mouth and tried. No sound issued. She wanted to tell them, but her voice wouldn't work. Tears trickled down her cheeks. She'd failed her husband. Would he be angry with her now? Would all his kindness turn to hate?

"Don't you worry." Glorianna took Chiquita's hands in hers and rubbed them. "The doctor here is very good. He'll fix your husband right up. Now you come with me."

Chiquita pulled back. She didn't want to leave. She wanted to be here with Eduardo. A wife's place was with her husband. He might need her. She had to see him.

As if she understood, Glorianna gave a gentle squeeze and smiled. "You can't do Eduardo any good if you get sick. After you're warm and dry, I'll bring you back. By then the doctor will be finished, and you can sit with your husband."

She could see the wisdom in this. She would go with Glorianna, but as soon as possible, she would come back to be with Eduardo. Thinking of the man who shot at them, she felt nauseous. Although she didn't want him to die in the flood, she hated the thought that he might still be after them. He wouldn't give up until she was dead, and she had no idea why he wanted to kill her.

⌒

Chiquita barely noticed the wet earth smell as she hurried back to the hospital. The bath warmed her, but she couldn't relax with the thought of Eduardo lying pale and chilled in the hospital. The fear that he might die made her rush to be back by his side. She pushed the door open and took a moment to get her bearings before setting off for Eduardo's room. When she arrived, he wasn't alone.

"Señora Villegas, I'm Dr. Elliot. Your husband is a lucky man. I didn't find any broken bones from him being wrapped around that tree." The doctor, a portly man who seemed to jiggle with every step he took, patted her on the shoulder. "The problem is the blow to the head."

Chiquita clenched her fingers together. What was this doctor trying to tell her? Would Eduardo die? Her heart ached. She wanted her husband to know that she loved him. She wanted him to hold her again. There were so many things she wanted to do for him.

"We can never tell about injuries to the skull. He still hasn't regained consciousness, but it's possible he will before morning. The longer he stays like he is, the less likely he will recover."

She felt the blood drain from her face.

Dr. Elliot grasped her arm. His face came close to hers. His eyes narrowed as he studied her. "Señora, you have to be strong. I might have a way you can help your husband. Let's sit down and talk." He led her to a chair, making the seat next to her creak in distress as he lowered his bulk onto it.

"I've heard that some doctors have success with head injuries when the patient hears a familiar voice. They say there have been cases where, after recovering their senses, the patient can repeat conversations they overheard while unconscious. I want you to sit with your husband and talk to him. I don't care what you say. That doesn't matter so much as him hearing your voice."

Panic closed her throat with icy fingers. How could she do this? Even if she could talk, Eduardo had never heard her speak and wouldn't recognize her voice. Maybe she could send for Pilar or Rico. He was familiar with them. She didn't know how she could do that though. Since she couldn't talk, she couldn't tell anyone what she needed. Tears burned her eyes.

"Excuse me, Dr. Elliot." Conlon stood in the open door. "I happened to overhear what you said to Señora Villegas. I'm afraid she won't be able to talk to Eduardo. I don't know the circumstances, but for some reason, she can't speak."

Dr. Elliot gave Chiquita a piercing look. "Is that right, young lady?"

She nodded, giving Conlon a look of gratitude.

"I want you to come with me to my office down the hall." Dr. Elliot put a hand under her elbow. "I want to examine your throat and ask a few questions about why you can't talk."

∽

Relief swept through Chiquita when she finally got to see Eduardo. A young man brought her a chair, placing it beside the head of the bed. Everyone left. She was alone with her husband.

His color, although pale, looked healthier. His lips didn't have the blue tinge anymore. He appeared to be warm and dry, resting peacefully. She put her hand over his chest, then lay her head there, listening to his steady heartbeat. Tears of gratitude traced a path down her cheeks.

She had been with the doctor a long time. Although she'd been nervous and wary of him at first, she soon relaxed because of his professional attitude.

Dr. Elliot seemed to understand what happened to her at home. With only a few questions, he'd found out about Papa beating her and that she had spoken when she was a very young child. He talked to her for a long time, assuring her that this wasn't a physical problem. When she learned to trust other people, she had a very good chance of speaking again.

Reaching under the edge of the blanket, Chiquita twined her fingers with Eduardo's. She ran her thumb over his callused palm, watching his face for any sign of a reaction. He didn't even twitch. Only the steady rising and falling of the sheet as he breathed let her know he lived.

She'd never felt so alone. No one here knew her. She couldn't talk to anyone and tell them she needed help. She couldn't even ask about the man who'd been shooting at them. Why had he been trying to kill her? When he'd come to the ranch the other day, he hadn't said why someone paid him to kill her. He'd only said that they did. She'd never done anything to hurt anyone, yet now her husband, a good man, might die because of her. Resting her forehead on the bed, she wept.

Jesus, I know I'm not worthy to ask anything of You, but I do this for Eduardo. Please, help him. Help me. I can't lose him. I'm so afraid. I don't know what to do. Lord, I've always been unworthy. I'm the worst of the sinners Eduardo told me about. I'm so sorry. Please, forgive me. Please, spare Eduardo.

Peace bathed her in a comforting embrace. An indescribable feeling flowed over her as if she were being washed clean of every wrong thing she'd ever done. She felt like she could float away as the burdens lifted. Her chest warmed, the heat spreading all the way up her throat until even her lips tingled.

She didn't know how long she rested on the edge of the bed. She wasn't even sure what happened to her. If Eduardo were awake and she could talk, she'd ask him. Brushing her fingers across his still face, she felt the need to try speaking once more.

"Ed. . .uar. . .do." The raspiness startled her. She glanced at the closed door, half expecting someone to have come in without her noticing. They were still alone in the room.

Touching her throat, she sat too stunned to do anything. Had that voice been hers? Opening her mouth, she fought back the fear of failure and tried again.

"Ed. . .uardo." This time she knew the voice was hers. Although stronger, the sound still carried a lot of hoarseness from long disuse. "Love. . .you." Delight raced through her to finally be able to say those words to her husband. Suddenly, she couldn't wait to talk more. Her heart felt full to bursting with gratitude for this gift.

∞

Terror clutched at Eduardo. He could hear the floodwaters racing past, but he couldn't see them. Someone needed his help. Chiquita? Had she fallen back in the wash when the torrent swept down? He didn't think so, yet he couldn't shake the sense of impending doom. He needed to see her. The light was too dim to make out anything. Sometimes voices pierced the mist, but they faded in and out. He couldn't understand any of them.

Pushing upward, he struggled to find a way through the fog surrounding him. Pieces of memory pierced him. The man shooting. The raging waters. Chiquita's terrified face. The horses' screams. Pounding hooves. A crunch of wood. Blackness.

He couldn't fight any longer. His strength faded. Maybe after he rested, he could find a way out of this odd place. The darkness began to close around him once more.

"Eduardo."

Someone called his name. He'd never heard the voice before, yet for some reason, the sound tugged at him. A woman called him. Rising through the fog, he began to fight his way free. He had to respond. She needed him.

"Eduardo, love you. I'm afraid. Please, come back." Her voice ended in a sob.

He blinked. Someone lay with her head on his bed. This couldn't be Chiquita. She didn't speak. He closed his eyes. Her weeping drew him back. Opening his eyes again, everything looked clearer.

In the dim light, he could still see the pale strands running through the woman's hair. Chiquita's hair looked like that. Could she have spoken to him, or was he only dreaming? He licked at his dry lips. Now he could feel her fingers wrapped around his hand. Using every last bit of energy he possessed, he closed his fist, holding her hand tight.

CHAPTER 17

Two days later, Conlon and Eduardo headed for Tucson. Eduardo made Chiquita stay with Glorianna. His wife delighted in playing with Glorianna's twins and gave her some much-needed respite. A nagging ache from his wound still plagued Eduardo, the remains of his injury. Dr. Elliot assured him the headaches would pass in a few days.

The hazy memory of the soft voice that pulled him from the blackness still bothered him. He couldn't get over the feeling that he should know who called him. Somewhere inside, he'd had the wild hope that maybe Chiquita had spoken, but she remained silent. She hadn't left his side during his hospital stay. He warmed at the thought. Somehow, she seemed a little different, but he couldn't quite figure out how.

After relating the events of the past few weeks to Conlon, the lieutenant urged him to consult with Quinn. Maybe the deputy would have some helpful advice, even though the Villegas ranch was outside his jurisdiction. Hesitant to leave Chiquita, Eduardo only agreed when Conlon pointed out she would be surrounded by the whole cavalry. Also, he would alert his sergeant to watch for possible trouble.

The first buildings came into sight. Eduardo forced himself to relax. *Lord, You know how upset I am that this is happening. My wife is being threatened. I don't believe this anger is wrong. On the other hand, I don't want it to cloud my reasoning. Give me wisdom to do as You would have me do, Lord.* Peace flowed through him, the comfort that could only come from God. Somehow, he knew this would all work out.

Quinn pushed the door of his house open to let them in. "Good morning." Dark circles around his eyes gave him a haunted look.

"We stopped by the jail, but you weren't there yet." Conlon grinned. "Taking the day off?"

"Naw. Jonathan spent the whole night crying. Kathleen thinks he has colic." He led them into the kitchen and poured some coffee. "I stayed home a little late to see if I could let her get some rest. Right now, they're both asleep."

They all settled down at the table. Quinn took a long sip of coffee before speaking. "So, what brings you to town, Eduardo? Tired of married life already?"

When not even Conlon chuckled at the joke, Quinn turned serious. Eduardo didn't know how or what he wanted to ask his friend. Finally, he started at the beginning, with the discovery that someone on the hillside watched the ranch, to the final attack on the road to Tucson. With the retelling of each event, Quinn's expression looked grimmer.

"We left Chiquita with Glorianna and came here to see if you have any idea why someone is trying to kill my wife. I don't know if this is a grudge against me or my family. I can't imagine how Chiquita could have incurred someone's wrath. She'd never been away from home until we married."

"Do you think the man who chased you on the way to town is the same one who tried to kidnap Chiquita at the ranch?" Quinn asked.

"I never saw the man who tried to take Chiquita." Eduardo cradled the warm cup in his hands. "I did think to ask her if she recognized him. She thinks it was the same man."

"We need to try to find him, then." Quinn drummed his fingers on the table. "If we could talk to him, we could clear up this mystery. I haven't heard anything about someone being after you or your wife. It doesn't make sense to me either."

Conlon cleared his throat. "As soon as Eduardo told me what happened, I sent some men out looking. Last night, they reported finding the horse several miles downstream from the crossing where Eduardo and Chiquita were attacked. The horse was dead, tangled in brush and drowned. There was a boot still lodged in the stirrup but no sign of the rider."

"If the flood was that bad, he probably didn't survive either." Quinn frowned. He absently rubbed the badge pinned to his vest.

"I sent them back out again this morning with orders to go farther downstream. They have enough men to search along both sides of the wash. He may have only been injured and crawled into the brush to recover. If so, my men will find him."

Quinn nodded. "That's a good start. I'll ask around town. I have some sources who might help."

They were all silent as Quinn brought the coffeepot and refreshed their cups. Sitting back down, he tilted his head as if listening for something, then relaxed.

"I thought I heard Jonathan." He shrugged. "I think I'll go see Lavette Washington in a bit and ask if she'll help out Kathleen. Otherwise, I might never get any work done.

"Now, Eduardo, I want you to tell me everything you know about the man who's been watching your place. Any little clue you can remember will help. I haven't got any authority where you live, but that doesn't mean I can't help you."

"I know he smokes." Eduardo tried to picture the scenes he and Rico had examined. "His horse wears an unusual shoe on his left hind foot. It isn't curved quite right."

"That's good. I'll talk to Josiah Washington and see if any of the horses he's shod have that kind of shoe. What else?"

"The day they shot at Chiquita in the garden, there were two men."

"Two?" Quinn's eyebrows rose.

"There had to be two, because one couldn't fire the shots from those angles. He would have had to move, and Lucio would have seen him. When the boys trailed them, the riders went into the river. They lost the trail."

"What direction were they heading at that point?" Conlon asked.

"East." Eduardo didn't know if he should say more. Diego's place was east of his, but he hesitated to point a finger at his father-in-law without substantial proof.

"Diego lives east of you." Quinn's flat statement echoed Eduardo's thoughts.

"I have no way of proving he's involved in this. Besides, why would he trick me into marrying Chiquita, then try to kill her? That makes no sense."

"I've found murder rarely makes sense." Quinn's grim words sent a chill of dread through Eduardo.

"Eduardo, I have an idea. Why don't you bring Chiquita here? You can stay with us. She can help Kathleen with the baby while you and I look into this matter. Would she be willing to do that?"

"I think so." Eduardo finished the last of his coffee. "I wanted to take her to the mercantile, anyway, to pick out some material for a couple new dresses. She's having to tailor and wear my mother's old ones."

"Didn't she bring her clothes with her?" Quinn looked puzzled.

Anger crept into Eduardo's tone as he related all that had gone on the day he married Chiquita. "I burned the dress she wore. It wasn't even good enough to tear into rags."

Conlon's jaw tightened. "I have trouble finding a decent Christian thought when it comes to Diego Garcia. That man has a streak of meanness a mile wide."

"By the way, did you know Diego was in town last weekend?" Quinn walked with them to the door. "He was drunk, as usual, and bragging about some relative dying. He claimed he was going to inherit a fortune. He sure had plenty of friends all of a sudden."

∞

Chiquita tried not to cling to Eduardo's arm too tightly as they walked to the mercantile. She'd never imagined there could be so many people. Eduardo told her there were more than seven thousand residents in Tucson. How could so many people stand to be so close together? Just being in town made her long for the quiet of the ranch.

Tucson had to be the noisiest place. Dogs barked. Mules brayed. Men shouted. Sometimes she could even hear a gunshot. Last night, she'd been afraid, but Eduardo assured her the shots were only some men who'd had a little too much to drink. The ground shook as a couple of huge freight wagons lumbered past. They were so tall, she thought she could sit upright beneath them and never have them touch a hair on her head. The driver cracked his whip and let loose with a stream of words that made her want to hide her face.

Eduardo patted her hand and gave her a reassuring smile. Her breath caught. Even with the white bandage on his forehead, he was the handsomest man in all of Tucson. She thought back to the time when he'd been unconscious. She'd spoken to him then and hoped to be able to continue when he awoke. For some reason, she couldn't. Every time she tried, the words stuck in her throat. Fearing to say the wrong thing and make him angry with her, she'd kept quiet. A few times, she caught him looking at her with a strange expression—as if he knew she talked once and wondered why she didn't again.

The door of the mercantile creaked as Eduardo pushed it open. Chiquita stepped inside and halted. Her eyes widened. There were shelves full of different food items, things she'd never thought could be bought in a store. Along one wall were stacks of already-made clothing. Bolts of material in varying colors and patterns caught her eye. In her whole life, she'd never had a dress that no one else wore before her. She'd never imagined there could be so many choices.

Eduardo herded her to one side so other people could use the door. She flushed, embarrassed by her intent scrutiny of the store and her lack of courtesy to other people.

"Don't worry." Eduardo's breath tickled her ear as he spoke. "Take your time and look around. I have to talk to Sam over there about some things we need at the ranch." He motioned toward the man standing behind the counter. "After I'm done there, I want to help you pick out a pair of shoes and at least three lengths of material for new dresses."

Chiquita caught her breath. She stared up at Eduardo. Had he really said she could have new dresses? Her gaze flew to the bolts of material. Excitement made her shaky. She glanced back at Eduardo, and his smiling gaze held her. He made her feel so loved at times. Why couldn't she tell him that?

Eduardo spent a long time going over a list of items with the storeowner. At one point, they even traipsed outside to see something. Eduardo gave her a brief smile before leaving. For a while, Chiquita wandered past the tables and shelves of goods, puzzling over some items. She had no idea what they were.

At last, she stood before the material, her fingers brushing the different types of cloth. Many were darker colors, good for work clothes, but not very attractive. A few were a shiny material she'd never seen before. Those felt soft and rich to the touch but seemed impractical for everyday use. The more vivid colors caught her eye. One bolt of bright pink with tiny white flowers kept her enthralled. No matter how many others she looked at, her gaze always returned to that one. The material would never do for working in the garden, but the thought of wearing a dress out of that cloth thrilled her. She tried her best to examine only the more practical fabrics, but the pink seemed to draw her back again.

"We'll need a dress length in this pink one for sure." Eduardo's voice at her back startled her. She hadn't heard him or the shopkeeper approaching. Whirling around, she gazed at him wide-eyed and shook her head. He couldn't waste his money on something so frivolous.

"I want you to have something pretty, Chiquita. This one suits you. I can tell how much you like it. Antonio showed me the chapel he built near his house. He plans to have services there on Sundays as soon as he can get a pastor. I want you to have a pretty dress or two to wear then." His warm gaze made her wish they were alone. She thought he wanted to kiss her as much as she wanted to be kissed.

"Which other ones would you like?" Sam tugged the bolt of pink cloth from the pile.

Eduardo gestured at the stack. "Pick out two for everyday, Chiquita. They don't have to be dull, but they should be serviceable."

Trembling, she indicated her choices. This was too much. She didn't know how to react to Eduardo's being so kind and generous. Following the mercantile owner, she picked out the thread she needed and, at Eduardo's insistence, a packet of needles and other necessary notions.

"She also needs some new shoes, Sam. My mother's didn't fit her."

Chiquita longed to hide. She didn't want anyone to see the condition of the slippers she wore. Going barefoot was almost better than this. Her face filled with heat as Eduardo pulled her shoes off and helped her try on a new pair. This would be the first time she'd ever gotten a pair of shoes just for herself, too. She felt like a princess.

Loaded with packages, they left the mercantile. Eduardo carried most of them, but Chiquita insisted on carrying the package with her sewing items.

The new shoes were on her feet. Eduardo told Sam to throw out the old ones.

The afternoon sun was sinking behind the mountains as they headed back to Quinn's house. The streets were quieter as people quit work for the evening and went home for supper. Balancing the parcels in one arm, Eduardo kept his other hand on her elbow, guiding her around the various piles of refuse in the streets. She wrinkled her nose at the smell.

Across the street, a door slammed, accompanied by raucous laughter. Two men staggered around horses tied at the hitching post outside the saloon. They spotted Eduardo and Chiquita and halted. Swaying like a gale force wind blew on them, the pair stared openmouthed at them. With the sun setting behind them, Chiquita couldn't make out their faces, but something made her uncomfortable. She edged closer to Eduardo.

"Villegas."

The roar sent chills through Chiquita. In an instant, she was a child again. She wanted to whimper, run, and hide, but her spine stiffened. She faced her father as he wove his way across the street.

"What kind of man are you, Villegas?" Papa's words slurred. His breath stank of alcohol, a smell Chiquita would always hate. "I give you my daughter in marriage, but here you are with another woman, parading her through town."

From the moment her father spoke, Eduardo's grip on her elbow had become almost painful. She could feel the waves of anger rushing through him at the accusations.

"You're not making sense, Diego. This is your daughter."

"Are you saying I don't know my own girl?" Papa stumbled closer, the whites of his eyes red. His companion, a man Chiquita had never seen before, grabbed him by the arm.

"Diego, look at her." He waved a hand at Chiquita. "She looks just like Bella. This is her."

"Who is Bella?" Eduardo spoke the question Chiquita wanted to ask.

"Why, her mother, Bella Garcia de Noriega." The man continued to gaze at Chiquita as he braced her father.

Chiquita barely noticed the package falling from her hands. Her gaze flew to her father's face. He whirled on the man who'd spoken, his eyes blazing. She needed no further proof for the truth of the words. With a sob, she jerked free from Eduardo and raced away.

CHAPTER 18

C hiquita, no! Wait!" Eduardo almost raced after her, torn between catching his wife and finding out about this mystery. Chiquita's mother was Lupe Garcia. He'd never heard her called by this Bella name before. Besides, Chiquita looked nothing like her mother. In fact, she looked nothing like any of the others in her family.

Dropping his parcels, he grabbed Diego's shirt, dragging the drunken sot close. "Who is Bella?" Rage simmered inside him.

Diego's eyes rolled back in his head. He crumpled, his heavy weight pulling him from Eduardo's grasp. He sank into the dirt of the road, unconscious.

Before the other man could run, Eduardo caught hold of him. "Oh no you don't." He jerked the man back, glad that the street was fairly deserted. The few who were out didn't seem to care about this small altercation.

"Let me make this clear." Eduardo ignored the man's frightened gaze. Twisting the neck of the man's shirt, he gave a little shake. "I want to know who you are and how you know things about my wife that she doesn't seem to know. You have about one minute to start talking."

"Sí Señor." The man's voice shook almost as much as the rest of him. "I am Diego's cousin, José. From California." He swallowed. "I bring him news of his family there."

"Who is Bella?"

"She is the daughter of our uncle. I came to tell Diego that our uncle passed away a few months ago."

"Why did you say Bella is Chiquita's mother?"

"Please, Señor, I was mistaken. It is the drinking. I didn't think clearly. Lupe is her mother, and Diego is her father."

"You're lying." Eduardo shook the man again. "I want the truth."

"I'm telling the truth, Señor. Please don't hurt me." Jose tried to pry Eduardo's fingers loose. "You need to go and find your wife."

Glancing down the street where Chiquita had disappeared, Eduardo knew that was true. Where had she gone?

Dragging José a step closer, Eduardo gritted his teeth. "Are you and Diego staying in town?" José nodded. Eduardo released him, and he stumbled back a few steps. "I'll find you. Even if you leave town, I'll find you. I want some answers, and I can see I'll have to corner Diego to get them. Just remember:

You can't run far enough or fast enough to escape me." Picking up all the packages, Eduardo strode down the street.

He hoped Chiquita had found her way back to Quinn's house, but when he got there, Quinn and Kathleen hadn't seen her.

"I'll help you look." Quinn slapped a hat on his head. "Then, if you want, we'll go see Diego together." He gave Kathleen a quick kiss. "Don't wait to eat. We'll get something when we get back."

∞

Lies, Chiquita thought as she ran, *my whole life has been a lie. No wonder Lupe and Diego hated me. They didn't want me because I wasn't their child.*

She didn't know who the stranger was, but the instant he'd stated that Bella was her mother, Chiquita knew he told the truth. Now she understood the reason she never fit in at the Garcia household. This explained why her sisters were treated differently. She'd always been the outcast, the unworthy one. Even her real mother hadn't wanted her. Her mother thought it would be better to give her to someone like Diego than to be troubled with raising such an unworthy child. Hurt burned inside her.

She didn't know how long she ran. Even the direction didn't matter—she just had to escape. Too exhausted to take another step, Chiquita sank down on the steps of a building. The sun was down now, and the steps were in shadow. No one could see her here. She covered her face with her hands and sobbed. Now Eduardo would understand how awful and unacceptable she was as a wife. Would he make her leave? She wouldn't blame him if he did.

"Child, are you all right?"

The man's touch startled her. Chiquita gasped and scrambled away. A man in a plain brown robe knelt at the spot where she'd been. He didn't move but gave her a kind smile. Although she usually feared men, this one seemed different. Something in his expression and his eyes told her he wouldn't hurt her.

He held out a hand. "The wind is rising. You have no wrap. Come inside the church so you won't catch a chill."

She glanced up at the façade of the building. She hadn't realized these steps belonged to a chapel. Scrubbing at her cheeks, she tried to wipe away all traces of tears.

"Come, child." The priest stood and held out his hand.

All fear left her. She allowed him to help her up, then followed him inside the small church. She hadn't realized how harsh the wind was until she walked through the doors. Warmth enveloped her. The priest led her into

442

the wooden pew-lined sanctuary.

"Sit here." She sank down, still tired from her run. "Would you like to talk? I'm a very good listener."

His gentle voice soothed her ragged nerves. Urgency built within her. She needed to talk to someone. Maybe this man knew the Jesus Eduardo knew. Maybe he could tell her what to do to make herself worthy of such a Savior. She ducked her head. *Oh, please, let me be able to talk to him.*

He waited in silence. Without passing judgment, he appeared willing to give her all the time she needed. Once again, she could feel the warmth she'd felt the day she spoke to Eduardo when he'd been unconscious. Her throat relaxed. She knew she could talk again.

"I'm not worthy." Tears burned her eyes. That wasn't what she intended to say, but she couldn't seem to stop. "For Jesus. I want. . .so much. Need a Savior. Don't know how." She looked at the priest through a blur of tears.

"Ah child." He leaned back against the pew. "Tell me why you are unworthy."

She struggled for the words. This man of God ought to be able to tell just by looking at her. "They said I'm worthless."

"Who said that?"

"My. . ." She hesitated, not knowing what to call Diego and Lupe. They weren't her parents, but all her life she'd thought they were. "My family."

He frowned, his bushy eyebrows drawing together. She wanted to turn away. He must understand now and would tell her they were right. She would never have a Savior.

"I think there is a misunderstanding." Slipping his hands in his sleeves, the priest straightened. "In the book of Ephesians, the Apostle Paul tells us that salvation is through the grace of God. That way, we won't have anything to boast about." He pursed his lips in a thoughtful expression. "Do you know about Jesus and His death on the cross?"

Chiquita nodded. "My husband. He read the story."

"You see, if there were something we could do to earn our way to heaven, then Jesus died for nothing."

"There's no hope?" Her eyes burned. She blinked hard, trying to stop the tears.

"Oh, there is always hope, my child." He smiled. Kindness shone from his eyes. "You are no different from anyone else. We are all unworthy."

"But. . .my husband. . .he's good."

"According to the Bible, none of us are righteous on our own. In fact, we all have wicked hearts."

"How do people become saved?"

"It's really very simple. You have to admit your worthlessness. Once you do that and you see the truth of who Jesus is, then you simply ask Him to forgive you and be your Savior."

"But, I think I did that." Warmth filled Chiquita as she recalled the night in Eduardo's hospital room and the feeling of peace she experienced. She related the account to the priest, and his smile widened.

"I would say you already have Jesus as your Savior, child. Trust me, He loves you more than you'll ever believe or understand." He patted her shoulder as he stood. "I'll leave you alone now. Spend some time listening for Him to talk to you."

Tears of joy ran down her cheeks. Chiquita stumbled to the altar and knelt. With her head on the rail, she stayed quiet. There weren't words for the praise and thankfulness in her heart. Jesus loved her. She didn't have to become worthy on her own. He made her acceptable. Never again would she be a complete outcast. She would always have Jesus.

She didn't know how long she knelt there, basking in the tumultuous emotions pouring over her. The sense of utter joy and peace made her weep until she thought she couldn't cry another tear. When she heard the door open, she thought the priest must be returning to tell her she had to leave. Wiping the moisture from her face, she stood.

Eduardo faced her, his shoulders bowed as if he carried the weight of the world. His face looked haggard and worn. Even from across the room, she could see the despair in his eyes. As his gaze found her, the despair turned to relief, then joy.

"Chiquita, I've looked everywhere for you. I was so worried." In a few steps he held her in his arms, her face pressed to his shoulder. His hand caressed her hair while he murmured of his love.

"Eduardo."

He froze. His hand stilled. She thought he quit breathing.

"Eduardo, I love you." Her whisper filled the quiet chapel.

In a rush of movement, he pushed her back until he could cup her cheeks and gaze into her eyes. "It was you." Wonder filled his voice. "You talked to me in the hospital. I heard someone calling me, but I didn't recognize the voice. That's because I never heard you speak before."

"Forgive me." She brushed her fingers across his brow. "I want to talk, but I'm afraid. At first, I couldn't speak. After the hospital, I thought you would be angry. Maybe think I tricked you." She blinked. "I'm sorry."

"Oh sweetheart." He pulled her back into his embrace. "I can't promise to never be angry with you, but I don't want to be. I've prayed about this, and I believe God has helped me overcome my tendency to fly into a rage at the least little thing. I should be the one asking your forgiveness. I didn't mean to scare you."

He kissed her, a long, lingering kiss that made her pulse race. "Why did you run today, Chiquita?" He led her to a pew and snuggled her next to him.

"When the man said Lupe wasn't my mother, I knew the truth. I've always been different, but I didn't understand why." She leaned against Eduardo. "It hurt so much to know even my real mother didn't want me. She let Diego raise me. I felt like the whole world rejected me."

"Oh my love." He stroked her shoulder, letting her draw comfort from his closeness.

Taking a deep breath, Chiquita began to tell Eduardo about her experience with religion. Starting from her childhood and ending with her discussion with the priest, she told him all that had happened. Through it all, he stayed silent, holding her tight.

"My life is changed. I don't need approval. Jesus loves me. That's enough." She tilted her head back to gaze up at him. "So glad you love me, too."

He grinned. "I'm glad you love me." He stood and lifted her to her feet. "I hate to end this time together, but we need to get back to Quinn's house. He's been helping me look for you. They're worried." He kissed her nose. "Don't fret. They're not mad at you."

She shivered in the chilly wind as they walked out the door. He wrapped an arm around her, trying to share his warmth.

"Eduardo, please?"

"What, my love?"

"I want to go home." He stopped. She turned to face him, her gaze serious. "I've seen the city. I miss our house and garden. I want to see the horses."

"It may not be safe." His brow furrowed in concern. "We don't know that the gunman who got caught in the flood was working alone."

She traced the strong line of his jaw. "You can protect me."

Eduardo nodded. This afternoon, Conlon sent word to Quinn that the gunman's body had been found. According to Conlon, he was unidentifiable. Whoever he was, Eduardo prayed this was the end of the troubles. "Then let's go home."

☙

The first rays of the sun peeped through the window. Eduardo rolled over and looked at Chiquita, still sleeping. They'd been home from Tucson for three days—three peaceful, marvelous days, full of catching up as she told him about her childhood and all the dreams she had that she hadn't been able to share with anyone. They'd talked for hours. He'd been afraid to leave her alone, although he wanted to find Diego and discover what he and his cousin, José, were hiding. He'd tried to find them in Tucson, but they'd already left town. Today, he would ride over to the Garcia place and confront Diego.

Chiquita stirred, rolling toward him. Since she'd lost her fear of him, she'd proved to be very affectionate. She loved to snuggle up next to him at night. Many times during the day she would touch him, as if she couldn't get enough of the connection between them. He smiled. That went both ways. He loved touching her, too.

Her nose twitched. He almost laughed. Her lips pursed, and he resisted the temptation to lean down and kiss her. For a moment, her eyelids quivered. Soon she would open her eyes, and the first thing she would see would be him smiling at her. They'd done this the past few mornings. He loved to see her delight in such little things. She was like a child, discovering a whole new world.

Her eyes opened, shut, then opened again. She gave him a slow, sweet smile. He knew he would never tire of her tawny gaze. The yellow flecks in her eyes were a constant delight. He'd discovered gold, and this gold he could keep for his whole life.

"Good morning, my love." He gave her a tender kiss, wishing he didn't have to get up and do chores. He gave her another kiss before forcing himself to get out of bed.

When he came inside with the milk, she had breakfast ready for him. They held hands as he prayed over the food. He waited until after the meal was over to tell her his plans for the day.

"Chiquita, I'm riding over to visit Diego today." At her stricken expression, he hurried on. "I have to find out what he and his cousin were talking about. You need to know, too. Can you trust me on this?"

She bit her bottom lip and nodded. He wanted this pain to end for her. She deserved to know who her parents were and what Diego was hiding from her.

CHAPTER 19

The midmorning sun shone bright as Eduardo cantered away from the barn. El Rey, eager to run after being cooped up for the past two weeks, gave a couple of little jumps as he started off. Eduardo patted his copper neck, relishing the feel of the silken coat. As soon as they reached the smoother part of the road, he would let the stallion have his head for a few miles to run off his orneriness.

His gaze roved constantly over the hills as he rode. Since coming home, they hadn't seen any sign of anyone watching the ranch. On the trip back from Tucson, Conlon and Quinn both accompanied them. Nothing out of the ordinary happened. Eduardo did his best to convince Chiquita that the man swept away by the flood had been working alone. He couldn't explain why a stranger would want to kill her, but she seemed to accept his theory.

This morning, Eduardo had Tomás and Lucio work close to home. Rico and Jorge were off checking on some of the cattle, a job that had to be done. The niggling doubts that assailed Eduardo made him keep at least part of the crew where they would be close enough to help Chiquita should she need them.

El Rey snorted and tugged on the reins. During Eduardo's musing, they'd reached the road. The horse was eager to be off. Loosening the reins, Eduardo relaxed, letting his body move with the horse's easy gait. Although El Rey raced like the wind, he still flowed smoothly, rather than in a jerky motion some horses had at a dead run.

Over an hour later, Eduardo pulled El Rey to a stop on the hill overlooking Diego's small house. Although he'd alternated between walking and cantering to keep El Rey from overheating, a light sheen of sweat darkened the stallion's coat. Eduardo could see one of the girls hanging the wash on the line. Another worked in the garden. He couldn't see the other girls, Diego, or Lupe. He didn't know if Diego's cousin was staying with them still.

Nudging El Rey, he headed the horse down the rocky slope. He'd chosen to leave the road a ways back, hoping to surprise Diego. He didn't fully understand why he felt this was necessary, but the feeling was too intense to be ignored. All morning, he'd prayed that he wouldn't lose his temper here. He wanted to act in a godly manner, not according to his human nature.

The girl pinning the clothes on the line glanced up. She shaded her eyes with a hand to her brow trying to see him. Dropping a clean piece of clothing in the dirt, she raced for the house, shouting for her mother, followed by the sister who'd been in the garden. El Rey snorted a second time, shaking his head as if he were commenting on what might be happening inside the house.

Lupe stepped outside as Eduardo rode into the yard. Chickens scattered through the refuse cluttering the ground. A mangy dog gave a high-pitched sound, halfway between a bark and a yelp, before slinking under the sagging end of the porch. A scrawny cat hissed and batted at the retreating dog. Eduardo reined in El Rey and took his hat off, giving Lupe a nod.

"Is Diego at home, Señora Garcia?"

Lupe folded her arms across her chest and pinned Eduardo with a glare designed to make him uncomfortable. Although she stood less than five feet tall, the woman was formidable. Eduardo could only imagine how difficult a time Chiquita had living with this woman. Most likely, Diego wasn't the only one who abused her.

"My husband has no business with you anymore." Lupe's tone could have frozen boiling water. "He paid our debt to you when you stole our daughter. You aren't welcome here anymore."

"I have some other unfinished business with Diego. I need to see him." Eduardo refused to allow Lupe to intimidate him. "If he isn't home right now, I can wait." He swung down off his horse.

"He's gone." Lupe took a step back. "I'll tell him you were here. He can come to your house."

"That won't do. My wife doesn't need any reminders of what she suffered when she lived here." He took a step forward. "If Diego isn't here, may I speak with José?"

Lupe's confidence seemed to melt away. She gave a fearful glance toward the house as she took a couple of shuffling steps back.

"I met Diego's cousin, José, in Tucson a few days ago. I'd like to talk to him, too."

"He's not here." She grasped the post at the edge of the porch, causing it to creak as she hauled herself up a step. "Neither one of them is here. Now go away."

Eduardo stayed where he was as Lupe edged into the house. The woman was lying and scared to death about something. He would almost be willing to bet that José, at least, had stayed at home today. Eduardo swung up on El Rey. Staying here didn't make sense. Lupe wouldn't allow him in the house, and he couldn't force his way in. As he left, he deliberately followed the road until he couldn't be seen from the house. Then, he cut up into the hills until he had a perfect view of the place, yet couldn't be seen. Tying the stallion where he would be out of sight, Eduardo picked a good place and hunkered down to watch what Lupe would do.

He didn't have long to wait. About ten minutes passed before José exited the house in a hurry, Lupe on his heels. Even from this distance, Eduardo could see from her movements and gestures she was giving him orders about something. José saddled a horse, mounted, and raced down a path that would take him to the river. Eduardo scrambled back to El Rey. He would follow José, who would hopefully lead him to Diego. Maybe then he could get the truth from the two of them.

∽

Lucio had done a good job caring for her garden while they were in Tucson, but Chiquita was glad to be back. She carried water for the plants, moistening the ground where the weeds grew. After they soaked awhile, they would be easier to pull. In the dry ground, the roots merely broke off rather than coming up.

She carefully examined the plants for any bugs or worms that might do damage. The summer squash were already blooming. She touched a yellow blossom with her fingertip. In a few days, there would be enough flowers that she could afford to pull a few to fry for their supper. By tomorrow, one of the baby squash would be big enough to use for their meal. Her mouth watered at the thought.

Humming a wordless tune, Chiquita began to pull the weeds from around her tomatoes. When asked about them, Lucio shrugged and said tomato plants made him sneeze. He'd done well with the rest of the garden though. Pilar apologized for not helping. She hadn't been feeling well for the past week. Today, Rico said she felt better, but he insisted on her resting most of the time. Chiquita missed spending time with her friend.

Since marrying Eduardo, Chiquita couldn't believe how many friends she had. After spending her growing-up years virtually alone, having Eduardo and all his friends accept her made her happier than she thought possible. When they returned from Tucson, she realized, for the first time, that she belonged here. She had a bond to this place and these people.

A shout came from the direction of the barn. Chiquita sat back on her heels and shaded her brow, wondering what the commotion meant. From here, the big mesquite tree blocked her view, so she couldn't make out much. She heard Lucio shout again and decided to investigate. She needed a drink anyway.

After taking a long sip from the dipper beside the water bucket, Chiquita walked to the front of the house where she would have an unobstructed view of the barn. Lucio was running across the pasture where the mares and foals were kept. Tomás followed after him. Across the field, the horses stood in a group, facing away from the house. Chiquita couldn't see what they were looking at, but she knew something was wrong.

Picking up her skirt so she wouldn't trip, she trotted across the yard to the fence surrounding the pasture. Lucio and Tomás were pushing the mares to one side. In the center of the group something struggled on the ground. Dread crept through Chiquita. She hurried to the gate and dashed across the field.

Two foals were tangled together in a mass of rope and ocotillo fence. Their white-rimmed eyes reflected their panic. One began to struggle, and the other joined in, causing the thorny cactus to dig deeper into them.

"Hold this one still, Lucio." Tomás held a knife. With his knee and his left arm, he tried to hold the second foal.

"What happened?" Chiquita reached for the filly and tried to soothe her.

"The fence broke." Lucio's expression was grim. "Somehow these two got caught in the rope when they ran past. The whole thing wrapped around them."

"How could this happen? You just checked this fence." Chiquita knew Eduardo wouldn't allow any of the fences to be in disrepair.

"I walked this line myself, yesterday." Lucio ground out the words. "I'm not sure how this happened, but when I get the chance, I'll do some checking."

Tomás seemed to take forever before he began to cut. Chiquita found herself wanting to yell at him to hurry before the foals bled to death.

Tomás glanced at her. "If I cut the wrong way first, they're likely to struggle more. If the fence digs in too deep, they'll lose too much blood and die."

Chiquita stroked the small head. She thought of all the times she looked out her window and watched these babies buck and gallop around the pasture. Seeing them hurt made her heart ache. She knew Eduardo would feel the pain, too.

"Is there something I can do?"

"In the barn." Tomás motioned with his head. "In the tack room is a jar of salve. When I clip the rope, it will help if we put that on to slow the bleeding."

"I'll be right back." She raced across the field, into the tack area of the barn. Rummaging through the brushes and other equipment, she found a tin of salve. A loud clank echoed at the far end of the barn. She glanced that way but didn't have time to investigate. One of the dogs must be nosing through the stalls back there.

"Is this what you need?" Out of breath, she knelt slowly so she didn't startle the foals.

"That's it. Set the tin down over there, where it won't get trampled." Lucio had his hands full as the filly thrashed, trying to get free.

"Can you go fix a stall?" Tomás wiped the sweat from his forehead. The long ocotillo sticks were hard to work with. "When we get them free, we'll need a clean, dry place for them. If you could put down some straw in one of the empty stalls, that would help."

Chiquita trotted back to the barn. The tension exhausted her. She wished Eduardo would return. He would want to help with this. Midway down the aisle of the barn, she peered into an empty stall. The floor, clean-swept, would be easy to prepare. She only had to spread some fresh straw to have it ready.

"You won't get away this time."

Her breath caught at the voice behind her. Closing her eyes, she prayed for strength and help. Turning, she faced Diego. He stood close to her, an unlit torch in one hand, a cigarette dangling from the corner of his mouth. A tendril of smoke curled up past one eye.

"What do you want?"

His eyes widened. For a moment he stared at her. His eyes narrowed, turning his expression to one of hatred. "All those years, you pretended to be dumb. Now, you marry someone with a little money, and you think you're better than we are."

"You're the one who made me marry Eduardo. He thought he was marrying Teresa, but you tricked him with me, remember?"

"Shut up." He slapped her hard enough to knock her back a step. She resisted the urge to touch her stinging cheek.

"I'm here to take care of you myself. I sent that incompetent fool to get rid of you, and look what happened."

"What are you talking about?" Apprehension clutched at her. Had Diego been the one trying to kill her? Why?

His lips turned up in a sinister smile. "You have to die, you see. I should have gotten rid of you years ago, but you were a hard worker, so we kept you around. That was a mistake."

"I don't understand."

"I guess it doesn't matter if I tell you now. By the time those vaqueros get the foals loose, you'll be dead anyway."

She shuddered. He'd deliberately hurt the horses so he could get her alone. How could she have lived in the same house with this man and never realized how devious he was?

"You were brought to us when you were a little baby. Your mama, my uncle's daughter, wasn't married when she had you. Some drifter passing through caught her out alone and took advantage of her. After you were born, my uncle said she had to get rid of you." He took the cigarette from his mouth.

"Your mama knew she couldn't go against her papa. He was a hard man. She convinced José to bring you to us. She paid us to keep you. That's where we got the money for the place we have." He gave a malevolent chuckle. "You bought that for us.

"Everything went along just fine until right after you were married. José showed up saying my uncle died. Your mama, Bella, is now a wealthy woman. She's been looking for us since we disappeared years ago. We didn't want her to know how we used the money. I couldn't let you tell her how you've been raised. She wouldn't approve, and that means we wouldn't get any more money from her. That's why we hid from her years ago. We were only waiting to hear about her inheritance; then we would let her know where we were."

He touched the end of the cigarette to the torch, then dropped the cigarette in the dirt, grinding it out with the toe of his boot. The cloth smoldered, then caught. Chiquita's heart pounded. She wanted to scream that this couldn't be true.

"Now you understand. If we get rid of you, we can give her a sob story about how you died of disease a few years back. José and I even put in a grave with a marker so she can go there and cry awhile. Part of the bargain was that if we did our best by you, she would reward us handsomely when her father died. Her brother is in charge of the estate, but she received a large share under his authority."

The torch flame burned brighter, dark smoke spiraling upwards. The scent of fire made the few horses in stalls restless. Diego glanced at the door.

"I've talked enough." He took two strides and reached a lantern hanging from a nail in the wall. After twisting off the cap to the oil reservoir, he tossed the lid on the ground and plucked the lantern from the wall. She knew, without asking, what he intended to do as he walked toward her.

"Diego, no." She tried to stand strong against him, but the venomous gleam in his eye sent a tremor of fear through her. The fear of fire that plagued her since childhood overwhelmed her.

CHAPTER 20

Her senses heightened. She took in every detail—the dirt under Diego's fingernails, the faint crackling of the flames, the crunch of the straw littering the aisle as Diego walked toward her, the all-too-familiar smell of cigarettes that clung to him, the acrid taste of fear in her mouth. Faint thunder rumbled outside.

Catching the bottom of the lantern in his right hand, Diego lifted it high. Chiquita's skin began to prickle as terror shot through her. Unexpected energy washed over her. She jumped to the side as Diego began the downward motion intended to douse her with oil. Her hand jerked up, knocking his arm aside.

The thunder grew louder. Three horses raced up to the barn, their hooves sending a shower of dirt into the air as they slid to a stop. She heard Eduardo yell. She tried to turn and run to him. Her foot slipped. The fall knocked the air from her lungs. She could almost feel the heat from the torch. The stench of oil and smoke filled her nostrils as she finally drew in a breath. She rolled, trying to get away from Diego, praying for Jesus to help. Someone screamed, a horrible, fear-laden sound. The stench of burning flesh made her gag.

∞

Eduardo leaned over El Rey's neck, urging the stallion to run faster. Rico and Jorge followed behind him, their grim and determined expressions matching his own. The horses' hooves thundered on the road leading back to the ranch house.

When he left the Garcia place, following Diego's cousin, José, Eduardo hadn't gone far before he realized José was taking the back way to the Villegas ranch. Taking a shortcut, Eduardo came around in front of José and stopped him. The man tried to put up a front, but Eduardo had little trouble convincing him to tell the truth about Diego. While he was getting the answers he needed, Rico and Jorge rode up to see if he needed help. He couldn't have been more grateful when he found out that Diego had gone to find Chiquita in order to make sure she was out of the way.

Leaving José behind, the three rode hard and fast to the ranch. Eduardo couldn't remember when he'd prayed so hard. He knew Chiquita would be outside working in the garden or doing other chores. Diego would have little trouble getting to her. Even with Tomás and Lucio watching, any little distraction would keep them busy elsewhere long enough for Diego to harm Chiquita.

For the first time in years, Eduardo realized he wasn't filled with anger. He did feel concern and determination, but this had nothing to do with the unhealthy rage he would have felt a few weeks ago.

As they raced from the river road toward the barn, Eduardo could see Lucio and Tomás in the field with the horses. He wanted to shout at them. What were they doing there rather than watching over his wife? Lucio glanced up, saw the riders, and motioned wildly at Eduardo to join them. He knew he couldn't possibly see what Lucio wanted until he found Chiquita and made sure she was all right.

The rumble of hoofbeats echoed as they hit the hard-packed ground of the barnyard. Hauling in on the reins, Eduardo's gaze was drawn to the open barn doors. In an instant, he took in the scene. Chiquita stood with her back to a stall, facing Diego. Diego held a lantern over his head with one hand and a burning torch in the other. Eduardo's heart thudded. Even someone as cruel as Diego wouldn't do something this evil.

"No!" He hit the ground running almost before El Rey slid to a stop.

He saw Chiquita fall. Diego's arm, knocked aside by Chiquita, flew up. At the same time, Diego must have heard Eduardo's yell. He pivoted. The oil from the lantern splashed across his shirt and his face, then ran down his chest and back.

Squinting his eyes closed to keep the oil out, Diego began to wipe the liquid away. The torch, brushing by his face, flared. The flames touched the oil, igniting and spreading rapidly, following the trail across his body. Diego screamed. Dropping the torch and lantern, he ran from the barn. Eduardo tried to intercept him, but Diego moved too fast.

As Diego raced across the barnyard, the flames leapt higher, fueled on by the fresh air and wind. Rico and Jorge both ran after him. Eduardo turned back to the barn. The discarded torch had caught the straw-littered floor on fire. Snatching up a saddle blanket, Eduardo began to beat at the flames. The need to get to Chiquita urged him on. He had to get the fire out first before he checked to see if she was hurt. Finally, he knelt beside his wife. She lay curled in a ball on the ground.

"Chiquita." He touched her. She flinched. "It's me, my love."

Her tear-streaked face turned to him. "Eduardo?" She almost flung herself at him. He pulled her close, sitting down on the floor to rock her as she sobbed. An unbelievable peace stole over him. Despite all that had happened, he knew everything would work out just fine.

∞

"Come on, keep your eyes closed a minute longer." Eduardo led Chiquita by the hand, his pulse racing in excited anticipation. One of the things he recalled about his parents was their ability to have fun together. After all that had happened to him and Chiquita since they married, he knew they needed to find a way to laugh.

Chiquita had difficulty sleeping some nights. The image of Diego's burned body haunted her. She often struggled with guilt over not being the right kind of daughter that he could love, even though he wasn't her natural father. After Diego's death, Lupe insisted on returning to California with José, choosing to go home to relatives there. Eduardo made Lupe tell them the whole story. He wanted Chiquita to realize her mother, Bella, had to do what she'd done, and the deception and cruelty were Diego and Lupe's fault. Lupe admitted that Bella had been a virtual prisoner in her own home. Although Lupe said Chiquita could have the land and house she grew up in since they'd used her money to purchase the place, Eduardo still insisted on paying her something. He couldn't see leaving her destitute when she still had four daughters to raise.

"Can I open my eyes yet?"

"In one minute." Eduardo positioned her so she would have the best view when he let her look. He ignored the drops of sweat trickling down his back. Placing the bundle he carried in the soft grass, he stood to one side of his wife. He wanted to see her reaction to this place. She'd never been here before.

"Okay, you can look."

Her eyes flew open. She blinked. Her mouth dropped open, her eyes wide. A slow smile lit her face.

He glanced to the side, looking at the view she saw. This small, natural spring had been one of his parents' favorite places. Surrounded by cottonwood trees, the oval pond formed by the stream looked cool and inviting. Sunlight rippled in sparkling waves across the half of the water that wasn't shaded. Grass grew in abundance here, the blades reaching almost to his knees in spots.

"It's beautiful." Chiquita's voice held a note of awe. "I didn't know this was here."

He put an arm around her shoulders and tugged her close. "My parents used to come here quite a bit during the summer. This was their special place. I thought maybe we could make this our place now."

She looked up, her eyes shining. "I just can't believe a place like this exists here."

"Take off your shoes. The grass feels wonderful on your feet." Eduardo sat down and tugged his boots off. Chiquita giggled and removed her slippers. He could see her toes wiggling through the soft, green blades.

He clambered to his feet. "Now, I want to show you what my parents used to do here." She smiled up at him, totally unprepared for what he was about to do. He swept her into his arms and stepped to the edge of the water. Her eyes widened in shock as he swung her in the air and let go. The splash as she hit the water almost drowned out her gasp.

Spluttering, she floundered for a moment before discovering she could stand. He knew the water only came to her shoulders at the deepest part.

"Why did you do that? My clothes are soaked." She started for the bank.

"Don't you dare come out here, or I'll throw you back in again."

She glared at him. Tossing his hat on the ground, Eduardo jumped. Landing in the pond close to Chiquita, his resulting splash soaked her again. The shock of the cool water faded, replaced by sheer enjoyment. He laughed. Eduardo couldn't remember the last time he'd laughed like this.

Chiquita stared at him. Her braid had come partially undone. Strands of drenched hair streamed across her face and shoulders. Her eyes began to twinkle. He couldn't seem to stop laughing.

Drawing her hand back, she brought the palm forward through the water, lifting at the last minute to send a huge splash directly into his mouth. He sputtered.

"War it is, my love." He sent a splash back at her, making her squeal and stumble away.

In minutes, she was using both hands to get him as wet as he was getting her. Her melodic laugh startled him. He realized he'd never heard her laugh before. Diving for her, he pinned her arms to her body as she squealed and fought him. Catching both of her hands in one of his, he caught her face with his other hand. She quit laughing as he gave her a long, lingering kiss.

"This is what I want for us, Chiquita." His voice was husky with emotion. "We'll have a lot of hard work, but I want us to laugh and enjoy one another. Do you think we can do that?"

She tugged one hand free and caressed his cheek. "Yes. I love you so much, even when you try to drown me." She chuckled. "What if I couldn't swim?"

"I would have been your handsome prince and jumped in to save you."

She giggled. "I thought the prince always had his servant do the dangerous work."

"Then I'll be the servant who rescues you, my lady." They both dissolved in gales of laughter.

The afternoon sun was waning as they strolled, hand in hand, back to the house. Eduardo had brought a change of clothes for each of them so they didn't have to wear their wet things home. They waved to Lucio and Tomás, seeing the pair exercising the foals that'd been hurt. The babies would be fine after a few more days of pampering.

A buggy stood outside the house. Chiquita glanced up. "Were you expecting company?" Her hand lifted to her damp, loose hair.

He frowned in thought. "No, not that I know of. Whoever it is, Rico or Pilar must have let them inside."

The door creaked shut behind them. As they entered the living room, an older woman rose. Her well-made gown suggested money. She looked familiar, but it took a moment before Eduardo knew where he'd seen her before. She was an older, darker version of Chiquita. This must be Bella, her mother.

"Estrella?" The woman took a hesitant step forward. "I'm sorry. I hear you are called Chiquita now. I've always thought of you as Estrella."

Chiquita's eyes widened in understanding. She glanced at Eduardo. He smiled and nudged her forward.

"My name is Bella. I've waited so many years to see you." The woman's voice broke. She stretched out a slender, gloved hand to Chiquita. "I wanted you to know—I loved you so much. I'm so sorry your birth had to be kept a secret for so long." Tears glittered in her eyes.

Chiquita hesitated only a moment longer. With a cry, she flew across the room into her mother's arms. Eduardo left them to get acquainted. He would have time to join them later.

That evening, after supper, they sat together in the living room. Eduardo held his wife's hand as she snuggled next to him. After her mother retired, they sat for a while, enjoying the quiet and each other's company.

"I've tried to get used to calling you Estrella, but I can't." Eduardo spoke softly near her ear. "That's such a beautiful name for a beautiful woman. You do remind me of a shining star, but somehow you'll always be my Chiquita. Do you mind if I call you that?"

She shook her head. "I will always love you calling me Chiquita."

He kissed her. "Can you tell me what you and your mother talked about?"

Chiquita gazed up at him, her expression more peaceful than he could ever recall. "She's so beautiful, isn't she?"

Eduardo caressed her cheek. "You look just like her."

Chiquita lowered her gaze. "I don't know how I could. For so long I've thought of myself as ugly, it's hard to think otherwise." She gave a sad smile. "My mother felt so bad. She already talked to José and found out how Lupe and Diego treated me. It's nice to know she thought of me and wanted me all these years. Her father was a tyrant—almost as bad as Diego."

"I'm glad you're not angry at her." Eduardo couldn't seem to quit touching her.

"I think this is all such a shock. Maybe if I'd thought I had a choice, I might have been bitter. Although Jesus could take that bitterness away, I'm so glad that all I feel is love for her."

"Come here. I want to show you something." Eduardo pulled her up from the couch and led her to the mirror hanging on the wall. "Look." His hands on her shoulders, he made her face the looking glass.

She stared at the floor. "I can't. You know that."

"Please, for me." He brushed a strand of hair from her cheek.

Reluctantly, she glanced up. She'd never had the courage to look in a mirror. The young woman looking back caught her eye. She stared. The face was her mother's, only much younger. She had lighter hair and eyes, but her features resembled Bella's.

"You see." Eduardo's whispered words sent a shiver through her. "You are beautiful, just like your mother."

They were quiet a few minutes before Chiquita spoke again. "She told me about my father and what happened. She had been visiting a friend. While she was returning home, this man tricked her into thinking he was injured. She got off her horse to help him, and he attacked her." A tear slid down her cheek. "Even after all these years, she still carries the hurt from what he did."

"You mustn't think of him, though, my love. Consider the gift God's given you of such a great mother." He turned her to face him and put his arms around her.

She smiled up at him, her hand stroking his cheek. "And, what a gift I have in you."

He smiled. "All I wanted was someone to be here in the lonely evenings, and God blessed me with you. I love you so much."

Her eyes shone with love as she returned the kiss he gave her. "I love you, too."

LOVE'S SHINING HOPE

by JoAnn A. Grote

DEDICATION

To Sharon Olsen Falvey,
my sister, my friend.

CHAPTER 1

1893

"Marry you, Jason?" A sophisticated little laugh cut sharply through the early August twilight. "Don't be silly."

Pearl Wells caught her breath at her best friend's condescending tone. Dismay welled up in her chest. When she'd sat down to await Miranda thirty minutes earlier, she'd never intended to eavesdrop on a lovers' quarrel!

Her spine pressed her blue Eton jacket against the high back of the wooden porch bench. If only she could get away without being seen! But the couple was too close—just around the corner where the wide porch continued its journey about the pleasant two-story clapboard building.

"Silly? We've talked of marrying since we were children!"

The shock in Jason's voice echoed that in Pearl's mind. She could imagine his usually laughing, golden brown eyes widening beneath gleaming, russet brown hair.

"We *were* children," Miranda responded. "Until you went to school in Chicago three years ago and I went to Saint Paul last fall, we never left Chippewa City. Besides," a petulant note crept into her voice. "Our plans never included running your parents' farm on the Minnesota prairie and raising your brothers and sisters."

"Our plans didn't include my parents dying in a buggy accident three weeks ago either." Jason's bitter tone burned into Pearl's heart with the searing heat of a branding iron.

"Your parents were so proud of your plans to be an architect. Surely they wouldn't expect you to throw them away."

"Are you sure that your concern is for me? You seem to have developed the popular attitude that farmers are somehow less important than townspeople. Perhaps you just don't care to be a farmer's wife." His voice could have formed ice.

Pearl pressed her hands firmly over her ears. She wouldn't listen to any more of this private conversation! But her small hands couldn't shut out the embarrassing scene.

"You've always known I don't want to live on a farm. A farmer's wife has a hard life. I won't grow old before my time working my fingers to the bone when instead I can live as a lady is meant to live."

"You mean with less-deserving women performing your household chores?"

"You needn't sound so scornful. As an architect, you'll have a much different life as an adult than you did as a child. With your talent and personality, you are certain to be a success. Naturally your wife will be busy with social obligations."

"Sounds as though it's the architect you love rather than the man." Jason's low, sharp words almost didn't make it through the barrier Pearl had tried to erect. She wished fervently they hadn't.

Exasperation filled Miranda's sigh. "I simply want what is best for you."

"Trust me to know what that is. I'm asking you again to marry me. I give you fair warning that my plan to be an architect is behind me. I can't foresee a time I'll be leaving the farm or my family."

"Then my answer must be no."

A huge, burning rock seemed to replace Pearl's heart. How could Miranda say no?

"My answer will be yes when you give up this preposterous idea—"

"I'll not give it up. If you think so little of me that you believe I could walk away from my family when they need me, perhaps it's best that you refuse me."

A dog howled in the distance and was answered by another. Jason's horse snorted, and another horse's hooves plodded down a nearby street. The slight, sweet scent of the bushes in front of the porch railing drifted on the barely moving air. Pearl held her breath, waiting for the silence to end between the two who had loved each other for so many years. Her fingers slipped from their ineffectual place over her ears. She lowered them slowly to the wide arms of the bench, inadvertently brushing her jacket's leg-of-mutton sleeve against something on the small table beside her.

Too late she realized she had knocked over a porcelain pot of geraniums. She grasped for it as it fell and watched in horror as it crashed to pieces on the painted wooden floor.

Silence followed. Pearl closed her eyes tight and took a deep breath before standing up. There'd be no more hiding from Jason and Miranda.

"Who's there?"

Jason's bark is more of a demand than a question, Pearl thought, lifting her tailored blue serge skirt and stepping around the dirt, blossoms, and broken porcelain. She stopped short around the corner, just past the darkest shadows.

The couple stood in the yellow rectangle made by the sitting room lamp shining through the window. Jason was standing as straight and tall as ever, his shoulders broad beneath his long roll black suit, black crape wrapped around the crown of his derby in the traditional mourning manner.

"It's only me. I was waiting for Miranda."

"So you could eavesdrop on us?"

Anger fired through her at Jason's suspicion. It was embarrassing enough to be in this situation without being accused of having staged it. "Naturally, I could think of nothing more exciting to do with my evening than listen to the two of you quarrel!"

She regretted her sarcasm immediately. Jason's emotions must be raw from Miranda's treatment. It wasn't like him to attack her so rudely. She gripped her hands together behind her and forced her voice to a softer and lower level. "I apologize to you both. I truly didn't intend to eavesdrop. It's just that you were suddenly here, and quarreling, and there didn't seem to be a path of escape."

"It's all right, Pearl." Miranda pardoned her carelessly.

Pearl didn't care whether Miranda forgave her after the way she'd treated Jason. She glanced at him. He'd never been a handsome man, but definitely appealing with his ready grin and laughing eyes—eyes that could be so warm and steady. They'd reminded her of the sun the first time she'd looked into them across a sheet of gray ice the day he'd saved her life.

There was nothing warm about his eyes tonight.

"I guess you would have heard about it anyway. You and Miranda tell each other everything." Jason didn't sound as though he was forgiving her. Would he ever look at her without remembering that she'd heard Miranda refuse his proposal? If she lost his friendship. . . A shudder went through her at the thought.

Jason turned away from her. "Good-bye, Miranda."

The pain that throbbed in the short farewell brought instant tears to sting Pearl's eyelids. She bit her lip hard to keep from crying out as he crossed the porch, each step an exclamation point against the narrow wooden boards.

Pearl remained frozen until the buggy disappeared, then turned to Miranda. She was standing at the top of the steps with one black lace glove against a white wooden pillar. Her thick, dark hair was piled high above her slightly round face, beneath one of the hats she loved. A firefly flared and faded against the black silk gown she wore in sympathy with Jason's grieving.

"I cannot believe you refused him."

"When he's thought it over, he'll realize I'm right, and he'll come back."

Pearl doubted it. She'd known Jason as long as Miranda had known him.

He wouldn't be Jason Sterling if he left his family for her. "You mean when he realizes you're right about leaving his family to their own devices?"

Miranda settled gracefully into a white wooden rocker in front of the sitting room window. "You make it sound vile. With his fine, quick mind and talented fingers, Jason would be miserable as a farmer."

"He shall be miserable if he doesn't care for his family. Don't you know the man at all?"

The small glow of lamplight touched Miranda's lips in their condescending smile. "It may hurt him now, but eventually he'll realize that he has to pursue his career as an architect, has to live the life he was created to live. When that happens, you and Jason will both see that love for him is behind my refusal to marry him now."

Pearl shook her head slowly. "I shall never believe love behaves in such a manner—forcing the person one claims to love to abandon his principles. You should be proud that the man who loves you is God-fearing, unselfish, and fine."

Miranda's superior laugh rang through the evening air. "You've been reading too many romantic serials. Sacrifice seems noble in a story, but in true life, it is only painful and hard. Jason has always known what he wanted to do with his life, and it isn't farming."

"You always knew what you wanted to do with your life also. You wanted to be Jason's wife."

"Only after the manner we've planned, especially after the time I've spent in Saint Paul. I met fascinating people there, had entrance to elegant homes, was escorted to fine eating establishments, wore beautiful gowns."

"Are you certain you haven't fallen in love with one of your city-bred escorts?" Pearl was almost ashamed of her question. When Miranda wrote of the men she was seeing while in Saint Paul, Pearl had been horrified that she would treat her commitment to Jason so lightly. Miranda had insisted that her escorts were merely friends, and Pearl's loyalty had been quick to accept her explanation. Now she wondered anew.

Miranda's gaze dropped to her lap, where her lace-covered fingers played with her fine silk skirt. "I could hardly go about the city unescorted. Aunt Elsie was kind enough to insist I experience the benefits of culture the city provided, and arranged for her friends' sons to accompany me."

"They must have been weak examples of manhood if you no longer recognize the worth of a man like Jason."

"I won't apologize for liking life as I experienced it there. Jason and I can have a similar life. I don't intend to allow him to give it away in a moment of sentimental self-sacrifice."

Pearl took an impulsive step nearer, her hands balling into fists at her sides. "Sentimental! I do believe Jason's right. You aren't thinking of him at all. You're thinking of yourself, and a life filled with empty grasping instead of giving! Why, I can hardly believe you're the same sweet, innocent girl with whom I grew up!"

The rocker stopped short as Miranda's back stiffened. "I'm not that girl. I've become a woman during the year in Saint Paul, and I'm not a whit ashamed of that woman."

"I spent months advancing my music training at the Northwestern Conservatory of Music in Minneapolis, but I hope I haven't become as self-seeking and superior as you've grown. Jason's life is disintegrating around him. He's lost his parents and given up his career, and now he's lost you, too."

"He hasn't lost me. I told you, he'll be back."

Pearl shook her head so hard that some of her blond curls came unpinned and slid down her neck. "Not if he has to meet your demands. He has too much honor. How *could* you hurt him so unbearably when he needs your love and understanding now more than ever?"

A high little laugh escaped Miranda's heart-shaped lips, and her eyes widened in surprise. "Why, I do believe you are in love with Jason yourself!"

Pearl flushed. After all these years, had she given away her secret in a moment of anger? Although she and Jason were good friends, it was Miranda who had caught his heart. Never had she revealed her love to anyone, and now . . . It wouldn't do for Miranda to know of it now, when she'd become a stranger and treated Jason's love so lightly. "You're only attempting to change the subject because you know you cannot defend the way you've treated him."

Miranda shot out of the chair and stood quaking only inches away from Pearl. "What gives you the right to judge me, or to tell me how to deal with my fiancé?"

"The right of one who has been a friend to both of you since we were ten years old. And he's not your fiancé. You ended that tonight when you threw his love back in his face."

Miranda's hand streaked out to land a resounding slap on Pearl's cheek.

Pearl gasped, blinking against the sting of the unexpected blow. Turning sharply on her high-heeled, high-buttoned shoes, she grasped her slender skirt and hurried down the steps and away from the friend she'd loved like a sister. The burning in her cheek seemed minor compared to the fire in her chest.

To think anyone would treat Jason's love in such a trifling manner! He must be aching horribly over Miranda's refusal. One would think his love would die a sudden and merciful death upon realizing that the woman he cared for was selfish and wholly unworthy of that love. At eighteen, she wasn't so young and inexperienced as to believe love died so easily.

If it did, her own love for Jason would have died years ago when she discovered he was madly in love with her best friend. Instead it took root all the more fiercely and grew taller and stronger than an oak beside a river. She'd tried to care for other men, but every potential suitor had paled beside Jason Sterling. If he had asked *her* to marry him, she'd have accepted so quickly it would have set his head spinning.

CHAPTER 2

Pearl closed the door behind her last piano student and hurried to the shed to harness her horse, Angel, to her adoptive father's buggy. Large baskets of bread and apple pies she'd baked the night before were placed on the floor and seat, covered with towels to protect them from flies and the dust of the road.

Her conscience had been prickling for a day and a half—ever since that night on Miranda's porch. When Jason's parents died, she'd attended the funeral with her adoptive parents, Dr. Matthew Strong and his wife, whom Pearl had always called Mother Boston. She'd expressed her condolences, and Mother Boston had sent out a basket of food. Of course she'd been praying for Jason and his family, but she was ashamed to admit she hadn't realized they might need more substantial assistance.

She wasn't certain of what that assistance might consist. However, since the oldest woman in the home was now Maggie, Jason's twelve-year-old sister, she was sure baked goods would be appreciated.

Fields began almost before she left the prairie town. The hay crops were mostly garnered, and haystacks dotted the fields, along with men and horses beginning to harvest barley and early wheat. The heady smell of the ripe grains filled the air. She loved the way friendly clouds sent lilac shadows weaving over the golden fields.

The buggy's red wheels settled into the well-worn ruts in the dirt road, their rattle bringing curious prairie dogs from their holes. The *plop, plop* of Angel's hooves and the swish of the wind through the fields kept up a constant background to Pearl's thoughts.

She and her brother, Johnny, had lived with their adoptive parents since she was two and he was six. Although Dr. Matt and Mother Boston had surrounded them with all the love two children could ask, she and Johnny had maintained a special bond through the years.

Jason and Johnny had been good friends from the time Jason's family moved into the area eight years earlier. Perhaps it was Johnny's attitude that caused Jason to be so accepting toward her. She was so comfortable with him! He was like a second brother.

A yellow-breasted meadowlark lit on a weed top and trilled its song as Pearl turned off onto the lane leading to Jason's farmstead. The two-story, white clapboard house was dwarfed by the red barn, the machine shed, and corncribs. She recalled Jason speaking of the house being built in the '80s. Those had been profitable years for the farmers, and fine farm homes had replaced most of the sod huts and small homes that were common in the '70s.

Cottonwoods and maples had been planted around the house and beside the lane years ago, but they were still young. She smiled at the sound of the thick, shiny cottonwood leaves clapping in the wind, as if applauding her decision to come.

Smells of animal life assailed her, drawing her attention to the brown-and-white cows gazing idly at her over the fence and to the hogs lazily grunting in another fenced section near the farm building most distant from the house. She knew Jason's father had kept only a few cows and hogs to meet the family's needs, and considered the crops his livelihood, though dairy farming was the primary means of support for most area farmers.

As she tied Angel to the white fence enclosing the yard, she noticed the weed-infested garden off to one side, near the fields. The pansies lifting their cheery heads beside the porch, however, grew weed free, and she wondered at the inconsistency.

It was Maggie who responded to her knock on the kitchen screen door, her broad face pale and plain between two long brown braids. The girl's suspiciously red eyes opened wide at the sight of the piano teacher. "Miss Wells!"

Pearl politely ignored the signs of her grief and smiled cheerfully. "Hello. I overbaked and decided to share my bounty."

"How kind! Won't you come in?" Maggie held the screen door while Pearl entered the large square kitchen and placed the baskets on the rectangular oak table in the middle of the room.

Pearl had never been inside Jason's home, and she glanced eagerly about the high-ceilinged kitchen. There were windows on two walls, filling the room with late summer sunlight. The wainscoting was shiny white, and the walls above it a cheerful yellow. The furnishings were surprisingly up-to-date. Pale blue curtains fluttered at the open, screened windows.

It warmed her heart that Jason's mother had tried to make the workroom of the house such a welcoming place for the family. True, table, worktable, sink, and all other available space were filled with dirty dishes and failed baking attempts, but that only went to prove that she was justified in coming out here. "What a cheerful room!"

The pain in Maggie's white face brought her up short. She'd assumed the girl's red eyes were due to grieving over her parents. Now she saw that Maggie was cradling one arm carefully with her other.

Pearl winced at the long burn on the inside of Maggie's forearm, beneath a rolled-up sleeve. "From the stove?"

Maggie nodded, her teeth biting her bottom lip hard.

Pearl retrieved a chipped graniteware bowl and pitcher from the back porch and placed cold, wet cloths on the wound and on the girl's forehead. Inside the small oak refrigerator, she found butter, and under Maggie's guidance located a clean cloth in the pantry. Dirty clothes overflowed a wicker basket onto the pantry floor, making it difficult to walk in the small room.

"I was baking bread," Maggie explained while Pearl spread the wound with butter and wrapped it. With a feeble wave of her hand, she indicated an exceedingly flat loaf sitting on a square of wooden slats on the worktable. She sighed and slumped against the straight chair back. "I was hoping to have some bread and pie ready for when the neighbors and hired men help with the harvesting in a couple days. Today seemed like a good time, since my brothers are helping in Thor Lindstrom's fields—he's our neighbor—and there were only five-year-old Grace and me to make dinner for."

Is Maggie trying to run the household all by herself? Pearl tried to hide how the thought horrified her. "Don't you have a hired girl to help?"

Maggie's shaggy brown braids wiggled as she shook her head. "She married in December, and Jason hasn't found anyone to replace her." She rubbed a hand self-consciously over the dirty apron covering her wrinkled green-and-white dress. "I can't seem to keep up with everything around the house like Mom did. Baking is the worst. I'm pretty hopeless at it."

Pearl patted the younger girl's shoulder briskly. "No one is hopeless. I'll teach you to make wonderful bread." There were some things she planned to teach Jason, too, about expecting a girl to take over a woman's responsibilities.

Maggie looked up at her eagerly. "Do you really think I could learn? Frank and Andy make fun of my baking and cooking. Frank even brought home bread from Carl's Bakery last time he was in town. Jason tells them to quit teasing me, but even he doesn't clean his plate the way he did when Mom cooked."

"We'll show Frank and Andrew what a woman can do in a kitchen. In fact, I intend to stay the rest of the day and help you catch up on your housework a bit." She held an index finger up in a prim, piano-instructor manner as Maggie opened her mouth to object. "It's simply the neighborly thing to do, and I won't be put off."

A frown crinkled the girl's brow, and she rolled her hands in her dirty apron. "Jason may not like it if you help. He says it's my place to take care of the house now that Mom's gone."

"I'll see to Jason. Now, if you'll lend me an apron, we'll get busy with this kitchen." Pearl pulled the pins from her flower-covered straw hat. Hoping to cheer Maggie, she said, "Your flower bed looks nice."

Maggie's eyes clouded over again. "Jason weeded the flowers by lantern last night. He said he didn't want Mom's flowers to die." The hint of a sob caught in her sigh. "I can't seem to do everything he wants me to."

"I'm sure Jason thought no such thing when he tended to the flowers. It was only a way to comfort himself by doing something he thought your mother would like."

Hope relieved some of the tense lines in Maggie's face, but she said nothing.

The afternoon wasn't nearly long enough to accomplish all that needed to be done. The kitchen was hot from the growing heat of the early August day, and from the large cookstove that stood along the wall between the kitchen and the dining room—the better to offer heat to more of the home during the winter months. They used water heated in the reservoir at the back of the stove during Maggie's baking attempts to wash the myriad of dirty dishes and to scrub the floor.

Pearl was frying chicken for supper when Grace called excitedly from the post she'd taken up for the last thirty minutes beside one of the kitchen windows. "The boys are comin'!" She was out the door in a flash, racing to greet the men, her shoulder-length dark brown hair flying.

Pearl's heart leaped to her throat. *Jason! He'll be inside any minute now.* She wiped perspiration from her forehead with the back of a hand that still held the large fork she was using to turn the chicken, and she moaned slightly in dismay. She must look a wreck! Stray bits of her hair were curling wetly against her forehead and cheeks. Her trim chambray dress of tiny blue plaid with a plaited front—chosen to compliment her eyes—was no longer crisply fresh.

Through the nearest window she saw Jason stop beside her buggy. He scooped Grace up in his arms, and her giggle floated through the open window as Pearl turned back to the stove. Children always loved Jason, with his open, fun-loving manner. She envied Grace. She'd like to greet him so freely herself!

The men's responses to Grace's chatter mixed with the splashing of water as they washed up on the porch. The door slammed, and Frank's voice moved ahead of his heavy boots as he crossed the kitchen to stare over Pearl's shoulder. In spite of his recent washing, he smelled of earth and grain and the kerosene farmers used to discourage flies and mosquitoes.

"Pearl Wells, as I live and breathe, frying chicken on our cookstove. Are you real, or is this a dream?"

A laugh bubbled forth at the usually reserved Frank's teasing. They were the same age, and the two of them were quite good friends. With his black hair, thin black mustache, and normally somber dark eyes, he was handsome and brooding in a manner that won girls' sympathetic hearts easily, but it was Jason's laughing, golden brown eyes she preferred. At least they used to laugh most of the time, before his parents died.

"I'm definitely not a dream—assuming you were referring to me and not the chicken."

"Of course I was referring to you!" His eyes opened innocently wide. "Though I'm glad to see you're accompanied by the chicken."

"Me, too!" thirteen-year-old Andrew piped up from the other side of her. His face was a duplicate of Maggie's beneath straight, light brown hair. "We haven't had a decent meal around here in days."

"Thanks a bunch, Andy!" Maggie pushed him aside indignantly and held out a large platter for Pearl to place the chicken on.

"Neither of you shall have any supper until you've removed your boots. You should be ashamed of yourselves, walking over Maggie's clean floor in those filthy things."

Out of the corner of her eye, she saw Jason beside the door. She stifled a laugh at the sight of him guiltily removing his boots beside his chastened brothers.

Maggie pulled fresh rolls from the oven and took corn on the cob from the stove while Pearl made the gravy. When the food was on the table and everyone was standing impatiently behind their chairs waiting to sit down, she realized Jason was still standing at the door. He was staring at her grimly.

She smiled at him in spite of the lead ball that hit her stomach at the growl in his eyes. "Well, Mr. Head-of-the-House, aren't you going to join us?"

The veins stood out like cords on the darkly tanned forearms crossed over his sweaty work shirt. His voice was quiet and polite, but that didn't deceive her after the thunderclouds she saw in his eyes. "What are you doing here?"

"Who cares? Look at this feast!"

"I wasn't speaking to you, Andy." Jason's gaze didn't flicker from Pearl's face.

"She's just helping me, Jason. Don't be angry."

"I wasn't speaking to you either, Maggie."

"I just stopped by with some extra baked goods, and. . ."

" 'Just stopped by' three miles from your house?"

"And decided to stay for dinner. Which is getting cold, by the way."

They stared at each other, and Pearl wondered nervously what he would say next. Didn't he realize he was making everyone uncomfortable? This wasn't anything like the Jason she'd known so many years.

Her hands closed tightly around the top of the chair in front of her. "Well, I guess the way to your heart isn't through your stomach."

Frank and Andy guffawed, and even Maggie laughed. Pearl thought she saw a slight softening in the set of Jason's mouth, but decided a moment later that she'd never been more mistaken in her life.

His words lashed at her. "You have no right to come into my home and take over like this."

CHAPTER 3

Pearl swallowed her shock. She'd expected Jason to be uncomfortable with her after she'd witnessed Miranda refuse his proposal, but she hadn't expected him to react so rudely in front of his family.

"Jason!"

Frank's sharp bark of disapproval jerked Jason's gaze from hers, and he had the decency to flush hotly beneath his tan.

"I apologize," he muttered, his stance making it obvious that the words were a social requirement only.

She hoped no one noticed her lips trembling beneath her smile. "Won't you sit down to supper? We can continue this discussion later, if you wish."

One corner of his mouth lifted in the suspicion of a smile. "Well, it does smell mighty good."

Beside her, Maggie echoed Pearl's small sigh of relief as Jason pulled out a chair at the head of the table and slipped into it. The rest of the family quickly followed suit, and Pearl heard Andrew mutter a low "About time!" Following a brief prayer, the food was quickly passed around, and silence ensued as everyone began eating.

Evidently the silence was too much for Grace to bear. She held a greasy drumstick in one hand, looked everyone over calmly with large, chocolate brown eyes beneath hair that touched her eyebrows. "Maggie burned her arm t'day."

Everyone stopped eating and stared first at Grace and then at Maggie. Grace grinned with gratification at the disturbance her announcement caused and promptly began eating.

"Maggie?" Jason's forehead furrowed into a frown.

Maggie fidgeted slightly and looked down at her plate. "It's not too bad, honest." She slipped her arm to her lap.

The girl's fear and dread of Jason were disturbing to Pearl. Didn't Maggie understand that it wasn't she who made Jason angry but the pain of losing their parents?

"May I see it?"

At Jason's gruff request, Maggie held out her bandaged forearm. "Miss Wells looked after it for me."

"Maggie cwied," Grace announced with satisfaction, and Maggie scowled at her.

Jason gently unwrapped the bandage. Maggie gave a little gasp and dug her teeth into her bottom lip. His gaze darted to her face, then he peeked under the loosened end of the covering. His eyelids slammed shut.

"How did it happen?"

Maggie answered his tight question as he carefully retied the covering. "Burned it on the stove. I should have been more careful."

Jason leaned over to kiss her forehead. "I'm sorry, sweetie."

The guilt in his voice and face both hurt and comforted Pearl. His actions were much more in keeping with the Jason she'd always known than the stern man who frightened Maggie so terribly.

When the pie had been devoured among numerous and extreme compliments, Pearl rose and began to clear the table.

"Maggie will clean up." Jason's tone let it be known his decision was final.

"Her injured arm won't be able to endure the hot dishwater." Pearl tried to state the fact without sounding defensive.

"Then Andy can wash the dishes."

"Aw, Jase, that's women's work!"

"It needs doing, Andy. Maggie can wipe them for you."

"I don't mind helping Maggie," Pearl protested.

"I'm going to hitch up your horse and take you home. It's already late, and I have to be in the fields early."

"I don't need an escort."

He reached for the sweaty beige hat he'd hung on the peg behind the door. Settling it on his head, he turned to look at her. "No lady is leaving my home in the dark without an escort."

He left the house without waiting for her reply. *Wonderful,* she thought. *Now I'm feeling guilty for keeping him out late when he obviously isn't getting all the sleep he needs as it is!*

They'd traveled half a mile through the grain- and earth-scented night before she gave up hoping he would end the silence between them and spoke herself.

"You needn't act like such an ogre. I was only helping."

"I don't need your pity." His tone was harder than the rocks the wheels hit in the road. "You don't have to play nursemaid to me because Miranda turned me down."

"You...you...oh!" Pearl could hardly stop sputtering. "You think I pity you because of Miranda? On the contrary, I think you were fortunate to get out of her clutches!"

"Fortunate?" He drew hard on the lines, drawing Angel to an abrupt halt that set the carriage rocking precariously and brought a nervous whinny from his own horse, tied behind. Jason's eyes blazed in the light that darted over his face from the swinging lanterns. "You think I'm *fortunate* to lose her?"

"Yes! No. I don't know." Her arms clenched tightly over her chest. He wouldn't appreciate hearing how her heart went out to him when Miranda turned him down.

Her voice was only a throaty whisper the prairie night tried to snatch away. "I think we both lost her. I miss her, too."

After her quarrel with Miranda, she'd felt so empty. Now it appeared she was losing Jason's friendship also.

"I don't understand."

It was the friendliest his tone had been toward her all evening. Relief loosened the tightness in her chest. "I. . .I as much as told her she was a fool not to marry you."

"I don't know whether to thank you or upbraid you."

"I know it wasn't my affair, but. . ."

"But that's never stopped you before." The tremor of a laugh jiggled his words.

"You and Miranda are my best friends! If I can't be honest with you, with whom can I be?"

"I assume she wasn't pleased with your interference?"

"No." *Interference!* That put her in her place. "How could a year in Saint Paul have changed Miranda so?"

"I don't know." Hopelessness filled his voice.

The plopping of horses' hooves, the swishing of Angel's tail, the singing of crickets, and the thumping of moths against the lanterns all sounded incredibly loud in the night air. Pearl longed to reach out to Jason, to let him know that he wasn't alone or unloved because one woman had been fool enough to let him out of her life.

"You've never been to the farm before, so why now, two days after Miranda. . ." She heard him swallow hard. "If it's not out of pity, why come now?"

"I only meant to leave some baked goods. But when Maggie told me how she was trying to take your mother's place—and failing miserably—and I saw how much needed to be done, and worst of all how afraid she is of you. . ."

Jason swung to face her, his square jaw dropping. "Afraid?"

"Yes. She didn't say it in so many words, but she's terrified of displeasing you."

He snorted. "That's ridiculous."

"You've given her an adult's responsibilities before she's even through grieving for her parents. She isn't prepared for those duties."

"Someone has to take care of the cooking and laundry and such."

"Naturally. But a twelve-year-old?"

"There isn't anyone else. What do you expect me to do? Give up working in the fields or caring for the livestock? Give up sleeping to do the household chores?"

Pearl gritted her teeth and swallowed the anger that rose in her throat at his sarcasm. *He is impossible! Did I expect him to remain the easygoing boy with the constant grin and laughing eyes I've always known,* she reprimanded herself. Did she think a person could lose his parents, his fiancée's love and support, and the work he loved without being affected by his loss?

She took a deep breath and counted to ten, gripping her patience to keep her voice calm. "Maggie said you've already tried unsuccessfully to hire help. Until you can find someone, you might accept the help of friends."

Jason stared stonily ahead a moment longer, then brushed his floppy hat back farther on his head and wiped a hand down his face with a weariness that caught at Pearl's heart anew. "My family isn't your responsibility."

"We're friends. That makes us each other's responsibility."

He grabbed her arm, and she was forced to look into the eyes only inches from her own, eyes that looked stormy in the swaying lantern light. "Can't you understand? When the grieving time is over, there's still going to be the fieldwork and the animals to care for and the garden and the housework. That isn't going to change. So *we* have to change—me and Frank and Andy and Maggie and even Grace. We have to learn to rely on ourselves."

A chill swept through her at the raw pain in his fierce explanation. He was right; she hadn't understood.

He dropped her arm with a muttered apology.

It took a few minutes for Pearl to regain her courage, for she had no intention of letting the matter drop. "I understand now why you're so angry about my helping out. Just the same, Maggie is too young. . ." She held up a hand as if to ward him off as he turned toward her. "Let me finish! Maggie is too young and inexperienced to take on all your mother's responsibilities yet. If I. . .that is, if you *let* me. . .help out for a bit, I can teach her some of the things your mother hadn't time to teach her."

He took so long to respond that she almost thought he wouldn't answer. When he did, there was no anger left in his voice, only regret. "Is she really frightened of me?"

Impulsively, she laid a hand on his arm. "She's only afraid of disappointing you, not that you'll punish her."

"When I saw that burn, I felt so guilty." His groan seemed to echo through her chest. "I'd never realized the things that could happen to her and Grace while we're out in the fields."

"They could happen even if you're home."

He looked up at the expanse of dark blue above them, where a handful of stars were beginning to peek through. "It seems the last few weeks I can't leave anyone I care about for even a few minutes without wondering whether I'll ever see them alive again."

"I'm sure that's only natural." She wished there were something more soothing to say.

"If it's been hard for me, it must be more difficult for my brothers and sisters, being younger. How could Miranda think I would cause them additional pain by leaving them now?"

Would his heart never heal from Miranda's betrayal?

"Do you agree with her, Pearl?"

Her head snapped up. "No! Of course not. Your family needs you."

A sigh whooshed out of him. "That's what I believe, too."

"Jason," she started cautiously, "what if you sold the farm? Could you care for the family in town on what you can earn as an architect?"

"Farms are going dirt cheap with the hard times the country's experiencing. If we could sell it, we'd barely make enough to pay off Dad's banknotes. Then, too, I'd like to keep the farm in case Frank or Andy wants it one day. Besides, I was only beginning as an architect—haven't proven myself yet. Certainly couldn't guarantee making enough to support five people."

"I only thought if there was a way you could stay in architecture and live in town, perhaps Miranda. . ."

"She objected to my family as well as my vocation." From the tautness in his voice, she knew this had hurt him more than anything else in Miranda's rejection.

He reached for her hand, squeezing her fingers so tightly she had to clamp her lips together hard to keep from crying out. "You're a good friend, always have been. I'm afraid I took advantage of that friendship tonight and let a lot of the anger and frustration that's built up in me the last few weeks tumble out on you. I'm sorry."

The niggling fear that their friendship had been lost in the recent happenings released. Her eyelids pressed tightly closed as she lifted a quick prayer of thanksgiving heavenward. "Our friendship is strong enough to withstand some onslaughts. You've forgiven a few faults in me over the years."

Lantern light revealed the tender smile in Jason's eyes as he squeezed her hand once more, not so hard this time.

The matter of her helping out on the farm hadn't been settled, and when they'd entered Chippewa City and were nearing her adoptive parents' home, she broached the subject again.

"I promised Maggie I'd help with the laundry in the morning." She hoped her tone said this was as natural as the sun rising.

His chuckle was a relief. "Sometimes you're so stubborn you make a Missouri mule look downright amiable by comparison. Guess I knew I was beaten before we even began discussing the matter."

She wished she'd known it!

"But I'll only agree to your helping until you've taught Maggie a few things," he continued before she had time to savor her victory.

"Yes sir," she replied meekly, not about to let him know how her heart was racing with joy and anticipation.

He laughed outright this time. Pulling up in front of her house, he bounced a broad, callused index finger off the tip of her nose. "I can see I'm in trouble now. You never act so humble without some mischief up your sleeve."

She grinned from the sheer joy of seeing laughter back in his eyes once more.

His arm slipped around her shoulder, giving her a brief hug. "Thanks for standing by me, friend," he said in a low, gruff voice. It was all she could do to keep from throwing her arms about his neck and telling him she would always stand by him.

Over Pearl's protests, Jason unhooked Angel and took her to the shed behind the house to brush, feed, and water while Pearl went inside and lit a lamp.

Looking down from the saddle when he was ready to leave, he grinned at her. "That apple pie sure hit the spot tonight. Think you could teach Maggie how to make that, right off?"

Without waiting for a reply, he turned his mount and started out of town. Pearl could hardly believe her ears when a whistled tune floated back to her. When she could no longer see his shadow or hear his whistle, she tilted her head back to take in the stars twinkling in the dark blue bowl of the sky.

"Thank You, Lord, for beginning to heal him."

CHAPTER 4

Jason Sterling leaned against a wooden support on the porch, hands stuffed into the back pockets of his jeans, and watched the rain pouring over the fields. It was coming down good and steady, but not hard enough to damage the unharvested crops. If he was as good at reading the weather as he thought, they wouldn't be out of the fields more than a day or two.

He was almost glad for the reprieve. The harvester needed repairing. So did his muscles. He lifted his shoulders, then rolled them back in a stretch, wincing. He'd grown soft the last couple years, at school and working in town.

The wheat was good and plump. Harvest was going full blast. The hay crop was already mostly garnered and barley reaped. His father would have been more than satisfied with him and his brothers. *Still,* he thought, *you can never count your money until the crop is completely harvested. Nature might have a surprise or two up her sleeve yet.*

Through the open windows, Pearl's clear voice floated out to him in a sweet hymn accompanied by the parlor piano. The tension melted from his body as she sang. She'd been helping out for two weeks now, and he'd often heard her singing as she worked.

He was glad he'd agreed to her coming out to help them. She'd been good for everyone. His chuckle blended with the patter of the rain and with Pearl's clear voice. "Agreed" to her coming! It would be easier to stop a tornado than to stop Pearl once she'd set her mind on something.

She'd always been that way. Once her brother, John, had tried to patiently convince her that girls did not go fishing. It had been impossible to persuade her, even when he and John had insisted she find her own nightcrawlers and learn to bait her own hook. The relish with which she had chased down the 'crawlers amused them. She hadn't liked putting the worms on hooks, but she'd set her small pink lips in a determined line and done it anyway. John had told him early in their friendship that their parents were gone. Jason had admired the way John looked out for Pearl, and the two boys had formed an unspoken pact to always keep her under their wings. He wasn't sure she still needed their protection.

Beat all how a girl who looked so sweet and fragile could be so tough underneath. He'd learned the fact years ago. It still amused him when one of the young men in town was deceived by her femininity. To look at her, she was all frills and lace and golden curls, yet in a difficult place, he'd as soon have her on his side as a band of hardened cowboys.

His smile died. Well, he was in a difficult place now, and she was right here helping out as he should have expected. He detested himself for wishing it was Miranda instead.

It's not the real Miranda I want beside me. Surprise ripped through him at the thought. It was true. The woman he wanted was the woman he'd believed Miranda to be, not the woman she'd actually become.

With a weary sigh that came from the very tips of his mud-covered boots, he pushed himself away from the wooden support. He couldn't afford to waste his energy in self-pity. A woman who wouldn't stand by the man she loved wasn't worth all that regret anyway.

He tugged off his boots at the kitchen door and crossed the room to the parlor. Apple butter bubbling on the back of the stove made his mouth water. It was only the second year the apple trees, which had been planted in the '80s had borne fruit. His mother had been so proud of those apples last year.

Leaning against the doorframe, he slipped his thumbs beneath the suspenders at his waist. It was Maggie playing the piano, studiously concentrating on the pages in front of her. Grace was asleep on the plush forest green sofa that matched the tasseled draperies, one arm curled around her doll and the other thrown out in abandonment. Pearl was in his mother's high-backed, upholstered spring rocker beneath the large hanging lamp with the rose-colored glass shade, mending one of his socks as she sang softly to Maggie's accompaniment. The homey scene eased the familiar tightness in his chest caused by thoughts of Miranda.

His mother had loved this room. He could still hear his father telling him that a farmer's wife had a hard life and deserved whatever beauty a husband could give her in return. The up-to-date furnishings had cost his father plenty, but he'd never complained. Between the modern home and conveniences and the farm implements purchased during the affluent eighties, the bank held a good-sized note for Jason and his brothers to work off.

"Sounds good, Maggie," he encouraged when the song ended. "But don't you think you should be helping Pearl with the mending?"

Maggie flushed and stood quickly, setting the round top of the piano stool in a spin.

"I asked her to play. The music relaxes me." Pearl's gaze met his, her blue eyes challenging although her tone was friendly.

Maggie bent over the never-empty tapestry mending basket beside Pearl's rocker. "I'm almost through with mending for the afternoon," Pearl told her cheerily. "Perhaps you'd check the pantry to see whether there's any of your mother's wonderful rhubarb sauce to have with the pound cake you made for supper."

"Yes ma'am." Maggie smiled. The smile disappeared as she edged past Jason with her eyes averted, and the change twisted something sharply inside him.

"Maggie!" She stopped at his call, turning around slowly, apprehension filling her face. Was she always going to be afraid of him, he wondered in frustration? "You play well. Rev. Conrad will be asking you to play for church services soon."

The grin she flashed him was his reward.

He settled into the overstuffed chair opposite Pearl, his head resting wearily against the lace tidy. Remembering his sweaty work clothes, he dropped to the hassock near the rocker instead. Even though his mother had insisted on using the parlor for the family sitting room, she never allowed them on the furniture in their field clothes.

Elbows propped against his knees, he plowed his hands through his hair. "Did it again, didn't I? Frightened Maggie. Thought things between us were almost back to normal."

Pearl glanced up from her mending. "Remember how fragile one's pride is at that age? Besides, your compliment went a long way toward healing any bruises your earlier words may have caused."

He rubbed a hand across his jaw. "Don't know how parents manage to discipline their children without losing their love altogether. I sure haven't mastered the art."

"You've only been a parent for six weeks, and Maggie's been a child for twelve years. You're doing fine, Jason."

He studied the pattern of the Brussels carpet. "You were right about us needing you. We were all so wrapped up in our grief that we didn't know how to smile or help each other anymore. You respected our loss but brought back some of the warmth the house had when Mom and Dad were with us." He cleared his throat, thick from emotion. She glanced up at the oil painting of his parents over the settee. "I was admiring this painting of them earlier. I'm so glad you have it to remember them by. Johnny has a small picture of our parents on their wedding day. Sometimes I stare at their likenesses, trying to remember what they were like, how they spoke, how they moved. I never succeed."

Her lips trembled before she caught her bottom lip between her teeth, and the sight caught at his heart. He slipped a hand over one of hers. *How can he be so incredibly self-centered?* He could kick himself for being so stupid. "I'd forgotten that you lost your parents when you were two. Being here—it must bring back a lot of painful memories."

"It's not the same as your loss. Only Mother died then. Father just left us."

He felt as well as heard the slight sigh that escaped her, and his stomach clenched at the thought of the pain she'd gone through as a child. It was impossible for him to understand a man abandoning his children, even if he believed it would be better for the children without him, as Pearl's father had believed.

She turned toward him with a bright little smile, and her brave cheerfulness made his voice gruff. "You make me realize how blessed we've been to have had our parents with us all these years. Been pretty wrapped up in self-pity, I guess."

Her soft fingers squeezed his where they still rested over her hand and mending. "It's only natural to grieve for what might have been."

At her nearness and gentle sympathy, he had a sudden urge to draw her into his arms to seek comfort for his recent losses and to comfort her for old ones. In all the years of their friendship, he'd never experienced such a longing, and the intensity of it pushed all thought of conversation from his mind as he stared at her in wonder.

Footsteps galloping down the stairway broke the silence. Frank burst into the room, stopping short at the sight of them. He brushed back the lock of his black hair that always insisted on dropping over the middle of his forehead and grinned at his older brother. "Forgot to tell you the big news I heard the other night at the Grange meeting. Chippewa City is going to build a combination town hall and opera house next spring. Thought you might want to submit plans for the building."

Jason's chest felt like a bull had stomped on it. "No."

"It's a great opportunity to show the town what you can do," Frank urged.

"I can't be a successful architect and run a farm at the same time." Wouldn't he love to try to design that building! Sometimes his fingers positively itched for a pencil when a new design formed in his head. He couldn't allow himself to dwell on the desire. He wouldn't be able to get back to his career anytime soon, maybe never.

"So you meant it when you moved back here. You're really going to give up your vocation, after Dad saw to it you received the education you needed." Frank bounced his fist off the wall beside him. "I suppose that means I won't be able to attend Windom Academy in Chippewa City this fall, either, even though we both know it's what Dad intended."

Jason wished Frank had chosen another time for this discussion, rather than bringing all the dirty laundry out in front of Pearl. "Not this fall, no."

Frank's jaw jutted out. "Dad was willing to chance it."

"He wasn't aware of the extent of what the newspapers are now calling the Great Economic Depression of 1893. Silver continues to fall; banks are closing all over the country. Saint Paul started something they call the Public Employment Bureau—their mayor is urging farmers to hire unemployed Saint Paul men," he snorted, "and that with wheat at the lowest price ever."

His brother's black eyes snapped. "Even with the price of wheat low, we're not going to starve. Dad was always one of the wealthiest farmers around. Does it make you feel powerful, keeping your tight little fist on the purse strings?"

Jason spread his palms against his thighs, trying to keep calm. "I haven't the experience Dad had running the farm. Best to set aside what money we can. Harvest isn't over; we don't know what the future might hold." He stood and reached for the newspaper on the table beside them, hoping Frank would drop the subject. "I'm going to drive into town with Pearl after supper. Would appreciate it if you'd get to work on that broken harvester."

"Why should I have to spend the evening working while you're out for an evening drive?"

Jason's hands settled on his hips. "That harvester needs to be fixed before we can get back in the fields. As for my evening drive, I'm not about to let Pearl head back alone after an afternoon of rain. You know what that can do to the roads."

Frank's square jaw tightened, and Jason groaned inwardly at the battle his brother insisted on waging. "You make all the decisions around here. I can dig a buggy out of the mud as well as you, big brother. Why shouldn't you be the one to repair the machinery while I enjoy Pearl's company?"

"Fine, have it your way! *You* can spend the evening riding around in the mud and rain!"

Pearl stepped between them with a palm toward each one. "Please! I can drive myself back."

"We've had this argument before. You don't drive home alone."

A whimper broke through Jason's words, and he felt a tug on his jeans. "Why are you yellin'? I don't like it when you yell."

His heart caught in his throat as he lifted Grace. "Sorry, Pumpkin. Didn't mean to wake you."

"You were loud." She laid a soft little hand on his stubbly cheek, her pink lips in a pout. "I don't want you to be mad."

Jason forced a smile. The things this five-year-old did to his heartstrings! He turned his face and kissed one of the tiny fingertips. "How could anyone be mad with you around, Pumpkin?"

He hugged her close. How it cut into his soul whenever he saw her upset! He was doing a lousy job as a parent. If God was going to put him in his parents' place, it would have been nice if He'd sent him a primer on how to do the job! Setting Grace down, he gave her a tap on the back. "Go wash up for supper."

"All wight!" She hurried into the kitchen, slightly wobbly yet from her nap.

He swung his attention back to Frank. "I'll work on the harvester, and you drive Pearl back to town."

Frank turned toward Pearl somewhat sheepishly, Jason thought. "Is that acceptable to you, Pearl?"

"I always enjoy your company, Frank. In any case, it doesn't seem I have much to say about my escorts, even as to whether I shall have any."

Jason met her belligerent gaze as evenly as possible. He was tired of all the silly disagreements. *Did everyone think it was easy to run this place, to make all the decisions, to be the person responsible for all the lives the farm touched?* It made him weary all the way to his bones, and he lifted a silent prayer for continued strength.

∽

Pearl stood against the wall of the station house, wishing there were lamps in the area. She should probably have let her parents take the horse-drawn bus home, but they deserved a warmer welcome when they'd been gone for three weeks. She rather hated to meet the night train. Tramps had broken into nine boxcars last week. Another night tramp had fired shots at passengers on the midnight train, then stolen potatoes and chickens waiting for shipment.

What would Jason think of her meeting the midnight train, which was infinitely more dangerous than traveling alone at night across a few miles of barren prairie. A chuckle rose in her throat at the thought.

Strange, but the railroad that the early settlers had hoped for and worked to make a reality, which brought growth to the town and prosperity to the farmers and merchants, was one of the largest causes of crime and pain in Chippewa City. Accidents among the railway workers and between trains and buggies kept her father and other area doctors busy.

Were the things one hoped for always that way? Never the way one thought they would be when realized? Always accompanied by unexpected problems?

Her thoughts were interrupted by the train roaring and wheezing into town, the huge lamp on the engine lighting its way, its wheels grinding against the track as it slowed to a stop. Black coal smoke settled over the people waiting on the wide plank platform.

Lantern light framed her mother on the top step of the train in her gray traveling suit with a fashionable hat on her silver-striped chestnut hair. A moment later Pearl's father joined her, and they descended to the platform. For an instant Pearl lost them in the crowd. Then pushing forward, she came face-to-face with them.

"Mother Boston!" She pressed her face against her mother's soft cheek. "Dr. Matt! It's so good to see you both again. I can't wait to hear all about the world's fair."

The doctor gave her a quick, tight hug, almost dislodging her smart hat with its feathers dyed to match her suit. "Reckon we'd like to hear what's happening with you first, young lady."

She laughed up at him. Goodness, she'd forgotten how tall he was! With his silvering blond hair and fair coloring, he could almost have been mistaken for the man who had given her and Johnny birth. "Nothing so exciting as Chicago and the world's fair."

"You and Boston wait here for me. I'll get the baggage."

"Howdy, Young Doc!" An old settler greeted Dr. Matt with the affectionate term by which everyone called him since he had first come to the area. She and Mother Boston exchanged smiles. The doctor was a well-loved man in town. She and Johnny were fortunate he and Boston had raised them.

He returned a few minutes later loaded down with bags, and they were soon on their way home. Pearl smiled broadly from the buggy's backseat. "Remember when you brought me and Johnny down to see the first train arrive in town back in '78? I thought the engine looked like a dragon from our storybooks!"

Dr. Matt didn't return her smile. "More serious dragons than that around, I'll wager."

"Matthew," Boston whispered urgently with a shake of her head, and Pearl wondered what in the world they were sending signals about.

"Did you see the Minnesota exhibits?" Pearl asked eagerly.

"Yep. The local elevator won a medal for its grain."

"That's wonderful!" It was quite an honor for the small town. She couldn't wait to tell Jason.

"Going to tell us what's been going on 'round here while we've been gone, young lady?"

"Well, the oil tank we just passed is new. There's one on each end of town now, to make it more convenient for the night marshall to fill the lamps. And new street lamps have been placed on the hill."

"What's been happening with *you*?"

Pearl shook her head, bewildered by his unusually stern tone. "What do you mean?"

"We've been hearing tales for the last thirty miles about you and young Sterling."

"Jason?"

He nodded sharply. "Yep. Boston and I trust you, but when we hear the same tale from three different people—and respectable citizens at that. . . ."

Pearl could feel her backbone stiffening. "I haven't done anything to set people's tongues wagging."

"So you haven't been spending time at the Sterling farm?"

"Well, yes. Yes, I have."

He pulled Angel up short beneath a street lamp, and both he and Boston turned to look at her. She felt blood flooding her face as she met their searching gazes.

"We're listening."

In the light of the gas lamp, she could see the concern, almost fear, in his eyes beneath the determination to hear her side of the story. Boston and Dr. Matt had always played fair with her and Johnny, always trusted them to be truthful, and she knew they would listen to her now.

"So you can see it's all innocent," she finished her story. "Jason needed help, and there wasn't anyone else to give it."

"Yes, he'd tried to find a hired girl," she answered Dr. Matt's question. "And, yes, Jason refused to allow her to go out to the farm at first. But when harvest was claiming all his time and Maggie and Grace couldn't keep up with everything. . ."

"What about Serena?" Mother Boston asked, referring to the hired Scandinavian farm girl who helped at their own home a few mornings each week.

"I asked if she could help, but she'd already hired out to another farmer for the hours she had free."

Dr. Matt urged Angel out of the light and toward the steep road that climbed the bluff to the prairie where their home was located. "Well, I can see you were just being bighearted, like Boston here. However, a girl has to watch out for her reputation. I don't want you going out there unchaperoned anymore. Three people mentioned your visits to us tonight. *Three!*"

"But. . ."

"Matthew is right," Boston added in her soft voice that still had a touch of an Eastern accent after eighteen years on the Minnesota prairie—and was responsible for the nickname her husband had given her. "You'll be of no use to Jason and his family if you ruin your reputation and besmirch his also. Believe me, dear, I know how tempting it is to try to help him, but you'll have to find a more discreet manner in which to do so."

"I can't simply walk away from him now. Neither of you would pay any attention to gossip if it meant not helping a friend in need."

In the moonlight she saw Matthew's lips tighten. "You know how we've always tried to avoid making demands of you and John, but I can see no other way. I refuse to allow you to return to the Sterlings' farm."

Fury filled her chest at the injustice, and her eyes stung from the heat of her anger. "They *need* me!"

Boston reached over the low leather seat to take her hand, and Pearl's gaze bored into hers. "Please, Mother Boston. . ."

"Matthew is right. Proper decorum won't allow your visits. We'll have to ask the Lord to help Jason and his family some other way."

"But. . ."

"Surely you don't think God incapable of helping them without you?"

Mother Boston's question was gentle, but her voice held a spark of laughter, and Pearl had to look away. Of course God could help them without her. It was the one argument she couldn't possibly win out against.

"No." The whispered answer hurt her throat.

It wasn't that she didn't want God to help Jason. But with an unflattering, humbling glimpse into her own heart, she realized that she didn't want God to find a way to help him without her.

CHAPTER 5

Pearl smoothed her hands over the skirt of her new, butter yellow gown as she stood beside the buggy on Main Street. Laughter and gay voices mingled with music from the dance in the new Rollefson building a few doors down. Excitement swirled through the evening breeze, spicy with the scent of autumn leaves. She took a shaky breath and greeted a young couple passing by.

It wasn't the music and the crowd that sent shivers tripping along her nerves, she admitted to herself. It was the knowledge that Jason would be here tonight. Only last evening she'd been at his home, yet it seemed a lifetime since she'd seen him. What would it be like if she did as Dr. Matt commanded and stayed away from the farmhouse altogether?

If she had any regard at all for her heart, she'd welcome the excuse to stay away and protect herself from heartbreak. Always before she'd thought of Jason as belonging to Miranda. Sharing Jason's struggles, knowing Miranda had rejected his marriage offer, she'd opened her dreams to what it would be like to share his life forever. Now that she'd let the hope of experiencing his love slip inside her heart, she didn't know how to push it back out.

Whatever was she going to do when Jason took a wife? Yes, she should run from all association with him. But she wouldn't, even though it meant defying Dr. Matt. With the knowledge came a clenching about her heart at the vision of pain to come.

"Haven't seen you since church last Sunday," a familiar voice said in her ear, and she turned eagerly to grasp her brother's hand.

"Johnny! Is Jewell doing well?"

A grin split his wide face beneath the hair that was as blond as her own. "She's doing fine."

"I must stop by and see her soon." A sliver of guilt poked at her. Jewell, as was proper, only left home to attend church now that she was eight months along with their first child. Usually Pearl stopped by to visit her every couple days. She hadn't been there since she had begun helping at Jason's farmstead.

Johnny was nodding. "She'd like that. I wouldn't have come tonight, but she nearly pushed me out the door. Said to be sure to come back with all the news of the neighbors, knowing everyone and their brother would be here tonight."

"Did Billy come?" she asked, referring to the orphaned eleven-year-old boy Johnny and Jewell had taken into their home when they married two years earlier.

"Not tonight." He crossed his arms and watched the passersby as he said with an exaggerated attempt to be casual, "Boston and Dr. Matt stopped this afternoon. Dr. Matt wondered why I hadn't been watching out for you better while they were in Chicago." He glanced sidewise at her.

Heat flooded her cheeks. "I haven't done anything improper."

The warmth in his gaze calmed her somewhat. "I know that. But you know how some people will imagine the worst and glory in the telling of it. Boston and Dr. Matt are only concerned for your reputation."

She nodded glumly.

He glanced over her shoulder and waved. Turning, she saw Jason coming toward them with Grace in his arms. Fireworks seemed to go off in her stomach. Dressed for the dance, his shirt blazing white against his tan, Jason looked better than ever.

Johnny and Jason visited with a comfortable familiarity while Grace talked excitedly with her. She noticed Jason studying the new two-and-a-half-story brick building where the dance was being held as they talked. Was he admiring the design or thinking what he would have done differently?

"Good to see a number of brick buildings going up in town," she heard him say over Grace's chatter. "A lot safer in case of fire. Would hate to see Chippewa City lose most of its business section, like nearby Canby did recently—twenty-three business places gone overnight."

Johnny, a volunteer fireman, nodded. "Wouldn't mind seeing electrical service supplied to the town either. It was an exploding lamp that caused the Canby fire. On the other hand, when lightning struck just fifteen miles away in Granite Falls last month and lights burst in almost every home on the electrical service, there were no major fires."

Grace demanded her attention once more, and Pearl didn't hear any more of the men's conversation until the group decided to enter the dance.

Even with the cool August air and the open windows, it was hot from the swarm of people. Men's bay rum cologne battled with women's toilet water in fragrances of lavender, violet, and rose, and both competed with the always present cigars. Rustling gowns splashed the room with color.

Jason's laughter over a comment of Johnny's cut off sharply, his face suddenly taut. Following his shocked gaze, Pearl caught her breath. *Miranda!*

She couldn't take her eyes off her friend. Her escort, Grant Tyler, had Miranda's hand tucked intimately in the crook of his arm, and his possessive manner disgusted Pearl. Miranda's pointed chin was tilted up, and she smiled boldly into his face. She'd never seen Miranda with any escort but Jason, and Grant Tyler was the last man in Chippewa City she would have suspected Miranda would agree to see.

Grant must be five years older than she and Miranda. He'd come to Chippewa City two years ago and opened a hotel—a fine one. He dressed more elegantly than most men in town, always wearing flashy vests crossed by a gold watch chain. He loved to spin that chain while watching the ladies as they passed his business establishment. Pearl always thought his smile had an oily quality to it, beneath the carefully groomed mustache that was as shiny as freshly applied shoeblack. *How could Miranda refuse Jason only to turn up with this. . .this dandy?*

She darted a quick glance at Jason out of the corner of her eye. His jaw was rigid.

He set his little sister down carefully. "Will you watch Grace for a few minutes, John?" Without waiting for an answer, he took Pearl's hand. "Dance with me, Miranda."

It wasn't a question, and he didn't seem to realize he'd called her by his former fiancée's name. Pearl followed him onto the dance floor, her throat too swollen from holding back the sobs that suddenly filled her chest to protest.

The band was playing a waltz, and Jason drew her stiffly into his arms. He smelled of shaving soap, and his white shirt of fresh starch. She remembered ironing the shirt the day before, and a queer little tightening twisted in her stomach. It had seemed such an intimate thing to do for him. Now here she was, dancing with him, her face only inches from his broad chest covered by that same shirt, and he was thinking only of Miranda.

She stumbled, and Jason caught her, drawing her tight against his chest to prevent her from falling. "I'm sorry," she apologized at his look of surprise. "I've never danced a waltz before."

If he'd asked her to do him the honor of a dance, as was proper, she would have reminded him that her parents considered the waltz too intimate for unmarried couples. But he hadn't asked. He'd only assumed that, of course, she would dance with him, grabbed at her as a shield against the embarrassment of Miranda showing up with another man.

He grimaced. "Sorry. I forgot." The steel bands of his arms relaxed, and he guided her from the floor, his hand gentle against her back.

When they reached Johnny and Grace, the little girl held up both arms to Jason. "Dance with *me!*"

Pearl thought his smile looked forced as he lifted Grace. "I'll be honored to dance with the prettiest girl here."

Grace's tiny teeth flashed with pleasure.

Jason glanced over her shoulder at Johnny. "I'm sorry," he said through tight lips. "Don't know what I was thinking, dancing with Pearl like that."

Johnny nodded solemnly.

Frank slipped up beside her as one of the townspeople claimed Johnny's attention. "Must be hard on Jason, Miranda being here with Grant and all."

"Yes." She didn't want to talk about it. It seemed disloyal to Jason. He wouldn't want people pitying him.

"Never thought anything would come between those two. Can almost forgive him for being so touchy lately."

"It's awfully warm in here. Perhaps you'd accompany me to get some punch?" Her diversion was successful. Frank took her elbow, and they worked their way through the crowd to a table that had been set up to serve refreshments. After picking up their punch cups, they moved slowly about the edge of the dance floor, greeting a couple here, a group there. Scandinavian and German accents mixed with "American" accents to form a music that rivaled that of the band.

"Amy!"

Pearl heard Frank's strangled whisper at the same time she saw the willowy girl in a pink gown. Impulsively, she reached out to give her a quick hug. Next to Miranda, Amy was her dearest friend.

"I stopped by your house a few times this last week. Where have you been keeping yourself?" Amy asked in her soft voice.

The sly look that tall, skinny Ed Ray, Amy's escort, slanted at Frank did not escape Pearl, and anger heated her cheeks. She looked him straight in the eye. "I've been helping out the Sterlings. It's been difficult for Maggie, taking care of everything, with their parents gone and the men in the fields."

"Oh, I do wish you'd told me! Perhaps I could have helped." Her instant, sincere response poured oil on Pearl's anger, though she noticed the distaste with which Ed greeted her words. Evidently he didn't care for the idea of Amy helping at the Sterlings.

Before she could reply, Amy reached a hand in a lacy glove to gently touch Frank's hand. It lingered on his no longer than was proper, but Pearl noticed the flush that rushed across Frank's face. "I was so sorry to hear of your loss. I've been remembering you and your family in my prayers."

"Thank you, Miss Amy," Frank murmured, his dark eyes on hers.

Ed's hand closed over Amy's elbow, drawing her away from them slightly. "Yes, Sterling, sorry to hear about your parents. Wouldn't wish it on anyone. Let's dance, Amy."

She smiled at them over her shoulder as Ed led her away.

"I understand Mr. Ray is attending Windom Academy again this fall," Pearl said, attempting to make conversation.

Frank stared broodingly after the retreating couple. "Yes. He plans to go on to the university after that to get a law degree."

She remembered his insulting look and thought she wouldn't want such a man representing the law. Why was gentle Amy, with her high ideals, seeing him?

"Some people have all the luck." Frank's bitter tone surprised her. She assumed he was thinking of Jason's refusal to allow him to attend Windom Academy. *Or perhaps,* she thought, noticing his gaze still following Amy and Ed, *perhaps he is thinking of Amy.*

"What do you think of Miranda Sibley turning up on Grant Tyler's arm?" The words seemed to scream at Pearl and Frank as they passed a group of young men, although they were spoken no louder than any of the other comments and were not directed at them. Indeed, the speaker didn't seem aware that they were in the vicinity. Pearl and Frank exchanged glances of dismay.

"Can't blame a lady for accepting the attentions of an up-and-coming young man like Tyler. Too bad Sterling left his architectural practice to move back to the farm. What can a farmer offer her after all?"

The others in the group nodded agreement, and indignation rose in Pearl's throat. "Foolish men! Don't they know that it's farmers who keep this town and all the towns around alive?"

Frank's lips were drawn in a line so tight they might have been stitched together. "They're just repeating what they've heard."

"Dr. Matt says when the town was young, the farmers and townspeople were like a family, excited to build up this new land together. Now they act like enemies."

"Not all of them, but too many," he agreed. "Dad thought it was because the farmers are primarily Scandinavian immigrants, not Easterners like Dad and most of the townspeople. Did you read the letter in the newspaper written by a local farmer? Says the townspeople wouldn't be crying hard times so loudly if they lived like most of the farmers—taking their children out of school and putting them to work when they need money. It's those farmers' children who lose out in the end. And just when they need to know more than ever about new farming methods and improved machinery."

His vehemence surprised her. No wonder he was so upset at not attending Windom Academy.

"Some say if a man doesn't leave the farm for an education and a profession in town, he doesn't have any future at all," he continued. "Perhaps they're right. Perhaps that's why Miss Amy is with Ed Ray. Perhaps no woman thinks there's a future with a farmer."

The hopelessness in his tone dismayed her. "Frank Sterling, no woman of value would give up a man because he's a farmer."

"Are you speaking of Miranda?"

She whirled about at Jason's question, dismay flooding her. When had he come up behind them?

"We weren't speaking specifically of Miranda." Annoyance and surprise edged Frank's statement.

Jason's eyes probed Pearl's, searching their depths in the flickering lantern light. *Is he trying to decide whether Frank and I are telling the truth,* she wondered, returning his gaze steadily. "It seems I owe you a second apology." His words were soft, and she felt their sincerity.

Before she could respond, Jason strode away.

Pearl's hand slipped to her neck. She could feel the pulse beating there, fast as a typist beating out letters on one of those noisy little machines. Why did Jason have to overhear her comment? Surely he must feel that she'd insulted Miranda personally, even though she hadn't mentioned Miranda's name. First, she overheard Miranda refuse him, and now, he overheard her effectively say that Miranda was not a woman of value. It was as though she was determined to earn his scorn.

"Hey Sterling! What's this we hear 'bout you gettin' a new little filly out to your farm?"

Pearl's blood ran cold at the sneer in Ed Ray's voice as he called to Jason from the group of young men. She knew instinctively he was referring to her.

Amy was nowhere to be seen. *Perhaps another gentleman has claimed a dance with her,* Pearl thought irrelevantly.

Beside her, Frank muttered something she couldn't understand. Pushing his empty punch cup into her hands, he started toward the men.

Jason spoke to Ed in a low voice, but though she strained, she couldn't hear his words.

"What do I mean?" the heckler asked with a laugh. "Why, that pretty little music teacher. Don't have more than one lady calling on you regular, do you?"

Dread rooted her to the spot.

CHAPTER 6

She's just been helping out, you say? And what kind of favors does Miss Wells do for you boys?" the awful voice rang out again. It seemed to Pearl that everyone in the vicinity had stopped to listen.

Crass laughter put wings on her feet. Dropping the punch cups heedlessly, she grasped her skirt and rushed toward the group. If they were going to insult her, they could do so to her face.

She gasped and stopped short at the sight of Frank drawing back his fist and aiming it at Ed's surprised face. Jason shoved him aside before he could land his blow and grasped Ed's narrow lapels. Every plane and line of Jason's face were rigid as he demanded in a frighteningly even voice, "I'd take back those words if I were you."

Suddenly Dr. Matt was there, looking positively spectral in the lamplight. His normally laughing eyes were like volcanoes filled with fire and fury. He grabbed tight to Jason's arm, and his voice had the deceptive softness of the sheath that covers a hunter's deadly blade.

"Now Sterling, you don't want to hit these *gentlemen*. I'm sure they were just about to apologize for their mistaken comments. Isn't that right?"

Embarrassed, the young men couldn't mutter their apologies fast enough. Jason's hold on Ed's lapels slowly released, and Ed quickly followed the others in their retreat.

Would their reaction have been different if the adoptive father of the woman they were deriding had not been a prominent citizen like Dr. Matt? she wondered. He had come to Chippewa City twenty years ago, when the town was new and struggling. Like the other old settlers, he was held in awe by later citizens—the more so because of the community's love for the man who had given so much of himself to help their families over the years.

Jason's hands were balled into fists, she noticed as Dr. Matt released his arm. To think Jason had been intending to fight those—those poor excuses for men because of the statements they were making about her! Her stomach turned over at the thought. He and Frank against so many. They could have been seriously hurt because of her.

She walked toward them slowly, aware that Dr. Matt was staring at her but refusing to return his gaze. Disappointment for her loss of reputation would be in his face, and she didn't want to see it. The tip of her tongue ran lightly over her suddenly dry lips. She stopped in front of the two men, but it was Jason's gaze she met, quaking. Her hands wanted to grip her skirt, to grip anything to give her added courage. She made her fingers hang quietly at her sides. "I'm sorry."

"You've no reason to apologize. You've done nothing wrong. It's those men's minds that are evil. I should have realized what I was exposing you to when I allowed you to help us out."

He turned to Dr. Matt, straightening his broad shoulders and looking him in the eye with that steady gaze of his. "I'm the one to apologize, sir, to Pearl and to you. I should have had more sense. She's a fine woman. I assure you I've made no unseemly advances toward her in the time she's been helping us, and I have only the utmost respect for her. I should never have willingly exposed her to such vile speculations and comments." He swallowed hard, and Pearl saw his Adam's apple jerk. "If any man put my daughter in such a position, I expect I'd want to wallop the tar out of him."

Pearl felt her eyes widening. Why didn't Dr. Matt tell Jason he'd never consider any such thing? She wanted to speak, but her throat seemed paralyzed.

She'd never seen Dr. Matt's face so angry. What thoughts were going on beneath his scowl?

After what seemed hours, his scowl softened slightly. "I admit the thought of a thrashing crossed my mind, but I think we can get by without it."

She heard a soft *whoosh* and realized Jason had been holding his breath waiting for Dr. Matt's response.

"Thank you, sir. I will never again put your daughter in such an untenable position. You have my word."

Dr. Matt held out his hand, and Jason met it with his own in a solemn handshake. "I've asked her not to go to your farm again, but I appreciate your taking the decision out of my hands."

Both men seemed to have forgotten she was there. Pearl took an impulsive step nearer. "Your family still needs assistance, Jason. I want to continue helping."

Disbelief washed over Jason's face. He opened his mouth to reply, then snapped it shut. A second later he spoke, his voice rigidly under control. "I appreciate your good-hearted desire to help my family, Miss Wells, but it won't be necessary."

His cold dismissal sent chills down her spine.

Matthew seemed to relent slightly at the distress in Pearl's face. He rested his large hand on her shoulder. "The fact is, Boston and I did discuss the possibility of Boston accompanying Pearl on her trips out to your place until you could arrange to hire someone to help with the housework and all."

Pearl gave a little gasp. *They hadn't told her! What a wonderful solution!*

Matthew's brows met again. "But in light of what happened here tonight, I don't think that will be possible."

"But. . . !"

"Of course not, sir." Jason's smooth acceptance interrupted Pearl's protest. "It was kind of you and Mrs. Strong to even consider such a thing. Mighty kind."

He nodded at Pearl, and her heart ached at the stranger's face he wore. "I appreciate the help you've given more than I can say. Good night."

Dr. Matt's hand slid gently around her arm. "Come, dear. I'll walk with you to the buggy and then find Boston, so we can go home."

She stumbled once, walking as she was with her head turned over her shoulder so she could watch Jason. How could her desire to help Jason be turned into something so terrible by those young men? It seemed everything she did regarding Jason turned into a disaster lately.

∞

Anger seethed in Jason's chest as he walked through the dance hall. How could he have been so blind? He should have realized what would happen with Pearl coming out to his home daily. It would have been different if one of his parents were alive; their presence would have protected her. But as it was—he knew men's minds, should have known what people would say. What if he'd destroyed her reputation for good? To think it took something like this to make him aware! *Young men publicly ridiculing her, and she and her father there to hear it.*

His gaze darted about the room. He'd had more than enough "fun and relaxation" for one evening. He just wanted to find his family and start home.

Where was Frank? He'd been beside him facing that disgusting crowd outside. *When had he left?* He moved slowly about the room, but after an entire trip around it, he still hadn't located him. Heading for the door, he passed Dr. Matt, still looking for his wife.

Outside again he looked up and down the street, vainly hoping for a sight of Frank. Rows of buggies, wagons, and horses lined each side as far as he could see. People from the dance lingered in front of the building, getting some cool air.

He wandered a few feet down the plank walk, wondering where to look next, his patience growing thinner by the minute.

A scream tore through the night. *Pearl!* He raced toward the place he'd seen Dr. Matt's buggy before the dance, his shoes pounding on the wooden planks. Horses pranced and whinnied nervously, rocking buggies. A pistol shot rang out, and dread scorched through him. *Please, Lord. . .*

If only there were a lamp in this part of the street! He was vaguely aware of feet beating behind him. Another scream pierced the darkness, this time masculine.

A couple fell from the tangle of horses and buggies onto the walk, struggling wildly. Jason leaped for them, tearing the larger figure away and throwing him against the wall of a store.

"He has a gun!"

He saw the pistol glint in the attacker's hand at the same time he heard Pearl's warning. He caught the man's arm and threw it against the wall. The weapon clattered to the walk. Jason braced his body against the man, holding him captive, ignoring the oaths spewing from him on rancid breath.

In a moment other men from the dance were surrounding them. Jason gladly turned the tramp over to them, eager to see for himself whether Pearl had been harmed.

Someone lit one of the buggy's lanterns, and Jason's heart spun crazily at the sight of Pearl's torn dress and dirt-smudged face. She was assuring others that she was all right, but he pushed through them and grasped her arms, needing to prove it was true.

Her eyes sparked with anger, not the tears he'd been afraid he would see. She clutched the buggy whip in one hand. "Are you sure you're all right?" His voice shook.

"Yes, but. . . Jason, he was going to take the buggy, and—and Angel! I couldn't let him take Angel!"

He fought a losing battle with a smile. "Of course not."

"He didn't see me in the buggy at first. When he took Angel's harness and started to lead her into the street, I took this." She held up the buggy whip. "And jumped down. He had a p—pistol, and I hit his arm with the handle of the whip. I—I didn't know how to use the other end." A small laugh escaped her. "Haven't I been telling you I can take care of myself?"

Amusement fled. Relief fueled anger. "You could have been killed! No horse is worth risking your life!"

"I couldn't let him take Angel!"

He pulled her into his arms, exasperation flooding his chest. "I can't believe you took such a foolish chance," he whispered fiercely against her neck. "Thank the Lord you're safe!"

"Sterling!"

Jason started at Dr. Matt's bellow and felt a tremor run through Pearl. He released her immediately, allowing his hands to stop at her waist only long enough to steady her.

The crowd who had formed had been concerned with the tramp and been ignoring the couple. Now they turned their attention to Jason and the Strongs, curious.

Pearl quickly explained the situation to Dr. and Mrs. Strong, needing to begin again when middle-aged, Norwegian Sheriff Amundson arrived moments later. It didn't take long for the sheriff to haul the tramp off to the jail beside the large schoolhouse on the bluff.

Dr. Matt's anger diminished when he discovered Jason had captured the tramp, but Jason knew he wasn't completely forgiven for embracing Pearl in public.

When he returned to the dance to again look for Frank, he realized that the terror he'd felt for her had left him badly shaken. Or perhaps it was the relief of knowing she wasn't harmed.

Or the way she'd trembled in his arms and rested against him so trustingly. *Foolish thought!*

Still, the memory lingered. And when Miranda moved into his line of vision, laughing at something Grant Tyler said as they waltzed past, Jason's heart didn't miss a beat.

It was two hours before Frank stumbled into the hall. His eyes were unnaturally bright, and his breath smelled like a still. Jason helped him to their wagon in disgust. Just what he needed on top of everything else—a drunken brother. He'd never known Frank to drink before. Why did he have to begin now? Between that and the episode with Ed Ray, the Sterling family name was going to be mud in town after tonight.

∞

Pearl looked about at the ripe golden wheat on either side of the dusty road. Farmers were out in force today. Threshing machines hummed and whirred as numerous teams of weary draft horses circled. Chaff filled the air. Prairie chickens were everywhere, snuggling close to the wheat and wild grass or bursting into the sky in a brown rush of wings that startled Angel every time.

Almost to Jason's farm, Pearl leaned forward slightly to glide a hand down Angel's neck. Her heart beat quicker with every passing mile. Other than church last Sunday, she hadn't seen him in the two weeks since the dance.

She'd missed him and his family horribly. *Mostly him,* she admitted. She'd tried to pray for him and his family whenever he came to mind, instead of dwelling on the yearning for him that seemed a constant part of her now. When the prayers were done, he lingered in her thoughts in spite of her efforts to rid them of him.

The feel of his arms about her the night of the dance, of his breath warm on her neck, would steal through her other thoughts again and again. Working with her music students didn't keep him out of her head for long. With Jewell's baby due soon, she'd spent much of her free time helping her sister-in-law with errands that were far too heavy for a woman in her condition. Even then her thoughts would stray to Jason.

After his order to stay away from the farmstead, she didn't expect him to be glad to see her. He'd be less so when he heard the reason for her visit.

Angel wanted to turn down the lane to the farmstead, knowing oats and cool water waited there. Pearl urged her on and, a few acres farther, pulled her to a stop at the edge of a field where some men were working. Was Jason among them?

It was only a couple minutes before the men caught sight of her. One walked toward her, the wheat bending gracefully before him. It was Jason, she saw as he drew near, and her courage almost failed her. She slid off Angel's back before she could turn the horse and hurry away.

Grasshoppers jumped against her brown divided skirt, but she paid them no mind. She played anxiously with Angel's reins, wrapping the leather around her hands and unwrapping it again, watching Jason come closer.

He stopped a few feet from her and nodded a greeting. He smelled just as she'd remembered he did when he came in from the fields—of kerosene and sweat and rich earth.

His gaze was studying her face, every inch of it, as if he'd never seen her before. It didn't help her fleeing courage to have him watching her like that.

He took a step closer, and his tone was unexpectedly gentle. "Is something wrong?"

The concern in his eyes made her stomach turn over.

"It's Miranda," she blurted out. "She's engaged to marry Grant Tyler."

CHAPTER 7

Jason's feet seemed to have grown into the ground, as surely as the roots of the crops in his field. *Miranda actually engaged to someone else! It didn't seem possible.*

"I see."

He lifted his hat, wiped his gritty forearm across his sweaty brow, and ran a hand through his hair, giving himself time to absorb Pearl's news.

"I—I didn't want you to hear of it from town gossip or. . .or something."

Did she think he was going to crumble under the news? He reached out absently to brush a stray lock of her blond hair behind her ear where the fragrant prairie breezes couldn't catch it for the moment.

She'd risked her father's anger and her reputation in order that he would be prepared when faced publicly with Miranda's engagement. Strange, but the engagement seemed a small thing compared to this sacrifice of Pearl's for him. He couldn't seem to stop looking at her. Dark lashes silhouetted against her creamy skin framed her wide eyes. He had to swallow twice before he could speak, and then his voice sounded even to him as though it came from a cave.

"Thank you."

She nodded and leaned slightly against Angel, her hand against the horse's neck as though to steady herself.

"How is Maggie?"

Had his touch caused that breathlessness?

"Fine. Her cooking has improved considerably with your teaching."

Her smile seemed a bit feeble. "And Grace?"

Grace was another story. "She's started having nightmares. Bad ones. 'Most every night she wakes up at least once, screaming at the top of her lungs. Doesn't want any of us out of her sight during the day."

"Isn't there anything you can do?"

"Nothing we've tried has worked. Says she's afraid we'll go away and never come back, like the folks." *And like Pearl,* but he wasn't going to burden her with that knowledge. It wasn't her fault she wasn't here every day.

"I'll be praying for her. And your brothers?"

"At least they aren't having nightmares." He shrugged and tried to give a nonchalant grin.

"I've heard some rumors about Frank. . . ."

"If they're about his drinking, they're true. Don't seem to know what to do about that any more than I do Grace's nightmares."

"I'm sorry."

He was sorry, too. Seemed he was failing right and left at taking care of his family. His father would be mightily disappointed in him if he knew.

"I'd like to stop up at the house and say hello to everyone, but I'd best be getting back to town."

He nodded, wishing he had the right to ask her to stay awhile longer. But he'd promised her adoptive father he'd never do anything to hurt her reputation again, and he meant to keep that promise.

He watched as Pearl and Angel disappeared down the road between the wheat, barley, and corn that covered the prairie between his place and town. She'd thought he would be upset with her for telling him about Miranda and Grant Tyler; it was as plain as the turned-up little nose on her round little face.

His lack of emotion at her news surprised him. There was a time when he couldn't imagine his life without Miranda in it. It had only been a month since she'd turned him down. The longest month of his life, though not entirely because of her. He'd hardly thought of her since the dance. Only his pride had been hurt that night, not his heart. Until then, Miranda had never entered a social function on any man's arm but his or her father's.

He should have realized months ago that Miranda's feelings were changing. Whenever he'd brought up the subject of their future together, she'd become evasive. Her gaze had begun to follow other young men, particularly some of the strangers from the East who were attending the local Windom Academy.

The glimpse at Miranda's cold, selfish heart the night he proposed had destroyed the love he'd thought he had for her. It was as if she was an old habit he'd overcome. Miranda wasn't the same person she used to be, no doubt about it. She'd become someone else—someone he didn't love.

Pearl hadn't changed, except to become more of what she'd always been. More loyal, more idealistic, more beautiful. She was everything he'd wanted and expected Miranda to become.

The way she'd pitched in and helped around the house and garden—well, his family had fallen in love with her strong, cheerful spirit. Each of them complained over her absence.

He missed her, too. When he looked up a bit ago and saw her sitting atop Angel at the edge of the field, he'd thought for a moment he was daydreaming. He'd just been thinking how empty the house was without her welcoming smile when he came in from the fields.

He missed talking over little incidents of the day while he saw her home at night. He missed the comfort of knowing she was watching over his sisters and the house while he and his brothers took care of the fields and animals.

Again and again over the last two weeks, pictures of her in his home filled his mind. Standing over the cookstove, darning his socks, reading to Grace, laughing at his jokes at the dinner table, her eyes meeting his in a shared smile over the tops of his brothers' and sisters' heads. She'd given him strength and encouragement and the belief that eventually life was going to be good again— just by being there, standing by all of them, and being herself. And the terror he'd felt the night of the dance when he realized she was in danger still had the power to tighten his stomach.

He rubbed the palms of his hands briskly over his face, barely noticing the bristles of his evening whiskers or the smell of the earth and wheat. Why, he loved her! Loved his best friend's little sister, the tagalong who had followed him and John around as a child, and later accompanied him and Miranda more times than he could count.

"I love her." He said the words out loud, tasting the wonder of them on his lips.

His eyes followed the road down which Pearl had disappeared. He knew she cared for him, but as a friend or older brother. Could he possibly win the love he wanted from her—the love of a woman? Or would any attempt destroy the special friendship they already shared?

⚭

"You're a fool, Sterling," Jason admonished himself under his breath the following evening, knocking on the screen door of Pearl's home. "The world's biggest fool, that's what you are."

He was glad it was Mrs. Strong and not Dr. Matt who answered. After the fiasco at the dance, he wasn't certain Dr. Matt would look kindly on his desire to court Pearl. He declined Mrs. Strong's invitation to step inside while she went to find Pearl, electing to stay on the porch out of Dr. Matt's way.

He ran two fingers beneath his stiff white collar. It sure was tight.

Trying to keep his freshly shined boots from clunking too loudly on the narrow wooden floorboards, he paced nervously. What if she flat out told him she wouldn't allow him to court her?

No, she wouldn't do that. They'd been friends for eight years. Good friends. She had to care for him, and a lot, or she wouldn't have been helping out at his farm, or have argued with Dr. Matt, even after Ed Ray's disgusting comments, or have come out yesterday to tell him about Miranda and Grant, or. . .

"Good evening."

He whirled around. By Henry, she was more beautiful than he'd remembered. Her face glowed above her soft pink dress.

"Are you all right, Jason?"

With a start, he realized that he hadn't even said hello. He was acting like he'd never seen a girl before! "Hello." He swung the hat he'd been fiddling with toward the white wooden glider at one end of the porch. "Could we talk awhile?"

She preceded him to the glider, sitting down with a grace that made him all the more aware of her femininity. As if he needed a reminder! The lavender fragrance she wore contributed to the breakdown of his defenses. He slid his free hand down over his striped dress pants to wipe away the perspiration. He hadn't been this nervous since—he couldn't recall ever being this nervous.

He yanked his gaze away from hers. If he wasn't careful, he'd blurt out his love for her with no preamble. That would welcome a rejection for certain. He'd lost his parents, his career, the girl he'd once loved—his heart was too bruised to face loss again so soon.

"We've been friends a long time." The words came out in a squeaky voice that made him feel twelve years old again.

"Yes. Ever since you saved my life."

He darted a glance at her. She caught it and gave him a little smile. He forgot what he was going to say and stared at her until he felt foolish. Had her eyes always been such a rich shade of blue?

She looked down at her lap. "How is your family?"

"Fine." He didn't want to discuss his family. He wanted to talk about his feelings for her and find out if there was any hope of her returning his love. But he couldn't, not yet. Not without chasing her away before he even began trying to win her love. Maybe he should just say plain out that he wanted to court her. And then. . .

"You're lucky to have each other to lean on, with your parents gone."

"Yes, I suppose we are." He snorted softly. "I'm not doing such a good job of taking care of them. Frank is always belligerent, and now he's drinking every chance he gets. Maggie can't keep up with the house and garden, though she's improved after your instruction." He set his hat on the porch railing. Wouldn't be a brim left on it by the time he went home if he didn't stop rolling it up. "Fact is, the girls seem to need me more often than I can be available, and half the time, I don't know how to help them when I'm there."

"You're doing more for them than you realize, I'm sure." Her hand rested softly on his arm in a comforting gesture, and a bolt of energy scrawled through him.

He slipped his own hand over hers, playing his fingers over her soft skin.

I love you, Pearl. The words repeated over and over in his mind, and it was all he could do to keep from saying them aloud. He could tell by her tiny gasp that she was startled by his caressing touch. His declaration of love would frighten her even more. At the very least, she'd think he mistook his feelings because of his grief or that he was interested in her only because he was on the rebound from Miranda.

She cleared her throat, and he lifted his gaze to her face, only inches away from his in the fading twilight.

"I wish I could help your family, Jason."

"They all miss you. They need you."

Her lashes dropped, hiding her eyes from view. He wished she'd look at him again. He couldn't seem to get enough of her eyes tonight.

The words tumbled out before he could stop them. "*I* need you. Marry me, Pearl."

CHAPTER 8

M arry him! Surely she hadn't heard him correctly.

But the brown eyes with the golden lights that had been dear to her for so many years were real, pleading with her. Her free hand slipped to the high lace collar of her pink organdy gown. "I—I don't understand."

The glider stopped, and Jason turned to face her squarely, his hands on her shoulders. "I hadn't intended to blurt it out like that. I meant to ask to court you properly. But now that it's out in the open. . . I wouldn't ask if I thought there was a chance you were in love with someone else. You *don't* love anyone else, do you?"

"No." There'll never be anyone but Jason!

One hand cupped her cheek, and she cautiously leaned her head into it, glorying in his gentle touch. "You're certain, Jason?" Her voice trembled.

"Absolutely. We've always been good friends. We like each other, respect each other, share a commitment to keeping Christ first in our lives. We'd be good together."

"Yes." Did he honestly think she needed to be argued into marrying him? A smile hovered on her lips.

His grin filled his face, and something she'd never seen before sparked in his eyes, taking her breath. His hands cradled her face, making it impossible to look away from him. "Does that mean you'll marry me?"

She wondered if her smile was as wide as his. "Yes."

He took a deep breath, and its shakiness made her feel humble. Did he care for her so much? She ached to speak her love for him, but dared not unless he spoke first. "I wasn't expecting. . . I mean. . . You've always loved Miranda. We've only been friends."

Silence hung between them until she didn't think she could bear it any longer. One of his hands slipped to cover hers where they clasped in her lap. His skin was calloused and cut from working with the wheat, but even so she welcomed his touch.

He began to say something, then stopped and cleared his throat. Why, he was as nervous as she was! The thought brought a smile. She'd never seen him nervous before. Always he seemed so sure of himself. It was one of the things she admired in him. But to think he was nervous at proposing to her made her feel tender toward him, and she caressed the back of his hand with her thumb.

"You're right; we've only been friends. I want you to be my wife, but I'll not force my. . .attentions on you."

Something deep within her froze. He wasn't asking her to marry him because he loved her.

How was it possible to hurt so deeply when she felt completely empty inside? She made herself look him full in the face, hoping he wouldn't see her disappointment, willing her voice to be steady. "I understand. A friendly marriage. To look after your home and family."

Something flickered in his eyes and was gone. Was it regret? Surely not. She was being fanciful.

"Yes. A friendly marriage."

"Are. . .are you trying to use me to hurt Miranda?"

He touched her cheek again, caressing it lightly with his knuckles. "No. I need you."

His words were barely a whisper, and the urgency in them made her want to reach out to comfort him, but she couldn't move.

"Do you want to change your mind?"

He'd said he needed her. To turn him down would be unthinkable! "No."

"Sunday."

"What?"

"Let's get married Sunday."

"But that's only two days away!"

"Do you want a big wedding?"

Of course she did. Every girl she knew wanted a big wedding. But if he wanted to be married Sunday, that settled it. "Sunday will be fine. That is, is it possible to purchase the license and arrange for Uncle Adam to marry us by then?" She was amazed she could even consider such practical things.

"The license will be no problem, and I can't imagine Rev. Conrad not finding time to marry his favorite niece."

They talked for an hour, discussing their arrangements and when her things would be moved to the farmstead—her clothing, her hope chest, the few pieces of china that had belonged to her mother.

When he walked her to the door, he drew her close to him, and her hands trembled slightly on his shoulders. His lips touched her temple so lightly and quickly that she wondered if she'd imagined it. "I'll be a good husband to you, I promise."

A good husband, she thought as she watched him walk swiftly to his horse, *but not a husband who loves his wife.* The knowledge squeezed her heart unbearably.

The starry night surrounded Jason as he rode home. His saddle creaked, and the insects made prairie music, a background to the song in his heart. She'd promised to marry him. Forty-eight hours from now she'd be his wife.

A friendly marriage. He'd only wanted to reassure her that he wouldn't push her too quickly from the role of friend to that of wife. But one day, he'd win her love—the love of a woman for a man.

Anything less was unthinkable.

⚭

What could Miranda possibly want, Pearl wondered Saturday evening. She sat on the edge of the cushion at one end of the green velvet sofa in her parents' parlor and looked at Miranda sitting on the other end. They hadn't spoken to each other since the evening Miranda turned down Jason and slapped Pearl's face. She could feel the sting of it even now.

Miranda was dressed in a fashionable visiting suit of russet silk with tan shoes and matching bag. One of the wide hats she loved perched on her gleaming brown hair. She was beautiful, in a dark, vivid way with which her own pale beauty could never compete, Pearl realized with a twinge.

Her friend's gaze darted about the room curiously, and Pearl knew she was taking in the preparations for the wedding to be held in the parlor the next afternoon. She waited patiently for Miranda to state the purpose of her visit. Manners dictated that she offer Miranda some refreshment, but there were limits to her hospitality. She didn't want to encourage Miranda to stay any longer than necessary.

Miranda's brown eyes met hers, and she lifted her chin a trifle. "Even though we haven't been very friendly lately, I wanted to tell you my news myself. I'm engaged to be married. To Mr. Grant Tyler."

Her eyes held the look of a Roman conqueror, Pearl thought with distaste. "Yes, so I've heard."

Miranda's lips formed a little pout. "Oh dear, and I did so want you to hear the news from me." With a practiced feminine shrug that lifted the lace on the shoulders of her gown, she dropped her lashes in false modesty that tightened the corners of Pearl's mouth. "I suppose it's difficult for people not to speak of the wedding plans of one of the town's most eligible bachelors."

There was a time Miranda would have thought such behavior as unbecoming as she thought it herself, and Pearl couldn't help but wish her old sweet friend were with her now instead of this preening creature.

"I've heard rumors that you're engaged also. To Jason. Of course, I told the rumor bearer that was impossible." In spite of her attempt to appear unconcerned, her eyes peered sharply at Pearl.

"We're to be married tomorrow."

They stared at each other for a full minute. Sounds of the neighborhood filtered through the screens to enter on the breeze that lifted the lace-edged curtains: children laughing, horses' hooves plodding through the streets, buggy wheels creaking, dogs barking. But from the parlor, there was no sound at all.

"You can't be serious."

"Why?"

"Jason loves me! He's always loved me."

"You told him you wouldn't marry him. I heard you myself."

Miranda had also said that she still loved Jason, and would agree to marry him when he "came to his senses." Had Jason returned to her after that night, repeating his proposal? Would she ever know?

The buttons and lace on the front of Miranda's gown rose and fell rapidly. "What kind of friend are you, that you would marry him?"

"The kind of friend who will not turn him down because he plans to stay on his parents' farm and care for his family."

"Have you no pride? Jason would marry me even now if I'd have him."

She was right of course. The knowledge of it hadn't left Pearl for a moment since Jason admitted theirs was only to be a friendly marriage. She'd never give Miranda the satisfaction of knowing she believed it. "If you prefer Jason to Mr. Tyler, then I encourage you to tell Jason so. It's not kind to either man to marry Mr. Tyler if you love Jason."

Miranda rose swiftly. "And live on a farm with a ready-made family? I should say not!"

Pearl stood slowly, her gaze never leaving Miranda's flashing brown eyes. "No," she said quietly, relief mingling with her pain. "I didn't think you would."

CHAPTER 9

Boston patiently joined the myriad of tiny buttons that ran up the back of Pearl's white chiffon bodice while Pearl stared at her reflection in the freestanding, full-length mirror in her bedroom. Her fingers played with the orange blossoms that trailed down each side from the large bow at her neck to the hem of her skirt. The blossoms' scent surrounded her.

"The gown is lovely, Mother Boston."

Mrs. Strong turned her around and fussed with the pale yellow that edged the waist of the white brocade satin skirt. She stepped back, a satisfied smile slipping across her face beneath the coronet of still-thick chestnut brown hair streaked with gray. "Yes, I dare say it is."

Pearl gave her an impulsive hug. "Do you feel cheated out of planning a large wedding?"

"Not for myself. But a wedding planned on two days' notice. . ." Boston wrinkled her nose. "It's not what I have always wanted for you."

"You didn't have a grand wedding, and your marriage has weathered the years beautifully."

"Yes, life with Matthew has been very good." The tender, faraway look in her mother's eyes made Pearl's chest ache.

"Jason is a fine boy," Mrs. Strong continued, fitting a plain, filmy, floor-length veil on Pearl's head. She began anchoring a row of orange blossoms across the top with hairpins. "But your decision to marry was made in such haste."

Pearl kept her gaze determinedly on the high lace collar of the mauve gown that lent a lovely shade of rose to Boston's face.

"There!" Her mother stepped back. "What a beautiful bride!" She took Pearl's hands in her own. "I don't wish to pry, dear, but I do so desire your happiness. Do you love Jason?"

Pearl returned her gaze steadily. She didn't have to avoid the truth to give the answer she knew her mother wanted to hear. "Very much."

"Does he return your love?" Her voice held an apology.

Pearl picked up the bouquet that was laying on her bed. "He's never said so."

She heard Mrs. Strong's shaky breath. "Then why are you marrying him?"

"He needs me, he and his family."

Pearl could feel the love emanating from the woman who had raised her. "My dear, have you any idea how difficult life will be, married to a man who doesn't love you?"

Pearl picked at the blossoms of her bouquet restlessly. "You've always taught me to trust God's Word. Remember I Corinthians 13:7? Charity 'beareth all things, believeth all things, hopeth all things, endureth all things.'"

"The verse does not imply that these attributes of love come either easily or painlessly." Boston's lifeworn hands bracketed Pearl's face, and her voice gentled. "Marriage is sacred and meant to last a lifetime. That's a long time to be unhappy."

"I refuse to be unhappy with Jason. We've always been fond of each other. Perhaps one day that fondness will grow to love."

"Loving someone doesn't ensure that love will be returned. If it could, everyone on earth would return God's love."

Why won't she stop? Pearl wondered desperately. "Sometimes, loving someone *can* bring love in return. Doesn't the Bible tell us in I John 4:19 that 'We love him, because he first loved us'?"

The tears in her mother's eyes hurt her. She slipped her cheek next to the older one. "I want to be strong and cheerful for Jason always. With God's help, I can be. It's my wedding day. Be happy for me, please."

Boston gave her a quick squeeze before pulling back to look into her face. "When you and Johnny became part of our lives, I was afraid you would never heal from the pain of losing your parents so young. It became Matthew and my prayer that one day you would not only be healed, but that God would use you to heal other lives. Now Johnny helps heal lives by managing the poor farm, and you are to be part of God's healing for Jason and his family."

Pearl felt Boston's hands tremble as she ran her fingertips along the veil where it framed her cheeks. "It appears God has answered our prayers. But I wonder if I would have been brave enough to ask it if I'd known the cost it would demand of you."

Pearl's blue eyes met Boston's brown ones. "Would you have me be otherwise?"

Boston shook her head slowly. "No. Matthew and I couldn't be prouder of the lovely, Christlike woman you've become." A tender smile filled her eyes, and her hands rested on Pearl's shoulders. "If you can believe God will fill Jason's heart with love for you, then I will join you in your prayer and believe with you."

The ceremony was mercifully quick, Pearl thought, looking about at the small group of people chattering cheerfully in the flower-filled parlor. Except for her bridesmaid, Amy, only her own family, Jason's family, and Rev. Conrad's family had been invited. She was glad. It was difficult enough acting as though this was a normal wedding. The strain of it was getting on her nerves.

"You're the most beautiful bride I've ever seen!"

Pearl smiled at Maggie's wide eyes and eager compliment, remembering well that all brides look beautiful to a twelve-year-old girl.

"I'll second that."

Heat flooded her face at Jason's words. He laughed and raised his eyebrows. "A blushing bride. Now that's a pleasant sight."

She turned away amid Maggie's giggles. If she weren't the object of his jest, she'd be glad to see him teasing and laughing again, like the man she knew before his parents died. His arm slipped possessively about her waist, and her heart raced.

He'd been acting the part of the happy bridegroom since she'd joined him in front of Uncle Adam to exchange their vows. Why? Did he want people to think they were like any normal couple, wildly in love? If that was what he wanted, she would go along with it.

Johnny and Jewell were suddenly beside her. Jewell's blue gown was styled to demurely hide the evidence of the child she and Johnny expected soon. The couple glowed with love when they looked at each other. Pearl envied them that.

When Pearl first met Jewell, she'd thought her brother's quiet, gentle, brown-haired wife plain. Pearl had soon changed her opinion. Jewell's sweet nature won Pearl's heart and transformed Jewell from plain to beautiful in Pearl's eyes.

Now Johnny leaned down to give her a peck on the cheek. "My little sister married. Thought I'd never see the day."

"Well, I like that!" Pearl said indignantly, her hands propped at the waist of her satin skirt.

"Johnny!" Jewell reproved softly at the same time.

Johnny ignored their outbursts. "Remember a couple years ago when I tried to give you some advice on men, little sister?" He grinned broadly at Jason. "She told me in no uncertain terms that she could judge men just fine herself. Have to admit she's done a better job of it than I thought she would." He held out his hand to Jason. "Welcome to the family, old man. No one I'd rather see Pearl marry."

"Couldn't agree with that sentiment more." Jason pulled her even closer to his side. She forced herself to relax against him as though she was accustomed to being there. "I only hope we'll be as happy together as you two."

She wished that, too! If only he meant it. Of course he wanted them to be happy together, but not truly as man and wife.

"Are you ready to leave, Mrs. Sterling?"

Her new title on Jason's lips sent shivers dancing along her arms. He was smiling into her eyes, with a warmth tinged with laughter. Anyone who didn't know better would think he actually cherished her as a new husband would be expected to do.

At Pearl's suggestion, Maggie took Grace upstairs during the leave-taking. She and Jason feared the girl would be upset if she saw them driving away. Maggie had been told that Grace could have her choice of Pearl's dolls. They hoped the gift would keep the girl calm for the evening.

He guided her toward the door, family members from both sides stopping them every couple steps for a reminder or a hug or words of well wishes.

Rev. Conrad rested a hand on Jason's shoulder and held one of Pearl's hands. She looked up into his kind, deep-set eyes. His voice rumbled in its usual deep manner through the dark beard tinged with gray. "Proverbs 18:22 says that 'Whoso findeth a wife findeth a good thing, and obtaineth favour of the Lord.'" He gave them one of his rare smiles.

Mrs. Conrad, slightly plump but stylish, slipped a dainty hand through his arm. "Does the Bible say it's a good thing for a woman to find a husband?"

His large hand cupped hers, and the tender look he gave her caught at Pearl's heart. "Not that I've found, I'm afraid."

"I thought not. However." Mrs. Conrad glanced up at her husband from the corner of her eye. "I've found a husband to be a good thing, just the same."

Matthew leaned down to hug Pearl. "I hope you find it so, too," he said in a low voice. He straightened and reached to shake hands with Jason. "See you're good to her."

"I'll do my best to make her happy, sir."

It sounds like a solemn vow, the way he said it, Pearl thought. Her emotions had been swinging like a chandelier in the wind all day, but for the first time, tears filled her eyes.

"See that you do," Matthew said gruffly.

Pearl hugged Boston good-bye, and then Jason was helping her into the decorated carriage; and they were moving swiftly down the street behind Angel, the younger family members running along, calling cheers and good-byes.

They were at the edge of town before the well-wishers dropped back. The farther they moved out into the prairie, the more strained the silence became between the two. Pearl wished fervently that Jason hadn't arranged for his brothers and sisters to spend the evening at her home—that is, at her adoptive parents' home. More of his charade that their marriage was normal.

They hardly exchanged two words on the drive, and Pearl was glad when they finally arrived at the farmstead. Twilight had faded, and she remained in the carriage while Jason went inside to light some lamps.

When he returned, he helped her down, then reached for her alligator valise. Frank would bring the rest of her things when he and the others returned the next day. The valise looked so small, carried so few of her belongings, that she felt vulnerable.

"You'll have Mom and Dad's room," Jason said, leading the way upstairs. "Maggie readied it for you."

He held the door to the room, and she entered timidly. She'd never been in this room. Always when she'd been in the house, the door had been closed. Maggie had told her none of the family wanted to disturb it, feeling it would be too painful, too final.

"Are you sure you want me to stay in here?"

Jason set the valise on the end of the bed, not looking at her. "Yes."

The room was larger than the other bedchambers and had a matching set of fine cherry furniture. The bed was veiled in Nottingham lace and a lace scarf lay across the dressing table. A china pitcher trimmed in gold with delicately painted violets sat in a matching bowl on the stand beside the lace-covered windows. Mauve-colored, patterned paper warmed the walls.

"It's a lovely room." She recalled Jason telling her how his father had loved to give his mother beautiful things. He'd certainly filled their personal room with beauty.

Jason had lit the lamp on the dressing table, and the flame shone through the etched glass of the globe to reflect off the mirror, multiplying the light. A porcelain vase stood beside the lamp, filled with wildflowers whose fragrance scented the room. She touched one of the blossoms, aware of Jason standing in the doorway watching her. "Did Maggie pick these, too?"

"I did."

Something he'd done unbidden, just for her. Not to fool their families, but to welcome her. She wanted to gather the vaseful and hug the flowers close to her chest, burying her face in them. "Thank you."

He nodded and crossed the room to open the doors of the large clothespress. She was surprised to see it empty. "Maggie packed up Mom and Dad's things so you can put your clothes wherever you please. The room is entirely yours."

"It must have been difficult for Maggie, putting away your parents' things. I'd have helped her if I'd known."

Jason was beside her in two steps, sweeping her into his arms. "I think the reverend was right." His husky voice set her nerves tingling. "A wife is a good thing." She felt his lips press against her neck, and then he released her, moving to the door so quickly that she almost lost her balance.

He stood silhouetted there a moment, staring at her. "I'm sorry. It won't happen again. I'd best put Angel up."

But he didn't leave, and Pearl wished she could see his face clearly in the lamplit room. What had he meant by taking her in his arms that way, chasing her breath away?

"I'll be sleeping in the same room as always, with Frank and Andrew across the hall. If you need anything, just call."

He pulled the door shut behind him. She stood where she was, listening to his footsteps go down the stairs and fade. The outside door slammed a moment later.

Shakily she sat down on the edge of the bed, trying to catch her breath. Though his arms had been around her so briefly, she could still feel their warmth and strength. Was he sorry he'd embraced her so intimately in her bedchamber?

She reached for her valise and removed the white muslin bridal set her mother had purchased for her the day before. Her fingers drifted lightly over the tucks and fine embroidery and Hamburg lace. She hadn't had the courage to tell Mother Boston there wouldn't be any need for new nightwear.

Part of her was relieved that Jason was sleeping elsewhere, but she hadn't expected to feel so incredibly lonely. It was silly, considering she'd been sleeping alone most of her life.

Is Mother Boston right? Had she been a fool, marrying a man who didn't return her love?

She wrapped her arms about herself tightly, trying to relieve the pain inside her. "Please, Lord, help me. Help me to keep loving Jason, and hoping and believing and enduring, as Your Word says. Help me to be a good wife to him. And please, please take away some of this pain."

She brushed a tear from her cheek impatiently and began to change. It took her a full half hour to undo the six dozen tiny buttons at the back of her bridal gown. A number of times she considered asking Jason to assist her, but the memory of his lips against her neck warned her that it wouldn't be wise.

In her fine new chemise and drawers, she folded back the covers of Jason's parents' bed, then turned to put out the lamp. Something on the wall above the bed caught the corner of her eye, and she looked back.

It was a sampler. She leaned across the bed, trying to read it, but the lamplight didn't reach that far. Picking up the lamp, she lifted it in front of the embroidered piece.

" 'Charity hopeth all things,' " she read. A chill shivered through her, and the roots of her hair felt as though they were charged with lightning. A phrase from the verse she'd quoted to Mother Boston earlier that day!

She returned the lamp to the dressing table. Before putting it out, she pulled a stem from the vase of wildflowers. A sweet peace filled her as she slipped between the clean, crisp sheets and drew the soft, fragrant blossom lightly across her cheek.

The tightness that had made her insides feel like coiled wire all day long began to release. Surely God was showing her through Jason's mother's sampler that He would answer her prayer for Jason's love. She was to continue believing and hoping. God would make this strange, funny marriage right. She just had to continue hoping. . . .

CHAPTER 10

Jason tugged at Angel's lead, pulling her into a stall, oblivious to the crunching of straw beneath his best shoes, his work team's welcoming whinnies, or the sound of mice scurrying in the corners.

He'd had it all planned out—to go slowly, keep things casual and cheerful between himself and Pearl as they had always been, to allow her to become comfortable in his home and with his constant presence. Then slowly, let her know of his love, as though they were courting.

Instead he'd pulled her into his arms with no warning at all. Her eyes were huge when he looked back at her from the relative safety of the bedchamber door. Had he frightened her? Did she think he was going back on his word?

Well, he wouldn't. God help him, he'd stick to his original plan. He'd never take her to his bed unless she loved him as a wife loves a husband.

Leaning against the fence beside the barn, he stared moodily at the house. *My wife is there.* Wonder filled him at the thought. She'd been so beautiful in her wedding dress. Her eyes and voice hadn't wavered as she'd taken her vows. It was up to him to see she didn't regret those vows. Life wasn't going to be easy for them, but that didn't mean it couldn't be good.

Lord, please let her return my love. It was clear from the Scriptures that it was the Lord's will that husbands and wives love one another. Surely God would answer his prayer. Until then, Pearl would be in his home, sharing his life. He wanted more, he thought restlessly, but it was enough for now.

∞

Pearl slipped a final tomato into the bushel basket setting beside her between the garden furrows and stood, her hands against the small of her back as she unkinked her muscles. A red-winged blackbird lit on a plant, cocked his head at her, and darted off, his wing a crimson-and-black splash against the sky. A frown knit her brow beneath the wide straw hat she wore to protect her skin. Clouds rolled over and under each other like milk in a churn, constantly shifting shades of gray. It was going to rain, and hard. The only question was how soon. The stillness preceding the storm was eerie; winds were one of the constants on the prairie.

"Come along, Grace." Lifting the basket, she started for the house with Grace racing stumblingly through the garden row before her.

Funny how her attitude toward the weather changed after only a few days

516

on the farm. In town a storm was merely an inconvenience, causing errands and pleasure outings to be postponed and making the streets difficult to pass. Here, a storm could threaten her new family's livelihood.

A smile softened the tense muscles in her face. Her new family. Precious words.

On the porch, she turned and surveyed the fields. She knew the men would stay out until the storm struck, redeeming every available minute.

She set the basket down inside the pantry. Spices in round wooden boxes, coffee in its red tin, and the ever-present kerosene jug dwarfed the smell of the fresh vegetables. She'd have to find time to preserve what vegetables she could for the winter. Perhaps Boston would help her; it would give them a chance to visit.

As she re-entered the kitchen, Pearl's gaze rested briefly on the old cupboard her father had made for her mother. Mother Boston and Dr. Matt had saved the cupboard for Pearl from the Wells's sod house. Jason and Frank had brought it to the farm the day before Jason and Pearl's wedding. The few pieces of her mother's blue-and-white china which had survived the journey from the East to the homestead claim now rested safely on the shelves.

Had her mother and father been happy, Pearl wondered, a young married couple, poor, starting out their life together on the frontier? She hoped so. She hoped they'd been madly in love; so much in love that no hardship they faced together seemed impossible to endure.

Pearl moved to the screen door. The clouds seemed to meet the earth in a solid gray-blue wall not far past Thor Lindstrom's fields.

Jason had told her to expect some neighbors to join himself and the day laborers next week to help with the threshing. Thor's wife, Ellie, had stopped the day after the wedding, offering to assist Pearl in cooking for the large group of men. She was grateful for the offer and would return it when the threshers worked Thor's farm.

Jason's favorite team of draft horses, fly nets flapping, stomped rapidly into the yard pulling a load of grain and the three men. The wind was already increasing and whirled the wheat from the wagon in dusty sworls. Even as she watched Jason and Andrew leap down to open the barn doors so Frank could drive the wagon inside, darkness shut out the daylight.

Rain came pouring down, the wind whistling around the house with a ferocious intensity.

Boots rushed across the porch, and the kitchen door swung open before the men. They were soaked to the skin, and water poured from their hats and clothes. Pearl was surprised to find that the day laborers had already left, hoping to beat the storm home.

When the men had changed, Maggie poured fragrant coffee from the large graniteware pot and set out sugar cookies, and the family spent a few luxurious minutes visiting around the kitchen table. Grace sat on Frank's lap and happily dunked a cookie in his coffee cup until the cookie all but dissolved. The little girl always loved when the men returned from the fields.

So did she, Pearl admitted to herself.

Frank pulled out the latest edition of *The Progressive Farmer*, and Andy slipped away—*likely to bury his nose in another dime novel,* Pearl thought. Grace climbed on Maggie's lap in the rocking chair and listened entranced to *Black Beauty*.

Jason took his cup of coffee and went out on the porch, leaned against a pillar, and watched the rain still drenching the land. Pearl took her blue cotton shawl from its peg behind the kitchen door and followed him, pulling the door shut behind them. She tugged the shawl close about her shoulders as she went to stand beside him, tucking a hand in his arm in the comfortable, old familiar manner she'd had with him when they were young, and fiancés and marriages were far in their future.

"Will the rain damage the crops?"

Jason slipped his arm from her hand to drop it loosely about her shoulders. "Dad always said not to tally up your losses until the game was over, but it doesn't look good."

It felt warm and secure with his arm about her, and she leaned against him contentedly.

He sighed deeply. "A farmer's always at nature's mercy. How's a man supposed to care for a family, never knowing when some storm or insects might wipe out his crops?" His hand cupped her shoulder, drawing her closer against him. "And now I've dragged you into that life."

She slipped a hand cautiously over his, not wanting to let him know how intimate it felt to be so near him. "I wasn't dragged into this m–marriage kicking and screaming. I'm not meant to be a responsibility. Wives were created to be helpmates, if I remember the story of Adam and Eve correctly."

His chuckle rumbled in her ear. "That's a mean argument. Makes it difficult for me to stand up on my soapbox and orate on man's natural superiority."

"Good!"

"But I've made a commitment to my brothers and sisters, and they're counting on me."

"God has made a commitment to you, too."

He was silent a moment. "I needed that reminder to trust Him. I've felt like Atlas trying to carry the earth on his shoulders the last few weeks. And doing a poor job of it, too."

The door creaked open behind them. Pearl tried to ignore the disappointment that flickered through her at the interruption.

"Pearl, will you cut my hair tonight?" Maggie asked, frowning down at one of her braids. "You did promise, and school is starting soon."

Jason jerked around, and a lonely feeling settled in the pit of Pearl's stomach as his arm dropped from her shoulders. "Why are you cutting your hair?"

"I'm almost thirteen. Girls my age simply do not wear their hair in braids."

"If you wear your hair short, how are the guys at school going to stick your braids in the inkwells or pull on it to let you know they've got a hankering for you?"

Maggie's face flooded with color. "Boys! Really, Jason!"

Pearl fought back a smile. "I recall a certain young man dunking my braids in an inkwell. Ruined my favorite school dress." Her gaze darted accusingly to Jason, and she had the satisfaction of seeing him flush. "If you find some shears, I'll cut your hair now, Maggie."

She was back in a minute with a comb and shears, and they all moved to the kitchen.

Jason sat across the table from them, turning the pages of the Montgomery Ward implement catalog. "So what's this newfangled hairstyle like?"

"Didn't you notice that almost all the young misses at the dance were wearing their hair in loose curls just below their shoulders?"

"Can't say I did, sis."

"Men!"

"You have to remember, I'm a married man. I'm not supposed to be noticing other girls."

Pearl's hands stilled, and her gaze shot to Jason's. He'd been waiting for it, his eyes laughing at her. The comb trembled slightly as she began pulling it through Maggie's hair once more. "We weren't married then."

He chuckled, and she had to smile. She'd sounded like a prim, middle-aged housewife even to herself.

Maggie pulled a Jordan Marsh catalog from the stack of magazines Jason had brought into the room and showed him the current style.

Grace entered and dumped two dolls and an armload of homemade clothes on the wooden chair beside Jason. Picking up a curly-haired doll, she wrapped it with painstaking care in a soft flannel square, then leaned heavily against Jason's leg. "She needs you to hold her."

Jason took the doll in his arms as carefully as though it were a baby, and Pearl's heart turned over at his gentle care for his little sister's feelings. She well remembered how Johnny refused to have anything to do with her when she played with dolls. "Pretty baby. Don't remember seeing her before. Is she new?"

Grace nodded, her head bouncing repeatedly, her attention already on another doll she was awkwardly attempting to diaper with a flannel scrap. "Pearl gave her to me."

"What's her name?"

"Mawy."

"Mary? Nice name."

Would Grace never outgrow her difficulty with the *r* sound, Pearl wondered as the little girl answered Jason. "Yes. That's her name 'cause Peawl gave her to me on your mawy day."

A puzzled frown appeared on Jason's brow. "You mean the day Pearl and I got married?"

The bouncing nod repeated. "Maggie said Pearl won't ever leave us again. She said when people get mawwied, they stay together for always." Her eyes looked like big brown buttons as she raised them seriously to Jason's face, silently asking if it was true.

He pulled her into his lap. "That's right, Pumpkin. When people get married, they make promises to each other. You know what promises are, don't you?"

"Yes. That's when you can never change your mind."

Pearl saw a laugh twinkling in the eyes so like Grace's. "That's a pretty good way to look at a promise, I reckon."

"And you pwomised to stay with Pearl for always?"

"Yep."

"What else did you pwomise?"

His voice grew softer, and there was a hint of huskiness. "I promised to love Pearl, and honor her, and cherish her forever."

Grace tilted her head and poked a finger at his chest, accentuating each word. "And you can't ever change your mind."

Pearl's heart caught in her throat as he captured her gaze in his. "No, I won't ever change my mind."

"Good." Grace wriggled down from his lap and exchanged dolls with him. "Now you hold Molly for a while."

"Yes ma'am," he said meekly.

Pearl could hardly keep her mind on trimming Maggie's hair. Why was he doing this, repeating his vows as though he meant them with all his heart, when they both knew it was Miranda he loved?

Pain lanced through her. How sweet it would be if his vow to love her had been sincere! It must have been difficult for him to promise to love and cherish her, when his heart belonged to another. He wasn't a man to give his word lightly.

Grace seemed content to play silently beside Jason, and he turned back to teasing Maggie. "Almost thirteen sounds a little young to be interested in boys."

"I didn't say I was interested in boys!"

"My mistake."

Big brothers must all be cut from the same cloth, Pearl thought, remembering how Johnny had teased her through the years. About time she came to Maggie's rescue. "You weren't much older than Maggie when you met. . ."

"My wife." He smoothly cut off her reference to Miranda.

She stared at him over Maggie's head, her mouth open slightly. What had come over him today? Perhaps he was simply his normal teasing self and had no idea how her heart turned each word over and over, wishing for his love.

"Tell me how you met," Maggie demanded.

"It was the winter your family moved here." Pearl clipped at the long locks carefully. "We were skating on the river. I skated too far downstream and fell through some weak ice. Jason rescued me."

Maggie gasped and whirled around, her eyes huge and shining. "He saved your life? How *romantic!*"

"Your hair is going to be much shorter than you wish if you jerk like that again." She softened the words with a smile. "It wasn't romantic at all. I looked like a drowned rat."

"You didn't look quite *that* bad," Jason qualified gallantly.

"Anyway, it took me a minute to find the hole in the ice when I came back to the surface of the river. I tried to crawl out, but the ice was too thin and kept breaking off. My hands felt like icicles, and my body was growing numb quickly. Then I heard Jason telling me to keep fighting."

She stopped trimming, the memory so powerful she couldn't continue.

Jason shrugged. "It wasn't such a big thing."

"I could hear the other kids yelling at him to stay back or he'd fall in, too, but he didn't even take his eyes off me once. He just flattened himself against the ice and held out a stick and told me to grab on. My hands were too cold by then to close around something that small."

"What happened next?" Maggie asked breathlessly.

She looked at the eyes that had stared into hers that long-ago day, knowing her heart was in her gaze but not knowing how to prevent his seeing it. "He said not to worry, he wasn't going to let me die." *And then the sun came out.* She always remembered it that way. His eyes had been brown and warm and golden all at once, like the sun. She'd looked into them and known he wouldn't let her drown, and the panic inside her ebbed away.

"You're making me sound way too gallant. You should be writing serials."

Pearl ignored his modesty. "He crawled closer to the edge of the hole. We could hear the ice cracking with every movement. My brother, John, who had been too far away to get to us immediately, held onto Jason's skates in case Jason fell in, too. It was a good thing, as the ice broke two more feet around the hole before Jason pulled me out."

Maggie sighed and hugged her arms around her apron-covered chest. "It's just like the knights of the round table."

Jason choked on his coffee, and Pearl laughed at him over Maggie's head. "Knights! Do I look as if I wear armor?"

"You're a hero, just the same," Maggie said with a determined nod of her freckled round face. "Overalls and all."

Jason snorted and refused to meet either of their gazes.

"He's certainly a hero in my book. I tagged after him for months." *Years would be more accurate,* Pearl thought. She handed Maggie a hand mirror. "What do you think of your new look?"

Maggie lifted a hand to the wavy hair. "Is it really me?"

Jason picked up the catalog Maggie had shown him earlier. Pursing his lips, he looked critically from the page to Maggie and back again. "Yep. You look just like the young miss in the advertisement."

Maggie flushed with pleasure.

"We'll wrap your hair in rags this evening to make curls."

"Oh Pearl, I'm so glad you came to live with us!" She wrinkled her nose at Jason. "And I don't care what you say. I think it's the most romantic thing I've ever heard, meeting your wife by saving her life."

"Just hope your own life doesn't ever need saving," Jason grumbled as he stood up. "Far from being the fearless savior Pearl describes, I was scared out of my wits the whole time."

"I never knew that."

Pearl didn't realize she'd said the words aloud until he stopped beside her. "Any reasonable person would have been. I was shaking in my boots, scared stiff you were going to sink beneath the waterline and be gone forever." His trembling attempt at a smile made her throat ache. "And then who would have been my helpmate?"

Her knees lost their starch as he left the room, and she plopped into the chair beside Maggie. Jason had always been an irrepressible tease. If she didn't stop taking his comments seriously, she was going to make herself miserable.

But his words and intense gaze lingered in her mind the rest of the evening and followed her into her bed that night. *I promised to love Pearl. . .forever.*

CHAPTER 11

The night of the big storm was the last Pearl had time to dwell on Jason's behavior. The storm hadn't been as damaging as they'd feared. Crop losses were minimal, though they later learned that many farmers did lose crops and windows to hail—including the poor farm Johnny managed.

It was days before the land dried out enough for the men, horses, wagons, and machines to get back into the fields. Until then they spent their time repairing and maintaining fences and machinery, and cleaning out the barn. Once they were back in the fields, Pearl and the girls seldom saw the men other than at meals, or when they carried morning and afternoon snacks to them.

Preserving, cooking, baking, laundry, housekeeping, and gardening kept the women as busy as the men. The hired men merely added to Pearl's workload. She fell into bed each night so tired that she was asleep almost before she finished her prayers.

Sundays were the only times of rest. After church they would often visit with Dr. Matt and Boston or with Johnny and Jewell. Back at the farm the children loved to read. Sometimes they had hay fights in the barn or slid down the haystacks—which would set Grace to giggling nonstop. Pearl especially liked the times they went horseback riding. She missed riding Angel, and the horse was gaining weight from lack of exercise.

Rising before the sun was especially difficult for Pearl, but Jason always arose before her and had the fire in the kitchen stove started so she could prepare the usual huge breakfast. His thoughtfulness never failed to add cheer to her morning.

Pearl's hope dipped and swayed like the wheat in the wind the first few days of their marriage, and she asked the Lord to show her how to stay strong in the hope He'd given her on her wedding night. Soon after, she came across Romans 15:4 in her daily devotions: "For whatsoever things were written aforetime were written for our learning, that we through patience and comfort of the scriptures might have hope."

The verse excited her, and she determined that she would not miss her daily devotional time regardless of her busy days. Sometimes she could fit in no more than ten minutes. She decided to make hope the topic of her devotions. Reading of God's faithfulness in keeping His promises to His people throughout the centuries encouraged her to keep hoping for Jason's love.

In addition to her personal devotions, she and Jason continued the family devotional time after the evening meal which Jason had begun. They kept the time short, only reading a few verses and praying together, both feeling the family needed the daily time of looking to God together.

Frank was the only family member who seemed uncomfortable with the devotional time. When Pearl asked Jason about Frank's faith, his eyes became troubled. "Mom and Dad always saw to it the family was churchgoing and made no secret of the fact they believed faith in Christ was the most important part of a person's life. I just assumed Frank had committed his life to Christ, as I did. Afraid I was wrong, considering his actions lately. I tried to talk with him about it, but he just shrugged me off."

They agreed to pray for Frank to come to a realization of his need for Christ. It hurt to see him trying to deal with the changes in his life by leaning on liquor instead of the Lord.

Before long school began, and Pearl assumed some of Maggie's duties. The only item which made it easier for Pearl to complete her work was her freedom of time spent watching Grace. Grace turned six in early September and was attending school for the first time. She and Maggie walked the three miles to school in Chippewa City each day.

Grace's school attendance brought the need for new clothes and added another item to Pearl's growing list of duties. Jason brought his mother's sewing machine into the kitchen, where Pearl could work and still be available to answer Maggie's questions as she studied algebra, geography, and natural philosophy at the kitchen table.

As soon as he could be spared from the fields, Andy would be attending classes also. It had been his father's dream that all of his children graduate and the boys continue their education beyond the traditional eight years of school. It was an unusual dream in a land where few boys graduated. Those who did normally took more than eight years to reach that goal, and Jason and Frank were not exceptions.

One rainy Saturday afternoon when Jason and Andy returned from delivering grain to the elevator, Andy's eyes were as large as wagon wheels. "There were one hundred ponies from Wyoming on First Street! When I'm a man, I'm heading west to be a cowboy."

"I can remember when this *was* the West," Pearl said when Andy left the room.

Jason poured a cup of coffee from the large graniteware pot. "He wanted to join the circus when Oliver's World's Greatest Shows was in town in April."

Leaning against the table, he watched Pearl ironing. "I don't understand Frank anymore. He used to argue with Dad all the time about continuing his education. Said all he ever wanted was to be a farmer and couldn't see any reason to go back to school when he was perfectly happy right here. Now all he talks about is attending Windom Academy." Jason raked a hand through his hair. "Frank wants to become a businessman, and Andy wants to be a cowboy. Don't know who Dad thought he was building the farm up for."

Pearl placed the cooling iron on the stove to reheat and changed the wooden handle to a hot iron. She watched Jason's back through the window as he walked to the barn. He hadn't wanted the farm either. Her heart ached for him.

Grace's nightmares added to the family's exhaustion. They were diminishing in quantity but not in intensity. Pearl and Jason asked the Lord fervently to show them how to help the poor child.

One Tuesday night in mid-September, a bloodcurdling scream made Pearl bolt upright. Almost before she was awake, she'd slipped into the flannel wrapper she kept across the foot of her bed.

She collided with Jason in the hallway in front of Grace's door. Corduroy trousers stuck out beneath his night shirt. "I'll see to her. You need your sleep," she offered.

"We'll both take care of her."

It was a conversation they had every night. The result never changed. They stayed up together with the girl until the memory of the nightmare dulled enough for her to go back to sleep.

Pearl led the way downstairs with a lamp, and Jason followed, carrying the kicking and screaming child. They'd learned from painful and exhausting experience that the screaming wouldn't end for at least a half hour, and it would be a good deal longer before she quieted enough to allow them to leave her and return to bed.

Jason sat in the spring rocker in the parlor, whispering comforting words to the girl in his arms, ignoring the kicks and blows. Seeing the pain and concern for Grace etched deeply into Jason's dry, tanned skin added to the pain Pearl felt for Grace. Pearl sat on the settee, lifting silent prayers for both.

After a long time, the screams subsided into scattered, wrenching sobs that slowly disappeared into occasional shaky breaths. For the dozenth time, Pearl and Jason urged her to tell them about the dream that frightened her so, but as always, she was unable to describe it. All she would say was, "I'm 'fwaid you're goin' ta be mad and go away, like Mommy and Papa."

No amount of reassurances would convince her otherwise.

"Do you think your mommy and papa are angry with you, dear?" Pearl asked. Why hadn't she heard that part of Grace's cry before, instead of only hearing that the child was afraid they'd leave her?

She nodded, her wet little face brushing against Jason's flannel robe.

"Why?"

"If they weren't mad, why don't they come home?"

Pearl saw the sheen of tears in Jason's eyes before he bent his head over his sister. His groan ripped through her. "Mommy and Papa aren't staying away because they're mad at you, Pumpkin. They can't come home because they're in heaven. Heaven is a wonderful place, but people can't leave there."

"Why?"

"I don't know why; I only know they can't."

Pearl swallowed the sob that rose in her own throat at the hopelessness in Jason's husky answer.

"Why did they go there? Don't they love me anymore?"

"Of course they do, Pumpkin. They love you so much that Pearl and I were given special orders to stay with you and watch over you for them."

A thumb slipped into her mouth as she considered this, and she was silent for a minute. "Is special orders like a pwomise?"

Jason's lips stretched in a sad smile. "Yes. It's something we won't ever change our minds about."

"I want to talk to Mommy and Papa," she mumbled around her thumb.

Jason closed his eyes tight, but Pearl intervened before he could respond.

"When I was even smaller than you, my mommy died and went to heaven. My brother, Johnny, and I wanted to talk to her, too. Johnny finally came up with a way we could talk to her, even though we couldn't see her and she couldn't answer us."

Grace's big brown eyes searched her face for a full minute. "How?"

"When we prayed, we would ask God to give her our messages, and tell her we loved her and missed her."

"Did He do that?"

Pearl forced a bright smile. "Oh, I'm sure He did. God takes very good care of people when they go to heaven."

Grace looked at Jason for confirmation, and he nodded. Pearl saw his Adam's apple jerk before he said, "Sure as shootin', Pumpkin."

"I'm goin' to ask Him to tell Mommy and Papa I love them."

"Good idea."

They had just tucked her back in bed when Frank's slurred voice raised in song came through the windows.

"Drunk again!" Disgust drenched Jason's whisper.

"Don't argue with him now. You need your sleep. It's less than two hours until sunrise."

"Two hours won't be enough to sleep off that hangover."

"Fall term begins tomorrow at Windom Academy. I expect that's what brought this on in the middle of the week."

"Is that supposed to be an excuse? A man should be able to handle life's disappointments without resorting to the bottle."

"Getting angry won't help anything and will keep you from needed rest."

But he was already heading for the top of the stairs. "I'll have to put up his horse. He never remembers to take care of her when he comes home in this shape."

Pearl couldn't sleep right away when she went back to bed; she kept listening for Jason to return. She didn't mind the heavy workload so much, but the emotional tension of dealing with Grace night after night and the strain of Frank's belligerence and drinking made her weary. She'd told Jason she was meant to be his helpmate, but she didn't seem capable of dealing with the things with which he needed help the most. If she found these things wearying, how much more must they affect him?

∽

Pearl stood on the porch the next evening watching Frank herd the milk cows into the barn. Their bawling filled the air. *Complaining of the heat as much as of their full udders,* she thought, wiping the back of her hand over her brow. It would be hotter in the barn, but at least they would be free of the sand whipped around by the prairie winds. One hundred degrees in the shade. It certainly didn't feel like the middle of September.

In spite of their heavy workload, the men always milked the cows. Frank was handling the milking today because Jason refused to allow him in the fields due to last night's drinking. Her own work had kept her from even considering helping with the milking in the past. Not that she'd ever milked a cow before; but she'd seen it done, and it didn't look too hard.

She stuck her head in the kitchen door where Maggie was pumping water at the sink to fill the bedroom water pitchers. "I'm going to the barn. Keep an eye on Grace."

Frank was taking a milk pail down from its peg when she entered the barn, the air thick with the odors of cows and hay. "I've come to help."

Frank shook his head. "Jason wouldn't like that."

She reached for a pail. "Nonsense. Will you teach me, or shall I teach myself?"

Grinning, he took the pail from her. "Afraid it's the cows who wouldn't approve of you teaching yourself."

Almost two hours passed before she looked up from the three-legged stool beside a brown-and-white cow to see Jason looking down at her with a puzzled frown. "Maggie told me I'd find you in here. What are you doing?"

She giggled. "Well, if you can't tell, I'm obviously doing it wrong."

"I don't want you doing the milking."

A shrug lifted the shoulders of her damp blouse, and she continued her pulling. "I'm glad to do it. You and your brothers have more than you can handle already."

"You've been working sunup to sundown and beyond yourself, and you don't see me trying to take on any of your workload."

The cow's tail hit her full in the face. Pearl sputtered and shook her head. "It's not the same thing."

He grinned and grabbed the cow's tail to keep it from striking her again. "It's just the same thing. I don't want you doing this."

"But I like helping you."

"Let me finish." He took her arm just above the wrist and gently tugged. "Ouch!"

In a second he was kneeling in the straw beside her, holding her arm between his callused hands more gently than she would have believed possible. "Your wrists are swollen!"

He touched his lips to them, and her breath caught in a light gasp at the sweet, spontaneous gesture. "They. . .they're fine, truly. I just didn't realize milking was so hard."

He kept her arm in his hands as he turned his gaze to hers. The corners of his mouth tipped up. "Did I actually hear you admit there's something a man can do better than a woman? After all the times you told John and me that you could do anything we could do?"

"I didn't say a man could do it better; I only said it's hard. My muscles will become accustomed to it."

He stood, pulling her up with him. "No, they won't. You aren't to do it again."

It was the first time he'd given her an order. An order it definitely was, in spite of his tender tone.

When she opened her mouth to protest, he laid his fingers over her lips. "I spend all day in the field and around animals, until I can smell them in my sleep. I don't want my wife to smell like cows."

The gentleness in his eyes stilled any further protest. "I only meant to help. You've been so tired lately."

His hand cupped her chin lightly, his thumb tracing her cheekbone. She trembled at his touch. "You are so sweet." His husky whisper sent goose bumps down her spine. He was so close. Was he. . .was he going to kiss her?

"So what do you think of her first day's milking?"

Jason and Pearl jerked apart at Frank's voice. Jason frowned at him. "Was it you who taught her how to do this?"

Frank leaned against the stall and raised his eyebrows at Pearl. "Told you he wouldn't like it."

"You're right; I don't."

The coldness in his voice had the effect on Pearl of being dumped in ice water. "You needn't bellow at him. It was my idea."

He stepped around her and dropped down on the stool. "Well, I'm taking over now."

"Yes, so I see." She grasped her skirt to keep it from tripping her in the straw and hurried out of the barn. Whatever had she done to change his attitude so suddenly? Everything was wonderful, and then. . .

"Why do I keep forgetting, Lord?" she asked through clenched teeth, her shoes hitting the hard soil of the yard sharply with each step. "When am I going to learn not to read love into each kind word and look Jason gives me?"

∞

Jason barely noticed the white streams hissing into the pail. His heart felt like someone had plucked it out of his chest and stomped on it. He'd been so touched that Pearl wanted to spare him. In another moment he would have kissed her, told her that he loved her.

Then Frank had spoken, and the thought flashed through his mind that perhaps she had done this not to spare him further work but to help Frank.

She'd pleaded Frank's case to him last night, when he'd expected her to be as disgusted with the man as he was himself. She knew Frank had the responsibility for milking tonight. It was he she was assisting, not her husband.

Before they were married, when he and Frank had argued over escorting her home, she'd said she'd always enjoyed Frank's company. It was no secret his brother was considered wildly attractive by most of the single women in town, in spite of the fact he barely said hello to them. He wasn't shy with Pearl. He was as comfortable with her as he was with Maggie. *What if Pearl. . .?*

"No!"

The cow turned her head to look at him, and he patted her flank. "Sorry, Bessie. Wasn't yelling at you."

He picked up the pail and walked slowly across the barn, dreading going inside and facing Pearl.

Leaning against the barn door, he listened to piano music from the open windows mix with the music of the prairie insects and allowed the thought he'd stamped out a minute earlier to wriggle inside his mind in all its ugliness.

What if his wife was falling in love with his brother?

CHAPTER 12

Pearl returned smiles and greetings as she moved down the aisle of Windom Academy recitation hall, joining the rest of the audience during the intermission of the musicale.

She was glad to see it so well attended. With the economic depression, the school was having difficulty meeting its debts, the same as everyone else. Male students had offered to provide the labor required for a much-needed well, but the funds from the musicale would purchase the necessary supplies for the well and windmill.

"I'll be back in a minute," Jason said near her ear.

She felt absurdly lonely watching him move through the crowd to stop beside Amy Henderson. Always in public he played the devoted husband, and she cherished his touch at her elbow or back and his endearing looks, even knowing they were only for show. The first few days and weeks of their marriage, she'd wondered if he could possibly be falling in love with her. He was so sweet, and the way he would look at her sometimes—well, even now it made her heart skip a beat. But since the episode in the barn, he'd not touched her in their home unless it was accidental. He remained friendly and even joked as always, but there was a definite cooling in his attitude. She was at a loss to understand it.

Amy and Jason parted, and she watched for him to return to her. Jealousy burned through her when Miranda stopped him with a gloved hand on his arm, darting a triumphant look at Pearl.

She turned decidedly away. What right had she to be jealous? She knew when she married him that he loved Miranda. The knowledge did nothing to decrease her pain.

How had Miranda become so self-centered, she wondered for the hundredth time. With all the unmarried women today seeking employment, her desire for a life of leisure was particularly unseemly. Even Chippewa City was filled with women working beside men—proprietresses of boarding houses and hotels, waitresses, maids, milliners, seamstresses, clerks, secretaries serving the professional men, instructors in music, school teachers, even a banker. Look at the wife of the Windom Academy's headmaster—why, she taught, acted as housemother to the young women boarding there, and cooked for twenty to forty teachers and students daily! If a woman hadn't a family to care for, the world certainly had plenty of places for her to fill a need.

Restlessly she moved toward a painting on the wall, one of many in an exhibit by Amy. Frank was in a group of young men nearby, she noticed, discoursing on the need for area farmers to support the new grain house in town, which had already advanced the local market two cents above list.

"It's so good to see you again, Mrs. Sterling. You don't get into town nearly often enough." Pearl started at Amy's gentle voice.

She gave Amy an impulsive hug. "You're right. We must get together soon." Would her bright smile fool her friend, she wondered as she waved a hand toward the paintings. "Your work is wonderful. I understand your showing at the Minnesota Exhibition this fall went well?"

"Yes, thank you."

"We're all so proud of you."

With her typical modesty, Amy changed the subject from her own success. "And you? I do hope you are happy as a married woman."

As happy as she had any right to be, she thought, wedding a man she knew loved another. "I wouldn't give up life with Jason for anything under the sun." At least that was true.

Amy's smile was warm. "I'm so glad. He is a fine man."

"Are you still seeing Mr. Ray?"

"Occasionally."

Had Amy hesitated before replying? Pearl hoped that meant she had reservations about the man.

"I—I hate to give credit to gossip..." Amy stopped as though reconsidering, a frown touching her otherwise smooth forehead beneath upswept hair. "I wouldn't even mention it if we weren't close friends."

Pearl laid a hand on Amy's green velvet cape. "What is it?"

"Is it true that Frank has taken up drinking?"

"Yes."

Amy's gaze dropped to her gloved fingers, playing restlessly with the gold braid on her coat. "I was hoping the rumors were false. My contact with Frank has always left me with a favorable opinion of him."

"We'd appreciate your prayers for him."

"You will most certainly have them."

Jason stepped up beside Pearl and took her elbow, his touch causing her pulse to race, as always. "And just what are you giving my wife?"

Pearl looked up at his laughing eyes and felt life drain from her soul. Such a pleased expression hadn't passed his face in weeks. *Were those few minutes with*

Miranda responsible for it? She hoped her answering smile wasn't the miserable failure it felt to be. "You've misunderstood Amy's comment," she said as Frank joined them. "We were discussing the need for the women of Chippewa City to pray for the community's wild young men."

Frank's dark eyes grew almost black at her comment, but Jason just chuckled. "When it comes to taming men, it takes a powerful dose of prayer."

Amy's delicate chin lifted slightly. "The unmarried members of the Women's Christian Temperance League here are considering adopting the vow of the young women of nearby Madison. They have banded together in a vow to boycott young men who use tobacco. We would add to it those young men who use intoxicating liquors or frequent billiard halls."

Pearl noticed Amy's gaze rested fully on Frank as she spoke. Frank's lips spread in an uncompromising grimace, in spite of the fact that Amy's voice was strictly conversational.

Jason didn't seem to notice the tension between the two. "I should think that would get the men's attention, if anything will." His smile settled into normal proportions. "There's been a lot of talk around town that the drinking is getting out of hand, what with the number of horse-and-buggy accidents drunkards have had recently, not to mention injuries from saloon scuffles."

"Rev. Conrad is encouraging the townspeople to hold socials in their homes for the young people, hoping to keep them from less dangerous pursuits."

The delicate ringing of a handbell interrupted Amy as a male Academy student walked by indicating the end of the intermission.

Pearl settled gracefully into her chair between Jason and Frank. Rev. Conrad's wife—Aunt Millicent—and Boston had often spoken of fighting against liquor licenses when the town was young. It seemed every generation had to fight the battle for high ideals all over again.

Frank leaned close to whisper, "Miss Amy's sweet voice and manner make her Temperance ideas a might more palatable than when presented by some of her more forceful counterparts. I wonder if she'd feel so strongly if she knew that her precious Ed Ray enjoys his 'intoxicating liquors' as much as the next man—and that's one of his better habits. Why can't a woman see a man for what he is?"

Her gaze darted to him in surprise, but he'd turned back to the stage where the musicale was about to resume. Always when he spoke of Ed Ray, bitterness clogged his voice. *Did he dislike the man so, or was it that he cared for Amy?*

Jason's hand closed over hers, and her heart dove to her stomach. She stared at the stage, hoping he didn't notice the way his touch had set her trembling. Slowly she turned her head just enough to see his face. He was grinning at her as though he was the proverbial cat that caught the canary—the same pleased look he'd worn after speaking to Miranda. *Was his former fiancée's effect so strong that it would last the entire evening?*

She turned her attention back to the stage and did something she'd never done before. Gently but deliberately, she extricated her hand from his.

∞

Jason set the lamp he'd carried downstairs with him on the kitchen table. The room seemed warm after the unheated bedroom. Even so, he was glad he'd dressed. No sense trying to sleep any longer. Between worrying about Frank and thinking about Pearl, he'd been awake all night. Must be two o'clock by now.

He sat down heavily beside the table and rested his head in his hands. Would Frank get home before dawn? *I shouldn't have let him go sleighing with his Academy friends after the musicale,* Jason thought. He snorted. *Stupid thought.* Frank was eighteen; how could he have prevented him from going?

Besides, Jason admitted reluctantly, he'd been eager to be alone with Pearl on the sleigh ride home. He'd had such hopes for tonight, and it had been a disaster from beginning to end. It was the first time they'd been out together since their wedding, and he'd entertained the thought that perhaps it would be a new start for them.

He'd about convinced himself he'd let his imagination get away from him, thinking his wife was attracted to his brother. He'd stomped out of his memory the dozens of times he saw them together laughing or talking in this very room.

Was there any way after tonight that a reasonable man could believe anything but that his wife preferred his brother's company to his own?

When she'd turned from whispering with Frank to coldly draw her hand from his, the pain was so great he'd wished his heart would simply stop beating.

Immediately before that, he'd been thinking of the pleasure his gift would give her. Amy had agreed to do a painting for Pearl for Christmas, and he couldn't stop grinning from that moment until Pearl so uncharacteristically pulled away from him. Even Miranda's embarrassing flirtation hadn't taken away the joy of arranging something special for Pearl. It shamed him to think he could ever have cared for a woman who would behave so brazenly as Miranda did tonight toward a married man.

His groan seemed to echo off the walls. Pearl gave unstintingly of herself

535

to him and his family, never complaining, never refusing anyone. His love for her grew with every passing day, with her every act of kindness.

He never thought when he asked her to marry him that he might be stealing from her the opportunity to spend her life with a man she loved. He only knew he wanted her in his life and was sure God would bring her around to loving him.

True, he'd been grieving, had lost so much in a short time that his heart cried out for a loving and loyal touch. He knew better than to think that justified what he'd done. He hadn't been thinking of Pearl's needs at all when he proposed, only his own. Love wasn't like that—selfish and grasping. It was giving, like Pearl.

The clear jangle of bells came through the still air, breaking into his thoughts. Jason scraped back his chair and hurried to the window. By the light of the lanterns on the sleigh, he could see Frank all but fall from the cutter. The driver laughed, turned the horse about, and headed down the drive.

The sky had been clear earlier in the evening, a nice night for a sleigh drive. It was snowing now, and the wind was coming up. Relief flooded him that Frank had arrived home safe. The prairie during a snowy night was no place for a drunken man.

He opened the door and helped Frank inside, screwing up his face at the liquor odor that hung strongly about his brother.

Frank leaned heavily against him and hiccuped. "Howdy, big brother."

"Let's take off your coat and boots and get you to bed."

"Don't want ta go ta bed!" Frank pulled away from his hold, stumbling against the table.

Jason grabbed the lamp as it started to tilt. "Watch it!"

Frank's lips spread in a grin. "Don't need ta watch anythin'. You do all the watchin' fer both of us."

"You're drunk."

Frank waved his index finger back and forth in front of his face, then began following the motion with his head. "Yup. Big brother takes care of all of us, whether we want him to or not."

Jason tried to take his arm again, but he dodged. "Someone has to watch out for you when you're drunk like this."

"I kin watch out fer myself."

"Oh? You can't even talk straight, let alone walk or think straight. Isn't it about time you sobered up and started acting like a man?"

Frank weaved closer to him, and his breath smelled like spoiled yeast as he laughed in Jason's face. "That's funny, you tellin' me ta act like a man." He leaned heavily on Jason's shoulder. "You treat yer wife like a hired girl. Least I'm man enough ta expect ta share my wife's bed when I marry."

Fury poured through his veins like molten rock. He pushed Frank from him.

"Jason, don't!"

Pearl's scream reached him as Frank landed against the door with a sickening thud. He ignored her and jerked his brother up by the lapels of his woolen coat. "How dare you insult my wife that way?"

"Jason!" Pearl's hands clung to his arm, and he felt all her weight straining to pull him away.

He glanced at her to tell her to let go, but the fright in her eyes stopped him.

"I won't have you fighting with your brother over me."

With a growl he dropped his brother's lapels, and Frank fell back against the door. Jason watched as he picked himself up and stumbled outside.

Jason's breath was coming as fast as a horse's after a quarter-mile gallop. "You wouldn't have defended him if you heard what he said."

"He was only speaking the truth."

He clenched his fists at his sides, trying to ease the rage and pain inside him.

Her bottom lip trembled slightly, and she caught it between her teeth. She brushed back the hair that fell waist length over her shoulders, kinked from the braids that held it earlier. Her voice was soft and controlled when she continued, "How can he be expected to understand our unusual marriage? Have you explained it to him?"

Tell his brother he'd married a woman who didn't love him? "No." He all but hollered the word.

The pain in her eyes lanced through him. He reached for her. "Pearl. . ."

The wind howled around the corners of the house and whistled between the door and frame, pouring cold air over him. The chill sent slivers of terror through him. *How long had the wind been blowing like that?*

He swung open the door, only to close it quickly against the snow that swirled over the threshold. He stuffed his feet into the boots beside the door. "Better make some coffee."

"Where are you going?"

"To find Frank. A storm's coming up." Pulling on his jacket, he asked, "Is there a lantern in here?"

When she returned from the pantry a minute later with a rope, lantern, and matches, he was tying a muffler over his hat and around his throat.

His hand hesitated over hers on the handle of the lantern. At the sight of the terror in her face, his anger melted away. She was trying valiantly to hide her fear, but he'd known her too long and too well to be deceived. He couldn't bear her hurting so, even if it was for love of his brother.

His free hand cupped the back of her neck and pulled her against his jacket. "Don't worry," he whispered gruffly against her hair. "I'll find him. Likely he's in the barn, sleeping it off."

A moment later, he plunged into the wintery night.

CHAPTER 13

Jason pushed his shoulder against the kitchen door two hours later, shutting out the storm. It took all his strength. He leaned against the door, trying to catch his breath. His muscles felt like he'd been pushing mountains around instead of wind and snow.

His eyelids closed. He let them stay that way, ice-coated lashes resting on his numb cheeks. How was he going to tell Pearl he hadn't found Frank? Maybe he wouldn't have to; maybe Frank had come home himself.

"Jason! Thank God!"

He knew the minute he saw her face that his brother was still out in the storm.

Pearl's fingers tugged at the ice-covered knot of the rope around his waist.

"I didn't find him."

"I know." One of her fingernails snapped, and he saw her cringe; but she didn't stop working at the knot. "You need to get into something dry."

"I didn't want to quit looking, to leave him out there, but I couldn't see more than a couple inches in front of me and. . ."

"I know, dear. You did everything you could." She began to make progress with the knot. A minute later, she had it undone. "Get out of these wet things. I'll bring you some dry clothes."

She busied herself at the stove while he changed, keeping her back to him, then urged him into the sturdy oak rocking chair beside the stove.

She'd changed while he was out, into a simple flannel house gown that reminded him of the rich color of a blue jay's feathers. He liked the way it deepened the color of her eyes.

He had to force his fingers to hold the cup of coffee she handed him. They were still stiff and red, and burning from the cold. His feet were the same, but Pearl had heated the brick used in the buggy, and his feet sat warming upon it now. When she tucked a thick quilt over his lap, he wanted to pull her down on top of it and let their arms comfort each other.

Pearl knelt by his chair and took one of his hands in hers. Laying her cheek against it, she whispered brokenly, "Let's pray together for him."

His words of prayer came haltingly. It seemed he'd been praying the entire time he was searching, but to say the words out loud made the knowledge that Frank's life was completely out of his hands all too real. It didn't help knowing that if he hadn't blown up at his brother when he was drunk, Frank would be safe asleep upstairs right now.

He set the coffee mug on the stove beside him and laid his hand on Pearl's head where it rested on his knee. The stinging of the receding numbness in his body was insignificant beside the longing to take her pain on himself. "I'm sorry, Pearl."

"For what?" Puzzlement shone in her eyes.

"For arguing with him, forcing him out into the storm."

"You didn't force him to do anything. Frank is a man. He makes his own choices, even if they aren't wise."

He wished he could believe her. If Frank didn't make it—well, he wouldn't allow himself to think about that now. As long as there was a chance Frank was alive, he wouldn't give up hope.

Pearl rubbed his hand briskly between her own. "Drink your coffee. You need the warmth." She pushed to her feet and headed toward the freestanding cupboard which held the ironstone dishes. "I made some oatmeal while you were out, too. It won't be as good as if it had steamed all night, but it's nourishing."

"Thanks, but I'm not hungry." *Not for food anyway.* He wished he dared ask her to come back and simply sit holding his hand again.

"You haven't stopped shivering since you came inside." She handed him a steaming bowl. "Now, eat this."

He smiled meekly as he accepted it, the effort cracking his chapped lips. "Yes, nurse." He ate the oatmeal faithfully as she busied herself about the kitchen, setting the table for breakfast, then covering it with a cloth trimmed in red. He knew she was only trying to keep her mind as occupied as possible.

Likely she was constantly pushing away the picture of Frank lying somewhere with the snow piling over him, the same as he was. Silently he repeated the prayer for Frank's safety.

When he finished the oatmeal, she took the bowl from him. He caught her hand, and she stopped, looking down at him with a question in her eyes.

"I'm sorry. About the argument earlier, I mean." He didn't ever want to argue with her again. When he was out in the storm, two thoughts kept battling each other: the need to find Frank, and the regret that he and Pearl had parted angry.

His thumb played across the back of her hand, and he felt her fingers tighten around his. Unable to look her in the eye, he watched their hands instead. "Was Frank right? Do you feel like a hired girl?"

The lamplight glinted off her long blond hair as she shook her head. "No. I don't mind the work. I'm your helpmate, remember?"

She'd avoided the real question, but he let it pass. "Are you sorry you married me?" The words seemed to scratch his throat. His heartbeat throbbed in his ears. If only he could catch the words back! What if she said yes?

"No, only. . ."

He swallowed the lump in his throat. "Only what?"

Her lashes dropped and were framed against her cheek. It gave her a demure, vulnerable look he wasn't accustomed to seeing in her and did funny things to his heart.

"Only sometimes I'm afraid our marriage has ruined our friendship. You were always the dearest, most fun comrade," she rushed on as though eager to explain, lifting her lashes and looking earnestly into his eyes, "but now you so often draw away from me and seem almost angry." She took a shaky breath. "Are. . .are you sorry you married me?"

Was he? Yes, if she loved Frank. But sorry to have her here in his home, beside him every day? "No. No, I'm not sorry. I miss the close friendship we shared, too. How about if we make a pact to get it back?"

Her smile was brilliant. "I'd like that." She moved toward the pantry. "You need some glycerin for your chapped lips and hands."

The lamp on the table cast only a dim, mellow light in that part of the kitchen. Maybe that made it easier to ask. "Why did you agree to marry me?"

She stopped moving for a full ten seconds. Would she ignore the question? "You said you needed me."

It wasn't the answer he longed to hear, but he hadn't any choice but to accept it.

"I love being part of your family. Some moments I almost feel like a mother to the younger ones." She wrapped her arms over her chest, and he had the fleeting thought that she was trying to comfort herself. "Being here has made me wonder about my own mother—the one who died. I didn't think I remembered her well enough to miss her until I came here. Now I wonder whether she'd wanted to move here—to what was then the frontier—whether she loved my father, what her dreams were for Johnny and me, what she thought and feared and prayed for concerning us when she knew she was going to die and had to leave us."

"I've been wondering some of the same things about my own mother these last few months." He cleared the huskiness from his throat and reached a hand to her. "Come here." Did his request sound as much like begging to her

541

as it did to him?

She took his hand hesitantly, and he tugged gently. "Come here," he repeated softly.

He pulled her into his lap, cradling her in his arms, rejoicing in the feel of her head resting against his shoulder, even as he ached for her pain. Teardrops glistened on her lashes, but she didn't cry. He couldn't recall ever seeing her cry. If only his arms wrapped around her could draw her pain away!

One hand cupped the back of her head and slid down the length of golden hair. Never had he felt anything so silky. The only time he saw her hair down was during Grace's nightmares. It had been years since she'd worn it down in public. A tremor ran through her at his touch, and he regretfully forced his hands to be still.

Tentatively he rested his cheek against her hair. He'd wanted to give her comfort, and instead he was frightening her. "Dear Lord, we thank Thee for Pearl's parents and the love they must have had for the little girl they had to entrust into Thy care after having her with them for such a short time. Thank Thee for the hopes and prayers they had for Pearl, which are known only unto Thee. And for Dr. Matt and Boston, who love her as their own. In Thy Son's name. Amen."

"Oh Jason!" Her words were a half sob that wrenched his heart.

"I wish I could take away all your pain," he whispered hoarsely.

"And I yours."

At a noise from the floor above them, Pearl pushed herself quickly from his lap. "I'd best get breakfast. Andy and the girls will be rising soon."

Regret swept over him. Perhaps it was for the best. It had become more difficult every moment to keep from lifting her face to his and kissing her the way he'd longed to do for months.

"The kids all love you. Maggie thinks the sun rises and sets with you. And Grace—thanks to you, her nightmares are almost a thing of the past. The scrapbook you started for her was an inspiration, asking each of us to write down a memory of things Mom and Dad did that showed how much they loved her and then letting her draw pictures in the book to illustrate them. It's become her favorite storybook."

"It's your family's love that healed her. Love is stronger than any fear."

"Yes, I suppose it is." Gratitude for the blessing she was to his family warmed his soul. She'd given so much to all of them. For them it was worth the constant fire that raged inside him, the continual yearning for her love, regardless if she ever returned his affection. But for her? "You've been a great helpmate these last few months. I've sure made a mess of being the head of this family."

"That's not true. You've kept everyone together, kept the farm running, made the payments on your father's banknote, seen to it there was food on the table, and that all the family's needs have been met."

Sausage sizzled in a pan, its odor covering that of the kerosene lamp and the fire in the stove.

He propped his elbows on the rocker's oaken arms and clasped his hands together in front of him. "I've alienated Frank somehow. Can't understand his drinking and carousing and temper tantrums. He never used to do such things."

"Perhaps he's trying to find a way to deal with his grief."

"I would have sworn he knew better than to think a man could handle his problems that way." He ran a hand through his unkempt hair. "Sometimes I want to ask him to leave home and support himself. Maybe that would make him sober up and act responsibly. But the farm and house are as much his as mine, and I've no right to demand he leave."

"Remember your mother's sampler? 'Charity hopeth all things.' We need to keep believing in Frank and hoping for him, Jason. Eventually, God will show you a way to make peace with him."

If he's still alive. He pushed the thought from his mind.

"Our God is the God of hope," she reminded. Her smile warmed some of the ice around his heart.

The God of hope. The thought cheered him. Maybe God would see to getting Frank back on the right path. And maybe He'd even bring Pearl around to loving him. Maybe. The flame of hope he'd thought extinguished began to flicker once more.

"Is. . .is there any chance Frank might be able to go to Windom Academy for winter term?"

Arguing Frank's cause again! His heart constricted painfully. He wasn't about to remind her that the arguments might be meaningless if Frank. . . He swallowed, not allowing himself to complete the thought.

"Do you think giving in to him on Windom would stop his drinking? Even if it did, wouldn't he only resort to drinking again when he runs into life's next disappointment?"

"I wasn't thinking only of his drinking. I was thinking. . ." She hesitated, then rushed on, "I have so much admiration for you and your willingness to sacrifice for your family. Of course, I never thought for a moment you would do anything less, but. . ."

"Forget the flattery. What is the 'but'?"

"Perhaps God isn't asking the same sacrifices of Frank that He's asking of you."

It hadn't once occurred to him to ask God whether he should support Frank's wish to go to Windom this year. All this time he'd thought he was relying on God's strength to run the farm and keep the family together. Had he been kidding himself—only been relying on God to help him go his own way?

"I'll pray about it," came Jason's hoarse response.

Chapter 14

The storm buffeted the house all the next day. The Sterling family even had to keep lamps lit because of the heavy snow and cloud cover. But the quiet among the family was more stifling than the darkness or the howling wind. Everyone but Grace was painfully aware of the dangers of a prairie blizzard. Only five years earlier, the infamous blizzard of '88 had claimed many lives across the Upper Plains states, including the lives of some of their neighbors.

Two of the victims had been Billy Worth's parents. After their deaths, Billy had been taken in by his grandfather. Pearl's brother, Johnny, married about the time Billy's grandfather died. The boy now lived with Johnny and Jewell. Billy's loss in '88 made the danger of the present blizzard more real.

After Jason had explained the situation to Maggie and Andrew, no one had spoken of it. They all realized that until the wind died down, there was nothing any of them could do but pray. By unspoken agreement, they kept busy with work about the house, homework, or playing with Grace. Every few minutes, someone would go to stand beside a window or put on a coat and walk out on the porch, vainly seeking a moving figure in the blinding snow.

Jason and Andrew tied ropes around their waists and went to the barn to care for the animals and chickens. The temperature had dropped drastically, and Pearl felt sorry for the creatures. Their water would likely be frozen before they had a chance to drink more than a few swallows.

When they returned from the barn, Jason noticed Pearl had moved the sampler that had hung in his parents' bedroom to the wall above the kitchen table—a silent reminder not to give up on Frank.

The storm still blew that night, and it was almost morning before it calmed. Immediately after breakfast, Andrew and Jason put on snowshoes and began to search again for Frank. Maggie left for neighboring farms to inquire if anyone had seen Frank, and to request assistance in the search. For once, Jason allowed Pearl to care for the cows and chickens.

It was still early when Jason, Andrew, and Maggie returned with Frank. The relief at finding him alive filled all their faces.

It turned out Frank had lost his way in the storm, eventually stumbling against Thor Lindstrom's barn. Realizing it would be suicide to try to leave the building, he'd huddled in the hay beneath a horse blanket. Thor found him there the next morning when he worked his way to the barn with a rope around his waist to care for the animals. Frank knew his family would be worried sick about him, but there was nothing to be done except stay with Thor and Ellie until the storm wore itself out.

He'd set out this morning with Thor accompanying him. The good-hearted Scandinavian wanted to make certain Frank had the strength to make it home. On the way, they'd met the Sterlings. Pearl never heard whether any cross words were spoken between Frank and Jason at that meeting. She only knew that relief eased the lines of fatigue and fear that had been etched in Jason's face during the prior thirty-six hours, and her heart rejoiced with thanksgiving to God.

Two apple pies filled the kitchen with their delectable odor as Pearl pulled them from the oven a few hours later, reflecting on how quickly the household had settled back to normal. Frank's safe return had almost felt anticlimactic.

Jason and Andrew were now busy clearing a path from the house to the barn. That and clearing an area in the corral and in front of the chicken coop would take them most of the afternoon. A few minutes earlier, Maggie had taken a restless Grace outside to make a snowman. The little girl's happy squeals could be heard through the closed windows.

"Guess I caused a mess of trouble, huh?"

She set the pies carefully on the wooden rack of the freestanding cupboard and looked over at Frank. The dark, deep-set eyes that so many Chippewa City misses found romantic watched her broodingly.

"It's behind us. We're all just glad you're back safe and sound." Would this experience convince him to stop drinking? She fervently hoped so.

"I owe you an apology."

She lifted the cover of the Dutch oven on the stove top. The tantalizing scent of beef stew drifted into the room. "Oh?"

"For saying those things about you and Jason the other night."

She hoped he'd think it was the heat of the stove coloring her face.

His chapped hand brushed back his black hair impatiently. "I don't understand. You know more than anyone how much Jason loved Miranda. Why did you marry him?"

"I love him." She could hardly believe the calm with which she met his challenging look. The seconds grew long as they stared. She refused to look away first, as though loving Jason was something of which to be ashamed.

He plunged his hands into his pockets. "I know what it's like to love someone who cares for another. Seems I've loved Amy Henderson since I first began noticing girls."

Frank in love with Amy!

He cleared his throat. "Appreciate it if you wouldn't mention it to anyone. Haven't even told Jason."

There were biscuits to be made for dinner, but she didn't move. It wasn't easy for him to confess his love for Amy, and she didn't want to show disrespect for his admission. "Why haven't you courted her?"

He snorted. Anger filled the eyes he turned to her, making them look black. "Think she'd be interested in a farmer when the almighty Ed Ray, a man planning to be a lawyer, is courting her? If I'd ever entertained such a foolish notion, Miranda's refusal to marry Jason would have killed it."

"You do Amy a disservice, comparing her to Miranda. It's not a man's vocation that will win Amy's love; it's a man's character."

"Ed Ray hasn't a shred of character! Why are women so blind? Why can't she see that Ed's everything she says she detests? He can drink me under the table in no time."

"You needn't growl about it. The truth about a man's character always comes out in time."

"Hope it's before she marries the louse."

Pearl measured the flour into a sieve. "Is that why you want to go to Windom Academy? To impress Amy?"

She'd added soda, cream of tartar, salt, and sugar and run the mixture through the sieve before he answered. "Yes. Sounds downright stupid when you put it into words like that."

"She'd be more impressed if you quit drinking. At the musicale, she told me she was upset you'd turned to it."

Surprise flickered in his eyes. "She did?"

"Yes. She thought it a shame such a fine young man was acquiring such a destructive habit."

Hands on the oilcloth table covering, he leaned across to look into her face. "She called me a fine young man?"

"Yes." She didn't try to hide the twinkle in her eyes. "I give you fair warning, she's praying that you'll give up drinking."

"It would be worth it, for Amy."

His vehemence was almost convincing, but Jason's comment cut through her memory. If he gave up drinking for Amy, would he only return to it again the next time something difficult happened in his life?

She rolled out the dough and reached for the tin biscuit cutter. "There are many men who don't drink. While that's important to Amy, it isn't enough in itself to win her love."

"And what is?"

"A God-fearing man. A man with enough character to do what's right for no other reason but that it *is* right, regardless of the consequences."

With a mutter she couldn't decipher, he turned his back.

"If you want to go to Windom Academy so badly, why have you stayed on the farm? Why haven't you tried to find a position to earn the money to pay tuition?"

He jammed his hands into his pockets and walked to the window. "Jason and Andrew would have had to hire another man to help with the harvest and threshing. That would more than double the expense of my tuition. It wouldn't be fair to the family."

So he felt the burden of the family the same as Jason. "Amy would approve of that aspect of your character—as I do."

A flush spread over his high cheekbones. "I've already destroyed any chance I might have had with Amy. She'd never consider courting me, with my drinking and all."

"You can change. God doesn't give up on us because we make mistakes. If we ask Him to forgive us and help us change, He meets us where we are and gives us a new start. God's love couldn't hope all things for us without that, and we couldn't hope all things for each other."

He slouched against the window frame. "Once I had all kinds of dreams for the future. I don't believe in fairy tales anymore."

She placed the biscuits in the oven. "Dreams seldom fall into our lives like gifts all wrapped up in fancy bows. Hopes and dreams require effort; we must live like we believe they will happen.

"You're a farmer. You know you don't have a crop without plowing and planting and caring for the crops while they're growing. You can't make hopes and dreams happen any more than a farmer can make grain grow from a seed—only God can do that. But we can kill hope by not nurturing it, as a farmer can his crops."

Scorn curled his lips. "You're living in a rainbow world." His arm shot toward the window. "See that? It's winter—cold and barren and hard, just like life."

"Spring and summer and fall, with all their beauty, warmth, and abundant life are just as real as winter. Life doesn't stay hard forever."

He swung from the window, his gazes burning into hers. "Doesn't it?" he demanded. "How easy will life be for you, living out your years with a man who loves another woman?"

CHAPTER 15

How easy will life be for you, living out your years with a man who loves another woman?" Pearl rubbed her fingers against her temples, wishing she could rub Frank's words from her mind. His challenge had been slipping into her thoughts at least once every waking hour for the last week, taunting her faith.

"I won't believe Jason will never love me," she whispered fiercely. "I won't!"

She pulled a linen tablecloth for tomorrow's Thanksgiving dinner from the hope chest that sat at the end of her bed. Sinking down on top of the chest, she rubbed a hand along the smooth finish. Dr. Matt and Boston had given the chest to her for Christmas one year. She'd always loved it.

How silly to think something as intangible as hope could be kept in a chest!

She stood and strode swiftly to the door. Paused. Or was it silly? Was making and storing things for the day one would marry a way of making hope real, helping it grow, keeping it alive—as she'd told Frank one must do?

Of course, one couldn't hope for just anything and expect God to produce it. But if the desired object was God's will—such as husbands and wives loving each other—could it be wrong to encourage that hope?

A picture flashed in her mind—a picture of herself filling the hope chest with acts of love for Jason. She'd call that picture to mind to replace Frank's ugly words whenever they assailed her.

⚭

Warmth wrapped around Jason's heart as he looked down the long table to where Pearl sat at the other end. This was the way it should be, the two of them surrounded by happy family. All the leaves had been added to the dining room table to accommodate the guests: Dr. Matt, Boston, Johnny, Jewell, and curly haired Billy. Having Pearl's family with them for the first holiday since his parents died made it easier for him and his brothers and sisters.

The kitchen had been busy as a beehive all day with the women chattering away while making all the traditional Thanksgiving foods. The smell of roasting turkey filled the house and brought the men to the kitchen time and again hoping for something to satisfy their tempted appetites.

"Would anyone like another piece of pumpkin pie?" Pearl asked.

"Sara doesn't have any pie." Grace giggled at her own humor, her large brown eyes spilling over with laughter.

Everyone smiled at her enjoyment of her joke. Only two months old,

Johnny and Jewell's little Sara wouldn't be having any pie this Thanksgiving Day.

"No more pie for me. I'm going to have my hands full." Jason reached into the basket setting between him and Jewell, and lifted the sleeping baby. *How could anything be so fragile,* he wondered, laying Sara gently against his shoulder. The feel of her trusting, tiny body against his chest created a yearning in the pit of his stomach.

Pearl set a piece of pie on Jewell's plate and smiled down at him, shaking her head. "Couldn't even wait until the child awoke."

Did Jason imagine it, or were her eyes misty? "Some temptations are impossible to resist."

"You can say that again. I never get my fill of holding her." Johnny grinned. "Maybe you'll have one of your own soon."

Pearl's gaze darted away from Jason's as though burned. He watched her continue dishing out pie. *What was she thinking?* "When we have our own," he replied softly, "I want to start just like you did, with a girl. A little replica of her mother."

Pearl's eyes flashed a surprised look at him. She turned away quickly but not before he'd seen the pain in her face and felt it sear through him. He hadn't intended to hurt her.

Did she think she would never have her own children? The thought almost stopped his heart. *Did she think she'd sacrificed that dream when she agreed to marry him?*

He rubbed his chin lightly against Sara's sweet-smelling head. Pearl's daughter—what an incredible gift that would be.

While the adults had a cup of coffee "to settle their meal," conversation covered a myriad of topics: the continuing political argument regarding silver versus other currencies, reports of the growing number of unemployed men across the nation, the effect of the depression on Chippewa City where "hard times" prices were becoming normal and sales were primarily for cash, the recent fire at the local mill—thought to be incendiary—and last week's blizzard in which a local woman died walking to her in-laws' farm.

Jason's gaze flew to Frank, and his throat suddenly felt thick. Seventy-five-miles-an-hour winds when Frank was out in that blizzard! *Thank You, Lord, for saving him.*

Maggie, Andrew, and Billy told of being sent home from school earlier in the week because the building was so cold that the ink was freezing in the ink-wells, of kids bringing their mothers' spoons and knives to plate silver in natural philosophy class, and of teachers requiring whisperers in class to memorize portions of the Constitution.

Dr. Matt leaned back in his chair, hooked one thumb under the lapel of his coat, adjusted the silver-edged spectacles he always wore now, and told about the trip to the World's Exposition in Chicago.

"Why don't we all tell something for which we're especially thankful this year?" Mother Boston suggested during a lull.

Jason's lips pressed a kiss on the top of Sara's head, and he winked at Johnny. "Bet I know what you and Jewell are most thankful for this Thanksgiving."

Johnny laughed and squeezed Jewell's hand. "Bet your guess is right."

"I'm most thankful that Pearl married Jason and came to live with us," Maggie volunteered.

"Me, too." Did Jason's voice sound as graveley to everyone else as it did to him?

Pearl smiled at Maggie, avoiding Jason's eyes. Had he angered her? Things had been so good between them again since the night of the storm. He couldn't go back to the tension they'd endured before. He wouldn't. He noticed Boston lift her eyebrows inquiringly at Pearl and the almost imperceptible answering shake of Pearl's head. What was that all about?

Frank scraped back his chair and threw down his napkin. "Far as I can see, Pearl's the only good thing that's happened to this family all year."

Jason's jaw was rigid in his effort to control his anger as Frank stormed from the room. He knew better than to act like that in front of company!

"Please excuse Frank," Pearl was saying. "Things have been rather difficult for him lately."

His anger grew. *Defending Frank again!*

Then it hit him like a lead ball to the stomach. It wasn't anger at all. It was fear. He was scared stiff that Frank's behavior today and the drinking binges he'd been going on didn't have anything to do with Windom Academy or their parents' deaths. *What if Frank's behavior was his way of dealing with his frustrated love for Pearl?*

Memories flashed through Jason's mind as though he looked at them through a stereoscope. Frank arguing for the right to drive Pearl home from their farm; Frank leaping to defend her honor against Ed Ray's vile comments; Frank getting drunk for the first time the night of the dance—was it because Jason had pushed him aside to defend Pearl's honor himself? Frank claimed he wanted to attend Windom Academy, but he stayed on the farm instead of finding a job that would pay his tuition. Was it to be nearer to Pearl?

Jason massaged baby Sara's back while the fear he'd been fighting for months burned inside him like acid. Were his wife and brother in love with each other?

∞

Eventually the others left the kitchen to the women. Maggie and Grace watched Sara so Jewell could help with the dishes. Andy and Billy went out to the barn, searching for something more exciting than adult company.

CHAPTER 16

The children chatted excitedly beneath heavy lap robes in the back of the wagon, listing the places they wanted to stop on the Christmas shopping trip. Pearl hadn't seen so much anticipation and joy in their faces since their parents died. The day away from the farm would be good for them.

Good for Jason, too. He and his brothers had been butchering this week. All of them hated the job, hated taking the lives of the animals they'd cared for so faithfully, but no one mentioned it. It had to be done. Perhaps today would wipe some of the memory of it from their minds.

Sunlight glinted off the snow, making the already bright day brighter. The runners which had replaced the wheels for easier travel squeaked as they glided over the snow. Clouds rushed from the horses' mouths, and frost coated the mufflers wrapped around the family members' faces.

The clear day offered a beautiful view of the river valley from the bluff which towered over the business section. Smoke from the store chimneys and the six stacks from the railroad roundhouse rose straight and tall in the crisp air. Jason and his large, shaggy, blanket-covered work team had all they could do to keep the wagon on its runners under control as they started down the steep street from the top of the bluff.

The town had changed radically during her lifetime, Pearl thought. Barely three hundred people lived in the town when she was born. Now there were almost two thousand. She'd been glad to read in the newspaper that tubular gaslights had been put in at the train station house last week. Her experience with the tramp back in August was one she didn't care to relive.

The millineries, pharmacies, clothing stores, hardware store, furniture store, jewelry stores, and general store all had their windows filled with Christmas displays, and nothing would do but they had to stop and admire each one. Maggie, Grace, and Pearl were captivated by the dolls and miniature furniture arranged in a Christmas party at Heiberg and Torgerson's, while the men preferred the carving of a Viking ship.

They stopped at Sherdahl Jewelers—not to purchase but to allow the children to see his electric lights. Maggie and Andrew peered closely at them, fascinated, but Grace hid behind Jason's legs and wanted nothing to do with the strange bulbs that held no flame or odor. Andrew tried to hide his excitement and pride when Mr. Sherdahl invited him along with Jason and Frank to view the two-horsepower engine that drove the lights and machinery in his store.

When they left, Jason spoke again of his desire to see the town establish an electrical service, listing its benefits as though the family hadn't already heard his arguments on the subject numerous times.

"You're a farmer now," Frank reminded him. "I'd think you'd be more interested in farmers rather than townspeople having electrical service."

That ended the conversation but sparked a strange thought for Pearl. It did seem Jason was born a city man. His conversations often centered on improvements for Chippewa City. He had dreams for the town, the same as Dr. Matt. It was Frank, although determined to continue his education, who went to the Grange meetings and read *The Progressive Farmer* until it was rags.

Jason and Frank had some business to attend to so they left the others for a bit. Jason promised to meet them at Dr. Matt's pharmacy in an hour.

The first stop for Pearl and the children was Bergh's General Store. Pearl wanted to find something for Jason before he returned.

Running a finger lightly over the top of a carved wooden collar box, she frowned and looked over a display: collar boxes, cuff boxes, workboxes, jewelry boxes. Jason wouldn't have much need of these now that he was on the farm instead of dressing daily as a rising young architect with a town office.

With Andrew's help, she decided on flannel slippers with lambs-wool liners. They would keep Jason's feet warm against the winter drafts that plagued their home, in spite of the hay piled around the foundation. Besides, the gift was thoughtful without being personal. With their unusual relationship, she felt her options were limited.

Before leaving the store, Pearl and the girls admired the silk and woolen mufflers, the latest novelties in dress goods and trimmings, plush cloaks and jackets, and ladies' shawls. Andrew was more interested in warm winter boots, hats, and gents' duck coats.

When they made their way to Dr. Matt's pharmacy, a crowd of children was huddled around the show window. The Sterling children were as fascinated as the rest at the reproduction of the world's fair Ferris wheel, its baskets in constant motion and loaded with dolls.

Bells chimed merrily as they entered. Jason entered right behind them. The warmth of the potbellied stove felt good to Pearl. Dr. Matt wasn't in, but Mr. Jenson, one of his clerks, greeted them cheerfully in his rolling Scandinavian accent.

"We want to look at dolls," Grace told Mr. Jenson importantly. Pearl and Jason exchanged delighted smiles over her head.

The clerk grinned from ear to ear. "You came to da right place, you betcha. Ve haf a t'ousand dolls—largest assortment ever brought to dis city." He looked at Jason. "Anyv'ere from one penny to two dollars. Everyt'ing in da store priced to suit da hard times, you betcha."

The toy department was a children's paradise. They passed tin toys, iron toys, wood toys, musical toys, mechanical toys, toy beds and cradles, toy trunks, drums, rocking horses, shooflies, tea sets, toy furniture, banks, games of every description, hand sleds, storybooks, picture books, scrapbooks, panorama books; the variety seemed endless.

Grace was unaffected by it all, heading straight for the wall covered with dolls. After fifteen minutes of carefully listening to her critical review of numerous samples, Pearl and Jason left her alone with them and looked about the rest of the store.

They found Maggie admiring a display of autograph albums and scrapbooks, so popular with young girls and ladies. Andrew was lost in the book department among the dime novels. Pearl smiled at Jason and shook her head. Would Andy's desire for adventure ever wane?

When they returned to the toy department, Grace was cradling a doll in her arms. It was porcelain, about eight inches long, with soft brown hair and eyes that opened and closed. It was difficult to convince her to leave the doll behind.

When the children finally drifted off to other stores to complete their own Christmas purchases, Maggie taking Grace with her, Jason and Pearl were free to do their shopping.

Of course, the doll with the eyes that opened and closed was a must for Grace. It was their first purchase.

At Pearl's question, Jason explained that their money wasn't so tight they would have to be "stingy" with their giving. The children had all been patient in asking for things for the last few months while Jason learned the basics of the family finances and running the farm. He felt they could afford a piece of clothing at a reasonable price for each child, and the doll for Grace. With the small gifts the children would be exchanging among themselves, it should be sufficient.

When they passed the lot where the town hall and opera house were to be built the following spring, Pearl noticed Jason's gaze linger over the sight and his lips tighten. She recalled happening upon him one evening in the parlor, sketching his idea of the future building. He'd flushed when he realized she'd recognized it and tossed the paper into the parlor stove, neither of them saying a word. She hurt for him but his willing sacrifice for his family only increased her love.

It was such fun shopping together, having friendly arguments over the most appropriate gifts, feeling Jason's hand at her elbow, shopkeepers nodding at them and calling them Mr. and Mrs. Sterling, as though they were one entity.

A stop at Kent's Confectionery and Bakery resulted in a few pieces of bright ribbon candy, oranges from California, and apples from New York to place in the Christmas stockings.

They chose a blouse of dainty French flannel for Maggie. Pearl was almost through making a school dress of the softest pale gray wool for Grace, and she purchased black braid for trim to complete it.

It was difficult to choose for Andrew. When Pearl moved to the farm in August, he was two inches shorter than Maggie. Now he was just barely taller and no telling how much more he'd grow. None of his clothes hung right on him anymore. They finally settled on a pair of leather boots, which were costly at just over five dollars but which were sorely needed. Pearl would try cutting down some of Frank's old slacks and shirts for the boy after the holidays.

When she asked about Frank, all Jason would say was that he'd already purchased his gift. His reticence made her curious.

A pictorial album of Chippewa City in blue leather with gold print, just published by a local photographer, was chosen for Dr. Matt. A porcelain heart pin, adorned with tiny painted pansies surrounding the word "Mother" in gold script, caught Pearl's attention. During the last few months she'd grown to appreciate Boston's sacrifices for her and Johnny in new ways. Perhaps this pin. . .

"Would you like it for Boston?" Jason asked.

She shifted her gaze to other pieces in the display case, not wanting him to see how badly she desired the piece. "We can find something else. The price is quite dear."

"We'll take it," he told the clerk.

She spun to face him, and he smiled at her with a tenderness that tugged at her heart. "We'll take it," he repeated.

"Thank you." Her gaze tangled with his. It wasn't until the clerk handed them the small package wrapped in brown paper and tied with red twine that she realized with an embarrassed start they were still staring at each other with silly smiles. The memory of it made her incredibly self-conscious through the dinner at a local restaurant. She queried the others about their shopping throughout the meal, glad for a reason to avoid Jason's eyes. An excitement that had nothing to do with Christmas buzzed beneath the surface, making her giddy.

After dinner, they stopped to watch kids sledding down the bluff, which dropped sharply from the prairie to the old river bottom where Main Street was built. It offered the only challenging sledding for miles. When one of the boys offered to let Andrew use his coaster for a run, he grasped at the chance. "Can I, Jase? I'll take Grace along."

Jason rubbed his chin, watching the kids whizzing past. The town fathers didn't approve of sledding in this part of town, with busy Main Street at the bottom of the hill filled with horses, delivery wagons, and buggies. Still, he was too close to boyhood himself not to remember the thrill of that bluff.

"All right. But don't forget what Dr. Matt said about all the loose teeth and broken bones he's seen from sledding the last few weeks."

It wasn't but a few minutes before Grace's laughing face zoomed past, Andy's arms shielding her from any possible harm. When the girl ran up to them, Pearl straightened her red crotcheted bonnet. "Was that fun?"

"Yes! We went fast! Faster than horses! And snow came up and splashed on my face!" She raised mittened hands in the air to demonstrate, giggling until her sparkling eyes and red lips seemed to meet.

The new Shakespearean Ice Rink beside the mill was next. It was fun to be on ice skates again. Grace was new to the sport, and her eyes were huge as Pearl and Jason skated along with her between them. When she was finally brave enough to try it on her own, she was on her chin or her bottom as often as on her skates, but those falls did nothing to dent her spirits.

If only people could keep that unconquerable zest throughout the true difficulties in life, Pearl thought, watching Grace once again struggle laughing to her feet. Some people did, people like Jason.

Her gaze drifted to Frank, who was gloomily watching Amy skate past with Ed Ray. Why was it that Frank took the easy road of complaint and excuses? Why did he refuse to hope and work for a better time?

Her thoughtful wanderings were cut short when Jason caught her hands as he darted past, pulling her about in a whirling circle and laughing down at her. "Skate with me, Mrs. Sterling," he implored, slowing to draw her against his side, taking one of her gloved hands in his own.

They skated perfectly together, a unison born of skating together many times in the past. His breath was a gentle warm rush against her cheek when he leaned closer to share a thought or a comment on one of the other skaters.

It made her heart race and her legs threaten to weaken if he removed his arm.

"By Henry! Frank's actually loosened up and is skating with a girl. I don't believe it!"

She quickly found the couple in the crowd. Amy Henderson was smiling up at Frank's slender face, her hand tucked securely in his. Pearl's breath caught in a happy little gasp.

Jason went stiff beside her and pulled away a fraction. Pearl looked up at him in surprise. Chilly air sliced between them where before there had been only warmth. His brow furrowed into a scowl as he watched Frank and Amy.

Confused, she looked back at the couple. Another couple was skating nearby. Miranda and Grant. So that was the reason for the change in Jason! Hopelessness wiped away the joy that filled her only moments before. Would Jason never get over loving Miranda?

She lifted her chin and swallowed the tears that formed a large knot in her throat. Hadn't she been admiring Grace's pluck only an hour ago? Had she so soon forgotten "Charity hopeth all things"? They'd only been married a few months. God hadn't put a time limit on hope, saying one could give up hoping when it seemed difficult or unendurably long. She wouldn't let herself quit hoping for her husband's love!

Pearl leaned into Jason's side, ignoring the pain that flashed through her at the way he seemed to stiffen further at her action.

"Today has been wonderful."

The look he gave her held no joy.

She forced herself to continue smiling. "We'd best be getting home soon. We'll all be exhausted tomorrow if we stay much longer."

Without comment, he stopped near the bonfire where Andy was eating popcorn with a number of other skaters. Leaving her, he gathered up Maggie and Grace. Frank had decided to attend a soap bubble party and taffy pulling at the banker's residence—one of the community's attempts to follow Rev. Conrad's advice to draw the town's young people away from the saloons and billiard halls.

"How will he get home?" Pearl asked.

"He'll find a way," was Jason's curt reply.

Her heart sank. After the friendliness of the last few weeks, were they going to be drawn into another period of silent hostility?

Without physical activity to keep them warm, the winter cold penetrated their clothing and the robes covering them in the sleigh. Even the bricks that they'd warmed beside the bonfire before leaving didn't keep Pearl warm. But then, her heart was frozen.

Once at home, Andy stirred up the embers in the kitchen stove while Jason took care of the horses. Then everyone hurried about hiding their purchases from possible prying eyes. When the stove was hot enough, Pearl made hot chocolate, and everyone gathered about the kitchen table.

She put bricks and irons on the stove to warm while they visited, as she did every night, to be wrapped in clean rags and used to warm the beds, as there was no heat in the bedrooms other than that which rose from the first story through small square registers in the bedroom floors.

Soon the household was in bed. After the stimulation of the day, Pearl couldn't sleep. She mixed buckwheat batter and set it on the back of the stove to rise for breakfast. Still restless, she took the school dress she was working on for Grace into the kitchen and stitched the braid in a fancy pattern along the hem and sleeves by the light of the kerosene lamp.

Two hours later, she heard Jason's step on the stairs. He stood beside her chair awkwardly. "Couldn't sleep?"

She shook her head. Was he sorry, too, for the stiffness between them this evening?

He reached out to touch a sleeve of the dress, which looked especially delicate next to his large, callused hands. "It's pretty. I saw you teaching Grace to sew the other night."

"She's six; it's time she learned. She's trying to hemstitch a handkerchief and is determined to give it to Mother Boston for Christmas."

"You do a lot for my family."

His family. The definition hurt her.

His eyes searched hers, and she wondered what he was trying to find there. She didn't realize she was holding her breath until she released it when he moved to a window.

"Worrying about Frank?" he asked.

She shook her head. "No. At least tonight there's no storm for him to get lost in. Actually, I'd forgotten he was still out."

"Forgotten?" His one word exploded with accusation. What had she done now?

He ran a hand through his already tousled hair in the gesture that had become so familiar to her. The despair in his face cut into her chest. "I don't remember when I've been as terrified as I was the night of the storm, wondering if he was lying dead out there. Hoped the experience would be enough to stop his drinking." He spread his hands helplessly. "What should I do for him?

What would Dad have done? I just don't know what to do."

She looked down at her stitches. "We can only keep praying for him until God shows us something He wants us to say or do." *What else was there to do? We are both too young and inexperienced with life to know the answers to things like this,* she thought.

Jason dropped into a kitchen chair and rested his head in his hands, dejection in every line of his body. "Sometimes I think God must get downright weary of hearing me ask Him about Frank."

"Proverbs says, 'Hope deferred maketh the heart sick: but when the desire cometh, it is a tree of life.' It's natural to become discouraged waiting for the things we hope for. That doesn't mean we'll never see what we desire. God will answer our prayers for Frank."

Jason propped his chin on the palm of his hand. "You've been studying scripture verses on hope for some time now. What is it you're hoping for so hard?"

A smile started on her lips and grew until she wondered whether it would ever stop. Could he read the answer in her eyes?

"I'll tell you when my hope is fulfilled."

∞

The morning chores were completed, breakfast eaten, the dishes done, and the children off to school before Frank came home in the company of Sheriff Amundson the next day.

Jason and Pearl hurried out to meet the wagon as it pulled up at the gate, Pearl pulling a shawl about her shoulders on the way.

Frank's angry eyes challenged Jason's from beneath black brows when the sheriff said in his Norwegian accent, "Frank here has been fined five dollars. Didn't haf the money to pay, but I figgered you'd be good fer it, Yason."

"What's the charge?"

"He vas arrested vit a number of ot'er men last night—some of t'em prominent businessmen—in a raid on the gambling den over Plummer's Saloon."

CHAPTER 17

Tears sprang to Pearl's eyes, and she caught her breath in a gasp. First drinking and now gambling! Hadn't the Lord heard their prayers at all?

She shoved the thought away from her immediately. Of course, He had. It was Frank who hadn't been listening to God.

Her gaze collided with Jason's. His face was stiff with restrained emotion. "I'll get the money."

Pearl watched him walk swiftly to the house, hating the pain this latest revelation was causing him.

When the sheriff left, the three remained standing in tense silence in the snow-filled yard. Frank's eyes smoldered, refusing to back down from Jason's steady gaze.

"Why don't you say it?" he finally blazed. "Tell me what a failure I am, how I've dirtied the family name!"

Jason didn't say a word. His silence curdled like fear in Pearl's stomach.

Frank shifted his feet. "It was just a friendly game of cards."

Pearl knew his anger would only increase if she or Jason reminded him that any form of gambling, including cards, was illegal in Chippewa City.

"With the low price of wheat making money hard to get and stores refusing to give credit, it's no wonder folks are resorting to gambling."

Jason dug his hands into his coat pockets. "Would seem spending money on liquor and gambling might not be a wise investment in hard times."

She could hardly believe Jason's voice was so calm. He'd always flared at Frank's indiscretions in the past.

"*You* can say that? When farming is the biggest gamble of all?" Frank challenged.

"If that's true, I shouldn't think you'd have need of any other kind."

Frank made a sound for all the world like a growl, turned on his heels, and stalked toward the house.

Pearl stared after him, rubbing her hands over her arms beneath her shawl, wondering miserably what she could say to comfort Jason.

"You'd better go inside, too, Pearl. You must be freezing."

The look in his eyes stopped the words on her lips. Was it pity she saw there? Pity for Frank she could understand, but for her?

His worn suede work glove rested on her cheek, and the gentleness in his voice almost hurt her. "Don't give up on him. We'll keep hoping for him, just like you said."

Later Jason drove into town for supplies. The day seemed long with him away. Frank spent the day husking corn. Pearl was glad to have Frank and his grumpy mood out of the house.

She was surprised to find Miranda on her doorstep in the early afternoon. Her smile did nothing to ease the apprehension Pearl felt at her presence. "May I come in?"

Pearl wanted to refuse, but decorum wouldn't allow it. She lifted her chin a trifle and stood back to allow her to pass. Silly to wish the door opened into a lovely entryway instead of the kitchen, when the visitor was the dearest friend from her childhood and had entered her adoptive parents' home by the kitchen hundreds of times!

When she took her guest's coat, dismay rippled through her at Miranda's fashionable Nile green costume. Loops of ribbon edged the narrow plaitings, waist, and wrists. The yoke of faille in front of the waist was trimmed with passementarie. The leg-of-mutton sleeves exaggerated her already tiny waist. Pearl's own checked gray flannel housedress seemed inordinately dowdy in comparison, and she hoped fervently that Jason wouldn't return until the visitor left.

She hung Miranda's cloak on a peg behind the kitchen door and indicated the rocking chair beside the stove. "Won't you sit down? If I'd expected you, I'd have started a fire in the parlor stove. I'll just put on some coffee for us."

"My, but you are the domestic little woman, aren't you?"

Her glance darted suspiciously at Miranda, who was gracefully adjusting her skirt. Had she imagined the sarcastic undertone?

Miranda looked up at her innocently and smiled. "What do you do with your days out here?"

"The same thing most housewives do with their days—care for the home and family."

"Does it seem terribly dreary after living in town? I seldom see you at the socials or dances."

Why, oh why had she come? Her very presence seemed to taint the atmosphere of their home. "Dreary?" She kept her voice light and smiled airily back at her guest. "Spending time with my new husband?"

Miranda's lips stiffened slightly. "Ah, but there are so many others underfoot." Her fingers moved to play with the delicate cameo pin at her neck. The brooch Jason had given Miranda for Christmas only last year! Pain and fury twisted feverishly in Pearl's stomach. No true lady would flaunt such a gift in front of a man's wife.

Frank's taunt rang in her thoughts—"*How easy will life be for you, living out your years with a man who loves another woman?*" She slammed the door of her mind against the words, and brought to mind a picture of herself tucking into her hope chest the memory of Jason and herself praying together for his family.

It calmed her. "This is Jason's family's home. We do not consider his family an imposition and do not allow our guests to speak of them as such."

In spite of Miranda's assurance that she had stopped to call in order to repair their friendship—"it is the Christmas season after all"—Pearl found the visit most uncomfortable and impatiently wished Miranda would leave.

"Have you and Mr. Tyler set your wedding date?"

"Not yet." Miranda dropped her gaze self-consciously to her lap. "Grant does pester me to agree to a date until his insistence is almost improper, but I feel it isn't wise for a woman to agree to marry so quickly. Don't you feel the same?"

"Yes, I do. Providing the couple doesn't know each other well."

Miranda's fingertips flew to her pursed lips. "Oh my dear, I do apologize. I'd forgotten you and Jason married so impulsively."

Of course she hadn't forgotten! Pearl looked demurely down at the fine china cup in her lap. "When two people are very much in love. . ." She shrugged daintily.

She had the satisfaction of noticing Miranda's lips tighten momentarily.

"I was disappointed not to receive an invitation to your wedding. But I forgive you, dear. Grant and I hope that you and Jason will attend our wedding, just the same."

Pearl set her cup and saucer on the table, avoiding an answer. If Miranda called her "dear" once more, she would scream!

"Since I wasn't at your wedding, won't you show me your wedding gown?"

"I don't think. . ."

Miranda was already standing. "I do so love beautiful gowns. The master bedchamber is this way, is it not?"

Pearl hurried behind her, furious at Miranda's brazen manner.

Miranda didn't hesitate at the bedchamber door, but walked in as though it were her own.

She looks like she's cataloging every detail, Pearl thought angrily as Miranda's eyes darted about the room.

The unwelcome guest stopped beside the dressing table and ran the tip of her index finger along Pearl's mother-of-pearl hand mirror. "All your lovely toiletries. Does your husband have none of his own?"

Their eyes met in the mirror, Pearl refusing to look away from Miranda's amused gaze.

"The gown must be in here." Miranda pulled open the doors of the handsome cherry clothespress and ran her hand along the gowns hanging there. "Why, this holds only your clothing." She turned to face Pearl, a self-satisfied smile spreading across her round face. "Jason isn't sharing your bedchamber, is he?"

CHAPTER 18

"I believe it's time you left, Miss Sibley."

Pearl almost went limp in relief and gratitude at the sound of Frank's voice, rigid with constrained fury. When had he come up behind them?

He strode across the room and grabbed Miranda by the arm. "Allow me to escort you out."

"Frank, let go of me this instant!" She jerked her arm, but he only tightened his grasp on the voluminous Nile green sleeve and hurried her toward the stairway. "You're hurting me!"

Pearl hurried along behind them telling herself she should insist Frank unhand their guest, but she couldn't get the words out.

Frank grabbed Miranda's lovely cloak from the peg and threw it into her arms. Yanking open the door, he shoved her through it. "Don't ever come to this house again."

The door slammed between them, closing off Miranda's indignant face.

"I don't know how to thank you. I couldn't think how to stop her, and . . . and. . . How could anyone be so dreadful?" To her horror, tears shook her last words.

Frank propped his fists against his hips. "Why didn't you tell that imitation of a lady to leave yourself?"

She wiped her fingers across her cheeks to catch any stray tears. "I'm surprised at you. A lady would never do such a thing."

His guffaw brought a trembling smile to her lips, and she hiccuped. "Jason mustn't know what she said."

"He won't hear it from me," he promised. "My big brother should thank God daily that he's not in that woman's clutches. Imagine spending your life with someone like that!"

"She isn't all bad," Pearl defended automatically.

"Well, he got a much better deal with you. He's a good man. He deserves a good wife."

"You're no longer angry with him?" Surprise tinged her question.

He shrugged. "Not his fault Mom and Dad died or that the country is so strapped financially." He ducked his head self-consciously. "I just wish he'd quit treating me like a kid or a hired hand. I'm only a couple years younger than he is, and I was raised on the farm, too. Do you think he ever asks my opinion about how anything should be handled around here? He does not! Why he even talks things over with you, and you're just a woman!" He flushed. "I'm sorry. I didn't mean. . ."

"I understand." Another time she would have argued that women have as much intelligence as men, but she didn't want to stop his confidence. It was true Jason discussed the business of the farm with her often. His sharing meant a great deal to her. She knew how uncommon it was for a man to discuss business with a woman.

"I just wish he'd treat me like an equal," Frank was saying.

She linked her fingers loosely in front of her. "I don't believe Jason realizes the way you feel. Taking on the burden of the farm and the family is the only tangible way Jason knows to deal with the grief of losing your parents. It's the last thing he can give them—the only thing he can give them now."

Frank's deep-set brown eyes met hers. "How does he expect me to deal with my grief?"

She had no answer.

He leaned back until the chair stood on only two legs. "I've been doing a lot of thinking. Figured Jason would be ready to wallop me when the sheriff brought me home, but the only thing I saw in his face was disappointment." He shook his head slowly. "Hurt me a lot more than anything he could say or do."

A flush spread up his neck, and the chair dropped back to all four legs. "What you said about being a man Amy could love—well, I've been considering that. You're right. With every passing week I've become more like men I don't respect—men like Ed Ray. Amy deserves a man of strong character, like Jason."

Thank You, Lord! her heart cried. "Jason isn't perfect," she said cautiously. "He makes mistakes like everyone else. I believe the strength he does have comes from leaning on Christ's strength."

Frank propped his elbows on his knees and examined his fingertips as though they held the secret of life. "Along with being angry at Jason, I've been pretty mad at God, too. Couldn't stop thinking about the things you said a few weeks back about God meeting us where we are and forgiving us—though, believe me, I tried to forget! This afternoon I told Him I was sorry. I mean to follow Him from now on, with His help."

Knowing an emotional display would only embarrass him, she refrained from grasping his hands as she wanted to do and settled for a simple "I'm glad." One hope that had become a tree of life!

"I realized it wasn't Jason or God who was messing up my life. I'm doing a pretty bang-up job of it all by myself. If I was attending Windom Academy right now, I would have been suspended after last night. Using intoxicating drinks and frequenting saloons and billiard halls is cause for expulsion."

"Yes, I know."

"Heard Amy with my own ears saying she wouldn't court any young men who drink, and even that didn't stop me. Figured I hadn't a chance with her anyway, so what did it matter? After she hears I've added gambling to my vices. . ."

"Shouldn't that be past tense?"

He snorted. "It's definitely past tense. Only good thing about last night is that Ed Ray was hauled in by the sheriff, too. At least Amy will know the truth about him now."

He sucked in his lips beneath his thin black mustache and took a deep breath. "Do you think I have any chance with Amy, after all the dumb things I've done?"

"Only she can answer that."

The chair almost fell over when he stood up. He slid the palms of his hands nervously down his jean-covered thighs and back up again. "Think I'll ride into town tonight. I'd kind of like to tell her about last night myself before she hears it from someone else. Maybe then she'll believe me when I tell her I'm turning over a new leaf."

This time she gave in to her impulse and gave him a quick hug. "Welcome back, Frank."

"Welcome back to what?" Jason's words were colder than the winter air that whistled through the open door behind him.

Chapter 19

Oh no!" Pearl yanked the oven door open with a hand loosely wrapped in her voluminous apron. Waving away the smoke, she grabbed the cookie sheet and dropped it on top of the stove. Every cookie was as black as coal—almost as black as Jason's eyes when he'd found her standing with her hands on Frank's shoulders yesterday afternoon. For a moment, she'd thought he was jealous. Ridiculous thought! More likely, his militant expression was the result of meeting Miranda on his way back from town. There wasn't any way they could have missed passing each other.

Joy and relief had routed the anger from his eyes when Frank told him he'd decided to mend his ways and had committed his life to Christ. Still, his gaze held some doubt after Frank left the room. Didn't he think Frank would stick by his decision?

How had Amy responded to Frank's news last evening, she wondered, dropping teaspoonfuls of gingersnap dough on a greased pan. She wasn't about to broach such a potentially delicate subject, despite her curiosity.

As though on cue, Frank came inside. Yanking off his boots, he dropped his work gloves on the table and came over to hold his hands out to the stove's warmth. He cleared his throat and said as though in answer to her thoughts, "Saw Amy last night."

"Oh?"

"She was incredible."

Pearl's throat contracted at the awe in his voice. If only Jason cared for her so much!

"I wasn't certain she'd even allow me the chance to speak, with the rumors about my drinking going around. But she invited me into their parlor, and I told her all the stupid things I've done the last few months—didn't dare leave anything out. Figured I'd rather she heard it from me than from someone else.

"Then I told her about my decision to live the way I thought Christ would want. She seemed pretty glad about that, so I packed up my courage and told her I'd like to court her. Could have knocked me off that dainty little parlor chair with a feather when she agreed to it."

"I'm so glad for you, Frank!"

He gave her an embarrassed smile. "It seems her father has other ideas. Said no way a man with my rotten reputation was going to be seen with his daughter. I tried to explain that I've changed my ways, but he wouldn't believe it."

"I'm sorry."

"Finally he said he'll reconsider. . . ."

"Frank!"

He grimaced. "In a year. If I stay sober and out of trouble for a year, he'll reconsider allowing me to see Amy—if Amy is still willing."

Poor boy! It had taken a lot of courage to make the decision to turn his life around and to tell Amy everything before he even knew whether she cared for him. The disappointment must seem devastating.

"A year sounds like a long time, but at least there's hope."

"I don't understand. God has forgiven me. Why can't Amy's father?" His eyes searched her face for an answer.

She slid her hands into her apron pockets. "God can see your heart, but Amy's father can only judge you by your actions."

A long minute passed while he stared gloomily at the stove. "I hate to admit it, but you're right."

Would he take offense at her next question? It came out haltingly. "You. . . you didn't decide to become a Christian only to please Amy, did you?"

His gaze met hers steadily, and a smile warmed his eyes. "No. That decision stands, no matter what else happens."

∽

The week before Christmas went by in a whirl of activities that put a sparkle of anticipation in everyone's eyes. Maggie and Andrew reluctantly fit studying for an algebra examination into their already full days of classes, studying, and chores. There were no complaints, however, when asked to help with the baking, candy making, or corn popping!

Grace's favorite holiday preparation was making cornucopias. The pride in her smile when she completed her first paper cone, complete with ribbon for hanging and trim of braid from a dress Pearl had made, was a memory Pearl was sure would live in her heart for the rest of her life. No one mentioned that the cornucopia was slightly lopsided or that any small items would be in danger of slipping out the bottom.

The six year old's help increased the time it took to do the Christmas baking, but neither Pearl nor Maggie minded in the least, as Grace's obvious enjoyment added to their own Christmas joy.

One evening Jason brought out a round wooden box and carefully removed three roughly carved wooden figures—Joseph, Mary, and the baby Jesus. When Pearl exclaimed over them, Jason said, "Dad carved these when I was no older than Grace. He said many times a house should have a reminder of what we're celebrating at Christmas."

The figures were placed on the round, marble-topped table in the middle of the parlor. Grace often abandoned her dolls to play with the wooden family over the next few days and never tired of listening to the Christmas story—or repeating it, though her interpretations varied slightly each time!

Friday, December 22nd, kept the entire family busy with the last-minute holiday cleaning, including polishing the nickel and cleaning the fancy parlor stove, strewing tea leaves over the parlor carpet and brushing it well, trimming wicks, and washing lamp chimneys.

As soon as the supper dishes were done, Jason brought in the barrels of greens from New York which he'd purchased in town, along with fine wire and twine. In a gesture that had warmed Pearl's heart, he'd purchased a barrel for the poor farm, also.

The greens were piled on top of the table, spilling the delightful pine fragrance into the air. The family gathered around to form the branches into garlands and wreaths. They chatted eagerly while they worked, teasing each other about the gifts Santa Claus would bring, the children sharing recitations from the Christmas program presented at school that day.

Jason looked across the spicy, forest green pile, and his fingers stopped wrapping the wire with which he'd been working. Pearl's face was filled with a sweet contentment that constricted his heart. If only he could believe she was truly happy here in his home!

The day they'd gone Christmas shopping, his heart had almost burst with happiness at being with her, at her sweet, unusually shy smile, at the way she'd fit so naturally into his arms when they'd skated. Then he'd pointed out Frank and Amy, and Pearl's gasp reminded him that he didn't hold his wife's heart.

After Grace had been tucked in bed, the rest of the family gathered to decorate the parlor. They wouldn't have a Christmas tree, but they had the greens to put up. They all wanted the sight of the decorated room to be a surprise for Grace.

Under Maggie and Pearl's direction, the men hung the garlands, swagging them from the hanging lamp to the corners of the room, attaching them to the picture rail next to the ceiling. More garlands were roped like trim along the fringed edges of the velvet draperies. The pictures on the wall didn't escape. Greenery was hung over the tops of the frames and wound around the wires attaching the pictures to the picture rail.

Jason and Andrew were assigned the task of hanging the roping over the doorway between the dining room and parlor. Frank and Pearl were laughing as they trimmed the railing of the staircase. The sound cut Jason to the quick and made him strangely tired.

Had he ever felt as young and carefree as the two of them seemed tonight, laughing and teasing together? He felt ninety years old, with the weight of six lives and a farm on his shoulders.

Did Pearl feel that way, too? *What a gift to her this marriage has been,* he thought bitterly. He'd loaded her young life with responsibilities and done precious little to relieve her load. Perhaps that was what Frank gave her— laughter and youth and freedom and dreams. She needed that; everyone did.

Pearl had given that to him. Jason's hands froze on the prickly pine. It was true. By becoming his wife and helping him carry his load, she'd given him the freedom to be true to himself and his values. The desire to win her love had given him a dream to replace Miranda and the career he'd given up.

He stepped off the stool. Picking up some of the remaining greens, he moved into the dining room, urging Andrew to join him. There wasn't enough garland left to trim that room as elaborately as the parlor, but they could place the greens about the picture frames and on top of the china closet and doorways.

Escaping the room didn't allow him the luxury of escaping his thoughts. He'd been unfair to Pearl, marrying her as he did. Not that he didn't love her. But he knew better than to think love justified such a selfish action as marrying someone who didn't return his love.

He should have been honest with her, admitted his love for her. Instead, he'd tried to manipulate her heart and her life as surely as Miranda had tried to manipulate his with her announcement that she wouldn't marry him unless he let his family fend for themselves.

Miranda. At the thought of her, he jerked the garland apart more savagely than he'd intended. What had she meant to accomplish, coming out to the farmstead the other day? She'd been turning from the farm lane onto the road when he met her as he returned from town. The sight of her had sent a combination of fear and fury rushing through his veins, and he'd passed her by with only a nod.

When the others retreated to the kitchen, he remained behind to bank the fire in the parlor stove and put out the lamps. One had to be especially careful of fire hazards with greens in the house.

Frank was in his boots and buttoning his coat when Jason entered the kitchen. His younger brother grinned at him with a friendliness that gripped his heart. It was good to have the bitterness gone from Frank's face and voice. "I'm going to run out and check on the animals one last time before turning in."

Jason watched him from between the blue curtains of the kitchen window, hands in his pockets. Pearl joined him, and his heart pumped faster. When he glanced down, her eyes were shining up at him. "It's wonderful to see him so happy, isn't it?"

He couldn't get his throat to work, so he only nodded. Did she love Frank so much that his happiness could bring such joy to her face? Had he destroyed all chance of happiness for himself—and Pearl and Frank, too—by tying Pearl to him with their "friendly" marriage?

He should have the courage to ask whether she and Frank loved each other, but he didn't. Something inside him would shrivel up and die if she admitted to loving Frank.

He forced his gaze away from her. "At least some apparent good has come from the raid Frank was arrested in last week—in addition to his commitment to Christ. Did you see the new town ordinance in the paper?"

Her hair brushed his arm as she shook her head, sending shivers along his nerves. "No."

"The ordinance prohibits saloons and other public places from having pool tables, billiard tables, pigeonhole tables, or cards, dice, musical instruments, or other entertainment where liquor is sold. No chairs, tables, stands, counters, or seats will be allowed in establishments that sell liquor—only a bar and seats for employees behind the bar."

She slipped her hand beneath his arm and squeezed it excitedly, and he stuffed his hands deeper into his pockets to avoid drawing her into his arms. "That's wonderful! At least young men won't be so blatantly tempted to gamble any longer. God can make good come out of anything, can't He?"

A small smile tugged at the edges of his mouth. "Yes, out of anything." Even out of the marriage he'd botched?

The wish to have her with him like this always, the joy in her eyes due to her love for him instead of Frank, was like a physical pain. She was fine and wonderful; he'd never believe anything less of her. If she did love Frank, she'd never act on that love and be unfaithful. Frank wouldn't be dishonorable either, not in that way, despite the drinking and gambling he'd fallen into—especially now that he'd decided to change.

But he wanted more than Pearl's faithfulness; he wanted her love.

His gaze slipped to the sampler on the wall above Pearl's head. *"Charity hopeth all things."* How many times had he heard or read that over the years? He hadn't known living the verse would be so painful. In his youth, he'd been foolish enough to believe that loving made all things easy. It only made them possible.

When he'd asked Pearl to marry him, she'd said she wasn't in love with anyone. If she'd grown to love Frank, it was because Jason had brought her to his home.

He'd believed God would cause Pearl to love him. But could God work in a situation that was a result of selfishness such as his?

He can if one asks forgiveness. The thought was like a bright light in the darkness that had filled his heart. Had his failure to ask forgiveness for his selfish actions stood in God's way of answering his prayers and fulfilling his hope?

Jason's prayer was simple and direct, and left him feeling relieved. He didn't know what, if any, changes would result from his prayer, but at least his unforgiveness would no longer stand in God's path as He worked in all of their lives.

∞

Early afternoon sunshine poured through the kitchen window Christmas Eve day to play on the packages and bright coffee tins filled with baked goods piled high on the table. Everyone but Jason was dressed and ready to leave.

Pearl grabbed a buttery sugar cookie from Grace's hand. "Be careful not to get anything on your pretty dress. You don't want it dirtied before Mother Boston and Dr. Matt see it, do you? It's so pretty!"

Grace grasped the edge of the table, shoulder high on her, with both hands and grinned up at Pearl, the sparkle in Grace's eyes showing plainly that she, too, thought her new dress was lovely.

It was. The ruby red silk accentuated the excited flush of her cheeks. The Mother Hubbard styling with the high standing ruffled neck and puffed sleeves made her look deceptively angelic.

Pearl had thought she'd never get the child dressed and ready. Frank had taken her with him to hang suet on tree branches and sheaves of grain on fence posts for the birds and wild animals. It was a Christmas custom he'd learned from their Norwegian neighbors, Thor and Ellie, when he was just a child. *Trust Frank with his love of animals to embrace the custom,* Pearl thought.

The door opened, allowing Frank and crisp winter air to enter together. "Horses are harnessed." He indicated the items on the table with a slight wave of his gloved hand. "These ready to put in the sleigh?"

Pearl raised her hands to her cheeks and shook her head. "I hope so. What if I've forgotten something?"

"No harm done. Your family will be here tomorrow for dinner, anyway," he reassured her.

"I do wish you could be with us for dinner at my parents' tonight, Frank."

"Someone has to see to it the cows are milked this evening. But I'll try to meet you for church services afterward."

"Good." She turned about, only to find herself face-to-face with Jason, who had just entered the room, freshly shaved and dressed in his best black suit, a high, round linen collar at his throat.

"My, you look handsome!"

A pleased look followed surprise across Jason's face. She wanted to melt right through the floor. Surely she hadn't said that! The snickers in the background assured her she had.

She watched his gaze swiftly take in her own turquoise silk with the dainty ribbon bow at the throat topping the jabot of cream-colored lace, and the wide ribbon accentuating her slender waist with a large bow in front.

"You're beautiful, Pearl."

The huskiness in his voice sent shivers skittering along her nerves.

"Aren't you two going to follow tradition?"

Perplexed, Pearl turned toward Maggie. "Follow...?"

Looking wide-eyed and innocent, Maggie pointed above Pearl's head.

Her heart sank to her stomach and beyond when she glanced up. Andrew had wired a kissing ball with mistletoe onto the end of a broom and was standing behind Jason, holding the abominable thing over their heads.

A quick glance at Jason showed he was as flustered as she. Andrew, Maggie, and Grace were wearing grins as wide as the Minnesota prairie.

"C'mon, Jase, kiss her!" Andrew taunted.

Jason would never kiss her without her consent, she was certain. Still her glance darted about the room, anywhere but Jason's face. Frank was leaning against the door, arms crossed over his chest, amusement in his eyes. The memory of his ridicule of Jason for not sharing her bedchamber flashed through her mind. She couldn't allow Jason to be embarrassed like that again.

She rested a hand on Jason's woolen sleeve. The smile she gave him when she lifted her face to meet his gaze was a triumph of courage over sheer terror.

"Merry Christmas, Jason."

For a moment she feared he would reject her offer. Then the surprise in his eyes turned to wonder, and his hands gently cradled her waist.

"Merry Christmas, my love." The words were for her ears only. His gaze didn't leave hers as he bent to touch her lips with his.

Her eyelids drifted shut. His kiss was a thousand times sweeter than any of her dreams.

CHAPTER 20

The children's hoots and applause slowly filtered through Jason's consciousness. Reluctantly he released Pearl's sweet lips. He tried to read her reaction in her eyes, but she shielded her gaze from his with her lashes and moved swiftly to retrieve her cape from one of the kitchen chairs, avoiding looking at anyone.

Had his kiss embarrassed her frightfully? He recalled how she'd always hated parlor game kisses, believing kisses should be reserved for those one dearly loved and given reverently. He moved behind her and took her cape, helping her into it. She stiffened when he rested his hands on her shoulders. The delicate scent of lavender surrounded him, and the soft touch of her hair against his cheek was like a taste of heaven as he whispered in her ear, "Thank you for not embarrassing me in front of my family."

He'd hoped she'd turn around into his arms. Instead, she merely nodded and moved through the door.

Was it only to save his pride that she'd kissed him? For she had returned his kiss, he thought, following her to the sleigh, returned it warmly and sweetly.

At the sight of Frank helping her into the conveyance, Jason's jaw all but locked. He forced it to relax as he moved around the back of the vehicle and climbed up himself. He even managed to smile as he waved good-bye to his brother.

The feel of Pearl's lips against his own was still with him. The sweet, willing manner in which she'd leaned against him and offered her kiss rekindled the hope and determination he'd allowed fear to almost extinguish. Pearl was his wife. He was going to do everything in his power to win her love. If Frank loved her—well, that would have to be between Frank and God. Surely God meant another woman for Frank. It couldn't be God's will that he love his brother's wife.

He'd tell Pearl that evening, get his love out in the open, and trust the Lord to help them through whatever the future held.

∽

Pearl had eagerly looked forward to spending Christmas Eve dinner with her parents and Johnny's family. Boston and Dr. Matt's home was decorated in greens, with large, floppy red bows accentuating the forest color. Fresh red carnations in the middle of the linen-covered dining room table added fragrant cheer.

Bayberry from the tapers lighting the table blended with the scents of pine and carnations, only to be lost with them to the smell of oyster soup, and later, succulent roast beef and gravy. Boston's best china, silver, and crystal reflected back the flickering light.

Anticipation of the church service and gift exchanging to come made everyone talkative during the meal. Yet Pearl had difficulty keeping her mind from straying to Jason's kisses. Once she even found her fingertips resting against her lips. Mortified, she removed them immediately, wondering whether Jason, seated beside her, had noticed and realized her thoughts.

Had she only imagined that he seemed especially solicitous and kind this evening? And the way he'd looked into her eyes and smiled—deliberately and warmly—as though she was the most special person in his world. At one point she'd had to catch herself from whispering, "I love you."

That was when she became truly nervous. He'd asked for her to be his wife and housekeeper; he'd not asked for her love. It would only make things more uncomfortable for them both if she confessed her feelings for him.

But what of the words he'd whispered against her lips, her heart argued? What of those impossibly sweet whispered words—*"Merry Christmas, my love?"* They hovered in her thoughts like a promise throughout the evening.

She understood now what Boston had tried to tell her on her wedding day—understood that sacrificing and hoping and believing for one who doesn't return your love meant living with constant pain.

She was tired of hurting inside, tired of the continual longing for his love. Still, given the chance to marry him again, knowing what she knew now, her answer would be the same.

The families had agreed to exchange gifts among themselves before the service; Jason's family would exchange their own gifts in the morning.

Watching Grace's delight in her gifts gave Pearl a welcome reprieve from the emotions that had held her captive since Andrew appeared with the kissing ball. Johnny and Jewell gave Grace a lovely apron of India lawn with lace edging the square neckline, and nothing would do but that she try it on immediately over her red silk Christmas dress.

Boston and Dr. Matt's gift to Grace surprised everyone. It was the reproduction of the world's fair Ferris wheel Dr. Matt had displayed in his pharmacy window, along with a tiny doll that fit in the wheel's baskets. Grace laughed and squealed, clapped and jumped up and down, unable to contain her excitement. Jason, Johnny, Billy, and Andrew were as taken with it as the little girl, and spent half an hour on the floor with the toy and Grace.

Pearl's most precious memory of the evening would be when Boston first saw the heart pin. From the tears that filled her eyes, Pearl knew she understood that from now on, she would always be Mother to her, and not Mother Boston. The love that had grown in Pearl's heart for Jason's brothers and sisters over the last few months had taught her how special Boston's devotion had been to her and Johnny.

True to his word, Frank joined them for church. Pearl knew it would be especially meaningful to him this year.

She loved hearing Rev. Conrad read the Christmas story in his rumbling deep voice. The Christmas service was always one of her favorites, the hope for the world becoming reality in the person of the baby Jesus.

Christ—the promised Messiah and Savior. Another hope that took a long time for fulfillment. She thought of the thousands of years that passed from the time of the promise to Christ's birth. Had people grown weary watching for the hope of a Savior to arrive?

Grace tugged on the leg-of-mutton sleeve of Pearl's turquoise dress and whispered loudly, "I know that story."

Pearl nodded, holding a finger to her lips. Grace faced forward again, sliding to the edge of the wooden pew, silently mouthing the words along with Rev. Conrad. Over her head, Jason and Pearl shared a smile that wrapped Pearl in a warm feeling of family and belonging.

After the services, the family scattered about the chapel, each seeking out special friends for a Christmas greeting. Maggie took Grace along with her, allowing Pearl to slip out to the wagon for the tins of cookies to exchange with friends.

The church was almost empty when she had distributed her gifts, and received *julekake*—a Scandinavian Christmas bread—and delicate golden rolls of lacy Scandinavian cookies called *krumkake* in return from Swedish and Norwegian friends. She hurried down the aisle to where Frank was speaking with Amy and her father.

"I don't blame you for not wanting me to court your daughter, Mr. Henderson," she heard Frank say. "I'd feel the same if I were her father. But. . ."

She'd intended to ask Frank if he'd seen Jason, but realizing the seriousness of his conversation, she slipped past without being noticed by the three. A quick prayer rose from her heart for Frank as she entered the narthex.

Hearing Jason's voice coming from the cloakroom, she started toward it. Her feet and heart came to an abrupt halt at Miranda's honeyed voice.

"Jason, I made an awful mistake when I called off our engagement. I only agreed to marry Grant to make you jealous. It's you I love, not Grant. If you have your marriage to Pearl annulled, I will still marry you."

CHAPTER 21

The three miles home were the longest miles of Pearl's life. She tried valiantly to act as though she hadn't heard Miranda's offer to Jason, and smiled and laughed with the rest of the family. If her laughter seemed strained and pitched higher than usual, no one mentioned it. The jingling bells Frank had tied to the horses' harnesses and the Christmas hymns the family sang couldn't chase away her pain.

What had Jason answered Miranda? She hadn't stayed around to find out. She knew Jason's beliefs would never allow him to dissolve their marriage, but those beliefs didn't prevent him from loving Miranda.

When he'd joined the rest of the family at the sleigh, his jaw was set so firmly it could have been chiseled in ice. Was he thinking that he could have married Miranda if he hadn't been so hasty in asking Pearl to be his wife?

She didn't wait to be helped from the sleigh when they arrived home but climbed down herself and hurried inside, lighting the lamp with the bit of red flannel in it that sat on the kitchen table. A moment later, she was stirring up the fire in the kitchen stove and announcing to those coming in behind her that she would be heating apple cider to warm them before they retired.

While Frank and Andy unharnessed the horses, Maggie and Grace warmed themselves beside the stove. Their cheeks and noses were red from the cold and wind, and their eyes sparkled with holiday joy.

Pearl entered the pantry to retrieve the cider and almost jumped when Jason's hands cupped her shoulders from behind. He took her cloak and whispered, "I'm going to start a fire in the parlor stove. Don't forget we have the stockings to fill after the others are in bed." He carried the cider jug to the kitchen for her.

Her hands were unsteady as she carried the cups to the table. Tonight of all nights, she did not want to be alone with him! How could she possibly keep to herself the knowledge of the conversation she'd overheard? She needed time alone to pray and compose herself.

She warmed the julekake while the cider heated. The cardamom from the frosted bread and cinnamon sticks added a festive scent to the air as the group enjoyed the warmth of the apple cider.

"Hardly seems like Christmas without Mom and Dad." Andy's eyes glinted suspiciously.

The mood in the room changed drastically at his words.

"We all feel that way," Jason admitted.

There was a sheen in his eyes, too, and it shamed Pearl. She'd been so concerned with her own desire for Jason's love that she'd forgotten this was the family's first Christmas without their parents.

"Before we go off to bed," Jason was saying, "maybe we should all share our favorite Christmas memories of Mom and Dad. Kind of like Grace's scrapbook stories with a Christmas theme."

By the time everyone had shared a memory, tears brightened every eye and smiles touched every face.

"Dear Lord, our Father, thank Thee for making each of us a member of this family." Everyone's head bowed as Jason began the unexpected prayer. "Thank Thee for giving us parents who loved us and Thee, and for the years Thou lent them to us, and for the wonderful memories they've left us. We thank Thee, also, for bringing Pearl into our lives and making us one family. In Jesus' name. Amen."

Tears misted her eyes at Jason's inclusion of her in his prayer. Grace drove away the somber mood with an eager question: "Do we get to open more pwesents now?"

Maggie shook her head. "Not until tomorrow morning."

"Why?"

"You have to go to bed so Santa Claus can bring your presents. He can't come when you might see him, you know," Maggie explained patiently.

"He could have come when we were at church. We couldn't see him then."

Pearl grinned at the child's nimble reasoning.

Jason shook his head. "I was just in the parlor, and there are no presents. Of course it might be because there aren't any stockings hung up yet."

Grace gasped, her eyes huge. "My stocking!"

Maggie and Grace retrieved stockings for everyone. Maggie held up her long ribbed wool stocking. "At last this ugly, itchy, baggy thing will serve a purpose other than humiliating me."

Pearl smiled in sympathy from her own experiences with the uncomfortable necessity.

Grace frowned as the stockings were passed out to the appropriate family members. "Mine is the smallest." Her bottom lip jutted out, and she sat down in the rocker, throwing herself in a slump against the back.

Jason picked up her stocking and held it alongside his, pursing his lips and pretending to study them seriously. "Guess mine is the biggest stocking here.

How about if we trade? I didn't ask Santa for anything very big anyway."

Her pout rolled away, and she threw out her arms in a silent offer of a hug. Jason complied, lifting her into his arms. "Thank you, Jason!"

He kissed her cheek. "You're welcome." His brows met. "Who do you think is more important, Pumpkin—Jesus or Santa?"

Grace's face scrunched in serious concentration. "Jesus." Her head bounced in a decided nod.

"Why?"

"Well, Santa comes only at Chwistmas to bwing pwesents if we've been good. Jesus came at Chwistmas, too. But the pastor says Jesus stays with us all the time, in our hea'ts, and loves us even if we fo'get to be good."

Jason smiled. "That's exactly right."

Frank dug his hands into the pockets of his wool trousers. "Best sermon I've heard in a long time."

Jason grinned at him over Grace's head. "Now how about if you go up to bed with Maggie, Pumpkin? Sooner you're asleep, the sooner Santa will come."

"Will you and Pearl come listen to my pwayers when I'm in bed?"

"Don't we always?"

She nodded vigorously. "But this is Chwistmas, and I was afwaid you might fo'get."

He gave her an extra squeeze before setting her down. "We never forget you, Pumpkin."

"Never," Pearl repeated, smiling at the little girl.

By the time they'd listened to Grace's prayers, Maggie and Andrew were ready to retire, also, and Pearl was dreading that the time alone with Jason was drawing near. She felt reprieved when they returned to the kitchen to find Frank still there.

She panicked immediately when Frank stood, raised his arms high over his head in a stretch, and said he was ready to turn in, too.

"I saw you speaking with Amy this evening," she said, hoping to delay him. "Did you give her a Christmas gift?"

Jason's head jerked toward her so swiftly she couldn't keep her gaze from meeting his. The shock in his eyes sent despair tumbling through her. How could she have been so thoughtless of Frank's confidence?

"I'm sorry, Frank. I forgot you hadn't told Jason."

Frank shrugged, and the startled look in his own eyes slipped away. "It's all right. No reason he shouldn't know, I guess."

Jason's brows met above troubled eyes. "Know what?"

He sounds as though he wasn't at all certain he wants to hear the answer, Pearl thought.

Frank gripped the back of the kitchen chair in front of him. With a rather sheepish look, he said, "About Amy Henderson. I. . .kind of like her. A lot."

Jason looked thunderstruck. He stared at his brother, his jaw hanging open. "You mean you. . .and Amy?"

Frank grimaced. "Well, there isn't any me and Amy yet." Succinctly, Frank told him the story.

Before he was done, Jason had lowered himself into one of the chairs, and Pearl thought curiously that it looked for all the world as though his knees trembled in the process.

"Anyway, after church tonight, her father allowed me to speak with her." Frank took a deep breath, his grip on the chair tightening. "I told her I intended to follow through on my commitment not to drink or gamble but it is going to be mighty hard waiting a year to court her."

"What did she say?" Pearl asked.

"She said, 'Mr. Sterling, I'd be pleased to have you escort me to next year's Christmas Eve service. We can then thank the Lord together for giving you the strength to keep that commitment.' "

Frank's almost black eyes lifted to Pearl's. "It's like you told me. God meets us where we are. I wish I'd never tried the drinking and gambling route. Deep inside I knew it wouldn't help anything, but I tried it anyway. Now I have to live with the consequences, including a year of not courting Amy." His grin was strained. "Guess if Jacob waited seven years for Rachel, I can make it through one year. With the Lord to lean on and with Amy's faith in me, there's no way I'm going to backslide."

Pearl envied Amy such a love! It took her two attempts to speak. "You can trust Amy not to promise herself to another before you court her. She'll be waiting for you next Christmas and will give you the chance to win her heart forever."

Frank's eyes were hungry with the desire to believe her.

The legs of Jason's chair squeaked across the linoleum as he pushed it back and stood. He clapped a hand on his brother's shoulder. "Amy Henderson is a good woman. I hope you win her."

Pearl thought Frank's grin endearingly self-conscious.

"Why didn't you tell me about her before?" Jason demanded, giving his brother a friendly shake.

Frank brushed his hair off his forehead. "Guess I didn't want anyone feeling sorry for me or laughing at me if she wasn't interested."

"I'd be the last one to laugh at that."

Is he thinking of Miranda? Pearl wondered at his husky admission.

Jason pulled an envelope from an inner suit pocket. "Your gift from Pearl and me."

Questions filled Frank's eyes when he lifted them from the opened paper moments later. "A receipt for the winter term at Windom Academy."

Jason jammed his hands into his wool trouser pockets and nodded briskly. "I figure I can handle most of the work around here during the next few months, with you and Andrew helping out weekends and after school. We can reevaluate in the spring, but we'll try to keep you in school as long as you want."

Frank reached out a hand, and Jason gripped it. "Thanks, big brother. Way I see it, with the way the railroads and other businessmen keep taking chunks of profit from grain and livestock the farmers raise, a farmer's got to have a good education today in order to stand a fighting chance. Then, too, there's the changing agricultural methods and farm machinery. Farmers've got to keep up."

Jason's brow furrowed. "Reckon you're right."

"When I get out of school, I'm going to do my share by this family so you can get back to being an architect." He looked down at the slip of paper in his hands and took a deep breath. "I've been trying to get up the courage to tell you. If things work out the way I hope, I'd like to run this farm one day."

She saw Jason swallow, and she had to restrain herself from hugging her brother-in-law. This was Frank's true Christmas gift to Jason, no matter what tangible item he would give him.

When Frank went upstairs a couple minutes later, Pearl could no longer avoid Jason. The time spent with Frank had lessened the tension between them. Perhaps it wouldn't be as bad as she'd feared.

She picked up the stockings from the table and started toward the parlor. "I guess it's time to play Santa Claus."

He stopped her with a hand on her arm. "How long have you known Frank cared for Amy?"

"I don't recall exactly." Why did he look worried?

"You. . .won't mind if they court?"

"I think it would be wonderful. Don't you?"

His grin routed every trace of concern from his face. "I sure do, Mrs. Sterling."

He played with the tiny bow at her neck, and she stepped nervously away.

"You were right about Frank, I think," he said. "I was so busy being the boss that it never occurred to me to ask God what He wanted anyone else here to do."

He took the woolen stockings from her, then tugged gently at her hand. "Come with me. I want to give you your gift tonight, too. It's in the parlor."

A shaky laugh tripped out at the eagerness in his face. "You're like a child when it comes to Christmas."

He stopped at the archway between the dining room and parlor, where the air was rich with the fragrance of pine. "Stay right here, and close your eyes."

She started to protest, then subsided. "Yes sir."

She heard the straw crunch beneath the carpet as he crossed the room, and smelled the sulfur of a lit match, the kerosene of a lamp before he said, "Open your eyes."

He stood near the hanging lamp with its large rose-colored shade. The lamp's light illuminated the two paintings in their oval, tortoiseshell frames over the green velvet settee.

Her hand flew to her throat. *Two* paintings. Beside the painting of his parents was a painting of *her* parents.

She walked toward it slowly, stopping at the settee. "It's perfect. How. . . when. . ."

He slipped behind her and slid his arms around her waist. "Amy Henderson painted it for me, copied from your brother's picture of your parents on their wedding day. I asked Amy to do it the night of the play. It seems only right that your parents' picture should hang beside my parents' picture. After all, our families are joined forever by our marriage."

Forever. The word brought back Mother Boston's words from Pearl and Jason's wedding day—*a lifetime is a long time to be unhappy.* Had she sentenced Jason to a lifetime of unhappiness?

She shivered as his lips touched the side of her neck softly. "Merry Christmas, Mrs. Sterling."

At his husky whisper, longing and terror joined forces to spiral through her. What was happening between them tonight? She freed herself from his arms and moved to the opposite side of the round marble-topped table in the middle of the room. At least now there would be something between them, and perhaps she could keep her mind clear.

"Jason, I'm sorry." Her fingers twisted the turquoise bow at her waist. "I should never have married you. I meant to make your life easier; instead, I only brought you pain."

"Pain?" A frown emphasized the lines the wind and sun had already worked into his young skin. "You've filled my home with cheerfulness and hope. If it weren't for you, Maggie would still be frightened of me, Grace would still be having nightmares, and Frank would still be drinking and gambling and running away from God. How can you possibly think you've hurt me?"

"Tonight at church. . ." It was so degrading to put it into words. She tried to swallow the lump in her throat. She tried again. "I was looking for you. I overheard Miranda tell you. . .tell you. . ."

Even in the mellow lamplight, his face looked suddenly pale. His hands fell to his sides in fists. "I'd give everything I own if you hadn't heard that."

She ran the tip of her tongue over her lips, which felt as parched as if she'd spent a week in the desert. "If I hadn't agreed to marry you, you'd be free to marry Miranda now."

His lips narrowed into a line as taut as a bowstring. His voice was just as taut. "I don't want to marry Miranda."

"Don't! Don't lie to me. You've never made any secret of your love for her."

He rubbed a hand over his mouth. "How much of my conversation with Miranda did you hear?"

She lowered herself onto the edge of the settee cushion. "Enough to know she claims she still loves you, and would marry you if. . .if. . ."

Jason sat down beside her and took her hands in a gentle hold that refused to allow her to pull them back. "Did you hear my answer?"

She turned her gaze to the ornate parlor stove, watching the firelight through the grate. "I didn't need to. I know you'd never break your marriage vows, regardless of your love for her."

"Thank God you have that much faith in me, anyway."

She caught her bottom lip between her teeth at his fervent words. Didn't he know she would never believe he could do anything dishonorable?

"The boy I *was* loved the girl who *was* Miranda. The man I've become doesn't love the woman Miranda has become." He paused, and she fought the temptation to look at him. "It shames me to think I could ever have cared for a woman who has such little regard for another's marriage vows made before God that she'd. . ."

Her gasp at his suddenly tightened hold stopped his words. He touched his lips to her hands in apology before taking a ragged breath and continuing, "When I asked you to marry me, I told you I needed you. It was true but not because I needed a housekeeper. I needed you because my house and heart were empty without you. I needed you because I'd fallen in love with you."

Her heart trembled within her, not daring to believe what he was saying.

He trapped the gaze that darted to his.

"I thought if we lived together in a friendly marriage, you might grow to love me. I would never force my. . .my affections. . .on you, but I think it's only fair to let you know where I stand. I've been praying for your love. And I give you fair warning that from this moment on, I intend to court my wife good and hard."

It was the tremor in his voice that gave him away. Why, he was scared stiff! As frightened as she'd been of not having love returned. The knowledge loosened her throat. "I'm afraid your courting shall prove exceedingly short."

Disappointment dropped over his face like a mask. "I see." He stood. "I guess. . ."

"Because," she interrupted with a tiny smile, "your wife has always loved you."

The glory in his face as he pulled her into his arms humbled her. "You dear!" His whisper was rough with love.

Joy shimmered through her. *What a lovely Christmas gift!* And to think that after all the months of trusting God for her husband's love, she almost hadn't recognized the fulfillment of her hope when it came. "Do you remember asking what I hoped for so much that I studied Bible verses on hope?" she asked shyly.

He nodded.

"I was hoping for your love."

"It's yours, my dearest. Always."

His hands slipped up to cradle her face. It seemed to her he studied every inch of it before he slowly lowered his lips to touch hers in a kiss so tender that her heart ached.

Resting his chin against her hair, his arms wrapped around her. "It's quite a life I've tied you to, a hard life with a ready-made family—at least until Frank's ready to take over the farm."

"I'm not complaining."

She shivered as he drew his thumb lightly over her cheek and along her jawline. "No, you never have complained."

"If we love each other and the Lord, we can handle anything. Love 'beareth all things, believeth all things, hopeth all things, endureth all things.' "

He kissed her lightly. "Love 'never faileth,' " he whispered. His golden brown eyes filled with promises.

"Never." A smile tugged at her lips. "Or as Grace would say, 'You can't ever change your mind.' "

His chuckle was lost in her kiss.

KIOWA HUSBAND

by DiAnn Mills

Dedicated to Roberta and Wesley Morgan

PROLOGUE

Independence, Missouri, April 1848

"Lydia, Sarah Jane, are we ready to pull out in the morning?" Papa wiped the sweat from his brow with a dirty sleeve and sunk the dipper into a bucket of cool water for a drink.

"Very soon," Mama said. "Sarah Jane and I want to make one last check."

He leaned against the side of the narrow, canvas-covered wagon. "The sooner we leave, the sooner we get to Oregon. Is that not right, Sarah Jane?"

"Yes, Papa." She struggled to push the heavy flour sacks next to the trunk containing their clothes. Beside this rested bolts of gingham and an extra pair of shoes for each of them. Papa had decided they'd make the four- to five-month journey to Oregon, and she and Mama had been working extra hard ever since. "Do you have a little time to read me the list from the guidebook?" Sarah Jane asked.

Mama pulled the book from her apron pocket and handed it to Papa. He studied the list of suggested supplies before calling out what they needed for the journey. "Six hundred pounds of flour," he began.

Sarah Jane counted the bags. "Yes, we have them."

"One hundred fifty pounds of lard, two hundred forty pounds of bacon, one hundred fifty pounds of beans, looks like plenty of dried fruit, thirty pounds of sugar, ten pounds of salt, and twenty pounds of coffee." He peered inside the shadowed wagon. "There's the cookstove, fry pan, kettle, knives, spinning wheel, rope, ax, and my shotgun." He peered closer. "In the corner I see the grindstone, my shovel, and the water keg. Are the sewing supplies, medicine, and clothes in the trunk?"

"Along with blankets and the Bible," Mama said. "We still need to pack many of the provisions into wooden boxes on the wagon bed. I need the coop attached to the side of the wagon for the chickens, and don't forget the tar when we ford the rivers."

Despite the wearisome day, Sarah Jane felt excitement tickle her stomach. "We won't want for a thing."

"I might squeeze in my fiddle." Papa gulped the rest of the water. "What do you say, daughter?" His mustache widened with the smile beneath it. She'd never seen him so happy.

"That would be glorious. We can send merriment into the heavens. In fact, we might have a singing fest tonight."

"After the prayer meeting." Mama stared down her long nose at him. Many times she'd shared her bad feelings about the trip, and Sarah Jane had seen Mama weep on more than one occasion.

Papa wrapped his arms around Mama's shoulders. "Of course, Lydia, after we ask the Lord to bless us with safe passage to Oregon."

"And no Indians to bother us, only to trade," Mama said.

Papa glanced at Sarah Jane. "We'll say extra prayers for God to keep us safe from marauding Indians. It doesn't please me one bit that a white man who's been raised by them heathens is scouting for the wagon train."

Mama gasped. "Surely not! Is he Christian?"

Papa shrugged. "I'm praying the wagon master knows what's best." He glanced at Sarah Jane. "Mind you stay away from him. I don't trust him—no, not for one minute."

"Yes, Papa." Sarah Jane had seen Painted Hands. His skin was as light as Papa's and his beard the color of walnuts, but he dressed like an Indian. She'd heard he'd lived years with the Kiowa and committed horrible atrocities against the whites.

Sarah Jane shivered. She prayed God would keep them all in the palms of His hands.

CHAPTER 1

Papa had warned that the hardships of traveling to Oregon would bring about the worst in the emigrants. Until today, Sarah Jane refused to believe his words. They had good friends among the folks in the wagon train. Everyone pitched in to help in times of trouble, and some evenings were filled with singing and dancing to the tune of Papa's fiddle. During the day, she often walked with the Robinson girls. If their parents knew how they giggled about the single men showing off at every opportunity, the girls would have received a good scolding; but the chatter helped ease the monotony.

"We're all marrying age," Martha Robinson, the oldest, had said three days ago. "I bet by the time we get to Oregon, we'll all have our husbands picked out. Might even be married."

"I won't." Sarah Jane nodded with her words. "I promised Papa I'd help him put in the first spring crop and harvest it before I up and marry."

"Let your new husband help," Amelia said. "How could your papa object to that?"

Sarah Jane laughed. "I imagine he'd be glad for two able-bodied people instead of one." The sound of horse hooves pounding into the prairie dirt captured her attention. Papa reined in his mare and called her name.

"I need you to drive the wagon for your mama." A frown tugged at his mustache. "She's feeling poorly."

Sarah Jane hurried back to the wagon, her heart pounding with worry over Mama. When she lifted her skirts and climbed onto the wagon seat, she inwardly gasped at her mother's pale cheeks. The journey so far had been hard on everyone, but Sarah Jane didn't mind the toilsome days, only the way Mama never seemed to be content. She seldom spoke to Papa and Sarah Jane, and she didn't show any interest in the other womenfolk either. In a far corner of Sarah Jane's mind, she feared Mama had allowed her apprehension of the trail to possess her soul.

Since they'd crossed the Kansas River and headed in a northwest direction, the wagon train had battled hailstorms, lightning displays that lit up the sky as though God had torched the heavens, and the ever-present flash floods. Once a piercing crack of thunder had sent over fifteen hundred head of cattle stampeding into the night. The wagon train lost two days rounding up the cattle and burying four people who had gotten in the way of the frightened animals. The unpredictable weather and the hand of death trailed them all the way to the

Platte River, a little over three hundred miles across the prairie. They'd passed two landmarks, according to the wagon master—Courthouse Rock and Scotts Bluff—and in a matter of days, they'd pass Chimney Rock, which marked five hundred miles from Independence, Missouri. From there they'd move on to Fort Laramie at the foothills of the Rockies. Fortunately, they could rest a little before heading on across the mountains. It was mid-June. Good timing, according to the wagon master, to beat the snowfall in the treacherous Rockies.

One night, after a little boy riding on the tongue of a wagon fell under the wagon wheels and died, she heard the wagon master, Charles Greenham, make a statement. "We're averaging one person dead every eighteen miles."

Papa had turned to Sarah Jane, more serious than she'd ever seen him. "Should we head back, daughter? I have money to purchase another farm."

"But where are your dreams?" Knowing Papa's growing concern for Mama, she added, "Mama will love Oregon. I'm praying for her every day."

Now, as Sarah Jane took the reins from Mama, she wondered if Papa had been right. Mama looked frail, like a fine piece of delicate china ready to shatter. Gazing into her once-sparkling brown eyes reminded Sarah Jane of a cloudy sky—no hope or joy, only the anticipation of one more dismal day. Perspiration dotted Mama's forehead, and the morning had barely begun.

"Mama, why don't you sleep for a while? I'm sure you'll feel better soon."

"I should drive the wagon." Mama's breathing came in short gasps. "You already cook the meals and do the washing and mending."

Sarah Jane smiled into her mother's face. If not for both hands steadying the reins, she'd have hugged and kissed her. "I don't mind. When you're feeling better, we'll do the work together."

Tears welled up in Mama's eyes, and her lips quivered. "I hope so. I'm ready to feel better. I'm ashamed of the bitterness and complaining. My family deserves my best." With those words, she crawled beneath the canopy of the wagon onto a straw-filled mattress and drew the front flaps into a pucker.

Sarah Jane tried not to dwell on Mama's failing health but rather on her encouraging words. Perhaps a little peppermint tea and some castor oil would add color to Mama's cheeks. She used to laugh and urge Papa to play his fiddle and sing. Those days and weeks vanished when the wagon train pulled out of Elm Grove, a mere thirty-three miles outside Independence.

Sometimes she allowed herself to dream about happier days in Nebraska. They'd all left behind treasured friends and cherished memories, but Sarah Jane felt the same enthusiasm as Papa about the Oregon Territory. She loved singing the trail songs and dreaming about the beautiful land awaiting them over the mountains.

When she thought about it, Mama had endured several difficult weeks. First Papa decided he wanted to open a mercantile in Independence. He felt that with the wagon trains heading for California and Oregon, he'd get rich in no time at all. Once they arrived in Independence, something took over Papa, and all he talked about was Oregon. Then he decided that's where he wanted to live. Sarah Jane looked at the situation as an adventure, but Mama had lived enough days on the trail to want a home of her own. To her, Papa shouldn't have dragged them all the way from Nebraska to Missouri, then back out onto the prairie again.

He traded their heavy Conestoga wagon for a lightweight, narrower one and purchased four oxen for the journey and fifty head of cattle. They'd have fresh milk along the way, and he imagined they'd find a way to churn butter, too. Papa claimed bountiful friends awaited them in the parade of wagons and even more once they arrived in the new territory. He planned to have a small farm on the free land, then open a mercantile. A twinge of excitement fluttered through Sarah Jane, but first Mama had to get well.

The day wore on. Mama began to moan in her sleep, and once she called out for Papa. The delirious cries mingled with the creaks of the wagon wheels, prompting Sarah Jane's prayers. Anxiety rose with the prairie heat. The familiar sounds of bawling cows and the shouts of men echoed against her fears. She hadn't seen Papa for quite a while, and she needed him—his wide smile and reassurance. If only someone would ride by, she could ask them to fetch him.

Painted Hands came into view, the man Papa didn't trust. He rode alongside her as if escorting the wagon. Nervousness snaked up her spine. If Papa saw the scout, he might think she was encouraging him. Sarah Jane studied Painted Hands through the corner of her eye, a formidable man dressed in buckskin. He wore his walnut brown hair parted down the middle and tied on both sides with pieces of rawhide woven with brightly colored beads. If he'd have looked more like a white man or ridden a horse other than a spotted one, perhaps she wouldn't have trembled so.

"Miss Benson," he said, his words slow and distinct.

She turned toward him and willed her nerves to steady. Just as Papa had described him, he showed no trace of emotion. "Yes, sir."

"Can you tell me where I might find Mrs. Benson?"

"She's resting right now." Sarah Jane moistened her lips. "Have you seen my papa? I need to talk to him."

"Your father is why I'm here."

Sarah Jane weakened while her heart drummed in her chest. "Is something wrong, sir?"

He rode a little closer, and for the first time, she saw his eyes, blue like a cloudless sky, and they looked calm, not at all wild or evil. "Your father seems to have taken ill. He fell off his horse. Mr. Greenham and a few other men are with him now, but he needs to rest in the wagon."

She squeezed the reins until the leather dug into her palms. Without another word, she pulled out of the line of wagons and followed Painted Hands. *Please, Lord. Let Papa be all right. With Mama sick and Papa not faring well, this is more than I can bear.*

Up ahead, Papa's horse, a fine mare, stood with no rider. Some men had dis-mounted their horses and hunkered over a man lying on the ground. *It must be Papa.* The oxen moved at such a slow pace when she needed to tend to her father. Sarah Jane willed herself to stop thinking the worst. Perhaps he'd gotten too much sun.

Painted Hands swung back alongside her. "Easy, Miss Benson. I'm sure your father will be fine."

"Do you know what's wrong?" she asked.

"He's feverish. Mr. Robinson said he complained of a bad headache before he fell off his horse."

Her thoughts tumbled into more prayers. Too many folks had not survived illnesses along the way. "Sir, what do you think it is?" she asked.

"I'm not sure. The sun could have gotten the best of him."

Although she had considered the same thing, something told her Painted Hands knew more than he claimed. Despite the heat, a chill raced up her arms as though warning her of what she'd find. At the site, Mr. Greenham helped her down from the wagon.

"Where's your ma?" he asked.

Sarah Jane avoided his gaze. "She's resting in the wagon." Suddenly, the dirt and dust from the trail settled on her lips, or perhaps the strange sensation sweeping over her was the awareness of impending adversity.

Her gaze flew to where Papa lay so still on the hard ground that she feared he'd died.

"Miss Benson," Mr. Greenham said. "Your pa's real sick. I'll help him get into the wagon, and then the committee needs to meet."

She glanced up. "What do you mean?"

"Look closer. See for yourself."

Kneeling beside Papa and blinking back tears, she searched his pale face. His closed eyes and faint breathing alarmed her. She held her breath. He was unconscious.

"Has he been feeling poorly?" Mr. Greenham asked.

"No sir." Her mind raced. "Well, Papa's been tired and hasn't felt like eating—been fretting over Mama."

"This doesn't look good. Might be contagious." He nodded at the wagon. "I'd best take a look at your ma." He strode to the rear of the wagon while Sarah Jane stayed beside her father. She lifted his hot hand into hers—waiting, praying, willing Papa to open his eyes and speak to her.

The thud of boots alerted her to Mr. Greenham's return. "Your mother's unconscious, too. She's breathing powerful hard."

A lump rose in Sarah Jane's throat. "I need to go to her."

"Miss Benson, you've got your pa to look after, too. Do you feel all right?"

His calloused words angered her. "I'm fine, and I can take care of Mama and Papa."

Mr. Greenham rubbed his graying beard. "Miss, let's get your pa inside before any of these other folks stop to help." A couple of additional men rode their way. "We have this handled," he called. "Thanks for offering."

Painted Hands dismounted. "I'll help you. Miss Benson doesn't need to get any more worn out."

"You're most likely right." Mr. Greenham pushed back his hat. With Painted Hands, they carried Papa to the wagon and laid him beside Mama.

"Thank you," Sarah Jane said. "I'm sure they'll be fine in a few days." She walked around them to the wagon front. "I have some medicine."

"Miss Benson, you need to stay right here. I don't need healthy folks coming down with fever. After the committee decides what's best, I'll be riding back."

Again he'd mentioned the committee—the group of ten men who'd been elected before the wagons crossed the Kansas River. They served as judges and jury on the journey to Oregon. Realization settled on her heart. "Are you thinking of leaving us out here?"

Again the wagon master tugged at his beard. "I'm responsible for getting these people to Oregon safely. No one will get there if everyone's wiped out in an epidemic."

"But you don't know if what Mama and Papa have is really bad."

He peered at her a moment. "How old are you, Miss Benson?"

"Seventeen, sir."

"I recollect a good many women your age are married with families. I'll be expecting you to act respectful of the committee's decision. I'll gather the men together for a meeting at noon."

Sarah Jane stared at the wagon master. With no more words between them, she knew the verdict would be against her. These fine people who sang and danced to Papa's fiddle would leave her behind without thinking twice about her plight.

"Will you be all right?" Painted Hands asked.

Startled, she swung her attention to the Indian scout. "I believe so. I have water to cool them off. I can make a broth—and medicine—" Embarrassed at rambling, she took a deep breath. "We'll be fine."

She followed Painted Hands's gaze to the other wagons rolling by. Women and children asked what was wrong, but she only waved back. The Benson wagon trailed near the end, and she'd soon be alone.

"I'm not afraid," she said and lifted her chin.

He nodded and mounted his horse. Together, Mr. Greenham and Painted Hands rode ahead, no doubt to summon the ten men who'd decide the Benson family's fate.

Lord, I lied to Painted Hands. I'm scared, real scared.

CHAPTER 2

Painted Hands kept his distance from the ten men who would settle the fate of the Bensons. Most of them were as skittish as new colts when he stood in their midst. His buckskins, moccasins, beaded hair, and knowledge of living in the wilderness seemed to intrigue and frighten them at the same time. He'd heard the barbaric stories of how he'd murdered innocent folks, and he'd chosen to let them believe the lies. The Kiowa ways had become a part of Painted Hands.

He understood the grave matter before them. These men had been entrusted with the burden of justice and well-being for the people of the wagon train. To allow the Bensons to continue endangered everyone, including their own families. To leave them behind meant certain death. He doubted if Mr. and Mrs. Benson would survive the fever. To Painted Hands, their shallow breathing marked a clear indication that death would soon claim their spirits. He'd seen the fever before, a sickness that knew neither age nor gender when it came to claiming lives. Typhoid fever. Painted Hands well recognized the symptoms.

"What do you think ails the Bensons?" one man asked Greenham.

"Like I said before—fever, no appetite, and just plain tired," he replied. His graying hair and weathered skin amounted to more than a small token of wisdom, and those under his charge valued his words.

"Do you think it's smallpox?" The same man spoke of the dreaded plague softly, as though saying it made it true.

"No, absolutely not," Greenham said. "They don't have spots. I have a good idea though. I've seen enough cases of them."

"Then tell us," the same man said. "We have a right to know."

"What if it's an epidemic that could wipe us out?" another man asked. "Do we want our families sick and dying?"

"I'll tell you what I think, and Painted Hands agrees with me," Greenham said. "We ain't doctors. We could be wrong, but it looks like typhoid."

A hush fell over the men.

"I'm a Christian man," another man said. "I'd hate to leave them folks out here to die when we could have done something to help."

"We're here to vote on that matter." Greenham stared into the faces of the committeemen. "We need to get this taken care of now. How many of you vote for the Bensons to leave the train?"

Some of the men talked among themselves. A heated discussion rose between a man who wanted the family to stay and another who felt it best for the Bensons to lag behind. Typhoid was a cruel master.

"Quarreling won't solve a thing." Greenham raised his voice. The men quieted, and seven of them raised their hands. A grim look deepened across his brow. "All right—I'll let their daughter know."

Painted Hands couldn't keep the sad face of Sarah Jane Benson from his mind. She was young and naive, destined to die on the lonely trail. Earlier, her haunting green eyes had pierced his soul when she attempted to sound brave. He admired that trait, especially when weeping and regret would not solve the problem. She stood apart from the other young women with her hair the color of sun and red clay. Loose curls framed her face, and when she walked, the prairie wind teased her hair like wildflowers tossed to and fro. And the freckles, the same color of her hair, disguised her womanhood with the look of a child. Unfortunately, her innocence was about to be taken by the committee's verdict.

"Are we going to leave anyone with them?" Mr. Robinson, a hearty man, asked. "Looks to me like we're nailing down all of their coffins. If not for my family, I'd offer."

"I like that idea. And who would be volunteering?" Greenham asked.

"We'd be fools," Sanders said. He was a thin wisp of a man with a soul to match. "Whoever stays will get that fever and die; then one of us has to look after the families left behind."

"Aren't you our preacher?" Greenham asked.

Sanders stepped back. He'd just condemned himself.

"Robinson has a point," Greenham said. "Do any of you feel led to stay with the Bensons? You can join up later."

No one volunteered. The thought of Sarah Jane nursing and burying her parents sat hard on Painted Hands's mind.

"We've got loved ones who need us," another man said. "I agree with Preacher Sanders."

Greenham shook his head. "So that's your vote? The Benson wagon is cut, and none of you fine men plans to stay with them." When no one commented, he continued. "I'll be riding out to the Bensons."

"If God heals them folks, then they're welcome back," Sanders said.

Now he talks of God? I don't hear of grace or mercy. Painted Hands refused to still the anger rising in him. He knew why the men made their choice, but he didn't have to agree with it. "I'll stay with the Bensons." Painted Hands stepped forward. "Greenham taught me about scouting, and I can catch up with the wagons when the sickness is over."

Silence fell around the small group. He had no intentions of asking for their permission—didn't matter anyway. He'd made a decision just as they had.

Sanders cleared his throat. "I don't approve—a young woman with a single man. Looks bad."

A knot twisted in Painted Hands's stomach. "Greenham just asked for volunteers."

"But he didn't mean single men." Sanders shook a bony finger at him. "The Bible says for folks not to be led into temptation."

"It also says do not kill." Painted Hands sensed the old familiar hatred churning through his stomach. He moved closer to the skinny form of Sanders. "Your vote to leave these folks most likely sends them to their death, but if a single man offers to help, that's a sin? Sounds like you're a hypocrite to me."

"What do you know about the Bible?" Sanders clenched his fists.

Painted Hands sneered at the pitiful creature before him. "Looks like a sight more than you do."

"That's enough!" Greenham raised his hand. "If Painted Hands wants to help these folks, that's his business. He knows this trail, been through it four times before. I can lead and scout this train all the way to Oregon if I have to."

"Take a vote," Sanders said. "I say if we leave him behind, then he must marry the Benson girl proper." He turned to face the other men. "What do you say?"

"All right—we'll take another vote." Greenham expelled a labored breath. "We need to get back on the trail, and this bickering is doing nothing but slowing us down."

"Wait a minute," Painted Hands said. "You're telling me that I have to marry Miss Benson or I can't help them?"

The men grew quiet; murmuring rose like the sound of a bunch of clucking chickens.

"No need to vote." Painted Hands now remembered another reason he chose Kiowa ways instead of the white man's. They were a stupid lot—made up rules to suit themselves and claimed to be God-fearing. In truth, they were selfish. "I'd rather bury all three of them than continue one more day with the likes of you." He whirled around and headed for his horse.

"Who's going to marry you two proper?" Sanders called. "I'm a preacher."

Painted Hands didn't attempt to hide his disgust. "How generous of you to offer your services, but I think the young woman needs to be informed since you good men are planning her future."

"Let's ride there together," Greenham said. "You men go on home. I think you've made enough decisions for one day."

Painted Hands grabbed his horse's reins and swung himself up onto the saddle. He couldn't get away from Sanders and the rest of the committeemen fast enough. *Marry Sarah Jane Benson?* What was he thinking? All of this because he felt sorry for the family? He knew how most folks felt about him. He lived somewhere in the world between Kiowa and white man, and the Indian side of him rubbed them like fleas in a blanket. Sarah Jane wouldn't be any different. She'd choose to take care of her folks without his help instead of marrying him. No doubt her folks had warned her about him before the wagon train left Independence. He wondered which she'd fear more, the sickness or being bound to him for life.

Images from the past floated through his mind. His brothers, the Kiowa, saved him from a tragic fire that killed his parents, three sisters, and a brother when he was six years old. That fire permanently scarred his hands and earned him his name. Painted Hands loved his life with the Kiowa, but soldiers removed him at the age of sixteen and placed him in the home of the Reverend Crandle, a godly man who lived and loved his faith. The Crandles lived near Independence and were childless. They doted on him with all the devotion they would have given to their own son. From the Reverend Crandle, Painted Hands learned about God.

Painted Hands embraced the Christian faith, but unhappiness with the white people caused him to abandon God, His commands, and His Word. At the age of eighteen, he learned his Kiowa family had been killed in a military raid. Anger and bitterness, plus confusion as to where he belonged, confronted him every day. He left the Crandles, and for four years, he'd helped guide Greenham's wagons over the prairie and mountains to Oregon.

Prior to leaving Independence this last time, the Reverend Crandle told him about his brother, Jacob, who had survived the fire and settled in Willamette, Oregon. Painted Hands hoped his brother was a key to the past and hope for the future.

"You don't have to do this," Greenham said once they were beyond earshot of the wagons. "I wouldn't blame you for riding as far away from this group as you can get. I say they're crazy. In fact, this is the last wagon train I'm leading. I'm tired of dealing with all the troubles."

Painted Hands laughed. "It's my last." He paused. "Miss Benson may be repulsed at the idea of marriage."

"I know, but she'd be foolish to turn you down. You're a fine man, Painted Hands, and I've been honored to make your acquaintance and work with you these past years."

Painted Hands whipped his gaze toward the wagon master. Greenham rarely did much more than bark orders, but Painted Hands respected him. "Thank you."

"I meant every word. I can see you're torn between living as an Indian or a white; but either way you decide, the other side loses."

Sarah Jane paced along the outside of the wagon. She'd washed down Mama and Papa with cool water and tried to get them to drink ginger tea, but neither one could swallow it. They drifted between sleep and unconsciousness, both eaten up with fever and delirium.

She stared in the direction of the wagon train and pondered the committee's decision. Deep within, she sensed the lone wagon would be abandoned. And she understood their way of thinking. They had families who faced enough danger without adding an epidemic. She sighed and crossed her arms over her chest in an effort to ease the aching in her heart. *What am I going to do? What can I give Mama and Papa to stop the fever? How long will they be sick? What if they don't survive?*

The thought of burying them or getting the fever caused her to shudder. When would Mr. Greenham be here? Not knowing left a queasy feeling in the pit of her stomach. How could she settle things in her mind with such an uncertain future?

She studied the outline of two riders heading her way. One part of her wanted them to hurry, and the other part dreaded the decision.

"Please don't let them abandon us, dear Lord," she whispered. "I don't know what I will do." She swiped at a tear. Mr. Greenham and Painted Hands would not see her cry.

She checked one more time on Mama and Papa before the two men arrived. She prayed to see them awake and her fears arrested, but their condition had not changed. She dabbed the perspiration on their faces and offered another prayer before stepping from the wagon and hearing their fate.

Mr. Greenham and Painted Hands dismounted and led their horses toward her. Sarah Jane searched their faces for signs of a good word. Both men were stoical.

"What did they say?" She rubbed her hands together, anxiety weaving cobwebs in her mind.

Mr. Greenham cleared his throat. "Miss Benson, I hate being the bearer of bad news, but the committee feels it's best if you don't join back up with the others until your parents are better."

She swallowed her tears while a simmering of anger started to rise. "So we're left to fend for ourselves."

"You won't be alone," Mr. Greenham said.

I know God is with us. . . .

"Painted Hands has volunteered to help you through this troublesome time."

She focused her attention on the scout, not sure what to say, not sure if she should be grateful or terrified. Stories whispered around the campfires wove an unknown path through her bleak future, but Mama and Papa's care came first.

"I appreciate your help, sir. I admit I'm at a loss as to what plagues my parents."

"We think we know the cause of the fever, Miss Benson," Painted Hands said.

Sarah Jane glanced from him to the wagon master. "Please tell me."

Mr. Greenham removed his hat. "Typhoid. Painted Hands and I are in agreement."

Chills rolled over her. *Typhoid killed.* Her mind roared with the deadly implication. They must be wrong. Another realization struck her, and she centered her attention on Painted Hands. "You could very well get this by helping me."

Not a muscle moved in his face. "I fully understand the risk."

If she could simply read the man's eyes, see how he truly felt, learn his motivation for wanting to help. "As soon as they are better, then we can join back up with the wagons?" she asked.

"I see no reason why you can't continue with the others," Mr. Greenham said. "But the committee will have to vote again. They did have one specific request."

"I'm confused. What else am I supposed to do? Burn the wagon or pay a fee?"

Mr. Greenham hesitated.

"I'll tell her." Painted Hands looped his thumbs in the top of his buckskins. "In order for me to stay with you, the committeemen say we must marry. They claim it's not fitting for a single man and woman to travel together."

A murderer. He ate his victims. Dear Lord in heaven, those things can't be true! She struggled to maintain her composure. "But they'll leave us alone to die? What if I refuse?"

Mr. Greenham touched her shoulder. "Painted Hands would still stay with you, but you couldn't join the wagons."

Bewilderment and helplessness twisted around her heart. If she'd been given to a sensitive constitution, she'd have fainted to avoid thinking about the committee's ultimatum. Marriage to Painted Hands? What would Papa say when he recovered? He'd be so angry that he might never forgive her. Sarah Jane held her breath. If the scout didn't help her, Mama and Papa would die for sure. This way they had a chance, and for them, she'd do anything.

"I'll marry Painted Hands." Sarah Jane swallowed so hard she nearly choked. She peered into her husband-to-be's face. "Thank you, sir, for your kindness. I appreciate the sacrifice you're making to help me and my folks, and I'll forever be indebted to you."

Painted Hands kept his impassive stance. This man before her had committed to spending the rest of his life with her, and she knew not why. She had neither the time nor the wisdom to discern his reasons.

Mama and Papa used to laugh and talk. For hours they'd sit in front of their sod house back in Nebraska and talk about everything from the farm to deadly twisters to the scriptures. Sarah Jane had always dreamed of the same qualities in a man. The scout before her held no resemblance to Papa. He could be spiteful, looking forward to hurting her once they were alone. Dare she live a life so miserable?

With a shudder, she realized the thoughts seizing control of her mind were selfish. Mama and Papa had given their best to her, and now she repaid their love and devotion with worrisome concerns about herself. She would honor her husband and nurse her parents back to health.

If only she could calm her quivering heart.

CHAPTER 3

With trembling fingers, Sarah Jane removed her soiled apron and attempted to smooth back her wayward curls, damp with perspiration. Glancing at her hands, she saw they were dirty and wiped them the best she could on the apron. Tossing it to the ground, she'd gather it up after the ceremony.

I'm about to marry, and I don't even have clean hands or a clean dress.

With unsteady legs, she walked alongside Painted Hands to the spot where Mr. Sanders awaited them. She and Mama had talked about her wedding day since she was a little girl—and none of this resembled their aspirations. Certainly not the groom. Certainly not these circumstances. And certainly not while Mama and Papa lay so gravely ill.

Painted Hands avoided looking at her, and she couldn't criticize him for it. The thought of beginning her married life with a stranger filled her with emptiness. Surely he must feel the same dread, as though judged and sentenced. She knew of couples who married sight unseen and parents who arranged marriages, but this had never been a consideration for her.

"We need to get on with this," Mr. Sanders said. He opened his Bible and read the story of Adam and Eve so fast that she could barely understand him.

Sarah Jane tried to concentrate on Mr. Sanders's reading of the vows. Her mind wandered to what the Robinson girls must be saying about her fate.

"Miss Benson," Mr. Sanders said, obviously irritated. "Do you take this man to be your husband? I've asked you twice before."

The idea of crumpling into a pool of emotion held merit, but she could not. Would not. "Yes. . .yes, I do."

"I know your folks are sick, but you are making a promise to God here, and I advise you to pay attention. The wages of sin is death."

Suddenly, Sarah Jane realized how much she detested Mr. Sanders. Her God and his were not the same. "I understand God's Word quite well, and I pray for your enlightenment as well."

∽

Painted Hands fought hard not to release his temper on Sanders. The self-righteous preacher refused to venture toward the Benson wagon for fear he'd contract typhoid and demanded Sarah Jane and Painted Hands walk several yards for the marriage ceremony. Painted Hands itched to lay his fists on the bony man's jaw and leave him sprawling in the dirt.

Greenham agreed to stay with the sick couple while Sanders married Sarah Jane and Painted Hands. Even then, the preacher shifted from one foot to the other and rushed through the ceremony in the time it took to breathe in and out.

Unlike the Reverend Crandle, the man who wore the peace of God on his face and God's love in his heart, Sanders interpreted the Bible according to his whim. The preacher might be surprised at how much Painted Hands knew about the Bible, even if he hadn't found the words meaningful to his life.

Anger chiseled at his good sense every time Painted Hands recalled the callous approach of so many men toward the Bensons.

"Cut their wagon."

"We have our own to think about."

The real believers on the wagon train recognized the burden of typhoid and yet were willing to take a risk to help. Mr. and Mrs. Benson had been among these folks for days, and the others were bound to get the sickness no matter where they situated themselves. Painted Hands vowed never to forget the believers' kindness. They brought food, blankets, herbs, and prayers for Sarah Jane. Those men reminded him of some of the folks back in Missouri, who were gentle and good when the situation called for it but strong and determined when righteousness required a firm stand.

Beside him, Sarah Jane quivered so that the skirt of her dress shook. Painted Hands wished something else could have been done to help her and her parents. She feared him and rightfully so. His looks and mannerisms set him apart as a man to avoid, one with a sordid past. He'd heard one toothless old man state that Painted Hands murdered a whole family, but no one could prove it. Another tale drifting through the wagons told of his living with wolves and drinking the blood of the animals' prey. As soon as he and Sarah Jane grew more acquainted, he'd tell her the truth about those tales—those vicious lies concocted by wagging tongues.

He hoped she wasn't the type of woman who made useless prattle or pestered folks with questions. He'd grown used to listening to the sounds of nature—the quiet of earth, the songs of birds and insects. There his spirit calmed the restless part of him that remembered his dark secret. Maybe in finding his brother, Jacob, Painted Hands would find peace.

Jacob was two years older; he'd been a lively boy who loved to hunt and fish. The Reverend Crandle found out Jacob had escaped the flames and run to get help. All these years, and at last, Painted Hands had found a link to his real family. Some memories had been blocked out about that night; others forged ahead like heavy boots in a muddy riverbed. He wanted to pull his feet out of the muck, but they'd been stuck for longer than he cared to remember. Some days he looked forward to the reunion with his brother. Some days he dreaded the image of a grown man calling him brother, then accusing him of murder. The screams of his family trapped inside the burning cabin preyed on his heart like a stalking cougar.

Among the Kiowa, the medicine men had tried to rid Painted Hands of the nightmares, but always they came back, each one worse than the last.

Painted Hands stared into his wife's young face. He beheld a distinct loveliness about her. He'd noticed her before because she always seemed to be laughing. He liked the part-girl, part-woman look about her, a combination of innocence and wisdom. Dare he hope they might grow to be friends? He didn't expect a real marriage between them. Sarah Jane already feared, maybe even loathed, him. Right now, she looked like a frightened deer. Why make the relationship any worse by consummating their vows or letting her inside his heart to learn the wretched truth?

"Most folks give the preacher something for marrying them," Sanders said, stretching out his hand.

Painted Hands considered the statement with as much gratefulness as a rattler's bite. "I'll make sure you keep your scalp."

Sanders snapped his Bible shut and headed toward his mule. "May God have mercy on your heathen soul, Mr. Painted Hands."

He wanted to take a few long steps to the preacher and wipe the smirk off his face, but he contained himself with Sarah Jane before him. He stole a look at her, and she pressed her lips firmly together. No doubt she agreed with Sanders.

"Miss Benson, we should get back to your folks," Painted Hands said.

She lifted her chin and gave him a faint smile. "I'm Mrs. Painted Hands now, and my given name is Sarah Jane."

"Yes ma'am."

"I. . .want to thank you for all you've done." She lifted her shoulders with a deep breath, and a few yellow-red curls slipped from under her bonnet. "I'll do my best to be a good wife."

Touched by her kind words, he wanted to respond with the same tenderness, but instead, a haunting voice rose in him—one that said she'd trick him, use him, despise him like all the other whites. Painted Hands kept his stance. He'd not be made to look like a fool. Sarah Jane needed him to nurse her parents, nothing more. When Mr. and Mrs. Benson recovered or died, she'd be on her way and he'd venture on to Oregon.

"I'm not expecting anything. We were both forced into this because of the committee. I won't be taking advantage of you."

She stepped back, her eyes full of apprehension. Good, Sarah Jane needed to keep her distance. In the next moment, he decided not to tell her the truth about the gossip. Let her think what she wanted. He cared neither way.

CHAPTER 4

Long after dark, Sarah Jane bedded down beneath the wagon for a precious hour of sleep. Papa's fifty head of cattle surrounded the wagon, and they acted uneasy. Maybe they sensed the trouble from the wagon train. Painted Hands and Mr. Greenham had separated them from the large herd and driven them back. The smell of the cattle almost felt comforting, as though nothing had changed.

Painted Hands had stacked his provisions in the wagon alongside Mama's spinning wheel, although he'd sold about half of them to Mr. Robinson. The day's troubles thundered in her ears, and a tear slipped over her cheek.

She prayed for God to multiply the time she slept before she crawled back into the wagon to nurse Mama and Papa. From here, the sounds from inside the wagon were vivid. If Mama or Papa rolled over or called out, she'd hear them. They drifted in and out of consciousness and often cried out from a confused world. Sarah Jane attempted to comfort them, only to realize they didn't know or care she stayed by their side.

Exhaustion seized Sarah Jane's body and mind. The day had been harder than the ones before, and the fever tearing through Mama and Papa caused a longing she couldn't describe. How could one day hold so much turmoil? This morning she woke with a prayer on her lips for Mama to renew her health. Tonight she prayed for Mama and Papa's healing—and for strength to endure her marriage to Painted Hands.

In all her girlish dreams, she'd never anticipated a wedding like today's. Mr. Sanders spoke the words that sealed her to Painted Hands until death met them face-to-face. Her husband said they were forced into marriage, and he didn't expect anything in return. Sarah Jane knew precious little about married couples, but what she did know bewildered her. To be relieved of wifely duties came as a blessing when her every waking moment centered on Mama and Papa's care. Except...what would the future bring?

Again she worried about Papa when he learned about the circumstances surrounding her marriage. She'd seen him enraged only twice: once when a man in Nebraska beat his wife and the second time when a twister destroyed their crops. The memory of unbridled anger made her cringe. Surely he'd understand. Of course he would. Staring up at the wagon bottom, she wondered when Painted Hands planned to sleep—and where.

Tears slipped unbidden from her eyes and slid over her cheeks. Papa always said God allowed things to happen for a reason—and a good reason for folks who loved Him. *Why this? What good could come from Mama and Papa suffering with typhoid?* If the wagon train traveled at the same fifteen miles per day, how would she and Painted Hands catch up once they could travel again? They must get to the mountains before the winter snows, and every day lost weakened their chances. Would Painted Hands remain as her husband, or once Mama and Papa regained their health, would he ride out?

Oh, how she ached for release from this burden of not knowing or understanding the future. On the farm in Nebraska, Papa set traps for wolves. The sight of an animal's foot caught and bleeding in the snare of metal jaws and the sound of the animal's mournful cries tore at her heart. Now she understood how the wolves felt; only her bleeding came from the inside.

Sarah Jane turned to stare into the fire. Painted Hands sat there on the hard ground with his legs crossed, motionless, gazing into the embers as though spellbound. She observed him, this strange man who had promised to love and cherish her. How could he maintain no emotion during all of this? His life had been changed forever, too. She wished she could master the same nonfeeling demeanor. Maybe in doing so she'd grow numb and not suffer any of the pain.

Studying him more closely, she saw he was a little taller than most men, stocky with broad shoulders. He wore a heavy beard along with his long, beaded hair, which most likely caused more folks to fear him. And his hands—they'd been burned and scarred. The discoloration must be the reason for his Indian name. In her next breath, she wondered about the name his parents gave him. Someday she'd ask.

As though he sensed her scrutiny, he swung his gaze from the fire to where she lay beneath the wagon. "You should be asleep." No compassion for the day's event. No sympathy for the plight of her parents.

"So should you."

"Tomorrow will be hard, and the days to come won't give you a reprieve."

"It's been that way since Independence," she said. "And I expect you're right about hard times with the wagon train leaving us behind." If he'd been Papa, she'd have scrambled from under the wagon to join him. They enjoyed long talks. "I'm sorry about today."

His hard stare sent her heart pounding, as though he hated her. "I made my choice."

She took a deep breath. "I suppose being married will change your plans."

"I won't let it. I've got important things to do."

"Is scouting your job?"

"Yes, but I'm heading to Oregon like the rest of 'em."

"What will you do there?"

"No more talk. I need time to think."

Sarah Jane gasped. His stinging response told fathoms of how he preferred a solitary life. Papa groaned and shifted above her, sending waves of guilt over her for attempting a brief reprieve. She rolled out from under the wagon. "You don't have to stay here," she said. "I can nurse Mama and Papa and later catch up with the other wagons. No point in you sitting here all miserable."

Painted Hands stood. He reminded her of a huge bear ready to pounce. "I keep my word. You'd die out here alone."

"I may die anyway." She'd not be bullied into thinking Painted Hands was her only chance of survival.

"That's right."

As soon as he hurled those words, she stepped to the rear of the wagon and climbed inside. If tonight gave any indication of how they'd get along for the rest of their married life, they'd most likely destroy each other.

Papa's ravings seized her attention. He called out for his ma, uttering childlike phrases. Sarah Jane touched his head. She jerked back her hand as alarm raced through her. *The lantern. I want to see his face.* In her haste to climb down, she caught her dress and fell backward. Her head hit the ground with a thud. For a moment, she lay there stunned, her head throbbing and her eyes flashing streaks of light. Strong arms lifted her from behind and righted her.

"Are you all right?" Painted Hands asked without a trace of emotion.

She nodded slowly and remembered the urgency. "Papa's worse," she said. "I need to see him and get some tea down him."

"I'll tend to him." Painted Hands urged her to sit down with a gentleness that surprised her.

In the shadows, she glanced up into Painted Hands's face. He didn't look nearly as ominous.

"He's talking out of his mind." Sarah Jane closed her eyes in hopes of settling the pain searing the back of her head.

"Typhoid does that." He stood and lifted the lantern from the side of the wagon, then disappeared inside.

While she waited for him to return, she struggled with what to do for Papa, and she hadn't checked on Mama. Earlier Sarah Jane had worked hard to get spoonfuls of tea down them and wipe their faces and necks with water. Nothing seemed to help.

God, please heal Mama and Papa. I've done all I can.

Sarah Jane braced herself with the side of the wagon and pulled herself to her feet. Her head spun, but after blinking several times, the dizziness faded. Holding on, she peered inside. Painted Hands blocked her view.

"Does he appear worse to you?" she asked.

"I'm afraid so. Your ma is unconscious, and she feels hotter."

She recalled Painted Hands's insistence on not wanting her to speak. Even so, she needed answers to her questions. "What can I do?"

"Wait and continue with what you've been doing." He eased back out of the wagon and stood beside her. "How's your head?"

"Better. What else can I expect?" She thought he might refuse to reply.

"Depends on each person. I'd say dysentery, more confusion, possibly a rash on the lower chest and stomach."

"How long will it all last?"

"Hard to tell, Sarah Jane. It could be days. It could be until morning." His voice sounded firm, and she wondered if he didn't think Mama and Papa would live.

"Do you think they're going to die?"

He leaned against the wagon. His relaxed stance took away from his Indian bearing. "Living and dying are not up to me. Your folks are real sick. They might pull through, and they might not."

"Mama's been poorly since we first started to Oregon. Leaving her friends behind made her sad." Sarah Jane pulled her shawl tighter around her shoulders. "The church women made her a friendship quilt just before we left. She loves that quilt, and I have it around her now."

"She needs to fight the fever. Tell her so even if you don't think she hears."

She sighed. "I'm afraid she'll give up. Papa has always been strong. Loved to work outside. Loved to play his fiddle. Loved talking to people. It's real hard seeing him. . .like this."

"Indian medicines would help, but I have none with me. I could ride out and look or search out the Indians in the area." He hesitated. "But you'd be left alone, and I don't know how long I'd be gone."

"I have no idea what is best."

He rubbed the top of his hand as though trying to remove the scars. "I knew a man who believed in prayer. He said it changes a man from the inside out. I see you're a believer, and, well, I think you need to hold on to your God."

"I've been praying until there are no more words."

"My friend said God hears our hearts."

"Are you a believer, too?"

He shook his head and pressed his lips together. "Kiowa believe in many spirits, not just one God like you. I reckon I'm more Kiowa than white."

Sarah Jane remembered Papa saying in order to reach folks with the Gospel of Jesus Christ, a man must understand what the other person believes. "I hope one day you will tell me about those spirits."

"You make a strange comment for a Christian."

"I want to know what's important to you. I'm your wife now."

Immediately, Painted Hands stiffened. "I want you to understand the truth here. I never wanted a wife. I have important business in Oregon, matters that don't involve a woman or a family. Once we're there, I'll take care of undoing what Sanders insisted was proper."

A wisp of a breeze blew back her hair. To Sarah Jane, the wind felt like a touch of God, letting her know of His love and provision. A woman who lived wary of her husband might never be happy as God intended for married folk. "I'd like for us to be friends," she said.

"I'm a loner."

Papa used to say a man who didn't want friends had something to hide. "Maybe in the weeks to come you'll change your mind."

"Too many men have tried."

But they weren't your wife.

CHAPTER 5

Sarah Jane prayed constantly for the strength and courage to withstand the hours and days to come. She feared for her stricken parents and the stranger who was now her husband. She no longer thought about taking a respite to sleep or eat; instead, she kept a vigil over Mama and Papa, doing all she could to keep them comfortable. At times, she talked to them. Her words moved from the hope and promise of the Northwest Territory, reminding them of the wondrous stories of rich earth and thick green forests, to the sweet memories left behind in Nebraska but alive in their hearts.

Painted Hands tended to cooking and making certain a plentiful supply of water was at hand. Camping beside the Platte River assured them they wouldn't run out. Sarah Jane and Painted Hands said little more than those things necessary in passing. She didn't have the stamina to encourage the friendship she deemed important, and she understood he preferred to be left alone. Later, when Mama and Papa were well, she'd concentrate on her husband. Odd that her new status took some getting used to, even if they were married in name only. For that concession, she thanked God. Outwardly, she refused to show signs of apprehension around Painted Hands. Inwardly, she quivered at the thought of his touching her. Never one given to gossip, she repeatedly pushed the stories about him from her mind, but in dark moments, they haunted her.

A strange predicament, this marriage to a stranger. She recalled his offer to search out medicine from the prairie or from neighboring Indians. She appreciated his willingness to do whatever might help Mama and Papa, even if she'd be left alone. God was always her companion; yet she feared the dangers of predators both animal and human. In the past, Indians had viewed the wagon train from a distance or stopped to trade with the hundreds of sojourners. The Sioux were ferocious looking, and she prayed they never approached the lone wagon.

Sarah Jane held the distinction of a woman defenseless against those who could easily overpower her. What good would she do Mama and Papa if she were abducted by Indians? Unwelcome thoughts tramped miles of fears and insecurities. For certain, she didn't want Painted Hands to venture out for the medicine; neither did she want to be accused of being selfish. What if Mama and Papa died when the Indian remedies could have healed them?

Precious Father in heaven, help me discern Your will. I am so confused.

The Twenty-third Psalm, the verses often spoken over graves, broke into her ponderings.

"Yea, though I walk through the valley of the shadow of death, I will fear no evil: for thou art with me; thy rod and thy staff they comfort me."

Tell me how not to be afraid, Father.

"Trust, My daughter. My will is woven into your life."

In the darkness, Sarah Jane heard a rustle and turned to see Painted Hands at the rear of the wagon.

"How are they?" he asked.

She wiped her forehead, then focused on Mama and Papa. "I believe they're worse. The rash has thickened on their stomachs and the lower part of their chests." Swallowing the emotion threatening to overcome her, she took a deep breath and whispered, "Tell me what to do."

"Climb down and let me take a look." He held out his hand, and she took it. His touch felt strong and secure, and she needed something solid to hold on to.

Outside, she grabbed the coffeepot and filled a tin cup. The hot liquid tasted bitter, but it helped settle her fragile emotions. She should ask Painted Hands to look for medicine in the morning. God promised never to leave her or forsake her. Her selfishness dare not steal the life from Mama and Papa.

Moments later, Painted Hands joined her at the fire. He poured coffee for himself and kicked at a cow chip, sending it into the smoldering fire. "Sarah Jane, I'm thinking you need to talk about your folks."

"Why is that?" She sensed the color drain from her face. The answer lay in the shadows of truth, a dark place where she refused to walk.

"Your ma and pa—they aren't going to live." Unlike in the past, Painted Hands spoke with tenderness. "Their spirits are giving in to the typhoid."

"No." Sarah Jane covered her mouth to hide the weeping.

"You've done all you can. Be brave now." He paused and took her hand. "Let's talk."

She swiped at her eyes. Prayer. Yes, more prayer and God would heal Mama and Papa. God wanted her to trust Him—not the words of a heathen who refused to believe in God. "I must pray harder. God must not have heard me." She pulled back her hand and started toward the wagon, but Painted Hands swung her around to face him.

"Listen to me. There is nothing you can do. If you insist upon sitting with them, I'll go with you."

She longed to give in to the hysteria, but Mama and Papa needed her.

Later, no matter what happened, she'd allow herself to feel the pain. Sarah Jane nodded. Inside the wagon, he held up the lantern. Gasping, she saw exactly what Painted Hands meant. Their shallow breathing and gray pallor indicated the beginnings of death. But she would not give up until Mama and Papa breathed their last.

"Are you the only child?" Painted Hands asked.

Forcing back the weeping, she found the strength to answer Painted Hands's question. "The only living child. Two little girls died of summer complaint before I was born."

"You are their legacy."

Legacy? A strange word for Painted Hands. "I'd never thought of it that way."

"Their blood flows through your body. They will never really die but will live on in you and your children and your grandchildren."

She glanced at him curiously, yearning to hear more. His words, like rich poetry, took her mind off the inevitable.

"The seeds here in this wagon are for planting when you arrive in Oregon. Did they come from good plants?"

Sarah Jane nodded, and he continued. "Only at the end of harvest when the beauty and usefulness of a plant are gone can one gather seeds. The plant lives on in its seed to accomplish the same as the parent plant."

"'Verily, verily, I say unto you, Except a corn of wheat fall into the ground and die, it abideth alone: but if it die, it bringeth forth much fruit.'" She recited the scripture as though it were a prayer.

Painted Hands smiled, the first she'd seen. "I've read the passage."

Yet Painted Hands did not believe. The Kiowa gods had a firm grip on him, and she vowed to pray for his release.

"What you've told me makes this easier to bear." She studied Mama and Papa, touching one cheek, then the other, and lingering on Mama's. "I understand, but life without them will be so hard."

"We are all dying from the moment life is breathed into us."

"Papa said our days on earth are to prepare us for the hereafter."

"Your father spoke with wisdom."

She twisted to see Painted Hands's face. "You, too, speak with wisdom. I wish I knew what to do while we wait. Prayer alone seems so feeble."

"You will honor them best by being strong. What is your pa's name?" he asked.

"John William, and Mama's name is Lydia Jane."

"And you are named after her."

"Mama and my grandmother Benson, Papa's mother."

"Where are you from?" Painted Hands leaned into the rear of the wagon. His voice echoed across the darkness as though he belonged with the night creatures.

"Near Lincoln, Nebraska. We lived in a sod house on a farm. Papa kept hearing about how he could get rich operating a mercantile in Independence, where wagon trains left for out west. He couldn't resist, not with his adventurous streak. Mama didn't like the idea, but she finally agreed. Once we arrived in Independence, talk of Oregon got into his blood, and before long, he caught the fever, too." She took a deep breath at the utterance of the word *fever*.

"Go on," he urged.

"Then Papa abandoned the idea of purchasing a mercantile for the territory beyond the mountains. Not much more to tell. He signed on with Mr. Greenham's wagon train, and we purchased the provisions needed. Mama fretted over Papa's plans, but he believed we should go."

"Did you want to come?"

Sarah Jane tilted her head in remembrance. "Oh, I wanted to go, although the preparations were more work than I thought. I inherited Papa's desire to see and do new things."

"And now?" His words were barely above a whisper.

She touched a cloth to Papa's face while pondering the question. "I can't turn around and go back. If I gave up, I wouldn't be my father's child."

"And your ma? What are you going to carry on about her?"

Sarah Jane probed her mind in search of the special something she wanted to treasure about Mama. "Your questions make me think, but that's good. I need to have purpose and meaning in my life. Before Mama started feeling poorly, she used to laugh a lot. She looked for the good in folks and never tired in helping others. She enjoyed taking food to those who needed it or visiting the sick."

"Your life will be full, Sarah Jane."

She bit down hard on her lip to keep from breaking down into sobs. "I hope so." Sarah Jane's fingers caressed her mother's cheek. The skin felt hard, cooler. "Oh no." She buried her face in her hands, no longer able to hide the unfathomable grief.

∞

Painted Hands thought Lydia Benson had died some moments before while Sarah Jane talked. He'd felt the woman's wrist for a steady beat and discovered none existed, but he hadn't wanted to interrupt. The memories of Sarah Jane's parents were more important than the precise moment of death. If he was not mistaken, Mr. Benson had passed away, too. He stepped down from the wagon to let her deal with the loss. He gripped the side of the wagon and watched, not sure what he should do.

Many new graves would lead the way to Oregon, all belonging to the wagons that had abandoned the Bensons. Typhoid. He'd seen it wipe out half a population, leaving widows and orphans to limp through life with only the memories of their loved ones to console them. He'd seen cholera and smallpox, too, but Painted Hands had escaped them and hoped to again. Now he wondered about Sarah Jane. His wife.

Her quiet weeping broke into his thoughts. Her shoulders rose and fell. He wrestled with comforting her, but he fought the intimacy it invited. A long time ago, he vowed never to feel the pain of losing loved ones again. If he attempted to console her, he risked growing close. If he grew close, he'd feel the agony of loss. Typhoid could attack Sarah Jane this very night. She could die in the next few days. Why allow himself to feel?

"Papa!"

He held his breath, certain Sarah Jane must have discovered her father no longer lived. He well remembered the terror of losing both parents at the same time.

The gruesome memories washed over him once more, bringing to the surface the cold night that a raging fire destroyed his family. The flames snatched up those he loved and left him to hear their screams forever. He'd done nothing to help until it was too late, and the scars on his hands were ever-present reminders.

Releasing his hold on the wagon, Painted Hands made his way back to the fire. For Sarah Jane to find strength, she must toughen in this barren land. If he allowed her to depend on him, he'd delay the process. Once his obligation was fulfilled, she'd be on her own. This night marked the beginning of her training ground. Let her harden like the sun baking the ground around them. It had worked for him. Painted Hands stared up into the starlit night. A gnawing sensation bit at his stomach, a mixture of guilt and regret. The thought of Sarah Jane living years of misery as he had was cruel. Did he really want her to exist alone and fearful of love?

Painted Hands heard the Reverend Crandle's voice whispering around him. "*You need to love, Painted Hands. Without it, we are nothing. For this commandment which I command thee this day, it is not hidden from thee, neither is it far off.*"

⟶

Miles from the kindly man who showed him the mark of a true believer, Painted Hands still heard the lessons. He ran from the Reverend Crandle in search of answers to his miserable existence, away from the one man who had loved him even when Painted Hands fled from God. Reverend Crandle had been more than a father and a friend; but what he asked was too difficult, and his spirit cried out for release. Turning from the young woman who needed him in her hour of sorrow was wrong, but he couldn't comfort her. The past pain consumed him, the barrier around his heart too tall and too wide.

Sarah Jane's sobs roared in his ears, not the loudness of her cries, but the depths of despair. The teachings of Reverend Crandle urged him to go to her, and yet he stayed still, silently begging her to cease. He poured another cup of coffee and allowed his wretched soul to feed his tortured mind. A raw part of him remembered the little boy who pulled the charred remains of his sister from the burning home. The sound of his own wails had been heard by a Kiowa hunting party.

At last, Sarah Jane's weeping stopped. He breathed relief and wiped perspiration streaming down his face—certainly not a result of the chilly night air but the result of tremors from his past. He faced the wagon. Preparing the bodies for burial was a task he could accomplish. A breeze caught the canvas flap and whisked it back and forth as though the spirits of Mr. and Mrs. Benson escaped from their beds.

"Sarah Jane," he called. "Are you all right?"

In the next instant, she climbed down from the wagon. Even in the shadows, he could see her tear-stained face and swollen eyes. "I'm not all right, but I'm sure God in His mercy will make each moment a little easier to bear."

"I'm sorry."

She half-nodded. "They are in the arms of Jesus."

The words sounded as though they were memorized and appropriate rather than how she honestly felt.

"I'll prepare them and dig the holes for burial."

She tugged her shawl tighter around her shoulders and ventured closer to the dying fire. "I can help."

"I think you should sleep, and there is only one shovel."

"Sleep will evade me, I'm sure."

"Then consider what you want to say over your parents in the morning."

She nodded, then shivered. "I do regret that your kind heart has been repaid with these dire circumstances."

"There is nothing kind about me, Sarah Jane. But what of you?"

She sighed, her thin shoulders shaking. "I will live for the legacy you spoke of. Without your wisdom, I'd die this very night. God bless you, Painted Hands, for allowing our Father to use you in my hour of distress."

CHAPTER 6

Sarah Jane woke the following morning with tears dried on her cheeks and feeling very much alone. She'd fallen asleep begging God for an answer to why her parents were taken. Now she felt guilty for sleeping when a needling voice told her she should stay awake and record all of the pleasant memories about her parents in Mama's journal. Did God think she didn't love them enough—that she was a selfish daughter who fell asleep on the eve of their funeral?

Today the remains of Mama and Papa would be laid to rest in an earthen hole. Their spirits had fled their sickened bodies and now waited with the Lord until she joined them. Sarah Jane didn't know how she'd go on. The sound of Mama's musical laughter would linger with her always. Back in Nebraska, ladies from all around came to quilt with Mama. Her perfect stitching and the way she pieced pattern sections into unique designs made Sarah Jane and Papa proud, but Mama never took the credit. She said God guided her needle. Papa's wisdom helped Sarah Jane understand the scriptures and how to apply them to her life. Their days had been good in Nebraska despite the blizzards in winter, the twisters in summer, and the unpredictable weather during planting and harvesting. But they had all been happy.

As much as she treasured Papa, he must not have heard God's direction in the journey to Oregon.

A part of Sarah Jane would always dwell in the past, where she felt secure and loved. Now she faced an uncertain future with Painted Hands. She had a husband; she was a wife, but she did not possess a real marriage. At the moment, she appreciated his not insisting she take a wifely role. Once they reached Oregon, he'd make the arrangements to dissolve the marriage. As much as she understood their union was in name only, the thought of not being fit for him made her feel worthless. She wasn't the plainest woman on the wagon train; maybe he had his eye on someone else. Sarah Jane remembered the scriptures said the man was the head of the household, so he must know best about going their own ways in Oregon.

What is wrong with me? Here I am pondering Painted Hands's displeasure with me on the morning of Mama and Papa's funeral.

In the way lay all the things Mama and Papa needed to begin homesteading and later open a mercantile. The daunting task frightened her, for she knew little about cultivating the land and even less about operating a business. In the trunk, Papa had made notes about both endeavors. She needed to find the written instruction and study it at nights.

"God has equipped us for this world," Papa had said. "We look to Him for direction, and He guides our paths."

"I'll not disappoint you," she whispered. "I'll simply look for God's messenger to light my way."

Glancing about, Sarah Jane wondered where Painted Hands had gone. She rolled from underneath the wagon and stood. The smell of coffee brought her to the present. Her mental despair had masked the otherwise enticing smell. He must have brewed it earlier, but where could he be? She turned her attention to the rear of the wagon. He could be digging the graves—a job with which she should help, although Papa had but one shovel. *Breakfast.* She must prepare a good meal for Painted Hands. She needed the bacon and flour stored inside the wagon, beside Mama and Papa. That meant seeing them again—lifeless. Eating did not appeal to her, but she had a duty to her husband.

Another thought clutched her heart. What if he had ridden off? Left her to fend for herself?

Terror twisted up her spine. She hurried to the opposite side of the wagon and saw his horse grazing on a single tuft of grass. Releasing a heavy sigh, she willed the queasy sensation in the pit of her stomach to vanish. Too many things must be done, whether she felt ill or well. Moving back to the fire, she poured a cup of coffee, then stared in an easterly direction. Painted Hands bent over, digging into the hard earth. A shovel of dirt, then another, was dumped onto a heap beside him. Obviously, he'd been working for some time. Guilt assaulted her again for sleeping while he labored on the hard prairie.

Last night she needed him to offer her comfort. He chose to let her grieve in privacy. When they were on the trail again, she'd ask him if the Kiowa mourned the dead alone. Another thought occurred to her. Mama's and Papa's deaths could remind him of his family's tragic deaths.

He had urged her to talk and remember, but oh, how she craved the arms of another human being. Perhaps she was weak. Shaking her head to dispel the nagging thought of the undesirable trait, she elected to take him a canteen of water at the grave site. She didn't want to look at Mama and Papa; rather, she preferred to see them in her mind where they were happy and whole.

Sarah Jane moved slowly, not sure what to say or how to help. The barbaric stories told about Painted Hands crept through her mind, yet she believed they were false. Her husband had been raised by Indians, and he preferred their ways; that made him an oddity. Folks tended to criticize what they didn't know or understand—another one of Papa's sayings. Or was she attempting to convince herself? Papa had warned her about Painted Hands. Why? Did he simply not know the man and fall prey to the consensus of most of the other folks on the wagon train? She hoped so; she prayed so.

Painted Hands glanced up when she arrived. She handed him the canteen, and he thanked her with a nod. Sweat dotted his brow with a trickle down the side of his face. If not for the beads woven in his hair, he'd look like a mountain man. When she gathered her wits to see the burial holes, she saw only one, and it was being widened to hold a second body.

"Good morning," she said, studying his face. "How early did you rise?"

He leaned on the shovel and released a labored sigh. "I didn't go to bed."

Stunned, she grasped for words. "You shouldn't have done all this alone. I could have helped."

"Sarah Jane, you were exhausted from caring for your folks. With only one shovel, what would you have done?"

She shrugged. "Kept you in coffee? Let you rest while I dug awhile?"

He stepped on the shovel and lifted another heap of dirt. "I am hungry."

"I can prepare food. I'll tend to it right away."

Silence separated them, as it had before. She'd have to climb into the wagon for the food—and see Mama and Papa.

"Thank you for all you've done. I'll have breakfast ready shortly." Sarah Jane turned to leave.

"I've covered your parents' bodies. There's no need for you to look at them."

She stopped and whirled around. He knew her thoughts. "Truly you are a gift from God."

Painted Hands continued his work. Without lifting his head, he appeared to speak his words to the empty grave. "I think not."

"You have been ever so kind."

"You've heard the tales. Don't tell me you haven't." He thrust the shovel into the hard ground with such force that she sucked in a breath.

She crossed her arms over her chest. "Are you saying they are true?"

He peered up at her, his emotionless face offering no indication of the man inside. "You should be frightened."

Anger rose within Sarah Jane. "Frightened? My parents are dead. I have no choice but to move on to Oregon. The wagon train is surely plagued with typhoid victims, which tells me Mama and Papa will always be blamed because they were the first to be ill. My husband can't wait to be rid of me." With each word, she spat fury and grief. Selfishness clouded her thinking, but at the moment she didn't care. "I thank you for what you've done, then you bully me? What is left for me to fear? Ridicule? Abandonment? Disease? Death?" She clamped her lips together before tossing another word. Lifting her chin, she started back to the wagon. "Your breakfast will take but a short while."

"Sarah Jane."

She had no intentions of letting him see her weep and marched ahead. "I owe you an apology, but not now—later."

"Would you rather bury them before eating? The sun will be hot before long."

The familiar lump rose in her throat. She blinked several times before responding. "Yes, please."

"I'm nearly finished here. I suggest you retrieve your Bible from the wagon before I return for your folks."

She paused to gain control. "I've been thinking about that very thing." She kept on walking, despising herself for not apologizing for her outburst and believing Painted Hands deserved her wrath in the same breath.

His mannerisms, so cold and unfeeling, swept over her like a wintry chill. Did the man have no compassion? Was this the Indian part of him? If so, they were truly barbaric and heathen. No wonder women clutched their children to their breast and men reached for their shotguns at the mention of Indians. The fear of hostiles murdering and torturing their captives made sense. Horrible, perfect sense.

She didn't need Painted Hands's sympathy. His backbreaking work would suffice, and once they caught up to the wagon train—providing they were permitted—he could go back to scouting for Mr. Greenham, and she'd take care of herself.

"He's your husband. You made a promise to God."

She held her breath. Must she be reminded? After all, the marriage hadn't been consummated.

"You promised God to bind yourself to this man until death."

Maybe she'd contract typhoid and die like Mama and Papa. The grave would solve everything. Maybe she'd pray for that very thing.

"Are you a child or a woman?"

The voice of the One who ruled the universe would not release her. *Why, God? I don't understand. Do You despise me? Is that why my life has fallen to the depths? Do You even care?* Always the questions and no answers. Papa always quoted scripture when folks didn't understand adversity. She could hear his booming voice still. " 'And we know that all things work together for good to them that love God, to them who are the called according to His purpose.'"

What was the purpose of loving God if He chose to destroy everything she held dear? How could any good come of this? *Just tell me, Lord. I see nothing ahead but more heartache.*

Her body numb and her heart broken, Sarah Jane trudged ahead until she reached the rear of the wagon. Paralyzed, she simply couldn't bring herself to fetch the Bible. Upon peering inside, she saw Painted Hands had covered the bodies with Mama's friendship quilt. The embroidered words *"Remember me"* seemed to lift off the coverlet and wrap their message around her heart. Mama and Papa were no longer there but in heaven. But touching them in order to fetch Papa's Bible made her cringe.

"I'll get the Book for you," Painted Hands said.

She hadn't heard him approach. Indians were silent, so Papa had said. They learned to walk without making a sound. Sarah Jane stepped aside and made her way back to the fire. "It's inside the trunk, on the top."

She listened to the creak of the lid's hinge, realizing he'd unfastened the leather straps. A moment later, he handed her the Bible.

"I can read, if it's too difficult for you." His voice sounded gentle.

Rubbing her fingers over the rough grain of the cover, she wanted to cry again. Painted Hands did have a tad of decency. She turned her attention to the site of her parents' final resting place. "Papa's favorite passage was Psalm One. Mama had several."

"The man I lived with after the soldiers took me from the Kiowa used to read Psalm Twenty-three at funerals. He thought the passage befited those who were grieving."

"Can we read both?"

"Yes ma'am."

Sarah Jane tore her gaze from the graves to his face. To her comfort, she saw a touch of compassion in his blue eyes. "Thank you."

"You will be able to endure this day, Sarah Jane. You're a strong woman."

She shrugged. "I feel like the crumbled dirt beneath our feet."

"Dirt packed together is what forms the earth. Come—let's get this thing done."

She agreed with him on that matter. "What shall I do?" she asked.

Painted Hands pointed to the fire. "Sit and wait for me. I'm going to hitch up the oxen and take your parents to their graves. Then I'll call for you."

She glanced at the smoldering chips, then back to him. "Seems like I need to do something more."

"You loved and nursed them while they were alive. I'll do what I can for them in death."

His simple words made sense; she nodded her compliance.

"I do know the sadness in your heart," Painted Hands said. "My family still lives inside me, and I see their faces lit with joy."

"How old were you?"

"Six. I thought for many years that I was the only survivor, but the Reverend Crandle learned of an older brother. He lives in Oregon."

"That is why you're with the wagon train," she said. If he'd have mentioned this part of his life before, she wouldn't have been so quick to criticize.

"Scouting kept me separated from the other folks who don't care for my ways." He repositioned his hat.

"I'm sure they'll feel differently since we're married and you helped me with Mama and Papa."

"I'm still the same man." The coldness whispered through his reply. "Typhoid has probably spread through the rest of them by now."

"Should we travel alone?" She braced herself, knowing how he preferred solitude.

"I could make it fine, but it would be lonesome for you." He headed toward the oxen.

Taking Papa's Bible, she opened it to the worn pages where he'd penned his thoughts or written dates that meant nothing to her. Again she asked to see God's power in this. Only silence, the dreadful finality of silence.

While she busied herself around the fire, Painted Hands wrapped Mama in the friendship quilt and Papa in another, then tied their bodies with rope and lifted them back into the wagon.

"I'll call for you after I lower them."

He drove away, leaving her more alone than she could ever remember. Bile rose in her throat, and she thought for certain she'd be ill. A short while later, Painted Hands called for her. At the grave site, he read Psalms One and Twenty-three, then a passage from First Corinthians chapter fifteen.

" 'In a moment, in the twinkling of an eye, at the last trump: for the trumpet shall sound, and the dead shall be raised incorruptible, and we shall be changed.' "

Sarah Jane listened to every word as he continued to read.

" 'O death, where is thy sting? O grave, where is thy victory?' "

God spoke to her in those words. Her rebellious stand against God shamed her. *Please forgive me, Father. I know Mama and Papa are with You. My tears are for myself.* How strange that God should choose to speak His words through a man who did not trust in Him. Maybe Painted Hands did believe but had chosen to run.

" 'Therefore, my beloved brethren, be ye stedfast, unmoveable, always abounding in the work of the Lord, forasmuch as ye know that your labour is not in vain in the Lord.' "

I will, Father. I will not forget my marriage vows or the lessons Mama and Papa taught me.

CHAPTER 7

Painted Hands pounded dirt into the graves by repeatedly running the wagon wheels over the final resting place of John and Lydia Benson. The procedure deterred animals from digging up the bodies for food and some unscrupulous folks—both white man and Indian—from stealing their clothes. Once he finished, he needed to talk to Sarah Jane about breaking camp and catching up with the wagon train.

He'd avoided the stares and barbs aimed in his direction and now enjoyed the solitude away from people. Those who singled him out were more heathen than any Kiowa he ever knew. If an Indian brother despised you, you understood the reason why, and you could choose an opportunity to prove yourself worthy. Among too many white people, the judgment was made without consideration of the heart of a man. Not all whites were this way, but far too many were, just as some Kiowa did not represent their race well.

The Reverend Crandle honored every man through his faith. He'd shown Painted Hands kindness and lived his teachings in the respect and dignity he showed to others. The reverend's manner of life had led the way for many folks to want to live like him. Sarah Jane also modeled integrity. Her honesty and willingness to extend herself unselfishly had affected Painted Hands. She'd touched him more than he cared to admit. He had yet to understand why her presence bristled and warmed him at the same time.

Yesterday and today he wanted to comfort her, but physically placing his arms around her grieving body and allowing her to weep against his chest battled against his vow to keep people away. When he closed his eyes at night, he saw Sarah Jane's face and lived the longing to protect her against those forces that threatened to hurt or sadden her. How many times had he lost himself in those green eyes? She had a beauty about her that rivaled nature. Her reddish-blond hair and matching freckles projected youth and a glimpse of honey sweetness, but Sarah Jane's true loveliness came from within. If he didn't keep a shield over his emotions, she'd melt his resolve to let nothing stand in the way of reaching Jacob.

He vaguely remembered his older brother. At the time of the fire, Jacob already worked with their pa on the farm and did most of the milking. Painted Hands looked up to him, but the older boy didn't have much need for a younger brother tagging along behind. Painted Hands quickly earned the nickname

"Puppy." What a nuisance he'd been, crying to Ma when Jacob shooed him away like a pesky fly. Those distant memories brought a smile to his lips. Once he found Jacob, he hoped the two of them could find the time to establish a lost relationship.

He stole a look at Sarah Jane. She bent to turn a slab of sizzling bacon in the frying pan. She had the faith he wished he'd succumbed to. Reverend Crandle had shown him the way, and Painted Hands even prayed for forgiveness and a new life in Jesus Christ, but that was before.

Nightmarish recollections stole the joy wanting to break through his rough exterior. The same day Painted Hands realized he needed God to lead and direct his life, various townsfolk visited Reverend Crandle with a false accusation about Painted Hands murdering a family outside town. The sheriff arrested him with no more proof than his Indian style of clothes and the way he wore his hair. Reverend Crandle and his wife prayed continuously. The law found the killer, but in the meantime, gossip about Reverend Crandle housing a murderer spread through the town. The church asked the reverend to resign. That's when Painted Hands decided he wanted no part of the Christian faith. He turned from God with a vow never to return.

"Don't let the weakness of man destroy your faith," the reverend had said. "All believers are saints who sin."

"I can't have faith in a God who allows unjust punishment," Painted Hands said.

"What of Jesus? Remember His death?"

Painted Hands shook his head. "I don't know. I think God will have to show me His power, because all I see is evil."

That had happened over seven years ago. Painted Hands continued to live with the Reverend Crandle awhile longer to try to sort out his future. Then he elected to join up with Greenham's wagon train as a scout. Painted Hands already had the skills, and Greenham gave him direction. Then some months ago came the unexpected. Painted Hands never tired of recalling every word.

"I have good news for you," the reverend had said. "I've located your brother, Jacob."

Painted Hands at last sensed hope. "Are you sure?"

The man grinned. "I'm certain. He listed parents Timothy and Elizabeth Carlson as perished in a fire along with three sisters: Rose Alice, Leah Mae, and Mary Elizabeth. He also named a deceased brother, Toby William. They were all from near Council Bluffs along the Missouri River."

"Where is Jacob?" Painted Hands could barely contain his excitement.

Pictures of the older brother flashed through his memories.

"He left about ten months ago for Oregon. His friends said he planned to start a logging camp north of the Willamette Valley."

"I have to find him." Painted Hands laughed. "My brother is alive."

"And it's an answer to prayer," Reverend Crandle said. "God's hand is in this. I can feel His presence."

Painted Hands didn't want to attribute the good news to God, but he sensed an exhilaration in his whole body. Not a single day since then had the desire wavered to reunite with Jacob. If he could have climbed on the wings of an eagle, he'd have flown to Oregon, but one obstacle after another lengthened the miles between them. The reverend said the journey to the Northwest meant a fresh start—one without malicious tongues. On this last trip to Oregon, Painted Hands wanted to make friends among the travelers, except someone already knew the old stories and spread them through the camp faster than a prairie fire. He hoped things would be different when he reached his brother.

Once more, Painted Hands knew the pain of isolation. This time he'd learned his lesson. No one would venture close; no one but Jacob, although his brother might shun him.

Shaking aside the thoughts that repeated in his head, Painted Hands moved his ponderings to the present.

"We need to decide about what to do next," he said after he'd unhitched the oxen and the two ate their meal.

She lifted her gaze; a curly wisp of reddish-blond hair trailed down the side of her face. Innocence and a sense of trust greeted him. He had to be strong and fight his growing feelings.

"I think joining back up with the wagon train makes good sense."

"You mean if they will have us," she said.

"Don't think on it that way. If they are dying of typhoid, we don't want them either."

She nodded. "But they treated you shamefully."

"I'm used to it."

"I still want to go to Oregon."

A wolf howled in the distance and grasped his attention. He waited for another one, but it never came. Hostile Indians sometimes spoke to each other through bird and animal calls. "My plans haven't changed."

She tilted her head and looked about. "There's nothing keeping us here. When do you want to leave?"

"As soon as we can get started." He searched her face for signs of remorse;

when her placid features revealed nothing, he finished his bacon and biscuits. "Can we leave in an hour?"

∞

At the designated time, Sarah Jane climbed onto the wagon seat, and Painted Hands rode alongside. Papa's horse was tied to the rear of the wagon. Mama and Papa lay behind them without so much as a wooden box to cradle their bodies. The stretch of road ahead provided time to think and plan. In the bottom of the trunk, hidden in the folds of one of Mama's dresses, was money to purchase land in Oregon and the beginnings of a mercantile. She considered selling Papa's horse and saddle at Fort Laramie and hiding the money, too.

Her gaze swung to Painted Hands. This should be a matter she discussed with her husband—if he were a real husband. Since he chose a loveless existence, then she'd keep financial matters to herself. What would stop him from taking the money, leaving her penniless? If only they were friends, like Mama and Papa used to be. Her parents often talked late into the night, never running out of topics. Sarah Jane wanted to learn about Painted Hands—his life with the Kiowa, their customs and language.

Painted Hands preferred not to talk. He'd told her so. Wishing for a friend in him was futile at best, and she wasted her efforts and faced disappointment every time she tried. Slapping the reins over the backs of the oxen, she chose to dwell on life once she got to Oregon. Operating a mercantile assured her of wonderful friends. Just thinking about the goods she'd carry and the customers she'd assist made her tingle. Bolts of beautiful cloth, bonnets, food, tools for the men, and jars of penny candy would line the shelves. She'd need a clever name for the store, maybe Sarah Jane's Supplies or Benson's Mercantile.

A realization seized her. She couldn't open a Benson's Mercantile; her name was. . .Mrs. Painted Hands. Peering at her husband, she decided to ask him.

"What do I tell folks my name is?"

He said nothing, and she wondered if he'd heard her. She opened her mouth to speak again, then he rode closer.

"My name?"

She nodded. "Yes. When folks ask me."

"I suppose my white-man name."

"Which is?"

"Toby Carlson."

Sarah Jane had learned something about her husband. *Sarah Jane Carlson.* She rolled the name on her tongue. It went together nicely—for as long as she was his wife. And he had a first name, too—Toby. "That's a good name."

"I don't imagine you'll have much of a chance to use it, since I intend to get a divorce as soon as we get to Oregon. Might be best if you continue using your pa's name."

She didn't respond. What could she say? But the anger grew. Was she simply the wrong race? Maybe he didn't like the color of her hair or her freckles. She wasn't happy with her looks either, especially the unruly curls. Her eyes—yes, that must be the problem. She knew she looked like a cat, but those things weren't supposed to matter. Mama said beauty had to come from the inside. She said comely people one day grew old, but the important traits only got better—the things you learned by living life and honoring God. How would Painted Hands ever see anything worthwhile in her when he kept his distance as though she embarrassed him?

Startled, she threw a seething look his way. He could use a shave and a haircut. Of course, he might be so ugly that everyone would run.

"Are you ashamed of me?" She hadn't intended to blurt out the question. It simply fell from her mouth.

"What are you talking about?" The deep tone of his voice fueled her fury. The sound by no means frightened her, especially when rage simmered near the surface.

"I understand you married me because of the committee. I understand you're a humble man to help me take care of Mama and Papa, and I'm grateful. I understand we don't know each other, but I'm not *that* ugly."

Painted Hands adjusted his hat. "What are you talking about? Are you sick?"

"No, I'm not sick. I'm asking you what's wrong with me."

He stared straight ahead as if she'd gone mad. "I'm riding ahead for a camping site."

"Of course. Put miles between us as if there aren't enough right now. While you're out there scouting around, see if you can find a watering hole where I can take a bath."

He pressed his heels into the horse's side. "Yes ma'am. I'll do my best."

The man didn't even have the sense to participate in an argument.

"Go ahead and be by yourself," she called after him.

The moment his figure faded, Sarah Jane regretted her childish temper tantrum. This wasn't like her. She always held her tongue and looked on the bright side of things. What if he kept right on riding? Everything he owned was stuffed in his saddlebag, except the provisions in the wagon. Why should he stay? Those Indian customs would keep him alive all the way to Oregon.

Sarah Jane's mind raced with how she might do the same thing. If the committeemen said she couldn't come back, then she'd find her way to Fort Laramie. There she'd join the next wagon train that rolled through. She wasn't a man, but she certainly had the means to look out for herself.

The afternoon wore on, the sun hotter than she could remember, and still no sign of Painted Hands. He really had left her. The sound of creaking wagon wheels scraped at her scrambled thoughts. A pair of buzzards flew overhead, creating a wave of uneasiness in the pit of her stomach. She watched their flight to make certain the vultures didn't head back toward Mama and Papa's grave.

They could be feasting on me in a few days. Forcing the gruesome image from her mind, she shielded her eyes in hopes of seeing Painted Hands. Nothing rose in her view but miles and miles of sparse grass beaten down by the cattle moving with the wagon train ahead.

"We'll catch up to Mr. Greenham's wagons," she said to the oxen. "They won't refuse me. After all, I didn't get the typhoid."

The echo of her voice proved how easy it would be to lose her mind in this desolate country. Now she understood Mama's desperation. All her mother had experienced was the loneliness and nothing of the promise.

"Isn't that what you're doing?"

Sarah Jane swung her head from side to side, looking for the source of the voice. So real, so clear. The silence repeated, and she shrugged.

"What good is a promise without trust?"

Did God think Mama didn't trust Him? She was one of the most faithful of all the believers Sarah Jane had ever seen.

"You, My child. Where is your faith? Where is your trust?"

She wanted desperately to have those things, but all she could see came in the form of Mama and Papa's grave and a husband who didn't want her.

"Painted Hands is a good man."

How would she ever know? He despised her.

"He is a child astray."

"What can I do?" she whispered.

"Trust Me for the promises. Loneliness is for those in darkness."

Sarah Jane repeated the words she recognized as from the Father. Lately, she'd been incredibly selfish—fretting over things about herself instead of trusting God. He had a plan for her and for Painted Hands. The mysterious future was laid out by God like a huge feast waiting to be tasted. She craved joy in the engulfing sorrow. She pleaded for direction in the way of her husband and courage to complete the journey to Oregon. Undoubtedly, obedience to God's directives proved more difficult than she'd ever imagined. *"Loneliness is for those in darkness."*

Sarah Jane sniffed back a sob.

Forgive me for my faithless heart. I'll apologize to Painted Hands, and I promise to be a good wife—no matter what happens.

Her gaze lifted, and she saw a lone rider. Painted Hands had not deserted her. If not for fear of driving him even farther away, she'd have jumped from the wagon and run to him. Asking his forgiveness for her wild tongue meant humbling herself and possibly facing his rejection. From now on, she'd look at Painted Hands as Jesus saw him—totally loved and cherished.

The closer he rode, the more anxious she became. Once again, loneliness and insecurity washed over her, but she had not been abandoned. God had His hand on her shoulder, gently guiding her.

"Hello." She waved and forced a smile. "I am so sorry, Painted Hands, for the mean things I said. Will you forgive me?"

"No." He spit his words at her like an angry rattler. "The wagon train is not far ahead. From the tracks I see, maybe three days beyond us. I'll take you there; then I'm riding on."

CHAPTER 8

Painted Hands hated the way he treated Sarah Jane. She'd apologized to him and even smiled when he rode her way. Still, he had little choice. What kind of life did he have to offer? He'd become set in his ways—probably as mean as most folks liked to think. Best he lived a life of solitude. Everywhere he went, every person he learned to care about met with disaster: his family, the Kiowa, the Reverend Crandle, and now Sarah Jane. In an isolated part of his mind, he wondered if the Bensons would have lived if he'd not stepped up to help. God had cursed him and anyone who drew close. As much as he wanted to see Jacob, he questioned the wisdom of exposing his brother to the inevitable.

An unquenchable thirst to put miles between him and Sarah Jane consumed him. She pressed against his heart, more so than any other person ever had. He wanted to know her, open his scars that seemed to fester with age, and pray, really pray, for healing. But he dare not—the reminders of what always happened were as evident as his discolored hands. Reverend Crandle said Painted Hands bore the fire-bitten scars like a breastplate, a shield against freeing himself from pain.

Nothing could shake his determination as far as Sarah Jane was concerned. Every time he looked at her, his heart weakened. He had to take action fast before he gave in and something happened to her. For too many years, he'd told himself he didn't need anyone. Most days he'd believed it, but with Sarah Jane, his heart wrenched for a love that would not let him go. He sensed a weakening of his will, no matter how hard he tried to disguise it.

In the late afternoon they camped by the Platte River, where water was shallow and plentiful. The cattle drank their fill, and with the approaching sunset, the picturesque scene swelled in his chest. How he would have loved to take his wife by the hand and watch the sunset together. The talk he claimed he didn't want would happen naturally. They could make plans for the future—discuss their ambitions about what lay ahead at the end of their journey. He had never asked what she wanted to do upon reaching the Northwest, if friends or relatives awaited her arrival or if she was alone. As for him, he hoped things went well with Jacob, and there might even be a job for him at the logging camp.

Fool! What is wrong with you? You have no choice but a solitary life. You destroy everything you touch.

Shaken back to reality, Painted Hands rode ahead to scout out more of the trail. Sarah Jane had indicated she wanted a bath. A fitting man would disappear into the gathering dusk and give her privacy. Releasing a heavy sigh, he decided that by traveling on Sunday, they'd reach the wagon train in the allotted three days.

He'd seen the fresh graves, and by the number of them, typhoid had spread through the wagon train. The vengeful side of him claimed those folks had received their due, but the side of him that Reverend Crandle had touched felt sympathy for those who had lost loved ones. Which side of him was the real Toby Carlson, or would he eventually resign completely to Painted Hands—the half-crazed man who favored neither Indian nor white?

When darkness nearly enveloped him, he returned to the wagon. He'd stayed gone longer than he intended, but this way she would be ready for bed once they ate.

The smell of frying fish assaulted his senses. His stomach growled. She'd gone fishing, and he knew without dwelling on it further that she'd done it for him. By this time, he realized a lot about Sarah Jane, and her giving heart didn't seem to end. The realization made him feel like a snake—a rattler at best.

"I have food ready," she said when he entered the firelight.

I have to enjoy this while I can. The days without Sarah Jane would be long.

Another smell tugged at him—fresh biscuits and the scent of apples. How warm it felt to have a woman tending to him.

"You didn't have to go to this much trouble." Painted Hands masked the feelings ready to burst through his crusty exterior.

"I wanted to." Her sweet voice reverberated over the night air. She heaped a tin plate full of fish, biscuits, and warm apples and handed it to him. Next she poured a steaming cup of hot coffee and set it beside him on the ground.

They ate in the typical silence he'd demanded from the beginning, but it wasn't what he truly wanted. He finished his food and asked for more.

"Must we separate when we catch up to the wagon train?" she asked.

The food suddenly caught in his throat. "We aren't suited for each other."

"I don't know you very well, but I want to. I can change if you tell me what makes you comfortable—"

"Being alone. No one else around." He dared not look at her for fear he'd forgo his willpower at the sight of her angelic face.

"I would do whatever you ask."

"Why?" Painted Hands asked. "Is it your faith? Are you afraid of being alone for the rest of the journey? Is it the divorce?"

Her thin shoulders lifted and fell. "I'd be a liar if I said I wasn't afraid or that I didn't mind solitude. I'm not as strong as you. But I made a promise to

God to submit as your wife. I'm asking for a chance to fulfill my vow."

Frustrated at her, frustrated at himself, he squeezed the handle on his mug. "Marriage will never work between us, Sarah Jane. There's no point in discussing it any longer or ever again." Gritting his teeth, he set the plate and mug down and stomped away in the dark.

For the first time in years, tears trickled down his cheeks.

∞

Sarah Jane had seen the graves, more than she ever hoped to see again. Some held stones as markers, others crude crosses, and too many appeared to be mass burials. Always wheels had firmed the dirt heaped on top, and always she wondered who had fallen prey to the typhoid. A risk needled at her. By returning to the wagon train, she faced the possibility of getting the disease, too. With Painted Hands leaving, she had to endure whatever God saw fit.

Up ahead, speckles of cattle moved across the prairie. They'd caught up with Mr. Greenham.

"Painted Hands," she said, for he'd ridden his spotted horse beside her. "Would you please stay three days with me? I know you're set to go, but I'm begging."

He stared straight ahead. Long moments lingered in the quiet. No matter what he said, she'd not resort to tears.

"I can do that," he finally said.

Thank You, God. A smile tugged at her mouth. "I'll not be a burden to you. I need to talk to some folks about helping me on to Oregon, and the three days would give me time."

"You've never been trouble." He rode ahead then, always running from her as if she were distasteful.

You can't run forever, Painted Hands. Someday God will turn your heart back to Him.

As the wagon eased closer to the others, Painted Hands and Mr. Greenham rode to her. Their faces wore a grim expression. The news must not be good.

"Good afternoon," Mr. Greenham said, leaning on his saddle. "Sorry to hear about your parents."

Sarah Jane studied the lines on his face, more lines than she'd seen before. "How have you fared?"

"We lost lots of folks to the typhoid. Still have many folks down with it. The sickness spread the very night the committee voted you out."

That's why she and Painted Hands had caught up with the wagons so quickly. "Are the Robinsons all right?" She couldn't bear to think of Martha and Amelia fretting with fever.

"We lost all of 'em," Mr. Greenham replied. "Buried them in a mass grave."

Sarah Jane shuddered. Several moments went by before she regained her composure. "The girls were my dearest friends, and my parents often visited Mr. and Mrs. Robinson. I do hope they didn't suffer much."

Mr. Greenham nodded. "So many have passed on that I don't remember all the particulars. No new cases yesterday or today," he said. "Thank God, it must be over."

"I'll pray for all of them." Sarah Jane understood the bereavement of those families. "Perhaps I can help in the nursing."

"You're a mighty kind woman to offer help. I won't be refusing you and Painted Hands to join up with us again, although I wonder the good sense of it."

"Traveling alone is dangerous," Painted Hands said. "I want my wife to have the protection you offer."

"You're a wise man. This country hollows out enough graves without increasing the chances." Mr. Greenham straightened in the saddle. "Go ahead and drive your cattle back into the herd and pull the wagon to the end of the line. As you can see, we haven't been making good time with so many down sick."

"Fort Laramie isn't far ahead," Painted Hands said. "Will they let us in?"

"Doubt it," Mr. Greenham said. "That will disappoint a lot of folks. The healthy ones most likely can get us supplies, and we'll rest up a few days." He turned his horse back toward the wagons. "I've missed you, Painted Hands. Glad you're back."

A few days ago, Sarah Jane would have fought the urge to encourage her husband to stay longer than the three days, but not now. An unexplainable peace wrapped around her insecurities with a message of comfort. God's way was the best.

That evening, Painted Hands left her without a word. She'd grown used to his disappearances. Would he give her a final good-bye at the end of the three days? She doubted he'd even considered a proper farewell. Avoidance best described her husband.

A cook fire warmed apples from the previous evening along with fried bacon and a few precious potatoes. She hoped Painted Hands arrived soon, for the day had been particularly taxing, and she craved sleep. All day her head hurt, and no wonder with the burden bearing down on her. After straightening the inside of the wagon and filling the water keg, she opened the trunk to seek out the money Papa had set aside for Oregon. Resting the lantern on a sack of flour, she carefully pulled the bills from Mama's dress. To her amazement, the money amounted to over twice what Sarah Jane believed was hidden. She could open a mercantile right away. A note wrapped another bundle of money. She opened it and recognized the handwriting.

My beloved daughter,

If you are reading this, no doubt your papa and I perished along the journey to Oregon. I am sorry for abandoning you. Your papa and I prayed that God in His infinite wisdom would send someone to help you in the event of our deaths. Do not turn back. I know I protested leaving Nebraska, but your papa's dreams are far more important. Only you can fulfill his vision.

The amount of money here is far more than we told you. We wanted to keep a good portion for you in the event you married. Praise God there is plenty here for you to establish yourself in a new home.

My reason for this letter is to tell you how very much you are loved. The days and months ahead will be difficult, but I have no doubt you will see Oregon, the promised land, and it will be as beautiful as we dreamed.

Select your husband wisely. You have the means to take care of yourself, so a marriage out of necessity should not befall you. First, let him be a man of God. Second, pray together every day of your life, and third, understand that troubles will try to tear your love apart, but do not succumb to such evil. God is in His heaven all the days of your life, and He loves you dearly.

I love you.
Mama

Tears streamed down Sarah Jane's face. Oh, how she missed Mama and Papa. Sometimes she thought the ache would never go away. *"Select your husband wisely."*

Mama, I didn't choose Painted Hands. Circumstances chose us. I pray I never disappoint you, and as long as we are husband and wife, I will honor him.

With a deep breath, she replaced the money and thanked God for His provision. This blessing came at the right time in light of the upcoming departure of Painted Hands. But her husband had not left yet, and she would not give up until he rode away.

"Mrs. Painted Hands."

Sarah Jane heard the familiar male voice but couldn't quite place the name. "I'll be right with you." She quickly made certain the trunk was in order and climbed down from the wagon. Of all the people she wished to see, Preacher

Sanders was at the bottom of the list. He'd escaped the typhoid. *How sad.* Immediately, she chastised herself.

"Mr. Sanders, how are you?" She feigned cordiality.

"I saw, uh, your husband earlier."

"Yes, you married us, remember?"

He pressed his thin lips together. "Mr. Greenham said your parents died."

"Yes sir. I understand many other fine people have perished with the sickness."

"I spoke at more funerals than I care to recall."

"I'm sorry. Mr. Greenham said the epidemic is lessening," she said.

"That is my prayer."

Just speak your mind and be gone. "May I ask why you've paid me a visit? Or is this to express your condolences?" Why did peering into the man's face make her irate?

"I've called the committee to a meeting tonight, what's left of them."

"Why do I need to know this?" Exhaustion swept over her. Then she remembered hearing Mr. Greenham say the committeemen might need to meet again if she and Painted Hands returned. If Mr. Sanders simply got on with his business, she'd rest until her husband returned.

"Since your parents were the first to come down with typhoid, I believe you must be carrying it with you."

All thoughts of courtesy vanished. Respect for Mr. Sanders blew with the night breeze. "How dare you make such an accusation? I suggest you leave before I scream for help."

Mr. Sanders took a step back. He looked like the old tomcat that used to live in Papa's sod barn. He hissed and spit until a person took a step in his direction. "Considering the reputation of your husband, I doubt if anyone would listen."

Sarah Jane held her breath while her mind raced with rage. "My husband is a far better man than you could ever be. He knows the meaning of integrity and honor, whereas you hide behind a God whom I doubt you've ever met!"

"You will regret speaking to me in such a manner." His squeaky voice inched higher. "I have my means."

Sarah Jane attempted to calm her nerves. Papa always said anger never solved anything. "Mr. Sanders, you are not welcome here. I'm asking you to leave. If you refuse, I'll ask my husband to file a complaint with the committee."

"No need to ask me." Painted Hands stepped into view. The lantern lit up his reddened features.

"You two are a disgrace," Mr. Sanders said. "As I said earlier, your wagon brought misfortune and death to this wagon train, and I intend to put an end to it."

"Go ahead," Painted Hands said. "While you're at it, you can include this." He threw his fist alongside the man's jaw, sending him sprawling in the dirt. "That's for bullying my wife. When you get up, I'll give you another one for what you said about her parents."

Sarah Jane grabbed Painted Hands's arm. "He's not worth the trouble. Let him crawl back to his committee."

Mr. Sanders did indeed crawl backward, then shifted to his feet and took off in a dead run. Some of the other wagons had seen and heard the ruckus, but Sarah Jane didn't care. She still trembled.

"I'm so glad you came," she said, taking her breath in quick spurts.

"I've met his kind before. A hypocrite." A rare look of concern etched his brow. "Are you all right? Did he touch you?"

Her breathing refused to slow down. Her legs felt as if they were weighted down with rocks. "I'm tired. So very tired."

Blackness inched over her mind and body, and she gave into the overwhelming urge to sleep.

CHAPTER 9

Painted Hands caught Sarah Jane before she collapsed onto the ground. This was the first time he'd ever touched her, and she was burning with fever. *No, not Sarah Jane.* He swept her into his arms, noting how light and frail—and incredibly hot—she was. Once she lay on the straw-filled mattress in the back of the wagon, he tried to wake her. She mumbled about needing sleep, but he could not get her to acknowledge him.

You destroy everything you touch.

He ground his teeth against the backdrop of the accusations swirling about in his head. Not this time. Not if he could do anything to stop it. Sarah Jane would not die because of him.

Painted Hands buried his head in his hands. He should have left sooner. Selfishness over his growing feelings for her had ruled his better judgment.

Brushing back a damp curl from her cheek, his calloused fingers felt the smoothness of her skin. How he'd longed to be this close these past weeks, but not at the cost of Sarah Jane's health. How could he cool down the fever? Helpless and disoriented, he bit back bitter tears.

"I'll get some water," he said as if she comprehended every word.

Painted Hands scooted back and out of the wagon. Snatching up a towel, he filled a basin. For the next hour, he continuously wiped her face and listened to her occasional delirium. He answered when he could, assuring her she needed rest and he was there for her. He said the things he should have said from the first day of their marriage. What good would it have done, since the ultimate outcome was her lying ill with typhoid?

"I'm sorry," he said. "Sarah Jane, I never intended for you to fall prey to my curse."

"Painted Hands," she whispered and lifted her hand.

He grasped it and brought the slender fingers to his lips. Anxiously, he searched her face for signs of consciousness or more of the fever-ravaged confusion.

"Mama, Papa, don't leave me," she said. "He doesn't want me."

Painted Hands sucked in a breath. Guilt attacked him on every side. He'd refused her desire to be his wife. He'd been cruel and heartless in everything he said and did, neglecting to comfort her when her parents died and insisting she not talk to him. He'd wanted to guard her against his curse, and even then his efforts failed.

He remembered the tea she so diligently prepared and spoon-fed to her ma and pa. Lifting the trunk lid, he saw the small bag of dried ginger leaves. His experience with herbs told him ginger provided little aid for the fever, but it should help the stomach problem that often accompanied typhoid.

The sound of voices outside the wagon seized his attention. He whirled around, recognizing Sanders's high-pitched screech of excitement.

"Right here—he tried to kill me," Sanders said. "All I was doing was offering my sympathy and prayers in regard to his wife's family. We've heard the tales. He's a murderer, I say, and he's dangerous."

Painted Hands took a deep breath to control the bubbling fury. He took a longing glance at Sarah Jane and left her for the storm brewing outside the wagon.

"Sanders, when are you going to tell them the truth?" Painted Hands asked.

Greenham stood with a half dozen other men, but Painted Hands spurned any thought of using his friendship with the wagon master as leverage. "I walked into the campsite to find you accusing my wife's parents of carrying typhoid. You also claimed to have called a committee meeting to cut us out of the wagon train."

"Is this true?" Greenham asked.

Sanders rubbed his bony jaw. "He punched me before trying to kill me."

"I hit you, and I'd do it again, but I never threatened to kill you. Although I wish someone would do me the favor."

"Where's your wife?" Greenham asked. "If she backs up Painted Hands, then I'm for ending this right now."

Painted Hands realized lying about Sarah Jane made no sense. "She's inside the wagon. After I ran Sanders off, she took sick."

"Sick?" one of the men asked.

Staring straight into the man's eyes, Painted Hands saw the fear. "Yes, fever."

"Typhoid," Greenham stated more than asked.

"I think so." Painted Hands hurled an angry glance at Sanders. "What do you have to say now?"

"Cut 'em out," Sanders said, tossing his words to the men beside him.

Greenham stiffened. "After the Bensons, we didn't cut the other families when they came down sick."

"He's a wild man—can't trust 'im." Sanders's voice rose with each word.

"I'd hit you if you insulted my wife," another man said. "Sanders, you called me away from my family, saying this was an important meeting affecting the whole wagon train. This is nothing more than a personal vendetta." The man stepped in front of Sanders. "I hear you asked John Benson for his daughter to marry up with your son. Benson told you no. You want a vote? Fine. Let's do it now." The man stuck out his hand to Painted Hands. "You've never done me wrong, and my vote is for you to stay. I hope some of us can give help in nursing your wife."

Painted Hands shook the man's hand. He didn't even know his name.

"My name is Andrew. I'm feeling right bad about the way you've been treated."

"I appreciate what you've done here tonight," Painted Hands said, and he meant every word.

"Those of you in favor of Painted Hands and his wife staying with the wagons, raise your hand," Greenham said.

Three men voted for them to stay, which left three others opposed.

"I say this couple deserves a chance, especially since we kept the other sick folks," Greenham said.

Sanders sneered. "You don't have a vote."

"What if I quit right now? Then you don't have a scout or a wagon master."

"You'd desert all these people, leaving them to die in the wilderness because of a no-good crazy man?" Sanders tossed Painted Hands a triumphant sneer.

Painted Hands stepped forward. "I'll pull out in the morning with my wife and the fifty head of cattle." He nodded at the three men who had voted in their favor. "I appreciate what you tried to do here, but it won't ever be said that I was responsible for good folks dying." He turned around and headed back to Sarah Jane. For the first time since he'd agreed to marry, Painted Hands felt as if he'd conducted himself as a good man—not a selfish one.

"You take care of your wife," Greenham said. "I'll get your cattle."

"We'll round them up in the morning," Andrew said. "Would you like some company tonight? I could sit with your wife while you sleep a little."

"Thanks, but I don't think I could rest with her sick."

Andrew rammed his hands into his trouser pockets. "I lost my wife and baby boy to typhoid. Can't sleep anyway—might as well see what I can do for you."

Painted Hands studied the man before him. He looked not much older than Sarah Jane. From the haggard look about him, Andrew was hurting real bad. "Sorry about your family. Don't seem fair, does it?"

Andrew shook his head and stared into the darkness. "I reckon the Lord needed 'em, but I miss 'em. . .every minute of the day."

Painted Hands didn't respond, but he knew he'd remember Andrew for as long as he lived. A stranger had seen Painted Hands as a real man without knowing the person inside.

The rest of the night crept by. Painted Hands kept a vigil for Sarah Jane; the idea of sleep never crossed his mind. He thought back over how she'd tried to please him and done little things for him that he failed to acknowledge. So many times she smiled and appeared to be happy even when he was mean. Shame swept over him until he wept.

"I often wish I'd said and done things differently," Andrew said. "I reckon she knows how I'm grieving for her and our son." His voice cracked. "When your wife gets well, be sure to tell her how much you love her."

"I just hope it's not too late," Painted Hands said.

Andrew touched his shoulder. "I'll be praying for you."

Painted Hands wanted to tell him not to bother, but the man had faced enough bad luck in his life without adding to it.

Come morning, the wagon train pulled out, leaving behind Painted Hands and Sarah Jane along with a cloud of dust and bawling cows. They had plenty of water, grazing for the cattle, and provisions. But he longed for herbs to treat the typhoid. White men called the plant coneflower, and he'd seen it cool down the worst of fevers. That meant leaving her, and he feared she'd grow worse while he searched for the wildflowers. All day and through the night, he tended to her. At times he dozed off only to waken sharply with guilt piercing his heart worse than a jagged knife.

Sarah Jane's dress was soaked. He thought long and hard about removing it—wondering about the propriety of it all. Casting aside his doubts, he carefully slid it from her shoulders in hopes this made her more comfortable. She was thin, and he thought back since they'd married and didn't recall seeing her eat much. He stiffened. She'd been ill and either hadn't said a word or didn't pay attention to the symptoms. Pondering over his wife, he assumed she'd pay more attention to someone else's needs than her own. A few nights ago, she'd gone fishing—for him—and after he'd treated her so shamefully.

Maybe he should have tried to tell her the truth about his curse right from the beginning, but it took over a year for the Reverend Crandle to earn his confidence and open up to the truth. Painted Hands dabbed the cloth over Sarah Jane's face and expelled a labored breath. Right now he'd do anything to break this fever.

Coneflower.

The higher the sun climbed in the sky, the higher Sarah Jane's fever. She ranted about things Painted Hands thought were childhood matters, and he'd seen enough typhoid to understand how close she teetered to death. Once she called out for him, and it startled him. The sound of his name on her lips moved him to make a decision. He'd have to leave her long enough to find the reddish-purple wildflower with its healing powers.

"I won't be long, Sarah Jane," he said, caressing her limp hand. "Hold on and fight the typhoid."

In his rush against death, he slipped the bridle over his mare's neck and rode bareback. Digging his heels into the horse's side, he raced across the plain beyond where the cattle from the wagon train had beaten down the grasses. Not a single coneflower broke into his view.

Lord, please. I'm not asking for me but for Sarah Jane.

A stab of realization nearly staggered him. He'd *prayed.* How long had it been?

"I have loved you with an everlasting love."

The whisper reminded him of Reverend Crandle's voice but deeper, like the sound of a waterfall. He rolled the words around in his head, grasping and yet fighting their meaning.

"Then tell me what to do." Painted Hands stared up at a cloudless sky. "Take my life. Sarah Jane is innocent of my sins—the curse You have cast upon me."

"Sin and suffering do not come from Me."

"Then tell me how to stop it." Painted Hands's voice echoed around him. *"You can't."*

Sarah Jane deserved to live, to reach her dream of Oregon. She trusted God, even when her parents died. Desperation wrapped a strangling hold around him. Had he gone mad? He, too, must have typhoid. A feverish mind was the reason for the voice. God didn't talk to sinful folks, just good people like Reverend Crandle, Sarah Jane, Andrew, and other folks including his Kiowa family. They all had impressed him with their decency.

"Please don't take Sarah Jane."

"Trust Me."

Painted Hands hesitated. If trusting God was all it took to heal Sarah Jane, then he'd trust with every bit of strength in his body. But he'd called out too many times in the past, and God had been silent.

"I beg of You to spare her. Whatever You ask, I will do."

The sounds of insects chorusing over the heated prairie met his ears. The roar in his spirit ceased. Painted Hands relaxed. His hands loosened their grip on the reins, and he trembled. Sweat streamed down his face, more from the unexplainable encounter than from the afternoon sun. Sensing a need to walk, he slid from the mare's back and led her while he sorted through what had just happened.

Suddenly, the horse reared, and the reins were snatched from his grasp. Painted Hands had always prided himself in the way he handled horses, a skill learned from his Indian brothers. In the next instant, the horse broke free and galloped away in the opposite direction of the wagon.

Painted Hands shook his fist. Again he saw the curse of God. Sarah Jane lay dying in the wagon. He couldn't find the wildflowers that would aid in her healing, and now his horse had deserted him. *How can I trust You when You make a mockery of me?*

With grim determination, he headed toward the wagon. Nearly a mile passed with nothing in view but the prairie. Painted Hands continued to search for the coneflower, though he'd looked before his horse deserted him.

Then to the right of him he saw several reddish-purple flowers. They nodded their petaled heads in the warm breeze. Laughing like a boy, he hurried to them and pulled up all he could carry. The entire plant would be made into a tea.

"Thank You," he said, lifting his head to the heavens. He'd ridden right by them earlier, for hoofprints were embedded in the earth.

A surge of energy like fresh hope filled his body as he dashed toward Sarah Jane. And when he caught sight of that canvas-covered prairie schooner, he spotted his horse.

He'd found the coneflowers, and the mare had taken off in the opposite direction. How strangely odd and wonderful at the same time. God must love Sarah Jane. Painted Hands realized another peculiar matter. He loved her, too.

Inside the wagon, Sarah Jane lay still; her pallor frightened him. By habit, Painted Hands washed her face, neck, and arms from the basin of water he'd used earlier.

"I have medicine," he said. "Please hold on to life while I brew some tea."

He snatched up the flint and steel fireworks kit and slipped the striker over his finger. Soon he had water heating over a fire and the coneflower steeping, its healing powers spreading through the water. Grasping a mug and spoon, he stirred the tea and allowed it to cool.

Lord, You answered me today, and I thank You. Please heal her, I beg of You.

Inside the wagon, he lifted Sarah Jane's head and spooned the medicine into her mouth, allowing it to trickle down her throat. This had to break the fever—this and prayer.

CHAPTER 10

Sarah Jane fought to open her eyes. She attempted to gather her wits about her, but time and place eluded her. All she could remember was Painted Hands sending his fist into Preacher Sanders's face. She'd tried to stop her husband, but a part of her—a very wicked part of her—gained a sense of satisfaction from seeing the man run off into the night.

I'm sorry, Lord. Vengeance is wrong, and I know it.

Where was Painted Hands? The cloudy haze engulfing her mind started to lift. She remembered he went out into the night, and she kept supper waiting for him. Yes, now things were clearer. She'd found Mama's letter and the money, put it all back into the trunk, then heard Mr. Sanders calling for her. Suddenly, she remembered the irritating man wanting to cut their wagon again. Why couldn't she remember more?

"Sarah Jane?"

Her eyes fluttered. She desperately wanted to open them. Painted Hands spoke her name. Something must be terribly wrong, for his voice rang with tenderness.

"Sarah Jane, are you awake?"

She battled the urge to fall back to sleep, but Painted Hands had called her name in a way she'd dreamed. Slowly, Sarah Jane opened her eyes. The blur faded until she saw his face. He looked tired, and she forced a smile. The gesture stole her strength.

"How are you?" he asked.

She mouthed "sleepy," and he touched her cheek.

"Don't try to talk," he said. "Rest and get well. You've been very sick."

Sick? She remembered wanting to sleep but nothing else.

"You had typhoid, Sarah Jane, but the danger is gone. You need to get well."

She opened her mouth, but he laid a finger on her lips.

"Hush. Go to sleep, and we'll talk later. I have medicine, and it has helped."

Obediently, she allowed her eyelids to close. She'd survived typhoid? How long had she lain ill while Painted Hands cared for her? One question after another inched across her mind with no answers. She'd ask the questions later, when she wasn't so sleepy. Painted Hands had acted so kind. . . .

When Sarah Jane awoke the second time, evening shadows hugged the wagon. Again her husband sat beside her bed. Had he never left? How dear of him, as though he really cared.

A smile tugged at his lips. "Hello." He reached for her hand. "I've been watching you sleep."

"How long"—the words seemed to drag from her mouth—"have I been ill?"

"Five days."

His reply sent a note of panic throughout her body. Surely she should have died. God must have a reason for sparing her. Now she understood her weakened condition and lack of memory. How good of Painted Hands to nurse her.

"Thank you," she managed. "I'm. . .sorry."

He gathered up her hands into his, and she treasured the sweet gesture. "Sarah Jane, things are going to be different now. I'm the one who's sorry. You nearly died, just when I was about to run off again."

"I'll get well." Speaking pulled at what little strength she mustered. "I want to be a good wife."

"You are. It's me who has failed. Don't try to talk anymore. I have medicine for you, and I've made broth."

Humiliation crept through Sarah Jane as she realized what had been involved in having Painted Hands care for her. She'd been worse than a baby to tend to—spoon-feeding the medicine, bathing her when the dysentery tore through her body. He had ignored his own needs for her sake. Surely the humble task came under God's plan. She thanked God for her husband and for delivering her from the typhoid. Sarah Jane prayed this would be a new beginning for them.

Two days later, he carried her outside the wagon and laid her in the shade beneath the wide branches of a cottonwood tree overlooking the Platte River. While she gazed over the water and listened to the insects, birds, and an occasional cow, Painted Hands washed clothes and straightened the inside of the wagon. The smell of death lingered there, and he opened the flaps at both ends to allow fresh air to whisk away the reminders of typhoid.

While she slept, he found more coneflowers for the healing tea and hunted a rabbit for their supper. She cherished his doting. This was a side of Painted Hands he'd kept secret. He laughed and whistled, and she thought if they never moved from the prairie, she'd be perfectly fine.

"I think I've found a piece of paradise," she said as he climbed the small bank carrying a dress, shirt, and undergarments from the river.

"It is peaceful."

"Reminds me of Nebraska."

He stopped and gazed out over the prairie, beyond the grazing cattle to where the plains and the horizon met. "Do you want to go back?"

She considered his question. Friends were in Nebraska and a way of life she knew well. But Papa's dreams lay beyond the mountains, and her life was now with her husband. "Nebraska will always be home, but my future is in Oregon. How long before we can travel?"

"You need to grow stronger first."

"I'll drink the medicine all day long, if it will help."

He eased down beside her, holding the wet bundle against his chest. "I refuse to do anything that causes you to be ill again. Sometimes the fever can last for days or weeks. I've seen folks recover from the typhoid, then get something else because their bodies aren't strong."

She studied his blue eyes, matchless to the heavens. "I want us to get to Oregon before the winter snows. When I get tired, I can sleep in the wagon if you're willing to drive." She shrugged. "Providing the cattle keep up a good pace."

He dropped the washing between his legs to the grass below and leaned back on his hands. "I won't take any chances where you are concerned. The journey to Fort Laramie is right ahead, but the mountain pass is difficult for those who are hearty."

"Can't we make better time than the wagon train? We could start earlier in the mornings, and I could make extra bread and bacon so we wouldn't have to stop at noon but could move on till nightfall. And we wouldn't need a whole Sunday to wash clothes and hunt, but a half day."

He chuckled and combed his fingers through her curls. "Are you spending all your time fretting over this trip?"

His touch sent her heart racing. This had to be the real love Mama used to speak about. "I do have another idea."

"And what could it be, Sarah Jane? Shall we grow wings and fly like the eagle?"

"I'm serious." She punctuated her words with a nod. "We could sell the cattle at Fort Laramie, unless you want them."

He directed his gaze to the grazing animals. "It would be a sight easier and faster going over the mountains. Ought to keep a milk cow or two."

She smiled from the inside out. "Then we can go soon?"

He gathered up the washing. "I'll think on it, but you need to rest a few more days."

"Two?"

"Three, then we'll talk again."

She sighed. "I want you to see your brother as soon as you can."

He stood and seemed to study her. "Thank you, but Jacob knows I'm coming. Reverend Crandle sent word to him months ago, and my brother knows the perils of the journey."

"I don't want him worrying about you."

"Don't know many folks who've ever done that."

"You have me." When she saw her words left him uncomfortable, she ventured on. "Are you sad about not joining back up with Mr. Greenham?"

His laughter caused a nearby cow to perk her ears. "Only if I'd be missing Preacher Sanders and his committeemen."

"Oh, I declare he has the devil's wit. I'm not judging Mr. Sanders, really, but I feel sorry for him when he meets the Lord."

"True. He is one miserable man, although I met a man named Andrew who understood the meaning of living a Christian life. He stood up for us when the others were afraid of going against Sanders."

"What happened? Do you mind telling me?"

Painted Hands told her everything that occurred the night she fell to typhoid. "Andrew stayed with me until dawn, then helped cut out the cattle. I hope he reaches Oregon and finds a good future."

She thanked God for putting such a good man in their path. Her husband needed to see committed believers who put others before themselves—good folks who lived their faith. Painted Hands had obviously done that very thing while she suffered through typhoid.

In the past few days, she'd noted something wonderful about Painted Hands: a definite tenderness toward her beginning when she first opened her eyes from the typhoid. His new treatment of her had continued. Before, he had erected a barrier in front of him mortared with a fierce determination to keep others out. Now he no longer hid his emotions or said cruel things to her. She prayed it lasted. Earlier, she nearly told him of her feelings, but she feared he'd leave.

With an inner sigh, Sarah Jane watched her husband carry the washing to the wagon. He turned, and she waved. Becoming friends with Painted Hands held a bit of a risk and a challenge. Perhaps he felt the same.

∞

Painted Hands laid the washing over the brush and flat out on the grass to dry. He stole a look at Sarah Jane. Today the color had started to return to her cheeks. She was still weak, and he noticed she'd napped after spending but a few minutes brushing her hair. Such a small task to waste away her energy. He thought of asking if he could brush it for her. He would gladly while away the hours serving her needs. He craved every moment with Sarah Jane, like a calf trailing after its mother. Making her life easier in this harsh land became his sole purpose. Gazing into her green eyes became his passion. Without question, Painted Hands loved his wife.

A fierce protective instinct settled on him. He peered in every direction, keeping a guarded watch for any animal or bout of nature that might seek to do her harm. His brothers, the Kiowa, flashed across his mind. Some thought they were lazy, for their days were spent hunting, deepening their skills as warriors, and guarding their homes. Without those/traits, a Kiowa could not protect those he loved. Painted Hands understood his purpose as a man, and the realization made him proud and humble at the same time.

The thought of revealing his heart hammered incessantly. Although she held the title of his wife, he'd done nothing to consummate the marriage or encourage her about the relationship—quite the contrary. The spiteful things he'd said to her in the past aroused more guilt than he cared to admit. Tonight he'd apologize for the things he'd said and done. Confessing his heart was another matter. That would have to wait.

Dare he make plans to break camp and risk her health? Selfishly, he wanted nothing better than to head toward Oregon, but Sarah Jane's health was foremost. He'd speak of it again in three days hence. By then he could tell if she were strong enough to continue on to Fort Laramie. The thought of losing her made him shudder. He'd already lost so many before.

Everything you touch is destroyed.

The nagging, despised voice plagued him again. He longed for true peace, the kind he'd felt when he searched for the coneflower—when God spoke to him. Where did the condemning thoughts come from? Reverend Crandle said God loved him and the accusations came from Satan. If only he could believe those words.

That evening Painted Hands milked the cow and urged Sarah Jane to drink a full mug. He'd made butter earlier in the day, and it tasted good on hot biscuits. She even ate a little roasted rabbit with wild onions. Pleased with her determination to gain her strength, he praised her efforts.

"If we are to leave the prairie, then I must eat," she said. "I think you will have to show me how to cook. Your food is so much better than mine."

"You are simply hungry."

"And you prepared a feast."

He watched the firelight dance off her face and wondered how he'd ever managed without her, certainly a strange notion for a man who'd sworn he needed no one. She yawned. Sleepiness filled her eyes.

"Looks like you need some rest." Painted Hands took her plate and glanced at the bit of milk in the bottom of her mug. "Are you going to finish this?"

She covered her mouth to hide another yawn. "You sound like my mama."

"I've assumed a new role."

She drank the last bit and smiled. The mere sight of her warmed his soul.

"I'm looking forward to the day when you don't have to spend all your time taking care of me," she said.

He reached for her hands. "Until then, I'll be your mama. Let me help you to bed."

She slipped her frail fingers into his palms, and he pulled her to meet him. She stood close enough that he trembled at her nearness, and when she peered into his face with a look of trust and innocence, the urge to kiss her swept over him.

Sarah Jane lifted his hands to her lips, kissing each one. The gesture startled and embarrassed him.

"Why did you do that?" he asked a bit more gruffly than he intended.

"Because these hands took care of me. You fed me, gave me medicine, bathed me, and countless other things." Her melodious voice rang above the night sounds.

"The scars—"

She shook her head. "I feel awkward with how you nursed me, rather discomfited at times, and this is my way of thanking you."

Painted Hands hesitated. The thought of revealing his pain to this precious woman tugged at him. "They are ugly."

"I have never considered them as such. Were they burned?"

"Yes, a long time ago."

"Would you tell me what happened?"

He touched her cheek. He'd never told the whole story to anyone, not even to Reverend Crandle, but that didn't mean the need wasn't there.

"If it's too painful, I understand," she said. "I simply wondered."

Perhaps now the time had come for him to open up a small portion of his past. If he felt worse or she was repulsed, he'd never venture in that direction again. "Once you are in bed, I'll tell you." When she smiled at him again, he thought his heart would burst from his chest. "Do you need for me to help you?"

"I can manage," Sarah Jane said. "I'm getting stronger, you know, and I shan't take long."

CHAPTER 11

Sarah Jane nestled beneath the warmth of the quilt and called for Painted Hands. She was so very tired, but hearing him talk about himself meant more to her than sleep. They had come so far, and she refused to lose the closeness growing between them.

When he climbed into the wagon carrying the lantern, she couldn't help but admire the familiarity of him: the broad muscles spreading across his shoulders and his beaded hair. His buckskin clothes and moccasins no longer seemed foreign but welcome. A worried frown creased his forehead.

"Sit by me," she said. "I do want to hear your story. Every little bit I learn about you makes me feel as if we are deepening our friendship."

He sat beside the narrow mattress and drew up his knees. She pulled her hands from beneath the quilt to slip into his.

"This is not easy for me, Sarah Jane. I've lived with what happened the night of the fire for many years."

She glanced at the hand covering hers, then back to his face. "I'm listening. I don't want there ever to be anything you hesitate to tell me. After all, you discovered the very worst of me."

Painted Hands squeezed her hand lightly. "You are wrong to think those things. It was an honor to help you." He took a deep breath, and she prayed for his ability to relate the obviously painful memories. "My parents, three sisters, and an older brother—Jacob—lived in the western Kansas Territory. I was the youngest. Pa farmed, and we raised animals, and Ma and my sisters tended a garden. My job was to feed the pigs and chickens." He smiled with a look in his eyes that went beyond the here and now.

"I was six years old when I noticed several baby chicks running about the barnyard. In my mind I thought some wild animal would eat them, so I begged my folks to let me bring them inside. They said no, and I went to bed that night very upset. I couldn't sleep and got up to check on those chicks. Everyone else slept, and I knew better than to wake Ma or Pa. I crept out into the cold dark and made my way to the barn. Well, I found the mother hen and discovered her babies were snug and safe under her warm body. I decided to watch the mother hen awhile to make sure she didn't forget about those chicks, and I fell asleep. I woke sometime later to the sight of flames lapping up the cabin and screams from inside. I ran to the front of the cabin and cried out for my ma and pa. Horrible cries echoed around me. I hurried to the well, but the bucket sat inside the house. I remembered Ma asking me to take it outside earlier. I didn't know what to do, and I wanted to save my family. Every time I tried to get inside the cabin, a wall of hot flames stopped me.

"That's when a band of Kiowa on a hunting trip rode up. They were far from their normal territory. They pulled me from the fire, but my family died inside. My hands were burned, and that is how I received my name. For the next ten years, I lived with the Kiowa."

Tears filled Sarah Jane's eyes. "Why haven't you told anyone this? No one should live with this burden."

He released her hand and clenched his fists. "The bucket. I couldn't save any of them because I'd left it inside." He hesitated. "I've often wondered if I did something to start the fire before I left the cabin—knocked over the lantern or failed to see a stray spark from the cook fire."

"You were six years old." Compassion welled in her. "The fire, the deaths were not your fault."

He set his jaw. "I've never seen it that way." He rubbed his face. "I want to know how Jacob got out." Pain poured from his words.

"Now I understand even more about the urgency to get to Oregon. I'm sorry about your family. I wish I could say the right words to make you feel better, to help you see it wasn't your fault."

"I don't think it's possible."

"God can give you peace, Painted Hands. He wants to lift the burden—"

"I've been told the same thing before. I cried out to God that night, but He turned a deaf ear to me."

"He had a reason, although like you, I find it hard not to be angry."

"To send innocent people to a horrible death?" He lifted his hands. "I remember how my hands hurt, as though someone had taken a knife to them. To think their whole bodies were tortured like that. A loving, caring God would do this?"

The more he spoke, the louder his voice grew. Sarah Jane shivered. She well recalled the night Painted Hands took after Preacher Sanders. Fury hid beneath his soul, a frightening trait for a man she loved.

"I don't know why this terrible thing happened any more than I understand why Mama and Papa died, but I do know two things. Our families are in a better place where there is no pain or fear, and God has a plan for your life and mine. Because I trust in His wisdom and love, I can only serve Him the best way I can."

He said nothing, but the anger remained on his face like a rock etched with time. She hadn't seen this anger since before the fever, and she feared the pleasant days had disappeared. Painted Hands stood and left the wagon without a good-bye.

Sarah Jane longed to call after him, but she also recognized his need to work through the problems separating him from God. She couldn't be his savior; she could only live her life as Jesus desired and pray Painted Hands found God's grace and mercy.

The following morning, she awoke with a sense of renewed energy. She dressed and realized the simple task did not waste all of her strength. This morning she'd make coffee and breakfast for Painted Hands.

Stepping outside into a marvelous sunrise, Sarah Jane stopped to admire the dusky pink and gray-blue sky of dawn. It felt good to be alive, even with the hazards ahead and the grief of losing Mama and Papa. Her gaze swept about the area for Painted Hands. Normally, he slept under the wagon, but he was neither there nor at the river. She turned her attention toward the cattle and called for him.

Silence.

His spotted mare was nowhere to be found either. He'd gone hunting, she told herself and ignored the gnawing voice reminding her of last night. Her husband needed breakfast, and she would prepare it for him. When he returned from wherever he'd ridden, she'd ask him about leaving tomorrow. After all, he'd said three days and they'd talk about beginning the journey again.

The smell of fresh coffee tugged at her growling stomach, as well as the aroma of biscuits and frying bacon; yet Painted Hands was nowhere in sight. A twinge of fear wormed up her spine. All the old conversations and his desire to head alone for Oregon worried her. Finally, she sat in the grass and prayed for Painted Hands. She could not eat without him. He'd return shortly, she felt certain. Sleep tugged at her eyelids until they slid shut.

"Sarah Jane. Wake up. Are you ill?"

She opened her eyes to see Painted Hands kneeling beside her. He smelled of the outdoors, of fresh grass and leather. So happy to see him, she wrapped her arms around his neck and kissed his whiskered cheek. Immediately, his eyes widened, and a look of panic swept over him.

"I was frightened." She groped for words. "I...thought you'd gone on without me."

"And left you?" He sounded surprised, and she sighed with relief.

"Silly, aren't I?"

"I wouldn't just up and leave you, not without making provisions."

She released her hold on his neck. A sinking feeling settled in her stomach. She thought he'd abandoned the idea of going ahead alone. Fierce determination rose in her, and the words spilled out. "I want to go all the way to Oregon with you, Painted Hands. I'm well and able to drive the wagon. We can make good time as we talked about the other night. I promise not to slow you down."

"I'm not good company."

"You're the company I choose."

He crossed his arms. "You're a difficult woman to understand."

She lifted her chin. "Have you ever met a woman you did understand?"

He paused and moistened his lips. "Reckon not."

"This land is terribly hard, Painted Hands, but I know the dreams of Oregon are only weeks away. Please understand that if you want to set up homesteading here by the Platte River and not move another inch toward the mountains, then I want to be right here with you. If you decide to go back to Independence, I want to be with you. If you are ready to head on beyond Fort Laramie and wade through mud and the first signs of snow in the mountains, I'm ready."

He rubbed his whiskered chin. "You're a stubborn and courageous woman."

She shook her head and touched his arm. "I'm not brave, no, not at all. Too many times I feel Mama's desperation. But what I do know is I want to be with you, and I don't care where."

He stared at her for a moment longer. "We could put a few miles behind us day after tomorrow. We will stop at noon for you to rest, and I'll prepare something for us to eat. I'll be watching you, and at the first signs of your faltering, we'll not go a step farther until you sleep."

"So be it." She leaned over and kissed him once more on the cheek. "Thank you. I intend to be a helpmate, not a burden."

Painted Hands glanced away, as though ignoring her kiss. "I brought down another rabbit, but I want to hunt deer after breakfast."

∞

Painted Hands raised his shotgun and took aim at the buck in the distance. Meat wasn't his only motive in bringing down the animal. He wanted the hide to make clothes for Sarah Jane. He saw what she wore, and the rugged terrain of the Rockies called for more practical dress than long skirts that became weighed down with snow and mud—and proved a hindrance in climbing. If she'd slip into buckskin breeches once her feet hit the mountains, she'd fare much better. For that matter, so would every female journeying the narrow mountain passes.

He chuckled in remembering past wagon trains where proper ladies left Independence donned in heavy skirts, petticoats, and all their other wearisome layers. As the journey lengthened, one layer after another disappeared or was thread-thin the closer they got to Oregon. Sadly, he recalled the women who swished their skirts too close to the fire or fainted from heat on the prairie when the daytime temperatures soared to one hundred. Because of their choice of clothing, many took sick when the mountain cold chilled them to the bone.

Why a woman chose to make this trip puzzled him. Being separated from friends and family, realizing the death of loved ones, struggling with day-to-day survival, and facing their own female sensibilities were grim challenges. Sarah Jane's words inched across his mind. Did the hundreds of women who started out across the wilderness feel like her? Did being with their husbands mean more to them than danger? He was uncomfortable with Sarah Jane's feeling so strongly about him, but her commitment left him proud. Could he claim the same about her?

She'd be clothed properly, for sure, and he'd treat her as he wanted to be treated. Looks said more than words, and he'd seen something in her eyes, a light that seemed to say she cared for him. He had no idea why, unless his nursing her had brought about sentiments of gratitude. But if he thought back to before the typhoid, she'd tried to please him then, too.

Sarah Jane scared him worse than walking up on a she-bear with cubs.

After taking down the buck, Painted Hands positioned the animal atop his horse and led the mare back to the wagon. Again, as he had so many times in the past, he pondered the situation with his wife—his wife in name only. If he could fault her, he'd feel much better. If she had reacted to his story with anything but kindness, he could have justified leaving her at Fort Laramie. Sarah Jane wasn't perfect, but she stood on the border, causing him to wonder if she was an angel sent to make his miserable existence a little easier to bear. If he affixed his mind to that way of thinking, he'd have to acknowledge God.

CHAPTER 12

Sarah Jane had busied herself all morning, and now she read from Papa's Bible. Her perch beneath the cottonwood facing the river had become her favorite spot during her recuperation. She could become very lazy here, mesmerized by the gentle flow of the water and the placid scene of grazing cattle. She opened the Bible to one of Mama's favorite passages—the book of Ruth. The ancient Moabite woman's journey to a new home and her devotion to God filled Sarah Jane with renewed hope for her marriage.

Papa always said things happened for God's reason and not our own. At the time, Sarah Jane believed him; but since her marriage, she'd contemplated the wisdom of Papa's statement. One moment she was filled with despair and certain Painted Hands planned to leave her at Fort Laramie; in the next he acted as if he cared. She wanted to look expectantly to the future, but she wished God would give her a glimpse of it. Trust was a heavy dose of medicine to one who lacked patience.

Closing the Bible, she stood and headed back to the wagon. There, Painted Hands bent over a deer. He'd skinned the hide and set it aside, then deftly sliced up the meat. She could cure it with the extra salt, but her curiosity was piqued with what he intended to do with the hide.

"I'm going to tan it," he said. "You need some good buckskin for the mountains." He filled a second bucket with the venison. "We're going to stay here an extra two days to get it started."

Buckskin? Mama and Papa will roll over in their graves. "I have clothes, Painted Hands."

"I know, but they aren't suitable for the mountains." A smile greeted her. "Once you get used to them, you might never wear a dress again."

"So will I wear a buckskin dress like an Indian woman?"

He laughed long and loud. "No, Sarah Jane. These will be breeches and a shirt. They won't wear out, and the going will be easier."

I have to be excited about this. "No one will be able to tell us apart."

"Oh, I imagine there will be a few differences."

Sarah Jane flushed hot, and it had nothing to do with the heat of the day or a fever.

Sarah Jane wanted to leave the peaceful site by the Platte River, but she realized the need for a few extra days of rest, and the thought of watching her husband prepare a hide for clothing purposes sounded interesting. In fact, she decided to record each step in Mama's journal.

Painted Hands began the process once the meat had been sliced and salted. He prepared a mixture of the deer's brains and liver with a little fat in a kettle over a low fire.

"Are you going to eat that?" she asked.

"Did you want to?"

"Not exactly, although I guess if I was hungry enough, I'd eat anything."

He stirred the mixture before answering. "Once it's cooked for about an hour, it will be ready to use in the tanning."

She had so many questions, but she knew how he felt about them. "Will I bother you by wanting to learn how this is done?"

He stopped stirring. "I'll make you a deal. You watch me do this, and if there is something you don't understand, go ahead and ask."

She shrugged. "All right."

"The wisdom comes in knowing when to observe and when to pose your questions."

Her eyes widened.

Maybe the idea of recording the instructions could wait until another time, but she would at least begin now.

"It's very simple," he continued. "If you ask a good question, I'll answer. If you ask a bad one, then you have to eat the brains and liver mixture." Not a muscle moved in his face.

Sarah Jane hid her mirth. "Agreed, and I'll provide a spoon for you, too."

They laughed together, and it felt good. Really good.

In the late afternoon, Painted Hands staked the hide on the ground, stretching it taut as he worked. He divided the brain and liver mixture in half, rubbing it into one side and then the other with an old rag. With his hands and a smooth, rounded rock, he worked the mixture thoroughly over every part of the hide. He scooted back on his knees and appeared to study every inch of it. Then he released the stakes from the hide and folded it up.

"That's all I can do for today." He peered over her shoulder as she wrote. "Tomorrow I'll wash the hide and stake it again."

"Stretch it, too?" she asked, then immediately wondered if she should have waited.

"Yes, it will shrink if I don't." He grinned. "Are you going to write a book about the Oregon adventure?"

"I'm pondering the matter. Our children and grandchildren might find it interesting." The mention of children invited warmth to rise from her neck to her cheeks.

He said nothing, but the silence felt like a wall of rock between them.

"I'll fix our supper," she said. "The deer will be a welcome change."

"While you're tending to that, I need to make a travois, a wide one."

She lifted a questioning gaze.

"The hide will need to dry in the sun. I plan to stretch it out over a travois."

"Did you learn that from the Kiowa?"

"No." He chuckled. "I don't know if it's been done this way before. Tanning hides is done in a camp—and by the women."

"Then I'd better pay attention."

Once the meat started to sizzle in the pan, Sarah Jane milked the cow. She'd assumed most of her chores by now, but she appreciated that Painted Hands was concerned about her health. When they started on the trail again, she planned to share every bit of the work with him.

"The color is back in your face," he said, reaching for another biscuit.

Grateful for his notice, she responded with a smile.

"Sarah Jane," he began a few minutes later. "There's a matter between us we should talk about."

This was not his usual manner. She swallowed hard with the knowledge that he must have a serious topic of discussion. *Do not think the worst.*

"We're married, but we're not living like married folks."

She nodded and sensed her cheeks were aflame.

"I'm a man, and I could easily claim my rights as a husband, but I won't until I can see myself as a fitting person for you."

She blinked back a tear. He'd already proved to her that he was good and kind. What more did he dare accomplish? "To me you are more than I ever thought possible in a man or a husband."

"How many men have you known? Your pa and his acquaintances?"

"That's a fair amount." She twisted a loose thread on her apron hem. "Doesn't matter to me how many or whom. God knows best. You're a fine man, Painted Hands, and I'm proud to be your wife."

He set his plate on the ground and stood. With a heavy sigh, he turned and stalked away into the darkness.

Must he always run when things don't suit him? She wanted to shout at him to come back—to talk about the matter of their marriage—except the words refused to spill from her lips. Without asking, Sarah Jane realized he'd not make a move back to the wagon until she'd gone to bed. In the past, moments like these made her stomach churn, but not tonight. God had given her a peace about Painted Hands.

Mend his broken heart, God. He blames himself for his family's deaths and most likely too many other things.

The following morning, Painted Hands acted as though nothing had happened. He appeared friendly enough, but he'd put a definite distance between them.

After breakfast, he disappeared again without a word. Sarah Jane elected to bathe and wash her hair. An amazing calm cradled her, and she found herself singing.

At noontime, Painted Hands returned and announced he planned to work on the hide. She sat on the opposite side of him, relishing in his closeness while watching him work with his hands. Soon he had the hide washed to his perfection and staked in the sun to dry. Once more, he left on his horse.

Where does he go? What does he do?

∞

Painted Hands slipped his Bible from his saddlebag and found a soft place to sit and read. He hadn't told Sarah Jane where he'd been spending his time, and if he allowed himself to be honest, he'd confess his natural rebellious instinct was the reason. The ill-tempered side of him claimed he deserved his privacy. The tender side of him understood she'd worry, and he should spare her any discomfort.

Since her illness, he'd wanted to find reasons for his existence, answers to why his life had gone from one bad turn to another. All of Reverend Crandle's words flowed through him, which was why he'd sneaked away to read those passages important to his old friend. Always he came back to Psalm One. The words of David were like a guidebook to Painted Hands, and though he fought the power of God in his life, he couldn't discount the wisdom.

> *Blessed is the man that walketh not in the counsel of the ungodly, nor standeth in the way of sinners, nor sitteth in the seat of the scornful. But his delight is in the law of the LORD; and in His law doth he meditate day and night. And he shall be like a tree planted by the rivers of water, that bringeth forth his fruit in his season; his leaf also shall not wither; and whatsoever he doeth shall prosper. The ungodly are not so: but are like the chaff which the wind driveth away. Therefore the ungodly shall not stand in the judgment, nor sinners in the congregation of the righteous. For the LORD knoweth the way of the righteous; but the way of the ungodly shall perish.*

Painted Hands looked out over the prairie—quiet, peaceful, as he wanted to feel inside. God had answered his prayers on this very terrain and showed him the coneflowers. In turn, the tea made from the wildflowers helped save Sarah Jane's life. But the other tragedies of the past filled him with bitterness.

He couldn't deny God, but he couldn't give himself over to trust either—not as he once did. If the answers to his miserable life would miraculously appear, he could understand why. Was he cursed by the same God who said He loved all His creation?

"The way of the ungodly shall perish."

God said the way of sinners would perish, but sinners could receive forgiveness. Painted Hands remembered enough from his own Bible study and his years with the Reverend Crandle to know that acknowledgment of wrongdoings initiated confession. Then repentance had to occur before forgiveness could take place. What had he done so wrong that God chose to strike down him and the ones he loved? Always the same questions. Always the same silence.

And if he declared love for his wife, God would take her, too. That fear alone halted a move in Sarah Jane's direction. He ached to hold her, touch her smooth, soft cheeks the way he did when she lay burning up with fever. His mind sped with the words he wanted to say but couldn't. He recalled the treasured times he'd let himself enjoy her company. Those moments were sealed for the bleak future.

She wanted to record the events along the trail to Oregon for their children and grandchildren. Painted Hands desired the same and more. A longing deep and passionate assaulted him whenever he thought of a green-eyed child calling him Papa.

∽

After dusk, Painted Hands returned to the wagon site. He seated himself by the cook fire. His shoulders sagged; when the firelight illuminated his face, lines deepened around his eyes.

Compassion moved Sarah Jane, but she was weary from wrestling with her own emotions.

"Tomorrow is your last day before we leave this place." His gaze stayed fixed on the reddened embers.

"I'm ready." She hoped her words sounded optimistic.

"Nothing you want me to tend to?"

She shook her head. An urgency in her spirit moved her to say more. "I'm sorry I've said things that make you want to stay away."

663

He stared into the fire, his features like stone. "You, Sarah Jane, have always done what is good and right. I'm the restless, wild one."

"You're wrong." She spoke clearly in the night. "I pray you one day discover how blessed I am." As she expected, Painted Hands did not respond. "Think of what you've done for me. You volunteered to help strangers with deadly typhoid. You married me when Preacher Sanders demanded it. You helped me nurse Mama and Papa and spared me the pain of preparing them for burial. You took care of me when you could have left me behind. Every minute of the day, you ignore your needs for mine. If that is your description of restless and wild, then I hope someday to claim such honorable traits."

He rubbed his palms. "I am cursed, Sarah Jane. Whatever I touch is destroyed. I can't allow another human being to suffer because of me."

Folks were not cursed. What did he mean? How could she make him understand that life held many tragedies? Good and bad fell on everyone.

"I'm going to check on the cattle," he said. "Go on to bed when you're tired."

She stood and laid her hand on his arm. "You can do all you will to stop me from caring, but I'm determined. Run as far from me as you can, but I won't stop praying."

"You're a fool!"

His words pierced her heart. "Perhaps you're right. Some days I want to give up and resign myself to watching you leave me. But when I consider what I'd lose, I pray for more strength." Standing, she climbed into the wagon and willed herself to sleep.

On the morning of their last day along the Platte River, Painted Hands took a rough stone and rubbed it into the entire hide. Sarah Jane silently recorded his every move. In the late afternoon, he made a loop of rope and worked the hide back and forth through it. Once he finished, he heated water and lowered the hide into it.

"I'll take care of this before we leave."

"What's next? Can I help you?" She realized he abhorred unnecessary quizzing, but frustration in dealing with him worked at crushing her spirit.

"To do this properly, I have to make sure it's stretched out tight." He paused. "I hope my idea of using a travois is not a mistake."

She thought a minute. "Could you fix the hide to the top of the wagon?"

"Possibly." He was using his cold, unfeeling tone. She'd gotten rather used to it, but that didn't mean she liked it or embraced the silence.

Late that night, Sarah Jane woke to the sound of crashing thunder. The intensity shook the wagon. She glanced out at the night sky and gasped at the vivid display of jagged lightning across the dark heavens. In less than a second, thunder pounded again. High winds seized the canvas and whipped it to the outside. She heard Painted Hands stirring about the travois and hurried to join him.

"A bad storm is upon us," he said, releasing the deer hide and hoisting it into his arms. "Make sure everything is brought inside."

She hustled about to store their belongings from the impending storm. She remembered when they'd been scarcely out of Elm Grove and a prairie storm besieged the wagon train and sent the cattle stampeding. She and Mama had huddled inside like frightened chickens until it was over. Lightning had struck one of the wagons nearby and quickly set fire to the canvas top. This storm looked no less intimidating.

The wind wove its way across the land. The whole earth rumbled with no reprieve in sight. Sarah Jane and Painted Hands climbed into the wagon with the lighted lantern and sat on the mattress. The wind whistled, and the wagon rocked. Then the rains came as though the storm clouds desired to drown earth's inhabitants. This must be how the people felt outside Noah's ark.

"Sounds like we're under a waterfall." She refused to think about a swirl of floodwaters sweeping them away into the Platte River. "Are we on high enough ground?"

"I believe so," Painted Hands replied. He sounded neither hopeful nor downcast.

The cattle milled about, crying out with the upheaval in nature. As a little girl, she'd covered her ears during storms, but none of those frightful memories compared with the roar outside the wagon. Sarah Jane wrapped her arms about herself and shivered.

"I hope the cattle don't stampede," she said. "Are there any buffalo nearby?"

"There's nothing we can do if the cattle get spooked or a herd of buffalo runs us over."

"Well, I'm scared!"

"I figured as much." He picked up the quilt from the bed and draped it around her shoulders. "Keep warm, Sarah Jane, or you will have fever again."

Above the deafening roar of the storm, another drumming against the earth assaulted her ears. The cattle. They were running. She held her breath. Any moment she expected the wagon to topple over while she and Painted Hands faced the hooves of frightened cows.

The thunder and lightning finally ceased, but the downpour continued until dawn. This was supposed to be the day they'd pack up camp and move toward the Northwest, but instead, it would be spent in rounding up cattle on a water-soaked prairie. Luckily, the oxen were close by.

"I can ride Papa's horse and help you," she said.

"You stay here. The extra day of rest is a good thing." With those words, he tramped across the mud and rode out.

Somewhat agitated with his refusal, she easily fell back to sleep and dreamed of Oregon and its claim to being near heaven. Midmorning, she woke to the soft sounds of more rain. The longer it fell, the more it picked up momentum. The river had risen considerably last night. Would it reach the banks and sweep her away? Shaking her head, she vowed to push away the worrisome thoughts.

Painted Hands was a strong man, but his constant exposure to the elements gave her cause for alarm. As long as it continued to rain, she couldn't make him coffee. *Keep him safe, Father, and help him find the cattle.*

By late afternoon, the rain let up. Sarah Jane affixed her skirts to well above her ankles and stepped out beneath a cloudy sky. Her gaze flew to the river, where the water nearly crested. A hint of light attempted to peek through the dismal gray, but what she needed was a rainbow. She picked through the buffalo chips they had stacked inside the wagon last night to build a fire. Cooking for Painted Hands kept her mind and body occupied until he returned.

Just before dusk, she saw him ride in from the east. He drove a number of cows; not all had run into parts unknown.

"We lost five of your pa's cattle," he said, swinging down from his mare. Water dripped from his hat, beard, and clothes.

"They are our cattle," she said. "And I was more worried about you than the animals."

Painted Hands lifted a brow.

"Please don't doubt me. You're a sight more important than"—she waved her arm toward the cows—"those cattle."

"Are you always looking after other folks?" The strained muscles in his face challenged her.

Sarah Jane stiffened. "Yes, most times, even those who don't care one way or the other." She bent and poured him a mug of coffee. "This hasn't been made too long. It might thaw out your heart." She thrust the mug at him, and he chuckled.

"Guess I had that one coming."

"Good, because I'm in no mood to apologize."

Early the following morning, the day of their departure, Sarah Jane woke with anticipation to be gone again. She dressed and collected her journal, for already she smelled coffee and biscuits.

Painted Hands had mounted the hide, hair side down, on the wide travois with strips of leather. About every six inches, he'd fastened a piece of it to the travois. To Sarah Jane, the deer hide could not possibly shrink. With a knife, he began to scrape the pieces of flesh and fat still attached. Twice the hide nearly dried, but he added warm water to his work. Once he had finished, he stood back.

"It needs to dry for about two days. Then I'll soak it again and scrape the hair side."

"I see it takes awhile, like most things we value."

He set his jaw and cleaned his knife on the grass.

Sarah Jane decided tanning the deerskin was much like God's laboring over troubles that plagued Painted Hands. Every day He scraped off the ugliness from the past and worked on making a new man who would eventually step forward with purpose and direction. Maybe then he'd want to be a real husband.

CHAPTER 13

The first day on the trail came more easily than Sarah Jane anticipated. A tinge of bittersweetness enveloped her when she thought of leaving the peaceful spot on the prairie with its lush grasses and wildflowers. She could have easily lived out her years there—building a home by the Platte River and raising babies. Of course, harsh winters, summer twisters, and flash floods would soon give cause for regret. So would life almost anywhere she lived.

She shook her head. Longing for a life that might never be hers was foolish. First in order was her husband's spiritual life; all the other problems lagged sadly behind.

The oxen plodded ahead, and the sun grew hotter in the sky. She'd cast aside her petticoat for only her dress in the heat, not caring a bit if she came upon a gathering of women. My, how her priorities had changed. She grinned at the thought of wearing buckskin. Next she'd be in moccasins and living in a tepee. Preacher Sanders would hold a revival if he learned about her new way of life.

Over to her right, Painted Hands drove the cattle with an occasional holler. The scent of the animals had made Mama ill, but Sarah Jane didn't mind. After the stench of death, she could handle about anything. The tall grass made the cows fat, which should help bring a fair price at Fort Laramie. Then Painted Hands would be free to roam about as he pleased.

"Isn't it wonderful to be moving again?" she called to him.

He nodded and waved. At least he acknowledged her. The oxen trudged on ahead while the road bent and wound with the river. The solitary wagon ambled on, passing Chimney Rock with its single peak like an outstretched arm reaching to the sky and on to Scotts Bluff. Painted Hands figured it would take them about a week to reach Fort Laramie; he was certain Mr. Greenham had pulled out to the mountains by now. Not that she cared; she'd rather not see any of them again.

At noon, Painted Hands stopped the cattle to keep his word for her to rest while he prepared a meal. Today they planned to eat leftover biscuits and bacon from breakfast and drink water to wash it all down.

"I'm going to scout around while you nap," he said. "Do you know how to use your pa's shotgun?"

"Yes, Papa taught Mama and me before we left Nebraska."

"Good. I meant to ask you before. Don't be afraid to use it."

Why had he waited so long to find out? It wasn't as though he hadn't left her alone in the past. "Is there trouble ahead?"

He finished his food and set the tin plate on the ground. "Fort Laramie can be rough with white men and Indians."

Had he decided to leave her there? "I can take care of myself." Irritation crept into her thoughts. Painted Hands had more unexplainable moods than a woman.

He chuckled, fueling her frustration. "What's so funny?"

"Your stubborn attitude."

"Me?" Sarah Jane squeezed a fold of her skirt. "Sounds to me like you're ready to leave me at Fort Laramie, but first you have to make sure no one is going to pull a gun on me."

He swung a glare at her. "I haven't decided."

"I'm so glad you're in charge of my future. Let me tell you this, and don't you lose sight of it. I'm going to Oregon, and if you won't take me, then I'll find my way with another wagon train."

"I have no doubt you would take out over those mountains alone."

"Must you always be so smug?" Sarah Jane bit back another ugly remark, one that involved not needing any man to protect her.

"I know a few more things about this country than you do."

"Wonderful, but your knowledge doesn't make you an expert on what's best for me."

Painted Hands snatched up his shotgun and stood. He towered over her. "A husband is in charge of his household."

She struggled to her feet. Rage pushed through her veins. "You have to be a husband first."

Painted Hands whirled around and stomped off toward his spotted mare.

"You always run," she said. "For once, I'd like for us to talk through something."

He kept right on without hesitation. He slid onto his horse bareback and raced out across the flat terrain, leaving a cloud of mud spitting behind him. Let him ride until he fell off the edge of the earth. Making her own way to Fort Laramie and on to Oregon wasn't impossible, and she could take care of herself without him or anyone else.

Suddenly, remorse seized her for the impetuous words she'd flung at Painted Hands. After all he'd done for her, and she repaid him with sarcasm. She'd committed to reflect Jesus in her life, but her pride had stepped in and taken over. Sarah Jane focused her attention on the direction he'd ridden. A part of her wanted to saddle Papa's horse and go out after him. The longer she waited, the more impatience needled her. Guilt laced every thought. Watching the prairie didn't bring him any closer either.

∞

Sarah Jane's fury tore at Painted Hands. *"You always run."* He didn't know his wife was capable of such anger, and oddly enough, seeing her red-faced offered relief. His original opinion of her was that she'd allow him to domineer her every move. Today she'd proven otherwise.

"You always run."

She was right. He'd spent most of his life running from some kind of truth. When life gave him sorrow, he took off in the opposite direction. He'd started as a child with the Kiowa when their different ways frustrated him or when memories plagued his tormented mind, and he persisted in the habit with the Crandles and now Sarah Jane. They should have named him Runner.

The Reverend Crandle had told him a man faces his problems head-on and asks God to help him with the solution. Painted Hands understood the wisdom in those words, because the running labeled him less of a man. At one time, Reverend Crandle asked him to dwell on the good times in the past and give the bitterness to God. The idea of facing the problems and remembering the good sounded easy in one breath and insurmountable in the next. So he'd done nothing but continue in the same pattern. Now, feelings for Sarah Jane and the hope she built in him of being a whole man moved him to step out in faith—yes, faith in the God who refused to let him go. If Painted Hands pondered the matter, would his days with God be any more miserable than his current meaningless existence?

Once again giving his life to Jesus Christ, with the understanding there would be no turning back, frightened him. There—he'd admitted it. Fear of the unknown kept him bound tighter than a heavy rope.

"You are not alone."

Painted Hands recognized the voice, and it wasn't the one Reverend Crandle called the accuser.

Lord, forgive me for not having the strength to stay close to You. I'm a broken man, weak and lower than a snake, and I can't do this alone. So many questions pound my head and heart that I'd rather run forever than face them squarely. Help me, Lord, I beg of You.

A verse sprang to his mind, one he remembered reading many times in the past. This time the words held clarity, and he reached out to hold on to them with all his might.

"Come unto me, all ye that labour and are heavy laden, and I will give you rest."

"Thank You," he whispered.

Painted Hands stopped his horse and eased the mare back around. With a renewed commitment to God, he had to mend his relationship with Sarah Jane—his wife.

∞

Sarah Jane shielded her eyes. There, off to the southwest, someone approached. She studied the figure heading her way until she realized there were several riders. Her heart pounded hard against her chest.

Indians! She counted seven of them—seven fierce-looking men. *Papa's shotgun.* She had to dig it out from underneath some boxes. Why hadn't she done that sooner? By the time she found it, they'd be here. Her legs threatened to give way. Her mouth grew dry. Trembling, she grabbed the side of the wagon for support. Her gaze swept around the campsite. A knife lay just inside the wagon. She forced herself to release her grip and snatch up the weapon.

Dear Lord, is this the end?

The Indians wore breechcloths. One wore a sleeveless shirt, similar to the buckskin Painted Hands wore but with more beadwork and fringe. She'd seen the Sioux when still traveling with Mama and Papa, and these Indians looked different. One of the men wore a black animal-skin hat. Their bronzed bodies glistened in the sun, their muscles rippling like the flow of the Platte River. She recalled the horrific tales of warring Indians and shuddered.

While she leaned against the side of the wagon, they formed a half circle around her. The one who wore the hat laughed and slid from his horse. Sarah Jane raised the knife, although her hand shook so badly she almost dropped it.

"What do you want?" she asked in a voice that quivered like a leaf in the wind.

In a language foreign to her, the Indians exchanged words and grunts. They pointed at her, Papa's horse, and the cattle. Even if Painted Hands returned, what could he do? Maybe they were Kiowa. Why hadn't she asked Painted Hands to teach her the language? The one wearing the hat stepped closer. She lifted the knife higher. A sick feeling swept over her.

"Take the cattle." The sound of her voice wrapped fear around her heart. "I'll stab this knife into your heart if you come any closer."

The hat-wearing Indian yanked the weapon from her hand and grabbed her arm.

Sarah Jane screamed. She beat her fists against his chest, and when he lowered his grasp to her waist, she continued to pound any part of his body she could reach with her fists. Laughter rose from him and the other Indians. He pulled her toward his horse. He smelled of filth and animals. She kicked, then bit him before a dirty hand clamped over her mouth.

Dear God, help me!

The Indian carried her toward his horse, while the others rummaged through the wagon.

A shot fired.

She held her breath, praying.

The voice of Painted Hands rang out over the sultry air, but not in English. The Indians must be Kiowa, but Painted Hands had said the prairie was not their home. She cringed. There were too many of them to fight. He'd be hurt. *Help us, dear God.*

❧

Painted Hands had seen the tracks before he raced back to the wagon. The Indians were Cheyenne, and Sarah Jane was alone. They'd pick the place clean, drive away the cattle, and ride off with his wife—if they didn't choose to kill her. Panic twisted through him, then anger. This was his fault. He'd left her alone to face any danger, as he'd done so many times in the past. He had to get to her, fast.

"Please, God, no." His heels dug into the horse's side, urging the mare faster. He fired his shotgun into the air at the sound of her screams. The image of Sarah Jane abused by the Indians attacked his senses. "Sarah Jane!"

"Neaahtove!" Listen to me. Painted Hands spoke the words in Cheyenne. *"Éneoestse!"* Stop.

The warrior holding on to Sarah Jane laughed. "Emoonahe." *She is pretty.*

Painted Hands fought his anger. "She is my wife." They would not take her; he'd die trying.

"Why do you speak our language?" The warrior's eyes narrowed.

"I lived with the Kiowa for ten years. I learned your language through a Cheyenne brother."

The warrior held a firm grip on Sarah Jane. Fear etched her delicate features.

"Netonesevehe?" What is your name?

"Painted Hands." Perspiration trickled down his face.

The warrior glanced at the scarred hands of Painted Hands, then back to his face. "I want to buy this woman."

"She is not for barter." He took a step toward Sarah Jane and touched her stomach. *"Naneso."* My child. Painted Hands realized the warrior would not let Sarah Jane go easily. "You can have five of the cattle."

The warrior sneered. "The cattle are already mine."

"We are brothers."

The man stiffened. "For long time, Kiowa and Cheyenne at war."

"The Kiowa and Cheyenne made peace eight years ago."

The other warriors began to talk until the man silenced them. "You know our ways. Five of the cattle are not enough."

"Ten."

"And the horse."

Neither the horse nor the cattle were his to give away, but he had no choice. "Agreed."

"Twenty cattle."

"I said ten."

"Ten and the horse, and we leave the woman," the warrior said.

Painted Hands studied the Indian before him. If he hadn't bargained in Cheyenne, he'd have been killed, and they'd have Sarah Jane. He nodded at the warrior and headed back to retrieve John Benson's horse. When Painted Hands returned, he held out the bridled horse and eyed the warrior squarely.

"My wife," Painted Hands said. The warrior released her, and Painted Hands pulled her to him. "We are brothers. Let me have my woman cook for you."

The Indian nodded and motioned for the others to cut out the cattle.

"Are you hurt?" Painted Hands asked Sarah Jane.

"No." Sarah Jane trembled so that her skirt shook.

He drew her closer, and she laid her head on his chest. If he hadn't been watching the Indians taking the cattle, he'd have kissed her.

"They are taking ten head of cattle and your pa's horse," he said.

She nodded and pressed her lips together. "They can have all the cattle."

"I was ready to give them everything we have. And a bellyful of lead, if that's what it took."

"They're leaving?" she asked.

"They need food. Are you able to cook for them?"

"We have the salted deer. I'll cook plenty—anything to make sure they don't come back."

Sarah Jane sliced off hunks of the venison and fried them and baked biscuits. After the Cheyenne ate their fill, Painted Hands watched as the Indians made their way to their horses. The Indians shouted and took out across the plain with the cattle. Two of them held the chickens. In the next instant, they were a speck of dust disappearing over the prairie. He pulled his wife next to him.

"Thank you, Painted Hands," she said. "I'm sorry for what I said to you."

He rested his chin on her head. "I'm not. It was the truth. Tonight, after we've settled down from supper, I want to talk."

"Of course." Her eyes glistened with tears. "The Indians, are they Kiowa?"

"No, Cheyenne. I learned their language some years before."

"Praise God," she whispered. "I've never been so frightened."

"He wanted you for himself." Painted Hands expelled a heavy breath. What if he'd failed?

Her face paled. "I would have rather died. Why—why did you touch my stomach?"

"Sarah Jane, forgive me, but I told him you carried my child."

She wrapped her arm around his waist. "There is nothing to forgive. Once again you have saved my life." Her soft weeping tugged at his heart.

"You forget my anger is what put you in danger. I'll never leave you like that again. If I need to hunt, you will go with me."

She snuggled against his chest. If he died tonight, he'd keep this moment forever sealed in his mind.

"Let's leave this place," he said. "I wouldn't want those Indians to forget I called them brothers."

In a short time the wagon meandered in the opposite direction from where the Cheyenne drove the cattle. He couldn't keep his gaze off Sarah Jane, and whenever he stole a glimpse of her, she was looking at him. The desire to tell her of his love and his renewed faith nearly burst from his chest.

The afternoon hours sped by as Painted Hands relived the scene with the Cheyenne. Repeatedly, he praised God for rescuing his precious wife. Every time he considered what might have happened to her, a fierce, protective resolve shattered his past treatment of her.

"Do you want me to tie my horse to the wagon?" he asked. "I'd like to sit next to you."

She pulled back on the reins and called to the oxen. "Does that answer your question?"

CHAPTER 14

Sarah Jane prepared a dried-peach cobbler that night, adding a pinch of cinnamon and a hunk of the precious butter. Mama had always said the best way to keep a man happy was to feed him well.

"You're a good cook, Sarah Jane," he said, scooping up more of the peach cobbler.

"Thank you. I had a good teacher in Mama."

"You miss her badly, don't you?"

She blinked back the wetness. "Doesn't seem like they're really gone. I hope I don't ever forget the good times—and the love we shared."

"I understand. My family lives in my dreams."

"Oh, but soon you will be reunited with your brother."

He smiled. "Sometimes I wonder if Jacob will look at all as I remember."

"I'm excited for you." She poured him another mug of coffee. "Your meeting will be grand."

"He's not married, at least not yet. So he will have a brother and a sister."

His words touched her, and warmth flooded her face. She didn't know how to respond without becoming emotional. *He must have changed his mind about leaving me at Fort Laramie.*

"Sarah Jane," he began. "While I was gone today, I made a decision."

She met his gaze and studied him through the amber firelight.

"I haven't been good to you, and saying I'm sorry doesn't cover all the ways I've wronged you. But I am sorry. I told you about the fire. You should know other things about me, and I'll tell you of them someday. You already know I'm not a talkative man." He released a sigh and stared into the fire. "While living with Reverend Crandle, I made a decision to follow Christ, but I turned my back on Him. See, folks accused me of murdering a family, and the Reverend Crandle took up for me. Because of his commitment to me, he lost his church. It didn't seem right for God to allow it. I was bitter, angry, so I signed up as a scout for Greenham's wagon train. During that time, the reverend tracked down Jacob and found out he'd gone to Oregon."

"Have you seen the reverend since?"

Painted Hands nodded. "Just before the wagon train left Independence. He had a new church in Independence."

"How wonderful for him and his wife."

He paused for a moment. Should she have said nothing while he spoke, or should she prod him?

"What was your decision?" Sarah Jane pulled her shawl tighter around her shoulders.

"I figured since God hadn't given up on me, I needed to follow Him. He answered my prayers to help me find the coneflower when you were sick with typhoid, and He saw fit to save you."

"Oh, Painted Hands, I'm so glad."

"I'm a stubborn man, prone to keeping my troubles to myself, but with God's help, I'm going to change." He looked up at her through saddened eyes. "I want to be a good husband, Sarah Jane, if you'll have me and have patience. I nearly got you kidnapped or killed by those Cheyenne, and I'm powerful ashamed."

Her chest felt heavy, but she was determined not to cry. "I think we both learned a lot today." She hesitated. How did he feel about her beyond honoring his wedding vows? Love was a gift, a vow on her part, as well as his. "I love you, Painted Hands. I have for some time, but I was afraid to tell you."

His face tightened, and he inhaled deeply. He reached out for her. "And I love you." He held her close, and when she peered up at him, he lowered his head and brushed his lips against hers.

Sarah Jane had never been kissed by any man other than Papa, who had sometimes graced a kiss on the top of her head. Warm and sweet best described the tender embrace of Painted Hands. If she lived to see her great-grandchildren, she'd never forget his endearing words and touch of love.

"Tell me again," she whispered.

He chuckled and stroked her cheek with his finger. "I love you."

"Before or after the Cheyenne wanted to take me?"

"Before. I was coming back to tell you."

She reached up to plant a kiss on his lips, and his beard tickled her mouth. She giggled.

"Looks like I need to take a stand," he said.

"For what?" Had she angered him?

Painted Hands gently righted her to sit alone. "Can I borrow your scissors and your pa's razor?"

She started. "I need to get them from the trunk."

He laughed and hugged her to him. "If I want to kiss you all night, then I'd better be getting rid of these whiskers."

"All night?" Her pulse quickened.

"Until the sun climbs over the horizon."

∞

Painted Hands had worn his beard since the soldiers placed him in the Crandles' home. Full of loathing and longing for his Indian family, Painted Hands chose to blame himself for the tragedies around him. He despised himself so much that the only way he could cover his shame came in the form of a thick, wiry beard.

"You can hide from yourself, but you can't hide from God," the Reverend Crandle had said.

Painted Hands ignored him, and even when he stepped into the arms of Jesus, he couldn't bring himself to face the truth of his torment. As the years went by, the bitterness deepened until it became like a festered sore eating away at his spirit.

Those days were past. He'd become a new creation. And although he realized the accuser would continue to plague him, he prayed God would always guide him through the tough days.

Sarah Jane held a small mirror beside the lantern while he first cut the beard with scissors, then used the razor. Once he finished, his cheeks felt smooth, like soft buckskin. The exposed areas of his face looked darker, a rather amusing sight. As he further studied the transformation, he noted a peculiar likeness of his face to his hands; both were a mixture of light and tanned skin. Both had resulted in choices he'd made. Suddenly, the scars on his hands weren't so ugly; they represented the love he'd felt for his family and how he'd tried to save them, just as shaving his beard came as a desire not to scratch Sarah Jane's soft face.

"This is strange, indeed." He stole a look at Sarah Jane, searching for her reaction.

She gasped. "Painted Hands, you are quite handsome." She reached up and touched his cheek. "I'm glad we married before the other women on the wagon train saw you without your beard."

"I don't remember looking at anyone else but you." His words were void of teasing, for they were true.

"Me?" Her eyes widened.

He set aside the scissors and razor and drew her into his arms. "I thought you had the prettiest color of hair I'd ever seen." He combed his fingers through the curls gracing her forehead. "It's not red or yellow, as if God made a special wildflower." He kissed the tip of her nose. "Your freckles remind me of a mischievous little girl, as though I never know what to expect next. And your eyes—many times since we've married, I've been lost in your green eyes, the color of growing earth." With the lantern reflecting in her eyes and adding a soft glow to her skin, she looked lovelier than he'd ever imagined.

"Thank you for making me feel beautiful."

"You are, Sarah Jane, and I've been a fool not to tell you until now. God had to open my eyes to more than one thing today."

∽

As much as Painted Hands wanted to linger a few days with his precious bride, he saw the foolishness of wasting time with the mountains ahead. The determination to beat the first snows didn't stop him from stealing kisses from Sarah Jane or thanking God for the gift of love. Another concern kept him constantly alert. This was Cheyenne country, and with their allies the Sioux, they ran fear into every white man who embarked upon their land. He'd feel safer once they hit Fort Laramie.

He continued to work on tanning the deer hide by soaking it again overnight. The next day, he flipped it over to scrape off all the hair in the same manner he'd removed the flesh. Today marked the second day for the hide to dry and bleach out on the travois. Not many days from now, Sarah Jane could sew warm clothes for the mountain trek.

On the north bank of the Laramie River, close to where it met the North Platte River, sat Fort Laramie. Painted Hands stopped the wagon to caulk the sides with tar before crossing the river. He hated crossing rivers with a wagon, and the Laramie was a deep and ofttimes rough waterway. Whereas the lazy Platte seemed to cool off man and beast, the Laramie often plunged into waterfalls.

"I know we're anxious to get to the fort," he said. "But I'm taking the time to construct a raft of sorts. This is one of the most dangerous rivers on the trail."

"Can I help?"

"No ma'am, but you can watch. Record it in your journal."

She laughed, for it had become his way of teasing her. She'd much rather record their journey than mend and sew. "All right, and I'll be quiet while you work."

While he labored over the task before him, Sarah Jane wrote what she could before tending to her chores. He never tired of hearing her chat—not at all as he used to.

"Painted Hands, I need to tell you something." She lifted her needle from the pale yellow material.

"You want moccasins, too?" he asked, slinging the ax over his shoulder.

"No, I think boots will be fine. I'm serious. I want to tell you about the money Papa left us so you won't be fretting over how we'll live once we get to Oregon."

"That makes me feel a bit uneasy, Sarah Jane. You should be planning what to do with your parents' money."

"No, it's ours. Anyway, I told you before that Papa wanted to build a mercantile and take advantage of the free land for a farm. We have plenty—we're not rich, mind you, but there's enough for a venture."

He smiled. "I have no idea what we'll do for sure once we get there. From what Reverend Crandle told me, Jacob wanted to start a lumber camp near Willamette Falls, and maybe I could work for him. Then again, I might be a farmer. God hasn't told me yet."

She shrugged and started to mend again. "I wanted to tell you about the money. Along with selling the cattle, we should be fine."

"Don't you worry about a thing. I'm planning to take good care of you."

She laughed. "I simply wanted to offer something besides another pair of working hands."

"Prettiest hands I've ever seen."

∞

Sarah Jane believed the fifteen-foot adobe walls of Fort Laramie were the most welcome sight she'd ever seen. They stood as a link to civilization with the Black Hills in the background.

"This is beautiful," she said, drawing the oxen to a halt so she could savor the view. "I wish I knew how to paint so I could keep it forever—to look at it when my mind wandered back to our journey."

"Then memorize every inch of it." Painted Hands rode up close to her. "So someday you can tell our children."

"And our great-grandchildren." She'd kept writing in Mama's journal for the same reason. "Do we need many supplies from the fort?" she asked.

"I've taken inventory, and we need only a few. The cost of provisions here is expensive. I used some salt in preserving the deer, and I'd like to replace it. The wheels need repairing but little else. Not sure what kind of price I'll get for the cattle."

"I don't want to stay long." She glanced at him for a response. When he didn't reply, she continued. "I like being alone with my husband."

He chuckled, and she wrinkled her nose at him. The truth was, she did prefer his company. Oh, someday she'd want for womenfolk talk again, especially when children arrived.

"What's ahead for us?" she asked. "I mean, what can we expect after leaving the prairie behind?"

"The terrain will change, more barren with mostly sage and occasional cedar. Remember the times on the wagon train when we had to stop the cattle before they reached alkali-poisoned water holes?" When she nodded, he continued. "In addition to the water problem, we'll have water holes so full of salt that the animals won't drink it. It's going to be hot, and the air will be thick with dust."

"How hot? Worse than the prairie?"

"Mean, miserable heat. I'm not teasing you about the temperatures. I've seen cattle appear to go mad for water. We're lucky to have only a few to contend with."

"Just tell me what to do," she said. The road ahead would give any woman cause for alarm. She could do it—as long as she refused to think about Mama's fate and the others who had fallen prey to nature's fury.

"Simply endure it, understanding it won't last forever. Once we're through the heat and our skin sunburned, we'll hit Willow Springs. There we can enjoy fresh water and prettier country. I'd like to do a little hunting in that territory. Then we'll follow the Sweetwater River to Independence Rock. A day's travel from there is Devil's Gate and on to the mountains."

She nodded. "I'm ready—prayed up and looking forward to wearing my new clothes. I'll have them finished way before I need them."

"I'm sure every man who ventures into this area wishes his wife would be this excited."

"Those women don't have Painted Hands for a husband. Besides, you're so comely that I'm not so sure I want other women looking at you."

His laughter echoed across the countryside. "Shall I grow my beard to please my jealous wife?"

She stiffened and pretended anger. "You might have to." Then she remembered the cold mountains. "Won't you need it for warmth in the Rockies?"

"Yes ma'am. But I'll shave it once we're through them."

The bantering, the kisses, the nights snuggled in his arms. Sarah Jane never dreamed her husband could make her so happy. She still had her moments when she missed Mama and Papa; she'd not be a real person without those grieving times. Yet more often her thoughts dwelled on the memorable times with them.

Painted Hands had not said any more about his family and nothing about the years spent with the Kiowa. She would not press him. He'd tell her when he saw fit.

The Greenham wagon train was about two weeks ahead of them, and Painted Hands and Sarah Jane preferred to keep their distance. Once they sold all the cattle but two milk cows and purchased a few provisions, they left Fort Laramie. There were creeks to cross and lots of time for Sarah Jane to spend with her husband.

In the distance, she saw the vegetation change. A twinge of fear twisted in her stomach. The unknown. The prairie drew her back. Although it had been filled with death and ugliness, it also held her heart. The beautiful, fragrant wildflowers, the blue of the sky, the tall grass that in places soared above her head, and most of all, the place where she'd found the love of a good man.

The more she considered this journey to Oregon, the more she realized the trail was filled with uncertainty about the future. She had to trust God; she had no choice.

CHAPTER 15

Sarah Jane held her breath at the magnificence of the long, narrow gorge called Devil's Gate. Through the rock flowed the Sweetwater River with cliffs nearly four hundred feet high. She begged Painted Hands to go exploring, for she'd never seen such a magnificent sight.

"I wonder how it was made," she said, staring up at the steep rock.

Taking her hand, he guided her over rocks to the rushing sound of the river. "The Indians have a story, if you want to hear it."

"Need you ask?"

He laughed and helped her over a jagged rock. "The Arapaho and Shoshone Indians believe at one time a huge beast lived here and stopped the Indians from hunting and fishing along the river. They decided to attack and kill it, but when they sent arrows into the animal's side, it became angry and tore out the gorge to escape."

"How did you learn this?" Painted Hands always had the best stories.

He shrugged. "Good ears."

"What about the name?" Sarah Jane released his hand and climbed up a rock for a better view of the river.

"I have no idea—probably from the number of people who tried to climb the cliffs and plunged to their death."

She glanced down at the many jagged rocks and decided her husband might be right.

"Leave the climbing to the bighorn sheep," Painted Hands said. "I rather like my wife in one piece."

By mid-August, they reached the Big Sandy. The land around them held little but sage, and the water was filled with alkali, but Painted Hands showed her where to find good water and plump gooseberries to vary the everyday diet of biscuits and bacon. Together they ventured across streams until they reached the Green River. From there they ambled in a southwesterly direction.

"The trail to Fort Bridger is desertlike. Remember I spoke about this earlier," Painted Hands said. "Sandstorms and heat that will rival the fire and brimstone one hears from the best of preachers. Wish I knew a better way."

"We've managed before," Sarah Jane said.

He squeezed her hand. "Once we get to the fort, you'll see it sits in a green valley with plenty of water. No doubt we'll need wagon repairs before leaving."

She listened to every word, sealing the terrain in her mind so she could record it later in the journal. More important, she remembered his caution for potential hardships. She would not be a burden to her husband, not now or ever.

Beyond Fort Bridger, a small post with few extra supplies, they moved toward Bear River.

"This is another rough river to cross," Painted Hands said. "The current is swift, even in shallow water."

"I handled the others just fine," she said, although the thought of the wagon tumbling into the water and ruining provisions always frightened her.

"You don't sound so confident."

She offered a faint smile. "I'll not lie to you about it."

An hour later they pulled alongside the Bear. Painted Hands appeared to study its flow. Praise God, they'd done this twice before.

"I'll ride the horse across, and you follow me. Take it slow and easy, and we'll get safely across." He glanced at the river, then back to her. "Would you rather take the horse and go first?"

She shook her head and lifted the reins. "I'll drive these oxen."

Painted Hands took the lead, and the oxen stepped into the muddy river. A snake slithered by. Sarah Jane shuddered. The sooner they reached the far bank, the better. The going was slow, and she found herself gripping the reins and praying for courage. At midstream, one of the oxen balked.

She lifted the reins. "Giddyap. Let's get across."

Nothing.

Painted Hands whipped his horse around to help, and he called to the oxen, too.

The wagon started to lean to the right. "Haw! Haw!" she exclaimed in an effort to straighten it.

Painted Hands shouted the same command, but the oxen refused to move. "Jump! Get clear of the wagon!" he shouted.

She doubted if the water was over her head, but she feared the wagon would tip over on her. Her legs wouldn't move. Fear held her in a stranglehold.

"Sarah Jane, jump from the opposite side." Painted Hands's anxious voice rose above her harried thoughts. He urged his horse toward her, splashing water in every direction.

The wagon leaned farther to the right.

"You have to jump!"

She glanced up. *Lord, help me.* It took all of her strength to drop the reins and stand. Any second, the wagon would plunge into the swiftly moving water. Painted Hands shouted at her again. He sounded scared. *I won't be a burden. I won't be a burden.*

She stood and leaped from the left side of the wagon, catching her foot on the side and falling facefirst into the cold water. She came up sputtering and spitting. Water had filled her nose, and her head stung. She choked and coughed. Painted Hands reached down and pulled her up. In the next instant, the wagon fell. With his hand grasped around her waist, Painted Hands carried her safely to the other side and eased her onto the rocky bank.

"Are you hurt?" he asked.

"No." Glancing back into the river and the toppled wagon, she wiggled free and started back into the river.

"Stop, Sarah Jane. I'll get the wagon," he said. "Stay here."

She shook her head and kept wading in. Tears rolled down her cheeks. "This is my fault." She should have been able to drive the oxen across.

"Get back."

She ignored him until he hurried past her on his horse, and she slipped. Helplessly, Sarah Jane watched Painted Hands calm the oxen, then tie a rope to the wagon and somehow right it and urge the oxen to the other side.

"The food." Her voice came out as a feeble cry. With water dripping from every inch of her, she climbed into the rear of the wagon. The lump in her throat grew larger. They'd starve because of her.

Painted Hands was right behind her. Their clothes were soaked, and their breathing came in quick gasps. The mattress was ruined. Water covered everything. Her fingers clawed over the food. Water-soaked bacon could still be used. Most of the flour lay in a pasty clump, and a large portion of the sugar was dissolved, certain to make everything around it sticky and useless.

"We'll make it," Painted Hands said. "I can hunt, and we can ration what's left. Remember we had more than enough when we started out."

The tears flowed unchecked over her cheeks. "I'm sorry. Please forgive me."

He drew her close. "There's nothing to forgive. What's important is that we're alive, and we'll take care of things and move on." He touched her wet hair. "First thing I'm doing is building a fire so you can dry out. Praise God, you weren't hurt."

She nodded in a feeble attempt to be brave. Suddenly, exhaustion took hold of her, but she refused to give in. "I'll find some wood."

"You'll love Bear Valley," he said, helping her down from the wagon. His fingers grasped the bones beneath her waist. More than once he'd voiced his concern about her frail frame. "It's as close to paradise as you'll see in these parts. I've tasted some of the best fish and birds you'll ever find. There are wild goat, elk, and deer and so many berries you won't know what to do with them all. I imagine I'll fatten you up for sure."

"How will we make it? What can I do to help?"

"We have a little salt we can use to cure meat, and in the mountains, the cold will help preserve it all."

∞

Painted Hands lowered his aching back down next to the fire. Tomorrow he'd sit beneath a cottonwood tree and listen to the birds sing—after he tended to the many chores facing him. He thought back to the image of Sarah Jane too frightened to jump from the wagon. It could have crushed her. He'd seen it happen on past trips—watched women and children plunge to their death in water far deeper and colder than this. He remembered the wailing of grown men who had lost their families and children. Some were too stunned to cry. With a sigh, he pushed the thoughts away. Sarah Jane was safe. He needn't dig up old memories.

Back at Fort Laramie, some of the old-timers claimed they were in for an early winter, but sometimes weather predictions were stated to frighten travelers. Those who wanted to turn back needed an excuse and used signs of bad weather or the threat of hostile Indians to head east. He and Sarah Jane were a few weeks late moving up the mountain trail, and with the food shortage, he had cause for concern. He decided it was best not to voice his worries to her; she already blamed herself for losing their provisions.

The days and weeks ahead were treacherous. In the past, the Shoshone Indians had helped wagon trains in distress, and the warriors anticipated trading their horses for blankets and knives from the whites. Painted Hands had nothing to barter, but he'd like to hear about the weather farther up in the mountains.

They'd follow the Bear River to the Portneuf River that led to Fort Hall. The fort seldom had anything to offer, usually being short of provisions. From that site, he and Sarah Jane would move along the Snake River for about three hundred miles. This trek was rocky and wild. If his dear wife had been afraid today, she'd be petrified of the steep and narrow trail ahead.

Lord, help me guide us safely through these mountains. I don't have a good feeling about what lies ahead, not a good feeling at all.

CHAPTER 16

Sarah Jane had never known such treacherous terrain as that along the Snake River. The oxen tore their feet climbing over sharp rocks, and many times she led the horse while Painted Hands walked alongside the wagon in case it threatened to plummet down a mountainside. When the trail wove them into the Snake Valley, he steered the wagon clear of deep sand. The blinding dust storms bothered her the most. During those times, she couldn't even see the oxen in front of her. A kerchief and her scarf did little good to halt the cutting grit whipping around their bodies.

The mosquitoes must have been sent from Satan, for they settled on the oxen and horse like a fog of torment. Night after night, the horse cried out for relief. Once the sun went down, she and Painted Hands covered themselves completely to avoid the swarming insects. She wondered how many of them they drank in the coffee or ate with their food. Painted Hands led the wagon up the mountain as high as possible to avoid the mosquitoes, but that left them far from the water supply. Leading the animals down a steep path for a mile to secure water, then up again, was another arduous task.

Painted Hands and Sarah Jane talked little. Exhaustion took its toll, and when they could take advantage of rest, they were too tired even to mumble a few words. She noted her husband had slipped back into his black moods. He ignored her unless danger prevailed—no smiles or kind words. Some nights she cried herself to sleep, but if Painted Hands heard her weep, he said nothing. She realized he worried about the winter snows and the shortage of food, and when she repeatedly saw his gaze move to the higher mountains, she understood his trepidation. The plunge she'd taken into the Bear River proved how quickly life could be jeopardized.

The journey had to get easier. How could the hardships be much worse?

Twice the Shoshone visited them. They brought salmon and trout, and Sarah Jane cooked it for them all. The friendly Indians appeared grateful— her dealings with them were not at all like those with the Cheyenne. She still shuddered when she recalled that ordeal. Painted Hands communicated with them in their own language—something she resolved to learn when time allowed. From what she gathered, the Indians wanted to trade for blankets and knives, but the travelers could spare little. Their new friends no doubt realized the limited amount of food in the wagon. A few times, Painted Hands accompanied them to the fishing streams. While he was gone, Sarah Jane hurried through her chores so she could sleep.

The days blended together in a haze of exhaustion. Her existence with Painted Hands worsened. He resorted to not wanting her to speak, his foul temperament leaving her cold and miserable. She wondered what had become of his relationship with the Lord, but she often felt as surly. She hoped God understood these difficult days. Then the rains came—relentless sheets of water that chilled her to the bone. Some days she thought she'd never be warm or dry again. Her hair froze, but as Painted Hands had claimed, the buckskin suited the purpose more than her dresses. The rocky trails were slick, and she slipped in mud to her knees. At least during the downpours she could cry freely and he never saw.

If only Painted Hands would put his arms around her, hold her as he used to. Some days she wondered if they were growing to hate each other. She wondered if he remembered his previous words of love and affection, for he'd turned more inward than in the days after Mama's and Papa's deaths.

With depression settling around her and no end in sight, Sarah Jane gave up trying to please him. She no longer cared about Oregon or dreams or her husband. Most days she'd have sold her soul for a day of rest and a warm bed. Her whole body ached.

One afternoon, Sarah Jane believed she saw a mirage in the Powder River Valley. The path downward looked every bit as precarious as where they'd come from, but the green valley below took her breath away.

"Am I seeing things?" she asked. "Is there really a beautiful valley below?"

Painted Hands grunted affirmation. "Won't last long." He pointed to the snowcapped mountains ahead. "That's what's ahead."

Couldn't he be happy for a small blessing? "Can we rest for a few days?"

"We're already behind."

His granitelike demeanor angered her. "But the animals are worn out. Surely they need to eat for us to continue."

He said nothing in response, but she didn't expect him to.

"Their hooves need time to mend."

His silence angered her. She wanted to scream at him, but she didn't have the strength. His renewed dedication to God and his commitment to her seemed to have vanished miles behind.

"Well, I'm not forcing these oxen beyond the valley until they are rested."

∽

Painted Hands despised the man he'd become. Always the whispers of God urged him to be kind, to be considerate of Sarah Jane. Now, as he helped the oxen down into the Powder River Valley and thought back over his harsh words to Sarah Jane, he realized the truth of why he'd turned back to his black days.

He was afraid.

Simply and without a doubt, he was scared to the point he couldn't think clearly.

For ten years he lived with the Kiowa and learned their ways. He acquired the skills of hunting, surviving in the wilderness, and engaging in warfare, but he'd always been with his Indian brothers. With the Reverend Crandle and his wife, Painted Hands learned how to read, write, and ponder the scriptures. From his Indian life and his time among the whites, he discovered wisdom and truth. Four times before, he'd journeyed this path to Oregon with the best route, the purest water, food, and survival all sunk into his character.

But he hadn't made the trip to Oregon alone. Greenham led the wagons while Painted Hands scouted for those four trips across the prairies and mountains. Never had he been the sole man responsible for getting the wagons through safely. The fear raged inside him. Every inch of the trek depended on him. He woke in the mornings with a heavy heart at the thought of another day. He loved Sarah Jane so much, but he couldn't look at her or offer a kind word. Her life rested in the palm of his hand, and he refused to take his responsibility lightly.

Not so many weeks ago, Painted Hands believed he was a man, and that man gave his heart to Christ. For the first time in his life, he had felt true peace. With God's gift of love, he treasured Sarah Jane. That part of him seemed like another person.

His prayers for courage and strength went unanswered. He despised his weakness. Sarah Jane had begun to loathe him, and he understood why. In her position, he'd have given up, too.

During the past trips with the wagon trains, he didn't have God directing him. When he realized the importance of a relationship with the Lord of the universe, he embraced Him. Life looked hopeful, especially a future with Sarah Jane. Now, fear once more seemed to strangle him.

Taking a deep breath, he glanced back at his wife. Even with dirt woven through her hair and ground into her clothes, she was the most beautiful woman in the world. *Help me, Lord. I hate my heart of stone.*

"We can rest a few days," he said. "These last weeks have been hard on us. I need to wrap chains around the rear wheels to help us over the steep mountain passes, and you're right that the animals need rest."

"Thank you." Her words sounded lifeless, and he ached to make things right between them.

If not for leading the oxen, he'd have walked back to talk to her. But this time, like so many times in the past, other priorities took over. If God would take away his fears, then he could be a husband again.

Once the oxen were unhitched and allowed to feed and water, Painted Hands took to repairing wheels and examining every inch of the wagon. The trek across the Blue Mountains usually took four days, and the threat of snowstorms made him want to leave the next morning.

Sarah Jane fished trout from the river and fried it up for supper that night. She hadn't smiled in days, and he knew he was the problem. Sitting beside her on an old log with the fire crackling filled him with a deep longing for the closeness they'd once shared.

"If we had the provisions, this valley would be a beautiful place to stay," he said, feeling the agony of so many wearisome days in his bones.

Her gaze flew to him. No doubt these were the most civil words he'd spoken in too long. He captured her green pools; where once they sparkled like a mountain stream, now dull, dark circles cratered beneath them. "Sarah Jane, I warned you the going would be rough."

"That you did." She looked around her.

"Saying I'm sorry isn't enough, is it?" he asked.

She continued to study the land about them. "Does it matter?" He heard her release a sigh. "I'm so tired that if I could die this very minute, I would."

"You can't give up." He didn't mean just the dreams about Oregon but also their marriage, except those words stayed on his tongue.

"I believe I have. There's nothing left inside of me but a faint desire to get through another day. The hope is gone. For the first time, I understand how Mama felt."

"And your faith?"

"I'm not sure what faith is anymore." She stood up from the log and massaged her back with her fingertips. "I want to go to bed."

"Sleep until there is no sleep left in you," he said.

"If that were true, you'd need to dig another grave." She left without saying good night. Full of agony, he watched her climb into the rear of the wagon.

"You'll feel better when you're rested," he said.

She failed to reply. Could he blame her when he'd done the very thing to her? He'd turned her against him, destroyed her spirit if not her will to live.

The curse lived on.

The next two days, Sarah Jane stayed to herself. She washed clothes, bathed, and roamed the valley. She brought back gooseberries and wildflowers but offered no sign of peace. She looked extremely pale. Painted Hands had seen that look in women before, and he knew the end result. He saw her staring at the mountains and made his way to her side.

"Tomorrow is our last day here," he said. "I see you've taken a liking to the valley. We could spend the morning enjoying what we can of it."

"Go ahead without me." She kept her gaze fastened on the mountains. "I have chores to do."

"The time wouldn't be the same without you." There—he'd said it, the only words of affection he could muster.

"Nonsense, Painted Hands. You much prefer the company of nature to my prattle."

Desperate to find her spunk, he searched his mind for the words to spark some kind of emotion. "We need to get our lives back the way they were."

She tilted her head. "And why is that? Once we start up the mountains, things will go back to the same."

A fall breeze combed through her hair, teasing the reddish-yellow curls that matched the colorful foliage. What he wouldn't give for the music of her laughter.

"I'm sorry for what I've done to you," he said, but she failed to acknowledge him. "Sarah Jane, I wish I knew why I've hurt you over and over again, especially when you are the one person in this world I love. I'd do anything to win you back."

Her blank stare told him all he wanted to know. His morose ways had destroyed their love. And he deserved it.

The trail over the Blue Mountains began with no prayer or formal introduction. Silently, he asked God to guide them safely on to Oregon. The wagon simply climbed higher. Painted Hands remembered when the trees were so thick that he and Greenham, along with other men from the wagon train, had to use axes to hack a path through.

Toward late morning on the second day of the climb, the temperatures fell, and the sky grayed.

"We're in for snow," he said.

She nodded and shrugged. "What do we do?"

"Keep going for as long as we can. If it turns into a blizzard, then we'll have to find shelter."

In an hour's time, the snow started, first in featherlike softness and a rhythmic beauty that in other circumstances would have been beautiful. The intensity increased, and soon it blew fast and furious, reminding him of the tales of lost wagons that had fallen prey to wild blizzards.

"I see a cliff where we can find shelter," he said, pointing. "We'll have to wait this one out."

The snow-roofed rock offered only a bit of reprieve until the heavy fall ceased to blind them.

"I'm going after firewood," he said. "I won't be gone long. Will you be all right?"

For a moment, he saw a flash of something akin to longing. They stood side by side, near enough for him to pull her into his arms. "I'll unhitch the oxen and search for wood near the wagon," she said. "I'll have a fire going and food cooked when you return. There're a few kindling pieces in the wagon."

"Stay close, for there isn't much wood nearby. Don't wander off. Keep your sights on the wagon."

Sarah Jane shivered, and he drew her scarf close about her neck. "Later on, when we have a warm fire, I'd like to talk, really talk."

She moistened her chapped lips. If not sun-parched, they were cracked and bleeding from the cold. He wished their love had not taken the same beating.

"Don't fill me with hope again. I can't bear it anymore," she said.

"It's not your doing." Painted Hands touched her cheek with a gloved finger. He thought of telling her about the fear raging through his spirit. He'd missed her, and he wanted what they'd left behind.

Wetness pooled in her green eyes. She turned aside and blinked the tears back.

"Don't you think I know the nights you cried yourself to sleep?"

"I didn't believe you cared." She lifted her face to gaze into his, something she hadn't done in a long time.

He tugged on his scraggly beard. "I never stopped caring, and I'm not sure I can explain it all now."

"You have to try, or we'll never survive."

Painted Hands bent and brushed a kiss atop her head. "I understand."

With the ax on one shoulder and his shotgun slung over the other, he left her feeling warmer than he had all day. The tree line was directly above them, which meant he needed to descend the same path to find fallen branches. Once he gathered a sufficient supply, he'd store them under the wagon. There they'd dry out, for they might be holed up in the mountains for a while. Painted Hands pushed aside the needling stories of those found frozen to death and focused his attention on the broken limbs below. Some food lay in the wagon, and his shotgun would ward off wolves looking to sink their teeth into the oxen or his horse. He could take down a deer or mountain sheep for meat. They'd be fine for as long as it took.

He shielded his eyes from the snow, then took careful steps downward. Up ahead was a small grove of aspen trees, and farther on he saw pine and spruce. Suddenly, his foot slipped. Reaching down, he tried to stop from gliding down the snow, but he skimmed it like a child's sled on a snow-packed hill. Finding nothing to grab but more snow, he continued to fall. He dare not shout for fear of scaring Sarah Jane. The trees he'd sought loomed his way. Before he could plan how to reach for one and break his fall, his left leg caught on a tree trunk and threw him against another.

Painted Hands heard the snap of his leg, like a tree branch caught under the weight of ice and snow. Sucking in his breath, he assumed the pain would hit him hard, but only numbness met him. He looked to the side. His leg lay twisted in a grotesque shape. He breathed in and out, then attempted to move. And then it hit him. A moan escaped his lips with the excruciating pain from his broken leg. Glancing up, he saw the path he'd fallen down was steep, and the way up would be difficult for a whole man.

Swallowing hard, he fought the urge to slip into unconsciousness as easily as he'd descended the mountainside. He stared up at a white sky. Snowflakes dusted his face. He'd be a tasty find for a wolf—along with his wife and animals above him.

I have to find a way to get back up to the wagon.

The means of getting firewood left him defeated. One of his legs felt as if it were on fire, and the other he couldn't feel at all for the cold. He stared at the hand that still held the ax and thanked God he hadn't lost the tool. With it, he had a chance. Surely, in this cold, the pain in his leg might ease up.

I'll crawl up. On the way, I'll think of some way Sarah Jane and I can survive. Oh Lord, I don't care about myself, but please save my wife.

Painted Hands forced himself onto his belly. He studied the mountain. Somehow he'd make it.

CHAPTER 17

Sarah Jane built a fire, using the kindling from inside the wagon and the pieces of wood found not far from the campsite. As Painted Hands requested, she did not venture beyond sight of the wagon, for the snow blew at her back and whirled in front of her eyes. She continued to pick up every stick of wood, whether twigs or bigger pieces, and carry them back to the overhanging rock. Beneath the wagon, they'd dry out, for she assumed they'd be there for a couple of days—or longer. Some of the pieces were large, so she dragged them. Painted Hands could split them when he returned.

She'd admired the trees as they climbed the mountain path: the huge pines varying in size and type of cone, the spruce, the bright yellow foliage of the aspen, the tall fir, the scarlet-and-gold-leafed maple, and the gray-green-barked poplar. She wanted to know about each tree and referred to Papa's traveler's guide to help her identify them.

The afternoon wore on, and Sarah Jane looked anxiously toward the path Painted Hands had taken for wood. Every time she considered looking for him, the snow fell more heavily masking the dangerous downward path. He'd taken the shotgun. Maybe he'd followed the fresh tracks of a deer, but as the sun descended to the west, apprehension set in.

Her spirits lifted, and she sensed calmness in her heart. His parting words were filled with hope, and unless he'd deceived her, he sounded regretful for his actions. And she needed to tell him how the arduous days had darkened her mood. Painted Hands wanted to talk, a promising sign. Where was he now? Would he have gone on and left her alone to starve or freeze to death? She dug through the wagon and pulled out Papa's shotgun—just in case a hungry wolf took a liking to the animals. And grizzly bears—Sarah Jane rubbed her hands together; she didn't even want to think about wild animals. A moment later, she loaded Papa's shotgun.

The snow stopped. Stepping from beneath the ledge, she scanned the terrain for signs of Painted Hands. Nothing. Her gaze fell on a branch sticking through a mound of white. Every stick of dead wood she could find looked invaluable. During the next several minutes, she pulled and tugged the log to the wagon. Using her foot as leverage, she broke off as many of the smaller branches as possible, moving on to do the same with her other supply. She separated the pine from the other, understanding the soft wood made better kindling. Evening shadows crept across the mountainside. She was hungry but realized the food needed to be rationed, and she'd not eat without Painted Hands.

Hours had passed since her husband first left to gather wood. She stepped as far from the wagon as possible and again searched every portion of the area around her.

"Painted Hands!" Her voice echoed around her. "Painted Hands!"

A branch snapped behind her, and she whirled around to see nothing—and hear nothing but the rapid beat of her heart. She was utterly alone. Panic seized her mind and mocked her fears.

∽

The hours crept by, and the rush of sunset forced Painted Hands to crawl faster. The slightest movement sent knifelike jabs to his leg and tore at his strength. He clenched the ax in one hand and the shotgun in the other. Slamming the ax into the soft snow, he tried to anchor himself and move another inch, another foot. A glance behind him showed a trail of blood. Wolves would pick up the scent and be on his trail soon. As darkness edged around him, he thanked God for the gun.

His thoughts spun with worry about Sarah Jane. She knew nothing about surviving in the mountains. At least if she'd been stranded on the prairie, she'd have had a chance at survival.

If he died this very night, would she remember he loved her? Would God send someone to help her?

"Painted Hands! Painted Hands!"

His pain-dulled senses thought he heard her calling. He lifted his head and craned his neck, hoping he might be near the top. Quiet. Only the sounds of nature whispered around him. Disappointment nudged him.

Keep going, Painted Hands. Night had not settled on him yet, and as long as he had breath, he'd crawl on to the top.

"Painted Hands!"

He heard her voice again, echoing around him like the cries of a lost child. This could not be the makings of his mind.

He took a deep breath. "Sarah Jane."

Silence nestled in his ears—that and a grim reminder of the pain.

"Painted Hands! Where are you?"

"Sarah Jane, keep talking so I can find you." The effort to shout nabbed his strength.

"I don't see you. Are you hurt?"

Painted Hands heard the anxiety in her voice. "I've. . .broken my leg. I'm crawling up the mountain."

"Help me find you."

He peered about him, looking for something, anything, to mark where he lay. "I see three fir trees with a spruce on each side. The trees look like they're forming a tepee. Off to my left is a grove of tall pine."

"I'm looking hard, but the trees seem to blend together."

Her voice sounded raspy as though she were crying or her throat hurt from shouting. "Pray, Sarah Jane." But his words came out like a child's whimper.

"I see you!" she called.

He glanced up, and there she was, making her way down the steep grade, her coat flapping open to the buckskin hugging her body. Never had he seen such a beautiful sight. Tears froze on his cheeks.

Sarah Jane worked her way toward him at a good pace. She planted her feet sideways and half-slid down the slope. Praise God she knew how to move through the snow, even if her experience came from the Nebraska prairie.

"I'm coming. Don't give up on me."

He clung to her words of encouragement. His precious wife had become so thin. Her fragile body could not withstand much more. How would they get the rest of the way up? His gaze stayed fixed on her as he continued to crawl upward with her name on his lips.

When Sarah Jane finally reached him, she wrapped her arms around his shoulders and laid her head against his. He believed an angel had come to deliver him. Indeed, God in His mercy had shown her the way.

"Look at the trouble I've gotten us into," he said in a feeble attempt to sound light. She dared not read his anxiety.

She shook her head and hugged his shoulders. "Well, you didn't dump food into the river."

But I may have carved our tombstones. "We're a fine pair."

"I agree. We have to hurry," she said. "Night is gathering. Tell me how we're going to do this."

"I was hoping you'd have a plan." He shifted his weight and moaned.

"Just to hurry."

"Take the shotgun, and I'll use the ax to make my way up." His leg throbbed with every beat of his heart.

She moved to his right side. "Slip your hand around my shoulders." She grabbed his waist while gripping the shotgun in her right hand. "Do it! Time's a-wasting."

A surge of white-hot fire assaulted him.

"We have to make it up this hill," she said. "We have no choice."

Was it fear that made her insistent? No matter, his wife had her gumption back.

The two crawled up the incline together. When he groaned, she assured him they were almost there; she could see the light from the fire. "I want to get there and add another log," she said. "You need to get warm."

Painted Hands didn't try to talk. It was all he could do to cease his groanings, but the sound came without his realizing it.

"I love you, Painted Hands. We have a life ahead in Oregon."

He hurt too badly to say the same things, so he squeezed the hand holding on to him. Sarah Jane had to ache with the weight on her narrow shoulders.

"I see the fire," she said a few moments later. "I really do. Look ahead. Only a bit farther."

Indeed, they had made it. As much as he hurt, he attempted a laugh.

"Hold on to your sense of humor," she said. "You'll need it when I set your leg."

She'd have to find splints—or make them—and he'd have to tell her how to straighten it. "Tomorrow we'll set it, not tonight."

She nodded, then eased him down beside the fire. Hurrying to the wagon, she came back with a shovel and scooped out the snow that had gathered earlier. In the next instant, she had made a pallet for him. When at last he collapsed on the blankets and she covered him, she picked up the ax and split two logs for the fire. He hated to see her work so hard.

"There's nothing for pain." She sighed. "This will be a bad night for you."

"Not as long as you're here."

She smiled—the same smile he remembered from their more pleasant days. "I wish I could get you inside the wagon, but this will be warmer."

"The fire is good. Thank you for coming after me. I owe you my life."

She eased over by him. "We're constantly beholden to each other. Let me see your leg and where the blood's coming from."

He turned to see the twisted limb he called his leg. "I think it's scratched from one of the trees."

Sarah Jane melted snow in a pan, then gingerly dabbed at the gash exposed through his buckskin. In the dancing flames, he saw the weary lines around her eyes.

"Honey, you need to stop. Tomorrow we'll work through the damage I've done today."

She scooted back on her knees and gazed into the fire. "I'm going to treat it; then we should eat. It won't take me long to do either one."

He would not tell her he hurt too badly to taste anything, but both of them needed their strength. Watching her prepare trout that had been caught a few days ago kept his mind off the incessant pain. How beautiful his wife was. He feared this land would take her from him.

"Let's pray before we eat," he said. She took his hand. "Father, You saved me from death today, and I thank You. I also thank You for Sarah Jane. Keep us safe and direct our path. Amen."

The fish did taste good, but his worries about the future gripped him. He knew the sin of worry, but his thoughts raced ahead despite his spirit's warnings. They'd need firewood and saplings to make a splint. Food was another concern.

"You should try to sleep." Sarah Jane moved to his side and lifted his head into her lap. "Now you have a pillow."

"And what of you?"

"I have what makes me happy at my fingertips." She picked up a blanket warming near the fire and draped it across her shoulders. "Now I not only look like an Indian, but I'll sleep like one."

He feigned a chuckle. "Indians don't sleep sitting up."

"This one does."

Painted Hands slept fitfully that night. The torment in his leg consumed him. The care of his wife overwhelmed him. He prayed; he thought back over his life. God had delivered him too many times for this to be the end, or had he run out of chances? Sarah Jane dozed off from time to time, always waking to see to his needs. They talked little as they simply waited until dawn.

∞

Sarah Jane stood at the crack of sunrise and shrugged the blanket around her shoulders. She split a few logs and added them to the fire. While she made coffee and fried bacon, she listened to Painted Hands explain how to set his leg. The idea of hurting him caused her to tremble, but she pushed the thought aside and concentrated on his directives.

"You'll need three saplings cut the length of my leg and strips of leather or rope to tie the wood pieces to my leg. Pulling it straight is another matter."

After breakfast, she went in search of the wood for splints, making sure she didn't slip on the snow. Her mind raced with the immediate. *How will I put his leg into place? How can I tell if it's straight? What if I don't set it right and he's crippled? When can Painted Hands travel? Must life be so incredibly hard?*

Snow clouds lingered above, and she picked up her pace. Once she tended to his leg, she'd need to gather more wood. She focused her attention in every direction. If they didn't move on soon, they'd be trapped until spring. Praying for the snow to let up, she hurried her pace. Painted Hands couldn't ride in the wagon over the narrow paths. It was too dangerous.

Everything they'd attempted had been full of peril. Was Oregon worth the price?

At the campsite, Painted Hands lay in torment, but he refused to allow Sarah Jane to know the extent of his pain. He swallowed hard and approved of the splints. "The time is now to pull it into place."

Sarah Jane's stomach churned. "How will you stand the pain?"

He nodded toward the wagon. "I'm going to hold on to the wheel. I'd do it myself if I could."

She helped him to the wagon, then carried the sapling pieces and the leather straps and laid them beside him—anything to keep her from completing the task before her. The time had come; she had no more excuses. She cut the buckskin up to his thigh, the gnarled leg a swollen mass of purple and blue. Painted Hands reached over his head and grabbed the wheel behind him.

"Work fast." Sweat beaded his brow in the frigid temperatures. "You can do it, Sarah Jane. I only wish another man was here to hold me down."

"Help me, Jesus," she whispered. "Dull his pain and guide my hands." She knew better than to look at his face and know her hands caused the excruciating pain. Clenching her fists, she released her fingers and found her hold on both sides of his broken leg. In the next instant, she yanked it into a downward position. Painted Hands jerked and cried out, his voice echoing around them like that of a hurt animal. Sarah Jane bit her lip until she tasted blood, but she had to finish. Seeing the leg needed to be straightened further, she steadied her shaking hands and lined up his leg to match the other.

He gasped, and his face paled. Leaning his head back, Painted Hands closed his eyes. A moment later, he wet his lips and took several deep breaths before looking at the injured leg. "Good," he managed. "Now put the splints in place."

Sarah Jane worked fast, her pulse beating in her head and her fingers trembling like twigs on a dead branch. How could one man endure such pain? When the last leather strap was tied, she stared into his stricken face.

"You did a fine job," he said. "Thanks to you, I'll walk again."

She moistened her lips. "I'll be praying for this leg every morning, noon, and night until we remove those splints."

"I will, too." He closed his eyes and released his hold on the wagon wheel. "Sarah Jane," he said, "when you write about this for our children, don't tell them I nearly cried like a baby."

"I promise. I'll write that you were brave and never uttered a sound." She smiled.

She helped him crawl back to the fire and covered him snugly. Picking up the shotgun and ax, she headed away from the camp. Now she had to find wood.

CHAPTER 18

Painted Hands watched her leave until she disappeared in front of a rounded pine. Sarah Jane looked more like a little girl than a grown woman—a grown woman who carried a large burden. How he loved her. She held more strength in her little finger than most men ever achieved. Why she loved him went far beyond his understanding.

He glanced up at the sky; soon the snow would fall again. The old anxieties slapped his face. They'd faced a sad shortage of food before, but with him laid up and the impending weather, the gravity of the situation hit him harder. Helplessness settled on his shoulders.

He couldn't gather firewood; he'd already tried that and failed. He couldn't hunt with a broken leg. He couldn't lead the oxen through the narrow passageways. He couldn't ride his horse. He couldn't clear fallen branches from the trail. In fact, he was totally dependent on Sarah Jane. What irony. The tiny woman he wanted to protect had become his rock. To make matters worse, she was worn out. What if the typhoid attacked her again? For sure, once they reached Oregon, he'd never let her suffer like this.

Dear God, all I can do is trust in Your provision. Show me what I must do.

He exhaled a ragged breath. His leg hurt; the incessant pain offered no reprieve, always reminding him of their predicament. As intense as the agony was, it still didn't compare with her pulling it straight. He'd nearly passed out. He'd even begged God to blacken his mind. Sarah Jane had done a fine job of setting it, and he'd be forever grateful.

The present. He needed to do his share of the work. Until they were able to move the wagon ahead, they'd need firewood. Painted Hands glanced about. If Sarah Jane was able to find a limb or even a sapling, he'd have a crutch. He realized hobbling around today was next to impossible, but tomorrow. Yes, tomorrow he'd force himself to use a crutch. Being mobile meant he wasn't useless. Another thought occurred to him. He could drive the wagon, and when they reached those precarious places where the wagon risked a tumble over the side of a cliff, he'd limp alongside.

Painted Hands closed his eyes while he waited for his precious wife to return. Last night he lay awake hour after hour waiting for the pain to subside. Today the throb continued. If only he could sleep; a few hours' rest might clear his foggy mind. Maybe then he'd figure out a way to hunt with a crutch or lead the dangerously thin animals down to find grazing. If they died—Painted Hands shook his head and pushed his thoughts in another direction.

Lord, if I was scared before, it doesn't compare with now.

He opened his eyes with a start and realized he'd dozed off. Near the wagon lay a small pile of wood. He managed to smile. She'd left the camp again, but a pot of coffee rested by the fire, just beyond his reach, along with a mug. Dear, sweet Sarah Jane; she always put others first.

He tugged on his leg to help him grasp the mug. An unbidden moan broke the silence, and he fell back.

"Here, let me get the coffee for you," Sarah Jane said, stepping into his view. She carried wood in one arm and dragged a long limb with the other.

"I thought you were gone." He bit on his tongue to keep from crying out.

"I had an idea—something to help you get about." Her cheeks flushed red in the cold. She dumped the wood on top of the other and dropped the limb near him. In the next breath she poured him coffee and delivered it with a kiss. "How are you?"

"I'll live." He smiled at the nearness of her. Odd how love made him forget the danger threatening to take their lives. "Did you bring me that limb for a crutch?" he asked.

"Most certainly. I've been thinking on some other things, too." She sat beside him and drew her knees to her chest. No one ever looked as good as Sarah Jane in buckskins.

"I want to hear every thought."

"I saw two mountain sheep this morning. There's no reason why I can't bring one down." She grinned. "Papa said I had a good eye."

"Sarah Jane, if you can bring in meat, then do so."

She gave him another kiss, this one on his forehead. "And I wonder if I should try to build us a shelter—a cabin of sorts. I'd be slow in cutting down the trees, and I'd need you to tell me what to do."

He gathered her hand into his. "We're asking for trouble to spend the whole winter here. We'd need a solid cabin for that—and a supply of food and wood."

"What else can we do?"

"Find a way to get out of here. You and I will have to switch places for us to get ahead of the weather. I'll take the wagon and you the horse. That's the only way we can make it over the mountains."

Sarah Jane nodded slowly, as if taking in every word and pondering it. A dusting of snow started to fall around the perimeter of their site. "You're saying we'll freeze to death or starve if we try to stay?"

"Yes, and there's nothing here for the animals either. I want to travel a bit higher above the tree line. At least there we won't have to clear a path in front of us."

She stared into the fire. "I've been wondering if we ought to abandon the wagon. I don't want to, but with the snow and all—"

How much should Sarah Jane suffer? "We aren't at that point yet. We need the wagon to carry provisions and tools. When we make it to the Columbia River, we'll decide then what's best to do."

"Mama and Papa's things did mean more than I care to admit, but none of it is more important than life." Tiny lines were etched around her eyes.

"I saw women in Independence who insisted upon bringing their fine hats and extra petticoats. Unfortunately, their priorities changed when they faced the hardships of the trail and had to bury a family member. You aren't like any of them, Sarah Jane. You've always known what is important."

She smiled and patted the hand holding hers. "And you see more in me than I really am. When you are ready to leave, I'll ride the mare. I'll try very hard not to give up again; but if I do, please make me go on."

He needed to tell her the truth of why he'd failed her. "I never told you why I turned back to my old ways," Painted Hands said. "It wasn't right. I deserve to be shot for it, and telling you the reason doesn't make things right."

"I did my share," she said. "I ignored you, and when we were in the Powder River Valley, I stayed to myself."

"But you wouldn't have, if not for me. The truth is, I was scared, still am, Sarah Jane. I've been on this trail four times, but never by myself. Always someone rode alongside me. Two or three of us made decisions, and we led the wagon train together. Then all of a sudden I realized I was alone. I didn't have the sense to realize I had God as my personal guide."

"I'm sorry. I always thought of you as full of wisdom. I never doubted what you said or what you wanted to do."

He chuckled, moved his leg, then winced. "I'm glad to have your confidence." Having her close did wonders to his spirits. "Have I ever told you any of the tales about other women on the wagon train?"

"No, and I love your stories."

He held her hand and stared into her eyes. "Starting out on the trail, I saw women who were so quiet I had to look to make sure they were there; but as the hardships grew, they changed."

"You mean they started not to care about their families?"

"Worse." He took a gulp of his coffee. "Some got mean, spiteful. You could hear them hollering at their children and cursing their husbands. One woman set her wagon on fire. She said if her husband wouldn't take her back across the plains, then she'd make sure they all died."

Sarah Jane's eyes widened.

"Another woman held a shotgun to her husband's head until he pulled out of the wagon line. They never joined back up."

"And I'm sure there were women, like Mama, who gave up." Her sad gaze moved him, and he squeezed her hand a bit.

"For as many folks who make it to Oregon, there are that many graves along the way. You are brave, Sarah Jane. One day our children will tell our story, and you will be praised." He squeezed her hand. "I always appreciated your pa bringing out his fiddle. He made folks forget what was ailing them."

She closed her eyes. "When I'm missing Papa real bad, I think back on him playing a lively tune and Mama laughing. This has been hard, harder than I ever thought it could be, but despite the death and troubles, I'm a better person." She tilted her head. "And I feel as if it's the way God intended for me."

⟳

Sarah Jane thought she knew the meaning of fear and believed her worst nightmares came from not seeing the future. Yet setting out on a snow-laden trail with an injured husband and snow flying in her face made her question her sanity.

Now she understood the women in her husband's stories. If not for one hand grasping the horse's reins and the other holding on to God, she'd have said and done more unholy things herself.

Her husband's plan to venture higher might have been easier if not for the wind seemingly pushing them back. Her legs felt so numb that she no longer believed she had any at all. The crunch of snow beneath the wagon wheels said they made some progress, if even a few feet. With a scarf tied around her face, she urged the horse upward, yet when she looked behind, she could still see their previous campsite.

Have we only moved this short distance? Will we ever climb down from these mountains? The words *God help us* poured through her mind, spinning around and around lest she forget their true Providence. She turned to see Painted Hands, his face a ghastly white. In her next breath, she gathered the stubborn determination necessary to lead them over the top of the Blue Mountains and on to the Columbia River and the Willamette Valley in Oregon.

When shadows of late afternoon forced them to stop, she was ready to cook a slab of bacon. She'd gone looking for the mountain sheep she'd seen yesterday, but their trail led too far from the campsite, and she was afraid of getting lost. From now on, she always had to be ready with the shotgun.

"I think I'd make a good Indian wife," she said in an attempt to ease the gloom. Tomorrow the coffee would be gone. Perhaps she'd boil tree bark to warm them.

"Why is that?" Painted Hands asked through a thin smile.

"I dress like one. I'm learning how to survive in the wilderness, and I haven't thought about a pretty bonnet in weeks. Besides, the Cheyenne warrior thought so."

Her husband lifted a brow. "I think he had other matters on his mind."

She felt her cheeks grow hot, and his laughter bounced off the cliffs surrounding them. "That's what I get for being prideful." Suddenly, she noticed her nose bleeding.

"You're fine, Sarah Jane," Painted Hands said. "It happens when folks are up this high."

She released a pent-up breath and used her scarf to stop the blood's flow. The thought of getting sick and not being able to care for Painted Hands worried her.

"What do we have left for provisions?" he asked.

If it hadn't been ingrained in her not to lie, she'd have easily done so. "We have frozen berries and a little bacon and a few nuts we found some days ago. A couple of potatoes are left from when we traded with the Indians. There's coffee through tomorrow. No flour or sugar. The cows haven't given any milk for a while." She shrugged. "I promise to do better and try to bring down some meat for us."

"Sarah Jane, soon I'll be able to get around on the crutch. You don't need to feel responsible for keeping us alive. That's my job."

She added a small log to the fire. The wood, too, had to be rationed. "I've been so tired of biscuits, but right now, one sure would taste good," she said.

Sarah Jane toyed with the worries in her mind. Surprises were for children. "What are our chances of getting out of this alive?"

Painted Hands's gaze captured hers. "I never believed much in gambling."

"Papa said it was a sin. But he also valued the truth."

"As I said, I never believed much in gambling."

CHAPTER 19

The temperature dropped lower that night, and in the morning, Painted Hands and Sarah Jane woke to a blanket of snow. She claimed sleeping by the fire was a much warmer proposition than inside the wagon. Painted Hands understood his wife; she didn't want him alone with a broken leg. As he'd decided before, she carried too much weight on her shoulders.

And their dire circumstances were about to get worse. This morning laid out the dismal truth. They would either starve or freeze to death unless the weather calmed. How far could Sarah Jane venture out from the campsite to gather firewood before they were forced to use the wagon for fuel?

"Let's get going." He caressed her cheek. "Every step we take brings us closer to home." As much as he treasured his heavenly home, he so wanted to reach Oregon with his bride.

She rose from her sleeping position and brushed the snow from the quilt and her hair. "I agree. Shall I fix the last of the coffee?"

Painted Hands hesitated. "I can wait."

She nodded and folded one of the quilts. "I'm not very hungry. We could wait to eat. Maybe even tonight."

You ate so little yesterday. I know what you're doing, Sarah Jane.

"I wish you'd have something now. You need strength for the day," he said.

She stared into his face. Her gaze told fathoms about the anxiety rippling through her. "I'll fry up some bacon and one of the potatoes."

"A wise decision." He took a glimpse of the cattle.

"They can't go on much longer without food," she said. "I can keep melting the snow for water—"

"We'll do the best we can. We need to pray," he said, not taking his gaze from her tired face. "I believe it's time we started."

She knelt beside him, and they bowed their heads. Painted Hands took her hand in his. "God, we need Your help more than ever. We're low on food, and the cattle are growing weak. I'm moving slow, but I'm grateful to be alive. Thank You for Sarah Jane and her courage—and for giving her to me as my wife. Help us to honor You all the days of our lives. We're scared, God, and we're asking for guidance. In Jesus' name, amen."

Her cold lips brushed against his. "He hasn't brought us this far without a plan. We must have faith."

As soon as they had eaten and the animals were watered, Sarah Jane hitched up the oxen, and Painted Hands climbed onto the wagon seat. He'd almost grown accustomed to the pain in his leg.

"We'll make better time if we continue along the tree line," Painted Hands said. "Usually it takes about four days to get over these mountains." But that is without snow and half a man. "The valley below is beautiful."

"I look forward to that valley. There we'll rest, and I can fish for food."

Slowly the wagon inched along, the cattle straining against their yoke and the cold wind. Not far was a narrow passageway around the side of the mountain. He'd seen Conestoga wagons too wide to make it around and animals sensing the danger head straight over the side. Praise God for John Benson's wisdom in purchasing a narrow wagon. Still, uncertainty hung in his throat. He had never thought the gut-wrenching fear he saw in other men would affect him.

The closer they approached the site where the narrow trail clung to the mountain cliff, the more he realized the need for him to scout ahead. Painted Hands pulled the oxen to a halt.

"I need to see the trail," he said. "Sometimes it's washed out."

"I can do it."

Painted Hands gritted his teeth and climbed down from the wagon. "I can hobble up there."

With the wind crashing against his body, Painted Hands moved upward and around, noting the pathway was clear but slippery. He struggled to maintain his balance, stopping at several intervals to garner his strength. At the steep, angling curve, he breathed a deep sigh of relief that the wagon could round it and start its decline. Now, if the snow let up, they had a chance to make it.

An hour later, Painted Hands stood at the precipice and realized the oxen had to be led. How could he hold on to a crutch with one hand and the oxen with the other?

"I can lead them," Sarah Jane said as though reading his thoughts. She dismounted. "I'll tie the horse to the back of the wagon with the cows."

"I'll keep the horse with me." He despised the inability to do his share. He'd been over this pass four times and knew the pitfalls. "If the wagon starts to lean or slip backward, get out of its way."

"I learned my lesson the last time," she said.

Alarm registered in his mind. "This is not waist-high water, Sarah Jane. That wagon goes, and you're heading straight down."

She looked at him, startled. "I'll be careful. What about you?"

"I'll hug the side of the cliff."

She moved around to the back of the wagon and climbed inside. A few moments later, she pulled out a dress of her mama's, the Bible with her journal tucked inside, and a box containing the rest of the food. On a second trip, she brought the steel and flint and two boxes of shotgun shells and affixed the other shotgun and rope to his saddle. Inside his saddlebag were more shells. Finally, she carried out the quilts, which she piled beside the box of food. If need be, those could be tied to the horse.

"Have you gotten everything that's important out of the wagon?" he asked, scrutinizing the pile. "What about the ax?"

Sarah Jane shook her head. One more time, she climbed into the wagon and added the axe, shovel, and bucket to the items on the ground. "I'll come back and get these when we're safely around."

Painted Hands hated to see her work so hard. "I'm serious," he said, pointing to the small mound of supplies. "I can live without any of those things you have there, but I can't live without you."

She took her position with the oxen and started upward. The wagon creaked, and the oxen pulled on the yokes as they plodded forward against the wind and fought to keep from sliding backward. From where he limped in the rear nearest the cliff, it seemed headed for the sky. If there had been more wagons, they'd have used men and chains to pull each one up.

Slowly, they ascended to the top. Painted Hands forgot about the pain in his leg. He kept one eye on the wagon and the other on Sarah Jane. Each step became a prayer for the chains to dig into the slippery snow. He felt cold to the bone, but sweat dripped down the side of his face.

When at last they made it around the curve, the incline lay before them more menacing than the trek up. Painted Hands studied the trek down.

"Stay clear." Painted Hands had not felt so helpless since the childhood fire.

The moment the wagon started to slip, he shouted for Sarah Jane. He saw the tragedy coming, but he couldn't get to her fast enough. Painted Hands quickened his pace, slipped, and braced his fall.

"Sarah Jane, get out of the way. You can't stop the wagon."

She cried out to the oxen. But the wheels spun faster, and the wagon gained momentum, heading straight down the pass. Sarah Jane screamed.

Then he saw her, kneeling on the rock-hard ground, her face buried in her hands. In the next instant, the sound of the wagon and frightened animals crashing against the side of the cliff reverberated around them.

"It's all right," he repeated as he hobbled to her side. "You're safe."

Once he reached her, Painted Hands dropped his crutch and eased down beside her, holding her sobbing body next to his.

"I'm sorry," she managed, burying her face in his chest. "I tried. I really tried."

"You did better than any man, ten men."

"Twice I've failed."

He kissed the top of her head. "Twice you've escaped death. That's what's important."

"What will we do now?" she asked between sobs.

Painted Hands took a deep breath. "We're going to head down this mountain, put our supplies on a travois, and lead the horse to Oregon."

∞

Sarah Jane was cold, colder than she could ever remember, and she sat in front of a fire. Her eyes stung, and her head ached. No matter how hard she rubbed her hands together, they refused to thaw. She kept wiggling her toes for fear they'd be frostbitten. She and Painted Hands drank the last of the coffee and ate a little of the bacon. When her teeth chattered, he wrapped his arms around her and suggested she remember the heat on the prairie. Perhaps the memories would warm her body, but nothing helped. Sarah Jane wanted to cry, although it clearly upset him when she wept.

They couldn't hold out much longer. Traveling down the mountain was slow with Painted Hands limping on his crutch. He tried to move faster, but it hurt him so. If their days were numbered, then they needed to talk about their lives before they married. Sharing joys and sorrows sealed their love—even in death.

"I'd like to hear about the years with the Kiowa," she said, studying his face. "I see you cared for them very much."

His gaze softened. "I did. They became my family when I no longer had one. When the hunting party brought me to the village, I was scared. I grieved for my family, believing their deaths were my fault. My hands were badly burned, and in my mind, I deserved the pain. A Kiowa couple took me in. The woman coated my hands in a type of salve and wrapped them in cloth. At night, when I cried for my family, she held me. Later on, I learned she'd lost a son in a fire, and I became her replacement. All the love she had for him was now mine. When the other children teased me about my hands, she ran them off. She gave me the name of Painted Hands and told me I should be proud. I had fought the fire and won. The scars were a symbol of honor, and I should never be ashamed of them."

"A wise woman, Painted Hands."

"Her husband treated me like his own son. He taught me how to hunt buffalo and to show courage in battle. He was a member of the *Koitsenko*, one of the ten most highly respected warriors in the tribe. I remember he wore a red sash around his waist and carried a sacred spear when he went into battle. Those were the days when the Cheyenne and Kiowa were fierce enemies, and those warriors knew how to fight."

She gasped. "They could have killed you that day on the prairie."

He pressed his lips together and said nothing for several moments, as though his memories had carried him back to before the days of their marriage. "The two tribes made a peace treaty about eight years ago, and we're both lucky they honored it, especially since I'm white."

"How were you trained to show courage?"

He grinned. "By proving myself as a hunter and achieving war honors."

"Do I want to know about the war honors?"

He chuckled, the first time he'd laughed in a long time. "I stole a few horses from the enemy and charged their warriors in battle." He paused. "I was happy; content with life. I followed the many gods of the Kiowa and consulted the medicine men for guidance. My white parents had instilled the teachings of the Bible, but everything in that life had died. I no longer felt as if I belonged in the white man's world, neither did I want to. But still I had the nightmares about the fire."

Sarah Jane struggled to understand. "You didn't long for your own people?"

"I was a little boy who craved love and family. From the Kiowa, I learned respect and what it meant to be a respected warrior of honor. After ten years, the white man's ways were foreign."

"How did the soldiers find you?"

"Another man spotted me in a hunting party, and the soldiers rode out in search. None of them bothered to ask me if I wanted to stay."

"They took you against your will?"

He nodded. "The soldiers surrounded the hunting party and at gunpoint singled me out. I put up a good fight, but there were too many of them. I used to wonder why they found me so easily, but now I realize it was part of God's plan. They brought me to Independence, and the Reverend Crandle and his wife took me in."

"Weren't they afraid of you?"

"Sarah Jane, I would have slit every white man's throat within miles if given the chance. The soldiers brought me tied up like an animal to the Crandles, but as soon as they were gone, the reverend spoke kindly to me and cut me loose. He told me that if I wanted to go back to the Kiowa, he'd let me go, but he asked for a chance to show me the white man's way of living. I don't know why I agreed, except the Reverend Crandle trusted me not to hurt him. Two years later, I overheard a soldier telling him that most of my Kiowa village had been killed. It took a lot of talking on the reverend's part to convince me not to seek revenge.

"He's a great man of God. He believed in me when I gave up on myself. He taught me how to read and write and to trust God, not man. Unfortunately, it has taken me a long time to find the faith he lived. I'm not sure how he found out about Jacob. All I know is he met with him while I was on the trail with Greenham."

She rubbed her hands over the fire. "Once we get to Oregon, you two will be inseparable."

His face darkened. "I hope so. I pray so." A moment later, he glanced up at the sky lit with a thousand twinkling stars. "You had a good life with your folks?"

"For the most part, yes. Papa was a dreamer with grand plans. He laughed a lot and always had something witty to say. At least I thought his words were worth remembering. He always wanted something better for us, while Mama wanted to stay in the same place and be happy with what we had. At times they quarreled about it, especially when Papa sold the farm and moved us to Independence. Mama missed her friends, and living in a wagon did not sit well with her. The worst time between them happened when Papa decided we were going to Oregon. She cried and begged him to let us live in Independence. They talked things out right before she took to feeling poorly. They loved Jesus and understood the importance of following Him. I'm thinking all marriages have their mountains and valleys."

"We've had ours. The mountains can be a little cold though."

She managed a laugh.

He squeezed her a little tighter. "You're too thin. I'm afraid this wind will blow you away."

She was tempted to give in to the gloom, but she refused. "When we get to Oregon, I'll eat everything in sight. Most likely get fat. Then we'll have babies, and I'll get fatter."

"Babies," he whispered. "I'd like to be a father."

"Good, 'cause I want to be a mother."

"We can't give up, can we, Sarah Jane?"

She shook her head and swallowed the lump stopping her from speaking.

"I love you more than I ever thought possible." The gentleness in his voice made it even more difficult for her to hold her composure. "For as long as God gives us, I will be devoted to you," he said.

No longer able to keep her emotions hidden, she turned to him and buried her face in his chest. "You would have made it to Oregon if not for me. Dying up here is my fault. I'm so sorry."

"No one is to blame. We're part of God's plan, and I believe we will survive. Every step we take down brings us closer to warmer weather and a supply of food."

A wolf howled, then several more. Normally, their presence meant little to her when she sat in front of a fire. But tonight, as she faced the bleak outcome of cold and starvation, the wild animals frightened her. For a moment, she allowed the comforts of home in Nebraska to soothe her. Perhaps she needed to dwell on the promises of heaven instead.

CHAPTER 20

Another day's trek downward, and Painted Hands grieved with the slow progress. Four days over the mountains had turned to seven. Too often he had to stop and rest. The slippery incline and the debris that covered the path made the going difficult. The food was gone; Sarah Jane hadn't wanted to tell him about the shortage, but he saw the diminishing provisions. Hunting with his broken leg seemed nearly impossible unless an animal walked in front of him, and the idea of sending his wife out into the wilderness sounded just as menacing. They could melt snow for water, but how long could they continue without food?

Snow clouds loomed overhead. Everywhere he turned, life dealt another blow. *Why, Father? I'm trusting You, but our future looks grim.*

In the next hour, the snow started. The two walked as far as they could until the whirling white mass blinded them. They were forced to find shelter, this time under a pine tree. Sarah Jane gathered wood, and he started a fire. His stomach rumbled as it had for days. Tree bark had begun to look good.

Huddled together, they watched the snow drift and blow, each flake sealing their future. He'd lost all hope, but he dared not tell Sarah Jane. He melted snow over the fire and offered it to her, but she refused. Their destiny was freezing to death or starving, whichever came first.

"Talk to me," Sarah Jane said, snuggling closer. "I'm sleepy and can't get warm."

"Drink the warm water."

"I can't. I want to sleep."

"Stand up. Move around. Jump up and down." He tried to chase away the panic from his voice by replacing it with anger, but even he doubted his tone.

"No, I can't. I'm too tired."

He heard the resignation. "I won't let you give up. What can I do?"

"Tell me a story. I want to fall asleep listening to your voice."

His mind registered nothing. He couldn't remember anything. If she'd been a man, he'd have picked a fight. "As your husband, I'm telling you to stay awake."

"It doesn't matter. I can't go on." Her weak voice sent a streak of fear through him.

"But you must. We can wait out this storm and go on." Painted Hands searched for the words to keep her awake. "I'm asking for a favor, Sarah Jane. Look at me with those beautiful green eyes and call me by my given name."

He felt her frail frame shiver, and she positioned herself to face him. "Toby."

"Do you like the name?"

"Oh yes. It's pleasing to the ears." Her voice grew fainter.

"I want to name our first son Toby. What do you think of that?" His mind raced. Whatever it took, he could not let her fall asleep. *Please, God, slow down the snow. Let us walk down this mountain.*

"We won't have any children. We are going to die right here."

"No!" He shook her. "We are not."

"Please, Painted Hands—"

"The name is Toby." He shook her again.

"It's no use. Just let me be."

He felt tears and anger spur him on. "I thought you were your father's child. Fight this, I beg of you! Stand up and move."

She slumped against him. "I'll try." Slowly, she rose to her feet. She lifted her arms to the sky and wiggled them, then fell beside him. "It's too hard."

"All right, we'll talk. I want to name our children, a dozen of them. The first son is Toby. What will we call our first daughter?"

She sighed. "Lydia Jane, after my mother."

"Good. Another son we could call John William after your pa."

She nodded and relaxed against him.

"And another girl named after you and my mother—Sarah Elizabeth." When she didn't reply, he nudged her. "Sarah Jane, talk to me."

She didn't answer; her eyes were closed. He wanted to give up, too, but his thoughts raced in prayer. Only God could deliver them—either into His hands for eternity or through a miracle.

∞

Painted Hands woke with a start. He had no concept of time; he only knew the light glistening off the snow caused him to blink. Flames from the fire soared as though reaching up to the sky. The heat warmed him to the bone. How had this happened? Buffalo robes covered them. He glanced at Sarah Jane sleeping in his arms. She looked like an angel at peace, and a faint smile etched her delicate features. Her chest rose and lowered. He kissed her forehead, then her lips. Praise God, she still lived. But who had stoked the fire?

Then he saw them. Three Cayuse Indians, a tall race who moved with grace and agility. They were dressed warmly in shirts, fringed buckskin, and buffalo and deer robes. One brought out dried salmon and breadlike cakes made from camas bulbs. Painted Hands stared up. He hoped the gratitude shone from his eyes, because he didn't have the strength to pull out his arms to talk to them in sign language.

Cayuse Indians. Less than a year ago, in November 1847, they had killed Marcus and Narcissa Whitman and twelve others at the Whitman mission. Growing resentment that the whites intended to take over the Cayuse land escalated when a measles epidemic broke out and killed many of the Indians. They feared the whites had brought the disease to destroy the Indians. They blamed those at the Whitman mission and took revenge. Why were they helping him and Sarah Jane now? The reason didn't matter, only that they were there. This wasn't the first time God had sent Indians to deliver him.

Painted Hands attempted to move about. A Cayuse who wore a horned headdress handed him a cup of hot broth. It tasted of deer and root vegetables, like the finest of food. Slowly, his head began to clear as his body thawed. A short while later, he pulled his arms from beneath the buffalo robe and signed his gratitude to the four sitting beside the fire.

"We are glad to have found you," said the one who had given him the broth.

Odd how the Indian spoke perfect English. Perhaps he'd learned from the Whitmans.

"My wife and I had given up, believing only God in His providence could save us," Painted Hands said.

"God has answered your prayers." He pointed to Painted Hands's broken leg. "Your leg has been set straight. I believe you will walk upright when it heals."

A strange sensation settled on the back of his neck. By all rights, he and Sarah Jane should be dead, either from the cold, starvation, or the Cayuse—Indians who spoke excellent English and waged war against the whites. None of this made sense. Perhaps this was a dream or a passageway into heaven.

"How did you find us?" Painted Hands asked. He felt no fear, but he *should*.

"We found the remains of your wagon and searched you out," the Cayuse replied.

"I will be forever grateful."

"We will take you to the river. From there you can take a canoe to the white man's settlement."

"Why didn't you kill us? Have the Cayuse agreed to peace?"

"Your God led us to you. We respect His power."

In awe of what God had done through these Indians, Painted Hands realized no works of man, neither good nor evil, could stop God's purpose. Many would never believe this wondrous story, only those who also had experienced a miracle.

"I wish I had something to give you in return," Painted Hands said.

"A prayer for our people is enough. We fear the whites will kill us all, and yet we must fight for our way of life."

"I will pray for you as long as I have breath." Painted Hands understood the plight of these Indians, just as he'd understood the troubles of the Kiowa, Cheyenne, Pawnee, Sioux, and all the other Indians who faced the overwhelming odds of the whites seeking to occupy the Indians' lands. He saw both sides, and it grieved him.

"Your heart is good," the Cayuse said, his voice strong yet gentle. "Your wife, she must eat, too."

"Wake up, Sarah Jane." He kissed her forehead. "We have been delivered."

∞

For the next four days, Painted Hands and Sarah Jane stayed with the three Cayuse Indians. The couple regained their strength, then started down the mountain with the Indians guiding them. Some of the trails were familiar to Painted Hands, but others were only wide enough to accommodate a walking path. The Indians provided horses and food every step of the way.

"Where is their village?" Sarah Jane asked while they rode horses the Cayuse provided.

"I asked the one who wears the horn headdress, but he did not answer."

"I am amazed you speak their language, too," she said with a smile. "You are constantly surprising me."

Painted Hands was startled. "I don't speak their tongue. They speak English."

Sarah Jane peered at him oddly. "But I never heard English—it was something else."

Painted Hands realized another miracle had taken place. Forever, he'd praise God for blessing him far beyond what he deserved.

"Where are they taking us now?" she asked.

"To the Columbia River, where we'll take a raft all the way to the Methodist mission at the Dalles. The rapids are horrible, but God has brought us this far—and He will see us on to the Willamette River and the Willamette Valley."

"And to Jacob," she said. "Do I continue to call you Toby?"

He thought for a minute. "I am a white man who has been delivered by God through the Indians of this vast country time and time again. I'm proud of my experience with them, but I am Toby Carlson."

She reached out for his hand. "I'm so proud to be your wife. I love you no matter what you choose to be called."

"And I'm blessed to have the love of a fine woman."

On the shores of the sparkling Columbia River, the Cayuse helped Toby construct a raft. When it was completed, Toby and Sarah Jane bundled their few belongings together and turned to the Indians.

"Thank you again," Toby said, hearing his words swell with emotion. "You saved our lives." He grasped the shoulder of the man wearing the horned headdress—the one Toby called a friend.

"Remember to pray for our people." The man smiled.

"I give you my word. I do not even know your name."

"Names are of no purpose when God calls us brothers."

"I understand." Toby stared into the man's dark eyes. Peace and warmth radiated from the dark pools.

"Your leg will heal without a limp." The man paused. "God has healed your heart and your body. Show to others what He has done for you."

Toby nodded and swallowed hard. "God bless you, my friend and brother."

The Cayuse turned, and the men disappeared into the trees. Toby wrapped his arm around Sarah Jane. "God's ways are mysterious," he whispered and planted a kiss on her forehead. "With His guidance, I will never return to my black moods. I am a free man who knows his source of strength."

Sarah Jane leaned her head upon his chest as he balanced on his crutch. The rush of water whirled around them. "I am not afraid of what's ahead."

He pulled her closer. "Neither am I."

EPILOGUE

Toby, how will we know it's Jacob?" Sarah Jane asked. Her gaze flitted from one man to another among the small crowd in Oregon City.

"I don't know. Maybe I should be carrying a sign stating 'Looking for Jacob Carlson.'" He, too, searched all around them. Men, women, and children went about their business. "I wish I knew if he had a wife or what he looked like. We'll ask for the nearest logging camp, talk to everyone we meet, and keep looking until we find him."

Sarah Jane held her breath. There, not ten feet in front of them, stood a man who looked identical to Toby: the same walnut-colored hair and beard, the same broad shoulders and stocky build. She tugged on Toby's sleeve. He turned to the man.

"Jacob?"

The man stepped forward with outstretched arms. "Toby."

The two enveloped each other with hugs and laughter.

Jacob stood back and shook his head. Tears streamed down his face. "I've prayed twenty-three years for this day. I heard from a Charles Greenham that you'd been left behind on his wagon train. Since that day, every time I got word of new emigrants making their way into Oregon City, I've been here."

Toby wrapped his arm around Sarah Jane's waist. "This is my wife, Sarah Jane."

Jacob first grasped her hand, then pulled her into his arms. "Welcome, my sister. If the good Lord took me home this hour, I would live in gratitude for seeing Toby and his bride before me today."

"Thank you." Tears trickled down Sarah Jane's face, and she quickly whisked them away.

"We have years to catch up, little brother." Jacob turned to Toby and laughed long and hard. "I have so much to tell, and I want to hear about the years you spent with the Kiowa."

"When can we get started?" Toby asked. He paused and nodded as though pleased with life and everything in it.

"Tonight," Jacob said. He grasped Toby's shoulder. "And what are your plans now that you are here?"

Toby shrugged. "To find work, maybe farm."

"I could use a partner at the beginnings of a lumber camp—if it suits you."

Sarah Jane felt her emotions rise to the surface. She knew Toby's desire to work with his brother.

"That would suit me just fine. God does listen to the prayers of the heart," Toby said. He gazed into Sarah Jane's eyes, then looked at Jacob. "He's answered every one of mine."

ABOUT THE AUTHORS

ELAINE BONNER lives in north Texas where she works as a registered nurse. When not working or writing, she loves to spend time doting on her three grandchildren. Her goal is to portray through her writing the importance of having Christ in the center of life.

RAMONA K. CECIL is a wife, mother, grandmother, freelance poet, and award-winning inspirational romance writer. Now empty nesters, she and her husband make their home in Indiana. A member of American Christian Fiction Writers and American Christian Fiction Writers Indiana Chapter, her work has won awards in a number of inspirational writing contests. Over eighty of her inspirational verses have been published on a wide array of items for the Christian gift market. She enjoys a speaking ministry, sharing her journey to publication while encouraging aspiring writers. When not writing, her hobbies include reading, gardening, and visiting places of historical interest.

NANCY J. FARRIER is an award-winning author of numerous books, articles, short stories, and devotions living in Southern California. She is married and the mother of five children and one grandson. Nancy feels called to share her faith with other through her writing.

JOANN A. GROTE lives on the Minnesota prairie which is a setting for many of her stories. Once a full-time CPA, JoAnn now spends most of her time researching and writing. JoAnn has published historical nonfiction books for children and several novels with Barbour Publishing as well as the American Adventure and Sisters in Time series for children. Several of her novellas are included in CBA best-selling anthologies by Barbour Publishing. JoAnn's love of history developed when she worked at an historical restoration in North Carolina for five years. She enjoys researching and weaving her fictional characters' lives into historical backgrounds and events. JoAnn believes that readers can receive a message of salvation and encouragement from well-crafted fiction. She captivates and addresses the deeper meaning between life and faith.

DIANN MILLS is a bestselling author who believes her readers should expect an adventure. She combines unforgettable characters with unpredictable plots to create action-packed, suspense-filled novels.

Her titles have appeared on the CBA and ECPA bestseller lists; won two Christy Awards; and been finalists for the RITA, Daphne Du Maurier, Inspirational Readers' Choice, and Carol award contests. Library Journal presented her with a Best Books 2014: Genre Fiction award in the Christian Fiction category for Firewall.

DiAnn is a founding board member of the American Christian Fiction Writers; the 2015 president of the Romance Writers of America's Faith, Hope & Love chapter; and a member of Advanced Writers and Speakers Association and International Thriller Writers. She speaks to various groups and teaches writing workshops around the country. She and her husband live in sunny Houston, Texas.

DiAnn is very active online and would love to connect with readers on any of the social media platforms listed at www.diannmills.com.